THE BROADVIEW ANTHOLOGY OF SCIENCE FICTION

THE BROADVIEW ANTHOLOGY OF

Science Fiction

EDITED BY JASON HASLAM

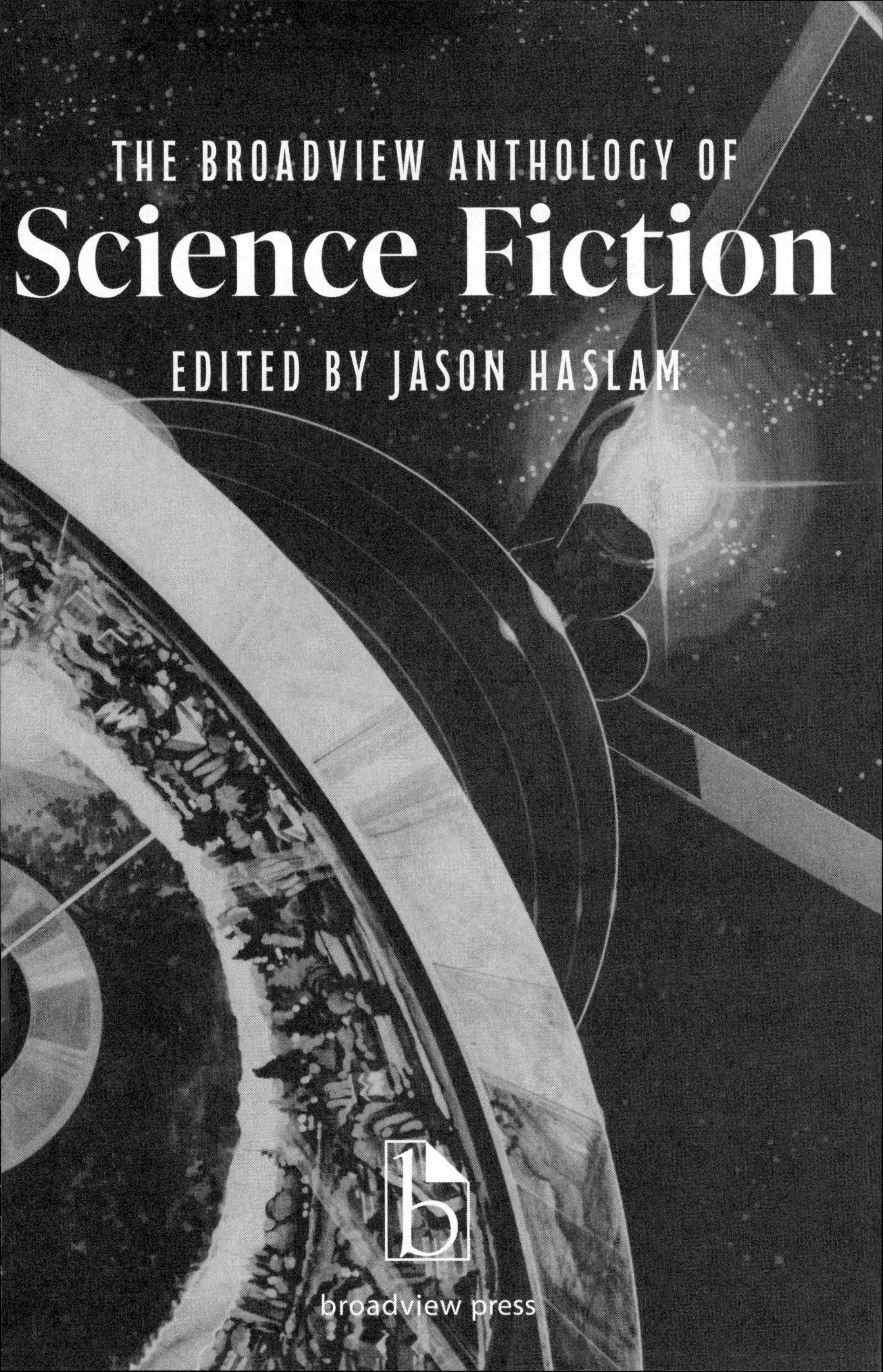

broadview press

BROADVIEW PRESS
Peterborough, Ontario, Canada

Founded in 1985, Broadview Press is a fully independent academic publishing house owned by approximately twenty-five shareholders—almost all of whom are either Broadview employees or Broadview authors. Broadview is supported by a collaboration with Trent University, a liberal arts university located in Peterborough, Ontario—the city where Broadview was founded and continues to operate. Broadview is committed to environmentally responsible publishing and fair business practices.

Library and Archives Canada Cataloguing in Publication

Title: The Broadview anthology of science fiction / edited by Jason Haslam.
Names: Haslam, Jason, 1971- editor.
Description: Includes bibliographical references.
Identifiers: Canadiana (print) 20250245213 | Canadiana (ebook) 20250247844 | ISBN 9781554816118 (softcover) | ISBN 9781460409596 (EPUB) | ISBN 9781037700507 (PDF)
Subjects: LCSH: Science fiction. | LCGFT: Science fiction. | LCGFT: Short stories.
Classification: LCC PN6120.95.S33 B76 2025 | DDC 823/.0876208—dc23

Broadview Press handles its own distribution in Canada and the United States:
PO Box 1243, Peterborough, Ontario K9J 7H5, Canada
555 Riverwalk Parkway, Tonawanda, NY 14150, USA
Tel: (705) 482-5915
email: customerservice@broadviewpress.com

Broadview Press books are imported and distributed in the United Kingdom and European Union by:
Gazelle Book Services Ltd.
White Cross Mills, Hightown, Lancaster, Lancashire, LA1 4XS
sales@gazellebookservices.co.uk

European Union – Responsible Person (for official use only):
eucomply OÜ
Pärnu mnt 139b14
11317 Tallinn, Estonia
hello@eucompliancepartner.com
+33757690241

Broadview Press acknowledges the financial support of the Government of Canada for our publishing activities.

Canada

Copy-edited by Michel Pharand
Book Design: George Kirkpatrick

PRINTED IN THE UNITED STATES

2 3 4 5 6 7 8 9 10   26 27 28 29 30

For my sister and brother, who always kept me in books,
and never minded when I stole theirs.

And, of course, for Julia, who always makes better worlds possible.

Contents

Period/Chronological Contents

Multiple Histories, Multiple Futures Contents

Afrofuturism, Africanfuturism, and Black Science Fiction

Asian and South Asian Science Fiction

Indigenous Futurisms

Feminist and Queer Futurisms

Thematic and Sub-Genre Contents

Climate Fiction, Nature, and Ecology

Colonialism, Invasion, and War

Gothic and Weird Science Fiction

Meta-SF: Science Fiction about Science Fiction

"Others": Aliens, Creatures, Robots, and Artificial Intelligence

Space and Interplanetary Travel

Speculative Poetry

Time Travel

Utopias and Future Histories

List of Figures

Acknowledgements

I've thought about doing a project like this for as long as I can remember, so to see it through is not just a dream come true, but also the result of support I've received from countless people throughout *many* decades (though of course any of its failings are my own). My family, to whom this is dedicated, are first among them (not least for supporting the kid who would rather reread *Hitchhiker's Guide to the Galaxy* for the tenth time than go outside), and my partner, Julia, who is always my first and best reader and supporter: without her, none of this is possible or nearly as fun.

The work on this anthology has also been supported by many wonderful and thoughtful colleagues and friends at Dalhousie and elsewhere; in addition to all my Department of English colleagues, and at the risk of leaving some out because of my own faulty memory, I need to mention those who have generously been willing to talk SF and related topics: James Allard, Becca Babcock, John Barnstead, Brent Bellamy, Steven Bruhm, Kathy Cawsey, Krista Collier-Jarvis, Brad Congdon, Dennis Denisoff, Leonard Diepeveen, Anthony Enns, Lynne Evans, Danine Farquharson, Brian Greenspan, Jessica Hawkes, Kala Hirtle, Asha Jeffers, Christopher Lockett, Shao-Pin Luo, Karen Macfarlane, Mary Beth MacIsaac, Rohan Maitzen, Ian McKergow and the whole family, Geordie Miller, Nicola Nixon, Isaac Saney, Stephen Schryer, Peter Schwenger, Stephen Snobelen, Xine Yao, T'ai Zimmer, and all the others who humoured me. A special thanks to those who continue to take part in and attend Hal-Con's "professor panels," and to their organizing team.

This project was also made possible with the help of the dedicated staff at the Killam Library, including Lindsay McNiff and our colleagues in document delivery, who found obscure works at almost faster-than-light speeds. Thanks, too, to the amazing staff in the Rare Books and Music Room at the British Library. Funding for that and related research was provided by the Social Sciences and Humanities Research Council of Canada, which provides vital research infrastructure and should be further supported at this time when public research bodies are so clearly necessary. SSHRC support also allowed me to work with my research assistants *par excellence*, Cher Hann and Helen Pinsent, who helped with the endless task of proofreading, as well as with notes and other research. A special thank you to copyeditor Michel Pharand, who helped immensely with both editing and chasing down editorial material. (Facts for the explanatory notes were gathered through the many resources at the libraries mentioned and others, as well as such digital sources as the *Encyclopedia Britannica*, the *Dictionary of National Biography*, the *Internet Speculative Fiction Database*, the *Stanford Encyclopedia of Philosophy*, and *SFE: The Encyclopedia of Science Fiction*. Sources for more specific details are referenced in the notes and further reading as appropriate.)

There is no way to praise highly enough Broadview Press. I've worked with Don LePan, Marjorie Mather, Christine Handley, Brett McLenithan, and others for decades now, and this independent, scholarly press is vital to the wider academic work of countless colleagues and students, across numerous fields and nations. That it's Canadian is only the butter tart on top.

Speaking of students, this project only exists because of the students who have, over the past two decades, brought their enthusiasm and brilliance to undergraduate and graduate SF courses, and because of the honours, masters, and doctoral students I've been lucky enough to work with. Some of these students are named above, since they went on to become colleagues working across our educational and cultural sectors. If you find a favourite part of this work—whether a story, image, or even a note—I guarantee that at some point a student made me think about it in brand new ways.

Introduction: The Broad Views of Science Fiction

By the mid 1950s, a new phrase had become popular in the lexicon of English-language newspapers: "like something out of science fiction." In 1953, the *Lurgan Mail* announced that a new method of "baby-sitting by electronics may sound like something out of science-fiction. Yet it's possible—and it works!" later reassuring their readers that "It's all done with two-way wireless, not robots" (12 June 1953, 6). Advertising also used the phrase: "Necchi push-button sewing is here," we're told in a large headline, and "It's like a 'human' machine out of science-fiction" (*Toronto Daily Star*, 14 Sept. 1955, 40). Science fiction was also appearing in the military realm: "A weird structure, looking like something out of a science fiction magazine, is rising in the Mojave Desert of California" for new US Air Force rockets (*Evening Express*, 3 Sept. 1956, 9). Public universities weren't spared the invasion of science fiction, either: a letter to the editor in the 1957 *Belfast News-letter* warns of the "menace of advanced technology masquerading as education," imploring universities to include material that "come[s] out of the past—not out of 'science fiction'" (15 Oct. 1957, 4). Not even the animal kingdom was spared: at an electronics exhibition in 1954, among the "meters, dials, flashing bulbs and jigging green lines flashing across viewing screens" that made the exhibition hall "look like something out of science fiction," one could find "the *apidictor* which tells the beekeeper exactly what the bees are doing in their hives"; or, as the headline puts it, the world had become a place where you could buy "MACHINES TO SPY ON THE BEES" (*Birmingham Gazette*, 24 Nov. 1954, 5).

These headlines tell us many things about the larger culture of the English-speaking North Atlantic world of the post-World War II period, certainly, but do they also tell us anything about science fiction? As we'll learn below, science fiction and the literary forms that gave rise to it existed long before this period. Starting in the late 1920s and especially in the 1930s, the term "science fiction" or variations thereon were being popularized by pulp magazines dedicated to such stories (though the phrase itself has been around since at least the mid-1800s).[1] But by the 1950s, Hollywood science fiction films had become a staple of cinemas, while comic books, with their myriad fantastic heroes and villains, were already nearing the end of their so-called golden age. Science fiction had become a common, pop-culture referent. Even so, these headlines may also tell us something about science fiction's wider readership and viewership in the era, as the range of newspaper items and their implied audiences speak to a form that crosses multiple demographics.

But do these stories and advertisements tell us anything about what science fiction actually is? Clearly many of them focus on new—or newly repurposed—technologies. A focus on the future is also evident, with "science

1 See H. Bruce Franklin, "What Is Science Fiction—And How It Grew," p. 24.

fiction" standing in for a future disconnected—sometimes radically—from the past and present. There's also an emphasis on design, on things looking *like* something out of science fiction: these are objects that appear to be futuristic, even when that appearance is ironic or lamentable. Lastly, there is an assumption that these technologies will reshape human life, from everyday activities to the grand sweep of global politics.

Technology, the future, and the transformation of societies all seem to join in this moment to create a world that was "like something out of science fiction." As you'll read below, these three concepts also lie at the centre of certain definitions of science fiction, though some ways of looking at the history—or, more accurately, the histor*ies*—of the field challenge such definitions. To help us understand the complex literary and cultural area known as science fiction (SF, for short), the rest of this introduction will focus on two central and inseparable methods for understanding SF as a literary and cultural form: Definitions of SF and Histories of SF, the latter of which is folded in with a discussion of the structure of this anthology and its editorial principles.

DEFINING SF

Nearly every book-length academic study of SF begins with, or is fully constituted by, a meditation on definitions—and almost as many begin by noting that the task is all but impossible. Two recent introductory works—Adam Roberts's *The History of Science Fiction* (2nd ed., 2016) and Gerry Canavan and Eric Carl Link's edited collection *The Cambridge History of Science Fiction* (2019)—address this issue directly. Roberts writes that there is "no single consensus as to what SF is" (2), while Canavan and Link write that, even if "all compelling attempts to define SF as 'the literature of *x*' seem to truly capture a core element of many of the texts [...], nonetheless they all fall short of being descriptive of everything we could conceivably associate with the category or they are so broad as to encapsulate far more than would typically associate with the category" (7).

Most critics, however, including these scholars, do consistently turn to a handful of critical definitions that "seem to truly capture a core element" of SF, and such definitions are especially useful for those just starting their journey into the study of the field. I'll turn now to a brief selection of those sometimes complementary, sometimes competing, definitions, and then discuss how it may be better to look to more contextual analyses of the ways SF has been used and read, and how the many possible histories of SF complicate things—in exciting ways—even further.

"The Literature of Cognitive Estrangement" and the "Novum"

Possibly the most foundational scholarly definition of science fiction was proposed by Darko Suvin in *Metamorphoses of Science Fiction: On the Poetics and History of a Literary Genre* (1979), a book that arguably launched a thousand university courses into the stars and beyond.

Suvin defines SF as "the *literature of cognitive estrangement*" (15; emphasis in original). He writes that the "subject matter" of literature has long ranged from the "extreme of exact reproduction of the author's empirical environment," on the one hand, "to exclusive interest in a strange newness," on the other (16). That is, literature has long wavered between a mimetic realism that tries to hold up a mirror to the world as it is, and a more imaginative fantasy that creates entirely new fictional worlds. The latter, he writes, can be called the literature of estrangement; in addition to SF, it could include forms like myth, folktales, and fantasy.

But, for Suvin, there is a distinction between the estranged worlds of SF and those of fantasy, and this distinction lies in the operation of their worlds. In what we now call "high fantasy," including such works as J.R.R. Tolkien's *Lord of the Rings* (1954–55), the worlds created are estranged—different from ours—*and* they do not obey logical forms of cause and effect, or physical laws as we understand them. Magic, sympathetic identification between a land and its rulers, and other primarily metaphysical relations govern how fantasy worlds work (and the same can be argued for the gothic, folktales, and other such forms). Suvin argues that SF is also different from mimetic literature: it is still estranged, because every SF text focusses on a "strange newness" about its world, a newness he calls the "novum." But for Suvin, the estrangements of SF, unlike those of fantasy, are *cognitive*; that is, they still follow basic empirical and logical rules. The worlds of such works are driven by certain laws of physics, for example, rather than metaphysics or "magic."

Unlike in fantasy, the non-realist element of the SF text—the novum—is thus one that is drawn from what we know of the way the world works. That novum could be a technological or scientific development that, while not currently extant in the author's material reality, can nonetheless be logically extrapolated from current technologies or scientific theories. Thus, transportation from one building to the next using a wand, with no explanation as to how the atoms and particles of one's physical body are moved, would be fantasy, but transportation via a sub-spatial "wormhole" from one galaxy to another, the existence of which could be loosely predicated on current developments in string theory, could be science fiction. Or, the novum could be a political or social formation that doesn't exist in the world as we know it, but that operates according to our understanding of social structures. So, a world like Camelot where the trees bloom because the land spiritually reflects the quality of the King's rule would be fantasy, but a world where trees have stopped growing due to the foreseeable effects of climate change would be science fiction, as in Dilman Dila's "The Last Storyteller," included in this anthology. Importantly, for Suvin, that new element must change the basic structure of the world; the novum is "a totalizing phenomenon or relationship deviating from the author's and implied reader's norm of reality," but it does so in ways that are cognitive or logically consistent with the world as we understand it (80).

In sum, for Suvin, SF has to be a non-realist form that is nonetheless logically extrapolated from ours, and so SF is fundamentally different from both realism and other such non-realist modes as fantasy or the gothic. Suvin notes in his book—fairly judgmentally, it must be said—that much of what is called "SF" doesn't meet this definition of a purely cognitive estrangement, at least not throughout its world-building, but is instead "metaphysical gobbledygook" that simply replaces the trappings of fantasy (like the magic carpet) with only the *appearance* of science (a shiny rocket ship) (37). This approach makes the category of "real" science fiction for Suvin a *very* narrow one, and one that excludes a lot of what most people call "science fiction." This narrowness was part of his attempt to delineate "a coherent poetics of SF" (16), and out of that to also create an academic canon of (the best) SF.

Science Fiction's Semantic and Lyric Possibilities

The concepts of the novum and estrangement do speak to the structure of many SF texts, especially to the ways in which they build on current or past realities in order to speculate on possible futures or alternate societies. Perhaps the best element of Suvin's work, and the one that holds even for works he might dismiss, is seeing in SF a form that allows for "an escape from constrictive old norms into a different and alternative timestream [...] and an at least initial readiness for new norms of reality" (101). It seems fitting, then, that scholars after Suvin also escape from what they see as the constrictive norms of his definition of SF, to discuss instead a wider body of work, while some have worked to adapt his approach to make it more widely applicable.[1]

Like Suvin, SF author and critic Samuel R. Delany is interested in certain formal elements of works that make them SF. Specifically, Delany argues that SF is characterized by an extension of semiotic possibilities in language: that is, he argues that words can simply mean *more* in science fiction than they can in realist fiction—or what he calls (*hilariously*, to my mind) "mundane fiction." Delany sees this semantic inflation as a function of what Suvin would call the cognitive elements of SF and the materialization of metaphor it involves. He uses the phrases "Then her world exploded" and "He turned on his left

1 Notable here is Carl Freedman's *Critical Theory and Science Fiction* (2000), in which Freedman expands Suvin's strictly extrapolative "cognitive" element to what he calls a "cognition effect," where the text can present something as "cognitively valid" even if it may not be the reader's understanding of the world (pp. 18–19). See also Istvan Csicsery-Ronay Jr., *The Seven Beauties of Science Fiction* (2008).

side" to demonstrate what he means: in "mundane fiction," he writes, the first phrase only makes sense as "an emotionally muzzy metaphor about the inner aspects of some incident in a female character's life," while the latter would imply a man rolling over. In SF, however, the first phrase could additionally mean that the woman's planet was just blown up, while the second could reference a cyborg "activating the circuitry" on the left side of his body ("Science Fiction and 'Literature,'" 68).[1] In other words, because these phrases can be read as *both* metaphor *and* material statements about the estranged world and technology in an SF novel, the genre allows for more meaning, more possibilities, than do realist works.

But there's an added layer to Delany's understanding of SF. Note that he focusses on the interpretation of these lines: some readers may only see the material side of these sentences, for example, while others may stumble—especially if they're not used to reading SF works—by understanding the phrases first and foremost as metaphor. For Delany, SF is as much a reading *practice* as it is a literary *form*. As Delany has written, it may even be possible "to read [Jane] Austen as if her novels were science fiction" ("Science Fiction and 'Literature,'" 81). He describes a conversation with a historian who had started reading more SF; this historian told Delany that when he went back to reading realist fiction, specifically *Pride and Prejudice*, he found himself asking "what kind of world would have had to exist for Austen's story to have taken place?" further stating that such a world would have had to have been one "completely different from the world as it actually was back then," in Austen's time (81). In other words, for Delany, the reading practice we call "science fiction" "gives us a way to construct worlds in clear and consistent dialogue with *the world* that *is*, alas, the case.... And in a world where an 'alas' has to be inserted into such a description of it, the dialectical freedom of science fiction has to be privileged" (81). For Delany, part of what distinguishes the real from the estranged and vice versa is the action of reading itself, and that act can lead us to the same form of freedom that Suvin sees in SF.

Delany further expands on this freedom when, in his book *American Shore* (1978), he defines SF as a form of "free-fall" between the gravity wells of dominant discourses, especially those that organize things into hierarchies of value.[2] As the character Michael Burnham puts it in *Star Trek: Discovery*, when explaining how Lewis Carroll's non-realist *Alice in Wonderland* shaped her worldview, "The real world doesn't always adhere to logic. Sometimes down is up, sometimes up is down. Sometimes when you're lost, you're found."[3] In any given context, certain forms of discourse are dominant in literary, social, political, or other arenas, leading to specific ways of looking at the world,

1 Delany also uses these examples, with the characters' genders reversed, in an appendix to his novel, *Trouble on Triton* (285), blurring the line between the "real" author and his SF.

2 See *American Shore* (159–61).

3 *Star Trek: Discovery*, "Context is for Kings," airdate 1 October 2017.

but SF can shake us out of those standard positions. To take an example relevant to much of Delany's work, in twentieth- and twenty-first-century North America, the dominant discourse of sexuality privileges heterosexual relations over queer ones, and likewise tends to deny certain social privileges to people of colour over those who are categorized as white. In creating estranged, or "dislocated" other worlds where binaries of "up and down" can be tossed aside, SF can, for Delany (a gay, black man) offer new ways of seeing the world, between or beyond those dominant ones, thus allowing the reader to float free of those dominant world views, opening up possibilities for others (his story "Among the Blobs," included here in a previously unpublished version, is a case in point).

Later scholars pick up on this type of disruptive analysis. Notably, Seo-Young Chu, in *Do Metaphors Dream of Literal Sheep?* (2010), argues that SF is a "high-intensity variety of realism" (7), expanding Delany's materialization of metaphor, as part of a larger argument that representation itself is inherently "science-fictional." For Chu, SF is an engagement with "lyric mimesis," in which "lyric and narrative forces" combine to create "mimetic accounts of cognitively estranging referents" (73). In other words, SF, like the lyric, can represent objects that are "impossible to represent in a straightforward manner" but are nonetheless "absolutely real" (3). One example of this type of representation is the object of "cyberspace," a term popularized by SF author William Gibson to describe the virtual world of interconnected computers. Cyberspace is an impossible object to assess empirically, Chu writes—"cyberspace cannot be weighed on a scale"—yet it is nonetheless real, and Gibson's SF work allows us to see that reality (7). SF, for Chu, is "distinguished by its capacity to perform the massively complex representational and epistemological work" of making such impossible-to-describe realities available for description. From this argument, she is able to read realism itself as a "'weak' or low-intensity variety of science fiction" (7), since its referents are more easily described and understood than the more complex realities SF offers. I'll return to Chu's argument when discussing the speculative poetry included in this anthology.

Mass Culture and "Communities of Practice"

As with Suvin's definition, there are some potential difficulties with Delany's and Chu's—if even *Pride and Prejudice* can be read as SF, or, as Chu writes, "If all representation is to some degree science-fictional, then what is not science fiction?" (75).[1] If Suvin's definition is too restrictive, then maybe there is a risk

1 Throughout this introduction, I reference SF as a genre. Chu makes a convincing case—one I and other scholars (notably Csicsery-Ronay Jr.) have also attempted—to read SF instead as a mode, a term that describes more a form of discourse than a specific set of textual conventions. Chu's larger argument, which also explores allegory, is beyond the scope of this introduction, but I strongly encourage you to read her work.

that Delany's and Chu's are too wide-reaching. Can there be a way of defining the genre that balances these? That question turns me to John Rieder's *SF and the Mass Cultural Genre System* (2017). Where Suvin takes a formalist approach (albeit one heavily informed by Marxist analysis), and Delany takes an interpretive approach, while Chu adds a lyrical and epistemological one, then Rieder builds on these through a primarily historicist focus. He sees SF as one among many different literary and cultural forms that arose with a transformation of the larger cultural market, which brought with it a redefinition of the very concept of genre:

> science fiction and the other genres usually associated with so-called genre fiction, such as the detective story, the modern romance, the western, horror, and fantasy, collectively compose a system of genres distinct from the preexisting classical and academic genre system that includes the epic, tragedy, comedy, satire, romance, the lyric, and so on. (1)

This "newer genre system," he continues, "can be firmly associated with large-scale commercial production and distribution of narrative fiction in print, film, and broadcast media" (1). SF, then, becomes a "differentially articulated position in a historical and mutable field of genres" (16). In a manner closer to Delany than Suvin, Rieder understands SF as a "way of using texts," but importantly sees SF, and other genres, as also being constituted by "drawing relationships among" texts, rather than arguing that all SF texts share an "essence" or "single unifying characteristic" (16).

Rieder's approach allows us to understand SF and other genre fictions in ways the other definitions do not. For one, it refuses to draw a distinction between what "academics" and "regular readers" call SF, a distinction that has, I would say, always depended on a form of what sociologist Pierre Bourdieu would call "cultural capital," which reinforces class- or caste-based social divisions (those "constrictive old norms" Suvin critiques even as his work arguably reinforces some of them).

Second, but arising from this insight, is the recognition that "the genre of SF is the product of multiple communities of practice" (11). In other words, when the figure of "science fiction" enters into cultural discussion, it almost immediately begins to change as it gets adopted by different communities—communities of authors and practitioners of SF, as well as multiple communities of readers, fans, academics, and so on—leading to related but differing definitions of what SF can be, including definitions not covered here (SF as invoking a "sense of wonder" through technology the way Romantic poetry invokes a transcendent sublime through representations of nature, for example). Those communities debate and alter SF as it moves between them, intersects with other, similar forms (like the other "genre fictions") and other communities, and so on. Likewise, the proliferation of "sub-genres" of SF, from space opera, to cyberpunk, to alternate histories, and so on, echoes this idea of overlapping but distinct SF practices. For Rieder, such developments mean that "despite its multiplicity and complexity," the history of SF "has a shape" (161). Rieder points out that there are ways to periodize SF that permit one to see connections among texts of a particular era and place, for example, while still recognizing that there will be differences within those same periods based on authors' and readers' personal and larger social contexts.

This anthology arguably expresses some of this "shape" in ways discussed below. Rieder divides the history of English language SF into an "early period" leading up to the development of mass culture following the industrial revolution, a pulp magazine period that runs from the 1920s through to the 1970s, and a late period that is ongoing in which SF is "bifurcated" between "the mature SF subculture" (associated implicitly with literature and music) and "the franchise fictions and endless serializations" (similarly associated with film) (162–68). This is a convincing argument, especially when Rieder analyzes the centrality of Black authors, Indigenous authors, and authors of colour, as well as feminist approaches to recent SF—discussions to which I return below. His larger model allows, importantly, for alternate histories to be discovered, or nuance to be added to the history he posits.

HISTORIES OF SF AND THE STRUCTURES OF *THE BROADVIEW ANTHOLOGY OF SCIENCE FICTION*

We now come, then, to this anthology's approach to the histories of SF.[1] There are strong arguments for several different starting points for SF. Some critics trace the origins of SF through utopian literature back to the work that gives the tradition its name, Thomas More's political satire *Utopia* (1516). It is, in fact, difficult not to see the traditions of SF and utopia as intertwined; this is a central point behind one of the major statements on SF and political theory, Fredric Jameson's *Archaeologies of the Future: The Desire Called Utopia and Other Science Fictions* (2005), where he argues, in part, that utopian desires are fundamentally—if complexly—related to social transformation (for good and ill). More's work details life on a fictional island called Utopia, a name he derives from the Greek *ou-topos*, for "no place," though it is also related to *eu-topos*, for "good place." *Utopia* thus engages in a form of estranging world-building, of the sort Suvin discusses, to extrapolate a vision of the world different from the one More lived in. More's text was published in what is known as the early modern period, but which has also been called the "Renaissance," traditionally seen as period when religious and spiritual world views were being supplanted by humanist and scientific ones, a debate arguably expressed in his work. So,

1 For extended versions of some of the discussions in this section, reframed specifically in terms of SF's relation to US politics, see my chapter "Science Fiction" in the *Cambridge Companion to the Twentieth-Century American Novel and Politics*, edited by Bryan M. Santin (2023).

depending on how one uses or defines SF, one could easily start a history of SF at this point.

There is another reason for starting a history of SF in the early modern period, and that is the very concepts of exploration and of contact between groups of people previously unknown to each other. This period is, in other words, the age of the advent of contemporary colonialism. In an earlier work, Rieder situates SF primarily as a literature of colonialism.[1] The concept of "first contact," so central to much of space-exploration SF, is also an element of imperial and colonial activity, after all. Likewise, Shakespeare's *The Tempest*, first performed in 1611, with its themes of colonialism, magic, and philosophy, articulates a similar set of concerns, and inspired several later SF works, including the film *Forbidden Planet* (1956). Moving further ahead in time, but still fully encapsulated in this colonial moment, a strong case can be made for reading Irish satirist Jonathan Swift's *Gulliver's Travels* (1726) as a primary origin for modern SF. Detailing its often bumbling hero's travels to "strange new worlds" where he finds "new life and new civilizations," to quote *Star Trek*, this satire serves not only to estrange but to offer trenchant critiques of eighteenth-century British society. The very first story in this collection, Washington Irving's satirical "The Men of the Moon" from his *History of New York* (1809), takes a similar approach, arguably critiquing the colonial oppression of Indigenous peoples in what is now called North America, while later Indigenous Futurist authors, including Drew Hayden Taylor and Richard Van Camp, articulate decolonizing and Indigenous approaches that challenge this colonial mindset.

Many other starting points for SF have been proposed. Adam Roberts traces various SF-like themes back to what he calls the Ancient Greek novel, discussing, for example, Plutarch's *On the Face Apparent in the Circle of the Moon* (c. 80 CE). There are similarities between contemporary SF and the Romance quests of medieval England, as well. After all, replace horses with spaceships, and dragons with aliens, and you basically have space opera. Perhaps, as Paul Kincaid writes, because there are so many possible origins, maybe "There is no starting point for science fiction" (409).

All these possible sources, though, point to the need for careful students and readers of science fiction to be open to finding echoes of multiple traditions, literary and cultural influences, and allusions and intertextualities in any given piece of science fiction. As SF critics Sherryl Vint and Mark Bould write, we need to "draw attention to the complexity of texts and the meanings they are able to sustain" (51). In other words, SF opens our worlds to contact with many others.

The current anthology—alas!—can't include everything. *The Broadview Anthology of Science Fiction* restricts its "communities of practice" to English-language works, with the majority of those being from North America and the UK, though it also turns, for example, to the Caribbean, the Indian

1 John Rieder, *Colonialism and the Emergence of Science Fiction* (2008).

subcontinent, and Uganda; more generally, authors from a variety of cultural and social backgrounds are included, thus emphasizing a wide range of SF in ways I'll discuss below.

Like many of the critics cited here, our *Anthology* also chooses the nineteenth century as its starting point. Despite the longer histories gestured to above, there are several good reasons for starting the anthology at this point. In addition to Irving's piece discussed above, the opening section of the anthology includes authors commonly associated with the "origin" of SF: Mary Wollstonecraft Shelley, whose *Frankenstein* (1818) is often seen to inaugurate the genre;[1] Edgar Allan Poe, whose influence on US, British, and French SF is well documented; and H.G. Wells, whose "scientific romances," inspired directly by Shelley, set many of the plots and devices of much of later SF. It would be wrong, however, to limit these precursors to SF to a handful of well-known works. Other texts also used non-realist modes, as well as devices like the novum and estrangement, to generate new worlds in ways that would help to shape, or find echoes in, later works. While the many book-length nineteenth-century utopias are not included here, still we see echoes of their forms—from feminist utopias, including Mary E. Bradley Lane's *Mizora: A Prophecy* (1880), to such socialist utopias as Edward Bellamy's *Looking Backward: 2000–1887* (1888)—in later sections. Included in the anthology, however, is early Black speculation, in the form of Charles Chesnutt's "Mars Jeems's Nightmare," which centres on changing someone's race, a device that would be expanded significantly in George Schuyler's satirical SF novel *Black No More* (1931). SF builds itself on multiple foundations, as we will continue to see.

From these nineteenth-century foundations, the anthology is divided into several subsequent periods that mark pronounced shifts in SF production, its forms, and the contexts within which the authors were writing and to which they respond. The second section turns to the early decades of the twentieth century, both a transitional and foundational period in the advent of modern SF. It's a transitional period because general literary pulp magazines of the time—notable among them *The Argosy* and *The All-Story*, both published by Frank Munsey—also publish recognizable "genre" fictions, from romance to detective fiction to fantasy and SF, including titles that are still known today (Edgar Rice Burroughs's *Tarzan of the Apes* first appeared in *All-Story* in 1912, for example). Other magazines, arising from specific communities, were also publishing such works: E.M. Forster published his modernist SF masterpiece "The Machine Stops" in *The Oxford and Cambridge Review*, published by students of those universities, while women's rights activist and Bengali political leader Rokeya Sakhawat Hossain published her feminist utopia "Sultana's Dream" in *The Indian Ladies' Magazine*. SF and its genre relations were being formed across the gamut of magazines in this time.

1 SF author Brian Aldiss makes a well-known case for *Frankenstein* as an origin of SF in his *Billion Year Spree: The History of Science Fiction* (1973).

It's perhaps not surprising, then, that SF becomes professionalized in this period. Variations on the term "science fiction" are solidified as the name for a genre, and SF and other genre fictions also begin to be published in widely distributed and popular magazines specifically dedicated to them.

The most important of these to the history of English-language SF is Hugo Gernsback's *Amazing Stories*, the first issue of which was published in 1926. In his introduction to that issue, Gernsback differentiates his magazine from the more general literary magazines by noting its focus is on a "new" genre, "scientifiction," even as he explicitly connects it to earlier work by such authors as Poe and Wells (both included in section 1), as well as French author Jules Verne:

> a magazine of "Scientifiction" is a pioneer in its field in America. [...] Two hundred years ago, stories of this kind were not possible. Science, through its various branches of mechanics, electricity, astronomy, etc., enters so intimately into all our lives today, and we are so much immersed in this science, that we have become rather prone to take new inventions and discoveries for granted. [...] For the best of these modern writers of scientifiction have the knack of imparting knowledge, and even inspiration, without once making us aware that we are being taught. And not only that! Poe, Verne, Wells, Bellamy, and many others have proved themselves real prophets. (Gernsback, "A New Sort of Magazine," 3)

Already present in this description are Suvin's "novum" and "cognitive estrangement," with the "new inventions" that radically reshape our lives. The works that populated Gernsback's and other pulp magazines in this period would shape the form of SF for decades to come, even to today.[1]

As with the years preceding *Amazing Stories*, however, SF continued to be published beyond the professional pulps, and through those works we get a glimpse of the wider aesthetic and political possibilities of SF. For example, early versions of what would later be called Afrofuturism, SF that centres Black perspectives, appear in the same period: Pauline Hopkins's novel, *Of One Blood*, serialized in *The Coloured American Magazine* (1902–03); "The Comet," by American civil rights leader, sociologist, and philosopher W.E.B. Du Bois, published in 1920 and included here; the recently recovered space-operas of Black author John P. Moore originally published in African American newspapers starting in 1930;[2] and Schuyler's *Black No More*. All of these and other worlds serve to explicitly critique the dominant discourses

1 For a detailed historical overview of the SF pulps of this period, and Gernsback's own successes and failures as an editor, see Brooks Landon.

2 A book version of these stories, with commentaries by many major SF scholars, is, as of this writing, forthcoming as *The Martian Trilogy: John P. Moore, Amazing Stories, Black Science Fiction, and The Illustrated Feature Section* (Amazing Stories, LLC, scheduled for release in 2025).

of white supremacy in America even as they implicitly challenge the narrow confines of Gernsbackian SF.

From this early pulp period, the anthology moves to the middle decades of the twentieth century. The third section encapsulates the so-called "Golden Age" of pulp SF, often associated in histories of English-language SF with John W. Campbell's editorship, starting in 1937, of *Astounding Stories* (the Golden Age's end date is more variable, but it's generally agreed to have melted by 1960). These two decades also provide a snapshot of the rise of US political and cultural dominance globally, as the end of the Great Depression and World War II give way to a US economic and cultural ascendancy, even as the world found itself embroiled in the early decades of the Cold War between the US and the USSR. In the early years of this period, we find some of the authors whose names are still instantly identifiable with SF: Isaac Asimov, Arthur C. Clarke, and Robert A. Heinlein first and foremost (collectively often referred to as "The Big Three"), as well as Ray Bradbury. Also present here are those authors equally famous within the field but perhaps less so outside of it: C.L. Moore and Henry Kuttner, Theodore Sturgeon, and Judith Merril, for example, the last of whom, through her editing, reviewing, fandom work, and the later founding of the Merril Collection of Science Fiction in Toronto, arguably has as much or more to do with the shape of contemporary SF than Campbell.

Beyond the pulp canon of the "Golden Age," however, equally important to the rise of SF are those who, again, published outside of the professional SF pulps, including prolific and widely read Black SF artists. Included here, possibly for the first time since its initial publication, is James H. Hill's "The Space Ship," initially published in the newspaper *The Afro-American*. Hill's truly monumental body of work was only recently recovered by scholar Brooks E. Hefner and discussed in his study, *Black Pulp: Genre Fiction in the Shadow of Jim Crow* (2021). Likewise, poetry by jazz musician, and oft-cited innovator of Afrofuturism, Sun Ra is included in this section, work that points to both the critical and liberatory function Afrofuturism and SF can serve.

The fourth section of this anthology, "Revolutions and New Waves: 1960–1980s," begins the focus on what we can call contemporary SF. Still dominated by the pulps, these two decades arguably signal the decline of the classic form of Gernsbackian SF that reached its apotheosis in the Golden Age. The central group of texts in this period are generally referred to as "The New Wave," most often associated with Michael Moorcock's period as editor of the British magazine *New Worlds*, starting in 1964. Characterized by formal experimentation in the vein of other (post)modernist texts, New Wave works also tend to emphasize psychological and character analysis, elements somewhat missing from the classic pulp formulas; author J.G. Ballard is often cited as the originator of the claim that such works move from outer space to "inner space," in his 1962 article in *New Worlds* "Which Way to Inner Space?" Equally important to this period is an expansion of the always present feminist approaches to SF, but which now become even more central to the form, even as many of the authors—such as Joanna Russ and Ursula K. Le Guin—revive and transform the earlier feminist utopian tradition. Delany's queer Afrofuturist and modernist aesthetic also helps to radically transform the genre. The ways in which such works differ from earlier forms cannot be exaggerated, but they can perhaps be framed by the literature itself, as William Gibson does in "The Gernsback Continuum."

The fifth and sixth sections—"The Digital Age and Its Discontents: 1980s–2000s" and "The Multiple Futures of Contemporary SF: 2000s–present"—conclude the anthology with what could be called the expansion and multiplication of SF perspectives. The fifth section covers a period that sees the rise of the digital revolution and the expansion of interconnected technologies across the planet, which are also directly tied to economic globalization as the USSR falls and the Cold War ends. With these developments, the discourse of SF also becomes the language of the age. US President Ronald Reagan deploys the Strategic Defense Initiative in orbit, which was nicknamed "Star Wars" after the 1977 film; the rise of interconnected computer technologies spawns a need for new ways of discussing that realm of interaction, which becomes "cyberspace," a term William Gibson coined in his novel *Neuromancer* to describe an interconnected virtual reality. Famously written on a manual typewriter, this work popularized a new subgenre of SF, coined "cyberpunk." At the end of the section, we see these themes updated for the turn of the millennium and to further the Afrofuturist tradition in Nalo Hopkinson's and N.K. Jemisin's stories, while legal scholar and Critical Race theorist Derrick Bell expands the use of SF for anti-racist arguments in "The Space Traders," building on the somewhat pessimistic ending of Du Bois's "The Comet." Thus, while cyberpunk aesthetics and digital landscapes appear throughout this section, we also begin to see how the field of SF is multiplying beyond the attempts to too easily define or constrain its experiments. While it might be tempting to say that the New Wave gave way to surfing the web, it may be more accurate to say it ushered in a tide of multiple voices.

The final section shows how the contemporary field of SF is expanding beyond any attempt to contain it. As the twentieth century ended and a new millennium began—not without its own dystopian fears—the twenty-first century has seen Black authors, and specifically Black women authors, Indigenous authors, Latinx authors, and other racialized and minoritized authors become more central to the field of SF, a collective development recently referred to as "CoFuturisms," to which I return below. While, as some texts in early sections of this anthology show, such voices have never been absent from the field, their visibility has been overshadowed by a largely white set of authors, editors, and publishers. Much work has been done in recent decades and years, however, to resurrect other genealogies of SF. Central to the efforts to recover and expand these currents has been a series of anthologies: Sheree R. Thomas's *Dark Matter* anthologies (2000 and 2004); Andrea L. Bell and Yolanda Molina-Gavilán's *Cosmos Latinos: An Anthology of Science Fiction from Latin America and Spain* (2003); Nalo Hopkinson and Uppinder Mehan's *So Long Been Dreaming: Postcolonial Science Fiction* (2004); Grace Dillon's *Walking the Clouds: An Anthology of Indigenous Science Fiction* (2012); Nisi Shawl's *New Suns: Original Speculative Fiction by People of Color* (2019); Mary Ellis Gibson's *Science Fiction in Colonial India, 1835–1905* (2019); *Latinx Rising: An Anthology of Latinx Science Fiction and Fantasy*, edited by Matthew David Goodwin (2020); Sonia Sulaiman's *Thyme Travellers: An Anthology of Palestinian Speculative Fiction* (2024); and many others. Likewise, Hopkinson, Jemisin, Ken Liu, Nnedi Okorafor, and Richard Van Camp, among many other Black and Indigenous writers and writers of colour, have seen their works rightly feted within and beyond SF circles in the past two decades of the twenty-first century. This expansion has not come without those "constrictive old norms," in Suvin's terms, trying to enforce their rigid and artificial boundaries, including within certain fandom circles,[1] but while SF has always had conservative forces ensconced in its gravity well, the form has a tendency to leave them in its wake, as the ever-widening field of its vision attests.

Afrofuturism is a primary example whose presence allows for an entirely different genealogy for twentieth-century SF, one that we can read back through as a history that influenced all of the SF that grew alongside it and that came later. But even here, some traditions risk being overwritten by others. Author Nnedi Okorafor, for example, coined the term africanfuturism[2] as a distinct speculative tradition centred in African nations and peoples, and has repeatedly clarified that this tradition is separate from that of Afrofuturism, which is centred in North America. Likewise, there have of course been long traditions outside of English-language and Eurocentric SF, but even within English SF there are other histories through which we can refocus our understandings of SF. One can look to the long history of both feminist and queer SF—whether focussing on authors, themes, or both: questioning the heterosexist world order has its own genealogy, from at least Mary Wollstonecraft Shelley forward, including Francis Stevens's early twentieth-century matriarchal and arguably queer ecologies, of course Delany's work, Theodore Sturgeon's "The World Well Lost," and many others. Again, other specific anthologies are important here. These include such early collections as *Women of Wonder: Science-fiction Stories by Women about Women*, edited by SF author Pamela Sargent (1975), which inaugurated a series; Lisa Yaszek's recent *The Future Is Female!* anthologies from the Library of America (2018 and 2022); *Worlds Apart: An Anthology of Lesbian and Gay Science Fiction and Fantasy*, edited by Camilla Decarnin, Eric Garber, and Lyn Paleo (1986); and the *Bending the Landscape* series, including

1 In science fiction fandom, reactionary voices reached public notice around a 2015 attempt to derail the Hugo awards. See David M. Higgins, *Reverse Colonization: Science Fiction, Imperial Fantasy, and Alt-Victimhood* (4–10).

2 Okorafor writes the term with a lower-case "a" except at the beginning of sentences or in titles: "Like the terms 'science fiction' and 'fantasy,' africanfuturism is a neutral word, therefore it is not capitalized" ("Africanfuturism").

a science fiction installment, edited by noted SF author Nicola Griffith and Stephen Pagel (1998). More recently, anthologies have expanded both their scope and focus with LGBTQ+ authors, including the multiple volumes of *Transcendent: The Year's Best Transgender Speculative Fiction* series, edited first by K.M. Sparza and then Bogi Takács (2016–19), and many more. If SF is a field defined in multifaceted ways by communities of readers and practitioners, then several genealogies must—and do—exist from its multiple beginnings forward.

The same can be said for the forms of SF. This anthology focusses primarily on short fiction—a singularly important form throughout the history of SF, though it began to be supplanted by the novel and then film as the twentieth century wore on. But prose fiction is also just one form among many. Others include SF poetry, commonly referred to in SF communities as "speculative poetry," and the related form of SF music. As Chu writes, "Poems are absent [...] from the majority of SF anthologies," and of those that do include them, most "are dedicated exclusively to SF verse" (12). And yet, as Chu argues, both lyrical poetry and SF are "frequently soliloquy-like," both "speak from beyond ordinary time," "are inhabited by situations and tableaux transcending ordinary temporality," "are charged with depictive intensity," are "musically expressive," and both "evoke heightened and eccentric states of consciousness" (14).

In addition to Chu's evocative analyses, though, several poets, lyricists, and musicians *explicitly* engage with SF discourse. Sun Ra is only one of dozens or more well-known artists from the middle of the twentieth century who presented a futurist aesthetic, persona, and performance, helping to form the tradition of Afrofuturist music. Ra inspired George Clinton and Parliament Funkadelic, for example, and Jimi Hendrix often explored a similar form of psychedelic world-building. Janelle Monáe has become a more recent transformative figure of Afrofuturism. Beyond the Afrofuturist tradition, David Bowie, especially in his Ziggy Stardust period, fully embraced and transformed popular SF. While only a few musicians are included here, there is an even longer tradition of speculative lyric that the anthology includes throughout the various historical periods covered. In some cases, these poetic voices include those who analyze dominant discourses of science and technology from perspectives often left out of such discussions (I think here especially of Gil Scott-Heron's spoken word poetry and music, as well as Canisia Lubrin's "Voodoo Hypothesis"). Visual art and cinema are, of course, also central; while difficult to reflect in a print text, the anthology also includes some images to reflect the wider SF media landscape at different points in time.

PRINCIPLES OF SELECTION AND STRUCTURE

The discussion of the multiple histories of SF brings me to the principles used to construct and organize this anthology. The first thing to note is that the anthology includes only complete stories and poems; with two (arguable) exceptions, no excerpts are used.[1] As noted above, short fiction *is* singularly important to SF. As importantly, though, focussing solely on complete works allows the anthology to cover more ground, so to speak, while still giving instructors and readers the freedom to supplement with longer works or novels (without the possible duplication of excerpts). Each selection includes a brief note on the text, but in general first publications have been preferred as the copy-texts, unless noted otherwise. Only obvious typos have been corrected, and where there is some doubt, notes have been added, along with the other explanatory matter.

With these principles in mind, the anthology is structured first following the historical outline above, for reasons that are made clear there. Within each section, though, and for the anthology overall, the primary goal is to provide if not a fully comprehensive group of texts (an impossible task), then one that is useful in both breadth and depth. Such a goal involves a difficult representational balancing act between providing well-known—and often taught—selections from each period, and providing instructors and students alike with a range of voices generally less well represented in comprehensive teaching anthologies, be it in terms of racialized or otherwise structurally marginalized authors, or those publishing outside of the major SF publishing venues, or those writing in forms like poetry, not often included in the discussion. I acknowledge there is a risk of tokenism here, especially in some of the earlier periods, but I have attempted to mitigate this by representing certain subfields not (or not only) through those authors most associated with them, but through those who represent the fields while also bringing more to the topic. For example, rather than turn to Gibson's or Neal Stephenson's cyberpunk stories, this anthology chooses to centre Pat Cadigan's "Angel" and Candas Jane Dorsey's "(Learning about) Machine Sex."

The multiple tables of contents are another way in which the anthology addresses the various histories and forms of SF, especially through the "Multiple Histories, Multiple Futures" table of contents. This approach to the anthology echoes recent developments in "CoFuturisms," a term used by the editors of *The Routledge Handbook of CoFuturisms* (2024), and the affiliated international CoFUTURES group. In Taryne Jade Taylor's words, CoFuturisms

> knits together work being done on the various forms of futurisms by people of color and Global South Futurisms, such as Afrofuturisms, Indigenous Futurisms, Latinx Futurisms, Asian Futurisms, and Gulf/Middle Eastern Futurisms. [...] CoFuturisms are more than simply subgenres of science fiction; they are also movements that offer us paths to internal and external colonization, modes that remind us that we belong in the future and of the importance of recovering our often suppressed

1 The Buck Rogers comics are necessarily excerpts from a longer weekly strip, but are included here as an early, massively influential though equally problematic, example of visual storytelling and SF art. Washington Irving's piece *is* an excerpt from the *History of New York*, but it is fully self-contained.

> pasts, aesthetics that coalesce these visions under a single, diverse umbrella, and also represent growing subgenres of science fiction. (1)

While the current anthology does not provide the comprehensive analysis of each tradition, as do the authors in that volume or the specific anthologies discussed above, it is hoped that the current text can be a starting point for readers' more in-depth journey into these multiple genealogies. The other thematic groupings offered also allow one to read this anthology through multiple authors' approach to SF devices that have proven especially enduring. Readers are encouraged to create their own maps through the anthology (and to let the editor know of them for possible later editions of the work!).

Lastly, the most challenging part of any anthology is not what to include, but what must be left out. In some cases, these decisions were extensions of the initial one to only include complete works combined with length restrictions—many of the early pulp texts by authors I had initially intended to add were simply too long to include, and would have led to even more drastic cuts elsewhere. In other cases, they were dictated by the permissions and rights process, which can be complicated in our current publishing environment, while some authors or estates only rarely give such permissions. Some of these unavoidable gaps—including such major authors as Heinlein and Okorafor—may be addressed by novels added to supplement the readings here.

AND NOW, TO OTHER WORLDS!

It's time to turn to the actual works in this anthology, but by way of conclusion let me continue to stress the need to never, finally, conclude. As Rieder writes, the complex history of SF and its many relations may not offer us any *single* definition of the genre, or any single canon of best works, but it does offer a *shape* to that larger field. In this view of SF, each text or set of texts is simply an individual moving part on a multi-dimensional clockwork mechanism, with an infinite series of various gears called "subgenres," "histories," "locations," "themes," "authors," "identities," and more, all of which constantly move and affect each other's movements in turn. SF is thus perhaps best defined as the set of transmogrifying toys in the story "Mimsy Were the Borogoves" by C.L. Moore and Henry Kuttner (writing under the pseudonym Lewis Padgett), included in this anthology. At once entertaining and educational to some readers, incomprehensible and (literally) shocking to others, and providing forms of escape to new worlds that might be radically different from ours, in some ways, and reassuringly (or painfully) the same in others, these toys, and the stories offered in this anthology, are still undeniably "like something out of science fiction." Hopefully, the anthology will give you a *broad view* of the many possible worlds offered by science fiction.

FOUNDATIONS OF SF I:
THE NINETEENTH CENTURY

Washington Irving (1783–1859)

Hailed as the first US-born literary celebrity, Irving was born just as the American Revolution came to an end and was named "Washington" after revolutionary general and first US president George Washington. He is best known for his series of satirical and fantastic stories, published in multiple volumes as *The Sketch Book of Geoffrey Crayon, Gent.* (1819–20), which include the still-popular stories "Rip Van Winkle" and "The Legend of Sleepy Hollow." *History of New York*, an earlier publication, satirizes academic histories of America and, in the chapter below, the racist and colonial logic of its "discovery."

Note on the text: The text here reproduces that of the first edition of *History of New York*, Vol. I, Book I, Chapter V (Innskeep and Bradford, 1809).

[The Men of the Moon] (1809)

from *History of New York*

In which the Author puts a mighty Question to the rout, by the assistance of the Man in the Moon—which not only delivers thousands of people from great embarrassment, but likewise concludes this introductory book.

THE writer of a history may, in some respects, be likened unto an adventurous knight, who having undertaken a perilous enterprize, by way of establishing his fame, feels bound in honor and chivalry, to turn back for no difficulty nor hardship, and never to shrink or quail whatever enemy he may encounter. Under this impression, I resolutely draw my pen and fall to, with might and main, at those doughty questions and subtle paradoxes, which, like fiery dragons and bloody giants, beset the entrance to my history, and would fain repulse me from the very threshold. And at this moment a gigantic question has started up, which I must take by the beard and utterly subdue, before I can advance another step in my historick undertaking—but I trust this will be the last adversary I shall have to contend with, and that in the next book, I shall be enabled to conduct my readers in triumph into the body of my work.

The question which has thus suddenly arisen, is, what right had the first discoverers of America to land, and take possession of a country, without asking the consent of its inhabitants, or yielding them an adequate compensation for their territory?

My readers shall now see with astonishment, how easily I will vanquish this gigantic doubt, which has so long been the terror of adventurous writers; which has withstood so many fierce assaults, and has given such great distress of mind to multitudes of kind-hearted folks. For, until this mighty question is totally put to rest, the worthy people of America can by no means enjoy the soil they inhabit, with clear right and title, and quiet, unsullied consciences.

The first source of right, by which property is acquired in a country, is DISCOVERY. For as all mankind have an equal right to any thing, which has never before been appropriated, so any nation, that discovers an uninhabited country, and takes possession thereof, is considered as enjoying full property, and absolute, unquestionable empire therein.[1]

This proposition being admitted, it follows clearly, that the Europeans who first visited America, were the real discoverers of the same; nothing being necessary to the establishment of this fact, but simply to prove that it was totally uninhabited by man. This would at first appear to be a point of some difficulty, for it is well known, that this quarter of the world abounded with certain animals, that walked erect on two feet, had something of the human countenance, uttered certain unintelligible sounds, very much like language, in short, had a marvelous resemblance to human beings. But the host of zealous and enlightened fathers, who accompanied the discoverers, for the purpose of promoting the kingdom of heaven, by establishing fat monasteries and bishopricks on earth, soon cleared up this point, greatly to the satisfaction of his holiness the pope, and of all Christian voyagers and discoverers.[2]

They plainly proved, and as there were no Indian writers arose on the other side, the fact was considered as fully admitted and established, that the two legged race of animals before mentioned, were mere cannibals, detestable monsters, and many of them giants—a description of vagrants, that, since the times of Gog, Magog, and Goliath,[3] have been considered as outlaws, and have received no quarter[4] in either history, chivalry or song; indeed, even the philosopher Bacon,[5] declared the Americans to be people proscribed by the laws of nature, inasmuch as they had a barbarous custom of sacrificing men, and feeding upon man's flesh.

Nor are these all the proofs of their utter barbarism: among many other writers of discernment, the celebrated Ulloa tells us "their imbecility is so

---

1 Grotius. Puffendorf, b. 4. c. 4. Vattel, b. 1. c. 18. et alii. (Irving's note); Grotius: Hugo Grotius (1583–1645), Dutch philosopher and author. Puffendorf: likely Samuel von Pufendorf (1632–94), German political philosopher who interpreted notions of natural law as defined by, for example, Grotius. Vattel: Emer de Vattel (1714–67), Prussian lawyer specializing in international law.

2 Irving here describes the so-called "Doctrine of Discovery," as defined by several papal bulls starting in 1452, which declared the New World "empty" of people because Indigenous inhabitants were not Christian. These bulls were later rescinded, but their larger use to justify colonization continued. The Vatican did not formally repudiate the Doctrine until 2023.

3 All Biblical figures. Gog and Magog figure in the Revelation of John as allies of Satan during the prophesised apocalypse (20.7–10). Goliath is described in Samuel as a Philistine giant who, during a battle with the Israelites, is killed by a young David, who goes on to become King of Israel.

4 Received no mercy.

5 Francis Bacon (1561–1626), English politician and philosopher; this particular discussion of cannibalism does not appear to be Bacon's, and is most likely part of Irving's satire of such histories as Bacon's *Sylva Sylvarum, or A Natural History in Ten Centuries* (1623).

visible, that one can hardly form an idea of them different from what one has of the brutes. Nothing disturbs the tranquillity of their souls, equally insensible to disasters, and to prosperity. Though half naked, they are as contented as a monarch in his most splendid array. Fear makes no impression on them, and respect as little."[1]—All this is furthermore supported by the authority of M. Bouguer.[2] "It is not easy," says he, "to describe the degree of their indifference for wealth and all its advantages. One does not well know what motives to propose to them when one would persuade them to any service. It is vain to offer them money, they answer that they are not hungry." And Vanegas[3] confirms the whole, assuring us that "ambition, they have none, and are more desirous of being thought strong, than valiant. The objects of ambition with us, honour, fame, reputation, riches, posts and distinctions are unknown among them. So that this powerful spring of action, the cause of so much *seeming* good and *real* evil in the world has no power over them. In a word, these unhappy mortals may be compared to children, in whom the development of reason is not completed."

Now all these peculiarities, though in the unenlightened states of Greece, they would have entitled their possessors to immortal honour, as having reduced to practice those rigid and abstemious maxims, the mere talking about which, acquired certain old Greeks the reputation of sages and philosophers;—yet were they clearly proved in the present instance, to betoken a most abject and brutified nature, totally beneath the human character. But the benevolent fathers, who had undertaken to turn these unhappy savages into dumb beasts, by dint of argument, advanced still stronger proofs; for as certain divines of the sixteenth century, and among the rest Lullus[4] affirm—the Americans go naked, and have no beards!—"They have nothing," says Lullus, "of the reasonable animal, except the mask."—And even that mask was allowed to avail them but little, for it was soon found that they were of a hideous copper complexion—and being of a copper complexion, it was all the same as if they were negroes—and negroes are black, "and black" said the pious fathers, devoutly crossing themselves, "is the color of the Devil!" Therefore so far from being able to own property, they had no right even to personal freedom, for liberty is too radiant a deity, to inhabit such gloomy temples. All which circumstances plainly convinced the righteous followers of Cortes and Pizarro,[5] that these miscreants had no title to the soil that they infested—that they were a perverse,

1 Antonio de Ulloa (1716–95), Spanish scientist and explorer, and governor of Louisiana. This and several of the following references are adapted by Irving from William Robertson's 1777 *History of America* (see, e.g., Scraba, "Quixotic History").

2 Pierre Bouguer (1698–1758), French scientist.

3 Miguel Venegas (1680–1764), Jesuit geographer and ethnographer, born in Puebla while it was under Spanish control.

4 Lullus appears to be Irving's invention, perhaps referencing Ramon Llull (1232–1315/16) as a means of satirizing the reliability of the academic sourcing he is engaged in here.

5 Hernán Cortés (1485–1547) and Francisco Pizarro (1475–1541), Spanish colonizers of the Americas.

illiterate, dumb, beardless, bare-bottomed *black-seed*—mere wild beasts of the forests, and like them should either be subdued or exterminated.

From the foregoing arguments therefore, and a host of others equally conclusive, which I forbear to enumerate, it was clearly evident, that this fair quarter of the globe when first visited by Europeans, was a howling wilderness, inhabited by nothing but wild beasts; and that the trans-atlantic visitors acquired an incontrovertible property therein, by the *right of Discovery*.

This right being fully established, we now come to the next, which is the right acquired by *cultivation*. "The cultivation of the soil" we are told

> is an obligation imposed by nature on mankind. The whole world is appointed for the nourishment of its inhabitants; but it would be incapable of doing it, was it uncultivated. Every nation is then obliged by the law of nature to cultivate the ground that has fallen to its share. Those people, like the ancient Germans and modern Tartars, who having fertile countries, disdain to cultivate the earth, and choose to live by rapine, are wanting to themselves, and *deserve to be exterminated as savage and pernicious beasts*.[1]

Now it is notorious, that the savages knew nothing of agriculture, when first discovered by the Europeans, but lived a most vagabond, disorderly, unrighteous life,—rambling from place to place, and prodigally rioting upon the spontaneous luxuries of nature, without tasking her generosity to yield them any thing more; whereas it has been most unquestionably shewn, that heaven intended the earth should be ploughed and sown, and manured, and laid out into cities and towns and farms, and country seats, and pleasure grounds, and public gardens, all which the Indians knew nothing about—therefore they did not improve the talents providence had bestowed on them—therefore they were careless stewards—therefore they had no right to the soil—therefore they deserved to be exterminated.

It is true the savages might plead that they drew all the benefits from the land which their simple wants required—they found plenty of game to hunt, which together with the roots and uncultivated fruits of the earth, furnished a sufficient variety for their frugal table;—and that as heaven merely designed the earth to form the abode, and satisfy the wants of man; so long as those purposes were answered, the will of heaven was accomplished.—But this only proves how undeserving they were of the blessings around them—they were so much the more savages, for not having more wants; for knowledge is in some degree an increase of desires, and it is this superiority both in the number and magnitude of his desires, that distinguishes the man from the beast. Therefore the Indians, in not having more wants, were very unreasonable animals; and it was but just that they should make way for the Europeans, who had a thousand wants to their one, and therefore would turn the earth to more

1 Vattel—B.i, ch. 17. See likewise Grotius, Puffendorf, et alii. (Irving's note)

account, and by cultivating it, more truly fulfil the will of heaven. Besides—Grotius and Lauterbach, and Puffendorf and Titius[1] and a host of wise men besides, who have considered the matter properly, have determined, that the property of a country cannot be acquired by hunting, cutting wood, or drawing water in it—nothing but precise demarcation of limits, and the intention of cultivation, can establish the possession. Now as the savages (probably from never having read the authors above quoted) had never complied with any of these necessary forms, it plainly follows that they had no right to the soil, but that it was completely at the disposal of the first comers, who had more knowledge and more wants than themselves—who would portion out the soil, with churlish boundaries; who would torture nature to pamper a thousand fantastic humours and capricious appetites; and who of course were far more rational animals than themselves. In entering upon a newly discovered, uncultivated country therefore, the new comers were but taking possession of what, according to the aforesaid doctrine, was their own property—therefore in opposing them, the savages were invading their just rights, infringing the immutable laws of nature and counteracting the will of heaven—therefore they were guilty of impiety, burglary and trespass on the case,—therefore they were hardened offenders against God and man—therefore they ought to be exterminated.

But a more irresistible right than either that I have mentioned, and one which will be the most readily admitted by my reader, provided he is blessed with bowels of charity and philanthropy, is the right acquired by civilization. All the world knows the lamentable state in which these poor savages were found. Not only deficient in the comforts of life, but what is still worse, most piteously and unfortunately blind to the miseries of their situation. But no sooner did the benevolent inhabitants of Europe behold their sad condition than they immediately went to work to ameliorate and improve it. They introduced among them the comforts of life, consisting of rum, gin and brandy—and it is astonishing to read how soon the poor savages learnt to estimate these blessings—they likewise made known to them a thousand remedies, by which the most inveterate diseases are alleviated and healed, and that they might comprehend the benefits and enjoy the comforts of these medicines, they previously introduced among them the diseases, which they were calculated to cure. By these and a variety of other methods was the condition of these poor savages, wonderfully improved; they acquired a thousand wants, of which they had before been ignorant, and as he has most sources of happiness, who has most wants to be gratified, they were doubtlessly rendered a much happier race of beings.

But the most important branch of civilization, and which has most strenuously been extolled, by the zealous and pious fathers of the Roman Church,

1 On Grotius and Puffendorf, see Irving's first note, above. It is unclear who, if anyone, Irving is referring to by Lauterbach and Titius, given the specific context of the passage.

is the introduction of the Christian faith. It was truly a sight that might well inspire horror, to behold these savages, stumbling among the dark mountains of paganism, and guilty of the most horrible ignorance of religion. It is true, they neither stole nor defrauded, they were sober, frugal, continent, and faithful to their word; but though they acted right habitually, it was all in vain, unless they acted so from precept. The new comers therefore used every method, to induce them to embrace and practice the true religion—except that of setting them the example.

But not withstanding all these complicated labours for their good, such was the unparalleled obstinacy of these stubborn wretches, that they ungratefully refused, to acknowledge the strangers as their benefactors, and persisted in disbelieving the doctrines they endeavoured to inculcate; most insolently alledging, that from their conduct, the advocates of Christianity did not seem to believe in it themselves. Was not this too much for human patience?—would not one suppose, that the foreign emigrants from Europe, provoked at their incredulity and discouraged by their stiff-necked obstinacy, would forever have abandoned their shores, and consigned them to their original ignorance and misery?—But no—so zealous were they to effect the temporal comfort and eternal salvation of these pagan infidels, that they even proceeded from the milder means of persuasion, to the more painful and troublesome one of persecution—Let loose among them, whole troops of fiery monks and furious blood-hounds—purified them by fire and sword, by stake and faggot; in consequence of which indefatigable measures, the cause of Christian love and charity were so rapidly advanced, that in a very few years, not one fifth of the number of unbelievers existed in South America, that were found there at the time of its discovery.

Nor did the other methods of civilization remain uninforced. The Indians improved daily and wonderfully by their intercourse with the whites. They took to drinking rum, and making bargains. They learned to cheat, to lie, to swear, to gamble, to quarrel, to cut each others throats, in short, to excel in all the accomplishments that had originally marked the superiority of their Christian visitors. And such a surprising aptitude have they shewn for these acquirements, that there is very little doubt that in a century more, provided they survive so long, the irrisistible effects of civilization; they will equal in knowledge, refinement, knavery, and debauchery, the most enlightened, civilized and orthodox nations of Europe.

What stronger right need the European settlers advance to the country than this. Have not whole nations of uninformed savages been made acquainted with a thousand imperious wants and indispensable comforts of which they were before wholly ignorant—Have they not been literally hunted and smoked out of the dens and lurking places of ignorance and infidelity, and absolutely scourged into the right path. Have not the temporal things, the vain baubles and filthy lucre of this world, which were too apt to engage their worldly and selfish thoughts, been benevolently taken from them; and have they not in lieu thereof, been taught to set their affections on things above—And finally, to use the words of a reverend Spanish father, in a letter to his superior in Spain—

> Can any one have the presumption to say, that these savage Pagans, have yielded any thing more than an inconsiderable recompense to their benefactors; in surrendering to them a little pitiful tract of this dirty sub-lunary planet, in exchange for a glorious inheritance in the kingdom of Heaven![1]

Here then are three complete and undeniable sources of right established, any one of which was more than ample to establish a property in the newly discovered regions of America. Now, so it has happened in certain parts of this delightful quarter of the globe, that the right of discovery has been so strenuously asserted—the influence of cultivation so industriously extended, and the progress of salvation and civilization so zealously prosecuted, that, what with their attendant wars, persecutions, oppressions, diseases, and other partial evils that often hang on the skirts of great benefits—the savage aborigines have, some how or another, been utterly annihilated—and this all at once brings me to a fourth right, which is worth all the others put together—For the original claimants to the soil being all dead and buried, and no one remaining to inherit or dispute the soil, the Spaniards as the next immediate occupants entered upon the possession, as clearly as the hang-man succeeds to the clothes of the malefactor—and as they have Blackstone,[2] and all the learned expounders of the law on their side, they may set all actions of ejectment at defiance—and this last right may be entitled, the RIGHT BY EXTERMINATION, or in other words, the RIGHT BY GUNPOWDER.

But lest any scruples of conscience should remain on this head, and to settle the question of right forever, his holiness Pope Alexander VI, issued one of those mighty bulls, which bear down reason, argument and every thing before them; by which he generously granted the newly discovered quarter of the globe, to the Spaniards and Portuguese; who, thus having law and gospel on their side, and being inflamed with great spiritual zeal, shewed the Pagan savages neither favour nor affection, but prosecuted the work of discovery, colonization, civilization, and extermination, with ten times more fury than ever.[3]

Thus were the European worthies who first discovered America, clearly entitled to the soil; and not only entitled to the soil, but likewise to the eternal thanks of these infidel savages, for having come so far, endured so many

1 No source has been identified for this passage, meaning it is likely part of Irving's larger satire on colonial sources.

2 Black. Com. B. II. c. i. (Irving's note); William Blackstone (1723–80), famed English jurist and politician, author of *Commentaries on the Laws of England* (1765).

3 Pope Alexander VI (1431–1503; in office 1492–1503). The bull is accurately described.

perils by sea and land, and taken such unwearied pains, for no other purpose under heaven but to improve their forlorn, uncivilized and heathenish condition—for having made them acquainted with the comforts of life, such as gin, rum, brandy, and the small-pox; for having introduced among them the light of religion, and finally—for having hurried them out of the world, to enjoy its reward!

But as argument is never so well understood by us selfish mortals, as when it comes home to ourselves, and as I am particularly anxious that this question should be put to rest forever, I will suppose a parallel case, by way of arousing the candid attention of my readers.

Let us suppose then, that the inhabitants of the moon, by astonishing advancement in science, and by a profound insight into that ineffable lunar philosophy, the mere flickerings of which, have of late years, dazzled the feeble optics, and addled the shallow brains of the good people of our globe—let us suppose, I say, that the inhabitants of the moon, by these means, had arrived at such a command of their *energies*, such an enviable state of *perfectability*, as to controul the elements, and navigate the boundless regions of space. Let us suppose a roving crew of these soaring philosophers, in the course of an aerial voyage of discovery among the stars, should chance to alight upon this outlandish planet.

And here I beg my readers will not have the impertinence to smile, as is too frequently the fault of volatile readers, when perusing the grave speculations of philosophers. I am far from indulging in any sportive vein at present, nor is the supposition I have been making so wild as many may deem it. It has long been a very serious and anxious question with me, and many a time, and oft, in the course of my overwhelming cares and contrivances for the welfare and protection of this my native planet, have I lain awake whole nights, debating in my mind whether it was most probable we should first discover and civilize the moon, or the moon discover and civilize our globe. Neither would the prodigy of sailing in the air and cruising among the stars be a whit more astonishing and incomprehensible to us, than was the European mystery of navigating floating castles, through the world of waters, to the simple savages. We have already discovered the art of coasting along the aerial shores of our planet, by means of balloons, as the savages had, of venturing along their sea coasts in canoes; and the disparity between the former, and the aerial vehicles of the philosophers from the moon, might not be greater, than that, between the bark canoes of the savages, and the mighty ships of their discoverers. I might here pursue an endless chain of very curious, profound and unprofitable speculations; but as they would be unimportant to my subject, I abandon them to my reader, particularly if he is a philosopher, as matters well worthy his attentive consideration.

To return then to my supposition—let us suppose that the aerial visitants I have mentioned, possessed of vastly superior knowledge to ourselves; that is to say, possessed of superior knowledge in the art of extermination—riding on Hypogriffs,[1] defended with impenetrable armour—armed with concentrated sun beams, and provided with vast engines, to hurl enormous moon stones: in short, let us suppose them, if our vanity will permit the supposition, as superior to us in knowledge, and consequently in power, as the Europeans were to the Indians, when they first discovered them. All this is very possible, it is only our self-sufficiency, that makes us think otherwise; and I warrant the poor savages, before they had any knowledge of the white men, armed in all the terrors of glittering steel and tremendous gun-powder, were as perfectly convinced that they themselves, were the wisest, the most virtuous, powerful and perfect of created beings, as are, at this present moment, the lordly inhabitants of old England, the volatile populace of France, or even the self-satisfied citizens of this most enlightened republick.

Let us suppose, moreover, that the aerial voyagers, finding this planet to be nothing but a howling wilderness, inhabited by us, poor savages and wild beasts, shall take formal possession of it, in the name of his most gracious and philosophic excellency, the man in the moon. Finding however, that their numbers are incompetent to hold it in complete subjection, on account of the ferocious barbarity of its inhabitants; they shall take our worthy President, the King of England, the Emperor of Hayti, the mighty little Bonaparte, and the great King of Bantam,[2] and returning to their native planet, shall carry them to court, as were the Indian chiefs led about as spectacles in the courts of Europe.[3]

Then making such obeisance as the etiquette of the court requires, they shall address the puissant man in the moon, in, as near as I can conjecture, the following terms:

"Most serene and mighty Potentate, whose dominions extend as far as eye can reach, who rideth on the Great Bear, useth the sun as a looking glass and maintaineth unrivaled controul over tides, madmen and sea-crabs. We thy liege subjects have just returned from a voyage of discovery, in the course of which we have landed and taken possession of that obscure little scurvy planet, which thou beholdest rolling at a distance. The five uncouth monsters, which we have brought into this august presence, were once very important chiefs among their fellow savages; for the inhabitants of the newly discovered globe are totally destitute of the common attributes of humanity, inasmuch as they

1 In Greek myth, hippogriffs are half-horse, half-eagle creatures.

2 Napoleon Bonaparte (1769–1821), French Emperor (1804–14); Jean-Jacques Dessalines (1758–1806) was the first Emperor of Haiti following Haiti's formerly enslaved population's successful revolution against France; the Sultan of Banten (also called Bantam) in 1808, Sultan Afiluddin, had a dispute with the colonial Dutch rulers, which led to the death of Dutch representative, Mr. Du Pui, which in turn led to significant Dutch military action and their effective abolition of the sultanate (see Dinar Boontharm's dissertation, *The Sultanate of Banten AD 1750–1808: A Social and Cultural History*).

3 There is a long and complex history of Indigenous people being taken to or otherwise going to Europe during the early colonial period. For a discussion, see, e.g., Caroline Dodds Pennock's *On Savage Shores* (2023).

carry their heads upon their shoulders, instead of under their arms—have two eyes instead of one—are utterly destitute of tails, and of a variety of unseemly complexions, particularly of a horrible whiteness—whereas all the inhabitants of the moon are pea green!

"We have moreover found these miserable savages sunk into a state of the utmost ignorance and depravity, every man shamelessly living with his own wife, and rearing his own children, instead of indulging in that community of wives, enjoined by the law of nature, as expounded by the philosophers of the moon. In a word they have scarcely a gleam of true philosophy among them, but are in fact, utter heretics, ignoramuses and barbarians. Taking compassion therefore on the sad condition of these sublunary wretches, we have endeavoured, while we remained on their planet, to introduce among them the light of reason—and the comforts of the moon.—We have treated them to mouthfuls of moonshine and draughts of nitrous oxide, which they swallowed with incredible voracity, particularly the females; and we have likewise endeavoured to instil into them the precepts of lunar Philosophy. We have insisted upon their renouncing the contemptible shackles of religion and common sense, and adoring the profound, omnipotent, and all perfect energy, and the extatic, immutable, immovable perfection. But such was the unparalleled obstinacy of these wretched savages, that they persisted in cleaving to their wives and adhering to their religion, and absolutely set at naught the sublime doctrines of the moon—nay, among other abominable heresies they even went so far as blasphemously to declare, that this ineffable planet was made of nothing more nor less than green cheese!"

At these words, the great man in the moon (being a very profound philosopher) shall fall into a terrible passion, and possessing equal authority over things that do not belong to him, as did whilome[1] his holiness the Pope, shall forthwith issue a formidable bull,—specifying, "That—whereas a certain crew of Lunatics have lately discovered and taken possession of that little dirty planet, called *the earth*—and that whereas it is inhabited by none but a race of two legged animals, that carry their heads on their shoulders instead of under their arms; cannot talk the lunatic language; have two eyes instead of one; are destitute of tails, and of a horrible whiteness, instead of pea green—therefore and for a variety of other excellent reasons—they are considered incapable of possessing any property in the planet they infest, and the right and title to it are confirmed to its original discoverers.—And furthermore, the colonists who are now about to depart to the aforesaid planet, are authorized and commanded to use every means to convert these infidel savages from the darkness of Christianity, and make them thorough and absolute lunatics."

In consequence of this benevolent bull, our philosophic benefactors go to work with hearty zeal. They seize upon our fertile territories scourge us from

1 "At some past time; some time before or ago; once upon a time" (*OED*).

our rightful possessions, relieve us from our wives, and when we are unreasonable enough to complain, they will turn upon us and say—miserable barbarians! ungrateful wretches!—have we not come thousands of miles to improve your worthless planet—have we not fed you with moon shine—have we not intoxicated you with nitrous oxide—does not our moon give you light every night and have you the baseness to murmur, when we claim a pitiful return for all these benefits? But finding that we not only persist in absolute contempt to their reasoning and disbelief in their philosophy, but even go so far as daringly to defend our property, their patience shall be exhausted, and they shall resort to their superior powers of argument—hunt us with hypogriffs, transfix us with concentrated sun-beams, demolish our cities with moonstones; until having by main force, converted us to the true faith, they shall graciously permit us to exist in the torrid deserts of Arabia, or the frozen regions of Lapland,[1] there to enjoy the blessings of civilization and the charms of lunar philosophy—in much the same manner as the reformed and enlightened savages of this country, are kindly suffered to inhabit the inhospitable forests of the north, or the impenetrable wildernesses of South America.

Thus have I clearly proved, and I hope strikingly illustrated, the right of the early colonists to the possession of this country—and thus is this gigantic question, completely knocked in the head—so having manfully surmounted all obstacles, and subdued all opposition, what remains but that I should forthwith conduct my impatient and wayworn readers, into the renowned city, which we have so long been in a manner besieging.—But hold, before I proceed another step, I must pause to take breath and recover from the excessive fatigue I have undergone, in preparing to begin this most accurate of histories. And in this I do but imitate the example of the celebrated Hans Von Dunderbottom, who took a start of three miles for the purpose of jumping over a hill, but having been himself out of breath by the time he reached the foot, sat himself quietly down for a few moments to blow, and then walked over it at his leisure.

1 Lapland is a historic term for the northern region of Finland, split between Sweden and Finland until 1809; it is the ancestral territory of the Sámi people, who refer to the area as Sápmi.

George Gordon Byron (1788–1824)

Commonly referred to using his title, Lord Byron was one of the foremost English poets of the Romantic period. While not often associated with science fiction, it is notable that he was present when Mary Wollstonecraft Godwin (later Mary Wollstonecraft Shelley) conceived of *Frankenstein*, at the house Byron rented in Geneva in 1816. That same summer, Byron wrote the poem "Darkness," which has variously been read as part of the "last man" tradition, of which Shelley's novel *The Last Man* (1826) is a prime example, and also as an early example of the dystopian, apocalyptic strain of SF.

Note on the text: The text here is reproduced from a first edition of *The Prisoner of Chillon and Other Poems* (James Murray, 1816).

"Darkness" (1816)

I had a dream, which was not all a dream.
The bright sun was extinguish'd, and the stars
Did wander darkling in the eternal space,
Rayless, and pathless, and the icy earth
Swung blind and blackening in the moonless air;
Morn came, and went—and came, and brought no day,
And men forgot their passions in the dread
Of this their desolation; and all hearts
Were chill'd into a selfish prayer for light:
And they did live by watchfires—and the thrones,
The palaces of crowned kings—the huts,
The habitations of all things which dwell,
Were burnt for beacons; cities were consumed,
And men were gathered round their blazing homes
To look once more into each other's face;
Happy were those who dwelt within the eye
Of the volcanos, and their mountain-torch:
A fearful hope was all the world contain'd;
Forests were set on fire—but hour by hour
They fell and faded—and the crackling trunks
Extinguish'd with a crash—and all was black.
The brows of men by the despairing light
Wore an unearthly aspect, as by fits
The flashes fell upon them; some lay down
And hid their eyes and wept; and some did rest
Their chins upon their clenched hands, and smiled;
And others hurried to and fro, and fed

Their funeral piles with fuel, and looked up
With mad disquietude on the dull sky,
The pall of a past world; and then again
With curses cast them down upon the dust,
And gnash'd their teeth and howl'd: the wild birds shriek'd
And, terrified, did flutter on the ground,
And flap their useless wings; the wildest brutes
Came tame and tremulous; and vipers crawl'd
And twined themselves among the multitude,
Hissing, but stingless—they were slain for food:
And War, which for a moment was no more,
Did glut himself again;—a meal was bought
With blood, and each sate sullenly apart
Gorging himself in gloom: no love was left;
All earth was but one thought—and that was death,
Immediate and inglorious; and the pang
Of famine fed upon all entrails—men
Died, and their bones were tombless as their flesh;
The meagre by the meagre were devoured,
Even dogs assail'd their masters, all save one,
And he was faithful to a corse, and kept
The birds and beasts and famish'd men at bay,
Till hunger clung them, or the dropping dead
Lured their lank jaws; himself sought out no food,
But with a piteous and perpetual moan
And a quick desolate cry, licking the hand
Which answered not with a caress—he died.
The crowd was famish'd by degrees; but two
Of an enormous city did survive,
And they were enemies; they met beside
The dying embers of an altar-place
Where had been heap'd a mass of holy things
For an unholy usage; they raked up,
And shivering scraped with their cold skeleton hands
The feeble ashes, and their feeble breath
Blew for a little life, and made a flame
Which was a mockery; then they lifted up
Their eyes as it grew lighter, and beheld
Each other's aspects—saw, and shriek'd, and died—
Even of their mutual hideousness they died,
Unknowing who he was upon whose brow
Famine had written Fiend. The world was void,
The populous and the powerful was a lump,
Seasonless, herbless, treeless, manless, lifeless—

A lump of death—a chaos of hard clay.
The rivers, lakes, and ocean all stood still,
And nothing stirred within their silent depths;
Ships sailorless lay rotting on the sea,
And their masts fell down piecemeal; as they dropp'd
They slept on the abyss without a surge—
The waves were dead; the tides were in their grave,
The moon their mistress had expired before;
The winds were withered in the stagnant air,
And the clouds perish'd; Darkness had no need
Of aid from them—She was the universe.

Edgar Allan Poe (1809–49)

Few other figures are as identified with the origins of various forms of "genre fiction" as American author Edgar Allan Poe. In his short life, he wrote numerous tales which have been identified as significantly influencing the genres of science and gothic fiction and poetry, and he is often credited as the progenitor of detective fiction. When Hugo Gernsback published the first issue of his "scientifiction" magazine, *Amazing Stories*, not only was Poe's work included but his name, along with those of H.G. Wells and French author Jules Verne, was included on the cover and his oeuvre identified as an early example of the type of work Gernsback would like to publish. Included here is an early example of speculative poetry, "Sonnet–To Science," which connects science to the more fantastic realm of myth, and arguably his most "scientific" story, "The Facts in the Case of M. Valdemar."

Note on the texts: "Sonnet–To Science" was originally published as the opening poem in *Al Aaraaf, Tamerlane and Minor Poems* (Hatch and Dunning, 1829); "The Facts in the Case of M. Valdemar" was first published simultaneously in *The American Review* and *Broadway Journal* in their respective December 1845 issues. Both texts here are based on the versions in *The Works of the Late Edgar Allan Poe: Notices of His Life and Genius*, vol. 1, *Tales*, edited by N.P. Willis, J.R. Lowell, and R.W. Griswold (Redfield, 1850). The story was later published in the collection *Tales of Mystery and Imagination*, illustrated by Irish artist Harry Clarke (1889–1931) for a 1919 edition published in London by George G. Harrap (see Fig. 1).

"Sonnet–To Science" (1829)

Science! true daughter of Old Time thou art!
  Who alterest all things with thy peering eyes.
Why preyest thou thus upon the poet's heart,
  Vulture, whose wings are dull realities?
How should he love thee? or how deem thee wise,
  Who wouldst not leave him in his wandering
To seek for treasure in the jewelled skies,
  Albeit he soared with an undaunted wing?
Hast thou not dragged Diana[1] from her car?
  And driven the Hamadryad[2] from the wood

1 Diana: Roman goddess of the woods and the hunt, associated with the moon and generally with nature; car: chariot.

2 Hamadryad: minor Greek nature goddesses, represented as living in trees.

To seek a shelter in some happier star?
  Hast thou not torn the Naiad[1] from her flood,
The Elfin from the green grass, and from me
The summer dream beneath the tamarind tree?

"The Facts in the Case of M. Valdemar" (1845)

Of course I shall not pretend to consider it any matter for wonder, that the extraordinary case of M. Valdemar has excited discussion. It would have been a miracle had it not—especially under the circumstances. Through the desire of all parties concerned, to keep the affair from the public, at least for the present, or until we had farther opportunities for investigation—through our endeavors to effect this—a garbled or exaggerated account made its way into society, and became the source of many unpleasant misrepresentations; and, very naturally, of a great deal of disbelief.

It is now rendered necessary that I give the *facts*—as far as I comprehend them myself. They are, succinctly, these:

My attention, for the last three years, had been repeatedly drawn to the subject of Mesmerism;[2] and, about nine months ago, it occurred to me, quite suddenly, that in the series of experiments made hitherto, there had been a very remarkable and most unaccountable omission:—no person had as yet been mesmerized *in articulo mortis*.[3] It remained to be seen, first, whether, in such condition, there existed in the patient any susceptibility to the magnetic influence; secondly, whether, if any existed, it was impaired or increased by the condition; thirdly, to what extent, or for how long a period, the encroachments of Death might be arrested by the process. There were other points to be ascertained, but these most excited my curiosity—the last in especial, from the immensely important character of its consequences.

In looking around me for some subject by whose means I might test these particulars, I was brought to think of my friend, M. Ernest Valdemar, the well-known compiler of the "Bibliotheca Forensica," and author (under the *nom de plume*[4] of Issachar Marx) of the Polish versions of "Wallenstein" and "Gargantua."[5] M. Valdemar, who has resided principally at Harlem, N. Y.,

1 Naiad: minor Greek nature Goddesses associated with bodies of water.

2 Named after its primary theorist and practitioner, German physician Franz Anton Mesmer (1734–1815), mesmerism (also called "magnetism") was a practice of manipulating "animal magnetism," a natural force that existed within and among all living beings. Often associated with the later psychological practice of hypnotism, mesmerism's claims went far beyond the psychological, claiming benefits to physical health and even connections to the metaphysical and spirituality.

3 At the point of death (Lat.).

4 Pseudonym (Fr.).

5 "Wallenstein": likely a reference to the trilogy of plays by Friedrick Schiller (1759–1805) about the Bohemian general, Albrecht von Wallenstein (1583–1634), noted for his role in the Thirty (*continued*)

UPON THE BED THERE LAY A NEARLY LIQUID MASS
OF LOATHSOME—OF DETESTABLE PUTRIDITY

Fig. 1: Harry Clarke. Illustration to "The Facts in the Case of M. Valdemar." *Tales of Mystery and Imagination*, by Edgar Allan Poe, Harrap, 1919.

since the year 1839, is (or was) particularly noticeable for the extreme spareness of his person—his lower limbs much resembling those of John Randolph;[1] and, also, for the whiteness of his whiskers, in violent contrast to the blackness of his hair—the latter, in consequence, being very generally mistaken for a wig. His temperament was markedly nervous, and rendered him a good subject for mesmeric experiment. On two or three occasions I had put him to sleep with little difficulty, but was disappointed in other results which his peculiar constitution had naturally led me to anticipate. His will was at no period positively, or thoroughly, under my control, and in regard to *clairvoyance*,[2] I could accomplish with him nothing to be relied upon. I always attributed my failure at these points to the disordered state of his health. For some months previous to my becoming acquainted with him, his physicians had declared him in a confirmed phthisis.[3] It was his custom, indeed, to speak calmly of his approaching dissolution, as of a matter neither to be avoided nor regretted.

When the ideas to which I have alluded first occurred to me, it was of course very natural that I should think of M. Valdemar. I knew the steady philosophy of the man too well to apprehend any scruples from *him*; and he had no relatives in America who would be likely to interfere. I spoke to him frankly upon the subject; and, to my surprise, his interest seemed vividly excited. I say to my surprise; for, although he had always yielded his person freely to my experiments, he had never before given me any tokens of sympathy with what I did. His disease was of that character which would admit of exact calculation in respect to the epoch of its termination in death; and it was finally arranged between us that he would send for me about twenty-four hours before the period announced by his physicians as that of his decease.

It is now rather more than seven months since I received, from M. Valdemar himself, the subjoined note:

"My dear P——,

"You may as well come *now*. D—— and F—— are agreed that I cannot hold out beyond to-morrow midnight; and I think they have hit the time very nearly.

Valdemar."

I received this note within half an hour after it was written, and in fifteen minutes more I was in the dying man's chamber. I had not seen him for ten

Years' War; "Gargantua": possibly a reference to the five-volume set of novels, *The Five Books of the Lives and Deeds of Gargantua and Pantagruel* (published between c. 1532 and 1564), written by François Rabelais (c. 1494–1534).

1 John Randolph (1773–1833), American politician whose childhood illness or disease had made him physically diminutive.

2 Clairvoyance refers to an ability to perceive things not physically present, including the future and the supernatural.

3 phthisis: a general term for a wasting disease or progressive pulmonary illness, such as tuberculosis.

days, and was appalled by the fearful alteration which the brief interval had wrought in him. His face wore a leaden hue; the eyes were utterly lustreless; and the emaciation was so extreme, that the skin had been broken through by the cheek-bones. His expectoration was excessive. The pulse was barely perceptible. He retained, nevertheless, in a very remarkable manner, both his mental power and a certain degree of physical strength. He spoke with distinctness—took some palliative medicines without aid—and, when I entered the room, was occupied in penciling memoranda in a pocket-book. He was propped up in the bed by pillows. Doctors D—— and F—— were in attendance.

After pressing Valdemar's hand, I took these gentlemen aside, and obtained from them a minute account of the patient's condition. The left lung had been for eighteen months in a semi-osseous or cartilaginous state,[1] and was, of course, entirely useless for all purposes of vitality. The right, in its upper portion, was also partially, if not thoroughly, ossified, while the lower region was merely a mass of purulent tubercles,[2] running one into another. Several extensive perforations existed; and, at one point, permanent adhesion to the ribs had taken place. These appearances in the right lobe were of comparatively recent date. The ossification had proceeded with very unusual rapidity; no sign of it had been discovered a month before, and the adhesion had only been observed during the three previous days. Independently of the phthisis, the patient was suspected of aneurism of the aorta; but on this point the osseous symptoms rendered an exact diagnosis impossible. It was the opinion of both physicians that M. Valdemar would die about midnight on the morrow (Sunday). It was then seven o'clock on Saturday evening.

On quitting the invalid's bed-side to hold conversation with myself, Doctors D—— and F—— had bidden him a final farewell. It had not been their intention to return; but, at my request, they agreed to look in upon the patient about ten the next night.

When they had gone, I spoke freely with M. Valdemar on the subject of his approaching dissolution, as well as, more particularly, of the experiment proposed. He still professed himself quite willing and even anxious to have it made, and urged me to commence it at once. A male and a female nurse were in attendance; but I did not feel myself altogether at liberty to engage in a task of this character with no more reliable witnesses than these people, in case of sudden accident, might prove. I therefore postponed operations until about eight the next night, when the arrival of a medical student, with whom I had some acquaintance, (Mr. Theodore L——l,) relieved me from farther embarrassment. It had been my design, originally, to wait for the physicians; but I was induced to proceed, first, by the urgent entreaties of M. Valdemar, and secondly, by my conviction that I had not a moment to lose, as he was evidently sinking fast.

1 Generally speaking, his lungs had developed bony masses or masses comprising cartilage.

2 Nodules filled with pus.

Mr. L——l was so kind as to accede to my desire that he would take notes of all that occurred; and it is from his memoranda that what I now have to relate is, for the most part, either condensed or copied *verbatim*.

It wanted about five minutes of eight when, taking the patient's hand, I begged him to state, as distinctly as he could, to Mr. L——l, whether he (M. Valdemar,) was entirely willing that I should make the experiment of mesmerizing him in his then condition.

He replied feebly, yet quite audibly, "Yes, I wish to be mesmerized"—adding immediately afterwards, "I fear you have deferred it too long."

While he spoke thus, I commenced the passes which I had already found most effectual in subduing him. He was evidently influenced with the first lateral stroke of my hand across his forehead; but although I exerted all my powers, no farther perceptible effect was induced until some minutes after ten o'clock, when Doctors D—— and F—— called, according to appointment. I explained to them, in a few words, what I designed, and as they opposed no objection, saying that the patient was already in the death agony, I proceeded without hesitation—exchanging, however, the lateral passes for downward ones, and directing my gaze entirely into the right eye of the sufferer.

By this time his pulse was imperceptible and his breathing was stertorous,[1] and at intervals of half a minute.

This condition was nearly unaltered for a quarter of an hour. At the expiration of this period, however, a natural although a very deep sigh escaped the bosom of the dying man, and the stertorous breathing ceased—that is to say, its stertorousness was no longer apparent; the intervals were undiminished. The patient's extremities were of an icy coldness.

At five minutes before eleven, I perceived unequivocal signs of the mesmeric influence. The glassy roll of the eye was changed for that expression of uneasy *inward* examination which is never seen except in cases of sleep-waking, and which it is quite impossible to mistake. With a few rapid lateral passes I made the lids quiver, as in incipient sleep, and with a few more I closed them altogether. I was not satisfied, however, with this, but continued the manipulations vigorously, and with the fullest exertion of the will, until I had completely stiffened the limbs of the slumberer, after placing them in a seemingly easy position. The legs were at full length; the arms were nearly so, and reposed on the bed at a moderate distance from the loins. The head was very slightly elevated.

When I had accomplished this, it was fully midnight, and I requested the gentlemen present to examine M. Valdemar's condition. After a few experiments, they admitted him to be in an unusually perfect state of mesmeric trance. The curiosity of both the physicians was greatly excited.

---

1 Laboured or congested breathing, creating snoring-like sounds. In the 1850 version, this and later instances of the word were spelled *stertorious*, but this is corrected in other versions; see Poe, *Tales and Sketches*, vol. 2, p. 1237, notes c, e, and f.

Dr. D—— resolved at once to remain with the patient all night, while Dr. F—— took leave with a promise to return at daybreak. Mr. L——l and the nurses remained.

We left M. Valdemar entirely undisturbed until about three o'clock in the morning, when I approached him and found him in precisely the same condition as when Dr. F—— went away—that is to say, he lay in the same position; the pulse was imperceptible; the breathing was gentle (scarcely noticeable, unless through the application of a mirror to the lips;) the eyes were closed naturally; and the limbs were as rigid and as cold as marble. Still, the general appearance was certainly not that of death.

As I approached M. Valdemar I made a kind of half effort to influence his right arm into pursuit of my own, as I passed the latter gently to and fro above his person. In such experiments with this patient, I had never perfectly succeeded before, and assuredly I had little thought of succeeding now; but to my astonishment, his arm very readily, although feebly, followed every direction I assigned it with mine. I determined to hazard a few words of conversation.

"M. Valdemar," I said, "are you asleep?" He made no answer, but I perceived a tremor about the lips, and was thus induced to repeat the question, again and again. At its third repetition, his whole frame was agitated by a very slight shivering; the eye-lids unclosed themselves so far as to display a white line of a ball; the lips moved sluggishly, and from between them, in a barely audible whisper, issued the words:

"Yes;—asleep now. Do not wake me!—let me die so!"

I here felt the limbs and found them as rigid as ever. The right arm, as before, obeyed the direction of my hand. I questioned the sleep-waker again:

"Do you still feel pain in the breast, M. Valdemar?"

The answer now was immediate, but even less audible than before:

"No pain—I am dying."

I did not think it advisable to disturb him farther just then, and nothing more was said or done until the arrival of Dr. F——, who came a little before sunrise, and expressed unbounded astonishment at finding the patient still alive. After feeling the pulse and applying a mirror to the lips, he requested me to speak to the sleep-waker again. I did so, saying:

"M. Valdemar, do you still sleep?"

As before, some minutes elapsed ere a reply was made; and during the interval the dying man seemed to be collecting his energies to speak. At my fourth repetition of the question, he said very faintly, almost inaudibly:

"Yes; still asleep—dying."

It was now the opinion, or rather the wish, of the physicians, that M. Valdemar should be suffered to remain undisturbed in his present apparently tranquil condition, until death should supervene—and this, it was generally agreed, must now take place within a few minutes. I concluded, however, to speak to him once more, and merely repeated my previous question.

While I spoke, there came a marked change over the countenance of the sleep-waker. The eyes rolled themselves slowly open, the pupils disappearing upwardly; the skin generally assumed a cadaverous hue, resembling not so much parchment as white paper; and the circular hectic spots which, hitherto, had been strongly defined in the centre of each cheek, *went out* at once. I use this expression, because the suddenness of their departure put me in mind of nothing so much as the extinguishment of a candle by a puff of the breath. The upper lip, at the same time, writhed itself away from the teeth, which it had previously covered completely; while the lower jaw fell with an audible jerk, leaving the mouth widely extended, and disclosing in full view the swollen and blackened tongue. I presume that no member of the party then present had been unaccustomed to death-bed horrors; but so hideous beyond conception was the appearance of M. Valdemar at this moment, that there was a general shrinking back from the region of the bed.

I now feel that I have reached a point of this narrative at which every reader will be startled into positive disbelief. It is my business, however, simply to proceed.

There was no longer the faintest sign of vitality in M. Valdemar; and concluding him to be dead, we were consigning him to the charge of the nurses, when a strong vibratory motion was observable in the tongue. This continued for perhaps a minute. At the expiration of this period, there issued from the distended and motionless jaws a voice—such as it would be madness in me to attempt describing. There are, indeed, two or three epithets which might be considered as applicable to it in part: I might say, for example, that the sound was harsh, and broken and hollow; but the hideous whole is indescribable, for the simple reason that no similar sounds have ever jarred upon the ear of humanity. There were two particulars, nevertheless, which I thought then, and still think, might fairly be stated as characteristic of the intonation—as well adapted to convey some idea of its unearthly peculiarity. In the first place, the voice seemed to reach our ears—at least mine—from a vast distance, or from some deep cavern within the earth. In the second place, it impressed me (I fear, indeed, that it will be impossible to make myself comprehended) as gelatinous or glutinous matters impress the sense of touch.

I have spoken both of "sound" and of "voice." I mean to say that the sound was one of distinct—of even wonderfully, thrillingly distinct—syllabification. M. Valdemar *spoke*—obviously in reply to the question I had propounded to him a few minutes before. I had asked him, it will be remembered, if he still slept. He now said:

"Yes;—no;—I *have been* sleeping—and now—now—*I am dead*."

No person present even affected to deny, or attempted to repress, the unutterable, shuddering horror which these few words, thus uttered, were so well calculated to convey. Mr. L——l (the student) swooned. The nurses immediately left the chamber, and could not be induced to return. My own impressions I would not pretend to render intelligible to the reader. For nearly an hour, we busied ourselves, silently—without the utterance of a word—in endeavors to revive Mr. L——l. When he came to himself, we addressed ourselves again to an investigation of M. Valdemar's condition.

It remained in all respects as I have last described it, with the exception that the mirror no longer afforded evidence of respiration. An attempt to draw blood from the arm failed. I should mention, too, that this limb was no farther subject to my will. I endeavored in vain to make it follow the direction of my hand. The only real indication, indeed, of the mesmeric influence, was now found in the vibratory movement of the tongue, whenever I addressed M. Valdemar a question. He seemed to be making an effort to reply, but had no longer sufficient volition. To queries put to him by any other person than myself he seemed utterly insensible—although I endeavored to place each member of the company in mesmeric *rapport* with him. I believe that I have now related all that is necessary to an understanding of the sleep-waker's state at this epoch. Other nurses were procured; and at ten o'clock I left the house in company with the two physicians and Mr. L——l.

In the afternoon we all called again to see the patient. His condition remained precisely the same. We had now some discussion as to the propriety and feasibility of awakening him; but we had little difficulty in agreeing that no good purpose would be served by so doing. It was evident that, so far, death (or what is usually termed death) had been arrested by the mesmeric process. It seemed clear to us all that to awaken M. Valdemar would be merely to insure his instant, or at least his speedy dissolution.

From this period until the close of last week—*an interval of nearly seven months*—we continued to make daily calls at M. Valdemar's house, accompanied, now and then, by medical and other friends. All this time the sleep-waker remained *exactly* as I have last described him. The nurses' attentions were continual.

It was on Friday last that we finally resolved to make the experiment of awakening, or attempting to awaken him; and it is the (perhaps) unfortunate result of this latter experiment which has given rise to so much discussion in private circles—to so much of what I cannot help thinking unwarranted popular feeling.

For the purpose of relieving M. Valdemar from the mesmeric trance, I made use of the customary passes. These, for a time, were unsuccessful. The first indication of revival was afforded by a partial descent of the iris. It was observed, as especially remarkable, that this lowering of the pupil was accompanied by the profuse out-flowing of a yellowish ichor (from beneath the lids) of a pungent and highly offensive odor.

It was now suggested that I should attempt to influence the patient's arm, as heretofore. I made the attempt and failed. Dr. F—— then intimated a desire to have me put a question. I did so, as follows:

"M. Valdemar, can you explain to us what are your feelings or wishes now?"

There was an instant return of the hectic circles on the cheeks; the tongue quivered, or rather rolled violently in the mouth (although the jaws and lips remained rigid as before;) and at length the same hideous voice which I have already described, broke forth:

"For God's sake!—quick!—quick!—put me to sleep—or, quick!—waken me!—quick!—*I say to you that I am dead!*"

I was thoroughly unnerved, and for an instant remained undecided what to do. At first I made an endeavor to re-compose the patient; but, failing in this through total abeyance of the will, I retraced my steps and as earnestly struggled to awaken him. In this attempt I soon saw that I should be successful—or at least I soon fancied that my success would be complete—and I am sure that all in the room were prepared to see the patient awaken.

For what really occurred, however, it is quite impossible that any human being could have been prepared.

As I rapidly made the mesmeric passes, amid ejaculations of "dead! dead!" absolutely *bursting* from the tongue and not from the lips of the sufferer, his whole frame at once—within the space of a single minute, or even less, shrunk—crumbled—absolutely *rotted* away beneath my hands. Upon the bed, before that whole company, there lay a nearly liquid mass of loathsome—of detestable putrescence.[1]

1 Poe later changed this to "putridity" (as in Fig. 1) in a manuscript version, but earlier published versions used putrescence (see Poe, *Tales and Sketches*, vol. 2, p. 1243, note a).

Mary Wollstonecraft Shelley (1797–1851)

Mary Wollstonecraft Shelley's *Frankenstein* (1818) is often read as the first science fiction novel. A prominent writer of the English Romantic movement, Shelley (at that time Mary Wollstonecraft Godwin) conceived the tale during the summer of 1816, when she, the poet Percy Shelley (whom she would later marry), Lord Byron, and John Polidori challenged each other to compose fantastic tales. While that novel is by far her most famous and influential, she would also write several other novels, including the post-apocalyptic *The Last Man* (1826), dozens of stories, and many other works. In "The Mortal Immortal," she returns to the "mad scientist" trope of her most famous work, but adds a lab assistant (a figure later identified with the "Igor" of the early *Frankenstein* films, though that character appears nowhere in the original novel).

Note on the text: The text below is based on the first publication in *The Keepsake for 1834*, edited by Frederic Mansel Reynolds (Longman, December 1833), with reference to the collected *Tales and Stories*, edited by Richard Garnett (William Paterson, 1891). The story was listed in the table of contents and the story's header as "by the author of Frankenstein" and was accompanied by an engraving, "Bertha," by Frederick Bacon (1803–1887), after a painting by Henry Perronet Briggs RA (1791/93–1844) (Fig. 2).

"The Mortal Immortal: A Tale"[1] (1833)

JULY 16, 1833.—This is a memorable anniversary for me; on it I complete my three hundred and twenty-third year!

The Wandering Jew?—certainly not.[2] More than eighteen centuries have passed over his head. In comparison with him, I am a very young Immortal.

Am I, then, immortal? This is a question which I have asked myself, by day and night, for now three hundred and three years, and yet cannot answer it. I detected a gray hair amidst my brown locks this very day—that surely signifies decay. Yet it may have remained concealed there for three hundred years—for some persons have become entirely white-headed before twenty years of age.

I will tell my story, and my reader shall judge for me. I will tell my story, and so contrive to pass some few hours of a long eternity, become so wearisome to me. For ever! Can it be? to live for ever! I have heard of enchantments, in which the victims were plunged into a deep sleep, to wake, after a

1 The title could reference lines from Book I of the poem *Endymion* (1818) by John Keats (1795–1821): "Now, if this earthly love has power to make / Men's being mortal, immortal."

2 Stories popularized in the medieval period portray the Wandering Jew, primarily an antisemitic figure, as a man who was present at the crucifixion of Jesus and who is now cursed to wander the earth until the prophesied Christian Second Coming.

Fig. 2: Frederick Bacon. "Bertha" (after a painting by Henry Perronet Briggs). *The Keepsake for 1834*, edited by Frederic Mansel Reynolds, Longman, 1833.

hundred years, as fresh as ever: I have heard of the Seven Sleepers[1]—thus to be immortal would not be so burthensome: but, oh! the weight of never-ending time—the tedious passage of the still-succeeding hours! How happy was the fabled Nourjahad![2]——But to my task.

All the world has heard of Cornelius Agrippa. His memory is as immortal as his arts have made me. All the world has also heard of his scholar, who, unawares, raised the foul fiend during his master's absence, and was destroyed by him.[3] The report, true or false, of this accident, was attended with many inconveniences to the renowned philosopher. All his scholars at once deserted him—his servants disappeared. He had no one near him to put coals on his ever-burning fires while he slept, or to attend to the changeful colours of his medicines while he studied. Experiment after experiment failed, because one pair of hands was insufficient to complete them: the dark spirits laughed at him for not being able to retain a single mortal in his service.

I was then very young—very poor—and very much in love. I had been for about a year the pupil of Cornelius, though I was absent when this accident took place. On my return, my friends implored me not to return to the alchymist's abode. I trembled as I listened to the dire tale they told; I required no second warning; and when Cornelius came and offered me a purse of gold if I would remain under his roof, I felt as if Satan himself tempted me. My teeth chattered—my hair stood on end:—I ran off as fast as my trembling knees would permit.

My failing steps were directed whither for two years they had every evening been attracted,—a gently bubbling spring of pure living waters, beside which lingered a dark-haired girl, whose beaming eyes were fixed on the path I was accustomed each night to tread. I cannot remember the hour when I did not love Bertha; we had been neighbours and playmates from infancy—her parents, like mine, were of humble life, yet respectable—our attachment had been a source of pleasure to them. In an evil hour, a malignant fever carried off both her father and mother, and Bertha became an orphan. She would have found a home beneath my paternal roof, but, unfortunately, the old lady of the near castle, rich, childless, and solitary, declared her intention to adopt her. Henceforth Bertha was clad in silk—inhabited a marble palace—and was looked on as being highly favoured by fortune. But in her new situation among her new associates, Bertha remained true to the friend of her humbler days; she often visited the cottage of my father, and when forbidden to go thither, she would stray towards the neighbouring wood, and meet me beside its shady fountain.

1 An early Christian story, popularized in the medieval period, depicts seven young men who escape persecution by the Roman empire by hiding in a cave, only to fall asleep and awaken years later to find Christianity ascendent.

2 *The History of Nourjahad* (1767) is a novel by Irish author Frances Sheridan (1724–76).

3 Heinrich Cornelius Agrippa von Nettesheim (1486–1535), German occultist often associated with alchemy.

She often declared that she owed no duty to her new protectress equal in sanctity to that which bound us. Yet still I was too poor to marry, and she grew weary of being tormented on my account. She had a haughty but an impatient spirit, and grew angry at the obstacles that prevented our union. We met now after an absence, and she had been sorely beset while I was away; she complained bitterly, and almost reproached me for being poor. I replied hastily,—

"I am honest, if I am poor!—were I not, I might soon become rich!"

This exclamation produced a thousand questions. I feared to shock her by owning the truth, but she drew it from me; and then, casting a look of disdain on me, she said—

"You pretend to love, and you fear to face the Devil for my sake!"

I protested that I had only dreaded to offend her;—while she dwelt on the magnitude of the reward that I should receive. Thus encouraged—shamed by her—led on by love and hope, laughing at my late fears, with quick steps and a light heart, I returned to accept the offers of the alchymist, and was instantly installed in my office.

A year passed away. I became possessed of no insignificant sum of money. Custom had banished my fears. In spite of the most painful vigilance, I had never detected the trace of a cloven foot;[1] nor was the studious silence of our abode ever disturbed by demoniac howls. I still continued my stolen interviews with Bertha, and Hope dawned on me—Hope—but not perfect joy; for Bertha fancied that love and security were enemies, and her pleasure was to divide them in my bosom. Though true of heart, she was somewhat of a coquette in manner; and I was jealous as a Turk. She slighted me in a thousand ways, yet would never acknowledge herself to be in the wrong. She would drive me mad with anger, and then force me to beg her pardon. Sometimes she fancied that I was not sufficiently submissive, and then she had some story of a rival, favoured by her protectress. She was surrounded by silk-clad youths—the rich and gay——What chance had the sad-robed scholar of Cornelius compared with these?

On one occasion, the philosopher made such large demands upon my time, that I was unable to meet her as I was wont. He was engaged in some mighty work, and I was forced to remain, day and night, feeding his furnaces and watching his chemical preparations. Bertha waited for me in vain at the fountain. Her haughty spirit fired at this neglect; and when at last I stole out during the few short minutes allotted to me for slumber, and hoped to be consoled by her, she received me with disdain, dismissed me in scorn, and vowed that any man should possess her hand rather than he who could not be in two places at once for her sake. She would be revenged!—And truly she was. In my dingy retreat I heard that she had been hunting, attended by Albert Hoffer. Albert Hoffer was favoured by her protectress, and the three passed

1 Satan has historically been depicted as having cloven hooves in place of feet.

in cavalcade before my smoky window. Methought that they mentioned my name—it was followed by a laugh of derision, as her dark eyes glanced contemptuously towards my abode.

Jealousy, with all its venom, and all its misery, entered my breast. Now I shed a torrent of tears, to think that I should never call her mine; and, anon, I imprecated a thousand curses on her inconstancy. Yet, still I must stir the fires of the alchymist, still attend on the changes of his unintelligible medicines.

Cornelius had watched for three days and nights, nor closed his eyes. The progress of his alembics was slower than he expected: in spite of his anxiety, sleep weighed upon his eyelids. Again and again he threw off drowsiness with more than human energy; again and again it stole away his senses. He eyes his crucibles wistfully. "Not ready yet," he murmured; "will another night pass before the work is accomplished? Winzy, you are vigilant—you are faithful—you have slept, my boy—you slept last night. Look at that glass vessel. The liquid it contains is of a soft rose-colour: the moment it begins to change its hue, awaken me—till then I may close my eyes. First, it will turn white, and then emit golden flashes; but wait not till then; when the rose-colour fades, rouse me." I scarcely heard the last words, muttered, as they were, in sleep. Even then he did not quite yield to nature. "Winzy, my boy," he again said, "do not touch the vessel—do not put it to your lips; it is a philter—a philter to cure love; you would not cease to love your Bertha—beware to drink!"

And he slept. His venerable head sunk on his breast, and I scarce heard his regular breathing. For a few minutes I watched the vessel—the rosy hue of the liquid remained unchanged. Then my thoughts wandered—they visited the fountain, and dwelt on a thousand charming scenes never to be renewed—never! Serpents and adders were in my heart as the word "Never!" half formed itself on my lips. False girl!—false and cruel! Never more would she smile on me as that evening she smiled on Albert. Worthless, detested woman! I would not remain unrevenged—she should see Albert expire at her feet—she should die beneath my vengeance. She had smiled in disdain and triumph—she knew my wretchedness and her power. Yet what power had she?—the power of exciting my hate—my utter scorn—my—oh, all but indifference! Could I attain that—could I regard her with careless eyes, transferring my rejected love to one fairer and more true, that were indeed a victory!

A bright flash darted before my eyes. I had forgotten the medicine of the adept; I gazed on it with wonder: flashes of admirable beauty, more bright than those which the diamond emits when the sun's rays are on it, glanced from the surface of the liquid; an odour the most fragrant and grateful stole over my sense; the vessel seemed one globe of living radiance, lovely to the eye, and most inviting to the taste. The first thought, instinctively inspired by the grosser sense, was, I will—I must drink. I raised the vessel to my lips. "It will cure me of love—of torture!" Already I had quaffed half of the most delicious liquor ever tasted by the palate of man, when the philosopher stirred. I started—I dropped the glass—the fluid flamed and glanced along the floor, while I felt Cornelius's gripe at my throat, as he shrieked aloud, "Wretch! you have destroyed the labour of my life!"

The philosopher was totally unaware that I had drunk any portion of his drug. His idea was, and I gave a tacit assent to it, that I had raised the vessel from curiosity, and that, frighted at its brightness, and the flashes of intense light it gave forth, I had let it fall. I never undeceived him. The fire of the medicine was quenched—the fragrance died away—he grew calm, as a philosopher should under the heaviest trials, and dismissed me to rest.

I will not attempt to describe the sleep of glory and bliss which bathed my soul in paradise during the remaining hours of that memorable night. Words would be faint and shallow types of my enjoyment, or of the gladness that possessed my bosom when I woke. I trod air—my thoughts were in heaven. Earth appeared heaven, and my inheritance upon it was to be one trance of delight. "This it is to be cured of love," I thought; "I will see Bertha this day, and she will find her lover cold and regardless; too happy to be disdainful, yet how utterly indifferent to her!"

The hours danced away. The philosopher, secure that he had once succeeded, and believing that he might again, began to concoct the same medicine once more. He was shut up with his books and drugs, and I had a holiday. I dressed myself with care; I looked in an old but polished shield, which served me for a mirror; methought my good looks had wonderfully improved. I hurried beyond the precincts of the town, joy in my soul, the beauty of heaven and earth around me. I turned my steps towards the castle—I could look on its lofty turrets with lightness of heart, for I was cured of love. My Bertha saw me afar off, as I came up the avenue. I know not what sudden impulse animated her bosom, but at the sight, she sprung with a light fawn-like bound down the marble steps, and was hastening towards me. But I had been perceived by another person. The old high-born hag, who called herself her protectress, and was her tyrant, had seen me, also; she hobbled, panting, up the terrace; a page, as ugly as herself, held up her train, and fanned her as she hurried along, and stopped my fair girl with a "How, now, my bold mistress? whither so fast? Back to your cage—hawks are abroad!"[1]

Bertha clasped her hands—her eyes were still bent on my approaching figure. I saw the contest. How I abhorred the old crone who checked the kind impulses of my Bertha's softening heart. Hitherto, respect for her rank had caused me to avoid the lady of the castle; now I disdained such trivial considerations. I was cured of love, and lifted above all human fears; I hastened forwards, and soon reached the terrace. How lovely Bertha looked! her eyes flashing fire, her cheeks glowing with impatience and anger, she was a thousand times more graceful and charming than ever—I no longer loved—Oh! no, I adored—worshipped—idolized her!

She had that morning been persecuted, with more than usual vehemence,

---

1 This passage echoes the engraving by Bacon (Fig. 2).

to consent to an immediate marriage with my rival. She was reproached with the encouragement that she had shown him—she was threatened with being turned out of doors with disgrace and shame. Her proud spirit rose in arms at the threat; but when she remembered the scorn that she had heaped upon me, and how, perhaps, she had thus lost one whom she now regarded as her only friend, she wept with remorse and rage. At that moment I appeared. "O, Winzy!" she exclaimed, "take me to your mother's cot; swiftly let me leave the detested luxuries and wretchedness of this noble dwelling—take me to poverty and happiness."

I clasped her in my arms with transport. The old lady was speechless with fury, and broke forth into invective only when we were far on our road to my natal cottage. My mother received the fair fugitive, escaped from a gilt cage to nature and liberty, with tenderness and joy; my father, who loved her, welcomed her heartily; it was a day of rejoicing, which did not need the addition of the celestial potion of the alchymist to steep me in delight.

Soon after this eventful day, I became the husband of Bertha. I ceased to be the scholar of Cornelius, but I continued his friend. I always felt grateful to him for having, unawares, procured me that delicious draught of a divine elixir, which, instead of curing me of love (sad cure! solitary and joyless remedy for evils which seem blessings to the memory), had inspired me with courage and resolution, thus winning for me an inestimable treasure in my Bertha.

I often called to mind that period of trance-like inebriation with wonder. The drink of Cornelius had not fulfilled the task for which he affirmed that it had been prepared, but its effects were more potent and blissful than words can express. They had faded by degrees, yet they lingered long—and painted life in hues of splendour. Bertha often wondered at my lightness of heart and unaccustomed gaiety; for, before, I had been rather serious, or even sad, in my disposition. She loved me the better for my cheerful temper, and our days were winged by joy.

Five years afterwards I was suddenly summoned to the bedside of the dying Cornelius. He had sent for me in haste, conjuring my instant presence. I found him stretched on his pallet, enfeebled even to death; all of life that yet remained animated his piercing eyes, and they were fixed on a glass vessel, full of a roseate liquid.

"Behold," he said, in a broken and inward voice, "the vanity of human wishes! a second time my hopes are about to be crowned, a second time they are destroyed. Look at that liquor—you remember five years ago I had prepared the same, with the same success;—then, as now, my thirsting lips expected to taste the immortal elixir—you dashed it from me! and at present it is too late."

He spoke with difficulty, and fell back on his pillow. I could not help saying,—

"How, revered master, can a cure for love restore you to life?"

A faint smile gleamed across his face as I listened earnestly to his scarcely intelligible answer.

"A cure for love and for all things—the Elixir of Immortality. Ah! if now I might drink, I should live for ever!"

As he spoke, a golden flash gleamed from the fluid; a well-remembered fragrance stole over the air; he raised himself, all weak as he was—strength seemed miraculously to re-enter his frame—he stretched forth his hand—a loud explosion startled me—a ray of fire shot up from the elixir, and the glass vessel which contained it was shivered to atoms! I turned my eyes towards the philosopher; he had fallen back—his eyes were glassy—his features rigid—he was dead!

But I lived, and was to live for ever! So said the unfortunate alchymist, and for a few days I believed his words. I remembered the glorious drunkenness that had followed my stolen draught. I reflected on the change I had felt in my frame—in my soul. The bounding elasticity of the one—the buoyant lightness of the other. I surveyed myself in a mirror, and could perceive no change in my features during the space of the five years which had elapsed. I remembered the radiant hues and grateful scent of that delicious beverage—worthy the gift it was capable of bestowing—I was, then, IMMORTAL!

A few days after I laughed at my credulity. The old proverb, that "a prophet is least regarded in his own country," was true with respect to me and my defunct master. I loved him as a man—I respected him as a sage—but I derided the notion that he could command the powers of darkness, and laughed at the superstitious fears with which he was regarded by the vulgar. He was a wise philosopher, but had no acquaintance with any spirits but those clad in flesh and blood. His science was simply human; and human science, I soon persuaded myself, could never conquer nature's laws so far as to imprison the soul for ever within its carnal habitation. Cornelius had brewed a soul-refreshing drink—more inebriating than wine—sweeter and more fragrant than any fruit: it possessed probably strong medicinal powers, imparting gladness to the heart and vigor to the limbs; but its effects would wear out; already were they diminished in my frame. I was a lucky fellow to have quaffed health and joyous spirits, and perhaps long life, at my master's hands; but my good fortune ended there: longevity was far different from immortality.

I continued to entertain this belief for many years. Sometimes a thought stole across me—Was the alchymist indeed deceived? But my habitual credence was, that I should meet the fate of all the children of Adam at my appointed time—a little late, but still at a natural age. Yet it was certain that I retained a wonderfully youthful look. I was laughed at for my vanity in consulting the mirror so often, but I consulted it in vain—my brow was untrenched—my cheeks—my eyes—my whole person continued as untarnished as in my twentieth year.

I was troubled. I looked at the faded beauty of Bertha—I seemed more like her son. By degrees our neighbours began to make similar observations, and I found at last that I went by the name of the Scholar bewitched. Bertha herself grew uneasy. She became jealous and peevish, and at length she began to question me. We had no children; we were all in all to each other; and though, as she grew older, her vivacious spirit became a little allied to ill-temper, and her beauty sadly diminished, I cherished her in my heart as the mistress I had idolized, the wife I had sought and won with such perfect love.

At last our situation became intolerable: Bertha was fifty—I twenty years of age. I had, in very shame, in some measure adopted the habits of a more advanced age; I no longer mingled in the dance among the young and gay, but my heart bounded along with them while I restrained my feet; and a sorry figure I cut among the Nestors of our village.[1] But before the time I mention, things were altered—we were universally shunned; we were—at least, I was—reported to have kept up an iniquitous acquaintance with some of my former master's supposed friends. Poor Bertha was pitied, but deserted. I was regarded with horror and detestation.

What was to be done? we sat by our winter fire—poverty had made itself felt, for none would buy the produce of my farm; and often I had been forced to journey twenty miles, to some place where I was not known, to dispose of our property. It is true we had saved something for an evil day—that day was come.

We sat by our lone fireside—the old-hearted youth and his antiquated wife. Again Bertha insisted on knowing the truth; she recapitulated all she had ever heard said about me, and added her own observations. She conjured me to cast off the spell; she described how much more comely grey hairs were than my chestnut locks; she descanted on the reverence and respect due to age—how preferable to the slight regard paid to mere children: could I imagine that the despicable gifts of youth and good looks outweighed disgrace, hatred, and scorn? Nay, in the end I should be burnt as a dealer in the black art, while she, to whom I had not deigned to communicate any portion of my good fortune, might be stoned as my accomplice. At length she insinuated that I must share my secret with her, and bestow on her like benefits to those I myself enjoyed, or she would denounce me—and then she burst into tears.

Thus beset, methought it was the best way to tell the truth. I revealed it as tenderly as I could, and spoke only of a *very long life*, not of immortality—which representation, indeed, coincided best with my own ideas. When I ended I rose and said,

"And now, my Bertha, will you denounce the lover of your youth?—You will not, I know. But it is too hard, my poor wife, that you should suffer from my ill-luck and the accursed arts of Cornelius. I will leave you—you have wealth enough, and friends will return in my absence. I will go; young as I seem, and strong as I am, I can work and gain my bread among strangers, unsuspected and unknown. I loved you in youth; God is my witness that I would not desert you in age, but that your safety and happiness require it."

---

1 In Greek myth, Nestor is the King of Pylos. In the *Iliad*, as an elderly man, he regularly tells stories of his youth and gives advice to younger men.

I took my cap and moved towards the door; in a moment Bertha's arms were round my neck, and her lips were pressed to mine. "No, my husband, my Winzy," she said, "you shall not go alone—take me with you; we will remove from this place, and, as you say, among strangers we shall be unsuspected and safe. I am not so very old as quite to shame you, my Winzy; and I dare say the charm will soon wear off, and, with the blessing of God, you will become more elderly-looking, as is fitting; you shall not leave me."

I returned the good soul's embrace heartily. "I will not, my Bertha; but for your sake I had not thought of such a thing. I will be your true, faithful husband while you are spared to me, and do my duty by you to the last."

The next day we prepared secretly for our emigration. We were obliged to make great pecuniary sacrifices—it could not be helped. We realised a sum sufficient, at least, to maintain us while Bertha lived; and, without saying adieu to any one, quitted our native country to take refuge in a remote part of western France.

It was a cruel thing to transport poor Bertha from her native village, and the friends of her youth, to a new country, new language, new customs. The strange secret of my destiny rendered this removal immaterial to me; but I compassionated her deeply, and was glad to perceive that she found compensation for her misfortunes in a variety of little ridiculous circumstances. Away from all tell-tale chroniclers, she sought to decrease the apparent disparity of our ages by a thousand feminine arts—rouge, youthful dress, and assumed juvenility of manner. I could not be angry—Did I not I myself wear a mask? Why quarrel with hers, because it was less successful? I grieved deeply when I remembered that this was my Bertha, whom I had loved so fondly, and won with such transport—the dark-eyed, dark-haired girl, with smiles of enchanting archness and a step like a fawn—this mincing, simpering, jealous old woman. I should have revered her gray locks and withered cheeks; but thus!——It was my work, I knew; but I did not the less deplore this type of human weakness.

Her jealousy never slept. Her chief occupation was to discover that, in spite of outward appearances, I was myself growing old. I verily believe that the poor soul loved me truly in her heart, but never had woman so tormenting a mode of displaying fondness. She would discern wrinkles in my face and decrepitude in my walk, while I bounded along in youthful vigour, the youngest looking of twenty youths. I never dared address another woman: on one occasion, fancying that the belle of the village regarded me with favouring eyes, she brought me a gray wig. Her constant discourse among her acquaintances was, that though I looked so young, there was ruin at work within my frame; and she affirmed that the worst symptom about me was my apparent health. My youth was a disease, she said, and I ought at all times to prepare, if not for a sudden and awful death, at least to awake some morning white-headed, and bowed down with all the marks of advanced years. I let her talk—I often joined in her conjectures. Her warnings chimed in with my never-ceasing speculations concerning my state, and I took an earnest, though painful, interest in listening to all that her quick wit and excited imagination could say on the subject.

Why dwell on these minute circumstances? We lived on for many long years. Bertha became bed-rid and paralytic: I nursed her as a mother might a child. She grew peevish, and still harped upon one string—of how long I should survive her. It has ever been a source of consolation to me, that I performed my duty scrupulously towards her. She had been mine in youth, she was mine in age, and at last, when I heaped the sod over her corpse, I wept to feel that I had lost all that really bound me to humanity.

Since then how many have been my cares and woes, how few and empty my enjoyments! I pause here in my history—I will pursue it no further. A sailor without rudder or compass, tossed on a stormy sea—a traveller lost on a widespread heath, without landmark or stone to guide him—such have I been: more lost, more hopeless than either. A nearing ship, a gleam from some far cot, may save them; but I have no beacon except the hope of death.

Death! mysterious, ill-visaged friend of weak humanity! Why alone of all mortals have you cast me from your sheltering fold? O, for the peace of the grave! the deep silence of the iron-bound tomb! that thought would cease to work in my brain, and my heart beat no more with emotions varied only by new forms of sadness!

Am I immortal? I return to my first question. In the first place, is it not more probable that the beverage of the alchymist was fraught rather with longevity than eternal life? Such is my hope. And then be it remembered, that I only drank *half* of the potion prepared by him. Was not the whole necessary to complete the charm? To have drained half the Elixir of Immortality is but to be half-immortal—my For-ever is thus truncated and null.

But again, who shall number the years of the half of eternity? I often try to imagine by what rule the infinite may be divided. Sometimes I fancy age advancing upon me. One gray hair I have found. Fool! do I lament? Yes, the fear of age and death often creeps coldly into my heart; and the more I live, the more I dread death, even while I abhor life. Such an enigma is man—born to perish—when he wars, as I do, against the established laws of his nature.

But for this anomaly of feeling surely I might die: the medicine of the alchymist would not be proof against fire—sword—and the strangling waters. I have gazed upon the blue depths of many a placid lake, and the tumultuous rushing of many a mighty river, and have said, peace inhabits those waters; yet I have turned my steps away, to live yet another day. I have asked myself, whether suicide would be a crime in one to whom thus only the portals of the other world could be opened. I have done all, except presenting myself as a soldier or duellist, an object of destruction to my—no, *not* my fellow-mortals, and therefore I have shrunk away. They are not my fellows. The inextinguishable power of life in my frame, and their ephemeral existence, places us wide as the poles asunder. I could not raise a hand against the meanest or the most powerful among them.

Thus I have lived on for many a year—alone, and weary of myself—desirous of death, yet never dying—a mortal immortal. Neither ambition nor avarice can enter my mind, and the ardent love that gnaws at my heart, never to be returned—never to find an equal on which to expend itself—lives there only to torment me.

This very day I conceived a design by which I may end all—without self-slaughter, without making another man a Cain[1]—an expedition, which mortal frame can never survive, even endued with the youth and strength that inhabits mine. Thus I shall put my immortality to the test, and rest for ever—or return, the wonder and benefactor of the human species.

Before I go, a miserable vanity has caused me to pen these pages. I would not die, and leave no name behind. Three centuries have passed since I quaffed the fatal beverage: another year shall not elapse before, encountering gigantic dangers—warring with the powers of frost in their home—beset by famine, toil, and tempest—I yield this body, too tenacious a cage for a soul which thirsts for freedom, to the destructive elements of air and water—or, if I survive, my name shall be recorded as one of the most famous among the sons of men; and, my task achieved, I shall adopt more resolute means, and, by scattering and annihilating the atoms that compose my frame, set at liberty the life imprisoned within, and so cruelly prevented from soaring from this dim earth to a sphere more congenial to its immortal essence.

1 In Genesis, Cain is son to Adam and Eve, the first humans, and brother to Abel, who he kills.

Florence McLandburgh (1850–1934)

Scant information exists on American author Florence McLandburgh. Volume 4 of *Appletons' Cyclopaedia of American Biography* (1888) notes that she moved to Chicago as a teenager with her family, and "was educated by her brother John, a critic and essayist." The entry lauds her writing, stating that "Several brilliant short stories that she contributed to periodicals gave her a reputation, and she afterward published a collection of them in book-form," before noting that "impaired health subsequently compelled her to abandon literary work, and she has spent several years in travelling" (Wilson and Fiske 138). More recently, McLandburgh has been identified as using the pseudonym McLandburgh Wilson (by, for example, Marshall [1985]). As Wilson, she was best known for patriotic poems lauding US involvement in World War I. "Automaton Ear" is currently her best-known work and is regularly discussed in terms of technology studies and science fiction.

Note on the text: The text was first published in *Scribner's Monthly: An Illustrated Magazine for the People* (vol. 5, no. 6, 1873) in a version that varies in several minor ways from the book publication, *The Automaton Ear and Other Sketches* (Jansen, McClurg, and Co., 1876). The book version's corrections to grammar and changes for consistency in spelling have been silently adopted, but otherwise the original magazine version is followed. Substantive differences are noted.

"The Automaton Ear" (1873)

THE day was hardly different from many another day, though I will likely recall it even when the mist of years has shrouded the past in an undefined hueless cloud. The sunshine came in at my open window. Out of doors it flooded all the land in its warm summer light—the spires of the town and the bare college campus, farther the tall bearded barley and rustling oats, farther still the wild grass and the forest, where the river ran and the blue haze dipped from the sky.

The temptation was greater than I could stand, and taking my book I shut up the "study," as the students called my small apartment, leaving it for one bounded by no walls or ceiling.

The woods rang with the hum and chirp of insects and birds. I threw myself down beneath a tall, broad-spreading tree. Against its moss-covered trunk I could hear the loud tap of the woodpecker secreted high up among its leaves, and off at the end of a tender young twig a robin trilled, swinging himself to and fro through the checkered sunlight. I never grew weary listening to the changeful voice of the forest and the river, and was hardly conscious of reading until I came upon this paragraph:—

"As a particle of the atmosphere is never lost, so sound is never lost. A strain of music or a simple tone will vibrate in the air forever and ever, decreasing according to a fixed ratio. The diffusion of the agitation extends in all directions, like the waves in a pool, but the ear is unable to detect it beyond a certain point. It is well known that some individuals can distinguish sounds which to others under precisely similar circumstances are wholly lost. Thus the fault is not in the sound itself, but in our organ of hearing, and a tone once in existence is always in existence."[1]

This was nothing new to me. I had read it before, though I had never thought of it particularly; but while I listened to the robin, it seemed singular to know that all the sounds ever uttered, ever born, were floating in the air *now*—all music, every tone, every bird-song—and we, alas! could not hear them.

Suddenly a strange idea shot through my brain—Why not? Ay, *why not hear?* Men had constructed instruments which could magnify to the eye, and—was it possible?—Why not?

I looked up and down the river, but saw neither it nor the sky nor the moss that I touched. Did the woodpecker still tap secreted among the leaves, and the robin sing, and the hum of insects run along the bank as before? I cannot recollect, I cannot recollect anything, only Mother Flinse, the deaf and dumb old crone that occasionally came to beg and sell nuts to the students, was standing in the gateway. I nodded to her as I[2] passed, and walked up her long, slim shadow that lay on the path. It was a strange idea that had come so suddenly into my head and startled me. I hardly dared to think of it, but I could think of nothing else. It could not be possible, and yet—why not?

Over and over in the restless hours of the night, I asked myself, I said aloud, Why not? Then I laughed at my folly, and wondered what I was thinking of, and tried to sleep—but if it *could* be done?

The idea clung to me. It forced itself up in class hours and made confusion in the lessons. Some said the professor was ill those two or three days before the vacation; perhaps I was. I scarcely slept; only the one thought grew stronger—Men had done more wonderful things; it certainly was possible, and I would accomplish this grand invention. I would construct the king of all instruments—I would construct an instrument which could catch these faint tones vibrating in the air and render them audible. Yes, and I would labor quietly until it was perfected, or the world might laugh.

The session closed and the college was deserted, save by the few musty students whom, even in imagination, one could hardly separate or distinguish

1 This quotation does not seem to appear in any extant text, though several critics have noted its similarity to the argument in Charles Babbage's "On the Permanent Impression of Our Words and Actions on the Globe We Inhabit" (1838). See, e.g., Melissa Dickson and John M. Picker.

2 The book publication reads "as she passed," but given the subsequent "and walked up ..." the original is kept here.

from the old books on the library shelves. I could wish for no better opportunity to begin my great work. The first thing would be to prepare for it by a careful study of acoustics, and I buried myself among volumes on the philosophy of sound.

I went down to London and purchased a common ear-trumpet.[1] My own ear was exceedingly acute, and to my great delight I found that, with the aid of the trumpet just as it was, I could distinguish sounds at a much greater distance, and those nearer were magnified in power. I had only to improve upon this instrument; careful study, careful work, careful experiment, and my hopes would undoubtedly be realized.

Back to my old room in the college I went with a complete set of tools. So days and weeks I shut myself in, and every day and every week brought nothing but disappointment. The instrument seemed only to diminish sound rather than increase it, yet still I worked on and vowed I would not grow discouraged.

Hour after hour I sat looking out of my narrow window. The fields of barley and waving oats had been reaped, the wheat too had ripened and gone, but I did not notice. I sprang up with a joyful exclamation—Strange never to have thought of it before! Perhaps I had not spent my time in vain, after all. How could I expect to test my instrument in this close room with only that little window? It should be removed from immediate noises, high up in the open air, where there would be no obstructions. I would never succeed here—but where should I go? It must be some place in which I would never be liable to interruption, for my first object was to be shielded and work in secret.

I scoured the neighborhood for an appropriate spot without success, when it occurred to me that I had heard some one say the old gray church was shut up. This church was situated just beyond the suburbs of the town. It was built of rough stone, mottled and stained by unknown years. The high square tower, covered by thick vines that clung and crept round its base, was the most venerable monument among all the slabs and tombs where it stood sentinel. Only graves deserted and uncared for by the living kept it company. People said the place was too damp for use, and talked of rebuilding, but it had never been done. Now if I could gain access to the tower, that was the very place for my purpose.

I found the door securely fastened, and walked round and round without discovering any way of entrance; but I made up my mind, if it were possible to get inside of that church I would do it, and without the help of keys. The high windows were not to be thought of; but in the rear of the building, lower down, where the fuel had probably been kept, there was a narrow opening which was boarded across. With very little difficulty I knocked out the planks and crept through. It was a cellar, and, as I had anticipated, the coal receptacle.

1 A form of hearing aid with a large, trumpet-like opening that leads to a tube that narrows to a small point inserted into the ear.

After feeling around, I found a few rough steps which led to a door that was unlocked and communicated with the passage back of the vestry-room. The tower I wished to explore was situated in the remote corner of the building. I passed on to the church. Its walls were discolored by green mould and blackened where the water had dripped through. The sun, low down in the sky, lit the tall arched windows on the west, and made yellow strips across the long aisles, over the faded pews with their stiff, straight backs, over the chancel rail, over the altar with its somber wood-work; but there was no warmth; only the cheerless glare seemed to penetrate the cold dead atmosphere,—only the cheerless glare without sparkle, without life, came into that voiceless sanctuary where the organ slept. At the right of the vestibule a staircase led to the tower; it ascended to a platform laid on a level with the four windows and a little above the point of the church roof. These four windows were situated one on each side of the tower, running high up, and the lower casement folding inward.

Here was my place. Above the tree-tops, in the free open air, with no obstacle to obstruct the wind, I could work unmolested by people or noise. The fresh breeze that fanned my face was cool and pleasant. An hour ago I had been tired, disappointed, and depressed; but now, buoyant with hope, I was ready to begin work again—work that I was determined to accomplish.

The sun had gone. I did not see the broken slabs and urns in the shadow down below; I did not see the sunken graves and the rank grass and the briers. I looked over them and saw the gorgeous fringes along the horizon, scarlet and gold and pearl; saw them quiver and brighten to flame, and the white wings of pigeons whirl and circle in the deepening glow.

I closed the windows, and when I had crawled out of the narrow hole, carefully reset the boards just as I had found them. In another day all the tools and books that I considered necessary were safely deposited in the tower. I only intended to make this my workshop, still, of course, occupying my old room in the college.

Here I matured plan after plan. I studied, read, worked, knowing, *feeling* that at last I must succeed; but failure followed failure, and I sank into despondency only to begin again with a kind of desperation. When I went down to London and wandered about, hunting up different metals and hard woods, I never entered a concert-room or an opera-house. Was there not music in store for me, such as no mortal ear had ever heard? *All* the music, every strain that had sounded in the past ages? Ah, I could wait; I would work patiently and wait.

I was laboring now upon a theory that I had not tried heretofore. It was my last resource; if this failed, then—but it would not fail. I resolved not to make any test, not to put it near my ear until it was completed. I discarded all woods and used only the metals which best transmitted sound. Finally it was finished, even to the ivory ear-piece. I held the instrument all ready—I held it and looked eastward and westward and back again. Suddenly all control over the muscles of my hand was gone, it felt like stone; then the strange sensation passed away. I stood up and lifted the trumpet to my ear—What! Silence? No, no—I was faint, my brain was confused, whirling. I would not believe it; I would wait a moment until this dizziness was gone, and then—then I would be able to hear. I was deaf now. I still held the instrument; in my agitation the ivory tip shook off and rolled down rattling on the floor. I gazed at it mechanically as if it had been a pebble; I never thought of replacing it, and mechanically I raised the trumpet a second time to my ear. A crash of discordant sounds, a confused jarring noise broke upon me and I drew back trembling, dismayed. Fool! O fool of fools never to have thought of this, which a child, a dunce would not have over-looked! My great invention was nothing, was worse than nothing, was worse than a failure. I might have known that my instrument would magnify present sounds in the air to such a degree as to make them utterly drown all others, and, clashing together, produce this noise like the heavy rumble of thunder.

The college reopened and I took up my old line of duties, or at least attempted them, for the school had grown distasteful to me. I was restless, moody, and discontented. I tried to forget my disappointment, but the effort was vain.

The spires of the town and the college campus glittered white, the fields of barley and oats were fields of snow, the forest leaves had withered and fallen, and the river slumbered, wrapped in a sheeting of ice. Still I brooded over my failure, and when again the wild grass turned green I no longer cared. I was not the same man that had looked out at the waving grain and the blue haze only a year before. A gloomy despondency had settled upon me, and I grew to hate the students, to hate the college, to hate society. In the first shock of discovered failure I had given up all hope, and the winter passed I knew not how. I never wondered if the trouble could be remedied. Now it suddenly occurred to me, perhaps it was no failure after all. The instrument might be made adjustable, so as to be sensible to faint or severe vibrations at pleasure of the operator, and thus separate the sounds. I remembered how but for the accidental removal of the ivory my instrument perhaps would not have reflected any sound. I would work again and persevere.

I would have resigned my professorship, only it might create suspicion. I knew not that already they viewed me with curious eyes and sober faces. When the session finally closed, they tried to persuade me to leave the college during vacation and travel on the continent. I would feel much fresher, they told me, in the fall. In the fall? Ay, perhaps I might, perhaps I might, and I would not go abroad.

Once more the reapers came unnoticed. My work progressed slowly. Day by day I toiled up in the old church-tower, and night by night I dreamed. In my sleep it often seemed that the instrument was suddenly completed, but before I could raise it to my ear I would always waken with a nervous start. So the feverish time went by, and at last I held it ready for a second trial.

Now the instrument was adjustable, and I had also improved it so far as to be able to set it very accurately for any particular period, thus rendering it sensible only to sounds of that time, all heavier and fainter vibrations being excluded.

I drew it out almost to its limits.

All the maddening doubts that had haunted me like grinning specters died. I felt no tremor, my hand was steady, my pulse-beat regular.

The soft breeze had fallen away. No leaf stirred in the quiet that seemed to await my triumph. Again the crimson splendor of sunset illumined the western sky and made a glory overhead—and the dusk was thickening down below among the mouldering slabs. But that mattered not.

I raised the trumpet to my ear.

Hark!—The hum of mighty hosts! It rose and fell, fainter and more faint; then the murmur of water was heard and lost again, as it swelled and gathered and burst in one grand volume of sound like a hallelujah from myriad lips. Out of the resounding echo, out of the dying cadence a single female voice arose. Clear, pure, rich, it soared above the tumult of the host that hushed itself, a living thing. Higher, sweeter, it seemed to break the fetters of mortality and tremble in sublime adoration before the Infinite. My breath stilled with awe. Was it a spirit-voice—one of the glittering host in the jasper city "that had no need of the sun, neither of the moon to shine in it?"[1] And the water, was it the river clear as crystal flowing from the great white throne?[2] But no! The tone now floated out soft, sad, human. There was no sorrowful strain in that nightless land where the leaves of the trees were for the healing of the nations.[3] The beautiful voice was of the earth and sin-stricken. From the sobbing that mingled with the faint ripple of water it went up once more, ringing gladly, joyfully; it went up inspired with praise to the sky, and—hark! the Hebrew tongue:—

"The horse and his rider hath he thrown into the sea."[4]

Then the noise of the multitude swelled again and a clash[5] of music broke forth from innumerable timbrels. I raised my head quickly—it was the song of Miriam after the passage of the Red Sea.

I knew not whether I lived.

I bent my ear eagerly to the instrument again and heard—the soft rustle, the breathing as of a sleeping forest. A plaintive note stole gently out, more solemn and quiet than the chant of the leaves. The mournful lay, forlorn, frightened, trembled on the air like the piteous wail of some wounded creature.

1 Revelation 21.23, describing the New Jerusalem.

2 "river clear as crystal": Revelation 22.1; "great white throne": Revelation 20.11.

3 Revelation 22.1.

4 Exodus 15.21; Miriam sings praise as the Red Sea, which had parted allowing the Jews to escape slavery in Egypt, closes and drowns the Pharaoh and his army.

5 "crash" in book version.

Then it grew stronger. Clear, brilliant, it burst in a shower of silver sounds like a whole choir of birds in the glitter of the tropical sunlight. But the mournful wail crept back, and the lonely heart-broken strain was lost, while the leaves still whispered to one another in the midnight.

Like the light of a distant star came to me this song of some nightingale, thousands of years after the bird had mouldered to nothing.

At last my labor had been rewarded. As sound travels in waves and these waves are continually advancing as they go round and round the world, therefore I would never hear the same sound over again at the same time, but it passed beyond and another came in its stead.

All night I listened with my ear pressed to the instrument. I heard the polished, well-studied compliments, the rustle of silks, and the quick music of the dance at some banquet. I could almost see the brilliant robes and glittering jewels of the waltzers, and the sheen of light, and the mirrors. But hush! a cry, a stifled moan. Was that at the—No, the music and the rustle of silk were gone.

"Mother, put your hand here,—I am tired, and my head feels hot and strange. Is it night, already, that it has grown so dark? I am resting now, for my book is almost done, and then, mother, we can go back to the dear old home where the sun shines so bright and the honeysuckles are heavy with perfume. And, mother, we will never be poor any more. I know you are weary, for your cheeks are pale and your fingers are thin; but they shall not touch a needle then, and you will grow better, mother, and we will forget these long, long, bitter years. I will not write in the evenings then, but sit with you and watch the twilight fade as we used to do, and listen to the murmur of the frogs. I described the little stream, our little stream, mother, in my book.—Hark! I hear the splash of its waves now. Hold me by the hand tight, mother. I am tired, but we are almost there. See! the house glimmers white through the trees, and the red bird has built its nest again in the cedar. Put your arm around me, mother, mother—"

Then single, echoless, the mother's piercing cry went up—"O my God!"

Great Heaven! It would not always be music that I should hear. Into this ear, where all the world poured its tales, sorrow and suffering and death would come in turn with mirth and gladness.

I listened again. The long-drawn ahoy!—ahoy!—of the sailor rang out in slumbrous musical monotone, now free, now muffled—gone. The gleeful laugh of children at play, then the drunken boisterous shout of the midnight reveler—What was that? A chime of bells, strange, sublime, swimming in the air they made a cold, solemn harmony. But even over them dashed the storm-blast of passion that sweeps continually up and down the earth, and the harmony that bound them in peace broke up in a wild, angry clamor, that set loose shrill screams which were swallowed up in a savage tumult of discord, like a mad carnival of yelling demons. Then, as if terrified by their own fiendish rage, they retreated shivering, remorseful, and hushed themselves in hoarse whispers about the gray belfry. It was the Carillonneur, Matthias Vander Gheyn, playing at Louvain on the first of July, 1745.[1]

Yes, my invention had proved a grand success. I had worked and worked in order to give this instrument to the world; but now when it was finished, strange to say, all my ambition, all my desire for fame left me, and I was anxious only to guard it from discovery, to keep it secret, to keep it more jealously than a miser hoards his gold. An undefinable delight filled my soul that I alone out of all humanity possessed this treasure, this great Ear of the World, for which kings might have given up their thrones. Ah! they dreamed not of the wonders I could relate. It was a keen, intense pleasure to see the public for which I had toiled live on, deaf forever save to the few transient sounds of the moment, while I, their slave, reveled in another world above, beyond theirs. But they should never have this instrument; no, not for kingdoms would I give it up, not for life itself.

It exerted a strange fascination over me, and in my eager desire to preserve my secret a tormenting fear suddenly took possession of me that some one might track me to the tower and discover all. It seemed as if the people looked after me with curious faces as I passed. I went no longer on the main road that led to the church, but, when I left my room, took an opposite direction until out of sight, and then made a circuit across the fields. I lived in a continual fear of betraying myself, so that at night I closed my window and door lest I might talk aloud in my sleep. I could never again bear the irksome duties of my office, and when the college reopened I gave up my situation and took lodgings in town. Still the dread of detection haunted me. Every day I varied my route to the church, and every day the people seemed to stare at me with a more curious gaze. Occasionally some of my old pupils came to visit me, but they appeared constrained in my presence and were soon gone. However, no one seemed to suspect my secret; perhaps all this was merely the work of my imagination, for I had grown watchful and reticent.

I hardly ate or slept. I lived perpetually in the past listening to the echoing song of the Alpine shepherd; the rich, uncultivated soprano of the Southern slave making strange wild melody. I heard grand organ fugues rolling, sweeping over multitudes that kneeled in awe, while a choir of voices broke into a gloria that seemed to sway the great cathedral. The thrilling artistic voices of the far past rang again, making my listening soul tremble in their magnificent harmony. It was music of which we could not dream.

Then suddenly I determined to try the opera once more; perhaps I was prejudiced: I had not been inside of a concert-room for more than a year.

I went down to London. It was just at the opening of the fall season. I could hardly wait that evening until the curtain rose; the orchestra was harsh and discordant, the house hot and disagreeable, the gas painfully bright. My

1 Matthias Vanden Gheyn (1721–85), Flemish musician; carillon: an organ-like instrument that plays church bells.

restlessness had acquired a feverish pitch before the prima donna made her appearance. Surely that voice was not the one before which the world bowed! Malibran's[1] song stood out in my memory clearly defined and complete, like a magnificent cathedral of pure marble, with faultless arches and skillfully chiseled carvings, where the minarets rose from wreaths of lilies and vine-leaves cut in bas-relief, and the slender spire shot high, glittering yellow in the upper sunlight, its golden arrow, burning like flame, pointing towards the East. But this prima donna built only a flat, clumsy structure of wood ornamented by gaudily painted lattice. I left the opera amid the deafening applause of the audience with a smile of scorn upon my lips. Poor deluded creatures! they knew nothing of music, they knew not what they were doing.[2]

I went to St. Paul's on the Sabbath. There was no worship in the operatic voluntary sung by hired voices; it did not stir my soul, and their cold hymns did not warm with praise to the Divine Creator, or sway the vast pulseless congregation that came and went without one quickened breath.

All this time I felt a singular, inexpressible pleasure in the consciousness of my great secret, and I hurried back with eager haste. In London I had accidentally met two or three of my old acquaintances. I was not over glad to see them myself: as I have said, I had grown utterly indifferent to society; but I almost felt ashamed when they offered me every attention within their power, for I had not anticipated it, nor was it deserved on my part. Now, when I returned, everybody in the street stopped to shake hands with me and inquire for my health. At first, although I was surprised at the interest they manifested, I took it merely as the common civility on meeting, but when the question was repeated so particularly by each one, I thought it appeared strange, and asked if they had ever heard to the contrary; no, oh no, they said, but still I was astonished at the unusual care with which they all made the same inquiry. I went up to my room and walked directly to the glass. It was the first time I had consciously looked into a mirror for many weeks. Good Heavens! The mystery was explained now. *I could hardly recognise myself.* At first the shock was so great that I stood gazing, almost petrified. The demon of typhus[3] fever could not have wrought a more terrific change in my face if he had held it in his clutches for months. My hair hung in long straggling locks around my neck. I was thin and fearfully haggard. My eyes, sunken far back in my head, looked out from dark deep hollows; my heavy black eyebrows were knit together by wrinkles that made seams over my forehead: my fleshless cheeks clung tight to the bone, and a bright red spot on either one was half covered by thick beard. I had thought so little about my personal appearance lately that I had utterly neglected my hair, and I wondered now that it had given me no annoyance. I smiled while I still looked at myself. This was the effect of the

1 Maria Malibran (1808–36), famous Spanish opera singer.

2 Luke 23.34: "Then said Jesus, Father, forgive them; for they know not what they do."

3 There were several epidemics ascribed to typhus in North America in the mid-nineteenth century.

severe study and loss of sleep, and the excitement under which I had labored for months, yes, for more than a year. I had not been conscious of fatigue, but my work was done now and I would soon regain my usual weight. I submitted myself immediately to the hands of a barber, dressed with considerable care, and took another look in the glass. My face appeared pinched and small since it had been freed from beard. The caverns around my eyes seemed even larger, and the bright color in my cheeks contrasted strangely with the extremely sallow tint of my complexion. I turned away with an uncomfortable feeling, and started on a circuitous route to the church, for I never trusted my instrument in any other place.

It was a sober fall day. Everything looked dreary with that cold, gray, sunless sky stretched overhead. The half-naked trees shivered a little in their seared garments of ragged leaves. Occasionally a cat walked along the fence-top, or stood trembling on three legs. Sometimes a depressed bird tried to cheer its drooping spirits and uttered a few sharp, discontented chirps. Just in front of me two boys were playing ball on the road-side. As I passed I accidentally caught this sentence:

"They say the professor ain't just right in his head."

For a moment I stood rooted to the ground; then wheeled round and cried out fiercely,

"What did you say?"

"Sir?"

"What was that you said just now?" I repeated still more fiercely.

The terrified boys looked at me an instant, then without answering turned and ran as fast as fright could carry them.

So the mystery now was really explained! It was not sick the people thought me, but crazy. I walked on with a queer feeling and began vaguely to wonder why I had been so savage to those boys. The fact which I had learned so suddenly certainly gave me a shock, but it was nothing to me. What did I care, even if the people did think me crazy? Ah! perhaps if I told my secret they would consider it a desperate case of insanity. But the child's words kept ringing in my ears until an idea flashed upon me more terrifying than death itself. How did I know that I was *not* insane? How did I know but that my great invention might be only an hallucination of my brain? Instantly a whole army of thoughts crowded up like ghostly witnesses to affright me. I had studied myself to a shadow; my pallid face, with the red spots on the cheeks and the blue hollows around the eyes, came before my mental vision afresh. The fever in my veins told me I was unnaturally excited. I had not slept a sound, dreamless sleep for weeks. Perhaps in the long, long days and nights my brain, like my body, had been over-wrought; perhaps in my eager desire to succeed, in my desperate determination, the power of my will had disordered my mind, and it was all deception: the sounds, the music I had heard, merely the creation of my diseased fancy, and the instrument I had handled useless metal. The very idea was inexpressible torture to me. I could not bear that a single doubt of its reality should exist; but, after once entering my head, how would I ever be able to free myself from distrust? I could not do it; I would be obliged to live always in uncertainty. It was maddening: now I felt as if I might have struck the child in my rage if I could have found him. Then suddenly it occurred to me for the first time that my invention could easily be tested by some other person. Almost instantly I rejected the thought, for it would compel me to betray my secret, and in my strange infatuation I would rather have destroyed the instrument. But the doubts of my sanity on this subject returned upon me with tenfold strength, and again I thought in despair of the only method left me by which they could ever be settled.

In the first shock, when the unlucky sentence fell upon my ear, I had turned after the boys, and then walked on mechanically towards the town. Now, when I looked up I found myself almost at the college gate. No one was to be seen, only Mother Flinse with her basket on her arm was just raising the latch. Half bewildered, I turned hastily round and bent my steps in the direction of my lodgings, while I absently wondered whether that old woman had stood there ever since, since—when? I did not recollect, but her shadow was long and slim—no, there were no shadows this afternoon; it was sunless. As I reached the stairs leading to my room, my trouble, which I had forgotten for the moment, broke upon me anew. I dragged myself up and sat down utterly overwhelmed. As I have said, I would sooner destroy the instrument than give it to a thankless world; but to endure the torturing doubt of its reality was impossible. Suddenly it occurred to me that Mother Flinse was mute. I might get her to test my invention without fear of betrayal, for she could neither speak nor write, and her signs on this subject, if she attempted to explain, would be altogether unintelligible to others. I sprang up in wild delight, then immediately fell back in my chair with a hoarse laugh—Mother Flinse was *deaf* as well as dumb. I had not remembered that. I sat quietly a moment trying to calm myself and think. Why need this make any difference? The instrument ought to, at least it was possible that it might, remedy loss of hearing. I too was deaf to these sounds in the air that it made audible. They would have to be magnified to a greater degree for her. I might set it for the present and use the full power of the instrument: there certainly would be no harm in trying, at any rate, and if it failed it would prove nothing, if it did not fail it would prove everything. Then a new difficulty presented itself. How could I entice the old woman into the church?

I went back towards the college expecting to find her, but she was nowhere to be seen, and I smiled that only a few moments ago I had wondered if she did not always stand in the gateway. Once, I could not exactly recall the time, I had passed her hut. I remembered distinctly that there was a line full of old ragged clothes stretched across from the fence to a decayed tree, and a bright red flannel petticoat blew and flapped among the blackened branches. It was a miserable frame shanty, set back from the Spring road, about half a mile out of town. There I went in search of her.

The blasted tree stood out in bold relief against the drab sky. There appeared no living thing about the dirty, besmoked hovel except one lean rat, that squatted with quivering nose and stared a moment, then retreated under the loose plank before the door, leaving its smellers visible until I stepped upon the board. I knocked loudly without receiving any reply; then, smiling at the useless ceremony I had performed, pushed it open. The old woman, dressed in her red petticoat and a torn calico frock, with a faded shawl drawn over her head, was standing with her back towards me, picking over a pile of rags. She did not move. I hesitated an instant, then walked in. The moment I put my foot upon the floor she sprang quickly round. At first she remained motionless, with her small, piercing gray eyes fixed upon me, holding a piece of orange-and-black spotted muslin; evidently she recognized me, for, suddenly dropping it, she began a series of wild gestures, grinning until all the wrinkles of her skinny face converged in the region of her mouth, where a few scattered teeth, long and sharp, gleamed strangely white. A rim of grizzled hair stood out round the edge of the turbaned shawl and set off the withered and watchful countenance of the speechless old crone. The yellow, shriveled skin hung loosely about her slim neck like leather, and her knotted hands were brown and dry as the claws of an eagle.

I went through the motion of sweeping and pointed over my shoulder, making her understand that I wished her to do some cleaning. She drew the seams of her face into a new grimace by way of assent, and, putting the piece of orange-and-black spotted muslin around her shoulders in lieu of a cloak, preceded me out of the door. She started immediately in the direction of the college, and I was obliged to take hold of her before I could attract her attention; then, when I shook my head, she regarded me in surprise, and fell once more into a series of frantic gesticulations. With considerable trouble I made her comprehend that she was merely to follow me. The old woman was by no means dull, and her small, steel-gray eyes had a singular sharpness about them that is only found in the deaf-mute, where they perform the part of the ear and tongue. As soon as we came in sight of the church she was perfectly satisfied. I walked up to the main entrance, turned the knob and shook it, then suddenly felt in all my pockets, shook the door over, and felt through all my pockets again. This hypocritical pantomime had the desired effect. The old beldam[1] slapped her hands together and poked her lean finger at the hole of the lock, apparently amused that I had forgotten the key. Then of her own accord she went round and tried the other doors, but without success. As we passed the narrow window in the rear I made a violent effort in knocking out the loose boards. The old woman seemed greatly delighted, and when I crawled through willingly followed. I gave her a brush, which fortunately one day I had discovered lying in the vestibule, and left her in the church to dust, while I went up in the tower to prepare and remove from sight all the tools

1 An old woman, often used pejoratively.

which were scattered about. I put them in a recess and screened it from view by a map of the Holy Land. Then I took my instrument and carefully adjusted it, putting on its utmost power.

In about an hour I went down and motioned to Mother Flinse that I wanted her up stairs. She came directly after me without hesitation, and I felt greatly relieved, for I saw that I would likely have no trouble with the old woman. When we got into the tower she pointed down to the trees and then upward, meaning, I presume, that it was high. I nodded, and taking the instrument placed my ear to it for a moment. A loud blast of music, like a dozen bands playing in concert, almost stunned me. She watched me very attentively, but when I made signs for her to come and try she drew back. I held up the instrument and went through all manner of motions indicating that it would not hurt her, but she only shook her head. I persevered in my endeavor to coax her until she seemed to gain courage and walked up within a few feet of me, then suddenly stopped and stretched out her hands for the instrument. As she did not seem afraid, provided she had it herself, I saw that she took firm hold. In my impatience to know the result of this experiment, I was obliged to repeat my signs again and again before I could prevail upon her to raise it to her ear. Then breathlessly I watched her face, a face I thought which looked as if it might belong to some mummy that had been withering for a thousand years. Suddenly it was convulsed as if by a galvanic shock,[1] then the shriveled features seemed to dilate, and a great light flashed through them, transforming them almost into the radiance of youth; a strange light as of some seraph[2] had taken possession of the wrinkled old frame and looked out at the gray eyes, making them shine with unnatural beauty. No wonder the dumb countenance reflected a brightness inexpressible, for the Spirit of Sound had just alighted with silvery wings upon a silence of seventy years.

A heavy weight fell unconsciously from my breast while I stood almost awed before this face, which was transfigured, as if it might have caught a glimmer of that mystical morn when in a moment, in the twinkling of an eye, we shall all be changed.[3]

My instrument had stood the test; it was proved forever. I could no longer cherish any doubts of its reality, and an indescribable peace came into my soul, like a sudden awakening from some frightful dream. I had not noticed the flight of time. A pale shadow hung already over the trees—yes, and under them on the slime-covered stones.—Ay! and a heavier shadow than the coming night was even then gathering unseen its rayless folds. The drab sky had blanched and broken, and the sinking sun poured a fading light through its ragged fissures.

The old woman, as if wrapped in an enchantment, had hardly moved. I tried

1 Electric shock.

2 Angel.

3 1 Corinthians 15.51–52.

vainly to catch her attention; she did not even appear conscious of my presence. I walked up and shook her gently by the shoulder, and, pointing to the setting sun, held out my hand for the instrument. She looked at me a moment, with the singular unearthly beauty shining through every feature; then suddenly clutching the trumpet tight between her skinny claws, sprang backward towards the stairs, uttering a sound that was neither human nor animal, that was not a wail or a scream, but it fell upon my ears like some palpable horror. Merciful Heaven! Was that thing yonder a woman? The shriveled, fleshless lips gaped apart, and a small pointed tongue lurked behind five glittering, fang-like teeth. The wild beast had suddenly been developed in the hag. Like a hungry tigress defending its prey, she stood hugging the trumpet to her, glaring at me with stretched neck and green eyes.

A savage fierceness roused within me when I found she would not give up the instrument, and I rushed at her with hands ready to snatch back the prize I valued more than my life—*or hers;* but, quicker than a hunted animal, she turned and fled with it down the stairs, making the tower ring with the hideous cries of her wordless voice. Swiftly—it seemed as if the danger of losing the trumpet gave me wings to fly in pursuit—I crossed the vestibule. She was not there. Everything was silent, and I darted with fleet steps down the dusky aisle of the church, when suddenly the jarring idiotic sounds broke loose again, echoing up in the organ-pipes and rattling along the galleries. The fiend sprang from behind the altar, faced about an instant with flashing eyes and gleaming teeth, then fled through the vestry-room into the passage. The sight of her was fresh fuel to my rage, and it flamed into a frenzy that seemed to burn the human element out of my soul. When I gained the steps leading into the coal-room she was already in the window, but I cleared the distance at a single bound and caught hold of her clothes as she leaped down. I crawled through, but she clutched the instrument tighter. I could not prize it out of her grasp; and in her ineffectual efforts to free herself from my hold she made loud, grating cries, that seemed to me rang and reverberated all through the forest; but presently they grew smothered, gurgled, then ceased. Her clasp relaxed in a convulsive struggle, and the trumpet was in my possession. It was easily done, for her neck was small and lean, and my hands made a circle strong as a steel band.

The tremor died out of her frame and left it perfectly still. Through the silence I could hear the hiss of a snake in the nettle-weeds, and the flapping wings of some night bird fanned my face as it rushed swiftly through the air in its low flight. The gray twilight had deepened to gloom and the graves seemed to have given up their tenants. The pale monuments stood out like shrouded specters. But all the dead in that church-yard were not under ground, for on the wet grass at my feet there was something stark and stiff, more frightful than any phantom of imagination—something that the daylight would not rob of its ghastly features. It must be put out of sight, yes, it must be hid, to save my invention from discovery. The old hag might be missed, and if she was found here it would ruin me and expose my secret. I placed the trumpet on the window-ledge, and, carrying the grim burden in my arms, plunged into the damp tangle of weeds and grass.

In a lonesome corner far back from the church, in the dense shade of thorn-trees, among the wild brambles where poisonous vines grew, slippery with the mould of forgotten years, unsought, uncared for by any human hand, was a tomb. Its sides were half buried in the tall under-brush, and the long slab had been broken once, for a black fissure ran zigzag across the middle. In my muscles that night there was the strength of two men. I lifted off one-half of the stone and heard the lizards dart startled from their haunt, and felt the spiders crawl. When the stone was replaced it covered more than the lizards or the spiders in the dark space between the narrow walls.

As I have said, the instrument possessed a singular fascination over me. I had grown to love it, not alone as a piece of mechanism for the transmission of sound, but like a *living* thing, and I replaced it in the tower with the same pleasure one feels who has rescued a friend from death. My listening ear never grew weary, but now I drew quickly away. It was not music I heard, or the ripple of water, or the prattle of merry tongues, but the harsh grating cries that had echoed in the church, that had rattled and died out in the forest—that voice which was not a voice. I shivered while I readjusted the instrument; perhaps it was the night wind which chilled me, but the rasping sounds were louder than before. *I could not exclude them.* There was no element of superstition in my nature, and I tried it over again: still I heard them—sometimes sharp, sometimes only a faint rumbling. Had the soul of the deaf-mute come in retribution to haunt me and cry eternally in my instrument? Perhaps on the morrow it would not disturb me, but there was no difference. I could hear only it, though I drew out the trumpet for vibrations hundreds of years old. I had rid myself of the withered wretch who would have stolen my treasure, but now I could not rid myself of her invisible ghost. She had conquered, even through death, and come from the spirit world to gain possession of the prize for which she had given up her life. The instrument was no longer of any value to me, though cherishing a vague hope I compelled myself to listen, even with chattering teeth; for it was a terrible thing to hear those hoarse, haunting cries of the dumb soul—of the soul I had strangled from its body, a soul which I would have killed itself if it were possible. But my hope was vain, and the trumpet had become not only worthless to me, but an absolute horror. Suddenly I determined to destroy it. I turned it over ready to dash it in pieces, but it cost me a struggle to crush this work of my life, and while I stood irresolute a small green and gold beetle crawled out of it and dropped like a stone to the floor. The insect was an electric flash to me, that dispelled the black gloom through which I had been battling. It had likely fallen into the instrument down in the church-yard, or when I laid it upon the window-sill, and the rasping of its wings, magnified, had produced the sounds which resembled the strange grating noise uttered by the deaf-mute.

Instantly I put the trumpet to my ear. Once more the music of the past surged in. Voices, leaves, water, all murmured to me their changeful melody; every zephyr[1] wafting by was filled with broken but melodious whispers.

Relieved from doubts, relieved from fears and threatening dangers, I slept peacefully, dreamlessly as a child. With a feeling of rest to which I had long been unused, I walked out in the soft clear morning. Everything seemed to have put on new life, for the sky was not gray or sober, and the leaves, if they were brown, trimmed their edges in scarlet, and if many had fallen, the squirrels played among them on the ground. But suddenly the sky and the leaves and the squirrels might have been blotted from existence. I did not see them, but I saw—*I saw Mother Flinse come through the college gateway and walk slowly down the road!*

The large faded shawl pinned across her shoulders nearly covered the red flannel petticoat, and the orange-and-black spotted muslin was wrapped into a turban on her head. Without breathing, almost without feeling, I watched the figure until at the corner it turned out of sight, and a long dark outline on the grass behind it ran into the fence. The shadow! Then it was not a ghost. Had the grave given up its dead? I would see.

At the churchyard the briers tore my face and clothes, but I plunged deeper where the shade thickened under the thorn-trees. There in the corner I stooped to lift the broken slab of a tomb, but all my strength would not move it. As I leaned over, bruising my hands in a vain endeavor to raise it, my eyes fell for an instant on the stone, and with a start I turned quickly and ran to the church; then I stopped—the narrow fissure that cut zigzag across the slab on the tomb was filled with green moss, and this window was nailed up, and hung full of heavy cobwebs.

And my instrument?

Suddenly, while I stood there, some substance in my brain seemed to break up—it was the fetters of monomania which had bound me since that evening long ago, when, by the river in the oak-forest, I had heard the robin trill.

No murder stained my soul: and there, beside the black waves of insanity through which I had passed unharmed, I gave praise to the great Creator—praise silent, but intense as Miriam's song by the sea.

1 "gentle, mild wind or breeze" (*OED*).

H.G. Wells (1866–1946)

Along with Mary Wollstonecraft Shelley and Edgar Allan Poe, English author H.G. Wells is the most significant nineteenth-century English-language author in the development of modern science fiction. He also bridged the nineteenth and twentieth centuries, pointing to the continuities in SF's longer history. Noted by Hugo Gernsback as one of the authors who defines the form of "scientifiction," Wells's "scientific romances" include many of the formal elements that are seen to define the form. *The Time Machine* (1895), *The Island of Doctor Moreau* (1896), and *The War of the Worlds* (1897) each popularized SF plots and devices—from time travel, to evolutionary transformations and medical experimentation, to alien invasion—that are still being explored. "The Star," published on Christmas Day near the turn of the century, explores millenarian fears about the end of the world, but also the social effects of global climate change, galactic physics, and the interaction (or lack thereof) between sympathy and science.

Note on the text: The text used here is that of the original publication in a Christmas issue of *The Graphic* newspaper, 25 December 1897.

"The Star" (1897)

It was on the first day of the new year that the announcement was made, almost simultaneously from three observatories, that the motion of the planet Neptune, the outermost of all the planets that wheel about the sun, had become very erratic. Ogilvy had already called attention to a suspected retardation in its velocity in December. Such a piece of news was scarcely calculated to interest a world the greater portion of whose inhabitants were unaware of the existence of the planet Neptune, nor outside the astronomical profession did the subsequent discovery of a faint remote speck of light in the region of the perturbed planet cause any very great excitement. Scientific people, however, found the intelligence remarkable enough, even before it became known that the new body was rapidly growing larger and brighter, that its motion was quite different from the orderly progress of the planets, and that the deflection of Neptune and its satellite was becoming now of an unprecedented kind.

Few people without a training in science can realise the huge isolation of the solar system. The sun with its specks of planets, its dust of planetoids, and its impalpable comets, swims in a vacant immensity that almost defeats the imagination. Beyond the orbit of Neptune there is space, vacant so far as human observation has penetrated, without warmth or light or sound, blank emptiness, for twenty million times a million miles.[1] That is the smallest

1 The first confirmed human observation of Neptune was in 1846. While there was long speculation of other planets, Pluto, once considered a planet, was not observed until 1930. The Kuiper (*continued*)

estimate of the distance to be traversed before the very nearest of the stars is attained. And, saving a few comets more unsubstantial than the thinnest flame, no matter had ever to human knowledge crossed this gulf of space, until early in the twentieth century this strange wanderer appeared, a vast mass of matter it was, bulky, heavy, rushing without warning out of the black mystery of the sky into the radiance of the sun. By the second day it was clearly visible to any decent instrument, as a speck with a barely sensible diameter, in the constellation Leo near Regulus. In a little while an opera glass could attain it.

On the third day of the new year the newspaper readers of two hemispheres were made aware for the first time of the real importance of this unusual apparition in the heavens. "A Planetary Collision," one London paper headed the news, and proclaimed Duchaine's opinion that this strange new planet would probably collide with Neptune. The leader writers enlarged upon the topic. So that in most of the large capitals of the world, on January 3rd, there was an expectation, however vague, of some imminent phenomenon in the sky; and as the night followed the sunset round the globe, thousands of men turned their eyes skyward to see—the old familiar stars just as they had always been.

Until it was dawn in London and Pollux[1] setting and the stars overhead grown pale. The Winter's dawn it was, a sickly filtering accumulation of daylight, and the light of gas and candles shone yellow in the windows to show where people were astir. But the yawning policeman saw the thing, the busy crowds in the markets stopped agape, workmen going to their work betimes, milkmen, the drivers of news-carts, dissipation going home jaded and pale, homeless wanderers, sentinels on their beats, and in the country, labourers trudging afield, poachers slinking home, all over the dusky quickening country it could be seen—and out at sea by seamen watching for the day—a great white star, come suddenly into the westward sky!

Brighter it was than any star in our skies; brighter than the evening star at its brightest. It still glowed out white and large, no mere twinkling spot of light, but a small round clear shining disc, an hour after the day had come. And where science has not reached, men stared and feared, telling one another of the wars and pestilences that are foreshadowed by these fiery signs in the Heavens. Sturdy Boers, dusky Hottentots, Gold Coast negroes,[2] Frenchmen, Spaniards, Portuguese, stood in the warmth of the sunrise watching the setting of this strange new star.

Belt—where Pluto and other objects now classified dwarf planets can be found—was hypothesized later in the twentieth century, and observed in 1992. NASA's "Solar System Exploration" website offers a useful overview.

1 Pollux is the brightest star in the constellation Gemini.

2 "Boer" is a dated term for an Afrikaner South African, while "Hottentot" is a racist Dutch term for the Khoekhoe people of southern Africa. The Gold Coast was the name for a British colony in West Africa. "Negro" would have been considered a generally inoffensive term at the time of the story's writing, though it is now dated and carries racist connotations.

And in a hundred observatories there had been suppressed excitement, rising almost to shouting pitch, as the two remote bodies had hurried together, and a hurrying to and fro, to gather photographic apparatus and spectroscope, and this appliance and that, to record this novel astonishing sight, the destruction of a world. For it was a world, a sister planet of our earth, far greater than our earth, indeed, that had so suddenly flashed into flaming death. Neptune it was, had been struck, fairly and squarely, by the strange planet from outer space and the heat of the concussion had incontinently turned two solid globes into one vast mass of incandescence. Round the world that day, two hours before the dawn, went the pallid great white star, fading only as it sank westward and the sun mounted above it. Everywhere men marvelled at it, but of all those who saw it none could have marvelled more than those sailors, habitual watchers of the stars, who far away at sea had heard nothing of its advent and saw it now rise like a pigmy moon and climb zenithward and hang overhead and sink westward with the passing of the night.

And when next it rose over Europe everywhere were crowds of watchers on hilly slopes, on house-roofs, in open spaces, staring eastward for the rising of the great new star. It rose with a white glow in front of it, like the glare of a white fire, and those who had seen it come into existence the night before cried out at the sight of it. "It is larger," they cried. "It is brighter!" And, indeed the moon a quarter full and sinking in the west was in its apparent size, indeed, beyond comparison, but scarcely in all its breadth had it as much brightness now as the little circle of the strange new star.

"It is brighter!" cried the people clustering in the streets. But in the dim observatories the watchers held their breath and peered at one another. "*It is nearer,*" they said. "*Nearer!*"

And voice after voice repeated, "It is nearer," and the clicking telegraph took that up, and it trembled along telephone wires, and in a thousand cities grimy compositors fingered the type. "It is nearer." Men writing in offices, struck with a strange realisation, flung down their pens, men talking in a thousand places suddenly came upon a grotesque possibility in those words, "It is nearer." It hurried along awakening streets, it was shouted down the frost-stilled ways of quiet villages, men who had read these things from the throbbing tape stood in yellow-lit doorways shouting the news to the passers-by. "It is nearer." Pretty women, flushed and glittering, heard the news told jestingly between the dances, and feigned an intelligent interest they did not feel. "Nearer! Indeed. How curious! How very, very clever people must be to find out things like that!"

Lonely tramps faring through the wintry night murmured those words to comfort themselves—looking skyward. "It has need to be nearer, for the night's as cold as charity. Don't seem much warmth from it if it *is* nearer, all the same."

"What is a new star to me?" cried the weeping woman kneeling beside the dead.

The schoolboy, rising early for his examination work, puzzled it out for himself—with the great white star, shining broad and bright through the frost-flowers of his window. "Centrifugal, centripetal," he said, with his chin on his fist. "Stop a planet in its flight, rob it of its centrifugal force, what then? Centripetal has it, and down it falls into the sun! And this—!"

"Do *we* come in the way? I wonder—"

The light of that day went the way of its brethren, and with the later watches of the frosty darkness rose the strange star again. And it was now so bright that the waxing moon seemed but a pale yellow ghost of itself, hanging huge in the sunset. In a South African city a great man had married, and the streets were alight to welcome his return with his bride. "Even the skies have illuminated," said the flatterer. Under Capricorn, two negro lovers, daring the wild beasts and evil spirits, for love of one another, crouched together in a cane brake where the fire-flies hovered. "That is our star," they whispered, and felt strangely comforted by the sweet brilliance of its light.

The master mathematician sat in his private room and pushed the papers from him. His calculations were already finished. In a small white phial there still remained a little of the drug that had kept him awake and active for four long nights. Each day, serene, explicit, patient as ever, he had given his lecture to his students, and then had come back at once to this momentous calculation. His face was grave, a little drawn and hectic from his drugged activity. For some time he seemed lost in thought. Then he stood up, went to the window, and the blind went up with a click. Half way up the sky, over the clustering roofs, chimneys and steeples of the city, hung the star.

He looked at it as one might look into the eyes of a brave enemy. "You may kill me," he said after a silence. "But I can hold you—and all the universe for that matter—in the grip of this little brain. I would not change. Even now."

He looked at the little phial. "There will be no need of sleep again," he said. The next day at noon, punctual to the minute, he entered his lecture theatre, put his hat on the end of the table as his habit was, and carefully selected a large piece of chalk. It was a joke among his students that he could not lecture without that piece of chalk to fumble in his fingers, and once he had been stricken to impotence by their hiding his supply. He came and looked under his grey eyebrows at the rising tiers of young fresh faces, and spoke with his accustomed studied commonness of phrasing. "Circumstances have arisen—circumstances beyond my control," he said and paused, "which will debar me from completing the course I had designed. It would seem, gentlemen, if I may put the thing clearly and briefly, that—Man has lived in vain."

The students glanced at one another. Had they heard aright? Mad? Raised eyebrows and grinning lips there were, but one or two faces remained intent upon his calm grey-fringed face. "It will be interesting," he was saying, "to devote this morning to an exposition, so far as I can make it clear to you, of the calculations that have led me to this conclusion. Let us assume—"

He turned towards the blackboard, meditating a diagram in the way that was usual to him. "What was that about lived in vain?" whispered one student to another. "Listen," said the other, nodding towards the lecturer.

And presently they began to understand.

That night the star rose later, for its proper eastward motion had carried it some way across Leo towards Virgo, and its brightness was so great that the sky became a luminous blue as it rose, and every star was hidden in its turn, save only Jupiter near the zenith, Capella, Aldebaran, Sirius and the pointers of the Bear.[1] It was very white and beautiful. In many parts of the world that night a pallid halo encircled it about. It was perceptibly larger; in the clear refractive sky of the tropics it seemed as if it were nearly a quarter the size of the moon. The frost was still on the ground in England, but the world was as brightly lit as if it were midsummer moonlight. One could see to read quite ordinary print by that cold clear light, and in the cities the lamps burnt yellow and wan.

And everywhere the world was awake that night, and throughout Christendom a sombre murmur hung in the keen air over the country side like the belling of bees in the heather, and this murmurous tumult grew to a clangour in the cities. It was the tolling of the bells in a million belfry towers and steeples, summoning the people to sleep no more, to sin no more, but to gather in their churches and pray. And overhead, growing larger and brighter, as the earth rolled on its way and the night passed, rose the dazzling star.

And the streets and houses were alight in all the cities, the shipyards glared, and whatever roads led to high country were lit and crowded all night long. And in all the seas about the civilised lands, ships with throbbing engines, and ships with bellying sails, crowded with men and living creatures, were standing out to ocean and the north. For already the warning of the master mathematician had been telegraphed all over the world, and translated into a hundred tongues. The new planet and Neptune, locked in a fiery embrace, were whirling headlong, ever faster and faster towards the sun. Already every second this blazing mass flew a hundred miles, and every second its terrific velocity increased. As it flew now, indeed, it must pass a hundred million of miles wide of the earth and scarcely affect it. But near its destined path, as yet only slightly perturbed, spun the mighty planet Jupiter and his moons sweeping splendid round the sun. Every moment now the attraction between the fiery star and the greatest of the planets grew stronger. And the result of that attraction? Inevitably Jupiter would be deflected from its orbit into an elliptical path, and the burning star, swung by his attraction wide of its sunward rush, would "describe a curved path" and perhaps collide with, and certainly pass very close to, our earth. "Earthquakes, volcanic outbreaks, cyclones, sea waves, floods, and a steady rise in temperature to I know not what limit"—so prophesied the master mathematician.

1 Capella, Aldebaran, and Sirius are all stars. The Bear refers to the constellation Ursa Major, in which two stars (Dubhe and Merak) are called "the pointers" because extending a line between them "points" to the North Star (Polaris).

And overhead, to carry out his words, lonely and cold and livid, blazed the star of the coming doom.

To many who stared at it that night until their eyes ached, it seemed that it was visibly approaching. And that night, too, the weather changed, and the frost that had gripped all Central Europe and France and England softened towards a thaw.

But you must not imagine because I have spoken of people praying through the night and people going aboard ships and people fleeing towards mountainous country that the whole world was already in a terror because of the star. As a matter of fact, use and wont still ruled the world, and save for the talk of idle moments and the splendour of the night, nine human beings out of ten were still busy at their common occupations. In all the cities the shops, save one here and there, opened and closed at their proper hours, the doctor and the undertaker plied their trades, the workers gathered in the factories, soldiers drilled, scholars studied, lovers sought one another, thieves lurked and fled, politicians planned their schemes. The presses of the newspapers roared through the nights, and many a priest of this church and that would not open his holy building to further what he considered a foolish panic. The newspapers insisted on the lesson of the year 1000—for then, too, people had anticipated the end. The star was no star—mere gas—a comet; and were it a star it could not possibly strike the earth, there was no precedent for such a thing. Common sense was sturdy everywhere, scornful, jesting, a little inclined to persecute the obdurate fearful. That night, at seven-fifteen by Greenwich time, the star would be at its nearest to Jupiter. Then the world would see the turn things would take. The master mathematician's grim warnings were treated by many as so much mere elaborate self-advertisement. Common sense at last, a little heated by argument, signified its unalterable convictions by going to bed. So, too, barbarism and savagery, already tired of the novelty, went about their nightly business, and save for a howling dog here and there, the beast world left the star unheeded.

And yet, when at last the watchers in the European States saw the star rise, an hour later it is true, but no larger than it had been the night before, there were still plenty awake to laugh at the master mathematician—to take the danger as if it had passed.

But thereafter the laughter ceased. The star grew—it grew with a terrible steadiness hour after hour, a little larger each hour, a little nearer the midnight zenith, and brighter and brighter, until it had turned night into a second day. Had it come straight to the earth instead of in a curved path, had it lost no velocity to Jupiter, it must have leapt the intervening gulf in a day, but as it was it took five days altogether to come by our planet. The next night it had become a third the size of the moon before it set to English eyes, and the thaw was assured. It rose over America near the size of the moon, but blinding white to look at, and *hot*; and a breath of hot wind blew now with its rising and gathering strength, and in Virginia, and Brazil, and down the St. Lawrence valley, it shone intermittently through a driving reek of thunder-clouds, flickering violet lightning, and hail unprecedented. In Manitoba was a thaw and devastating floods. And upon all the mountains of the earth the snow and ice began to melt that night, and all the rivers coming out of high country flowed thick and turbid, and soon—in their upper reaches—with swirling trees and the bodies of beasts and men. They rose steadily, steadily in the ghostly brilliance, and came trickling over their banks at last, behind the flying population of their valleys.

And along the coast of Argentina and up the South Atlantic the tides were higher than had ever been in the memory of man, and the storms drove the waters in many cases scores of miles inland, drowning whole cities. And so great grew the heat during the night that the rising of the sun was like the coming of a shadow. The earthquakes began and grew until all down America from the Arctic Circle to Cape Horn, hillsides were sliding, fissures were opening, and houses and walls crumbling to destruction. The whole side of Cotopaxi[1] slipped out in one vast convulsion, and a tumult of lava poured out so high and broad and swift and liquid that in one day it reached the sea.

So the star, with the wan moon in its wake, marched across the Pacific, trailed the thunderstorms like the hem of a robe, and the growing tidal wave that toiled behind it, frothing and eager, poured over island and island and swept them clear of men. Until that wave came at last—in a blinding light and with the breath of a furnace, swift and terrible it came—a wall of water, fifty feet high, roaring hungrily, upon the long coasts of Asia, and swept inland across the plains of China. For a space the star, hotter now and larger and brighter than the sun in its strength, showed with pitiless brilliance the wide and populous country; towns and villages with their pagodas and trees, roads, wide cultivated fields, millions of sleepless people staring in helpless terror at the incandescent sky; and then, low and growing, came the murmur of the flood. And thus it was with millions of men that night—a flight nowhither, with limbs heavy with heat and breath fierce and scant, and the flood like a wall swift and white behind. And then death.

China was lit glowing white, but over Japan and Java and all the islands of Eastern Asia the great star was a ball of dull red fire because of the steam and smoke and ashes the volcanoes were spouting forth to salute its coming. Above was the lava flood, hot gases and ash, and below the seething floods, and the whole earth swayed and rumbled with the earthquake shocks. Soon the immemorial snows of Thibet and the Himalaya were melting and pouring down by ten million deepening converging channels upon the plains of Burmah and Hindostan.[2] The tangled summits of the Indian jungles were aflame in a thousand places, and below the hurrying waters around the stems were dark objects that still struggled feebly and reflected the blood-red tongues of fire. And in

1 A volcano in the Andes mountain range in Ecuador.

2 Historical terms for Myanmar and India (or northern India), respectively.

a rudderless confusion a multitude of men and women fled down the broad river-ways to that one last hope of men—the sea.

Larger grew the star, and larger, hotter, and brighter with a terrible swiftness now. The tropical ocean had lost its phosphorescence, and the whirling steam rose in ghostly wreaths from the black waves that plunged incessently about the storm-tossed ships.

And then came a wonder. It seemed to those who in Europe watched for the rising of the star that the world must have ceased its rotation. In a thousand open spaces of down and upland the people who had fled thither from the floods and the falling houses and sliding slopes of hill watched for that rising in vain. Hour followed hour through a terrible suspense, and the star rose not. Once again men set their eyes upon the old constellations they had counted lost to them forever. In England it was hot and clear overhead, though the ground quivered perpetually, but in the tropics Sirius and Capella and Aldebaran showed through a veil of steam. And when at last the great star rose near ten hours late, the sun rose close upon it, and in the centre of its white heart was a disc of black.

Over Asia it was the star had begun to fall behind the movement of the sky, and then suddenly, as it hung over India, its light had been veiled. All the plain of India from the mouth of the Indus to the mouths of the Ganges was a shallow waste of shining water that night, out of which rose temples and palaces, mounds and hills, black with people. Every minaret was a clustering mass of people, who fell one by one into the turbid waters, as heat and terror overcame them. The whole land seemed a-wailing, and suddenly there swept a shadow across that furnace of despair, and a breath of cold wind, and a gathering of clouds, out of the cooling air. Men looking up, near blinded, at the star, saw that a black disc was creeping across the light. It was the moon, coming between the star and the earth. And even as men cried to God at this respite, out of the East with a strange inexplicable swiftness sprang the sun. And then, with a sickening swiftness, star, sun and moon rushed together across the heavens.

So it was that presently, to the European watchers, star and sun rose close upon each other, drove headlong for a space and then slower, and at last came to rest, star and sun merged into one glare of flame at the zenith of the sky. The moon no longer eclipsed the star but was lost to sight in the brilliance of the sky. And though those who were still alive regarded it for the most part with that dull stupidity that hunger, fatigue, heat and despair engender, there were still men who could perceive the meaning of these signs. Star and earth had been at their nearest, had swung about one another, and the star had passed. Already it was receding, swifter and swifter, in the last stage of its headlong journey downward into the sun.

And then the clouds gathered, blotting out the vision of the sky, the thunder and lightning wove a garment round the world; all over the earth was such a downpour of rain as men had never before seen, and where the volcanoes flared red against the cloud canopy there descended torrents of mud. Everywhere the waters were pouring off the land, leaving mud-silted ruins, and the earth littered like a storm-worn beach with all that had floated, and the dead bodies of the men and brutes, its children. For days the waters streamed off the land, sweeping away soil and trees and houses in the way, and piling huge dykes and scooping out Titanic gullies over the country side. Those were the days of darkness that followed the star and the heat. All through them, and for many weeks and months, the earthquakes continued.

But the star had passed, and so men, hunger-driven and gathering courage only slowly, might creep back to their ruined cities, buried granaries, and sodden fields. Such few ships as had escaped the storms of that time came stunned and shattered and sounding their way cautiously through the new marks and shoals of once familiar ports. And as the storms subsided men perceived that everywhere the days were hotter than of yore, and the sun larger, and that the moon, shrunk to a third of its former size, took now fourscore days between its new and new.

But of the new brotherhood that grew presently among men, of the saving of laws and books and machines, of the strange change that had come over Iceland and Greenland and the shores of Baffin's Bay, so that the sailors coming there presently found them green and gracious, and could scarce believe their eyes, this story does not tell. Nor of the movement of mankind now that the earth was hotter, northward and southward towards the poles of the earth. It concerns itself only with the coming and the passing of the Star.

The Martian astronomers—for there are astronomers on Mars, although they are very different beings from men—were naturally profoundly interested by these things. They saw things from their own standpoint of course. "Considering the mass and temperature of the missile that was flung through our solar system into the sun," one wrote, "it is astonishing what a little damage the earth, which it missed so narrowly, has sustained. All the familiar continental markings and the masses of the seas remain intact, and indeed the only difference seems to be a shrinkage of the white discolouration (supposed to be frozen water) round either pole." Which only shows how small the vastest of human catastrophes may seem, at a distance of a few million miles.

Charles Chesnutt (1858–1932)

An African American author best known for writing novels that deal with the racist social structures in both northern and southern states following the US Civil War and the failure of Southern Reconstruction plans, Chesnutt first came to prominence through a series of "local color" stories, published together as *The Conjure Woman and Other Stories* (1899). Set in the South, these stories are framed as being told by a formerly enslaved Black man, Julius, to a recently transplanted Northern businessman and his wife. With Julius's stories written in Southern dialect, they are stylistically similar to the so-called Uncle Remus stories by white author Joel Chandler Harris (1848–1908), but rather than stories told for children that tend to reinforce the stereotype of the "contented slave," Chesnutt's stories consistently highlight the agency of their Black characters, who often challenge the power of white society. Thus, the stories form a continuity with his more realist novels, including *The Marrow of Tradition* (1901), which directly represented the white supremacist terrorism of the Wilmington massacre of 1898. The *Conjure Woman* stories veer away from realism in their representation of "conjuring" and other magical or supernatural acts. "Mars Jeems's Nightmare," specifically, uses the trope of a race switching, here involving a white enslaver being transformed into a Black man. Inverted, this trope would become the centre of George Schuyler's later science fiction satire, *Black No More* (1931).

Note on the text: The copy-text used for the version here is the first US edition of *The Conjure Woman* (Houghton Mifflin, 1899).

"Mars Jeems's Nightmare" (1899)

We found old Julius very useful when we moved to our new residence. He had a thorough knowledge of the neighborhood, was familiar with the roads and the watercourses, knew the qualities of the various soils and what they would produce, and where the best hunting and fishing were to be had. He was a marvelous hand in the management of horses and dogs, with whose mental processes he manifested a greater familiarity than mere use would seem to account for, though it was doubtless due to the simplicity of a life that had kept him close to nature. Toward my tract of land and the things that were on it—the creeks, the swamps, the hills, the meadows, the stones, the trees—he maintained a peculiar personal attitude, that might be called predial rather than proprietary.[1] He had been accustomed, until long after middle life, to look upon himself as the property of another. When this relation was no longer possible, owing to the war,[2]

1 When used in the context of enslavement, "predial" means "attached to the land" (*OED*).

2 I.e., the American Civil War (1861–65), which began when several southern states seceded from the United States of America to form their own, briefly lived, country called the Confederate States of

and to his master's death and the dispersion of the family, he had been unable to break off entirely the mental habits of a lifetime, but had attached himself to the old plantation, of which he seemed to consider himself an appurtenance. We found him useful in many ways and entertaining in others, and my wife and I took quite a fancy to him.

Shortly after we became established in our home on the sand-hills, Julius brought up to the house one day a colored boy of about seventeen, whom he introduced as his grandson, and for whom he solicited employment. I was not favorably impressed by the youth's appearance,—quite the contrary, in fact; but mainly to please the old man I hired Tom—his name was Tom—to help about the stables, weed the garden, cut wood and bring water, and in general to make himself useful about the outdoor work of the household.

My first impression of Tom proved to be correct. He turned out to be very trifling, and I was much annoyed by his laziness, his carelessness, and his apparent lack of any sense of responsibility. I kept him longer than I should, on Julius's account, hoping that he might improve; but he seemed to grow worse instead of better, and when I finally reached the limit of my patience, I discharged him.

"I am sorry, Julius," I said to the old man; "I should have liked to oblige you by keeping him; but I can't stand Tom any longer. He is absolutely untrustworthy."

"Yas, suh," replied Julius, with a deep sigh and a long shake of the head, "I knows he ain' much account, en dey ain' much 'pen'ence ter be put on 'im. But I wuz hopin' dat you mought make some 'lowance fuh a' ign'ant young nigger,[1] suh, en gib 'im one mo' chance."

But I had hardened my heart.[2] I had always been too easily imposed upon, and had suffered too much from this weakness. I determined to be firm as a rock in this instance.

"No, Julius," I rejoined decidedly, "it is impossible. I gave him more than a fair trial, and he simply won't do."

When my wife and I set out for our drive in the cool of the evening,—afternoon is "evening" in Southern parlance,—one of the servants put into the rockaway[3] two large earthenware jugs. Our drive was to be down through the swamp to the mineral spring at the foot of the sand-hills beyond. The water of this spring was strongly impregnated with sulphur and iron, and, while not particularly agreeable of smell or taste, was used by us, in moderation, for sanitary reasons.

America. These states seceded in order to maintain the racist system of chattel slavery, which was eventually abolished following the US victory.

1 Chesnutt here has Julius use the deeply racist epithet for Black people even as Julius's story arguably works to undermine the very racism that the word invokes.

2 An allusion to the biblical book of Exodus, in which the Pharaoh of Egypt's heart is hardened multiple times as he refuses to let the enslaved Israelites go free.

3 A rockaway is a type of carriage.

When we reached the spring, we found a man engaged in cleaning it out. In answer to an inquiry he said that if we would wait five or ten minutes, his task would be finished and the spring in such condition that we could fill our jugs. We might have driven on, and come back by way of the spring, but there was a bad stretch of road beyond, and we concluded to remain where we were until the spring should be ready. We were in a cool and shady place. It was often necessary to wait awhile in North Carolina; and our Northern energy had not been entirely proof against the influences of climate and local custom.

While we sat there, a man came suddenly around a turn of the road ahead of us. I recognized in him a neighbor with whom I had exchanged formal calls.[1] He was driving a horse, apparently a high-spirited creature, possessing, so far as I could see at a glance, the marks of good temper and good breeding; the gentleman, I had heard it suggested, was slightly deficient in both. The horse was rearing and plunging, and the man was beating him furiously with a buggy-whip. When he saw us, he flushed a fiery red, and, as he passed, held the reins with one hand, at some risk to his safety, lifted his hat, and bowed somewhat constrainedly as the horse darted by us, still panting and snorting with fear.

"He looks as though he were ashamed of himself," I observed.

"I'm sure he ought to be," exclaimed my wife indignantly. "I think there is no worse sin and no more disgraceful thing than cruelty."

"I quite agree with you," I assented.

"A man w'at 'buses his hoss is gwine ter be ha'd on de folks w'at wuks fer 'im," remarked Julius. "Ef young Mistah McLean doan min', he 'll hab a bad dream one er dese days, des lack 'is grandaddy had way back yander, long yeahs befo' de wah."

"What was it about Mr. McLean's dream, Julius?" I asked. The man had not yet finished cleaning the spring, and we might as well put in time listening to Julius as in any other way. We had found some of his plantation tales quite interesting.

"Mars Jeems McLean," said Julius, "wuz de grandaddy er dis yer gent'eman w'at is des gone by us beatin' his hoss. He had a big plantation en a heap er niggers. Mars Jeems wuz a ha'd man, en monst'us stric' wid his han's. Eber sence he growed up he nebber 'peared ter hab no feelin' fer nobody. W'en his daddy, ole Mars John McLean, died, de plantation en all de niggers fell ter young Mars Jeems. He had be'n bad 'nuff befo', but it wa'n't long atterwa'ds 'tel he got so dey wuz no use in libbin' at all ef you ha' ter lib roun' Mars Jeems. His niggers wuz bleedzd ter slabe fum daylight ter da'k, w'iles yuther folks's did n' hafter wuk 'cep'n' fum sun ter sun; en dey did n' git no mo' ter eat dan dey oughter, en dat de coa'ses' kin'. Dey wa'n't 'lowed ter sing, ner dance, ner play de banjo w'en Mars Jeems wuz roun' de place; fer Mars Jeems say he would n' hab no sech gwines-on,—said he bought his han's ter wuk, en

1 I.e., had visited in a formal manner.

not ter play, en w'en night come dey mus' sleep en res', so dey 'd be ready ter git up soon in de mawnin' en go ter dey wuk fresh en strong.

"Mars Jeems did n' 'low no co'tin' er juneseyin' roun' his plantation,—said he wanted his niggers ter put dey min's on dey wuk, en not be wastin' dey time wid no sech foolis'ness. En he would n' let his han's git married,—said he wuz n' raisin' niggers, but wuz raisin' cotton. En w'eneber any er de boys en gals 'ud 'mence ter git sweet on one ernudder, he 'd sell one er de yuther un 'em, er sen' 'em way down in Robeson County[1] ter his yuther plantation, whar dey could n' nebber see one ernudder.

"Ef any er de niggers eber complained, dey got fo'ty;[2] so co'se dey did n' many un 'em complain. But dey did n' lack it, des de same, en nobody could n' blame 'em, fer dey had a ha'd time. Mars Jeems did n' make no 'lowance fer nachul bawn laz'ness, ner sickness, ner trouble in de min', ner nuffin; he wuz des gwine ter git so much wuk outer eve'y han', er know de reason w'y.

"Dey wuz one time de niggers 'lowed, fer a spell, dat Mars Jeems mought git bettah. He tuk a lackin' ter Mars Marrabo McSwayne's oldes' gal, Miss Libbie, en useter go ober dere eve'y day er eve'y ebenin', en folks said dey wuz gwine ter git married sho'. But it 'pears dat Miss Libbie heared 'bout de gwines-on on Mars Jeems's plantation, en she des 'lowed she could n' trus' herse'f wid no sech a man; dat he mought git so useter 'busin' his niggers dat he 'd 'mence ter 'buse his wife atter he got useter habbin' her roun' de house. So she 'clared she wuz n' gwine ter hab nuffin mo' ter do wid young Mars Jeems.

"De niggers wuz all monst'us sorry w'en de match wuz bust' up, fer now Mars Jeems got wusser 'n he wuz befo' he sta'ted sweethea'tin'. De time he useter spen' co'tin' Miss Libbie he put in findin' fault wid de niggers, en all his bad feelin's 'ca'se Miss Libbie th'owed 'im ober he 'peared ter try ter wuk off on de po' niggers.

"W'iles Mars Jeems wuz co'tin' Miss Libbie, two er de han's on de plantation had got ter settin' a heap er sto' by one ernudder. One un 'em wuz name' Solomon, en de yuther wuz a 'oman w'at wukked in de fiel' 'long er 'im—I fe'git dat 'oman's name, but it doan 'mount ter much in de tale nohow. Now, whuther 'ca'se Mars Jeems wuz so tuk up wid his own junesey[3] dat he did n' paid no 'tention fer a w'ile ter w'at wuz gwine on 'twix' Solomon en his junesey, er whuther his own co'tin' made 'im kin' er easy on de co'tin' in de qua'ters, dey ain' no tellin'. But dey's one thing sho', dat w'en Miss Libbie th'owed 'im ober, he foun' out 'bout Solomon en de gal monst'us quick, en gun Solomon fo'ty, en sont de gal down ter de Robeson County plantation, en tol' all de niggers ef he ketch 'em at any mo' sech foolishness, he wuz gwine ter skin 'em alibe en tan dey hides befo' dey ve'y eyes. Co'se he would

1 A county in the south of North Carolina.

2 I.e., they were whipped (given forty lashes).

3 Sweetheart. (Chesnutt's note); see Lisa Cohen Minnick (89).

n' 'a' done it, but he mought 'a' made things wusser 'n dey wuz. So you kin 'magine dey wa'n't much lub-makin' in de qua'ters fer a long time.

"Mars Jeems useter go down ter de yuther plantation sometimes fer a week er mo', en so he had ter hab a oberseah[1] ter look atter his wuk w'iles he 'uz gone. Mars Jeems's oberseah wuz a po' w'ite man name' Nick Johnson,—de niggers called 'im Mars Johnson ter his face, but behin' his back dey useter call 'im Ole Nick,[2] en de name suited 'im ter a T. He wuz wusser 'n Mars Jeems ever da'ed ter be. Co'se de darkies did n' lack de way Mars Jeems used 'em, but he wuz de marster, en had a right ter do ez he please'; but dis yer Ole Nick wa'n't nuffin but a po' buckrah,[3] en all de niggers 'spised 'im ez much ez dey hated 'im, fer he did n' own nobody, en wa'n't no bettah 'n a nigger, fer in dem days any 'spectable pusson would ruther be a nigger dan a po' w'ite man.

"Now, atter Solomon's gal had be'n sont away, he kep' feelin' mo' en mo' bad erbout it, 'tel fin'lly he 'lowed he wuz gwine ter see ef dey could n' be sump'n done fer ter git 'er back, en ter make Mars Jeems treat de darkies bettah. So he tuk a peck er co'n out'n de ba'n one night, en went ober ter see ole Aun' Peggy, de free-nigger cunjuh 'oman down by de Wim'l'ton Road.

"Aun' Peggy listen' ter 'is tale, en ax' him some queshtuns, en den tol' 'im she 'd wuk her roots, en see w'at dey 'd say 'bout it, en ter-morrer night he sh'd come back ag'in en fetch ernudder peck er co'n, en den she 'd hab sump'n fer ter tell 'im.

"So Solomon went back de nex' night, en sho' 'nuff, Aun' Peggy tol' 'im w'at ter do. She gun 'im some stuff w'at look' lack it be'n made by poundin' up some roots en yarbs wid a pestle in a mo'tar.

"'Dis yer stuff,' sez she, 'is monst'us pow'ful kin' er goopher.[4] You take dis home, en gin it ter de cook, ef you kin trus' her, en tell her fer ter put it in yo' marster's soup de fus' cloudy day he hab okra soup fer dinnah. Min' you follers de d'rections.'

"'It ain' gwineter p'isen 'im, is it?' ax' Solomon, gittin' kin' er skeered; fer Solomon wuz a good man, en did n' want ter do nobody no rale ha'm.

"'Oh, no,' sez ole Aun' Peggy, 'it's gwine ter do 'im good, but he 'll hab a monst'us bad dream fus'. A mont' fum now you come down heah en lemme know how de goopher is wukkin'. Fer I ain' done much er dis kin' er cunj'in' er late yeahs, en I has ter kinder keep track un it ter see dat it doan 'complish no mo' d'n I 'lows fer it ter do. En I has ter be kinder keerful 'bout cunj'in' w'ite folks; so be sho' en lemme know, w'ateber you do, des w'at is gwine on roun' de plantation.'

"So Solomon say all right, en tuk de goopher mixtry up ter de big house en gun it ter de cook, en tol' her fer ter put it in Mars Jeems's soup de fus' cloudy

1 Overseer.

2 "Old Nick" was a common name for the Devil.

3 White man.

4 "A curse, spell, or conjuration" (*OED*).

day she hab okra soup fer dinnah. It happen' dat de ve'y nex' day wuz a cloudy day, en so de cook made okra soup fer Mars Jeems's dinnah, en put de powder Solomon gun her inter de soup, en made de soup rale good, so Mars Jeems eat a whole lot of it en 'peared ter enjoy it.

"De nex' mawnin' Mars Jeems tol' de oberseah he wuz gwine 'way on some bizness, en den he wuz gwine ter his yuther plantation, down in Robeson County, en he did n' 'spec' he 'd be back fer a mont' er so.

"'But,' sezee, 'I wants you ter run dis yer plantation fer all it's wuth. Dese yer niggers is gittin' monst'us triflin' en lazy en keerless, en dey ain' no 'pen'ence ter be put in 'em. I wants dat stop', en w'iles I'm gone erway I wants de 'spenses cut 'way down en a heap mo' wuk done. Fac', I wants dis yer plantation ter make a reco'd dat 'll show w'at kinder oberseah you is.'

"Ole Nick did n' said nuffin but 'Yas, suh,' but de way he kinder grin' ter hisse'f en show' his big yaller teef, en snap' de rawhide he useter kyar roun' wid 'im, made col' chills run up and down de backbone er dem niggers w'at heared Mars Jeems a-talkin'. En dat night dey wuz mo'nin' en groanin' down in de qua'ters, fer de niggers all knowed w'at wuz comin'.

"So, sho' 'nuff, Mars Jeems went erway nex' mawnin', en de trouble begun. Mars Johnson sta'ted off de ve'y fus' day fer ter see w'at he could hab ter show Mars Jeems w'en he come back. He made de tasks bigger en de rashuns littler, en w'en de niggers had wukked all day, he 'd fin' sump'n fer 'em ter do roun' de ba'n er som'ers atter da'k, fer ter keep 'em busy a' hour er so befo' dey went ter sleep.

"About th'ee er fo' days atter Mars Jeems went erway, young Mars Dunkin McSwayne rode up ter de big house one day wid a nigger settin' behin' 'im in de buggy, tied ter de seat, en ax' ef Mars Jeems wuz home. Mars Johnson wuz at de house, and he say no.

"'Well,' sez Mars Dunkin, sezee, 'I fotch dis nigger ober ter Mistah McLean fer ter pay a bet I made wid 'im las' week w'en we wuz playin' kya'ds te'gedder. I bet 'im a nigger man, en heah 's one I reckon 'll fill de bill. He wuz tuk up de yuther day fer a stray nigger, en he could n' gib no 'count er hisse'f, en so he wuz sol' at oction, en I bought 'im. He's kinder brash, but I knows yo' powers, Mistah Johnson, en I reckon ef anybody kin make 'im toe de ma'k, you is de man.'

"Mars Johnson grin' one er dem grins w'at show' all his snaggle teef, en make de niggers 'low he look lack de ole debbil, en sezee ter Mars Dunkin:—

"'I reckon you kin trus' me, Mistah Dunkin, fer ter tame any nigger wuz eber bawn. De nigger doan lib w'at I can't take down in 'bout fo' days.'

"Well, Ole Nick had 'is han's full long er dat noo nigger; en w'iles de res' er de darkies wuz sorry fer de po' man, dey 'lowed he kep' Mars Johnson so busy dat dey got along better 'n dey 'd 'a' done ef de noo nigger had nebber come.

"De fus' thing dat happen', Mars Johnson sez ter dis yer noo man:—

"'W'at 's yo' name, Sambo?'

"'My name ain' Sambo,' 'spon' de noo nigger.

"'Did I ax you w'at yo' name wa'n't?' sez Mars Johnson. 'You wants ter be pa'tic'lar how you talks ter me. Now, w'at is yo' name, en whar did you come fum?'

"'I dunno my name,' sez de nigger, 'en I doan 'member whar I come fum. My head is all kin' er mix' up.'

"'Yas,' sez Mars Johnson, 'I reckon I 'll ha' ter gib you sump'n fer ter cl'ar yo' head. At de same time, it 'll l'arn you some manners, en atter dis mebbe you 'll say "suh" w'en you speaks ter me.'

"Well, Mars Johnson haul' off wid his rawhide en hit de noo nigger once. De noo man look' at Mars Johnson fer a minute ez ef he did n' know w'at ter make er dis yer kin' er l'arnin'. But w'en de oberseah raise' his w'ip ter hit him ag'in, de noo nigger des haul' off en made fer Mars Johnson, en ef some er de yuther niggers had n' stop' 'im, it 'peared ez ef he mought 'a' made it wa'm fer Ole Nick dere fer a w'ile. But de oberseah made de yuther niggers he'p tie de noo nigger up, en den gun 'im fo'ty, wid a dozen er so th'owed in fer good measure, fer Ole Nick wuz nebber stingy wid dem kin' er rashuns. De nigger went on at a tarrable rate, des lack a wil' man, but co'se he wuz bleedzd ter take his med'cine, fer he wuz tied up en could n' he'p hisse'f.

"Mars Johnson lock' de noo nigger up in de ba'n, en did n' gib 'im nuffin ter eat fer a day er so, 'tel he got 'im kin'er quiet' down, en den he tu'nt 'im loose en put 'im ter wuk. De nigger 'lowed he wa'n't useter wukkin', en would n' wuk, en Mars Johnson gun 'im anudder fo'ty fer laziness en impidence, en let 'im fas' a day er so mo', en den put 'im ter wuk ag'in. De nigger went ter wuk, but did n' 'pear ter know how ter han'le a hoe. It tuk des 'bout half de oberseah's time lookin' atter 'im, en dat po' nigger got mo' lashin's en cussin's en cuffin's dan any fo' yuthers on de plantation. He did n' mix' wid ner talk much ter de res' er de niggers, en could n' 'pear ter git it th'oo his min' dat he wuz a slabe en had ter wuk en min' de w'ite folks, spite er de fac' dat Ole Nick gun 'im a lesson eve'y day. En fin'lly Mars Johnson 'lowed dat he could n' do nuffin wid 'im; dat ef he wuz his nigger, he 'd break his sperrit er break 'is neck, one er de yuther. But co'se he wuz only sont ober on trial, en ez he did n' gib sat'sfaction, en he had n' heared fum Mars Jeems 'bout w'en he wuz comin' back; en ez he wuz feared he 'd git mad some time er 'nuther en kill de nigger befo' he knowed it, he 'lowed he 'd better sen' 'im back whar he come fum. So he tied 'im up en sont 'im back ter Mars Dunkin.

"Now, Mars Dunkin McSwayne wuz one er dese yer easy-gwine gent'emen w'at did n' lack ter hab no trouble wid niggers er nobody e'se, en he knowed ef Mars Ole Nick could n' git 'long wid dis nigger, nobody could. So he tuk de nigger ter town dat same day, en sol' 'im ter a trader w'at wuz gittin' up a gang er lackly niggers fer ter ship off on de steamboat ter go down de ribber ter Wim'l'ton en fum dere ter Noo Orleens.

"De nex' day atter de noo man had be'n sont away, Solomon wuz wukkin' in de cotton-fiel', en w'en he got ter de fence nex' ter de woods, at de een' er de row, who sh'd he see on de yuther side but ole Aun' Peggy. She beckon' ter 'im,—de oberseah wuz down on de yuther side er de fiel',—en sez she:—

"'W'y ain' you done come en 'po'ted ter me lack I tol' you?'

"'W'y, law! Aun' Peggy,' sez Solomon, 'dey ain' nuffin ter 'po't. Mars Jeems went away de day atter we gun 'im de goopher mixtry, en we ain' seed hide ner hair un 'im sence, en co'se we doan know nuffin 'bout w'at 'fec' it had on 'im.'

"'I doan keer nuffin 'bout yo' Mars Jeems now; w'at I wants ter know is w'at is be'n gwine on 'mongs' de niggers. Has you be'n gittin' 'long any better on de plantation?'

"'No, Aun' Peggy, we be'n gittin' 'long wusser. Mars Johnson is stric'er 'n he eber wuz befo', en de po' niggers doan ha'dly git time ter draw dey bref, en dey 'lows dey mought des ez well be dead ez alibe.'

"'Uh huh!' sez Aun' Peggy, sez she, 'I tol' you dat 'uz monst'us pow'ful goopher, en its wuk doan 'pear all at once.'

"'Long ez we had dat noo nigger heah,' Solomon went on, 'he kep' Mars Johnson busy pa't er de time; but now he 's gone erway, I s'pose de res' un us 'll ketch it wusser 'n eber.'

"'W'at 's gone wid de noo nigger?' sez Aun' Peggy, rale quick, battin' her eyes en straight'nin' up.

"'Ole Nick done sont 'im back ter Mars Dunkin, who had fotch 'im heah fer ter pay a gamblin' debt ter Mars Jeems,' sez Solomon, 'en I heahs Mars Dunkin has sol' 'im ter a nigger-trader up in Patesville,[1] w'at 's gwine ter ship 'im off wid a gang ter-morrer.'

"Ole Aun' Peggy 'peared ter git rale stirred up w'en Solomon tol' 'er dat, en sez she, shakin' her stick at 'im:—

"'W'y did n' you come en tell me 'bout dis noo nigger bein' sol' erway? Did n' you promus me, ef I 'd gib you dat goopher, you 'd come en 'po't ter me 'bout all w'at wuz gwine on on dis plantation? Co'se I could 'a' foun' out fer myse'f, but I 'pended on yo' tellin' me, en now by not doin' it I 's feared you gwine spile my cunj'in'. You come down ter my house ter-night en do w'at I tells you, er I 'll put a spell on you dat 'll make yo' ha'r fall out so you 'll be bal', en yo' eyes drap out so you can't see, en yo teef fall out so you can't eat, en yo' years grow up so you can't heah. W'en you is foolin' wid a cunjuh 'oman lack me, you got ter min' yo' P's en Q's er dey 'll be trouble sho' 'nuff.'

"So co'se Solomon went down ter Aun' Peggy's dat night, en she gun 'im a roasted sweet'n' 'tater.

"'You take dis yer sweet'n' 'tater,' sez she,—'I done goophered it 'speshly fer dat noo nigger, so you better not eat it yo'se'f er you 'll wush you had n',—en slip off ter town, en fin' dat strange man, en gib 'im dis yer sweet'n' 'tater. He mus' eat it befo' mawnin', sho', ef he doan wanter be sol' erway ter Noo Orleens.'

1 Patesville is a fictional North Carolina town that Chesnutt uses in both *The Conjure Woman* and the novel *The House Behind the Cedars* (1900).

"'But s'posen de patteroles[1] ketch me, Aun' Peggy, w'at I gwine ter do?' sez Solomon.

"'De patteroles ain' gwine tech you, but ef you doan fin' dat nigger, *I'm* gwine git you, en you 'll fin' me wusser 'n de patteroles. Des hol' on a minute, en I 'll sprinkle you wid some er dis mixtry out'n dis yer bottle, so de patteroles can't see you, en you kin rub yo' feet wid some er dis yer grease out'n dis go'd, so you kin run fas', en rub some un it on yo' eyes so you kin see in de da'k; en den you mus' fin' dat noo nigger en gib 'im dis yer 'tater, er you gwine ter hab mo' trouble on yo' han's 'n you eber had befo' in yo' life er eber will hab sence.'

"So Solomon tuk de sweet'n' 'tater en sta'ted up de road fas' ez he could go, en befo' long he retch' town. He went right 'long by de patteroles, en dey did n' 'pear ter notice 'im, en bimeby he foun' whar de strange nigger was kep', en he walked right pas' de gyard at de do' en foun' 'im. De nigger could n' see 'im, ob co'se, en he could n' 'a' seed de nigger in de da'k, ef it had n' be'n fer de stuff Aun' Peggy gun 'im ter rub on 'is eyes. De nigger wuz layin' in a co'nder, 'sleep, en Solomon des slip' up ter 'im, en hilt dat sweet'n' 'tater 'fo' de nigger's nose, en he des nach'ly retch' up wid his han', en tuk de 'tater en eat it in his sleep, widout knowin' it. Wen Solomon seed he 'd done eat de 'tater, he went back en tol' Aun' Peggy, en den went home ter his cabin ter sleep, 'way 'long 'bout two o'clock in de mawnin'.

"De nex' day wuz Sunday, en so de niggers had a little time ter deyse'ves. Solomon wuz kinder 'sturb' in his min' thinkin' 'bout his junesey w'at 'uz gone away, en wond'rin' w'at Aun' Peggy had ter do wid dat noo nigger; en he had sa'ntered up in de woods so 's ter be by hisse'f a little, en at de same time ter look atter a rabbit-trap he 'd sot down in de aidge er de swamp, w'en who sh'd he see stan'in' unner a tree but a w'ite man.

"Solomon did n' knowed de w'ite man at fus', 'tel de w'ite man spoke up ter 'im.

"'Is dat you, Solomon?' sezee.

"Den Solomon reco'nized de voice.

"'Fer de Lawd's sake, Mars Jeems! is dat you?'

"'Yas, Solomon,' sez his marster, 'dis is me, er w'at's lef' er me.'

"It wa'n't no wonder Solomon had n' knowed Mars Jeems at fus', fer he wuz dress' lack a po' w'ite man, en wuz barefooted, en look' monst'us pale en peaked, ez ef he 'd des come th'oo a ha'd spell er sickness.

"'You er lookin' kinder po'ly, Mars Jeems,' sez Solomon. 'Is you be'n sick, suh?'

"'No, Solomon,' sez Mars Jeems, shakin' his head, en speakin' sorter slow en sad, 'I ain' be'n sick, but I 's had a monst'us bad dream,—fac', a reg'lar, nach'ul nightmare. But tell me how things has be'n gwine on up ter de plantation sence I be'n gone, Solomon.'

1 Patteroles were patrols that "restrict[ed] the movement" of enslaved people, "especially at night" (see "Patteroller," for patroller, in the *OED*).

"So Solomon up en tol' 'im 'bout de craps, en 'bout de hosses en de mules, en 'bout de cows en de hawgs. En w'en he 'mence' ter tell 'bout de noo nigger, Mars Jeems prick' up 'is yeahs en listen', en eve'y now en den he 'd say, 'Uh huh! uh huh!' en nod 'is head. En bimeby, w'en he 'd ax' Solomon some mo' queshtuns, he sez, sezee:—

"'Now, Solomon, I doan want you ter say a wo'd ter nobody 'bout meetin' me heah, but I wants you ter slip up ter de house, en fetch me some clo's en some shoes,—I fergot ter tell you dat a man rob' me back yander on de road en swap' clo's wid me widout axin' me whuther er no,—but you neenter say nuffin 'bout dat, nuther. You go en fetch me some clo's heah, so nobody won't see you, en keep yo' mouf shet, en I 'll gib you a dollah.'

"Solomon wuz so 'stonish' he lack ter fell ober in his tracks, w'en Mars Jeems promus' ter gib 'im a dollah. Dey su't'nly wuz a change come ober Mars Jeems, w'en he offer' one er his niggers dat much money. Solomon 'mence' ter 'spec' dat Aun' Peggy's cunj'ation had be'n wukkin' monst'us strong.

"Solomon fotch Mars Jeems some clo's en shoes, en dat same eb'nin' Mars Jeems 'peared at de house, en let on lack he des dat minute got home fum Robeson County. Mars Johnson was all ready ter talk ter 'im, but Mars Jeems sont 'im wo'd he wa'n't feelin' ve'y well dat night, en he 'd see 'im ter-morrer.

"So nex' mawnin' atter breakfus' Mars Jeems sont fer de oberseah, en ax' 'im fer ter gib 'count er his styoa'dship. Ole Nick tol' Mars Jeems how much wuk be'n done, en got de books en showed 'im how much money be'n save'. Den Mars Jeems ax' 'im how de darkies be'n behabin', en Mars Johnson say dey be'n behabin' good, most un 'em, en dem w'at did n' behabe good at fus' change dey conduc' atter he got holt un 'em a time er two.

"'All,' sezee, ''cep'n' de noo nigger Mistah Dunkin fotch ober heah en lef' on trial, w'iles you wuz gone.'

"'Oh, yas,' 'lows Mars Jeems, 'tell me all 'bout dat noo nigger. I heared a little 'bout dat quare noo nigger las' night, en it wuz des too redik'lus. Tell me all 'bout dat noo nigger.'

"So seein' Mars Jeems so good-nachu'd 'bout it, Mars Johnson up en tol' 'im how he tied up de noo han' de fus' day en gun 'im fo'ty 'ca'se he would n' tell 'im 'is name.

"'Ha, ha, ha!' sez Mars Jeems, laffin' fit ter kill, 'but dat is too funny fer any use. Tell me some mo' 'bout dat noo nigger.'

"So Mars Johnson went on en tol' 'im how he had ter starbe de noo nigger 'fo' he could make 'im take holt er a hoe.

"'Dat wuz de beatinis' notion fer a nigger,' sez Mars Jeems, 'puttin' on airs, des lack he wuz a w'ite man! En I reckon you did n' do nuffin ter 'im?'

"'Oh, no, suh,' sez de oberseah, grinnin' lack a chessy-cat, 'I did n' do nuffin but take de hide off'n 'im.'

"Mars Jeems lafft en lafft, 'tel it 'peared lack he wuz des gwine ter bu'st. '*Tell* me some mo' 'bout dat noo nigger, oh, *tell* me some mo'. Dat noo nigger int'rusts me, he do, en dat is a fac'.'

"Mars Johnson did n' quite un'erstan' w'y Mars Jeems sh'd make sich a great 'miration 'bout de noo nigger, but co'se he want' ter please de gent'eman w'at hi'ed 'im, en so he 'splain' all 'bout how many times he had ter cowhide de noo nigger, en how he made 'im do tasks twicet ez big ez some er de yuther han's, en how he 'd chain 'im up in de ba'n at night en feed 'im on co'n-bread en water.

"'Oh! but you is a monst'us good oberseah; you is de bes' oberseah in dis county, Mistah Johnson,' sez Mars Jeems, w'en de oberseah got th'oo wid his tale; 'en dey ain' nebber be'n no nigger-breaker lack you roun' heah befo'. En you desarbes great credit fer sendin' dat nigger 'way befo' you sp'ilt 'im fer de market. Fac', you is sech a monst'us good oberseah, en you is got dis yer plantation in sech fine shape, dat I reckon I doan need you no mo'. You is got dese yer darkies so well train' dat I 'spec' I kin run 'em myse'f fum dis time on. But I does wush you had 'a' hilt on ter dat noo nigger 'tel I got home, fer I 'd 'a' lack ter 'a' seed 'im, I su't'nly should.'

"De oberseah wuz so 'stonish' he did n' ha'dly know w'at ter say, but fin'lly he ax' Mars Jeems ef he would n' gib 'im a riccommen' fer ter git ernudder place.

"'No, suh,' sez Mars Jeems, 'somehow er 'nuther I doan lack yo' looks sence I come back dis time, en I 'd much ruther you would n' stay roun' heah. Fac', I's feared ef I 'd meet you alone in de woods some time, I mought wanter ha'm you. But layin' dat aside, I be'n lookin' ober dese yer books er yo'n w'at you kep' w'iles I wuz 'way, en fer a yeah er so back, en dere's some figgers w'at ain' des cl'ar ter me. I ain' got no time fer ter talk 'bout 'em now, but I 'spec' befo' I settles wid you fer dis las' mont', you better come up heah ter-morrer, atter I 's look' de books en 'counts ober some mo', en den we 'll straighten ou' business all up.'

"Mars Jeems 'lowed atterwa'ds dat he wuz des shootin' in de da'k w'en he said dat 'bout de books, but howsomeber, Mars Nick Johnson lef' dat naberhood 'twix' de nex' two suns, en nobody roun' dere nebber seed hide ner hair un 'im sence. En all de darkies t'ank de Lawd, en 'lowed it wuz a good riddance er bad rubbage.

"But all dem things I done tol' you ain' nuffin 'side'n de change w'at come ober Mars Jeems fum dat time on. Aun' Peggy's goopher had made a noo man un 'im enti'ely. De nex' day atter he come back, he tol' de han's dey neenter wuk on'y fum sun ter sun, en he cut dey tasks down so dey did n' nobody hab ter stan' ober 'em wid a rawhide er a hick'ry. En he 'lowed ef de niggers want ter hab a dance in de big ba'n any Sad'day night, dey mought hab it. En bimeby, w'en Solomon seed how good Mars Jeems wuz, he ax' 'im ef he would n' please sen' down ter de yuther plantation fer his junesey. Mars Jeems say su't'nly, en gun Solomon a pass en a note ter de oberseah on de yuther plantation, en sont Solomon down ter Robeson County wid a hoss en buggy fer ter fetch his junesey back. Wen de niggers see how fine Mars Jeems gwine treat 'em, dey all tuk ter sweethea'tin' en juneseyin' en singin' en dancin', en eight er ten couples got married, en bimeby eve'ybody 'mence' ter say Mars

Jeems McLean got a finer plantation, en slicker-lookin' niggers, en dat he 'uz makin' mo' cotton en co'n, dan any yuther gent'eman in de county. En Mars Jeems's own junesey, Miss Libbie, heared 'bout de noo gwines-on on Mars Jeems's plantation, en she change' her min' 'bout Mars Jeems en tuk 'im back ag'in, en 'fo' long dey had a fine weddin', en all de darkies had a big feas', en dey wuz fiddlin' en dancin' en funnin' en frolic'in' fum sundown 'tel mawnin'."

"And they all lived happy ever after," I said, as the old man reached a full stop.

"Yas, suh," he said, interpreting my remarks as a question, "dey did. Solomon useter say," he added, "dat Aun' Peggy's goopher had turnt Mars Jeems ter a nigger, en dat dat noo han' wuz Mars Jeems hisse'f. But co'se Solomon did n' das' ter let on 'bout w'at he 'spicioned, en ole Aun' Peggy would 'a' 'nied it ef she had be'n ax', fer she 'd 'a' got in trouble sho', ef it 'uz knowed she 'd be'n cunj'in' de w'ite folks.

"Dis yer tale goes ter show," concluded Julius sententiously, as the man came up and announced that the spring was ready for us to get water, "dat w'ite folks w'at is so ha'd en stric', en doan make no 'lowance fer po' ign'ant niggers w'at ain' had no chanst ter l'arn, is li'ble ter hab bad dreams, ter say de leas', en dat dem w'at is kin' en good ter po' people is sho' ter prosper en git 'long in de worl'."

"That is a very strange story, Uncle Julius," observed my wife, smiling, "and Solomon's explanation is quite improbable."

"Yes, Julius," said I, "that was powerful goopher. I am glad, too, that you told us the moral of the story; it might have escaped us otherwise. By the way, did you make that up all by yourself?"

The old man's face assumed an injured look, expressive more of sorrow than of anger, and shaking his head he replied:—

"No, suh, I heared dat tale befo' you er Mis' Annie dere wuz bawn, suh. My mammy tol' me dat tale w'en I wa'n't mo' d'n knee-high ter a hopper-grass."

I drove to town next morning, on some business, and did not return until noon; and after dinner I had to visit a neighbor, and did not get back until supper-time. I was smoking a cigar on the back piazza in the early evening, when I saw a familiar figure carrying a bucket of water to the barn. I called my wife.

"My dear," I said severely, "what is that rascal doing here? I thought I discharged him yesterday for good and all."

"Oh, yes," she answered, "I forgot to tell you. He was hanging round the place all the morning, and looking so down in the mouth, that I told him that if he would try to do better, we would give him one more chance. He seems so grateful, and so really in earnest in his promises of amendment, that I'm sure you 'll not regret taking him back."

I was seriously enough annoyed to let my cigar go out. I did not share my wife's rose-colored hopes in regard to Tom; but as I did not wish the servants to think there was any conflict of authority in the household, I let the boy stay.

FOUNDATIONS OF SF II:
ENTER THE TWENTIETH CENTURY: 1900–1936

Rokeya Sakhawat Hossain (1880–1932)

Rokeya Sakhawat Hossain, commonly known as Begum Rokeya (where Begum refers to a woman of high rank, as in "Lady"), was a Bengali feminist and political activist in British-controlled India. She was a driving force in the push for formal education for women, founding "the Bengal branch of the Anjuman-i-Khawatin Islam (All-India Muslim Women's Association), the first such organization for Muslim women in Bengal" (Smith and Carroll 303). She was also active in the struggle against purdah, the official social segregation of women practised in some Muslim and Hindu communities. She takes up these issues of feminist political liberation in her writings, including numerous essays, a series of short pieces titled *Avarodhbasini* (*The Secluded Ones*, 1928), and the feminist utopian story included here, "Sultana's Dream." Rokeya Day is now celebrated annually in Bangladesh on 9 December, the date of both her birth and death.

Note on the text: The version below is from the first publication in *The Indian Ladies' Magazine* (vol. 5, no. 3, Sept. 1905). Typographic errors have been silently corrected, but other variations from later versions (including in punctuation) are retained. Some more ambiguous changes from the magazine to later editions—such as between two viable but closely related real words—follow the magazine version. This story appeared as the second of three pieces in the section "Our Special Indian Lady Contributors' Column"; the author was listed as Mrs. R.S. Hossein.

"Sultana's Dream" (1905)

One evening I was lounging in an easy chair in my bed-room and thinking lazily of the condition of Indian womanhood. I am not sure whether I dozed off or not. But, as far as I remember, I was wide awake. I saw the moonlit sky sparkling with thousands of diamond-like stars, very distinctly.

All of a sudden a lady stood before me; how she came in, I do not know. I took her for my friend, Sister Sara.

"Good morning!" said Sister Sara. I smiled inwardly as I knew it was not *morning*, but starry night. However, I replied to her, saying,

"How do you do?"

"I am all right, thank you. Will you please come out and have a look at our garden?"

I looked again at the moon through the open window, and thought there was no harm in going out at that time. The men servants outside were fast asleep just then, and I could have a pleasant walk with Sister Sara.

I used to have my walks with Sister Sara, when we were at Darjeeling. Many a time did we walk hand in hand and talk light-heartedly in the Botanical gardens there. I fancied, Sister Sara had probably come to take me to some such garden, and I readily accepted her offer and went out with her.

When walking, I found to my surprise that it was a fine morning! The town was fully awake and the streets alive with bustling crowds. I was feeling very shy, thinking I was walking in the street in broad daylight, but there was not a single man visible.

Some of the passers-by made jokes at me. Though I could not understand their language, yet I felt sure they were joking. I asked my friend, "What do they say?"

"The women say that you look very mannish."

"Mannish!" said I, "What do they mean by that?"

"They mean that you are shy and timid like men!"

"Shy and timid like a man!" It was really a joke! I became very nervous, when I found that my companion was not Sister Sara, but a stranger. Oh! what a fool had I been to mistake this lady for my dear old friend, Sister Sara!

She felt my fingers tremble in her hand, as we were walking hand in hand.

"What is the matter, dear?" she said affectionately.

"I feel somewhat awkward," I said in a rather apologising tone, "as being a purdahnishin woman[1] I am not accustomed to walking about unveiled."

"You need not be afraid of coming across a man here. This is Ladyland, free from sin and harm. Virtue herself reigns here."

By and by I was enjoying the scenery. Really it was very grand. I mistook a patch of grass for a velvet cushion! Feeling as if I were walking on soft carpet, I looked down and found the path covered with moss and flowers.

"How nice it is," said I.

"Do you like it?" asked Sister Sara. (I continued calling her "Sister Sara," and she kept calling me by my name.)

"Yes, very much; but I do not like to tread on the tender and sweet flowers!"

"Never mind, dear Sultana! Your treading will not harm them; they are street flowers."

"The whole palace looks like a garden," said I admiringly. "You have arranged every plant so skillfully."

"Your Calcutta[2] could become a nicer garden than this, if only your countrymen wanted to make it so."

"They would think it useless to give so much attention to horticulture, while they have so many other things to do."

"They could not find a better excuse!" said she with smile.

I became very curious to know where the men were. I met more than a hundred women, while walking there, but not a single man!

---

1 Purdah is a religious system practised by some Muslim and Hindu communities that segregates women within society physically, socially, and/or politically (see *OED*).

2 Now known as Kolkata, this city sits in what is now the Indian state of West Bengal, near the border with Bangladesh.

"Where are the men?" I asked her.

"In their proper places, where they ought to be."

"Pray let me know what you mean by 'their proper places.'"

"O! I see my mistake, you cannot know our customs, as you were never here before. We shut our men indoors."

"Just as we are kept in the zenana?"[1]

"Exactly so."

"How funny!" I burst into a laugh. Sister Sara laughed too.

"But dear Sultana! how unfair it is to shut in the harmless women and let loose the men."

"Why? It is not safe for us to come out of the zenana, as we are naturally weak."

"Yes, it is not safe so long as there are men about the streets! nor is it so when a wild animal enters a market-place!"

"Of course not."

"Suppose, some lunatics escape from the asylum and begin to do all sorts of mischief to men, horses and other creatures, in that case what will your countrymen do?"

"They will try to capture them and put them back into their asylum."

"Thank you! and you do not think it wise to keep sane people inside an asylum and let loose the insane?"

"Of course not!" said I laughing lightly.

"As a matter of fact in your country this very thing is done! Men, who do,—or at least are capable of doing no end of mischief, are let loose and the innocent women shut up in the zenana! How can you trust those untrained men out of doors?"

"We have no hand or voice in the management of our social affairs. In India man is lord and master. He has taken to himself all powers and privileges and shut up the women in the zenana."

"Why do you allow yourselves to be shut up?"

"Because it can not be helped as they are stronger than women."

"A lion is stronger than a man, but it does not enable him to dominate the human race. You have neglected the duty you owe to yourselves and you have lost your natural rights by shutting your eyes to your own interests."

"But my dear Sister Sara if we do everything by ourselves, what will the men do then?"

"They should not do anything, excuse me; they are fit for nothing! Only catch them and put them into the zenana!"

"But would it be very easy to catch and put them inside the four walls?" said I, "and even if this were done would all their business,—political and commercial also go with them into the zenana!"

1 "An area in a house reserved for the use of the women of the household" (*OED*).

Sister Sara made no reply. She only smiled sweetly. Perhaps she thought it useless to argue with one who was no better than a frog in a well![1]

By this time we reached Sister Sara's house. It was situated in a beautiful heartshaped garden. It was a bungalow with a corrugated iron roof, it was cooler and nicer than any of our rich buildings. I can not describe how neat and how nicely furnished and how tastefully decorated it was.

We sat side by side; she brought out of the parlour a piece of embroidery work and began putting on a fresh design.

"Do you know knitting and needle work?"

"Yes; we have nothing else to do in our zenana."

"But we do not trust our 'zenana' members with embroidery!" she said laughing, "as a man has not patience enough to pass thread through a needle-hole even!"

"Have you done all this work yourself?" I asked her pointing to the various pieces of embroidered teapoy[2] cloths.

"Yes."

"How can you find time to do all these? You have to do the office work as well? Have you not?"

"Yes. I do not stick to the laboratory all day long. I finish my work in two hours."

"In two hours! how do you manage? In our land the officers, magistrates,—for instance, work seven hours daily."

"I have seen some of them doing their work. Do you think they work all the seven hours?"

"Certainly they do!"

"No, dear Sultana! they do not. They dawdle away their time in smoking! Some smoke two or three cheroots[3] during the office time. They talk much about their work, but do little. Suppose one cheroot takes half an hour to burn off, and a man smokes twelve cheroots daily; then you see, he wastes six hours every day in sheer smoking."

We talked on various subjects; and I learned that they were not subject to any kind of epidemic disease,—nor did they suffer from mosquito-bites as we do! I was very much astonished to hear that in Ladyland no one died in youth except by rare accident.

"Will you care to see our kitchen?" she asked me.

"With pleasure," said I, and we went to see it. Of course the men had been asked to clear off when I was going there! The kitchen was situated in a beautiful vegetable garden. Every creeper, every tomato plant was itself an ornament. I found no smoke, nor any chimney either in the kitchen,—it was clean

1 "frog in a well": Sanskrit phrase (*kūpa-maṇḍūka*) meaning "a narrow-minded person with a limited view of the world" (Les B. Morgan and Ram Karan Sharma 129).

2 A teapoy is a small table which, in colonial India, was "used as a tea chest or tea caddy" (Gloag 665).

3 Cigars.

and bright; the windows were decorated with flower garlands. There was no sign of coal or fire.

"How do you cook?" I asked.

"With solar heat," she said, at the same time showing me the pipe, through which passed the concentrated sunlight and heat. And she cooked something then and there to show me the process.

"How did you manage to gather and store up the sun-heat?" I asked her in amazement.

"Let me tell you a little of our past history then. Thirty years ago, when our present Queen was thirteen years old, she inherited the throne. She was a Queen in name only, the Prime-minister really ruling the country.

"Our good Queen liked science very much. She circulated an order that all the women in her country should be educated. Accordingly a number of girls' schools were founded and supported by the Government. Education was spread far and wide among women. And early marriage also was stopped. No woman was to be allowed to marry before she was twenty-one. I must tell you that before this change we had been kept in strict purdah."

"How the tables are turned," I interposed with a laugh.

"But the seclusion is the same," she said. "In a few years we had separate Universities, where no men were admitted.

"In the capital, where our Queen lives, there are two Universities. One of these invented a wonderful balloon, to which they attached a number of pipes. By means of this captive balloon, which they managed to keep afloat above the cloud land, they could draw as much water from the atmosphere as they pleased. As the water was incessantly being drawn by the University people, no cloud could gather and the ingenious Lady-Principal stopped rain and storms thereby."

"Really! now I understand why there is no mud here!" said I. But I could not understand how it was possible to accumulate water in the pipes. She explained to me how it was done; but I was unable to understand her, as my scientific knowledge was very limited. However she went on,—

"When the other University came to know of this, they became exceedingly jealous and tried to do something more extraordinary still. They invented an instrument by which they could collect as much sun-heat as they wanted. And they kept the heat stored up to be distributed among others as required.

"While the women were engaged in scientific researches, the men of this country were busy increasing their military power. When they came to know that the female universities were able to draw water from the atmosphere and collect heat from the sun, they only laughed at the members of the universities and called the whole thing 'a sentimental nightmare!'"

"Your achievements are very wonderful indeed! But tell me, how you managed to put the men of your country into the zenana. Did you entrap them first?"

"No."

"It is not likely that they would surrender their free and open air life of their own accord and confine themselves within the four walls of the zenana! They must have been overpowered."

"Yes, they have been!"

"By whom?—by some lady-warriors, I suppose?"

"No, not by arms."

"Yes, it cannot be so. Men's arms are stronger than women's. Then?"

"By brain."

"Even their brains are bigger and heavier than women's. Are they not?"

"Yes, but what of that? An elephant also has got a bigger and heavier brain than a man has! Yet men can enchain elephants and employ them according to their own wishes."

"Well said, but tell me, please, how it all actually happened. I am dying to know it!"

"Women's brains are somewhat quicker than men's. Ten years ago, when the military officers called our scientific discoveries 'a sentimental nightmare,' some of the young ladies wanted to say something in reply to those remarks. But both the Lady-Principals restrained them and said, they should reply, not by word, but by deed, if ever that got an opportunity. And they had not long to wait for that opportunity."

"How marvelous!" I nearly clapped my hands. "And now the proud gentlemen are dreaming sentimental dreams themselves."

"Soon afterwards certain persons came from a neighbouring country and took shelter in ours. They were in trouble having committed some political offence. The King who cared more for power than for good government asked our kind-hearted Queen to hand them over to his officers. She refused, as it was against her principle to turn out refugees. For this refusal the King declared war against our country.

"Our military officers sprang to their feet at once and marched out to meet the enemy.

"The enemy, however, was too strong for them. Our soldiers fought bravely, no doubt. But in spite of all their bravery the foreign army advanced step by step to invade our country.

"Nearly all the men had gone out to fight; even a boy of sixteen was not left at home. Most of our warriors were killed, the rest driven back and the enemy came within twenty-five miles of the capital.

"A meeting of a number of wise ladies was held at the Queen's palace to advise as to what should be done to save the land.

"Some proposed to fight like soldiers; others objected and said that women were not trained to fight with swords and guns; nor were they accustomed to fighting with any weapons. A third party regretfully remarked that they were hopelessly weak of body.

"'If you cannot save your country for lack of physical strength,' said the Queen, 'try to do so by brain power.'

"There was a dead silence for a few minutes. Her Royal Highness said again, 'I must commit suicide if the land and my honour are lost.'

"Then the Lady-Principal of the second University, (who had collected sun-heat), who had been silently thinking during the consultation, remarked that they were all but lost; and there was little hope left for them. There was however, one plan which she would like to try, and this would be her first and last effort; if she failed in this, there would be nothing left but to commit suicide. All present solemnly vowed that they would never allow themselves to be enslaved, no matter what happened.

"The Queen thanked them heartily, and asked the Lady-Principal to try her plan.

"The Lady-Principal rose again and said, 'before we go out, the men must enter the zenanas. I make this prayer for the sake of purdah.' 'Yes, of course,' replied Her Royal Highness.

"On the following day the Queen called upon all men to retire into zenanas for the sake of honour and liberty.

"Wounded and tired as they were, they took that order rather for a boon! They bowed low and entered the zenanas without uttering a single word of protest. They were sure that there was no hope for this country at all.

"Then the Lady-Principal with her two thousand students marched to the battle-field; and arriving there directed all the rays of the concentrated sunlight heat towards the enemy.

"The heat and light were too much for them to bear! They all ran away panic-stricken, not knowing in their bewilderment how to counteract that scorching heat. When they had fled away leaving their guns and other ammunitions of war, they were burnt down by means of the same sun-heat.

"Since then no one has tried to invade our country any more."

"And since then your countrymen never tried to come out of the zenana?"

"Yes, they wanted to be free. Some of the Police Commissioners and District Magistrates sent word to the Queen to the effect that the military Officers certainly deserved to be imprisoned for their failure; but they never neglected their duty and therefore they should not be punished, and they prayed to be restored to their respective offices.

"Her Royal Highness sent them a circular letter[1] intimating to them that if their services should ever be needed they would be sent for, and that in the meanwhile they should remain where they were.

"Now that they are accustomed to the purdah system and have ceased to grumble at their seclusion, we call the system 'Murdana' instead of 'zenana.'"[2]

"But how do you manage," I asked Sister Sara, "to do without the Police or Magistrates in cases of theft or murder?"

"Since the 'Murdana' system has been established, there has been no more

1 A letter to be circulated to multiple people (see "circular" in *OED*).

2 "Murd," or "mard," means man, while "zan" means woman in Persian.

crime or sin; therefore we do not require a Police man to find out a culprit, nor do we want a Magistrate to try a Criminal case."

"That is very good, indeed. I suppose if there were any dishonest person, you could very easily chastise her. As you gained a decisive victory without shedding a single drop of blood, you could drive off crime and criminals too without much difficulty!"

"Now dear Sultana, will you sit here or come to my parlour?" she asked me.

"Your kitchen is not inferior to a queen's boudoir!" I replied with a pleasant smile, "but we must leave it now; for the gentlemen may be cursing me for keeping them away from their duties in the kitchen so long." We both laughed heartily.

"How my friends at home will be amused and amazed, when I go back and tell them that in the far-off Ladyland ladies rule over the country and control all social matters, while gentlemen are kept in the Murdanas to mind babies, to cook and to do all sorts of domestic work! and that cooking is so easy a thing that it is simply a pleasure to cook!"

"Yes, tell them about all that you see here."

"Please let me know, how you carry on land cultivation and how you plough the land and do other hard manual work."

"Our fields are tilled by means of electricity, which supplies motive power for other hard work as well and we employ it for our aerial conveyances too. We have no rail road nor any paved streets here."

"Therefore neither street nor railway accidents occur here," said I. "Do not you ever suffer from want of rainwater?" I asked.

"Never. You see the big balloon and pipes attached thereto. By their aid we can draw as much rain water as we require. Nor do we ever suffer from flood or thunderstorms. We are all very busy making nature yield as much as she can. We do not find time to quarrel with one another as we never sit idle. Our noble Queen is exceedingly fond of Botany; it is her ambition to convert the whole country into one grand garden."

"The idea is excellent. What is your chief food?"

"Fruits."

"How do you keep your country cool in hot weather? We regard the rain-fall in summer as a blessing from heaven."

"If the heat becomes unbearable, we sprinkle the ground with plentiful showers drawn from the artificial fountains. And in cold weather we keep our rooms warm with sun-heat."

She showed me her bathroom, the roof of which was removable. She could enjoy a shower bath whenever she liked by simply removing the roof (which was like the lid of a box) and turning on the top[1] of the shower pipe!

"You are a lucky people!" ejaculated I, "You know no want. What is your religion, may I ask?"

---

1 Other versions correct this to "tap" but the original is retained here.

"Our religion is based on Love and Truth. It is our religious duty to love one another and to be absolutely truthful. If any person lies, she or he is——"

"Punished with death?"

"No; not with death. We do not take pleasure in killing a creature of God,—specially[1] a human being. The liar is asked to leave this land for good and never to come to it again."

"Is an offender never forgiven?"

"Yes, if that person repents sincerely."

"Are you not allowed to see any man, except your own relations?"

"No one except sacred relations."

"Our circle of sacred relations is very limited, even first cousins are not sacred."

"But ours is very large; a distant cousin is as sacred as a brother."

"That is very good. I see, Purity itself reigns over your land. I should like to see the good Queen, who is so sagacious and far-sighted and who has made all these rules."

"All right," said Sister Sara.

Then she screwed a couple of seats onto a square piece of plank. To this plank she attached two smooth and well-polished balls. When I asked her what the balls were for, she said, they were hydrogen balls and they were used to overcome the force of gravity. The balls were of different capacities to be used according to the different weights desired to be overcome. She then fastened to the air-car two wing-like blades, which, she said, were worked by electricity. After we were comfortably seated she touched a knob and the blades began to whirl, moving faster and faster every moment. At first we were raised to the height of about six or seven feet and then off we flew! And before I could realize that we had commenced moving we reached the Garden of the Queen.

My friend lowered the air-car by reversing the action of the machine, and when the car touched the ground the machine was stopped and we got out.

I had seen from the air-car, the Queen walking on a garden path with her little daughter (who was four years old) and her maids of honour.

"Halloo! you here!" cried the Queen addressing Sister Sara. I was introduced to Her Royal Highness and was received by her cordially without any ceremony.

I was very much delighted to make her acquaintance. In the course of the conversation I had with her the Queen told me that she had no objection to permitting her subjects to trade with other countries. "But," she continued, "no trade was possible with countries where the women were kept in the zenanas and so unable to come and trade with us. Men, we find, are rather of lower morals and so we do not like dealing with them. We do not covet other people's land, we do not fight for a piece of diamond though it may

1 This was amended to "especially" in later versions.

be a thousand-fold brighter than the Koh-i-Noor[1] nor do we grudge a ruler his Peacock throne.[2] We dive deep into the ocean of knowledge and try to find out the precious gems, which Nature has kept in store for us. We enjoy Nature's gifts as much as we can."

After taking leave of the Queen, I visited the famous universities, and was shown over some of their manufactories, laboratories and observatories.

After visiting the above places of interest we got again into the air-car, but as soon as it began moving I somehow slipped down and the fall startled me out of my dream. And on opening my eyes, I found myself in my own bedroom still lounging in the easy chair!!

1 One of the largest cut diamonds in the world, the Kooh-i-noor was taken by Queen Victoria as part of the colonial appropriation of India by the British. It is still part of the British Crown Jewels.

2 A throne of the Mughal emperors, the Peacock Throne was reportedly jewelled with diamonds and other precious stones.

E.M. Forster (1879–1970)

E.M. Forster is best known for his realist novels, including *A Room with a View* (1908) and *A Passage to India* (1924). His short stories regularly engage science fiction or fantasy, however, including many published in his collection *The Eternal Moment and Other Stories* (1928). Forster, a gay man living when British law still prosecuted homosexuality as a crime, also explored issues of queer sexuality in later published works, including the novel *Maurice* (1971), published only after his death, and his final story, "Little Imber." Written in 1961, "Little Imber" is a science fiction tale depicting a future world in which men are used as breeding stock, but two men have sex with each other and are able to reproduce. "The Machine Stops," however, is his better-known foray into SF: an allegorical tale that touches on problems with utilitarianism, automation, and humanity's disconnection from nature, it can also easily be read as gesturing to issues of nation and empire (and even to much later concerns relating to social media, online teaching, and social isolation).

Note on the text: The copy-text here is the first publication in *The Oxford and Cambridge Review* (no. 8, 1909).

"The Machine Stops" (1909)

PART I
THE AIR SHIP

IMAGINE, if you can, a small room, hexagonal in shape, like the cell of a bee. It is lighted neither by window nor by lamp, yet it is filled with a soft radiance. There are no apertures for ventilation, yet the air is fresh. There are no musical instruments, and yet, at the moment that my meditation opens, this room is throbbing with melodious sounds. An arm-chair is in the centre, by its side a reading-desk—that is all the furniture. And in the arm-chair there sits a swaddled lump of flesh—a woman, about five feet high, with a face as white as a fungus. It is to her that the little room belongs.

An electric bell rang.

The woman touched a switch and the music was silent.

"I suppose I must see who it is," she thought, and set her chair in motion. The chair, like the music, was worked by machinery, and it rolled her to the other side of the room, where the bell still rang importunately.

"Who is it?" she called. Her voice was irritable, for she had been interrupted often since the music began. She knew several thousand people; in certain directions, human intercourse had advanced enormously.

But when she listened into the receiver, her white face wrinkled into smiles, and she said:

"Very well. Let us talk, I will isolate myself. I do not expect anything important will happen for the next five minutes—for I can give you fully five minutes, Kuno. Then I must deliver my lecture on 'Music during the Australian Period.'"

She touched the isolation-knob, so that no one else could speak to her. Then she touched the lighting apparatus, and the little room was plunged into darkness.

"Be quick!" she called, her irritation returning. "Be quick, Kuno; here I am in the dark wasting my time."

But it was fully fifteen seconds before the round plate that she held in her hands began to glow. A faint blue light shot across it, darkening to purple, and presently she could see the image of her son, who lived on the other side of the earth, and he could see her.

"Kuno, how slow you are."

He smiled gravely.

"I really believe you enjoy dawdling."

"I have called you before, mother, but you were always busy or isolated. I have something particular to say."

"What is it, dearest boy? Be quick. Why could you not send it by pneumatic post?"[1]

"Because I prefer saying such a thing. I want——"

"Well?"

"I want you to come and see me."

Vashti watched his face in the blue plate.

"But I can see you!" she exclaimed. "What more do you want?"

"I want to see you not through the Machine," said Kuno. "I want to speak to you not through the wearisome Machine."

"Oh, hush!" said his mother, vaguely shocked. "You mustn't say anything against the Machine."

"Why not?"

"One mustn't."

"You talk as if a god had made the Machine," cried the other. "I believe that you pray to it when you are unhappy. Men made it, do not forget that. Great men, but men. The Machine is much, but it is not everything. I see something like you in this plate, but I do not see you. I hear something like you through this telephone, but I do not hear you. That is why I want you to come. Come and stop with me. Pay me a visit, so that we can meet face to face, and talk about the hopes that are in my mind."

1 Pneumatic tubes, a system of communication popular in the nineteenth century, consisted of interconnected tubes that used compressed air or a partial vacuum to send cylinders containing messages between locations (often within an office building).

She replied that she could scarcely spare the time for a visit.

"The air-ship barely takes two days to fly between me and you."

"I dislike air-ships."

"Why?"

"I dislike seeing the horrible brown earth, and the sea, and the stars when it is dark. I get no ideas in an air-ship."

"I do not get them anywhere else."

"What kind of ideas can the air give you?"

He paused for an instant.

"Do you not know four big stars that form an oblong, and three stars close together in the middle of the oblong, and hanging from these stars, three other stars?"

"No, I do not. I dislike the stars. But did they give you an idea? How interesting; tell me."

"I had an idea that they were like a man."

"I do not understand."

"The four big stars are the man's shoulders and his knees. The three stars in the middle are like the belts that men wore once, and the three stars hanging are like a sword."[1]

"A sword?"

"Men carried swords about with them, to kill animals and other men."

"It does not strike me as a very good idea, but it is certainly original. When did it come to you first?"

"In the air-ship——." He broke off, and she fancied that he looked sad. She could not be sure, for the Machine did not transmit *nuances* of expression. It only gave a general idea of people—an idea that was good enough for all practical purposes, Vashti thought. The imponderable bloom, declared by a discredited philosophy to be the actual essence of intercourse, was rightly ignored by the Machine, just as the imponderable bloom of the grape was ignored by the manufacturers of artificial fruit. Something "good enough" had long since been accepted by our race.

"The truth is," he continued, "that I want to see these stars again. They are curious stars. I want to see them not from the air-ship, but from the surface of the earth, as our ancestors did, thousands of years ago. I want to visit the surface of the earth."

She was shocked again.

"Mother, you must come, if only to explain to me what is the harm of visiting the surface of the earth."

"No harm," she replied, controlling herself. "But no advantage. The surface of the earth is only dust and mud, no life remains on it, and you would need a respirator, or the cold of the outer air would kill you. One dies immediately in the outer air."

---

1 Kuno is describing the constellation Orion.

"I know; of course I shall take all precautions."

"And besides——"

"Well?"

She considered, and chose her words with care. Her son had a queer temper, and she wished to dissuade him from the expedition.

"It is contrary to the spirit of the age," she asserted.

"Do you mean by that, contrary to the Machine?"

"In a sense, but——"

His image in the blue plate faded.

"Kuno!"

He had isolated himself.

For a moment Vashti felt lonely.

Then she generated the light, and the sight of her room, flooded with radiance and studded with electric buttons, revived her. There were buttons and switches everywhere—buttons to call for food, for music, for clothing. There was the hot-bath button, by pressure of which a basin of (imitation) marble rose out of the floor, filled to the brim with a warm deodorised liquid. There was the cold-bath button. There was the button that produced literature. And there were of course the buttons by which she communicated with her friends. The room, though it contained nothing, was in touch with all that she cared for in the world.

Vashti's next move was to turn off the isolation-switch, and all the accumulations of the last three minutes burst upon her. The room was filled with the noise of bells, and speaking-tubes. What was the new food like? Could she recommend it? Had she had any ideas lately? Might one tell her one's own ideas? Would she make an engagement to visit the public nurseries at an early date?—say this day month.

To most of these questions she replied with irritation—a growing quality in that accelerated age. She said that the new food was horrible. That she could not visit the public nurseries through press of engagements. That she had no ideas of her own but had just been told one—that four stars and three in the middle were like a man: she doubted there was much in it. Then she switched off her correspondents, for it was time to deliver her lecture on Australian music.

The clumsy system of public gatherings had been long since abandoned; neither Vashti nor her audience stirred from their rooms. Seated in her armchair she spoke, while they in their armchairs heard her, fairly well, and saw her, fairly well. She opened with a humorous account of music in the pre-Mongolian epoch, and went on to describe the great outburst of song that followed the Chinese conquest. Remote and primæval as were the methods of I-San-So and the Brisbane school, she yet felt (she said) that study of them might repay the musician of to-day: they had freshness; they had, above all, ideas.

Her lecture, which lasted ten minutes, was well received, and at its conclusion she and many of her audience listened to a lecture on the sea; there were ideas to be got from the sea; the speaker had donned a respirator and visited it lately. Then she fed, talked to many friends, had a bath, talked again, and summoned her bed.

The bed was not to her liking. It was too large, and she had a feeling for a small bed. Complaint was useless, for beds were of the same dimension all over the world, and to have had an alternative size would have involved vast alterations in the Machine. Vashti isolated herself—it was necessary, for neither day nor night existed under the ground—and reviewed all that had happened since she had summoned the bed last. Ideas? Scarcely any. Events—was Kuno's invitation an event?

By her side, on the little reading-desk, was a survival from the ages of litter—one book. This was the Book of the Machine. In it were instructions against every possible contingency. If she was hot or cold or dyspeptic or at loss for a word, she went to the book, and it told her which button to press. The Central Committee published it. In accordance with a growing habit, it was richly bound.

Sitting up in the bed, she took it reverently in her hands. She glanced round the glowing room as if some one might be watching her. Then, half ashamed, half joyful, she murmured "O Machine! O Machine!" and raised the volume to her lips. Thrice she kissed it, thrice inclined her head, thrice she felt the delirium of acquiescence. Her ritual performed, she turned to page 1367, which gave the times of the departure of the air-ships from the island in the Southern Hemisphere, under whose soil she lived, to the island in the Northern Hemisphere, whereunder lived her son.

She thought, "I have not the time."

She made the room dark and slept; she awoke and made the room light; she ate and exchanged ideas with her friends, and listened to music and attended lectures; she made the room dark and slept. Above her, beneath her, and around her, the Machine hummed eternally; she did not notice the noise, for she had been born with it in her ears. The earth, carrying her, hummed as it sped through silence, turning her now to the invisible sun, now to the invisible stars. She awoke and made the room light.

"Kuno!"

"I will not talk to you," he answered, "until you come."

"Have you been on the surface of the earth since we spoke last?"

His image faded.

Again she consulted the book. She became very nervous and lay back in her chair palpitating. Think of her as without teeth or hair. Presently she directed the chair to the wall, and pressed an unfamiliar button. The wall swung apart slowly. Through the opening she saw a tunnel that curved slightly, so that its goal was not visible. Should she go to see her son, here was the beginning of the journey.

Of course she knew all about the communication-system. There was nothing mysterious in it. She would summon a car and it would fly with her down the tunnel until it reached the lift that communicated with the air-ship station: the system had been in use for thousands of years, long before the universal establishment of the Machine. And of course she had studied the civilisation that had immediately preceded her own—the civilisation that had mistaken the functions of the system, and had used it for bringing people to things, instead of for bringing things to people. Those funny old days, when men went for change of air instead of changing the air in their rooms! And yet—she was frightened of the tunnel: she had not seen it since her last child was born. It curved—but not quite as she remembered; it was brilliant—but not quite as brilliant as a lecturer had suggested. Vashti was seized with the terrors of direct experience. She shrank back into the room, and the wall closed up again.

"Kuno," she said, "I cannot come to see you. I am not well."

Immediately an enormous apparatus fell on to her out of the ceiling, a thermometer was automatically inserted between her lips, a stethoscope was automatically laid upon her heart. She lay powerless. Cool pads soothed her forehead. Kuno had telegraphed to her doctor.

So the human passions still blundered up and down in the Machine. Vashti drank the medicine that the doctor projected into her mouth, and the machinery retired into the ceiling. The voice of Kuno was heard asking how she felt.

"Better." Then with irritation: "But why do you not come to me instead?"

"Because I cannot leave this place."

"Why?"

"Because, any moment, something tremendous may happen."

"Have you been on the surface of the earth yet?"

"Not yet."

"Then what is it?"

"I will not tell you through the Machine."

She resumed her life.

But she thought of Kuno as a baby, his birth, his removal to the public nurseries, her one visit to him there, his visits to her—visits which stopped when the Machine had assigned him a room on the other side of the earth. "Parents, duties of," said the book of the Machine, "cease at the moment of birth. P. 422327483." True—but there was something special about Kuno—indeed there had been something special about all her children, and, after all, she must brave the journey if he desired it. And "something tremendous might happen." What did that mean? The nonsense of a youthful man, no doubt, but she must go. Again she pressed the unfamiliar button, again the wall swung back, and she saw the tunnel that curved out of sight. Clasping the Book, she rose, tottered on to the platform, and summoned the car. Her room closed behind her: the journey to the Northern Hemisphere had begun.

Of course it was perfectly easy. The car approached and in it she found arm-chairs exactly like her own. When she signalled, it stopped, and she tottered into the lift. One other passenger was in the lift, the first fellow creature she had seen face to face for months. Few travelled in these days, for, thanks to the advance of science, the earth was exactly alike all over. Rapid intercourse, from which the previous civilisation had hoped so much, had ended by defeating itself. What was the good of going to Pekin[1] when it was just like Shrewsbury? Why return to Shrewsbury when it would be just like Pekin? Men seldom moved their bodies; all unrest was concentrated in the soul.

The air-ship service was a relic from the former age. It was kept up, because it was easier to keep it up than to stop it or to diminish it, but it now far exceeded the wants of the population. Vessel after vessel would rise from the vomitories[2] of Rye or of Christchurch (I use the antique names), would sail into the crowded sky, and would draw up at the wharves of the South—empty. So nicely adjusted was the system, so independent of meteorology, that the sky, whether calm or cloudy, resembled a vast kaleidoscope whereon the same patterns periodically recurred. The ship on which Vashti sailed started now at sunset, now at dawn. But always, as it passed above Rheims, it would neighbour the ship that served between Helsingfors and the Brazils, and, every third time it surmounted the Alps, the fleet of Palermo would cross its track behind. Night and day, wind and storm, tide and earthquake, impeded man no longer. He had harnessed Leviathan. All the old literature, with its praise of Nature, and its fear of Nature, rang false as the prattle of a child.

Yet as Vashti saw the vast flank of the ship, stained with exposure to the outer air, her horror of direct experience returned. It was not quite like the air-ship in the cinematophote. For one thing it smelt—not strongly or unpleasantly, but it did smell, and with her eyes shut she should have known that a new thing was close to her. Then she had to walk to it from the lift, had to submit to glances from the other passengers. The man in front dropped his Book—no great matter, but it disquieted them all. In the rooms, if the Book was dropped, the floor raised it mechanically, but the gangway to the air-ship was not so prepared, and the sacred volume lay motionless. They stopped—the thing was unforeseen—and the man, instead of picking up his property, felt the muscles of his arm to see how they had failed him. Then some one actually said with direct utterance: "We shall be late"—and they trooped on board, Vashti treading on the pages as she did so.

Inside, her anxiety increased. The arrangements were old-fashioned and rough. There was even a female attendant, to whom she would have to announce her wants during the voyage. Of course a revolving platform ran the length of the boat, but she was expected to walk from it to her cabin. Some cabins were better than others, and she did not get the best. She thought the attendant had been unfair, and spasms of rage shook her. The glass valves had closed, she could not go back. She saw, at the end of the vestibule, the lift in which she had ascended going quietly up and down, empty. Beneath those corridors of shining tiles were rooms, tier below tier, reaching far into the

1 Older spelling of Peking, now Beijing.

2 A vomitory is the passage into and out of a theatre or similar building.

earth, and in each room there sat a human being, eating, or sleeping, or producing ideas. And buried deep in the hive was her own room. Vashti was afraid.

"O Machine! O Machine!" she murmured, and caressed her Book, and was comforted.

Then the sides of the vestibule seemed to melt together, as do the passages that we see in dreams, the lift vanished, the Book that had been dropped slid to the left and vanished, polished tiles rushed by like a stream of water, there was a slight jar, and the air-ship, issuing from its tunnel, soared above the waters of a tropical ocean.

It was night. For a moment she saw the coast of Sumatra edged by the phosphorescence of waves, and crowned by lighthouses, still sending forth their disregarded beams. These also vanished, and only the stars distracted her. They were not motionless, but swayed to and fro above her head, thronging out of one skylight into another, as if the universe and not the air-ship was careening. And, as often happens on clear nights, they seemed now to be in perspective, now on a plane; now piled tier beyond tier into the infinite heavens, now concealing infinity, a roof limiting for ever the visions of men. In either case they seemed intolerable. "Are we to travel in the dark?" called the passengers angrily, and the attendant, who had been careless, generated the light, and pulled down the blinds of pliable metal. When the air-ships had been built, the desire to look direct at things still lingered in the world. Hence the extraordinary number of skylights and windows, and the proportionate discomfort to those who were civilised and refined. Even in Vashti's cabin one star peeped through a flaw in the blind, and after a few hours' uneasy slumber, she was disturbed by an unfamiliar glow, which was the dawn.

Quick as the ship had sped westwards, the earth had rolled eastwards quicker still, and had dragged back Vashti and her companions towards the sun. Science could prolong the night, but only for a little, and those high hopes of neutralising the earth's diurnal revolution had passed, together with hopes that were possibly higher. To "keep pace with the sun," or even to outstrip it had been the aim of the civilisation preceding this. Racing aeroplanes had been built for the purpose, capable of enormous speed, and steered by the greatest intellects of the epoch. Round the globe they went, round and round, westward, westward, round and round, amidst humanity's applause. In vain. The globe went eastward quicker still, horrible accidents occurred, and the Committee of the Machine, at the time rising into prominence, declared the pursuit illegal, unmechanical, and punishable by Homelessness.

Of Homelessness more will be said later.

Doubtless the Committee was right. Yet the attempt to "defeat the sun" aroused the last common interest that our race experienced about the heavenly bodies, or indeed about anything. It was the last time that men were compacted by thinking of a power outside the world. The sun had conquered, yet it was the end of his spiritual dominion. Dawn, midday, twilight, the zodiacal path, touched neither men's lives nor their hearts, and science retreated into the ground, to concentrate herself upon problems that she was certain of solving.

So when Vashti found her cabin invaded by a rosy finger of light, she was annoyed, and tried to adjust the blind. But the blind flew up altogether, and she saw through the skylight small pink clouds, swaying against a background of blue, and as the sun crept higher, its radiance entered direct, brimming down the wall, like a golden sea. It rose and fell with the air-ship's motion, just as waves rise and fall, but it advanced steadily, as a tide advances. Unless she was careful, it would strike her face. A spasm of horror shook her and she rang for the attendant. The attendant too was horrified, but she could do nothing; it was not her place to mend the blind. She could only suggest that the lady should change her cabin, which she accordingly prepared to do.

People were almost exactly alike all over the world, but the attendant of the air-ship, perhaps owing to her exceptional duties, had grown a little out of the common. She had often to address passengers with direct speech, and this had given her a certain roughness and originality of manner. When Vashti swerved away from the sunbeams with a cry, she behaved barbarically—she put out her hand to steady her.

"How dare you!" exclaimed the passenger. "You forget yourself!"

The woman was confused, and apologized for not having let her fall. People never touched one another. The custom had become obsolete, owing to the Machine.

"Where are we now?" asked Vashti haughtily.

"We are over Asia," said the attendant, anxious to be polite.

"Asia?"

"You must excuse my common way of speaking. I have got into the habit of calling places over which I pass by their unmechanical names."

"Oh, I remember Asia. The Mongols came from it."

"Beneath us, in the open air, stood a city that was once called Simla."[1]

"Have you ever heard of the Mongols and of the Brisbane school?"

"No."

"Brisbane also stood in the open air."

"Those mountains to the right—let me show you them." She pushed back a metal blind. The main chain of the Himalayas was revealed. "They were once called the Roof of the World, those mountains."

"What a foolish name!"

"You must remember that, before the dawn of civilisation, they seemed to be an impenetrable wall that touched the stars. It was supposed that no one but the gods could exist above their summits. How we have advanced, thanks to the Machine!"

"How we have advanced, thanks to the Machine!" said Vashti.

---

1 A city in India, now Shimla.

"How we have advanced, thanks to the Machine!" echoed the passenger who had dropped his Book the night before, and who was standing in the passage.

"And that white stuff in the cracks?—what is it?"

"I have forgotten its name."

"Cover the window, please. These mountains give me no ideas."

The northern aspect of the Himalayas was in deep shadow: on the Indian slope the sun had just prevailed. The forests had been destroyed during the literature epoch for the purpose of making newspaper-pulp, but the snows were awakening to their morning glory, and clouds still hung on the breasts of Kinchinjunga.[1] In the plain were seen the ruins of cities, with diminished rivers creeping by their walls, and by the sides of these were sometimes the signs of vomitories, marking the cities of to-day. Over the whole prospect air-ships rushed, crossing and intercrossing with incredible *aplomb*, and rising nonchalantly when they desired to escape the perturbations of the lower atmosphere and to traverse the Roof of the World.

"We have indeed advanced, thanks to the Machine," repeated the attendant, and hid the Himalayas behind a metal blind.

The day dragged wearily forward. The passengers sat each in his cabin, avoiding one another with an almost physical repulsion and longing to be once more under the surface of the earth. There were eight or ten of them, mostly young males, sent out from the public nurseries to inhabit the rooms of those who had died in various parts of the earth. The man who had dropped his Book was on the homeward journey. He had been sent to Sumatra for the purpose of propagating the race. Vashti alone was travelling by her private will.

At midday she took a second glance at the earth. The air-ship was crossing another range of mountains, but she could see little, owing to clouds. Masses of black rock hovered below her, and merged indistinctly into grey. Their shapes were fantastic; one of them resembled a prostrate man.

"No ideas here," murmured Vashti, and hid the Caucasus behind a metal blind.

In the evening she looked again. They were crossing a golden sea, in which lay many small islands and one peninsula.

She repeated, "No ideas here," and hid Greece behind a metal blind.

PART II
THE MENDING APPARATUS

By a vestibule, by a lift, by a tubular railway, by a platform, by a sliding door—by reversing all the steps of her departure did Vashti arrive at her son's room, which exactly resembled her own. She might well declare that the visit was

1 A variant spelling of Kangchenjunga, the third highest mountain in the world, part of the Himalayas.

superfluous. The buttons, the knobs, the reading-desk with the Book, the temperature, the atmosphere, the illumination—all were exactly the same. And if Kuno himself, flesh of her flesh, stood close beside her at last, what profit was there in that? She was too well bred to shake him by the hand.

Averting her eyes, she spoke as follows:

"Here I am. I have had the most terrible journey and greatly retarded the development of my soul. It is not worth it, Kuno, it is not worth it. My time is too precious. The sunlight almost touched me, and I have met with the rudest people. I can only stop a few minutes. Say what you want to say, and then I must return."

"I have been threatened with Homelessness," said Kuno.

She looked at him now.

"I have been threatened with Homelessness, and I could not tell you such a thing through the Machine."

Homelessness means death. The victim is exposed to the air, which kills him.

"I have been outside since I spoke to you last. The tremendous thing has happened, and they have discovered me."

"But why shouldn't you go outside!" she exclaimed. "It is perfectly legal, perfectly mechanical, to visit the surface of the earth. I have lately been to a lecture on the sea; there is no objection to that; one simply summons a respirator and gets an Egression-permit. It is not the kind of thing that spiritually minded people do, and I begged you not to do it, but there is no legal objection to it."

"I did not get an Egression-permit."

"Then how did you get out?"

"I found out a way of my own."

The phrase conveyed no meaning to her, and he had to repeat it.

"A way of your own?" she whispered. "But that would be wrong."

"Why?"

The question shocked her beyond measure.

"You are beginning to worship the Machine," he said coldly. "You think it irreligious of me to have found out a way of my own. It was just what the Committee thought, when they threatened me with Homelessness."

At this she grew angry. "I worship nothing!" she cried. "I am most advanced. I don't think you irreligious, for there is no such thing as religion left. All the fear and the superstition that existed once have been destroyed by the Machine. I only meant that to find out a way of your own was—— Besides, there is no new way out."

"So it is always supposed."

"Except through the vomitories, for which one must have an Egression-permit, it is impossible to get out. The Book says so."

"Well, the Book's wrong, for I have been out on my feet."

For Kuno was possessed of a certain physical strength.

By these days it was a demerit to be muscular. Each infant was examined at birth, and all who promised undue strength were destroyed. Humanitarians may protest, but it would have been no true kindness to let an athlete live; he would never have been happy in that state of life to which the Machine had called him; he would have yearned for trees to climb, rivers to bathe in, meadows and hills against which he might measure his body. Man must be adapted to his surroundings, must he not? In the dawn of the world our weakly must be exposed on Mount Taygetus,[1] in its twilight our strong will suffer euthanasia, that the Machine may progress, that the Machine may progress, that the Machine may progress eternally.

"You know that we have lost the sense of space. We say 'space is annihilated,' but we have annihilated not space, but the sense thereof. We have lost a part of ourselves. I determined to recover it, and I began by walking up and down the platform of the railway outside my room. Up and down, until I was tired, and so did recapture the meaning of 'Near' and 'Far.' 'Near' is a place to which I can get quickly *on my feet*, not a place to which the train or the air-ship will take me quickly. 'Far' is a place to which I cannot get quickly on my feet; the vomitory is 'far,' though I could be there in thirty-eight seconds by summoning the train. Man is the measure.[2] That was my first lesson. Man's feet are the measure for distance, his hands are the measure for ownership, his body is the measure for all that is lovable and desirable and strong. Then I went further: it was then that I called to you for the first time, and you would not come.

"This city, as you know, is built deep beneath the surface of the earth, with only the vomitories protruding. Having paced the platform outside my own room, I took the lift to the next platform and paced that also, and so with each in turn, until I came to the topmost, above which begins the earth. All the platforms were exactly alike, and all that I gained by visiting them was to develop my sense of space and my muscles. I think I should have been content with this—it is not a little thing,—but as I walked and brooded, it occurred to me that our cities had been built in the days when men still breathed the outer air, and that there had been ventilation shafts for the workmen. I could think of nothing but these ventilation shafts. Had they been destroyed by all the food-tubes and medicine-tubes and music-tubes that the Machine has evolved lately? Or did traces of them remain? One thing was certain. If I came upon them anywhere, it would be in the railway-tunnels of the topmost story. Everywhere else, all space was accounted for.

"I am telling my story quickly, but don't think that I was not a coward or that your answers never depressed me. It is not the proper thing, it is not mechanical, it is not decent to walk along a railway-tunnel. I did not fear that I

1 According to Plutarch, Spartans would throw "weakly and deformed" infants into "a deep cavern near the mountain *Taygetus*" (*Plutarch's Lives*, vol. 1, p. 140).

2 The pre-Socratic philosopher Protagoras (c. 490–c. 420 BCE) argued that "man is the measure of all things," a statement taken variously to support empiricism or relativism.

might tread upon a live rail and be killed. I feared something far more intangible—doing what was not contemplated by the Machine. Then I said to myself, 'Man is the measure' and I went, and after many visits I found an opening.

"The tunnels, of course, were lighted. Everything is light, artificial light; darkness is the exception. So when I saw a black gap in the tiles, I knew that it was an exception, and rejoiced. I put in my arm—I could put in no more at first—and waved it round and round in ecstasy. I loosened another tile, and put in my head, and shouted into the darkness: 'I am coming, I shall do it yet,' and my voice reverberated down endless passages. I seemed to hear the spirits of those dead workmen who had returned each evening to the starlight and to their wives, and all the generations who had lived in the open air called back to me, 'You will do it yet, you are coming.'"

He paused, and, absurd as he was, his last words moved her. For Kuno had lately asked to be a father, and his request had been refused by the Committee. His was not a type that the Machine desired to hand on.

"Then a train passed. It brushed by me, but I thrust my head and arms into the hole. I had done enough for one day, so I crawled back to the platform, went down in the lift, and summoned my bed. Ah what dreams! And again I called you, and again you refused."

She shook her head and said:

"Don't. Don't talk of these terrible things. You make me miserable. You are throwing civilisation away."

"But I had got back the sense of space and a man cannot rest then. I determined to get in at the hole and climb the shaft. And so I exercised my arms. Day after day I went through ridiculous movements, until my flesh ached, and I could hang by my hands and hold the pillow of my bed outstretched for many minutes. Then I summoned a respirator, and started.

"It was easy at first. The mortar had somehow rotted, and I soon pushed some more tiles in, and clambered after them into the darkness, and the spirits of the dead comforted me. I don't know what I mean by that. I just say what I felt. I felt, for the first time, that a protest had been lodged against corruption, and that even as the dead were comforting me, so I was comforting the unborn. I felt that humanity existed, and that it existed without clothes. How can I possibly explain this? It was naked, humanity seemed naked, and all these tubes and buttons and machineries neither came into the world with us, nor will they follow us out, nor do they matter supremely while we are here. Had I been strong, I would have torn off every garment I had, and gone out into the outer air unswaddled. But this is not for me, nor perhaps for my generation. I climbed with my respirator and my hygienic clothes and my dietetic tabloids! Better thus than not at all.

"There was a ladder, made of some primæval metal. The light from the railway fell upon its lowest rungs, and I saw that it led straight upwards out of the rubble at the bottom of the shaft. Perhaps our ancestors ran up and down it a dozen times daily, in their building. As I climbed, the rough edges cut through my gloves so that my hands bled. The light helped me for a little, and then came darkness and, worse still, silence which pierced my ears like a sword. The Machine hums! Did you know that? Its hum penetrates our blood, and may even guide our thoughts. Who knows! I was getting beyond its power. Then I thought: 'This silence means that I am doing wrong.' But I heard voices in the silence, and again they strengthened me." He laughed. "I had need of them. The next moment I cracked my head against something."

She sighed.

"I had reached one of those pneumatic stoppers that defend us from the outer air. You may have noticed them on the air-ship. Pitch dark, my feet on the rungs of an invisible ladder, my hands cut; I cannot explain how I lived through this part, but the voices still comforted me, and I felt for fastenings. The stopper, I suppose, was about eight feet across. I passed my hand over it as far as I could reach. It was perfectly smooth. I felt it almost to the centre. Not quite to the centre, for my arm was too short. Then the voice said: 'Jump. It is worth it. There may be a handle in the centre, and you may catch hold of it and so come to us your own way. And if there is no handle, so that you may fall and are dashed to pieces—it is still worth it: you will still come to us your own way.' So I jumped. There was a handle, and——"

He paused. Tears gathered in his mother's eyes. She knew that he was fated. If he did not die to-day he would die to-morrow. There was not room for such a person in the world. And with her pity disgust mingled. She was ashamed at having borne such a son, she who had always been so respectable and so full of ideas. Was he really the little boy to whom she had taught the use of his stops and buttons, and to whom she had given his first lessons in the Book? The very hair that disfigured his lip showed that he was reverting to some savage type. On atavism the Machine can have no mercy.

"There was a handle, and I did catch it. I hung tranced over the darkness and heard the hum of these workings as the last whisper in a dying dream. All the things I had cared about and all the people I had spoken to through tubes appeared infinitely little. Meanwhile the handle revolved. My weight had set something in motion and I span slowly, and then——

"I cannot describe it. I was lying with my face to the sunshine. Blood poured from my nose and ears and I heard a tremendous roaring. The stopper, with me clinging to it, had simply been blown out of the earth, and the air that we make down here was escaping through the vent into the air above. It burst up like a fountain. I crawled back to it—for the upper air hurts—and, as it were, I took great sips from the edge. My respirator had flown goodness knows where, my clothes were torn. I just lay with my lips close to the hole, and I sipped until the bleeding stopped. You can imagine nothing so curious. This hollow in the grass—I will speak of it in a minute,—the sun shining into it, not brilliantly but through marbled clouds,—the peace, the nonchalance, the sense of space, and, brushing my cheek, the roaring fountain of our artificial air! Soon I spied my respirator, bobbing up and down in the current high above my head, and higher still were many air-ships. But no one ever looks out of air-ships, and in my case they could not have picked me up. There I was, stranded. The sun shone a little way down the shaft, and revealed the topmost rung of the ladder, but it was hopeless trying to reach it. I should either have been tossed up again by the escape, or else have fallen in, and died. I could only lie on the grass, sipping and sipping, and from time to time glancing around me.

"I knew that I was in Wessex, for I had taken care to go to a lecture on the subject before starting. Wessex lies above the room in which we are talking now. It was once an important state. Its kings held all the southern coast from the Andredswald to Cornwall, while the Wansdyke protected them on the north, running over the high ground.[1] The lecturer was only concerned with the rise of Wessex, so I do not know how long it remained an international power, nor would the knowledge have assisted me. To tell the truth I could do nothing but laugh, during this part. There was I, with a pneumatic stopper by my side and a respirator bobbing over my head, imprisoned, all three of us, in a grass-grown hollow that was edged with fern."

Then he grew grave again.

"Lucky for me that it was a hollow. For the air began to fall back into it and to fill it as water fills a bowl. I could crawl about. Presently I stood. I breathed a mixture, in which the air that hurts predominated whenever I tried to climb the sides. This was not so bad. I had not lost my tabloids and remained ridiculously cheerful, and as for the Machine, I forgot about it altogether. My one aim now was to get to the top, where the ferns were, and to view whatever objects lay beyond.

"I rushed the slope. The new air was still too bitter for me and I came rolling back, after a momentary vision of something grey. The sun grew very feeble, and I remembered that he was in Scorpio—I had been to a lecture on that too. If the sun is in Scorpio, and you are in Wessex, it means that you must be as quick as you can, or it will get too dark.[2] (This is the first bit of useful information I have ever got from a lecture, and I expect it will be the last.) It made me try frantically to breathe the new air, and to advance as far as I dared out of my pond. The hollow filled so slowly. At times I thought that the fountain played with less vigour. My respirator seemed to dance nearer the earth; the roar was decreasing."

He broke off.

"I don't think this is interesting you. The rest will interest you even less. There are no Ideas in it, and I wish that I had not troubled you to come. We are too different, mother."

1 Wessex was a kingdom, in what is now the south of Great Britain, which existed from the sixth to tenth centuries. Andredswald, or Andredsweald, is the Saxon term for an area of southeast England; today, it is called the Weald. The Wansdyke is a medieval defensive wall and ditch in England's West Country.

2 Kuno is referencing the astrological sign Scorpio, which the Sun passes in late Fall (late October to late November). In astronomy, the sun passes the constellation Scorpius in late November.

She told him to continue.

"It was evening before I climbed the bank. The sun had very nearly slipped out of the sky by this time, and I could not get a good view. You, who have just crossed the Roof of the World, will not want to hear an account of the little hills that I saw—low colourless hills. But to me they were living and the turf that covered them was a skin, under which their muscles rippled, and I felt that those hills had called with incalculable force to men in the past, and that men had loved them. Now they sleep—perhaps for ever. They commune with humanity in dreams. Happy the man, happy the woman, who awakes the hills of Wessex. For though they sleep, they will never die."

His voice rose passionately.

"Cannot you see, cannot all you lecturers see, that it is we that are dying, and that down here the only thing that really lives is the Machine? We created the Machine, to do our will, but we cannot make it do our will now. It has robbed us of the sense of space and of the sense of touch, it has blurred every human relation and narrowed down love to a carnal act, it has paralysed our bodies and our wills, and now it compels us to worship it. The Machine develops—but not on our lines. The Machine proceeds—but not to our goal. We only exist as the blood corpuscles that course through its arteries, and if it could work without us, it would let us die. Oh, I have no remedy—or, at least, only one—to tell men again and again that I have seen the hills of Wessex as Ælfrid saw them when he overthrew the Danes.[1]

"So the sun set. I forgot to mention that a belt of mist lay between my hill and other hills, and that it was the colour of pearl."

He broke off for the second time.

"Go on," said his mother wearily.

He shook his head.

"Go on. Nothing that you say can distress me now. I am hardened."

"I had meant to tell you the rest, but I cannot: I know that I cannot: goodbye."

Vashti stood irresolute. All her nerves were tingling with his blasphemies. But she was also inquisitive.

"This is unfair," she complained. "You have called me across the world to hear your story, and hear it I will. Tell me—as briefly as possible, for this is a disastrous waste of time—tell me how you returned to civilisation."

"Oh—that!" he said, starting. "You would like to hear about civilisation. Certainly. Had I got to where my respirator fell down?"

"No—but I understand everything now. You put on your respirator, and managed to walk along the surface of the earth to a vomitory, and there your conduct was reported to the Central Committee."

"By no means."

---

1 Alfred the Great (c. 849–899) was the King of Wessex who fought, and eventually defeated, the Vikings.

He passed his hand over his forehead, as if dispelling some strong impression. Then, resuming his narrative, he warmed to it again.

"My respirator fell about sunset. I had mentioned that the fountain seemed feebler, had I not?"

"Yes."

"About sunset, it let the respirator fall. As I said, I had entirely forgotten about the Machine, and I paid no great attention at the time, being occupied with other things. I had my pool of air, into which I could dip when the outer keenness became intolerable, and which would possibly remain for days, provided that no wind sprang up to disperse it. Not until it was too late, did I realise what the stoppage of the escape implied. You see—the gap in the tunnel had been mended; the Mending Apparatus; the Mending Apparatus, was after me.

"One other warning I had, but I neglected it. The sky at night was clearer than it had been in the day, and the moon, which was about half the sky behind the sun, shone into the dell at moments quite brightly. I was in my usual place—on the boundary between the two atmospheres—when I thought I saw something dark move across the bottom of the dell, and vanish into the shaft. In my folly, I ran down. I bent over and listened, and I thought I heard a faint scraping noise in the depths.

"At this—but it was too late—I took alarm. I determined to put on my respirator and to walk right out of the dell. But my respirator had gone. I knew exactly where it had fallen—between the stopper and the aperture—and I could even feel the mark that it had made in the turf. It had gone, and I realised that something evil was at work, and I had better escape to the other air, and, if I must die, die running towards the cloud that had been the colour of a pearl. I never started. Out of the shaft—it is too horrible. A worm, a long white worm, had crawled out of the shaft and was gliding over the moonlit grass.

"I screamed. I did everything that I should not have done, I stamped upon the creature instead of flying from it, and it at once curled round the ankle. Then we fought. The worm let me run all over the dell, but edged up my leg as I ran. 'Help!' I cried. (That part is too awful. It belongs to the part that you will never know.) 'Help!' I cried. (Why cannot we suffer in silence?) 'Help!' I cried. Then my feet were wound together, I fell, I was dragged away from the dear ferns and the living hills, and past the great metal stopper (I can tell you this part), and I thought it might save me again if I caught hold of the handle. It also was enwrapped, it also. Oh, the whole dell was full of the things. They were searching it in all directions, they were denuding it, and the white snouts of others peeped out of the hole, ready if needed. Everything that could be moved they brought—brushwood, bundles of fern, everything, and down we all went intertwined into hell. The last things that I saw, ere the stopper closed after us, were certain stars, and I felt that a man of my sort lived in the sky. For I did fight, I fought till the very end, and it was only my head hitting against the ladder that quieted me. I woke up in this room. The worms had vanished.

I was surrounded by artificial air, artificial light, artificial peace, and my friends were calling to me down speaking-tubes to know whether I had come across any new ideas lately."

Here his story ended. Discussion of it was impossible, and Vashti turned to go.

"It will end in Homelessness," she said quietly.

"I wish it would," retorted Kuno.

"The Machine has been most merciful."

"I prefer the mercy of God."

"By that superstitious phrase, do you mean that you could live in the outer air?"

"Yes."

"Have you ever seen, round the vomitories, the bones of those who were extruded after the Great Rebellion?"

"Yes."

"They were left where they perished for our edification. A few crawled away, but they perished, too—who can doubt it? And so with the Homeless of our own day. The surface of the earth supports life no longer."

"Indeed."

"Ferns and a little grass may survive, but all higher forms have perished. Has any air-ship detected them?"

"No."

"Has any lecturer dealt with them?"

"No."

"Then why this obstinacy?"

"Because I have seen them," he exploded.

"Seen *what*?"

"Because I have seen her in the twilight—because she came to my help when I called—because she, too, was entangled by the worms, and, luckier than I, was killed by one of them piercing her throat."

He was mad. Vashti departed, nor, in the troubles that followed, did she ever see his face again.

PART III.
THE HOMELESS

DURING the years that followed Kuno's escapade, two important developments took place in the Machine. On the surface they were revolutionary, but in either case men's minds had been prepared beforehand, and they did but express tendencies that were latent already.

The first of these was the abolition of respirators.

Advanced thinkers, like Vashti, had always held it foolish to visit the surface of the earth. Air-ships might be necessary, but what was the good of going out for mere curiosity and crawling along for a mile or two in a terrestrial motor? The habit was vulgar and perhaps faintly improper: it was unproductive of ideas, and had no connection with the habits that really mattered. So respirators were abolished, and with them, of course, the terrestrial motors, and except for a few lecturers, who complained that they were debarred access to their subject-matter, the development was accepted quietly. Those who still wanted to know what the earth was like, had after all only to listen to some gramophone, or to look into some cinematophote. And even the lecturers acquiesced when they found that a lecture on the sea was none the less stimulating when compiled out of other lectures that had already been delivered on the same subject. "Beware of first-hand ideas!" exclaimed one of the most advanced of them. "First-hand ideas do not really exist. They are but the physical impressions produced by love and fear, and on this gross foundation who could erect a philosophy? Let your ideas be second-hand, and if possible tenth-hand, for then they will be far removed from that disturbing element—direct observation. Do not learn anything about this subject of mine—the French Revolution. Learn instead what I think that Enicharmon thought Urizen thought Gutch thought Ho-Yung thought Chi-Bo-Sing thought Lafcadio Hearn thought Carlyle thought Mirabeau said about the French Revolution.[1] Through the medium of these ten great minds,[2] the blood that was shed at Paris and the windows that were broken at Versailles will be clarified to an Idea which you may employ most profitably in your daily lives. But be sure that the intermediates are many and varied, for in history one authority exists to counteract another. Urizen must counteract the scepticism of Ho-Yung and Enicharmon, I must myself counteract the impetuosity of Gutch. You who listen to me are in a better position to judge about the French Revolution than I am. Your descendants will be even in a better position than you, for they will learn what you think I think, and yet another intermediate will be added to the chain. And in time"—his voice rose—"there will come a generation that has got beyond facts, beyond impressions, a generation absolutely colourless, a generation

'seraphically free
From taint of personality,'[3]

1 The French Revolution (1789–99) was a series of democratic and anti-monarchist uprisings and conflicts, which ended when Napoleon Bonaparte and others seized power through a military coup. Of the names listed, Lafcadio Hearn (1850–1904, a literary translator), Thomas Carlyle (1795–1881, a writer and historian), and Honoré Gabriel Riqueti, Count of Mirabeau (1749–91, French writer and revolutionary) are real, while the others appear to be invented figures, the lecturer apparently tracing historians from his own time back to the Revolution itself. "Urizen" is also the name of a figure who represents reason in several works by William Blake (1757–1821).

2 This is corrected to "eight great minds" in the version published in *The Eternal Moment and Other Stories* (1928).

3 From "The Lark Ascending" (1881) by English poet George Meredith (1828–1909).

which will see the French Revolution not as it happened, nor as they would like it to have happened, but as it would have happened, had it taken place in the days of the Machine."

Tremendous applause greeted this lecture, which did but voice a feeling already latent in the minds of men—a feeling that terrestrial facts must be ignored, and that the abolition of respirators was a positive gain. It was even suggested that air-ships should be abolished too. This was not done, because air-ships had somehow worked themselves into the Machine's system. But year by year they were used less, and mentioned less by thoughtful men.

The second great development was the re-establishment of religion.

This, too, had been voiced in the celebrated lecture. No one could mistake the reverent tone in which the peroration had concluded, and it awakened a responsive echo in the heart of each. Those who had long worshipped silently, now began to talk. They described the strange feeling of peace that came over them when they handled the Book of the Machine, the pleasure that it was to repeat certain numerals out of it, however little meaning those numerals conveyed to the outward ear, the ecstasy of touching a button, however unimportant, or of ringing an electric bell, however superfluously.

"The Machine," they exclaimed, "feeds us and clothes us and houses us; through it we speak to one another, through it we see one another, in it we have our being. The Machine is the friend of ideas and the enemy of superstition: the Machine is omnipotent, eternal; blessed is the Machine." And before long this allocution was printed on the first page of the Book, and in subsequent editions the ritual swelled into a complicated system of praise and prayer. The word "religion" was sedulously avoided, and in theory the Machine was still the creation and the implement of man. But in practice all, save a few retrogrades, worshipped it as divine. Nor was it worshipped in unity. One believer would be chiefly impressed by the blue optic plates, through which he saw other believers; another by the mending apparatus, which sinful Kuno had compared to worms; another by the lifts, another by the Book. And each would pray to this or to that, and ask it to intercede for him with the Machine as a whole. Persecution—that also was present. It did not break out, for reasons that will be set forward shortly. But it was latent, and all who did not accept the minimum known as "undenominational Mechanism" lived in danger of Homelessness, which means death, as we know.

To attribute these two great developments to the Central Committee, is to take a very narrow view of civilisation. The Central Committee announced the developments, it is true, but they were no more the cause of them than were the Kings of the Imperialistic period the cause of war. Rather did they yield to some invincible pressure, which came no one knew whither, and which, when gratified, was succeeded by some new pressure equally invincible. To such a state of affairs it is convenient to give the name of Progress. No one confessed the Machine was out of hand. Year by year it was served with increased efficiency and decreased intelligence. The better a man knew his own duties upon it, the less he understood the duties of his neighbour, and in all the world there was not one who understood the monster as a whole. Those master brains had perished. They had left full directions, it is true, and their successors had each of them mastered a portion of those directions. But Humanity, in its desire for comfort, had over-reached itself. It had exploited the riches of nature too far. Quietly and complacently, it was sinking into decadence, and Progress had come to mean the Progress of the Machine.

As for Vashti, her life went peacefully forward until the final disaster. She made her room dark and slept; she awoke and made the room light. She lectured and attended lectures. She exchanged ideas with her innumerable friends and believed she was growing more spiritual. At times a friend was granted Euthanasia, and left his or her room for the Homelessness that is beyond all human conception. Vashti did not much mind. After an unsuccessful lecture, she would sometimes ask for Euthanasia herself. But the death-rate was not permitted to exceed the birth-rate, and the Machine had hitherto refused it to her.

The troubles began quietly, long before she was conscious of them.

One day she was astonished at receiving a message from her son. They never communicated, having nothing in common, and she had only heard indirectly that he was still alive, and had been transferred from the northern hemisphere, where he had behaved so mischievously, to the southern—indeed, to a room not far from her own.

"Does he want me to visit him?" she thought. "Never again, never. And I have not the time."

No, it was madness of another kind.

He refused to visualise his face upon the blue plate, and speaking out of the darkness with solemnity said:

"The Machine stops."

"What do you say?"

"The Machine is stopping, I know it, I know the signs."

She burst into a peal of laughter. He heard her and was angry, and they spoke no more.

"Can you imagine anything more absurd?" she cried to a friend. "A man who was my son believes that the Machine is stopping. It would be impious if it was not mad."

"The Machine is stopping?" her friend replied. "What does that mean? The phrase conveys nothing to me."

"Nor to me."

"He does not refer, I suppose, to the trouble there has been lately with the music?"

"Oh no, of course not. Let us talk about music."

"Have you complained to the authorities?"

"Yes, and they say it wants mending, and referred me to the Committee of the Mending Apparatus. I complained of those curious gasping sighs that disfigure the symphonies of the Brisbane school. They sound like some one in pain. The Committee of the Mending Apparatus say that it shall be remedied shortly."

Obscurely worried, she resumed her life. For one thing, the defect in the music irritated her. For another thing, she could not forget Kuno's speech. If he had known that the music was out of repair—he could not know it, for he detested music—if he had known that it was wrong, "the Machine stops" was exactly the venomous sort of remark he would have made. Of course he had made it at a venture, but the coincidence annoyed her, and she spoke with some petulance to the Committee of the Mending Apparatus.

They replied, as before, that the defect would be set right shortly.

"Shortly! At once!" she retorted. "Why should I be worried by imperfect music? Things are always put right at once. If you do not mend it at once, I shall complain to the Central Committee."

"No personal complaints are received by the Central Committee," the Committee of the Mending Apparatus replied.

"Through whom am I to make my complaint, then?"

"Through us."

"I complain then."

"Your complaint shall be forwarded in its turn."

"Have others complained?"

This question was unmechanical, and the Committee of the Mending Apparatus refused to answer it.

"It is too bad!" she exclaimed to another of her friends. "There never was such an unfortunate woman as myself. I can never be sure of my music now. It gets worse and worse each time I summon it."

"I too have my troubles," the friend replied. "Sometimes my ideas are interrupted by a slight jarring noise."

"What is it?"

"I do not know whether it is inside my head, or inside the wall."

"Complain, in either case."

"I have complained, and my complaint will be forwarded in its turn to the Central Committee."

Time passed, and they resented the defects no longer. The defects had not been remedied, but the human tissues in that latter day had become so subservient, that they readily adapted themselves to every caprice of the Machine. The sigh at the crisis of the Brisbane symphony no longer irritated Vashti; she accepted it as part of the melody. The jarring noise, whether in the head or in the wall, was no longer resented by her friend. And so with the mouldy artificial fruit, so with the bath water that began to stink, so with the defective rhymes that the poetry machine had taken to emit. All were bitterly complained of at first, and then acquiesced in and forgotten. Things went from bad to worse unchallenged.

It was otherwise with the failure of the sleeping apparatus. That was a more serious stoppage. There came a day when over the whole world—in Sumatra, in Wessex, in the innumerable cities of Courland[1] and Brazil—the beds, when summoned by their tired owners, failed to appear. It may seem a ludicrous matter, but from it we may date the collapse of humanity. The Committee responsible for the failure was assailed by complainants, whom it referred, as usual, to the Committee of the Mending Apparatus, who in its turn assured them that their complaints would be forwarded to the Central Committee. But the discontent grew, for mankind was not yet sufficiently adaptable to do without sleep.

"Some one is meddling with the Machine——" they began.

"Some one is trying to make himself king, to reintroduce the personal element."

"Punish that man with Homelessness."

"To the rescue! Avenge the Machine! Avenge the Machine!"

"War! Kill the man!"

But the Committee of the Mending Apparatus now came forward, and allayed the panic with well-chosen words. It confessed that the Mending Apparatus was itself in need of repair.

The effect of this frank confession was admirable.

"Of course," said a famous lecturer—he of the French Revolution, who gilded each new decay with splendour—"of course we shall not press our complaints now. The Mending Apparatus has treated us so well in the past that we all sympathise with it, and will wait patiently for its recovery. In its own good time it will resume its duties. Meanwhile let us do without our beds, our tabloids, our other little wants. Such, I feel sure, would be the wish of the Machine."

Thousands of miles away his audience applauded. The Machine still linked them. Under the seas, beneath the roots of the mountains, ran the wires through which they saw and heard, the enormous eyes and ears that were their heritage, and the hum of many workings clothed their thoughts in one garment of subserviency. Only the old and the sick remained ungrateful, for it was rumoured that Euthanasia, too, was out of order, and that pain had reappeared among men.

It became difficult to read. A blight entered the atmosphere and dulled its luminosity. At times Vashti could scarcely see across her room. The air, too, was foul. Loud were the complaints, impotent the remedies, heroic the tone of the lecturer as he cried: "Courage! courage! What matter so long as the Machine goes on? To it the darkness and the light are one." And though things improved again after a time, the old brilliancy was never recaptured, and humanity never recovered from its entrance into twilight. There was an hysterical talk of "measures," of "provisional dictatorship," and the inhabitants of

1 At the time of Forster's writing, the Courland Governorate was part of the Russian Empire. It is now part of an independent Latvia.

Sumatra were asked to familiarise themselves with the workings of the central power station, the said power station being situated in France. But for the most part panic reigned, and men spent their strength praying to their Books, tangible proofs of the Machine's omnipotence. There were gradations of terror—at times came rumours of hope—the Mending Apparatus was almost mended—the enemies of the Machine had been got under—new "nerve-centres" were evolving which would do the work even more magnificently than before. But there came a day when, without the slightest warning, without any previous hint of feebleness, the entire of the communication-system broke down, all over the world, and the world, as they understood it, ended.

Vashti was lecturing at the time and her earlier remarks had been punctuated with applause. As she proceeded the audience became silent, and at the conclusion there was no sound. Somewhat displeased she called to a friend who was a specialist in sympathy. No sound: doubtless the friend was sleeping. And so with the next friend whom she tried to summon, and so with the next, until she remembered Kuno's cryptic remark, "The Machine stops."

The phrase still conveyed nothing. If Eternity was stopping it would of course be set going shortly.

For example, there was still a little light and air—the atmosphere had improved a few hours previously. There was still the Book, and while there was the Book there was security.

Then she broke down, for with the cessation of activity came an unexpected terror—silence.

She had never known silence, and the coming of it nearly killed her—it did kill many thousands of people outright. Ever since her birth she had been surrounded by the steady hum. It was to the ear what artificial air was to the lungs, and agonising pains shot across her head. And scarcely knowing what she did, she stumbled forward and pressed the unfamiliar button, the one that opened the door of her cell.

Now the door of the cell worked on a simple hinge of its own. It was not connected with the central power station, dying far away in France. It opened, rousing immoderate hopes in Vashti, for she thought that the Machine had been mended. It opened, and she saw the dim tunnel that curved far away towards freedom. One look, and then she shrank back. For the tunnel was full of people—she was almost the last in that city to have taken alarm.

People at any time repelled her, and these were nightmares from her worst dreams. People were crawling about, people were screaming, whimpering, gasping for breath, touching each other, vanishing in the dark, and ever and anon being pushed off the platform on to the live rail. Some were fighting round the electric bells, trying to summon trains which could not be summoned. Others were yelling for Euthanasia or for respirators, or blaspheming the Machine. Others stood at the doors of their cells fearing, like herself, either to stop in them or to leave them. And behind all the uproar was silence—the silence which is the voice of the earth and of the generations who have gone.

No—it was worse than solitude. She closed the door again and sat down to wait for the end. The disintegration went on, accompanied by horrible cracks and rumbling. The valves that restrained the Medical Apparatus must have been weakened, for it ruptured and hung hideously from the ceiling. The floor heaved and fell and flung her from her chair. A tube oozed towards her serpent fashion. And at last the final horror approached—light began to ebb, and she knew that civilisation's long day was closing.

She whirled around, praying to be saved from this, at any rate, kissing the Book, pressing button after button. The uproar outside was increasing, and even penetrated the wall. Slowly the brilliancy of her cell was dimmed, the reflections faded from her metal switches. Now she could not see the reading-stand, now not the Book, though she held it in her hand. Light followed the flight of sound, air was following light, and the original void returned to the cavern from which it had been so long excluded. Vashti continued to whirl, like the devotees of an earlier religion, screaming, praying, striking at the buttons with bleeding hands.

It was thus that she opened her prison and escaped—escaped in the spirit: at least so it seems to me, ere my meditation closes. That she escapes in the body—I cannot perceive that. She struck, by chance, the switch that released the door, and the rush of foul air on her skin, the loud throbbing whispers in her ears, told her that she was facing the tunnel again, and that tremendous platform on which she had seen men fighting. They were not fighting now. Only the whispers remained, and the little whimpering groans. They were dying by hundreds out in the dark.

She burst into tears.

Tears answered her.

They wept for humanity, those two, not for themselves. They could not bear that this should be the end. Ere silence was completed their hearts were opened, and they knew what had been important on the earth. Man, the flower of all flesh, the noblest of all creatures visible, man who had once made god in his image, and had mirrored his strength on the constellations, beautiful naked man was dying, strangled in the garments that he had woven. Century after century had he toiled, and here was his reward. Truly the garment had seemed heavenly at first, shot with the colours of culture, sewn with the threads of self-denial. And heavenly it had been so long as it was a garment and no more, so long as man could shed it at will and live by the essence that is his soul, and the essence, equally divine, that is his body. The sin against the body—it was for that they wept in chief; the centuries of wrong against the muscles and the nerves, and those five portals by which we can alone apprehend—glosing[1] it over with talk of evolution, until the body was white pap, the home of ideas as colourless, last sloshy stirrings of a spirit that had grasped the stars.

1 Glossing, as in adding marginal commentary to a text.

"Where are you?" she sobbed.

His voice in the darkness said, "Here."

"Is there any hope, Kuno?"

"None for us."

"Where are you?"

She crawled towards him over the bodies of the dead. His blood spurted over her hands.

"Quicker," he gasped, "I am dying—but we touch, we talk, not through the Machine."

He kissed her.

"We have come back to our own. We die, but we have recaptured life, as it was in Wessex, when Ælfrid overthrew the Danes. We know what they know outside, they who dwelt in the cloud that is the colour of a pearl."

"But Kuno, is it true? Are there still men on the surface of the earth? Is this—this tunnel, this poisoned darkness—really not the end?"

He replied:

"I have seen them, spoken to them, loved them. They are hiding in the mist and the ferns until our civilisation stops. To-day they are the Homeless—to-morrow——"

"Oh, to-morrow—some fool will start the Machine again, to-morrow."

"Never," said Kuno, "never. Humanity has learnt its lesson."

As he spoke, the whole city was broken like a honeycomb. An air-ship had sailed in through the vomitory into a ruined wharf. It crashed downwards, exploding as it went, rending gallery after gallery with its wings of steel. For a moment they saw the nations of the dead, and, ere they joined them, scraps of the untainted sky.

Francis Stevens (Gertrude Barrows Bennett) (1883–1948)

Gertrude Barrows (Gertrude Bennett after marriage) published her first science fiction story, "The Curious Experience of Thomas Dunbar," in the March 1904 edition of the pulp magazine *The Argosy*. That story was published under "G.M. Barrows," but she adopted the pseudonym Francis Stevens later in her writing career, which began in earnest in 1917. Often associated with Weird fiction, Bennett published eight longer works and almost as many short stories, the last of which, "Sunfire," was published in 1923, which her daughter has referred to as a "renewed attempt at fiction-writing after surviving the influenza epidemic of 1920," as Douglas A. Anderson has noted (290). There is some debate over her birth year, with Anderson and others in various online forums noting that census data shows her born in 1883, while others cite 1884.

Note on the text: The text of "Friend Island" here follows the initial publication in the well-known pulp magazine *All-Story* (vol. 88, no. 2, 7 Sept. 1918). "Friend Island" was one of the multiple stories, across various issues, labeled as "A 'Different' Story"; it also received the tag, "Being the Veracious Tale of an Ancient Mariness, Heard and Reported in the Year A. D. 2100."

"Friend Island" (1918)

IT was upon the water-front that I first met her, in one of the shabby little tea shops frequented by able sailoresses of the poorer type. The up-town, glittering resorts of the Lady Aviators' Union were not for such as she.

Stern of feature, bronzed by wind and sun, her age could only be guessed, but I surmised at once that in her I beheld a survivor of the age of turbines and oil engines—a true sea-woman of that elder time, when woman's superiority to man had not been so long recognized. When, to emphasize their victory, women in all ranks were sterner than to-day's need demands.

The spruce, smiling young maidens—engine-women and stokers of the great aluminum rollers, but despite their profession, very neat in gold-braided blue knickers and boleros—these looked askance at the hard-faced relic of a harsher day, as they passed in and out of the shop.

I, however, brazenly ignoring similar glances at myself, a mere male intruding on the haunts of the world's ruling sex, drew a chair up beside the veteran. I ordered a full pot of tea, two cups and a plate of macaroons, and put on my most ingratiating air. Possibly my unconcealed admiration and interest were wiles not exercised in vain. Or the macaroons and tea, both excellent, may have loosened the old sea-woman's tongue. At any rate, under cautious questioning, she had soon launched upon a series of reminiscences well beyond my hopes for color and variety.

"When I was a lass," quoth the sea-woman, after a time, "there was none of this high-flying, gilt-edged, leather-stocking luxury about the sea. We sailed by the power of our oil and gasoline. If they failed on us, like as not 'twas the rubber ring and the rolling wave for ours."

She referred to the archaic practise of placing a pneumatic affair called a life-preserver beneath the arms, in case of that dreaded disaster, now so unheard of, shipwreck.

"In them days there was still many a man bold enough to join our crews. And I've knowed cases," she added condescendingly, "where just by the muscle and brawn of such men some poor sailor lass has reached shore alive that would have fed the sharks without 'em. Oh, I ain't so down on men as you might think. It's the spoiling of them that I don't hold with. There's too much preached nowadays that man is fit for nothing but to fetch and carry and do nurse-work in big child-homes. To my mind, a man who hasn't the nerve of a woman ain't fitted to father children, let alone raise 'em. But that's not here nor there. My time's past, and I know it, or I wouldn't be setting here gossipin' to you, my lad, over an empty teapot."

I took the hint, and with our cups replenished, she bit thoughtfully into her fourteenth macaroon and continued.

"There's one voyage I'm not likely to forget, though I live to be as old as Cap'n Mary Barnacle, of the Shouter. 'Twas aboard the old Shouter that this here voyage occurred, and it was her last and likewise Cap'n Mary's. Cap'n Mary, she was then that decrepit, it seemed a mercy that she should go to her rest, and in good salt water at that.

"I remember the voyage for Cap'n Mary's sake, but most I remember it because 'twas then that I come the nighest in my life to committin' matrimony. For a man, the man had nerve; he was nearer bein' companionable than any other man I ever seed; and if it hadn't been for just one little event that showed up the—the *mannishness* of him, in a way I couldn't abide, I reckon he'd be keepin' house for me this minute.

"We cleared from Frisco with a cargo of silkateen petticoats for Brisbane. Cap'n Mary was always strong on petticoats. Leather breeches or even half-skirts would ha' paid far better, they being more in demand like, but Cap'n Mary was three-quarters owner, and says she, land women should buy petticoats, and if they didn't it wouldn't be the Lord's fault nor hers for not providing 'em.

"We cleared on a fine day, which is an ill sign—or was, then when the weather and the seas o' God still counted in the trafficking of the humankind. Not two days out we met a whirling, mucking bouncer of a gale that well nigh threw the old Shouter a full point off her course in the first wallop. She was a stout craft, though. None of your feather-weight, gas-lightened, paper-thin alloy shells, but toughened aluminum from stern to stern. Her turbines drove her through the combers[1] at a forty-five knot clip, which named her a speedy craft for a freighter in them days.[2]

"But this night, as we tore along through the creaming green billows, something unknown went 'way wrong down below.

"I was forward under the shelter of her long over-scoop, looking for a hairpin I'd dropped somewheres about that afternoon. It was a gold hairpin, and gold still being might scarce when I was a girl, a course I valued it. But suddenly I felt the old Shouter give a jump under my feet like a plane struck by a shell in full flight. Then she trembled all over for a full second, frightened like. Then, with the crash of doomsday ringing in my ears, I felt myself sailing through the air right into the teeth o' the shrieking gale, as near as I could judge. Down I come in the hollow of a monstrous big wave, and as my ears doused under I thought I heard a splash close by. Coming up, sure enough, there close by me was floating a new, patent, hermetic, thermo-ice-chest. Being as it was empty, and being as it was shut up air-tight, that ice-chest made as sweet a life-preserver as woman could wish in such an hour. About ten foot by twelve, it floated high in the raging sea. Out on its top I scrambled, and hanging on by a handle I looked expectant for some of my poor fellow-women to come floating by. Which they never did, for the good reason that the Shouter had blowed up and went below, petticoats, Cap'n Mary and all."

"What caused the explosion?" I inquired curiously.

"The Lord and Cap'n Mary Barnacle can explain," she answered piously. "Besides the oil for her turbines, she carried a power of gasoline for her alternative engines, and likely 'twas the cause of her ending so sudden like. Anyways, all I ever seen of her again was the empty ice-chest that Providence had well-nigh hove upon my head. On that I sat and floated, and floated and sat some more, till by and by the storm sort of blowed itself out, the sun come shining—this was next morning—and I could dry my hair and look about me. I was a young lass, then,[3] and not bad to look upon. I didn't want to die, any more than you that's sitting there this minute. So I up and prays for land. Sure enough toward evening a speck heaves up low down on the horizon. At first I took it for a gas liner, but later found it was just a little island, all alone by itself in the great Pacific Ocean.

"Come, now, here's luck, thinks I, and with that I deserts the ice-chest, which being empty, and me having no ice to put in it, not likely to have in them latitudes, is of no further use to me. Striking out I swum a mile or so and set foot on dry land for the first time in nigh three days.

"Pretty land it were, too, though bare of human life as an iceberg in the Arctic.

1 Waves.

2 45 knots would have been a remarkable, record-breaking steamship speed at the time of the story's publication and beyond: "By the 1930s, passenger liner speeds were reaching 30 knots" (Barnes).

3 In the original, this is written as "ten," but later printings, including *Fantastic Novels Magazine* (vol. 4, no. 3, Sept. 1950, pp. 110–16), silently amend to "then."

"I had landed on a shining white beach that run up to a grove of lovely, waving palm trees. Above them I could see the slopes of a hill so high and green it reminded me of my own old home, up near Couquomgomoc Lake in Maine. The whole place just seemed to smile and smile at me. The palms waved and bowed in the sweet breeze, like they wanted to say, 'Just set right down and make yourself to home. We've been waiting a long time for you to come.' I cried, I was that happy to be made welcome. I was a young lass then, and sensitive-like to how folks treated me. You're laughing now, but wait and see if or no there was sense to the way I felt.

"So I up and dries my clothes and my long, soft hair again, which was well worth drying, for I had far more of it then than now. After that I walked along a piece, till there was a sweet little path meandering away into the wild woods.

"Here, thinks I, this looks like inhabitants. Be they civil or wild, I wonder? But after traveling the path a piece, lo and behold it ended sudden like in a wide circle of green grass, with a little spring of clear water. And the first thing I noticed was a slab of white board nailed to a palm tree close to the spring. Right off I took a long drink, for you better believe I was thirsty, and then I went to look at this board. It had evidently been tore off the side of a wooden packing box, and the letters was printed in lead-pencil.

"'Heaven help whoever you be,' I read. 'This island ain't just right. I'm going to swim for it. You better too. Good-by. Nelson Smith.' That's what it said, but the spellin' was simply awful. It all looked quite new and recent, as if Nelson Smith hadn't more than a few hours before wrote and nailed it there.

"Well, after reading that queer warning I begun to shake all over like in a chill. Yes, I shook like I had the ague,[1] though the hot tropic sun was burning down right on me and that alarming board. What had scared Nelson Smith so much that he had swum to get away? I looked all around real cautious and careful, but not a single frightening thing could I behold. And the palms and the green grass and the flowers still smiled that peaceful and friendly like. 'Just make yourself to home,' was wrote all over the place in plainer letters than those sprawly lead-pencil ones on the board.

"Pretty soon, what with the quiet and all, the chill left me. Then I thought, 'Well to be sure this Smith person was just an ordinary man, I reckon, and likely he got nervous of being so alone. Likely he just fancied things which was really not. It's a pity he drowned himself before I come, though likely I'd have found him poor company. By his record I judge him a man of but common education.'

"So I decided to make the most of my welcome, and that I did for weeks to come. Right near the spring was a cave, dry as a biscuit box, with a nice floor of white sand. Nelson had lived there too, for there was a litter of stuff—tin cans—empty—scraps of newspapers and the like. I got to calling him Nelson in my mind, and then Nelly, and wondering if he was dark or fair, and how

1 Fever; sometimes used to refer specifically to malaria.

he come to be cast away there all alone, and what was the strange events that drove him to his end. I cleaned out the cave, though. He had devoured all his tin-canned provisions, however he come by them, but this I didn't mind. That there island was a generous body. Green milk-coconuts, sweet berries, turtle eggs and the like was my daily fare.

"For about three weeks the sun shone every day, the birds sang and the monkeys chattered. We was all one big, happy family, and the more I explored that island the better I liked the company I was keeping. The land was about ten miles from beach to beach, and never a foot of it that wasn't sweet and clean as a private park.

"From the top of the hill I could see the ocean, miles and miles of blue water, with never a sign of a gas liner, or even a little government running-boat. Them running-boats used to go most everywhere to keep the sea-ways clean of derelicts and the like. But I knowed that if this island was no more than a hundred miles off the regular courses of navigation, it might be many a long day before I'd be rescued. The top of the hill, as I found when first I climbed up there, was a wore-out crater. So I knowed that the island was one of them volcanic ones you run across so many of in the seas between Capricorn and Cancer.[1]

"Here and there on the slopes and down through the jungly tree-growth, I would come on great lumps of rock, and these must have came up out of that crater long ago. If there was lava it was that old it had been covered up entire with green growing stuff. You couldn't have found it without a spade, which I didn't have nor want.

"Well, at first I was happy as the hours was long. I wandered and clambered and waded and swum, and combed my long hair on the beach, having fortunately not lost my sidecombs nor the rest of my gold hairpins. But by and by it begun to get just a bit lonesome. Funny thing, that's a feeling that, once it starts, it gets worse and worser so quick it's perfectly surprising. And right then was when the days begun to get gloomy. We had a long, sickly hot spell, like I never seen before on an ocean island. There was dull clouds across the sun from morn till night. Even the little monkeys and parrakeets, that had seemed so gay, moped and drowsed like they was sick. All one day I cried, and let the rain soak me through and through—that was the first rain we had—and I didn't get thorough dried even during the night, though I slept in my cave. Next morning I got up mad as thunder at myself and all the world.

"When I looked out the black clouds was billowing across the sky. I could hear nothing but great breakers roaring in on the beaches, and the wild wind raving through the lashing palms.

"As I stood there a nasty little wet monkey dropped from a branch almost on my head. I grabbed a pebble and slung it at him real vicious. 'Get away, you dirty little brute!' I shrieks, and with that there come a awful blinding flare

1 I.e., the Tropic of Capricorn and the Tropic of Cancer.

of light. There was a long, crackling noise like a bunch of Chinese fireworks, and then a sound as if a whole fleet of Shouters had all went up together.

"When I come to, I found myself 'way in the back of my cave, trying to dig further into the rock with my finger nails. Upon taking thought, it come to me that what had occurred was just a lightning-clap, and going to look, sure enough there lay a big palm tree right across the glade. It was all busted and split open by the lightning, and the little monkey was under it, for I could see his tail and his hind legs sticking out.

"Now, when I set eyes on that poor, crushed little beast I'd been so mean to, I was terrible ashamed. I sat down on the smashed tree and considered and considered. How thankful I had ought to have been. Here I had a lovely, plenteous island, with food and water to my taste, when it might have been a barren, starvation rock that was my lot. And so, thinking, a sort of gradual peaceful feeling stole over me. I got cheerfuller and cheerfuller, till I could have sang and danced for joy.

"Pretty soon I realized that the sun was shining bright for the first time that week. The wind had stopped hollering, and the waves had died to just a singing murmur on the beach. It seemed kind o' strange, this sudden peace, like the cheer in my own heart after its rage and storm. I rose up, feeling sort of queer, and went to look if the little monkey had came alive again, though that was a fool thing, seeing he was laying all crushed up and very dead. I buried him under a tree root, and as I did it a conviction come to me.

"I didn't hardly question that conviction at all. Somehow, living there alone so long, perhaps my natural womanly intuition was stronger than ever before or since, and so I *knowed*. Then I went and pulled poor Nelson Smith's board off from the tree and tossed it away for the tide to carry off. That there board was an insult to my island!"

The sea-woman paused, and her eyes had a far-away look. It seemed as if I and perhaps even the macaroons and tea were quite forgotten.

"Why did you think that?" I asked, to bring her back. "How could an island be insulted?"

She started, passed her hand across her eyes, and hastily poured another cup of tea.

"Because," she said at last, poising a macaroon in mid-air, "because that island—that particular island that I had landed on—had a heart!

"When I was gay, it was bright and cheerful. It was glad when I come, and it treated me right until I got that grouchy it had to mope from sympathy. It loved me like a friend. When I flung a rock at that poor little, drenched monkey critter, it backed up my act with an anger like the wrath o' God, and killed its own child to please me! But it got right cheery the minute I seen the wrongness of my ways. Nelson Smith had no business to say, 'This island ain't just right,' for it was a righter place than ever I seen elsewhere. When I cast away that lying board, all the birds begun to sing like mad. The green milk-coconuts fell right and left. Only the monkeys seemed kind o' sad like still, and no wonder. You see, their own mother, the island, had rounded on one of 'em for my sake!

"After that I was right careful and considerate. I named the island Anita, not knowing her right name, or if she had any. Anita was a pretty name, and it sounded kind of South Sea like. Anita and me got along real well together from that day on. It was some strain to be always gay and singing around like a dear duck of a canary bird, but I done my best. Still, for all the love and gratitude I bore Anita, the company of an island, however sympathetic, ain't quite enough for a human being. I still got lonesome, and there was even days when I couldn't keep the clouds clear out of the sky, though I will say we had no more tornadoes.

"I think the island understood and tried to help me with all the bounty and good cheer the poor thing possessed. None the less my heart give a wonderful big leap when one day I seen a blot on the horizon. It drawed nearer and nearer, until at last I could make out its nature."

"A ship, of course," said I, "and were you rescued?"

"'Tweren't a ship, neither," denied the sea-woman somewhat impatiently. "Can't you let me spin this yarn without no more remarks and fool questions? This thing what was bearing down so fast with the incoming tide was neither more nor less than another island!

"You may well look startled. I was startled myself. Much more so than you, likely. I didn't know then what you, with your book-learning, very likely know now—that islands sometimes float. Their underparts being a tangled-up mess of roots and old vines that new stuff's growed over, they sometimes break away from the mainland in a brisk gale and go off for a voyage, calm as a old-fashioned, eight-funnel steamer.[1] This one was uncommon large, being as much as two miles, maybe, from shore to shore. It had its palm trees and its live things, just like my own Anita, and I've sometimes wondered if this drifting piece hadn't really been a part of my island once—just its daughter like, as you might say.

"Be that, however, as it might be, no sooner did the floating piece get within hailing distance than I hears a human holler and there was a man dancing up and down on the shore like he was plumb crazy. Next minute he had plunged into the narrow strip of water between us and in a few minutes had swum to where I stood.

"Yes, of course it was none other than Nelson Smith!

"I knowed that the minute I set eyes on him. He had the very look of not having no better sense than the man what wrote that board and then nearly committed suicide trying to get away from the best island in all the oceans.

1 The number of funnels on a steamship has an interesting cultural history in addition to its engineering function: more funnels were associated with more power, but this was not always the case. In fact, by 1931, *The Literary Digest*, referencing the *London Times*, notes that as the need for multiple funnels disappeared, some ships were given fake funnels: "In posters and pictorial advertisements, it is noted, ship funnels have a value of their own" ("Those Fake Steamship Funnels" 13).

Glad enough he was to get back, though, for the coconuts was running very short on the floater what had rescued him, and the turtle eggs wasn't worth mentioning. Being short of grub is the surest way I know to cure a man's fear of the unknown.

"Well, to make a long story short, Nelson Smith told me he was a aeronauter. In them days to be an aeronauter was not the same as to be an aviatress is now. There was dangers in the air, and dangers in the sea, and he had met with both. His gas tank had leaked and he had dropped into the water close by Anita. A case or two of provisions was all he could save from the total wreck.

"Now, as you might guess, I was crazy enough to find out what had scared this Nelson Smith into trying to swim the Pacific. He told me a story that seemed to fit pretty well with mine, only when it come to the scary part he shut up like a clam, that aggravating way some men have. I give it up at last for just man-foolishness, and we begun to scheme to get away.

"Anita moped some while we talked it over. I realized how she must be feeling, so I explained to her that it was right needful for us to get with our kind again. If we stayed with her we should probably quarrel like cats, and maybe even kill each other out of pure human cussedness. She cheered up considerable after that, and even, I thought, got a little anxious to have us leave. At any rate, when we begun to provision up the little floater, which we had anchored to the big island by a cable of twisted bark, the green nuts fell all over the ground, and Nelson found more turtle nests in a day than I had in weeks.

"During them days I really got fond of Nelson Smith. He was a companionable body, and brave, or he wouldn't have been a professional aeronauter, a job that was rightly thought tough enough for a woman, let alone a man. Though he was not so well educated as me, at least he was quiet and modest about what he did know, not like some men, boasting most where there is least to brag of.

"Indeed, I misdoubt if Nelson and me would not have quit the sea and the air together and set up housekeeping in some quiet little town up in New England, maybe, after we had got away, if it had not been for what happened when we went. I never, let me say, was so deceived in any man before nor since. The thing taught me a lesson and I never got fooled again. This was the way of it.

"We was all ready to go, and then one morning, like a parting gift from Anita, come a soft and favoring wind. Nelson and I run down the beach together, for we didn't want our floater to blow off and leave us. As we was running, our arms full of coconuts, Nelson Smith stubbed his bare toe on a sharp rock, and down he went. I hadn't noticed, and was going on.

"But sudden the ground begun to shake under my feet, and the air was full of a queer, grinding, groaning sound, like the very earth was in pain.

"I turned around sharp. There sat Nelson, holding his bleeding toe in both fists and giving vent to such awful words as no decent sea-going lady would ever speak nor hear to!

"'Stop it, stop it!' I shrieked at him, but 'twas too late.

"Island or no island, Anita was a lady, too! She had a gentle heart, but she knowed how to behave when she was insulted.

"With one terrible, great roar a spout of smoke and flame belched up out o' the heart of Anita's crater hill a full mile into the air!

"I guess Nelson stopped swearing. He couldn't have heard himself, anyways. Anita was talking now with tongues of flame and such roars as would have bespoke the raging protest of a continent.

"I grabbed that fool man by the hand and run him down to the water. We had to swim good and hard to catch up with our only hope, the floater. No bark rope could hold her against the stiff breeze that was now blowing, and she had broke her cable. By the time we scrambled aboard great rocks was falling right and left. We couldn't see each other for a while for the clouds of fine gray ash that filled the air and covered the sea.

"It seemed like Anita was that mad she was flinging stones after us, and truly I believe that such was her intention. I didn't blame her, neither!

"Lucky for us the wind was strong and we was soon out of range. After that it wasn't long before my poor, outraged Anita was just a streak o' smoke on the horizon.

"'So!' says I to Nelson, after I'd got most of the ashes out of my mouth, and shook my hair clear of cinders. 'So, that was the reason you up and left sudden when you was there before! You aggravated that island till the poor thing druv you out!'

"'Well,' says he, and not so meek as I'd have admired to see him, 'how could I know the darn island was a lady?'

"'Actions speak louder than words,' says I. 'You should have knowed it by her ladylike behavior!'

"'Is volcanoes and slingin' hot rocks ladylike?' says he. 'Is snakes ladylike? T'other time I cut my thumb on a tin can, I cussed a little bit. Say—just a li'l' bit! An' what comes at me out o' all the caves, and out o' every crack in the rocks, and out o' the very spring o' water where I'd been drinkin'? Why snakes! *Snakes*, if you please, big, little, green, red and sky-blue-scarlet! What'd I do? Jumped in the water, of course. Why wouldn't I? I'd ruther swim an' drown than be stung or swallered to death. But how was I t' know the snakes come outta the rocks because I cussed?'

"'*You* couldn't,' I agrees, sarcastic. 'Some folks never knows a lady till she up and whangs 'em over the head with a brick. A real, gentle, kind-like warning, them snakes were, which you would not heed! Take shame to yourself, Nelly,' says I, right stern, 'that a decent, little island like Anita can't associate with you peaceable, but you must hurt her sacredest feelings with language no lady would stand by to hear!'

"He give up his high manners then, for he knowed them words was true.

"I never did see Anita again. She may have blew herself right out of the ocean in her just wrath at the vulgar, disgustin' language of Nelson Smith. I don't know. We was took off the floater at last, and I lost track of Nelson just as quick as I could when we was landed at Frisco.

"He had taught me a lesson. A man is just full of mannishness, and the best of 'em ain't good enough for a lady to sacrifice her sensibilities to put up with.

"Nelson Smith, he seemed to feel real bad when he learned I was not for him, and then he apologized. But apologies weren't no use to me. I never could abide him, after the way he went and talked right in the presence of me and my poor, sweet lady friend, Anita!"

Now I am well versed in the lore of the sea in all ages. Through mists of time I have enviously eyed wild voyagings of sea rovers who roved and spun their yarns before the stronger sex came into its own, and ousted man from his heroic pedestal. I have followed—across the printed page—the wanderings of Odysseus. Before Gulliver I have burned the incense of tranced attention; and with reverent awe considered the history of one Munchausen, a baron.[1]

But alas, these were only men!

In what field is not woman our subtle superior?

Meekly I bowed my head, and when my eyes dared lift again, the ancient mariness had departed, leaving me to sorrow for my surpassed and outdone idols. Also with a bill for macaroons and tea of such incredible proportions that in comparison therewith I found it easy to believe her story!

1 Odysseus is the hero of the ancient Greek poem the *Odyssey*, which traces his adventures during his journey home to Ithaca following the Trojan War. Gulliver is the protagonist of Jonathan Swift's satirical work *Gulliver's Travels* (1726), which similarly tells the tales of his travels to various fantastic lands; Munchausen is the likewise adventurous fictionalized Baron from Rudolf Erich Raspe's novel *Baron Munchausen's Narrative of his Marvellous Travels and Campaigns in Russia* (1785).

W.E.B. Du Bois (1868–1963)

W.E.B. Du Bois was one of the foremost US civil rights activists, philosophers, sociologists, and historians of his day. He helped found the National Association for the Advancement of Colored People (NAACP) in 1909, and edited their journal, *The Crisis*. In terms of his writing, he is best known today for his book *The Souls of Black Folk* (1903), a series of essays exploring the lives and cultures of Black people in the US, simultaneously providing a philosophical analysis of race in the US that is still influential today. Among the most important contributions of that work is the concept of "double consciousness," which he defines as "this sense of always looking at one's self through the eyes of others, of measuring one's soul by the tape of a world that looks on in amused contempt and pity. One ever feels his two-ness,— an American, a Negro; two souls, two thoughts, two unreconciled strivings; two warring ideals in one dark body, whose dogged strength alone keeps it from being torn asunder" (364-65).

Note on the text: "The Comet" appeared as the concluding story in Du Bois's book *Darkwater: Voices from within the Veil* (1920). The text used here follows the first British edition of that book published by Constable and Company (1920).

"The Comet" (1920)

HE stood a moment on the steps of the bank, watching the human river that swirled down Broadway. Few noticed him. Few ever noticed him save in a way that stung. He was outside the world—"nothing!" as he said bitterly. Bits of the words of the walkers came to him.

"The comet?"

"The comet ——"

Everybody was talking of it. Even the president, as he entered, smiled patronizingly at him, and asked:

"Well, Jim, are you scared?"

"No," said the messenger shortly.

"I thought we'd journeyed through the comet's tail once," broke in the junior clerk affably.

"Oh, that was Halley's,"[1] said the president; "this is a new comet, quite a stranger, they say—wonderful, wonderful! I saw it last night. Oh, by the way, Jim," turning again to the messenger, "I want you to go down into the lower vaults today."

---

1 The orbit of Halley's comet repeatedly and predictably brings it close enough to Earth to be visible in the sky. Its most recent appearance before this story was in 1910.

The messenger followed the president silently. Of course, they wanted *him* to go down to the lower vaults. It was too dangerous for more valuable men. He smiled grimly and listened.

"Everything of value has been moved out since the water began to seep in," said the president; "but we miss two volumes of old records. Suppose you nose around down there,—it isn't very pleasant, I suppose."

"Not very," said the messenger, as he walked out.

"Well, Jim, the tail of the new comet hits us at noon this time," said the vault clerk, as he passed over the keys; but the messenger passed silently down the stairs. Down he went beneath Broadway, where the dim light filtered through the feet of hurrying men; down to the dark basement beneath; down into the blackness and silence beneath that lowest cavern. Here with his dark lantern he groped in the bowels of the earth, under the world.

He drew a long breath as he threw back the last great iron door and stepped into the fetid slime within. Here at last was peace, and he groped moodily forward. A great rat leaped past him and cobwebs crept across his face. He felt carefully around the room, shelf by shelf, on the muddied floor, and in crevice and corner. Nothing. Then he went back to the far end, where somehow the wall felt different. He sounded and pushed and pried. Nothing. He started away. Then something brought him back. He was sounding and working again when suddenly the whole black wall swung as on mighty hinges, and blackness yawned beyond. He peered in; it was evidently a secret vault—some hiding place of the old bank unknown in newer times. He entered hesitatingly. It was a long, narrow room with shelves, and at the far end, an old iron chest. On a high shelf lay the two missing volumes of records, and others. He put them carefully aside and stepped to the chest. It was old, strong, and rusty. He looked at the vast and old-fashioned lock and flashed his light on the hinges. They were deeply incrusted with rust. Looking about, he found a bit of iron and began to pry. The rust had eaten a hundred years, and it had gone deep. Slowly, wearily, the old lid lifted, and with a last, low groan lay bare its treasure—and he saw the dull sheen of gold!

"Boom!"

A low, grinding, reverberating crash struck upon his ear. He started up and looked about. All was black and still. He groped for his light and swung it about him. Then he knew! The great stone door had swung to. He forgot the gold and looked death squarely in the face. Then with a sigh he went methodically to work. The cold sweat stood on his forehead; but he searched, pounded, pushed, and worked until after what seemed endless hours his hand struck a cold bit of metal and the great door swung again harshly on its hinges, and then, striking against something soft and heavy, stopped. He had just room to squeeze through. There lay the body of the vault clerk, cold and stiff. He stared at it, and then felt sick and nauseated. The air seemed unaccountably foul, with a strong, peculiar odor. He stepped forward, clutched at the air, and fell fainting across the corpse.

He awoke with a sense of horror, leaped from the body, and groped up the stairs, calling to the guard. The watchman sat as if asleep, with the gate swinging free. With one glance at him the messenger hurried up to the sub-vault. In vain he called to the guards. His voice echoed and re-echoed weirdly. Up into the great basement he rushed. Here another guard lay prostrate on his face, cold and still. A fear arose in the messenger's heart. He dashed up to the cellar floor, up into the bank. The stillness of death lay everywhere and everywhere bowed, bent, and stretched the silent forms of men. The messenger paused and glanced about. He was not a man easily moved; but the sight was appalling! "Robbery and murder," he whispered slowly to himself as he saw the twisted, oozing mouth of the president where he lay half-buried on his desk. Then a new thought seized him: If they found him here alone—with all this money and all these dead men—what would his life be worth? He glanced about, tiptoed cautiously to a side door, and again looked behind. Quietly he turned the latch and stepped out into Wall Street.

How silent the street was! Not a soul was stirring, and yet it was high-noon—Wall Street? Broadway? He glanced almost wildly up and down, then across the street, and as he looked, a sickening horror froze in his limbs. With a choking cry of utter fright he lunged, leaned giddily against the cold building, and stared helplessly at the sight.

In the great stone doorway a hundred men and women and children lay crushed and twisted and jammed, forced into that great, gaping doorway like refuse in a can—as if in one wild, frantic rush to safety, they had crushed and ground themselves to death. Slowly the messenger crept along the walls, wetting his parched mouth and trying to comprehend, stilling the tremor in his limbs and the rising terror in his heart. He met a business man, silk-hatted and frock-coated, who had crept, too, along that smooth wall and stood now stone dead with wonder written on his lips. The messenger turned his eyes hastily away and sought the curb. A woman leaned wearily against the signpost, her head bowed motionless on her lace and silken bosom. Before her stood a street car, silent, and within—but the messenger but glanced and hurried on. A grimy newsboy sat in the gutter with the "last edition" in his uplifted hand: "Danger!" screamed its black headlines. "Warnings wired around the world. The Comet's tail sweeps past us at noon. Deadly gases expected. Close doors and windows. Seek the cellar." The messenger read and staggered on. Far out from a window above, a girl lay with gasping face and sleevelets on her arms. On a store step sat a little, sweet-faced girl looking upward toward the skies, and in the carriage by her lay—but the messenger looked no longer. The cords gave way—the terror burst in his veins, and with one great, gasping cry he sprang desperately forward and ran,—ran as only the frightened run, shrieking and fighting the air until with one last wail of pain he sank on the grass of Madison Square and lay prone and still.

When he arose, he gave no glance at the still and silent forms on the benches, but, going to a fountain, bathed his face; then hiding himself in a corner away from the drama of death, he quietly gripped himself and thought the thing through: The comet had swept the earth and this was the end. Was everybody dead? He must search and see.

He knew that he must steady himself and keep calm, or he would go insane. First he must go to a restaurant. He walked up Fifth Avenue to a famous hostelry and entered its gorgeous, ghost-haunted halls. He beat back the nausea, and, seizing a tray from dead hands, hurried into the street and ate ravenously, hiding to keep out the sights.

"Yesterday, they would not have served me," he whispered, as he forced the food down.

Then he started up the street,—looking, peering, telephoning, ringing alarms; silent, silent all. Was nobody—nobody—he dared not think the thought and hurried on.

Suddenly he stopped still. He had forgotten. My God! How could he have forgotten? He must rush to the subway—then he almost laughed. No—a car; if he could find a Ford. He saw one. Gently he lifted off its burden, and took his place on the seat. He tested the throttle. There was gas. He glided off, shivering, and drove up the street. Everywhere stood, leaned, lounged, and lay the dead, in grim and awful silence. On he ran past an automobile, wrecked and overturned; past another, filled with a gay party whose smiles yet lingered on their death-struck lips; on past crowds and groups of cars, pausing by dead policemen; at 42nd Street he had to detour to Park Avenue to avoid the dead congestion. He came back on Fifth Avenue at 57th and flew past the Plaza[1] and by the park with its hushed babies and silent throng, until as he was rushing past 72nd Street he heard a sharp cry, and saw a living form leaning wildly out an upper window. He gasped. The human voice sounded in his ears like the voice of God.

"Hello—hello—help, in God's name!" wailed the woman. "There's a dead girl in here and a man and—and see yonder dead men lying in the street and dead horses—for the love of God go and bring the officers——" And the words trailed off into hysterical tears.

He wheeled the car in a sudden circle, running over the still body of a child and leaping on the curb. Then he rushed up the steps and tried the door and rang violently. There was a long pause, but at last the heavy door swung back. They stared a moment in silence. She had not noticed before that he was a Negro. He had not thought of her as white. She was a woman of perhaps twenty-five—rarely beautiful and richly gowned, with darkly-golden hair, and jewels. Yesterday, he thought with bitterness, she would scarcely have looked at him twice. He would have been dirt beneath her silken feet. She stared at him. Of all the sorts of men she had pictured as coming to her rescue she had not dreamed of one like him. Not that he was not human, but he dwelt in a world so far from hers, so infinitely far, that he seldom even entered her thought. Yet

1 A luxury hotel near Central Park in New York.

as she looked at him curiously he seemed quite commonplace and usual. He was a tall, dark workingman of the better class, with a sensitive face trained to stolidity and a poor man's clothes and hands. His face was soft and slow and his manner at once cold and nervous, like fires long banked, but not out.

So a moment each paused and gauged the other; then the thought of the dead world without rushed in and they started toward each other.

"What has happened?" she cried. "Tell me! Nothing stirs. All is silence! I see the dead strewn before my window as winnowed by the breath of God,—and see——" She dragged him through great, silken hangings to where, beneath the sheen of mahogany and silver, a little French maid lay stretched in quiet, everlasting sleep, and near her a butler lay prone in his livery.

The tears streamed down the woman's cheeks and she clung to his arm until the perfume of her breath swept his face and he felt the tremors racing through her body.

"I had been shut up in my dark room developing pictures of the comet which I took last night; when I came out—I saw the dead!

"What has happened?" she cried again.

He answered slowly:

"Something—comet or devil—swept across the earth this morning and—many are dead!"

"Many? Very many?"

"I have searched and I have seen no other living soul but you."

She gasped and they stared at each other.

"My—father!" she whispered.

"Where is he?"

"He started for the office."

"Where is it?"

"In the Metropolitan Tower."[1]

"Leave a note for him here and come."

Then he stopped.

"No," he said firmly—"first, we must go—to Harlem."

"Harlem!" she cried. Then she understood. She tapped her foot at first impatiently. She looked back and shuddered. Then she came resolutely down the steps.

"There's a swifter car in the garage in the court," she said.

"I don't know how to drive it," he said.

"I do," she answered.

In ten minutes they were flying to Harlem on the wind. The Stutz[2] rose and raced like an airplane. They took the turn at 110th Street on two wheels and slipped with a shriek into 135th.

---

1 Most likely the Metropolitan Life Insurance Company Tower.

2 Stutz was a US car company, active from the 1910s to 1930s, that specialized in luxury sports cars (the best known of which was the Stutz Bearcat).

He was gone but a moment. Then he returned, and his face was gray. She did not look, but said:

"You have lost—somebody?"

"I have lost—everybody," he said, simply—"unless——"

He ran back and was gone several minutes—hours they seemed to her.

"Everybody," he said, and he walked slowly back with something film-like in his hand which he stuffed into his pocket.

"I'm afraid I was selfish," he said. But already the car was moving toward the park among the dark and lined dead of Harlem—the brown, still faces, the knotted hands, the homely garments, and the silence—the wild and haunting silence. Out of the park, and down Fifth Avenue they whirled. In and out among the dead they slipped and quivered, needing no sound of bell or horn, until the great, square Metropolitan Tower hove in sight. Gently he laid the dead elevator boy aside; the car shot upward. The door of the office stood open. On the threshold lay the stenographer, and, staring at her, sat the dead clerk. The inner office was empty, but a note lay on the desk, folded and addressed but unsent:

> Dear Daughter:
>
> I've gone for a hundred mile spin in Fred's new Mercedes. Shall not be back before dinner. I'll bring Fred with me.
>
> J. B. H.

"Come," she cried nervously. "We must search the city."

Up and down, over and across, back again—on went that ghostly search. Everywhere was silence and death—death and silence! They hunted from Madison Square to Spuyten Duyvel; they rushed across the Williamsburg Bridge; they swept over Brooklyn; from the Battery and Morningside Heights they scanned the river.[1] Silence, silence everywhere, and no human sign. Haggard and bedraggled they puffed a third time slowly down Broadway, under the broiling sun, and at last stopped. He sniffed the air. An odor—a smell—and with the shifting breeze a sickening stench filled their nostrils and brought its awful warning. The girl settled back helplessly in her seat.

"What can we do?" she cried.

It was his turn now to take the lead, and he did it quickly.

"The long distance telephone—the telegraph and the cable—night rockets and then—flight!"

She looked at him now with strength and confidence. He did not look like men, as she had always pictured men; but he acted like one and she was content. In fifteen minutes they were at the central telephone exchange. As they came to the door he stepped quickly before her and pressed her gently back as he closed it. She heard him moving to and fro, and knew his burdens—the

1 Locations and neighbourhoods across New York. The river referenced is the Hudson River.

poor, little burdens he bore. When she entered, he was alone in the room. The grim switchboard flashed its metallic face in cryptic, sphinx[1]-like immobility. She seated herself on a stool and donned the bright earpiece. She looked at the mouthpiece. She had never looked at one so closely before. It was wide and black, pimpled with usage; inert; dead; almost sarcastic in its unfeeling curves. It looked—she beat back the thought—but it looked,—it persisted in looking like—she turned her head and found herself alone. One moment she was terrified; then she thanked him silently for his delicacy and turned resolutely, with a quick intaking of breath.

"Hello!" she called in low tones. She was calling to the world. The world *must* answer. Would the world *answer*? Was the world—

Silence!

She had spoken too low.

"Hello!" she cried, full-voiced.

She listened. Silence! Her heart beat quickly. She cried in clear, distinct, loud tones: "Hello—hello—hello!"

What was that whirring? Surely—no—was it the click of a receiver?

She bent close, she moved the pegs in the holes, and called and called, until her voice rose almost to a shriek, and her heart hammered. It was as if she had heard the last flicker of creation, and the evil was silence. Her voice dropped to a sob. She sat stupidly staring into the black and sarcastic mouthpiece, and the thought came again. Hope lay dead within her. Yes, the cable and the rockets remained; but the world—she could not frame the thought or say the word. It was too mighty—too terrible! She turned toward the door with a new fear in her heart. For the first time she seemed to realize that she was alone in the world with a stranger, with something more than a stranger,—with a man alien in blood and culture—unknown, perhaps unknowable. It was awful! She must escape—she must fly; he must not see her again. Who knew what awful thoughts—

She gathered her silken skirts deftly about her young, smooth limbs—listened, and glided into a side-hall. A moment she shrank back: the hall lay filled with dead women; then she leaped to the door and tore at it, with bleeding fingers, until it swung wide. She looked out. He was standing at the top of the alley,—silhouetted, tall and black, motionless. Was he looking at her or away? She did not know—she did not care. She simply leaped and ran—ran until she found herself alone amid the dead and the tall ramparts of towering buildings.

She stopped. She was alone. Alone! Alone on the streets—alone in the city—perhaps alone in the world! There crept in upon her the sense of deception—of creeping hands behind her back—of silent, moving things she could not see,—of voices hushed in fearsome conspiracy. She looked behind and

1 In Greek myth, the sphinx (a creature part human woman, part lion, and part bird) asks travellers riddles and does not let them pass unless they answer correctly.

sideways, started at strange sounds and heard still stranger, until every nerve within her stood sharp and quivering, stretched to scream at the barest touch. She whirled and flew back, whimpering like a child, until she found that narrow alley again and the dark, silent figure silhouetted at the top. She stopped and rested; then she walked silently toward him, looked at him timidly; but he said nothing as he handed her into the car. Her voice caught as she whispered:

"Not—that."

And he answered slowly: "No—not that!"

They climbed into the car. She bent forward on the wheel and sobbed, with great, dry, quivering sobs, as they flew toward the cable office on the east side, leaving the world of wealth and prosperity for the world of poverty and work. In the world behind them were death and silence, grave and grim, almost cynical, but always decent; here it was hideous. It clothed itself in every ghastly form of terror, struggle, hate, and suffering. It lay wreathed in crime and squalor, greed and lust. Only in its dread and awful silence was it like to death everywhere.

Yet as the two, flying and alone, looked upon the horror of the world, slowly, gradually, the sense of all-enveloping death deserted them. They seemed to move in a world silent and asleep,—not dead. They moved in quiet reverence, lest somehow they wake these sleeping forms who had, at last, found peace. They moved in some solemn, world-wide *Friedhof*,[1] above which some mighty arm had waved its magic wand. All nature slept until—until, and quick with the same startling thought, they looked into each other's eyes—he, ashen, and she, crimson, with unspoken thought. To both, the vision of a mighty beauty—of vast, unspoken things, swelled in their souls; but they put it away.

Great, dark coils of wire came up from the earth and down from the sun and entered this low lair of witchery. The gathered lightnings of the world centered here, binding with beams of light the ends of the earth. The doors gaped on the gloom within. He paused on the threshold.

"Do you know the code?" she asked.

"I know the call for help—we used it formerly at the bank."

She hardly heard. She heard the lapping of the waters far below,—the dark and restless waters—the cold and luring waters, as they called. He stepped within. Slowly she walked to the wall, where the water called below, and stood and waited. Long she waited, and he did not come. Then with a start she saw him, too, standing beside the black waters. Slowly he removed his coat and stood there silently. She walked quickly to him and laid her hand on his arm. He did not start or look. The waters lapped on in luring, deadly rhythm. He pointed down to the waters, and said quietly:

"The world lies beneath the waters now—may I go?"

She looked into his stricken, tired face, and a great pity surged within her heart. She answered in a voice clear and calm, "No."

---

1 Cemetery (Ger.).

Upward they turned toward life again, and he seized the wheel. The world was darkening to twilight, and a great, gray pall was falling mercifully and gently on the sleeping dead. The ghastly glare of reality seemed replaced with the dream of some vast romance. The girl lay silently back, as the motor whizzed along, and looked half-consciously for the elf-queen to wave life into this dead world again. She forgot to wonder at the quickness with which he had learned to drive her car. It seemed natural. And then as they whirled and swung into Madison Square and at the door of the Metropolitan Tower she gave a low cry, and her eyes were great! Perhaps she had seen the elf-queen?

The man led her to the elevator of the tower and deftly they ascended. In her father's office they gathered rugs and chairs, and he wrote a note and laid it on the desk; then they ascended to the roof and he made her comfortable. For a while she rested and sank to dreamy somnolence, watching the worlds above and wondering. Below lay the dark shadows of the city and afar was the shining of the sea. She glanced at him timidly as he set food before her and took a shawl and wound her in it, touching her reverently, yet tenderly. She looked up at him with thankfulness in her eyes, eating what he served. He watched the city. She watched him. He seemed very human,—very near now.

"Have you had to work hard?" she asked softly.

"Always," he said.

"I have always been idle," she said. "I was rich."

"I was poor," he almost echoed.

"The rich and the poor are met together," she began, and he finished:

"The Lord is the Maker of them all."[1]

"Yes," she said slowly; "and how foolish our human distinctions seem—now," looking down to the great dead city stretched below, swimming in unlightened shadows.

"Yes—I was not—human, yesterday," he said.

She looked at him. "And your people were not my people," she said; "but today——" She paused. He was a man,—no more; but he was in some larger sense a gentleman,—sensitive, kindly, chivalrous, everything save his hands and—his face. Yet yesterday——

"Death, the leveler!"[2] he muttered.

"And the revealer," she whispered gently, rising to her feet with great eyes. He turned away, and after fumbling a moment sent a rocket into the darkening air. It arose, shrieked, and flew up, a slim path of light, and scattering its stars abroad, dropped on the city below. She scarcely noticed it. A vision of the world had risen before her. Slowly the mighty prophecy of her destiny overwhelmed her. Above the dead past hovered the Angel of Annunciation.[3] She

1 Proverbs 22.2.

2 Possibly a reference to the poem "Death the Leveller" by playwright James Shirley (1596–1666).

3 The angel Gabriel who, in Christian tradition, tells Mary she will give birth to the son of God.

was no mere woman. She was neither high nor low, white nor black, rich nor poor. She was primal woman; mighty mother of all men to come and Bride of Life. She looked upon the man beside her and forgot all else but his manhood, his strong, vigorous manhood—his sorrow and sacrifice. She saw him glorified. He was no longer a thing apart, a creature below, a strange outcast of another clime and blood, but her Brother Humanity incarnate, Son of God and great All-Father of the race to be.

He did not glimpse the glory in her eyes, but stood looking outward toward the sea and sending rocket after rocket into the unanswering darkness. Dark-purple clouds lay banked and billowed in the west. Behind them and all around, the heavens glowed in dim, weird radiance that suffused the darkening world and made almost a minor music. Suddenly, as though gathered back in some vast hand, the great cloud-curtain fell away. Low on the horizon lay a long, white star—mystic, wonderful! And from it fled upward to the pole, like some wan bridal veil, a pale, wide sheet of flame that lighted all the world and dimmed the stars.

In fascinated silence the man gazed at the heavens and dropped his rockets to the floor. Memories of memories stirred to life in the dead recesses of his mind. The shackles seemed to rattle and fall from his soul. Up from the crass and crushing and cringing of his caste leaped the lone majesty of kings long dead. He arose within the shadows, tall, straight, and stern, with power in his eyes and ghostly scepters hovering to his grasp. It was as though some mighty Pharaoh lived again, or curled Assyrian lord. He turned and looked upon the lady, and found her gazing straight at him.

Silently, immovably, they saw each other face to face—eye to eye. Their souls lay naked to the night. It was not lust; it was not love—it was some vaster, mightier thing that needed neither touch of body nor thrill of soul. It was a thought divine, splendid.

Slowly, noiselessly, they moved toward each other—the heavens above, the seas around, the city grim and dead below. He loomed from out the velvet shadows vast and dark. Pearl-white and slender, she shone beneath the stars. She stretched her jeweled hands abroad. He lifted up his mighty arms, and they cried each to the other, almost with one voice, "The world is dead."

"Long live the——"

"Honk! Honk!" Hoarse and sharp the cry of a motor drifted clearly up from the silence below. They started backward with a cry and gazed upon each other with eyes that faltered and fell, with blood that boiled.

"Honk! Honk! Honk! Honk!" came the mad cry again, and almost from their feet a rocket blazed into the air and scattered its stars upon them. She covered her eyes with her hands, and her shoulders heaved. He dropped and bowed, groped blindly on his knees about the floor. A blue flame spluttered lazily after an age, and she heard the scream of an answering rocket as it flew.

Then they stood still as death, looking to opposite ends of the earth.

"Clang—crash—clang!"

The roar and ring of swift elevators shooting upward from below made the great tower tremble. A murmur and babel of voices swept in upon the night. All over the once dead city the lights blinked, flickered, and flamed; and then with a sudden clanging of doors the entrance to the platform was filled with men, and one with white and flying hair rushed to the girl and lifted her to his breast. "My daughter!" he sobbed.

Behind him hurried a younger, comelier man, carefully clad in motor costume, who bent above the girl with passionate solicitude and gazed into her staring eyes until they narrowed and dropped and her face flushed deeper and deeper crimson.

"Julia," he whispered; "my darling, I thought you were gone forever."

She looked up at him with strange, searching eyes.

"Fred," she murmured, almost vaguely, "is the world—gone?"

"Only New York," he answered; "it is terrible—awful! You know,—but you, how did you escape—how have you endured this horror? Are you well? Unharmed?"

"Unharmed!" she said.

"And this man here?" he asked, encircling her drooping form with one arm and turning toward the Negro. Suddenly he stiffened and his hand flew to his hip. "Why!" he snarled. "It's—a—nigger—Julia! Has he—has he dared——"

She lifted her head and looked at her late companion curiously and then dropped her eyes with a sigh.

"He has dared—all, to rescue me," she said quietly, "and I—thank him—much." But she did not look at him again. As the couple turned away, the father drew a roll of bills from his pockets.

"Here, my good fellow," he said, thrusting the money into the man's hands, "take that,—what's your name?"

"Jim Davis," came the answer, hollow-voiced.

"Well, Jim, I thank you. I've always liked your people. If you ever want a job, call on me." And they were gone.

The crowd poured up and out of the elevators, talking and whispering.

"Who was it?"

"Are they alive?"

"How many?"

"Two!"

"Who was saved?"

"A white girl and a nigger—there she goes."

"A nigger? Where is he? Let's lynch the damned——"

"Shut up—he's all right—he saved her."

"Saved hell! He had no business——"

"Here he comes."

Into the glare of the electric lights the colored man moved slowly, with the eyes of those that walk and sleep.

"Well, what do you think of that?" cried a bystander; "of all New York, just a white girl and a nigger!"

The colored man heard nothing. He stood silently beneath the glare of the light, gazing at the money in his hand and shrinking as he gazed; slowly he put his other hand into his pocket and brought out a baby's filmy cap, and gazed again. A woman mounted to the platform and looked about, shading her eyes. She was brown, small, and toil-worn, and in one arm lay the corpse of a dark baby. The crowd parted and her eyes fell on the colored man; with a cry she tottered toward him.

"Jim!"

He whirled and, with a sob of joy, caught her in his arms.

Leland S. Copeland (1886–1973)

An American amateur astronomer, Copeland published a number of poems, including the collection *Whimsical Rimes* (1921; expanded ed. 1922). Some of these poems were then reprinted in Hugo Gernsback's *Amazing Stories* (as well as a few in *Amazing Stories Quarterly*, and one in *Science Fiction Adventure Classics*), cementing their place in the pulp period of SF and in the tradition of speculative poetry. NASA cites Copeland as giving the nickname "The Lost Galaxy" to galaxy NGC 4535 in the constellation Virgo (NASA Hubble Mission Team, "Hubble Takes Portrait").

Note on the texts: Both poems use Copeland's initial book publication in *Whimsical Rimes* as their copytext; "Alone" appeared in both the 1921 and 1922 editions of *Whimsical Rimes*, while "Planet Neptune to Mother Sun" first appeared in the expanded 1922 book. Both were printed by Schauer Printing Studios, with the 1922 edition listing Sunflower Press as the publisher. Both poems were reprinted in *Amazing Stories* (vol. 2, no. 4, July 1927).

"Alone" (1921)

I often think how lonely the Lord of Life must be,
Who made the pneumococcus[1] and poured the starry sea;
Who built a brontosaurus[2] and locked its bones in earth
Ere anthropoid or human had Cenozoic[3] birth.

How lonely, how forsaken, the God of Suns must be,
With neither wife nor comrade to share Eternity!
His home quintillions measure, but every else too small,
For suns themselves are motes that dust the Empty All.

I sometimes think how sated the King of Kings must be,
Whose microscopic vision records Infinity—
The toils and wars of trillions, while hunger, love, and hope
Unreel the old, old dramas through which the midges grope.

1 Streptococcus pneumoniae, the bacteria that causes pneumococcal disease (including pneumonia and meningitis).

2 A dinosaur from the Jurassic period.

3 The Cenozoic era is our current geological era.

"Planet Neptune to Mother Sun" (1922)

Mother of Worlds,[1] you shine afar
With the feeble light of an evening star;
Your smile is faint as I glimpse your face
Across the millions of miles of space.

Can you recall that destined day
When I left your arms and sped away
To spin my life in the lonely wide? —
Alone till a child moved by my side.[2]

Smaller you grew and dimmer yet
As eons dawned and millennia set,
Till you lived for midgets, Mars and Earth,
Older than I, but younger in birth.

Ages of ages have passed since then,
And time must die ere we meet again,
Yet I send my longing across the night
To dust of my dust and light of my light.

1 In the *Amazing Stories* version, "World" is used.

2 Various astronomical hypothesis from the early twentieth century posited that the planets were formed when material was ejected from the sun. The most detailed of these was from 1917, when astronomer James Jeans hypothesized that our sun interacted with another "massive star" such that tidal forces pulled material out from the sun, which eventually cooled to become the planets (Woolfson 3).

Philip Francis Nowlan (1880–1940) and Dick Calkins (1894–1962)

Philip Francis Nowlan is best known now as the creator of Anthony (later William) "Buck" Rogers, a character who would become synonymous with science fiction through much of the early part of the twentieth century. Dick Calkins is likewise best remembered for his artwork for the Buck Rogers comic strip. First appearing in Nowlan's novella *Armageddon 2419 A. D.*, published in the August 1928 issue of *Amazing Stories*, Rogers would be revisited in Nowlan's sequel *Airlords of Han* in the March 1929 issue of the same magazine (where it would be given the cover illustration). The character quickly escaped prose fiction, launching as a comic strip on 7 January 1929; along with the *Tarzan of the Apes* comic, which debuted the same day, it inaugurated the continuing-narrative daily adventure strip. From there, Buck Rogers would move to comic books, radio plays, film, and television to help spawn the multi-media SF franchise. The phenomenon even changed the language, being often credited with inventing the word "zap" as the sound of Buck's ray-gun. The Rogers franchise also had a more pernicious influence on American SF, however: fully immersed in—and helping to shape—the racist tradition of the "Yellow Peril" narrative, Nowlan's novellas and the initial strip (which largely follows *Armageddon*'s storyline) imagines the US invaded by China (whose rulers would later be revealed as space aliens). These works traded in racist, Orientalist stereotypes of the sort later critiqued by such SF authors as William F. Wu (see his story in this anthology). This makes the Buck Rogers stories an early and influential example of what David M. Higgins would term the "reverse colonization" narrative of American SF, a function of larger reactionary and racist politics.

Note on the text: The comics reproduced here are the first four daily strips, scanned from issues of *The Washington Post* published from 7 to 10 January 1929.

Buck Rogers, 2429 A. D. (1929)

BUCK ROGERS, 2429 A. D. — *The Sleeper* — By Phillip Nowlan and Richard Calkins

BUCK ROGERS, 2429 A. D. — *The Awakening* — By Phillip Nowlan and Richard Calkins

BUCK ROGERS, 2429 A. D. — *Falling Upward* — By Phillip Nowlan and Richard Calkins

BUCK ROGERS, 2429 A. D. — *The Raider* — By Phillip Nowlan and Richard Calkins

Leslie F. Stone (1905–91)

Leslie Frances Rubenstein (later Silverberg) published science fiction under the pseudonym Leslie F. Stone from the late 1920s through to the early 1940s. One of the earliest women to publish regularly in the pulps, she wrote stories and novels that often followed space opera structures. "The Conquest of Gola" is her best-known work, building on earlier matriarchal utopias, anticipating later feminist writers, and taking an explicitly anti-imperialist, if somewhat isolationist, position, all while telling a first-contact tale from the position of the "alien" contactee rather than the human explorer.

Note on the text: The version below reproduces the original text in *Wonder Stories* (vol. 2, no. 11, April 1931), though several minor typographical errors have been corrected after consulting later versions. The original publication includes an illustration of Stone and the following editorial "blurb":

> Americans are fond of ridiculing the customs, habits and temperaments of people of other nations. Similarly other nations pick our peculiarities as a source of amusement. We all think that what we do, think or say is natural and inevitable, and that the actions of others are "queer."
>
> Similarly if we were to travel to a strange world, and find different forms of intelligent life, we would be monstrosities to those people, as much as they would be to us. We would find it more difficult than we imagine to even establish the most elementary form of communication, because our mental processes would have practically nothing in common. That is all assuming that our mission is friendly. But if it is hostile, there is no doubt but that our career on that strange world, would be, as our author shows here, short and sweet. Here is a different and unusual story that you cannot help but enjoy and chuckle over. (1280)

"The Conquest of Gola" (1931)

HOLA, my daughters (sighed the Matriarch) it is true indeed, I am the only living one upon Gola who remembers the invasion from Detaxal, I alone of all my generation survive to recall vividly the sights and scenes of that past era. And well it is that you come to me to hear by free communication of mind to mind face to face with each other.

Ah, well I remember the surprise of that hour when through the mists that enshroud our lovely world, there swam the first of the great smooth cylinders of the Detaxalans, fifty *tas*[1] in length, as glistening and silvery as the soil of our

1 Since there is no means of translating the Golan measurements of either length or time we can but guess at these things. However, since the Detaxalan ships each carried a thousand (*continued*)

land, propelled by the man-things that on Detaxal are supreme even as we women are supreme on Gola.

In those bygone days, as now, Gola was enwrapped by her cloud mists that keep from us the terrific glare of the great star that glows like a malignant spirit out there in the darkness of the void. Only occasionally when a particularly great storm parts the mist of heaven do we see the wonders of the vast universe, but that does not prevent us, with our marvelous telescopes handed down to us from thousands of generations before us, from learning what lies across the dark seas of the outside.

Therefore we knew of the nine planets that encircle the great star and are subject to its rule. And so are we familiar enough with the surfaces of these planets to know why Gola should appear as a haven to their inhabitants who see in our cloud-enclosed mantle a sweet release from the blasting heat and blinding glare of the great sun.

So it was not strange at all to us to find that the people of Detaxal, the third planet of the sun, had arrived on our globe with a wish in their hearts to migrate here, and end their days out of reach of the blistering warmth that had come to be their lot on their own world.

Long ago we, too, might have gone on exploring expeditions to other worlds, other universes, but for what? Are we not happy here? We who have attained the greatest of civilizations within the confines of our own silvery world. Powerfully strong with our mighty force rays, we could subjugate all the universe, but why?

Are we not content with life as it is, with our lovely cities, our homes, our daughters, our gentle consorts? Why spend physical energy in combative strife for something we do not wish, when our mental processes carry us further and beyond the conquest of mere terrestrial exploitation?

On Detaxal it is different, for there the peoples, the ignoble male creatures, breed for physical prowess, leaving the development of their sciences, their philosophies, and the contemplation of the abstract to a chosen few. The greater part of the race fares forth to conquer, to lay waste, to struggle and fight as the animals do over a morsel of worthless territory. Of course we can see why they desired Gola with all its treasures, but we can thank Providence and ourselves that they did not succeed in "commercializing" us as they have the remainder of the universe with their ignoble Federation.

Ah yes, well I recall the hour when first they came, pushing cautiously through the cloud mists, seeking that which lay beneath. We of Gola were unwarned until the two cylinders hung directly above Tola, the greatest city of that time, which still lies in its ruins since that memorial day. But they have paid for it—paid for it well in thousands and in tens of thousands of their men.

men it can be seen that the ships were between five hundred and a thousand feet in length. (Stone's note)

We were first apprised of their coming when the alarm from Tola was sent from the great beam station there, advising all to stand in readiness for an emergency. Geble, my mother, was then Queen of all Gola, and I was by her side in Morka, that pleasant seaside resort, where I shall soon travel again to partake of its rejuvenating waters.

With us were four of Geble's consorts, sweet gentle males, that gave Geble much pleasure in these free hours away from the worries of state. But when the word of the strangers' descent over our home city, Tola, came to us, all else was forgotten. With me at her side, Geble hastened to the beam station and there in the matter transmitter we dispatched our physical beings to the palace at Tola, and the next moment were staring upward at the two strange shapes etched against the clouds.

What the Detaxalan ships were waiting for we did not know then, but later we learned. Not grasping the meaning of our beam stations, the commandants of the ships considered the city below them entirely lacking in means of defense, and were conferring on the method of taking it without bloodshed on either side.

It was not long after our arrival in Tola that the first of the ships began to descend toward the great square before the palace. Geble watched without a word, her great mind already scanning the brains of those whom she found within the great machine. She transferred to my mind but a single thought as I stood there at her side and that with a sneer "Barbarians!"

Now the ship was settling in the square and after a few moments of hesitation, a circular doorway appeared at the side and four of the Detaxalans came through the opening. The square was empty but for themselves and their flyer, and we saw them looking about surveying the beautiful buildings on all sides. They seemed to recognize the palace for what it was and in one accord moved in our direction.

Then Geble left the window at which we stood and strode to the doorway opening upon the balcony that faced the square. The Detaxalans halted in their tracks when they saw her slender graceful form appear and removing the strange coverings they wore on their heads they each made a bow.

Again Geble sneered for only the male-things of our world bow their heads, and so she recognized these visitors for what they were, nothing more than the despicable males of the species! And what creatures they were!

Imagine a short almost flat body set high upon two slender legs, the body tapering in the middle, several times as broad across as it is through the center, with two arms almost as long as the legs attached to the upper part of the torso. A small column-like neck of only a few inches divides the head of oval shape from the body, and in this head only are set the organs of sight, hearing, and scent. Their bodies were like a patch work of a misguided nature.

Yes, strange as it is, my daughters, practically all of the creature's faculties had their base in the small ungainly head, and each organ was perforce pressed into serving for several functions. For instance, the breathing nostrils also served for scenting out odors, nor was this organ able to exclude any disagreeable odors that might come its way, but had to dispense to the brain both pleasant and unpleasant odors at the same time.

Then there was the mouth, set directly beneath the nose, and here again we had an example of one organ doing the work of two for the creature not only used the mouth with which to take in the food for its body, but it also used the mouth to enunciate the excruciatingly ugly sounds of its language forthwith.

Guests From Detaxal

Never before have I seen such a poorly organized body, so unlike our own highly developed organisms. How much nicer it is to be able to call forth any organ at will, and dispense with it when its usefulness is over! Instead these poor Detaxalans had to carry theirs about in physical being all the time so that always was the surface of their bodies entirely marred.

Yet that was not the only part of their ugliness, and proof of the lowliness of their origin, for whereas our fine bodies support themselves by muscular development, these poor creatures were dependent entirely upon a strange structure to keep them in their proper shape.

Imagine if you can a bony skeleton somewhat like the foundations upon which we build our edifices, laying stone and cement over the steel framework. But this skeleton instead is inside a body which the flesh, muscle and skin overlay. Everywhere in their bodies are these cartilaginous structures—hard, heavy, bony structures developed by the chemicals of the being for its use. Even the hands, feet and head of the creatures were underlaid with these bones, ugh, it was terrible when we dissected one of the fellows for study. I shudder to think of it.

Yet again there was still another feature of the Detaxalans that was equally as horrifying as the rest, namely their outer covering. As we viewed them for the first time out there in the square we discovered that parts of the body, that is the part of the head which they called the face, and the bony hands were entirely naked without any sort of covering, neither fur nor feathers, just the raw, pinkish-brown skin looking as if it had been recently plucked.

Later we found a few specimens that had a type of fur on the lower part of the face, but these were rare. And when they doffed the head coverings which we had first taken for some sort of natural covering, we saw that the top of the head was overlaid with a very fine fuzz of fur several inches long.

We did not know in the beginning that the strange covering on the bodies of the four men, green in color, was not a natural growth, but later discovered that such was the truth, and not only the face and hands were bare of fur, but the entire body, except for a fine sprinkling of hair that was scarcely visible except on the chest, was also bare. No wonder the poor things covered themselves with their awkward clothing. We arrived at the conclusion that their lack of fur had been brought about by the fact that always they had been exposed to the bright rays of the sun so that without the dampness of our own planet the fur had dried up and fallen away from the flesh!

Now thinking it over I suppose that we of Gola presented strange form to the people of Detaxal with our fine circular bodies, rounded at the top, our short beautiful lower limbs with the circular foot pads, and our short round arms and hand pads, flexible and muscular like rubber.

But how envious they must have been of our beautiful golden coats, our movable eyes, our power to scent, hear and touch with any part of the body, to absorb food and drink through any part of the body most convenient to us at any time. Oh yes, laugh though you may, without a doubt we were also freaks to those freakish Detaxalans. But no matter, let us return to the tale.

On recognizing our visitors for what they were, simple-minded males, Geble was chagrined at them for taking up her time, but they were strangers to our world and we Golans are always courteous. Geble began of course to try to communicate by thought transference, but strangely enough the fellows below did not catch a single thought. Instead, entirely unaware of Geble's overture to friendship, the leader commenced to speak to her in most outlandish manner, contorting the red lips of his mouth into various uncouth shapes and making sounds that fell upon our hearing so unpleasantly that we immediately closed our senses to them. And without a word Geble turned her back upon them, calling for Tanka, her personal secretary.

Tanka was instructed to welcome the Detaxalans while she herself turned to her own chambers to summon a half dozen of her council. When the council arrived she began to discuss with them the problem of extracting more of the precious tenix from the waters of the great inland lake of Notauch. Nothing whatever was said of the advent of the Detaxalans for Geble had dismissed them from her mind as creatures not worthy of her thought.

In the meantime Tanka had gone forth to meet the four who of course could not converse with her. In accordance with the Queen's orders she led them indoors to the most informal receiving chamber and there had them served with food and drink which by the looks of the remains in the dishes they did not relish at all.

Leading them through the rooms of the lower floor of the palace she made a pretence of showing them everything which they duly surveyed. But they appeared to chafe at the manner in which they were being entertained.

The creatures even made an attempt through the primitive method of conversing by their arms to learn something of what they had seen, but Tanka was as supercilious as her mistress. When she thought they had had enough, she led them to the square and back to the door of their flyer, giving them their dismissal.

But the men were not ready to accept it. Instead they tried to express to Tanka their desire to meet the ruling head of Gola. Although their hand motions were perfectly inane and incomprehensible, Tanka could read what passed through their brains, and understood more fully than they what lay in their minds. She shook her head and motioned that they were to embark in their flyer and be on their way back to their planet.

Again and again the Detaxalans tried to explain what they wished, thinking Tanka did not understand. At last she impressed upon their savage minds that there was nothing for them but to depart, and disgruntled by her treatment they reentered their machine, closed its ponderous door and raised their ship to the level of its sister flyer. Several minutes passed and then, with thanksgiving, we saw them pass over the city.

Told of this, Geble laughed. "To think of mere man-things daring to attempt to force themselves upon us. What is the universe coming to? What are their women back home considering when they sent them to us? Have they developed too many males and think that we can find use for them?" she wanted to know.

"It is strange indeed," observed Yabo, one of the council members. "What did you find in the minds of these ignoble creatures, O August One?"

"Nothing of particular interest, a very low grade of intelligence, to be sure. There was no need of looking below the surface."

"It must have taken intelligence to build those ships."

"None aboard them did that. I don't question it but that their mothers built the ships for them as playthings, even as we give toys to our 'little ones,' you know. I recall that the ancients of our world perfected several types of space-flyers many ages ago!"

"Maybe those males do not have 'mothers' but instead they build the ships themselves, maybe they are the stronger sex on their world!" This last was said by Suiki, the fifth consort of Geble, a pretty little male, rather young in years. No one had noticed his coming into the chamber, but now everyone showed their surprise at his words.

"Impossible!" ejaculated Yabo.

Geble however laughed at the little chap's expression. "Suiki is a profound thinker," she observed, still laughing, and she drew him to her gently hugging him.

A Nice Business Deal

And with that the subject of the men from Detaxal was closed. It was reopened, however, several hours later when it was learned that instead of leaving Gola altogether the ships were seen one after another by the various cities of the planet as they circumnavigated it.

It was rather annoying, for everywhere the cities' routines were broken up as the people dropped their work and studies to gaze at the cylinders. Too, it was upsetting the morale of the males, for on learning that the two ships contained only creatures of their own sex they were becoming envious, wishing for the same type of playthings for themselves.

Shut in, as they are, unable to grasp the profundities of our science and thought, the gentle, fun-loving males were always glad for a new diversion, and this new method developed by the Detaxalans had intrigued them.

It was then that Geble decided it high time to take matters into her own hands. Not knowing where the two ships were at the moment it was not difficult with the object-finder beam to discover their whereabouts, and then with the attractor to draw them to Tola magnetically. An *ous* later we had the pleasure of seeing the two ships rushing toward our city. When they arrived about it, power brought them down to the square again.

Again Tanka was sent out, and directed the commanders of the two ships to follow her in to the Queen. Knowing the futility of attempting to converse with them without mechanical aid, Geble caused to be brought her three of the ancient mechanical thought transformers that are only museum pieces to us but still workable. The two men were directed to place them on their heads while she donned the third. When this was done she ordered the creatures to depart immediately from Gola, telling them that she was tired of their play.

Watching the faces of the two I saw them frowning and shaking their heads. Of course I could read their thoughts as well as Geble without need of the transformers, since it was only for their benefit that these were used, so I heard the whole conversation, though I need only to give you the gist of it.

"We have no wish to leave your world as yet," the two had argued.

"You are disrupting the routine of our lives here," Geble told them, "and now that you've seen all that you can there is no need for you to stay longer. I insist that you leave immediately."

I saw one of the men smile, and thereupon he was the one who did all the talking (I say '"talking" for this he was actually doing, mouthing each one of his words although we understood his thoughts as they formed in his queer brain, so different from ours).

"Listen here," he laughed, "I don't get the hang of you people at all. We came to Gola (he used some outlandish name of his own, but I use our name of course) with the express purpose of exploration and exploitation. We come as friends. Already we are in alliance with Damin (again the name for the fourth planet of our system was different, but I give the correct appellation), established commerce and trade, and now we are ready to offer you the chance to join our federation peaceably.

"What we have seen of this world is very favorable, there are good prospects for business here. There is no reason why you people as those of Damin and Detaxal can not enter into a nice business arrangement congenially. You have far more here to offer tourists, more than Damin. Why, except for your clouds this would be an ideal paradise for every man, woman and child on Detaxal and Damin to visit, and of course with our new cloud dispensers we could clear your atmosphere for you in short order and keep it that way. Why you'll make millions in the first year of your trade.

"Come now, allow us to discuss this with your ruler—king or whatever you call him. Women are all right in their place, but it takes the men to see the profit of a thing like this—er—you are a woman aren't you?"

The first of this long speech, of course, was so much gibberish to us, with his prate of business arrangements, commerce and trade, tourists, profits, cloud dispensers and what not, but it was the last part of what he said that took my breath away, and you can imagine how it affected Geble. I could see straightaway that she was intensely angered, and good reason too. By the looks of the silly fellow's face I could guess that he was getting the full purport of her thoughts. He began to shuffle his funny feet and a foolish grin pervaded his face.

"Sorry," he said, "if I insulted you—I didn't intend that, but I believed that man holds the same place here as he does on Detaxal and Damin, but I suppose it is just as possible for woman to be the ruling factor of a world as man is elsewhere."

That speech naturally made Geble more irate, and tearing off her thought transformer she left the room without another word. In a moment, however, Yabo appeared wearing the transformer in her place. Yabo had none of the beauty of my mother, for whereas Geble was slender and as straight as a rod Yabo was obese, and her fat body overflowed until she looked like a large dumpy bundle of *yat* held together in her furry skin. She had very little dignity as she waddled toward the Detaxalans, but there was determination in her whole manner and without preliminaries she began to scold the two as though they were her own consorts.

"There has been enough of this, my fine young men," she shot at them. "You've had your fun, and now it is time for you to return to your mothers and consorts. Shame on you for making up such miserable tales about yourselves. I have a good mind to take you home with me for a couple of days, and I'd put you in your places quick enough. The idea of men acting like you are!"

For a moment I thought the Detaxalans were going to cry by the faces they made, but instead they broke into laughter, such heathenish sounds as had never before been heard on Gola, and I listened in wonder instead of excluding it from my hearing, but the fellows sobered quickly enough at that, and the spokesman addressed the shocked Yabo.

"I see," said he, "it's impossible for your people and mine to arrive at an understanding peaceably. I'm sorry that you take us for children out on a spree, that you are accustomed to such a low type of men as is evidently your lot here.

"I have given you your chance to accept our terms without force, but since you refuse, under the orders of the Federation I will have to take you forcibly, for we are determined that Gola become one of us, if you like it or not. Then you will learn that we are not the children you believe us to be.

"You may go to your supercilious Queen now and advise her that we give you exactly ten hours in which to evacuate this city, for precisely on the hour we will lay this city in ruins. And if that does not suffice you we will do the same with every other city on the planet! Remember ten hours!"

And with that he took the mechanical thought transformer from his head and tossed it on the table. His companion did the same and the two of them strode out of the room and to their flyers which arose several thousand feet above Tola and remained there.

The Triumph of Gola

Hurrying into Geble, Yabo told her what the Detaxalan had said. Geble was reclining on her couch and did not bother to raise herself.

"Childish prattle," she conceded and withdrew her red eyes on their movable stems into their pockets, paying no more heed to the threats of the men from Detaxal.

I, however, could not be as calm as my mother, and I was fearful that it was not childish prattle after all. Not knowing how long ten hours might be I did not wait, but crept up to the palace's beam station and set its dials so that the entire building and as much of the surrounding territory it could cover were protected in the force zone.

Alas that the same beam was not greater. But it had not been put there for defense, only for matter transference and whatever other peacetime methods we used. It was the means of proving just the same that it was also a very good defensive instrument, for just two *ous* later the hovering ships above let loose their powers of destruction, heavy explosives that entirely demolished all of Tola and its millions of people and only the palace royal of all that beauty was left standing!

Awakened from her nap by the terrific detonation, Geble came hurriedly to a window to view the ruin, and she was wild with grief at what she saw. Geble, however, saw that there was urgent need for action. She knew without my telling her what I had done to protect the palace. And though she showed no sign of appreciation, I knew that I had won a greater place in her regard than any other of her many daughters and would henceforth be her favorite as well as her successor as the case turned out.

Now, with me behind her, she hurried to the beam station and in a twinkling we were both in Tubia, the second greatest city of that time. Nor were we to be caught napping again, for Geble ordered all beam stations to throw out their zone forces while she herself manipulated one of Tubia's greatest power beams, attuning it to the emanations of the two Detaxalan flyers. In less than a *ous* the two ships were seen through the mists heading for Tubia. For a moment I grew fearful, but on realizing that they were after all in our grip, and the attractors held every living thing powerless against movement, I grew calm and watched them come over the city and the beam pull them to the ground.

With the beam still upon them, they lay supine on the ground without motion. Descending to the square Geble called for Ray C, and when the machine arrived she herself directed the cutting of the hole in the side of the flyer and was the first to enter it with me immediately behind, as usual.

We were both astounded by what we saw of the great array of machinery within. But a glance told Geble all she wanted to know of their principles. She interested herself only in the men standing rigidly in whatever position our beam had caught them. Only the eyes of the creatures expressed their fright, poor things, unable to move so much as a hair while we moved among them untouched by the power of the beam because of the strength of our own minds.

They could have fought against it if they had known how, but their simple minds were too weak for such exercise.

Now glancing about among the stiff forms around us, of which there were one thousand, Geble picked out those of the males she desired for observation, choosing those she judged to be their finest specimens, those with much hair on their faces and having more girth than the others. These she ordered removed by several workers who followed us, and then we emerged again to the outdoors.

Using hand beam torches the picked specimens were kept immobile after they were out of reach of the greater beam and were borne into the laboratory of the building Geble had converted into her new palace. Geble and I followed, and she gave the order for the complete annihilation of the two powerless ships.

Thus ended the first foray of the people of Detaxal. And for the next two *tels* there was peace upon our globe again. In the laboratory the thirty who had been rescued from their ships were given thorough examinations both physically and mentally and we learned all there was to know about them. Hearing of the destruction of their ships, most of the creatures had become frightened and were quite docile in our hands. Those that were unruly were used in the dissecting room for the advancement of Golan knowledge.

After a complete study of them which yielded little we lost interest in them scientifically. Geble, however found some pleasure in having the poor creatures around her and kept three of them in her own chambers so she could delve into their brains as she pleased. The others she doled out to her favorites as she saw fit.

One she gave to me to act as a slave or in what capacity I desired him, but my interest in him soon waned, especially since I had now come of age and was allowed to have two consorts of my own, and go about the business of bringing my daughters into the world.

My slave I called Jon and gave him complete freedom of my house. If only we had foreseen what was coming we would have annihilated every one of them immediately! It did please me later to find that Jon was learning our language and finding a place in my household, making friends with my two shut-in consorts. But as I have said I paid little attention to him.

So life went on smoothly with scarcely a change after the destruction of the ships of Detaxal. But that did not mean we were unprepared for more. Geble reasoned that there would be more ships forthcoming when the Detaxalans found that their first two did not return. So, although it was sometimes inconvenient, the zones of force were kept upon our cities.

And Geble was right, for the day came when dozens of flyers descended upon Gola from Detaxal. But this time the zones of force did not hold them since the zones were not in operation!

And we were unwarned, for when they descended upon us, our world was sleeping, confident that our zones were our protection. The first indication that I had of trouble brewing was when awakening I found the ugly form of Jon bending over me. Surprised, for it was not his habit to arouse me, I started up only to find his arms about me, embracing me. And how strong he was! For the moment a new emotion swept me, for the first time I knew the pleasure to be had in the arms of a strong man, but that emotion was short lived for I saw in the blue eyes of my slave that he had recognized the look in my eyes for what it was, and for the moment he was tender.

Later I was to grow angry when I thought of that expression of his, for his eyes filled with pity, pity for me! But pity did not stay, instead he grinned and the next instant he was binding me down to my couch with strong rope. Geble, I learned later, had been treated as I, as were the members of the council and every other woman in Gola!

That was what came of allowing our men to meet on common ground with the creatures from Detaxal, for a weak mind is open to seeds of rebellion and the Detaxalans had sown it well, promising dominance to the lesser creatures of Gola.

That, however, was only part of the plot on the part of the Detaxalans. They were determined not only to revenge those we had murdered, but also to gain mastery of our planet. Unnoticed by us they had constructed a machine which transmits sound as we transmit thought and by its means had communicated with their own world, advising them of the very hour to strike when all of Gola was slumbering. It was a masterful stroke, only they did not know the power of the mind of Gola—so much more ancient than theirs.

Lying there bound on my couch I was able to see out the window and trembling with terror I watched a half dozen Detaxalan flyers descend into Tubia, guessing that the same was happening in our other cities. I was truly frightened, for I did not have the brain of a Geble. I was young yet, and in fear I watched the hordes march out of their machines, saw the thousands of our men join them.

Free from restraint, the shut-ins were having their holiday and how they cavorted out in the open, most the time getting in the way of the freakish Detaxalans who were certainly taking over our city.

A half *ous* passed while I lay there watching, waiting in fear at what the

Detaxalans planned to do with us. I remembered the pleasant, happy life we had led up to the present and trembled over what the future might be when the Detaxalans had infested us with commerce and trade, business propositions, tourists and all of their evil practices. It was then that I received the message from Geble, clear and definite, just as all the women of the globe received it, and hope returned to my heart.

There began that titanic struggle, the fight for supremacy, the fight that won us victory over the simple-minded weaklings below who had presumptuously dared to conquer us. The first indications that the power of our combined mental concentration at Geble's orders was taking effect was when we saw the first of our males halt in their wild dance of freedom. They tried to shake us off, but we knew we could bring them back to us.

At first the Detaxalans paid them no heed. They knew not what was happening until there came the wholesale retreat of the Golan men back to the buildings, back to the chambers from which they had escaped. Then grasping something of what was happening the already defeated invaders sought to retain their hold on our little people. Our erstwhile captives sought to hold them with oratorical gestures, but of course we won. We saw our creatures return to us and unbind us.

Only the Detaxalans did not guess the significance of that, did not realize that inasmuch as we had conquered our own men, we could conquer them also. As they went about their work of making our city their own, establishing already their autocratic bureaus wherever they pleased, we began to concentrate upon them, hypnotizing them to the flyers that had disgorged them.

And soon they began to feel of our power, the weakest ones first, feeling the mental bewilderment creeping upon them. Their leaders, stronger in mind, knew nothing of this at first, but soon our terrible combined mental power was forced upon them also and they realized that their men were deserting them, crawling back to their ships! The leaders began to exhort them into new action, driving them physically. But our power gained on them and now we began to concentrate upon the leaders themselves. They were strong of will and they defied us, fought us, mind against mind, but of course it was useless. Their minds were not suited to the test they put themselves to, and after almost three *ous* of struggle, we of Gola were able to see victory ahead.

At last the leaders succumbed. Not a single Detaxalan was abroad in the avenues. They were within their flyers, held there by our combined wills, unable to act for themselves. It was then as easy for us to switch the zones of force upon them, subjugate them more securely and with the annihilator beam to disintegrate completely every ship and man into nothingness! Thousands upon thousands died that day and Gola was indeed revenged.

Thus, my daughters, ended the second invasion of Gola.

Oh yes, more came from their planet to discover what had happened to their ships and their men, but we of Gola no longer hesitated, and they no sooner appeared beneath the mists than they too were annihilated until at last

Detaxal gave up the thought of conquering our cloud-laden world. Perhaps in the future they will attempt it again, but we are always in readiness for them now, and our men—well they are still the same ineffectual weaklings, my daughters ...

H.P. Lovecraft (1890–1937)

H.P. Lovecraft is often—erroneously—characterized as the originator of Weird Fiction, though there is no doubt he is the author most often associated with the term, and his particular form of "cosmic horror" continues to be influential. All these facts are due both to his early prominence in *Weird Tales* magazine, and more importantly to his world-building, and specifically "the mythos." This mythical structure, which focussed on a series of "Old Gods," notably Cthulhu, who form the source of power in a universe where humans exercise very little agency (and are often no more than cult worshippers or food for the Old Ones), would be used by other authors in what came to be called the Lovecraft circle (including Conan-creator Robert E. Howard, Henry Kuttner, Fritz Leiber, and others). A bust of Lovecraft was used as the model for the World Fantasy Award until 2015, when it was changed after prolonged criticism of Lovecraft's grotesquely racist, white supremacist beliefs, which he often espoused in his writings. Later authors, such as Charles R. Saunders (included in this anthology), would deploy Lovecraft's mythos directly against such racism.

Note on the text: One of the more concise articulations of Lovecraftian weird, "From Beyond" first appeared in the fanzine *Fantasy Fan* in June 1934. The copy-text here derives from its later publication in *Weird Tales* (vol. 31, no. 2, Feb. 1938), where the story is introduced with the teaser, "If Tillinghast was really a madman, then what became of the bodies of the servants whom the police said he had murdered?" (227).

"From Beyond" (1934)

Horrible beyond conception was the change which had taken place in my best friend, Crawford Tillinghast. I had not seen him since that day, two months and a half before, when he had told me toward what goal his physical and metaphysical researches were leading; when he had answered my awed and almost frightened remonstrances by driving me from his laboratory and his house in a burst of fanatical rage, I had known that he now remained mostly shut in the attic laboratory with that accursed electrical machine, eating little and excluding even the servants, but I had not thought that a brief period of ten weeks could so alter and disfigure any human creature. It is not pleasant to see a stout man suddenly grown thin, and it is even worse when the baggy skin becomes yellowed or grayed, the eyes sunken, circled, and uncannily glowing, the forehead veined and corrugated, and the hands tremulous and twitching. And if added to this there be a repellent unkemptness; a wild disorder of dress, a bushiness of dark hair white at the roots, and an unchecked growth of white beard on a face once clean-shaven, the cumulative effect is quite shocking.

But such was the aspect of Crawford Tillinghast on the night his half-coherent message brought me to his door after my weeks of exile; such was the specter that trembled as it admitted me, candle in hand, and glanced furtively over its shoulder as if fearful of unseen things in the ancient, lonely house set back from Benevolent Street.

That Crawford Tillinghast should ever have studied science and philosophy was a mistake. These things should be left to the frigid and impersonal investigator, for they offer two equally tragic alternatives to the man of feeling and action; despair, if he fail in his quest, and terrors unutterable and unimaginable if he succeed. Tillinghast had once been the prey of failure, solitary and melancholy; but now I knew, with nauseating fears of my own, that he was the prey of success. I had indeed warned him ten weeks before, when he burst forth with his tale of what he felt himself about to discover. He had been flushed and excited then, talking in a high and unnatural, though always pedantic, voice.

"What do we know," he had said, "of the world and the universe about us? Our means of receiving impressions are absurdly few, and our notions of surrounding objects infinitely narrow. We see things only as we are constructed to see them, and can gain no idea of their absolute nature. With five feeble senses we pretend to comprehend the boundlessly complex cosmos, yet other beings with a wider, stronger, or different range of senses might not only see very differently the things we see, but might see and study whole worlds of matter, energy, and life which lie close at hand yet can never be detected with the senses we have. I have always believed that such strange, inaccessible worlds exist at our very elbows, *and now I believe I have found a way to break down the barriers.* I am not joking. Within twenty-four hours that machine near the table will generate waves acting on unrecognised sense-organs that exist in us as atrophied or rudimentary vestiges. Those waves will open up to us many vistas unknown to man, and several unknown to anything we consider organic life. We shall see that at which dogs howl in the dark, and that at which cats prick up their ears after midnight. We shall see these things, and other things which no breathing creature has yet seen. We shall overleap time, space, and dimensions, and without bodily motion peer to the bottom of creation."

When Tillinghast said these things I remonstrated, for I knew him well enough to be frightened rather than amused; but he was a fanatic, and drove me from the house. Now he was no less a fanatic, but his desire to speak had conquered his resentment, and he had written me imperatively in a hand I could scarcely recognise. As I entered the abode of the friend so suddenly metamorphosed to a shivering gargoyle, I became infected with the terror which seemed stalking in all the shadows. The words and beliefs expressed ten weeks before seemed bodied forth in the darkness beyond the small circle of candle-light, and I sickened at the hollow, altered voice of my host. I wished the servants were about, and did not like it when he said they had all left three days previously. It seemed strange that old Gregory, at least, should desert his master without telling as tried a friend as I. It was he who had given me all the information I had of Tillinghast after I was repulsed in rage.

Yet I soon subordinated all my fears to my growing curiosity and fascination. Just what Crawford Tillinghast now wished of me I could only guess, but that he had some stupendous secret or discovery to impart, I could not doubt. Before I had protested at his unnatural pryings into the unthinkable; now that he had evidently succeeded to some degree I almost shared his spirit, terrible though the cost of victory appeared.

Up through the dark emptiness of the house I followed the bobbing candle in the hand of this shaking parody on man. The electricity seemed to be turned off, and when I asked my guide he said it was for a definite reason.

"It would be too much … I would not dare," he continued to mutter. I especially noted his new habit of muttering, for it was not like him to talk to himself.

We entered the laboratory in the attic, and I observed that detestable electrical machine, glowing with a sickly, sinister violet luminosity. It was connected with a powerful chemical battery, but seemed to be receiving no current; for I recalled that in its experimental stage it had sputtered and purred when in action. In reply to my question Tillinghast mumbled that this permanent glow was not electrical in any sense that I could understand.

He now seated me near the machine, so that it was on my right, and turned a switch somewhere below the crowning cluster of glass bulbs. The usual sputtering began, turned to a whine, and terminated in a drone so soft as to suggest a return to silence. Meanwhile the luminosity increased, waned again, then assumed a pale, outré color or blend of colors which I could neither place nor describe. Tillinghast had been watching me, and noted my puzzled expression.

"Do you know what that is?" he whispered. "*That is ultra-violet.*" He chuckled oddly at my surprize. "You thought ultra-violet was invisible, and so it is—but you can see that and many other invisible things *now.*

"Listen to me! The waves from that thing are waking a thousand sleeping senses in us; senses which we inherit from eons of evolution from the state of detached electrons to the state of organic humanity. I have seen *truth,* and I intend to show it to you. Do you wonder how it will seem? I will tell you."

Here Tillinghast seated himself directly opposite me, blowing out his candle and staring hideously into my eyes.

"Your existing sense-organs—ears first, I think—will pick up many of the impressions, for they are closely connected with the dormant organs. Then there will be others. You have heard of the pineal gland?[1] I laugh at the shallow

1 A small gland in the brain that secretes hormones. Tillinghast's theory shares much with French philosopher René Descartes (1596–1650), who (along with many others) thought the pineal gland housed the soul or consciousness and played a role in the function of the senses (see Lokhorst and Kaitaro).

endocrinologist, fellow-dupe and fellow-parvenu of the Freudian.[1] That gland is the great sense-organ of organs—*I have found out.* It is like sight in the end, and transmits visual pictures to the brain. If you are normal, that is the way you ought to get most of it … I mean get most of the evidence *from beyond.*"

I looked about the immense attic room with the sloping south wall, dimly lit by rays which the everyday eye cannot see. The far corners were all shadows, and the whole place took on a hazy unreality which obscured its nature and invited the imagination to symbolism and phantasm. During the interval that Tillinghast was silent I fancied myself in some vast and incredible temple of long-dead gods; some vague edifice of innumerable black stone columns reaching up from a floor of damp slabs to a cloudy height beyond the range of my vision.

The picture was very vivid for a while, but gradually gave way to a more horrible conception; that of utter, absolute solitude in infinite, sightless, soundless space. There seemed to be a void, and nothing more, and I felt a childish fear which prompted me to draw from my hip pocket the revolver I always carried after dark since the night I was held up in East Providence.[2] Then, from the farthermost regions of remoteness, the *sound* softly glided into existence. It was infinitely faint, subtly vibrant, and unmistakably musical, but held a quality of surpassing wildness which made its impact feel like a delicate torture of my whole body. I felt sensations like those one feels when accidentally scratching ground glass. Simultaneously there developed something like a cold draft, which apparently swept past me from the direction of the distant sound. As I waited breathlessly I perceived that both sound and wind were increasing; the effect being to give me an odd notion of myself as tied to a pair of rails in the path of a gigantic approaching locomotive.

I began to speak to Tillinghast, and as I did so all the unusual impressions abruptly vanished. I saw only the man, the glowing machine, and the dim apartment. Tillinghast was grinning repulsively at the revolver which I had almost unconsciously drawn, but from his expression I was sure he had seen and heard as much as I, if not a great deal more. I whispered what I had experienced, and he bade me remain as quiet and receptive as possible.

"Don't move," he cautioned, "for in these rays *we are able to be seen as well as to see.* I told you the servants left, but I didn't tell you *how.* It was that thick-witted housekeeper—who turned on the lights downstairs after I had warned her not to, and the wires picked up sympathetic vibrations. It must have been frightful—I could hear the screams up here in spite of all I was seeing and hearing from another direction, and later it was rather awful to find those empty heaps of clothes around the house. Mrs. Updike's clothes were close to the front hall switch—that's how I know she did it. It got them all.

1 Sigmund Freud (1856–1939), founder of psychoanalysis and the psychoanalytic theory of the human mind.

2 A city in the state of Rhode Island.

But so long as we don't move we're fairly safe. Remember we're dealing with a hideous world in which we are practically helpless ... *Keep still!*"

The combined shock of the revelation and of the abrupt command gave me a kind of paralysis, and in my terror my mind again opened to the impressions coming from what Tillinghast called "*beyond*." I was now in a vortex of sound and motion, with confused pictures before my eyes. I saw the blurred outlines of the room, but from some point in space there seemed to be pouring a seething column of unrecognizable shapes or clouds, penetrating the solid roof at a point ahead and to the right of me. Then I glimpsed the temple-like effect again, but this time the pillars reached up into an aerial ocean of light, which sent down one blinding beam along the path of the cloudy column I had seen before.

After that the scene was almost wholly kaleidoscopic, and in the jumble of sights, sounds, and unidentified sense-impressions I felt that I was about to dissolve or in some way lose the solid form. One definite flash I shall always remember. I seemed for an instant to behold a patch of strange night sky filled with shining, revolving spheres, and as it receded I saw that the glowing suns formed a constellation or galaxy of settled shape; this shape being the distorted face of Crawford Tillinghast. At another time I felt the huge animate things brushing past me and occasionally *walking or drifting through my supposedly solid body*, and thought I saw Tillinghast look at them as though his better-trained senses could catch them visually. I recalled what he had said of the pineal gland, and wondered what he saw with this preternatural eye.

Suddenly I myself became possessed of a kind of augmented sight. Over and above the luminous and shadowy chaos arose a picture which, though vague, held the elements of consistency and permanence. It was indeed somewhat familiar, for the unusual part was superimposed upon the usual terrestrial scene much as a cinema view may be thrown upon the painted curtain of a theatre. I saw the attic laboratory, the electrical machine, and the unsightly form of Tillinghast opposite me; but of all the space unoccupied by familiar objects not one particle was vacant. Indescribable shapes both alive and otherwise were mixed in disgusting disarray, and close to every known thing were whole worlds of alien, unknown entities. It likewise seemed that all the known things entered into the composition of other unknown things, and vice versa.

Foremost among the living objects were inky, jellyish monstrosities which flabbily quivered in harmony with the vibrations from the machine. They were present in loathsome profusion, and I saw to my horror that they *overlapped*; that they were semi-fluid and capable of passing through one another and through what we know as solids. These things were never still, but seemed ever floating about with some malignant purpose. Sometimes they appeared to devour one another, the attacker launching itself at its victim and instantaneously obliterating the latter from sight. Shudderingly I felt that I knew what had obliterated the unfortunate servants, and could not exclude the things from my mind as I strove to observe other properties of the newly visible world that lies unseen around us. But Tillinghast had been watching me, and was speaking.

"You see them? You see them? You see the things that float and flop about you and through you every moment of your life? You see the creatures that form what men call the pure air and the blue sky? Have I not succeeded in breaking down the barrier; have I not shown you worlds that no other living men have seen?"

I heard his scream through the horrible chaos, and looked at the wild face thrust so offensively close to mine. His eyes were pits of flame, and they glared at me with what I now saw was overwhelming hatred. The machine droned detestably.

"You think those floundering things wiped out the servants? Fool, they are harmless! But the servants *are* gone, aren't they? You tried to stop me; you discouraged me when I needed every drop of encouragement I could get; you were afraid of the cosmic truth, you damned coward, but now I've got you! What swept up the servants? What made them scream so loud? … Don't know, eh? You'll know soon enough. Look at me—listen to what I say—do you suppose there are really any such things as time and magnitude? Do you fancy there are such things as form or matter? I tell you, I have struck depths that your little brain can't picture! I have seen beyond the bounds of infinity and drawn down demons from the stars.… I have harnessed the shadows that stride from world to world to sow death and madness … space belongs to me, do you hear? Things are hunting me now—the things that devour and dissolve—but I know how to elude them. It is you they will get, as they got the servants.…

"Stirring, dear sir? I told you it was dangerous to move; I have saved you so far by telling you to keep still—saved you to see more sights and to listen to me. If you had moved, they would have been at you long ago. Don't worry, they won't *hurt* you. They didn't hurt the servants—it was the *seeing* that made the poor devils scream so. My pets are not pretty, for they come out of places where esthetic standards are—*very different.* Disintegration is quite painless, I assure you—*but I want you to see them.* I almost saw them, but I knew how to stop.

"You are not curious? I always knew you were no scientist. Trembling, eh? Trembling with anxiety to see the ultimate things I have discovered? Why don't you move, then? Tired? Well, don't worry, my friend, *for they are coming.…* Look, look, curse you, look … it's just over your left shoulder …"

What remains to be told is very brief, and may be familiar to you from the newspaper accounts. The police heard a shot in the old Tillinghast house and found us there—Tillinghast dead and me unconscious. They arrested me because the revolver was in my hand, but released me in three hours, after they found it was apoplexy which had finished Tillinghast and saw that my shot had been directed at the noxious machine which now lay hopelessly shattered on the laboratory floor. I did not tell very much of what I had seen, for I feared the coroner would be skeptical; but from the evasive outline I did give, the doctor told me that I had undoubtedly been hypnotised by the vindictive and homicidal madman.

I wish I could believe that doctor. It would help my shaky nerves if I could dismiss what I now have to think of the air and the sky about and above me. I never feel alone or comfortable, and a hideous sense of pursuit sometimes comes chillingly on me when I am weary. What prevents me from believing the doctor is this one simple fact—that the police never found the bodies of those servants whom they say Crawford Tillinghast murdered.

THE DAWN AND SETTING OF THE GOLDEN AGE: 1937–1959

43

LIAR!

By Isaac Asimov

A beautifully logical tale of a robot who simply couldn't tell the truth!

Illustrated by Schneeman

ALFRED LANNING lit his cigar carefully, but the tips of his fingers were trembling slightly. His gray eyebrows hunched low as he spoke between puffs.

"It reads minds all right—damn little doubt about *that!* But why?" He looked at Mathematician Peter Bogert, "Well?"

Bogert flattened his black hair

Fig. 3: Charles Schneeman. Illustration to "Liar!" *Astounding Science-Fiction*, vol. 27, no. 3, 1941.

Isaac Asimov (1920–92)

Born in Russia before emigrating, as a child, with his parents to the United States, Isaac Asimov would become one of the best-known authors of science fiction, one who is nearly synonymous with the so-called Golden Age. Asimov had a storied career both in and beyond the pulps, but he is best known for two, occasionally interconnected, series of works—the *Foundation* series and the *Robot* series. He also wrote in other genres, notably mysteries, but these never became as popular as his SF. Asimov also figures significantly in discussions of robotics and artificial intelligence due to his invention of the "Three Laws of Robotics," the first of which appears for the first time in the story below; the story also arguably details the early computer programming axiom "garbage in/garbage out," which dictates that any error—or bias—that humans knowingly or otherwise encode into computer programs will also appear in the outputs of those programs.

Note on the text: The copy-text used here is the first publication in *Astounding Science-Fiction* (May 1941). It was later reprinted in Asimov's "fix-up" novel *I, Robot* (1951); a fix-up novel is created by stitching together short stories, including previously published ones. In the table of contents for the issue of *Astounding*, the story is described as follows: "Herbie was a robot; he was also a mistake. Somewhere in assembly, an accident made him telepathic, with inevitable and disturbing consequences!" The story itself is preceded by the tagline, "A beautifully logical tale of a robot who simply couldn't tell the truth!" (43). The original publication included an illustration, listed as "By Schneeman"—Charles Schneeman (1912–72)—before the title (Fig. 3).

"Liar!" (1941)

ALFRED LANNING lit his cigar carefully, but the tips of his fingers were trembling slightly. His gray eyebrows hunched low as he spoke between puffs.

"It reads minds all right—damn little doubt about *that!* But why?" He looked at Mathematician Peter Bogert, "Well?"

Bogert flattened his black hair down with both hands, "That was the thirty-fourth RB model we've turned out, Lanning. All the others were strictly orthodox."

The third man at the table frowned. Milton Ashe was the youngest officer of U. S. Robot & Mechanical Men, Inc., and proud of his post.

"Listen, Bogert. There wasn't a hitch in the assembly from start to finish. I guarantee that."

Bogert's thick lips spread in a patronizing smile, "Do you? If you can answer for the entire assembly line, I recommend your promotion. By exact count, there are seventy-five thousand, two hundred and thirty-four operations necessary for the manufacture of a single positronic[1] brain, each separate operation depending for successful completion upon any number of factors, from five to a hundred and five. If any one of them goes seriously wrong, the 'brain' is ruined. I quote our own information folder, Ashe."

Milton Ashe flushed, but a fourth voice cut off his reply.

"If we're going to start by trying to fix the blame on one another, I'm leaving." Susan Calvin's hands were folded tightly in her lap, and the little lines about her thin, pale lips deepened, "We've got a mind-reading robot on our hands and it strikes me as rather important that we find out just *why* it reads minds. We're not going to do that by saying, 'Your fault! My fault!'"

Her cold gray eyes fastened upon Ashe, and he grinned.

Lanning grinned too, and, as always at such times, his long white hair and shrewd little eyes made him the picture of a biblical patriarch, "True for you, Dr. Calvin."

His voice became suddenly crisp, "Here's everything in pill-concentrate form. We've produced a positronic brain of supposedly ordinary vintage that's got the remarkable property of being able to tune in on thought waves. It would mark the most important advance in robotics in decades, *if* we knew how it happened. We don't, and we have to find out. Is that clear?"

"May I make a suggestion?" asked Bogert.

"Go ahead!"

"I'd say that until we *do* figure out the mess—and as a mathematician I expect it to be a very devil of a mess—we keep the existence of RB 34 a secret. I mean even from the other members of the staff. As heads of the departments, we ought not to find it an insoluble problem, and the fewer know about it—"

"Bogert is right," said Dr. Calvin. "Ever since the Interplanetary Code was modified to allow robot models to be tested in the plants before being shipped out to space, anti-robot propaganda has increased. If any word leaks out about a robot being able to read minds before we can announce complete control of the phenomenon, Tyrone and his demagogues could make pretty effective capital out of it."

Lanning sucked at his cigar and nodded gravely. He turned to Ashe, "I think you said you were alone when you first stumbled on this thought-reading business."

"I'll say I was alone—I got the scare of my life. RB 34 had just been taken off the assembly table and they sent him down to me. Obermann was off somewheres, so I took him down to the testing rooms myself—at least I

1 A positron is the antimatter particle equivalent to the electron; theoretically proposed in 1928, it was discovered in 1932. Asimov's fictional formulation of the "positronic brain" would be used in other SF works, including *Star Trek: The Next Generation*.

started to take him down." Ashe paused, and a tiny smile tugged at his lips, "Say, did any of you ever carry on a thought conversation without knowing it."

No one bothered to answer, and he continued, "You don't realize it at first, you know. He just spoke to me—as logically and sensibly as you can imagine—and it was only when I was most of the way down to the testing rooms that I realized that *I hadn't said anything*. Sure, I had *thought* lots, but that isn't the same thing, is it? I locked that thing up and ran for Lanning. Having it walking beside me, calmly peering into my thoughts and picking and choosing among them gave me the willies."[1]

"I imagine it would," said Susan Calvin thoughtfully. Her eyes fixed themselves upon Ashe in an oddly intent manner. "We are so accustomed to considering our own thoughts private."

Lanning broke in impatiently, "Then only the four of us know. All right! We've got to go about this systematically. Ashe, I want you to check over the assembly line from beginning to end—everything. You're to eliminate all operations in which there was no possible chance of an error, and list all those where there were, together with its nature and possible magnitude."

"Tall order," grunted Ashe.

"Naturally! Of course, you're to put the men under you to work on this—every single one if you have to, and I don't care if we go behind schedule, either. But they're not to know why, you understand."

"Hm-m-m, yes!" The young technician grinned wryly. "It's still a lulu of a job."

Lanning swiveled about in his chair and faced Calvin, "You'll have to tackle the job from the other direction. You're the robopsychologist of the plant, so you're to study the robot itself and work backwards. Try to find out how he ticks. See what else is tied up with his telepathic powers, how far they extend, how they warp his outlook, and just exactly what harm it has done to his ordinary RB properties. You've got that?"

Lanning didn't wait for Dr. Calvin to answer.

"I'll co-ordinate the work and interpret the findings mathematically." He puffed violently at his cigar and mumbled the rest through the smoke, "Bogert will help me there, of course."

Bogert polished the nails of one pudgy hand with the other and said blandly, "I dare say. I know a little in the line."

"Well! I'll get started." Ashe shoved his chair back and rose. His pleasantly youthful face crinkled in a grin, "I've got the darnedest job of any of us, so I'm getting out of here and to work."

---

1 "The willies" is "a strong feeling of nervous discomfort" (*OED*). The origin is disputed, but one possibility is that it was popularized by the ballet *Giselle* (1841), also titled "*Giselle, or, The Willis,*" where the latter are the ghosts of betrayed women.

He left with a slurred, "B' seein' ye!"

Susan Calvin answered with a barely perceptible nod, but her eyes followed him out of sight and she did not answer when Lanning grunted and said, "Do you want to go up and see RB 34 now, Dr. Calvin?"

RB 34's photoelectric eyes lifted from the book at the muffled sound of hinges turning and he was upon his feet when Susan Calvin entered.

She paused to readjust the huge "No Entrance" sign upon the door and then approached the robot with a friendly smile.

"I've brought you the texts upon hyperatomic motors, Herbie—a few anyway. Would you care to look at them?"

RB 34—otherwise known as Herbie—lifted the three heavy books from her arms and opened to the title page of one:

"Hm-m-m! 'Theory of Hyperatomics.'" He mumbled inarticulately to himself as he flipped the pages and then spoke with an abstracted air, "Sit down, Dr. Calvin! This will take me a few minutes."

The psychologist seated herself and watched Herbie narrowly as he took a chair at the other side of the table and went through the three books systematically.

At the end of half an hour, he put them down, "Of course, I know why you brought these."

The corner of Dr. Calvin's lip twitched, "I was afraid you would. It's difficult to work with you, Herbie. You're always a step ahead of me."

"It's the same with these books, you know, as with the others. They just don't interest me. There's nothing *to* your textbooks. Your science is just a mass of collected data plastered together by makeshift theory—and all so incredibly simple, that it's scarcely worth bothering about.

"It's your *fiction* that interests me. Your studies of the interplay of human motives and emotions"—his mighty hand gestured vaguely as he sought the proper words.

Dr. Calvin whispered, "I think I understand."

"I see into minds, you see," the robot continued, "and you have no idea how complicated they are. I can't begin to understand everything because my own mind has so little in common with them—but I try, and your novels help."

"Yes, but I'm afraid that after going through some of the harrowing emotional experiences of our present-day sentimental novel"—there was a tinge of bitterness in her voice—"you find real minds like ours dull and colorless."

"But I don't!"

The sudden energy in the response brought the other to her feet. She felt herself reddening, and thought wildly, "He must know!"

Herbie subsided suddenly, and muttered in a low voice from which the metallic timber departed almost entirely, "But, of course, I know about it, Dr. Calvin. You think of it always, so how can I help but know."

Her face was hard. "Have you—told anyone?"

"Of course not!" This, with genuine surprise. "No one has asked me."

"Well, then," she flung out, "I suppose you think I'm a fool."

"No! It is a normal emotion."

"Perhaps that's why it's so foolish." The wistfulness in her voice drowned out everything else. Some of the woman peered through the layer of doctorhood. "I am not what you would call—attractive."

"If you are referring to mere physical attraction, I couldn't judge. But I know, in any case, that there are other types of attraction."

"Nor young." Dr. Calvin had scarcely heard the robot.

"You are not yet forty." An anxious insistence had crept into Herbie's voice.

"Thirty-eight as you count the years; a shriveled sixty as far as my emotional outlook on life is concerned. Am I a psychologist for nothing?"

She drove on with bitter breathlessness, "And he's barely thirty and looks and acts younger. Do you suppose he ever sees me as anything but … but what I am?"

"You are wrong!" Herbie's steel fist struck the plastic-topped table with a strident clang. "Listen to me—"

But Susan Calvin whirled on him now and the hunted pain in her eyes became a blaze, "Why should I? What do you know about it all, anyway, you … you machine. I'm just a specimen to you; an interesting bug with a peculiar mind spread-eagled for inspection. It's a wonderful example of frustration, isn't it? Almost as good as your books." Her voice, emerging in dry sobs, choked into silence.

The robot cowered at the outburst. He shook his head pleadingly. "Won't you listen to me, please? I could help you if you would let me."

"How?" Her lips curled. "By giving me good advice?"

"No, not that. It's just that I know what other people think—Milton Ashe, for instance."

There was a long silence, and Susan Calvin's eyes dropped. "I don't want to know what he thinks," she gasped. "Keep quiet."

"I think you *would* want to know what he thinks."

Her head remained bent, but her breath came more quickly. "You're talking nonsense," she whispered.

"Why should I? I'm trying to help. Milton Ashe's thoughts of you—" he paused.

And then the psychologist raised her head, "Well?"

The robot said quietly, "He loves you."

For a full minute, Dr. Calvin did not speak. She merely stared. Then, "You're mistaken! You must be. Why should he?"

"But he does. A thing like that cannot be hidden—not from me."

"But I am so … so—" she stammered to a halt.

"He looks deeper than the skin, and admires intellect in others. Milton

Ashe is not the type to marry a head of hair and a pair of eyes."

Susan Calvin found herself blinking rapidly and waited before speaking. Even then her voice trembled, "Yet he certainly never in any way indicated—"

"Have you ever given him a chance?"

"How could I? I never thought that—"

"Exactly!"

The psychologist paused in thought and then looked up suddenly. "A girl visited him here at the plant half a year ago. *She* was pretty, I suppose—blond and slinky. And, of course, could scarcely add two and two. He spent all day puffing out his chest, trying to explain how a robot was put together." The hardness had returned, "Not that she understood! Who was she?"

Herbie answered without hesitation, "I know the person you're referring to. She's his first cousin, and there is no romantic interest there, I assure you."

Susan Calvin rose to her feet with a vivacity almost girlish, "Now isn't that strange? That's exactly what I used to pretend to myself sometimes, though I never *really* thought so. Then it all must be true."

She ran to Herbie and seized his cold, heavy hand in both hers. "Thank you, Herbie." Her voice was an urgent, husky whisper. "Don't tell anyone about this. Let it be our secret—and thank you again." With that, and a convulsive squeeze of Herbie's unresponsive metal fingers, she left.

Herbie turned slowly to his neglected novel, but there was no one to read *his* thoughts.

Milton Ashe stretched slowly and magnificently, to the tune of cracking joints and a chorus of grunts, and then glared at Peter Bogert, Ph.D.

"Say," he said, "I've been at this for a week now with just about no sleep. How long do I have to keep it up? I thought you said the positronic bombardment in Vac Chamber D was the solution."

Bogert yawned delicately and regarded his white hands with interest, "It is! I'm on the track."

"I know what *that* means when a mathematician says it. How near the *end* are you?"

"It all depends."

"On what?" Ashe dropped into a chair and stretched his long legs out before him.

"On Lanning. The old fellow disagrees with me." He sighed, "A bit behind the times, that's the trouble with him. He clings to matrix mechanics as the all in all, and this problem calls for more powerful mathematical tools. He's so stubborn."

Ashe muttered sleepily, "Why not ask Herbie and settle the whole affair."

"Ask the robot?" Bogert's eyebrows climbed.

"Why not? Didn't the old girl tell you?"

"You mean Calvin?"

"Yeah! Susie herself. That robot's a mathematical wiz. He knows all about everything plus a bit on the side. He does triple integrals in his head and eats up tensor analysis[1] for dessert."

The mathematician stared skeptically, "Are you serious?"

"So help me! The catch is that the dope doesn't like math. He'd rather read slushy novels. Honest! You should see the tripe Susie keeps feeding him: 'Purple Passion' and 'Love in Space.'"

"Dr. Calvin hasn't said a word of it to us."

"Well, she hasn't finished studying him. You know how she is. She likes to have everything just so before letting out the big secret."

"She's told *you*."

"We sort of got to talking. I've been seeing a lot of her lately." He opened his eyes wide and frowned, "Say, Bogie, have you been noticing anything queer about the dame lately?"

Bogert relaxed into an undignified grin, "She's using lipstick, if that's what you mean."

"Hell, I know that. Rouge, powder and eye shadow, too. She's a sight. But it's not that. I can't put my finger on it. It's the way she talks—as if she were happy about something." He thought a little, and then shrugged.

The other allowed himself a leer, which, for a scientist past fifty, was not a bad job, "Maybe she's in love."

Ashe allowed his eyes to close again, "You're nuts. Bogie. You go speak to Herbie; I want to stay here and go to sleep."

"Right! Not that I particularly like having a robot tell me my job, nor that I think he can do it!"

A soft snore was his only answer.

Herbie listened carefully as Peter Bogert, hands in pockets, spoke with elaborate indifference.

"So there you are. I've been told you understand these things, and I'm asking you more in curiosity than anything else. My line of reasoning, as I've outlined it, involves a few doubtful steps, I admit, which Dr. Lanning refuses to accept, and the picture is still rather incomplete."

The robot didn't answer, and Bogert said, "Well?"

"I see no mistake," Herbie studied the scribbled figures.

"I don't suppose you can go any further than that?"

"I daren't try. You are a better mathematician than I, and—well, I'd hate to commit myself."

There was a shade of complacency in Bogert's smile, "I rather thought that would be the case. It *is* deep. We'll forget it." He crumpled the sheets, tossed them down the waste shaft, turned to leave, and then thought better of it.

"By the way—"

---

1 Triple integrals: used in three-dimensional calculus; tensor analysis: a form of calculus used in, for example, Einstein's general theory of relativity.

The robot waited.

Bogert seemed to have difficulty, "There is something—that is, perhaps you can—" He stopped.

Herbie spoke quietly, "Your thoughts are confused, but there is no doubt at all that they concern Dr. Lanning. It is silly to hesitate, for as soon as you compose yourself, I'll know what it is you want to ask."

The mathematician's hand went to his sleek hair in the familiar smoothing gesture. "Lanning is past seventy," he said, as if that explained everything.

"I know that."

"And he's been director of the plant for almost thirty years."

Herbie nodded.

"Well, now," Bogert's voice became ingratiating, "you would know whether … whether he's thinking of resigning. Health, perhaps, or some other—"

"Quite," said Herbie, and that was all.

"Well, *do* you know."

"Certainly."

"Then—uh—could you tell me?"

"Since you ask, yes." The robot was quite matter-of-fact about it. "He has already resigned!"

"*What!*" The exclamation was an explosive, almost inarticulate, sound. The scientist's large head hunched forward, "Say that again!"

"He has already resigned," came the quiet repetition, "but it has not yet taken effect. He is waiting, you see, to solve the problem of—er—myself. That finished, he is quite ready to turn the office of director over to his successor."

Bogert expelled his breath sharply, "And this successor? Who is he?" He was quite close to Herbie now, eyes fixed fascinatedly on those unreadable dull-red photoelectric cells that were the robot's eyes.

Words came slowly, "*You* are the next director."

And Bogert relaxed into a tight smile, "This is good to know. I've been hoping and waiting for this. Thanks, Herbie."

He was still smiling as he closed the door behind himself, but what Herbie's feelings were, there was no way of telling.

Peter Bogert was at his desk until five that morning and he was back at nine. The shelf just over the desk emptied of its row of reference books and tables, as he referred to one after the other. The pages of calculations before him increased microscopically and the crumpled sheets at his feet mounted into a hill of scribbled paper.

At precisely noon, he stared at the final page, rubbed a bloodshot eye, yawned and shrugged. "This is getting worse each minute. Damn!"

He turned at the sound of the opening door and nodded at Lanning, who entered, cracking the knuckles of one gnarled hand with the other.

The director took in the disorder of the room and his eyebrows furrowed together.

"New lead?" he asked.

"No," came the defiant answer. "What's wrong with the old one?"

Lanning did not trouble to answer, nor to do more than bestow a single cursory glance at the top sheet upon Bogert's desk. He spoke through the flare of a match as he lit a cigar. "Has Calvin told you about the robot? It's a mathematical genius. Really remarkable."

The other snorted loudly, "So I've heard. But Calvin had better stick to robopsychology. I've checked Herbie on math, and he can scarcely struggle through calculus."

"Calvin didn't find it so."

"She's crazy."

"And *I* don't find it so." The director's eyes narrowed dangerously.

"You!" Bogert's voice hardened. "What're you talking about?"

"I've been putting Herbie through his paces all morning, and he can do tricks you never heard of."

"Is that so?"

"You sound skeptical!" Lanning flipped a sheet of paper out of his vest pocket and unfolded it. "That's not my handwriting, is it?"

Bogert studied the large angular notation covering the sheet, "Herbie did this?"

"Right! And if you'll notice, he's been working on your time integration of Equation 22. It comes"—Lanning tapped a yellow fingernail upon the last step—"to the identical conclusion I did, and in a quarter the time. You had no right to neglect the Linger Effect in positronic bombardment."

"I didn't neglect it. For Heaven's sake, Lanning, get it through your head that it would cancel out—"

"Oh, sure, you explained that. You used the Mitchell Translation Equation, didn't you? Well—it doesn't apply."

"Why not?"

"Because you've been using hyper-imaginaries,[1] for one thing."

"What's that to do with it?"

"Mitchell's Equation won't hold when—"

"Are you crazy? If you'll reread Mitchell's original paper in the *Mathematical Journal*—"

"I don't have to. I told you in the beginning that I didn't like his reasoning, and Herbie backs me in that."

"Well, then," Bogert shouted, "let that clockwork contraption solve the entire problem for you. Why bother with nonessentials?"

"That's exactly the point. Herbie *can't* solve the problem. I've asked him. And if he can't, *we* can't—alone. I'm submitting the entire question to the National Board. It's gotten beyond us."

1 While hyper-imaginary numbers are discussed in mathematics, this dialogue largely serves as "technobabble."

Bogert's chair went over backward as he jumped up asnarl, face crimson. "You're doing nothing of the sort."

Lanning flushed in his turn, "Are you telling *me* what I can't do."

"Exactly," was the gritted response. "I've got the problem beaten and you're not to take it out of my hands, understand? Don't think I don't see through you, you desiccated fossil. You'd cut your own nose off before you'd let me get the credit for solving robotic telepathy."

"You're a damned idiot, Bogert, and in one second I'll have you suspended for insubordination"—Lanning's lower lip trembled with passion.

"Which is one thing you won't do, Lanning. You haven't any secrets with a mind-reading robot around, so don't forget that I know all about your resignation."

The ash on Lanning's cigar trembled and fell, and the cigar itself followed, "What … what—"

Bogert chuckled nastily, "And I'm the new director, be it understood. I'm very aware of that; don't think I'm not. Damn your eyes, Lanning, *I'm* going to give the orders about here or there will be the sweetest mess that *you've* ever been in."

Lanning found his voice and let it out with a roar. "You're suspended, d'ye hear? You're relieved of all duties. You're broken, do you understand?"

The smile on the other's face broadened, "Now what's the use of that? You're getting nowhere. I'm holding the trumps. I *know* you've resigned. Herbie told me, and he got it straight from you."

Lanning forced himself to speak quietly. He looked an old, old man, with tired eyes peering from a face in which the red had disappeared, leaving the pasty yellow of age behind, "I want to speak to Herbie. He can't have told you anything of the sort. You're playing a deep game, Bogert, but I'm calling your bluff. Come with me."

Bogert shrugged, "To see Herbie? Good! Damned good!"

It was also precisely at noon that Milton Ashe looked up from his clumsy sketch and said, "You get the idea? I'm not too good at getting this down, but that's about how it looks. It's a honey of a house, and I can get it for next to nothing."

Susan Calvin gazed across at him with melting eyes. There had been a preliminary self-consciousness when she had first forced her hair into curls and lacquered her fingernails a bright red—a silly everyone-is-snickering-at-me feeling—but it always vanished when she was with *him*. There was nothing then but the hard, metallic voice of Herbie whispering in her ear—

"It's really beautiful," she sighed. "I've often thought that I'd like to—" Her voice trailed away.

"Of course," Ashe continued briskly, putting away his pencil, "I've got to wait for my vacation. It's only two weeks off, but this Herbie business has everything up in the air." His eyes dropped to his fingernails, "Besides, there's another point—but it's a secret."

"Then don't tell me."

"Oh, I'd just as soon. I'm just busting to tell someone—and you're just about the best—er—confidante I could find here." He grinned sheepishly.

Susan Calvin's heart bounded, but she did not trust herself to speak.

"Frankly," Ashe scraped his chair closer and lowered his voice into a confidential whisper, "the house isn't to be only for myself. I'm getting married!"

And then he jumped out of his seat, "What's the matter?"

"Nothing!" The horrible spinning sensation had vanished, but it was hard to get words out. "Married? You mean—"

"Why sure! About time, isn't it? You remember that girl who was here last summer. That's she! But you *are* sick. You—"

"Headache!" Susan Calvin motioned him away weakly. "I've ... I've been subject to them lately. I want to ... to congratulate you, of course. I'm very glad—" The inexpertly-applied rouge made a pair of nasty red splotches upon her chalk-white face. Things had begun spinning again. "Pardon me—please—"

The words were a mumble, as she stumbled blindly out the door. It had happened with the sudden catastrophe of a dream—and with all the unreal horror of a dream.

But how could it be? Herbie had said—

And Herbie *knew*! He could see into minds!

She found herself leaning breathlessly against the door jamb, staring into Herbie's metal face. She must have climbed the two flights of stairs, but she had no memory of it. The distance had been covered in an instant, as in a dream.

As in a dream!

And still Herbie's unblinking eyes stared into hers and their dull red seemed to expand into dimly-shining nightmarish globes.

He was speaking, and she felt the cold glass pressing against her lips. She swallowed and shuddered into a certain awareness of her surroundings.

Still Herbie spoke, and there was an agitation in his voice—as if he were hurt and frightened and pleading.

The words were beginning to make sense. "This is a dream," he was saying, "and you mustn't believe in it. You'll wake into the real world soon and laugh at yourself. He loves you, I tell you. He does, he *does!* But not here! Not now! *This* is all illusion."

Susan Calvin nodded, her voice a whisper, "Yes! Yes!" She was clutching Herbie's arm, clinging to it, repeating over and over, "It isn't true, is it? It isn't, is it?"

Just how she came to her senses, she never knew—but it was like passing from a world of misty unreality to one of harsh sunlight. She pushed him away from her, pushed hard against that steely arm, and her eyes were wide.

"What are you trying to do?" Her voice rose to a harsh scream. "*What are you trying to do?*"

Herbie backed away, "I want to help."

The psychologist stared, "Help? By telling me this is a dream? By trying to push me into schizophrenia?" A hysterical tenseness seized her, "This is no dream! I wish it were!"

She drew in her breath sharply, "Wait! Why ... why, I understand. Merciful heavens, it's so obvious."

There was horror in the robot's voice, "I *had* to!"

"And I *believed* you! I never thought—"

Loud voices outside the door brought her to a halt. She turned away, fists clenching spasmodically, and when Bogert and Lanning entered, she was at the far window. Neither of the men paid her the slightest attention.

They approached Herbie simultaneously; Lanny angry and impatient, Bogert coolly sardonic. The director spoke first.

"Here now, Herbie. Listen to me!"

The robot brought his eyes sharply down upon the aged director, "Yes, Dr. Lanning."

"Have you discussed me with Dr. Bogert?"

"No, sir." The answer came slowly, and the smile on Bogert's face flashed off.

"What's that?" Bogert shoved in ahead of his superior and straddled the ground before the robot. "Repeat what you told me yesterday."

"I said that—" Herbie fell silent. Deep within him his metallic diaphragm vibrated in soft discords.

"Didn't you say he had resigned?" roared Bogert. "*Answer me!*"

Bogert raised his arm frantically, but Lanning pushed him aside, "Are you trying to bully him into lying?"

"You heard him, Lanning. He began to say 'Yes' and stopped. Get out of my way! I want the truth out of him, understand!"

"*I'll* ask him!" Lanning turned to the robot. "All right, Herbie, take it easy. Have I resigned?"

Herbie stared, and Lanning repeated anxiously, "Have I resigned?" There was the faintest trace of a negative shake of the robot's head. A long wait produced nothing further.

The two men looked at each other, and the hostility in their eyes was all but tangible.

"What the devil," blurted Bogert, "has the robot gone mute? Can't you speak, you monstrosity?"

"I can speak," came the ready answer.

"Then answer the question. Didn't you tell me Lanning had resigned? *Hasn't he resigned?*"

And again there was nothing but dull silence, until from the end of the room, Susan Calvin's laugh rang out suddenly, high-pitched and semihysterical.

The two mathematicians jumped, and Bogert's eyes narrowed, "You here? What's so funny?"

"Nothin's funny." Her voice was not quite natural. "It's just that I'm not the only one that's been caught. There's irony in three of the greatest experts in robotics in the world falling into the same elementary trap, isn't there?" Her voice faded, and she put a pale hand to her forehead, "But it isn't funny!"

This time the look that passed between the two men was one of raised eyebrows. "What trap are you talking about?" asked Lanning stiffly. "Is something wrong with Herbie?"

"No," she approached them slowly, "nothin's wrong with *him*—only with us." She whirled suddenly and shrieked at the robot, "Get away from me! Go to the other end of the room and don't let me look at you."

Herbie cringed before the fury of her eyes and stumbled away in a clattering trot.

Lanning's voice was hostile, "What is all this, Dr. Calvin?"

She faced them and spoke wearily, "You know the fundamental law impressed upon the positronic brain of all robots, of course."

The other two nodded together. "Certainly," said Bogert. "On no conditions is a human being to be injured in any way, even when such injury is directly ordered by another human."

"How nicely put," sneered Calvin. "But what kind of injury?"

"Why—any kind."

"Exactly! Any kind! But what about hurt feelings? What about deflation of one's ego? What about the blasting of one's hopes? Is that injury?"

Lanning frowned, "What would a robot know about—" And then he caught himself with a gasp.

"You've caught on, have you? *This* robot reads minds. Do you suppose it doesn't know everything about mental injury? Do you suppose that if asked a question, it wouldn't give exactly that answer that one *wants* to hear. Wouldn't any other answer hurt us, and wouldn't Herbie know that?"

"Good heavens!" muttered Bogert.

The psychologist cast a sardonic glance at him, "I take it you asked him whether Lanning had resigned. You *wanted* to hear that he had resigned and so that's what Herbie told you."

"And I suppose that is why," said Lanning, tonelessly, "it wouldn't answer a little while ago. It couldn't answer either way without hurting one of us."

There was a short pause in which the men looked thoughtfully across the room at the robot, crouching in the chair by the bookcase, head resting in one hand.

Susan Calvin stared steadfastly at the floor, "*He* knew of all this. That … that devil knows everything—including what went wrong in his assembly." Her eyes were dark and brooding.

Lanning looked up, "You're wrong there, Dr. Calvin. He doesn't know what went wrong. I asked him."

"What does that mean?" cried Calvin. "Only that you didn't want him to give you the solution. It would puncture your ego to have a machine do what you couldn't. Did *you* ask him?" she shot at Bogert.

"In a way." Bogert coughed and reddened. "He told me he knew very little about mathematics."

Lanning laughed, not very loudly, and the psychologist smiled caustically. She said, "*I'll* ask him! A solution by him won't hurt my ego." She raised her voice into a cold, imperative "Come here!"

Herbie rose and approached with hesitant steps.

"You know, I suppose," she continued, "just exactly at what point in the assembly an extraneous factor was introduced or an essential one left out."

"Yes," said Herbie, in tones barely heard.

"Hold on," broke in Bogert angrily. "That's not necessarily true. You want to hear that, that's all."

"Don't be a fool," replied Calvin. "He certainly knows as much math as you and Lanning together, since he can read minds. Give him his chance."

The mathematician subsided, and Calvin continued, "All right, then, Herbie, give! We're waiting." And in an aside, "Get pencils and paper, gentlemen."

But Herbie remained silent, and there was triumph in the psychologist's voice, "Why don't you answer, Herbie?"

The robot blurted out suddenly, "I cannot. You know I cannot! Dr. Bogert and Dr. Lanning don't want me to."

"They want the solution."

"But not from me."

Lanning broke in, speaking slowly and distinctly, "Don't be foolish, Herbie. We *do* want you to tell us."

Bogert nodded curtly.

Herbie's voice rose to wild heights, "What's the use of saying that? Don't you suppose that I can see past the superficial skin of your mind? Down below, you don't want me to. I'm a machine, given the imitation of life only by virtue of the positronic interplay in my brain—which is man's device. You can't lose face to me without being hurt. That's deep in your mind and *won't* be erased. I *can't* give the solution."

"We'll leave," said Dr. Lanning. "Tell Calvin."

"That would make no difference," cried Herbie, "since you would know anyway that it was I that was supplying the answer."

Calvin resumed, "But you understand, Herbie, that despite that, Drs. Lanning and Bogert want that solution."

"By their own efforts!" insisted Herbie.

"But they want it, and the fact that you have it and won't give it hurts them. You see that, don't you?"

"Yes! Yes!"

"And if you tell them, that will hurt them, too."

"Yes! Yes!" Herbie was retreating slowly, and step by step Susan Calvin advanced. The two men watched in frozen bewilderment.

"You can't tell them," droned the psychologist slowly, "because that would hurt and you mustn't hurt. But if you don't tell them, you hurt, so you *must* tell them. And if you do, you will hurt and you mustn't, so you can't tell them; but if you don't, you hurt, so you must; but if you do, you hurt, so you mustn't; but if you don't, you hurt, so you must; but if you do, you—"

Herbie was up against the wall, and here he dropped to his knees. "Stop!" he shrieked. "Close your mind! It is full of pain and frustration and hate! I didn't mean it, I tell you! I tried to help! I told you what you wanted to hear. I had to!"

The psychologist paid no attention, "You must tell them, but if you do, you hurt, so you musn't; but if you don't, you hurt, so you must; but—"

And Herbie screamed!

It was like the whistling of a piccolo many times magnified—shrill and shriller till it keened with the terror of a lost soul and filled the room with the piercingness of itself.

And when it died into nothingness, Herbie collapsed into a huddled heap of motionless metal.

Bogert's face was bloodless, "He's dead!"

"No!" Susan Calvin burst into body-racking gusts of wild laughter, "not dead—merely insane. I confronted him with the insoluble dilemma, and he broke down. You can scrap him now—because he'll never speak again."

Lanning was on his knees beside the thing that had been Herbie. His fingers touched the cold, unresponsive metal face and he shuddered. "You did that on purpose." He rose and faced her, face contorted.

"What if I did? You can't help it now." And in a sudden access of bitterness, "He deserved it."

The director seized the paralyzed, motionless Bogert by the wrist, "What's the difference. Come, Peter." He sighed, "A thinking robot of this type is worthless anyway." His eyes were old and tired, and he repeated, "Come, Pete!"

It was minutes after the two scientists left that Dr. Susan Calvin regained part of her mental equilibrium. Slowly, her eyes turned to the living-dead Herbie and the tight smile returned to her face. Long she stared while the triumph faded and the helpless frustration returned—and of all her turbulent thoughts only one infinitely bitter word passed her lips.

"Liar!"

Fig. 4: William A. Kolliker. Illustration to "Mimsy Were the Borogoves." *Astounding Science-Fiction*, vol. 30, no. 6, 1943.

Lewis Padgett [C.L. Moore (1911–87) and Henry Kuttner (1915–58)]

Lewis Padgett was one of the pseudonyms used by writing partners and married couple C.L. Moore and Henry Kuttner. One of the most significant writers of the pulp period, Moore is best recognized for her stories about the Western-inspired hero Northwest Smith, who features in her first story, "Shambleau," and who could serve, in many ways, as the model for the swashbuckling hero of many space operas and other SF works. Kuttner was a well-known author, but he published under more than a dozen pseudonyms, making his overall influence difficult to trace. In some ways, his solo work is best remembered for his involvement in the Lovecraft circle as well as his contributions to comedic SF. His influence was significant on other authors, with Richard Matheson dedicating his foundational zombie-*cum*-vampire novel, *I Am Legend* (1954), to him. After Kuttner's untimely death in 1958, Moore pivoted to writing for television.

Note on the text: The story here comes from its first publication in *Astounding Science-Fiction* (1943), which is introduced as follows: "This is the first science-fiction story that I know of which has considered the children's toys of the far future. Simple little item—a time-machine inventor trying out his gadget sending back a few discarded children's toys. But—what toys!" (52). The original publication included the illustration (Fig. 4) on the second page of the story, listed as being by Kolliker, identified elsewhere as William A. Kolliker (1905–95). Typographical errors were corrected against later editions.

"Mimsy Were the Borogoves" (1943)

THERE'S no use trying to describe either Unthahorsten or his surroundings, because, for one thing, a good many million years had passed since 1942 Anno Domini, and, for another, Unthahorsten wasn't on Earth, technically speaking. He was doing the equivalent of standing in the equivalent of a laboratory. He was preparing to test his time machine.

Having turned on the power, Unthahorsten suddenly realized that the Box was empty. Which wouldn't do at all. The device needed a control, a three-dimensional solid which would react to the conditions of another age. Otherwise Unthahorsten couldn't tell, on the machine's return, where and when it had been. Whereas a solid in the Box would automatically be subject to the entropy and cosmic ray bombardment of the other era, and Unthahorsten could measure the changes, both qualitative and quantitative, when the machine returned. The Calculators could then get to work and, presently, tell Unthahorsten that the Box had briefly visited 1,000,000 A.D., 1,000 A.D., or 1 A.D., as the case might be.

Not that it mattered, except to Unthahorsten. But he was childish in many respects.

There was little time to waste. The Box was beginning to glow and shiver. Unthahorsten stared around wildly, fled into the next glossatch, and groped in a storage bin there. He came up with an armful of peculiar-looking stuff. Uh-huh. Some of the discarded toys of his son Snowen, which the boy had brought with him when he had passed over from Earth, after mastering the necessary technique. Well, Snowen needed this junk no longer. He was conditioned, and had put away childish things.[1] Besides, though Unthahorsten's wife kept the toys for sentimental reasons, the experiment was more important.

Unthahorsten left the glossatch and dumped the assortment into the Box, slamming the cover shut just before the warning signal flashed. The Box went away. The manner of its departure hurt Unthahorsten's eyes.

He waited.

And he waited.

Eventually he gave up and built another time machine, with identical results. Snowen hadn't been annoyed by the loss of his old toys, nor had Snowen's mother, so Unthahorsten cleaned out the bin and dumped the remainder of his son's childhood relics in the second time machine's Box.

According to his calculations, this one should have appeared on Earth, in the latter part of the nineteenth century, A.D. If that actually occurred, the device remained there.

Disgusted, Unthahorsten decided to make no more time machines. But the mischief had been done. There were two of them, and the first—

Scott Paradine found it while he was playing hooky from the Glendale Grammar School. There was a geography test that day, and Scott saw no sense in memorizing place names—which in 1942 was a fairly sensible theory. Besides, it was the sort of warm spring day, with a touch of coolness in the breeze, which invited a boy to lie down in a field and stare at the occasional clouds till he fell asleep. Nuts to geography! Scott dozed.

About noon he got hungry, so his stocky legs carried him to a nearby store. There he invested his small hoard with penurious care and a sublime disregard for his gastric juices. He went down by the creek to feed.

Having finished his supply of cheese, chocolate, and cookies, and having drained the soda-pop bottle to its dregs, Scott caught tadpoles and studied them with a certain amount of scientific curiosity. He did not persevere. Something tumbled down the bank and thudded into the muddy ground near the water, so Scott, with a wary glance around, hurried to investigate.

It was a box. It was, in fact, the Box. The gadgetry hitched to it meant little to Scott, though he wondered why it was so fused and burnt. He pondered.

1 1 Corinthians 13.11: "When I was a child, I spake as a child, I understood as a child, I thought as a child: but when I became a man, I put away childish things."

With his jackknife he pried and probed, his tongue sticking out from a corner of his mouth— Hm-m-m. Nobody was around. Where had the box come from? Somebody must have left it here, and sliding soil had dislodged it from its precarious perch.

"That's a helix," Scott decided, quite erroneously. It was helical, but it wasn't a helix, because of the dimensional warp involved. Had the thing been a model airplane, no matter how complicated, it would have held few mysteries to Scott. As it was, a problem was posed. Something told Scott that the device was a lot more complicated than the spring motor he had deftly dismantled last Friday.

But no boy has ever left a box unopened, unless forcibly dragged away. Scott probed deeper. The angles on this thing were funny. Short circuit, probably. That was why—*uh!* The knife slipped. Scott sucked his thumb and gave vent to experienced blasphemy.

Maybe it was a music box.

Scott shouldn't have felt depressed. The gadgetry would have given Einstein a headache and driven Steinmetz raving mad.[1] The trouble was, of course, that the box had not yet completely entered the space-time continuum where Scott existed, and therefore it could not be opened. At any rate, not till Scott used a convenient rock to hammer the helical non-helix into a more convenient position.

He hammered it, in fact, from its contact point with the fourth dimension, releasing the space-time torsion it had been maintaining.[2] There was a brittle snap. The box jarred slightly, and lay motionless, no longer only partially in existence. Scott opened it easily now.

The soft, woven helmet was the first thing that caught his eye, but he discarded that without much interest. It was just a cap. Next he lifted a square, transparent crystal block, small enough to cup in his palm—much too small to contain the maze of apparatus within it. In a moment Scott had solved that problem. The crystal was a sort of magnifying glass, vastly enlarging the things inside the block. Strange things they were, too. Miniature people, for example—

They moved. Like clockwork automatons, though much more smoothly.[3] It was rather like watching a play. Scott was interested in their costumes, but

1 Albert Einstein (1879–1955), theoretical physicist who developed the theory of relativity and the equation that explains the relation of energy to mass, $E=mc^2$; Charles Proteus Steinmetz (1865–1923), mathematician, electrical engineer, professor, and inventor.

2 The idea that time constituted a fourth dimension (in addition to three dimensions of space) has been proposed since the eighteenth century and was popularized by H.G. Wells in his early SF novel, *The Time Machine* (1895). It gained new attention in the twentieth century with Hermann Minkowski (1864–1909), who proposed a four-dimensional spacetime, connected to Einstein's special relativity.

3 Mechanical devices operated by clockwork, often in the shape of people, that appear to move of their own accord after the device is wound.

fascinated by their actions. The tiny people were deftly building a house. Scott wished it would catch fire, so he could see the people put it out.

Flames licked up from the half-completed structure. The automatons, with a great deal of odd apparatus, extinguished the blaze.

It didn't take Scott long to catch on. But he was a little worried. The manikins would obey his thoughts. By the time he discovered that, he was frightened, and threw the cube from him.

Halfway up the bank, he reconsidered and returned. The crystal block lay partly in the water, shining in the sun. It was a toy; Scott sensed that, with the unerring instinct of a child. But he didn't pick it up immediately. Instead, he returned to the box and investigated its remaining contents.

He found some really remarkable gadgets. The afternoon passed all too quickly, Scott finally put the toys back in the box and lugged it home, grunting and puffing. He was quite red-faced by the time he arrived at the kitchen door.

His find he hid at the back of a closet in his own room upstairs. The crystal cube he slipped into his pocket, which already bulged with string, a coil of wire, two pennies, a wad of tinfoil, a grimy defense stamp,[1] and a chunk of feldspar. Emma, Scott's two-year-old sister, waddled unsteadily in from the hall and said hello.

"Hello, Slug," Scott nodded, from his altitude of seven years and some months. He patronized Emma shockingly, but she didn't know the difference. Small, plump, and wide-eyed, she flopped down on the carpet and stared dolefully at her shoes.

"Tie 'em, Scotty, please?"

"Sap," Scott told her kindly, but knotted the laces. "Dinner ready yet?"

Emma nodded.

"Let's see your hands." For a wonder, they were reasonably clean, though probably not aseptic. Scott regarded his own paws thoughtfully and, grimacing, went to the bathroom, where he made a sketchy toilet. The tadpoles had left traces.

Dennis Paradine and his wife Jane were having a cocktail before dinner, downstairs in the living room. He was a youngish, middle-aged man with gray-shot hair and a thinnish, prim-mouthed face; he taught philosophy at the university. Jane was small, neat, dark, and very pretty. She sipped her Martini and said:

"New shoes. Like 'em?"

"Here's to crime," Paradine muttered absently. "Huh? Shoes? Not now. Wait till I've finished this. I had a bad day."

"Exams?"

1 US postage stamps issued starting on 16 October 1940, when the US began a military draft before entering World War II.

"Yeah. Flaming youth aspiring toward manhood. I hope they die. In considerable agony. *Insh'Allah!*"[1]

"I want the olive," Jane requested.

"I know," Paradine said despondently. "It's been years since I've tasted one myself. In a Martini, I mean. Even if I put six of 'em in your glass, you're still not satisfied."

"I want yours. Blood brotherhood. Symbolism. That's why."

"Paradine regarded his wife balefully and crossed his long legs. "You sound like one of my students."

"Like that hussy Betty Dawson, perhaps?" Jane unsheathed her nails. "Does she still leer at you in that offensive way?"

"She does. The child is a neat psychological problem. Luckily she isn't mine. If she were—" Paradine nodded significantly. "Sex consciousness and too many movies. I suppose she still thinks she can get a passing grade by showing me her knees. Which are, by the way, rather bony."

Jane adjusted her skirt with an air of complacent pride. Paradine uncoiled himself and poured fresh Martinis. "Candidly, I don't see the point of teaching those apes philosophy. They're all at the wrong age. Their habit-patterns, their methods of thinking, are already laid down. They're horribly conservative, not that they'd admit it. The only people who can understand philosophy are mature adults or kids like Emma and Scotty."

"Well, don't enroll Scotty in your course," Jane requested. "He isn't ready to be a *Philosophiae Doctor.* I hold no brief for child geniuses, especially when it's my son."

"Scotty would probably be better at it than Betty Dawson," Paradine grunted.

"'He died an enfeebled old dotard at five,'"[2] Jane quoted dreamily. "I want your olive."

"Here. By the way, I like the shoes."

"Thank you. Here's Rosalie. Dinner?"

"It's all ready, Miz Pa'dine," said Rosalie, hovering. "I'll call Miss Emma 'n' Mista' Scotty."[3]

"I'll get 'em." Paradine put his head into the next room and roared, "Kids! Come and get it!"

---

1 "God willing" (Arabic).

2 The last line of the humorous song "The Precocious Baby: A Very True Tale," by W.S. Gilbert (of Gilbert and Sullivan fame), published in *Fun* magazine (23 Nov. 1867) under the pseudonym Bab. The song recounts a story of an old man who married a young woman; they then have a child, who is born wiser than his years, who designs to marry his "elderly nurse," but he dies. A moral is added to the end of the song, warning "elderly men" not to marry, because their children will be "elderly too."

3 Kuttner and Moore here reproduce a dialect associated with stereotypes of Black servants in the US.

Small feet scuttered down the stairs. Scott dashed into view, scrubbed and shining, a rebellious cowlick aimed at the zenith. Emma pursued, levering herself carefully down the steps. Halfway she gave up the attempt to descend upright and reversed, finishing the task monkey-fashion, her small behind giving an impression of marvelous diligence upon the work in hand. Paradine watched, fascinated by the spectacle, till he was hurled back by the impact of his son's body.

"Hi, dad!" Scott shrieked.

Paradine recovered himself and regarded Scott with dignity. "Hi, yourself. Help me in to dinner. You've dislocated at least one of my hip joints."

But Scott was already tearing into the next room, where he stepped on Jane's new shoes in an ecstasy of affection, burbled an apology, and rushed off to find his place at the dinner table. Paradine cocked up an eyebrow as he followed, Emma's pudgy hand desperately gripping his forefinger.

"Wonder what the young devil's been up to?"

"No good, probably," Jane sighed. "Hello, darling. Let's see your ears."

"They're *clean*. Mickey licked 'em."

"Well, that Airedale's tongue is far cleaner than your ears," Jane pondered, making a brief examination. "Still, as long as you can hear, the dirt's only superficial."

"Fisshul?"

"Just a little, that means." Jane dragged her daughter to the table and inserted her legs into a high chair. Only lately had Emma graduated to the dignity of dining with the rest of the family, and she was, as Paradine remarked, all eat up with pride by the prospect. Only babies spilled food, Emma had been told. As a result, she took such painstaking care in conveying her spoon to her mouth that Paradine got the jitters whenever he watched.

"A conveyer belt would be the thing for Emma," he suggested, pulling out a chair for Jane. "Small buckets of spinach arriving at her face at stated intervals."

Dinner proceeded uneventfully until Paradine happened to glance at Scott's plate. "Hello, there. Sick? Been stuffing yourself at lunch?"

Scott thoughtfully examined the food still left before him. "I've had all I need, dad," he explained.

"You usually eat all you can hold, and a great deal more," Paradine said. "I know growing boys need several tons of foodstuff a day, but you're below par tonight. Feel O.K.?"

"Uh-huh. Honest, I've had all I need."

"All you *want?*"

"Sure. I eat different."

"Something they taught you at school?" Jane inquired.

Scott shook his head solemnly.

"Nobody taught me. I found it out myself. I use spit."

"Try again," Paradine suggested. "It's the wrong word."

"Uh … s-saliva. Hm-m-m?"

"Uh-huh. More pepsin? Is there pepsin in the salivary juices, Jane? I forget."

"There's poison in mine," Jane remarked. "Rosalie's left lumps in the mashed potatoes again."

But Paradine was interested. "You mean you're getting everything possible out of your food—no wastage—and eating less?"

Scott thought that over. "I guess so. It's not just the sp … saliva. I sort of measure how much to put in my mouth at once, and what stuff to mix up. I dunno. I just do it."

"Hm-m-m," said Paradine, making a note to check up later. "Rather a revolutionary idea." Kids often get screwy notions, but this one might not be so far off the beam. He pursed his lips. "Eventually I suppose people will eat quite differently—I mean the *way* they eat, as well as what. What they eat, I mean. Jane, our son shows signs of becoming a genius."

"Oh?"

"It's a rather good point in dietetics he just made. Did you figure it out yourself, Scott?"

"Sure," the boy said, and really believed it.

"Where'd you get the idea?"

"Oh, I—" Scott wriggled. "I dunno. It doesn't mean much, I guess."

Paradine was unreasonably disappointed. "But surely—"

"S-s-s-spit!" Emma shrieked, overcome by a sudden fit of badness. "*Spit!*" she attempted to demonstrate, but succeeded only in dribbling into her bib.

With a resigned air Jane rescued and reproved her daughter, while Paradine eyed Scott with rather puzzled interest. But it was not till after dinner, in the living room, that anything further happened.

"Any homework?"

"N-no," Scott said, flushing guiltily. To cover his embarrassment he took from his pocket a gadget he had found in the box, and began to unfold it. The result resembled a tesseract,[1] strung with beads. Paradine didn't see it at first, but Emma did. She wanted to play with it.

"No. Lay off, Slug," Scott ordered. "You can watch me." He fumbled with the beads, making soft, interested noises. Emma extended a fat forefinger and yelped.

"Scotty," Paradine said warningly.

"I didn't hurt her."

"Bit me. It did," Emma mourned.

Paradine looked up. He frowned, staring. What in—

"Is that an abacus?" he asked. "Let's see it, please."

Somewhat unwillingly Scott brought the gadget across to his father's chair. Paradine blinked. The "abacus," unfolded, was more than a foot square, composed of thin, rigid wires that interlocked here and there. On the wires

---

1 A four-dimensional hypercube, or an analogue of a cube extended to the fourth dimension.

the colored beads were strung. They could be slid back and forth, and from one support to another, even at the points of jointure. But—a pierced bead couldn't cross *interlocking* wires—

So, apparently, they weren't pierced. Paradine looked closer. Each small bead had a deep groove running around it, so that it could be revolved and slid along the wire at the same time. Paradine tried to pull one free. It clung as though magnetically. Iron? It looked more like plastic.

The framework itself— Paradine wasn't a mathematician. But the angles formed by the wires were vaguely shocking, in their ridiculous lack of Euclidean[1] logic. They were a maze. Perhaps that's what the gadget was—a puzzle.

"Where'd you get this?"

"Uncle Harry gave it to me," Scott said on the spur of the moment. "Last Sunday, when he came over." Uncle Harry was out of town, a circumstance Scott well knew. At the age of seven, a boy soon learns that the vagaries of adults follow a certain definite pattern, and that they are fussy about the donors of gifts. Moreover, Uncle Harry would not return for several weeks; the expiration of that period was unimaginable to Scott, or, at least, the fact that his lie would ultimately be discovered meant less to him than the advantages of being allowed to keep the toy.

Paradine found himself growing slightly confused as he attempted to manipulate the beads. The angles were vaguely illogical. It was like a puzzle. This red bead, if slid along *this* wire to *that* junction, should reach *there*—but it didn't. A maze, odd, but no doubt instructive. Paradine had a well-founded feeling that he'd have no patience with the thing himself.

Scott did, however, retiring to a corner and sliding beads around with much fumbling and grunting. The beads *did* sting, when Scott chose the wrong ones or tried to slide them in the wrong direction. At last he crowed exultantly.

"I did it, dad!"

"Eh? What? Let's see." The device looked exactly the same to Paradine, but Scott pointed and beamed.

"I made it disappear."

"It's still there?"

"That blue bead. It's gone now."

Paradine didn't believe that, so he merely snorted. Scott puzzled over the framework again. He experimented. This time there were no shocks, even slight. The abacus had showed him the correct method. Now it was up to him to do it on his own. The bizarre angles of the wires seemed a little less confusing now, somehow.

1 Euclid, mathematician in classical Greece best known today for his work on geometry, *The Elements* (c. 300 BCE). Non-Euclidian geometries began to be formalized in the nineteenth century.

It was a most instructive toy—

It worked, Scott thought, rather like the crystal cube. Reminded of that gadget, he took it from his pocket and relinquished the abacus to Emma, who was struck dumb with joy. She fell to work sliding the beads, this time without protesting against the shocks—which, indeed, were very minor—and, being imitative, she managed to make a bead disappear almost as quickly as had Scott. The blue bead reappeared—but Scott didn't notice. He had forethoughtfully retired into an angle of the chesterfield and an overstuffed chair and amused himself with the cube.

There were little people inside the thing, tiny manikins much enlarged by the magnifying properties of the crystal, and they moved, all right. They built a house. It caught fire, with realistic-seeming flames, and stood by waiting. Scott puffed urgently. "Put it *out!*"

But nothing happened. Where was that queer fire engine, with revolving arms, that had appeared before? Here it was. It came sailing into the picture and stopped. Scott urged it on.

This was fun. Like putting on a play, only more real. The little people did what Scott told them, inside of his head. If he made a mistake, they waited till he'd found the right way. They even posed new problems for him—

The cube, too, was a most instructive toy. It was teaching Scott, with alarming rapidity—and teaching him very entertainingly. But it gave him no really new knowledge as yet. He wasn't ready. Later—later—

Emma grew tired of the abacus and went in search of Scott. She couldn't find him, even in his room, but once there the contents of the closet intrigued her. She discovered the box. It contained a treasure-trove—a doll, which Scott had already noticed but discarded with a sneer. Squealing, Emma brought the doll downstairs, squatted in the middle of the floor, and began to take it apart.

"Darling! What's that?"

"Mr. Bear!"

Obviously it wasn't Mr. Bear, who was blind, earless, but comforting in his soft fatness. But all dolls were named Mr. Bear to Emma.

Jane Paradine hesitated. "Did you take that from some other little girl?"

"I didn't. She's mine."

Scott came out from his hiding place, thrusting the cube into his pocket. "Uh—that's from Uncle Harry."

"Did Uncle Harry give that to you, Emma?"

"He gave it to me for Emma," Scott put in hastily, adding another stone to his foundation of deceit. "Last Sunday."

"You'll break it, dear."

Emma brought the doll to her mother. "She comes apart. See?"

"Oh? It … *ugh!*" Jane sucked in her breath. Paradine looked up quickly.

"What's up?"

She brought the doll over to him, hesitated, and then went into the dining room, giving Paradine a significant glance. He followed, closing the door. Jane had already placed the doll on the cleared table.

"This isn't very nice, is it Denny?"

"Hm-m-m." It was rather unpleasant, at first glance. One might have expected an anatomical dummy in a medical school, but a child's doll—

The thing came apart in sections, skin, muscles, organs, miniature but quite perfect, as far as Paradine could see. He was interested. "Dunno. Such things haven't the same connotations to a kid—"

"Look at that liver. Is it a liver?"

"Sure. Say, I ... this is funny."

"What?"

"It isn't anatomically perfect, after all." Paradine pulled up a chair. "The digestive tract's too short. No large intestine. No appendix, either."

"Should Emma have a thing like this?"

"I wouldn't mind having it myself," Paradine said. "Where on earth did Harry pick it up? No, I don't see any harm in it. Adults are conditioned to react unpleasantly to innards. Kids don't. They figure they're solid inside, like a potato. Emma can get a sound working knowledge of physiology from this doll."

"But what are those? Nerves?"

"No, these are the nerves. Arteries here; veins here. Funny sort of aorta—" Paradine looked baffled. "That ... what's Latin for network? Anyway ... huh? *Rita? Rata?*"

"*Rales*," Jane suggested at random.

"That's a sort of breathing,"[1] Paradine said crushingly. "I can't figure out what this luminous network of stuff is. It goes all through the body, like nerves."

"Blood."

"Nope. Not circulatory, not neural—funny! It seems to be hooked up with the lungs."

They became engrossed, puzzling over the strange doll. It was made with remarkable perfection of detail, and that in itself was strange, in view of the physiological variation from the norm. "Wait'll I get that Gould,"[2] Paradine said, and presently was comparing the doll with anatomical charts. He learned little, except to increase his bafflement.

But it was more fun than a jigsaw puzzle.

Meanwhile, in the adjoining room, Emma was sliding the beads to and fro in the abacus. The motions didn't seem so strange now. Even when the beads vanished. She could almost follow that new direction—almost—

Scott panted, staring into the crystal cube and mentally directing, with

1 Paradine may be looking for the Latin word "rete," meaning "net." "Rales" in medicine refers to "An abnormal breath sound heard with the stethoscope [...] esp. a crackling or bubbling sound" (*OED*).

2 Likely a reference to *Gould's Medical Dictionary*, the fifth edition of which was published in 1941.

many false starts, the building of a structure somewhat more complicated than the one which had been destroyed by fire. He, too, was learning—being conditioned—

Paradine's mistake, from a completely anthropomorphic standpoint, was that he didn't get rid of the toys instantly. He did not realize their significance, and, by the time he did, the progression of circumstances had got well under way. Uncle Harry remained out of town, so Paradine couldn't check with him. Too, the midterm exams were on, which meant arduous mental effort and complete exhaustion at night; and Jane was slightly ill for a week or so. Emma and Scott had free rein with the toys.

"What," Scott asked his father one evening, "is a wabe, dad?"

"Wave?"

He hesitated. "I ... don't *think* so. Isn't wabe right?"

"Wab is Scot for web. That it?"

"I don't see how," Scott muttered, and wandered off, scowling, to amuse himself with the abacus. He was able to handle it quite deftly now. But, with the instinct of children for avoiding interruptions, he and Emma usually played with the toys in private. Not obviously, of course—but the more intricate experiments were never performed under the eye of an adult.

Scott was learning fast. What he now saw in the crystal cube had little relationship to the original simple problems. But they were fascinatingly technical. Had Scott realized that his education was being guided and supervised—though merely mechanically—he would probably have lost interest. As it was, his initiative was never quashed.

Abacus, cube, doll—and other toys the children found in the box—

Neither Paradine nor Jane guessed how much of an effect the contents of the time machine were having on the kids. How could they? Youngsters are instinctive dramatists, for purposes of self-protection. They have not yet fitted themselves to the exigencies—to them partially inexplicable—of a mature world. Moreover, their lives are complicated by human variables. They are told by one person that playing in the mud is permissible, but that, in their excavations, they must not uproot flowers or small trees. Another adult vetoes mud *per se*. The Ten Commandments[1] are not carved on stone; they vary, and children are helplessly dependent on the caprice of those who give them birth and feed and clothe them. And tyrannize. The young animal does not resent that benevolent tyranny, for it is an essential part of nature. He is, however, an individualist, and maintains his integrity by a subtle, passive fight.

Under the eyes of an adult he changes. Like an actor on-stage, when he remembers, he strives to please, and also to attract attention to himself. Such attempts are not unknown to maturity. But adults are less obvious—to other adults.

---

1 In Jewish and Christian traditions, the list of laws given by God to Moses.

It is difficult to admit that children lack subtlety. Children are different from the mature animal because they think in another way. We can more or less easily pierce the pretenses they set up—but they can do the same to us. Ruthlessly a child can destroy the pretenses of an adult. Iconoclasm is their prerogative.

Foppishness, for example. The amenities of social intercourse, exaggerated not quite to absurdity. The gigolo—

"Such *savoir faire!* Such punctilious courtesy!" The dowager and the blond young thing are often impressed. Men have less pleasant comments to make. But the child goes to the root of the matter.

"You're *silly!*"

How can an immature human understand the complicated system of social relationships? He can't. To him, an exaggeration of natural courtesy is silly. In his functional structure of life-patterns, it is rococo.[1] He is an egotistic little animal, who cannot visualize himself in the position of another—certainly not an adult. A self-contained, almost perfect natural unit, his wants supplied by others, the child is much like a unicellular creature floating in the blood stream, nutriment carried to him, waste products carried away—

From the standpoint of logic, a child is rather horribly perfect. A baby may be even more perfect, but so alien to an adult that only superficial standards of comparison apply. The thought processes of an infant are completely unimaginable. But babies think, even before birth. In the womb they move and sleep, not entirely through instinct. We are conditioned to react rather peculiarly to the idea that a nearly-viable embryo may think. We are surprised, shocked into laughter, and repelled. Nothing human is alien.[2]

But a baby is not human. An embryo is far less human.

That, perhaps, was why Emma learned more from the toys than did Scott. He could communicate his thoughts, of course; Emma could not, except in cryptic fragments. The matter of the scrawls, for example—

Give a young child pencil and paper, and he will draw something which looks different to him than to an adult. The absurd scribbles have little resemblance to a fire engine, but it *is* a fire engine, to a baby. Perhaps it is even three-dimensional. Babies think differently and see differently.

Paradine brooded over that, reading his paper one evening and watching Emma and Scott communicate. Scott was questioning his sister. Sometimes he did it in English. More often he had resource to gibberish and sign language. Emma tried to reply, but the handicap was too great.

Finally Scott got pencil and paper. Emma liked that. Tongue in cheek, she laboriously wrote a message. Scott took the paper, examined it, and scowled.

---

1 An eighteenth-century artistic and architectural style associated with significant, even excessive, decoration.

2 A shortened version of a Latin passage from the work of Roman playwright Terence (c. 195–c. 159 BCE): "Homo sum, humani nihil a me alienum puto": "I am man, nothing human is alien to me."

"That isn't right, Emma," he said.

Emma nodded vigorously. She seized the pencil again and made more scrawls. Scott puzzled for a while, finally smiled rather hesitantly, and got up. He vanished into the hall. Emma returned to the abacus.

Paradine rose and glanced down at the paper, with some mad thought that Emma might abruptly have mastered calligraphy. But she hadn't. The paper was covered with meaningless scrawls, of a type familiar to any parent. Paradine pursed his lips.

It might be a graph showing the mental variations of a manic-depressive cockroach, but probably wasn't. Still, it no doubt had meaning to Emma. Perhaps the scribble represented Mr. Bear.

Scott returned, looking pleased. He met Emma's gaze and nodded. Paradine felt a twinge of curiosity.

"Secrets?"

"Nope. Emma … uh … asked me to do something for her."

"Oh." Paradine, recalling instances of babies who had babbled in unknown tongues and baffled linguists, made a note to pocket the paper when the kids had finished with it. The next day he showed the scrawl to Elkins at the university. Elkins had a sound working knowledge of many unlikely languages, but he chuckled over Emma's venture into literature.

"Here's a free translation, Dennis. Quote. I don't know what this means, but I kid the hell out of my father with it. Unquote."

The two men laughed and went off to their classes. But later Paradine was to remember the incident. Especially after he met Holloway. Before that, however, months were to pass, and the situation to develop even further toward its climax.

Perhaps Paradine and Jane had evinced too much interest in the toys. Emma and Scott took to keeping them hidden, playing with them only in private. They never did it overtly, but with a certain unobtrusive caution. Nevertheless, Jane especially was somewhat troubled.

She spoke to Paradine about it one evening. "That doll Harry gave Emma."

"Yeah?"

"I was downtown today and tried to find out where it came from. No soap."

"Maybe Harry bought it in New York."

Jane was unconvinced. "I asked them about the other things, too. They showed me their stock—Johnson's a big store, you know. But there's nothing like Emma's abacus."

"Hm-m-m." Paradine wasn't much interested. They had tickets for a show that night, and it was getting late. So the subject was dropped for the nonce.

Later it cropped up again, when a neighbor telephoned Jane.

"Scotty's never been like that, Denny. Mrs. Burns said he frightened the devil out of her Francis."

"Francis? A little fat bully of a punk, isn't he? Like his father. I broke Burns' nose for him once, when we were sophomores."

"Stop boasting and listen," Jane said, mixing a highball. "Scott showed Francis something that scared him. Hadn't you better—"

"I suppose so." Paradine listened. Noises in the next room told him the whereabouts of his son. "Scotty!"

"Bang," Scott said, and appeared smiling. "I killed 'em all. Space pirates. You want me, dad?"

"Yes. If you don't mind leaving the space pirates unburied for a few minutes. What did you do to Francis Burns?"

Scott's blue eyes reflected incredible candor. "Huh?"

"Try hard. You can remember, I'm sure."

"Uh. Oh, that. I didn't do nothing."

"Anything," Jane corrected absently.

"Anything. Honest, I just let him look into my television set, and it … it scared him."

"Television set?"

Scott produced the crystal cube. "It isn't really that. See?"

Paradine examined the gadget, startled by the magnification. All he could see, though, was a maze of meaningless colored designs.

"Uncle Harry—"

Paradine reached for the telephone. Scott gulped. "Is … is Uncle Harry back in town?"

"Yeah."

"Well, I gotta take a bath." Scott headed for the door. Paradine met Jane's gaze and nodded significantly.

Harry was home, but disclaimed all knowledge of the peculiar toys. Rather grimly, Paradine requested Scott to bring down from his room all of the playthings. Finally they lay in a row on the table, cube, abacus, doll, helmetlike cap, several other mysterious contraptions. Scott was cross-examined. He lied valiantly for a time, but broke down at last and bawled, hiccupping his confession.

"Get the box these things came in," Paradine ordered. "Then head for bed."

"Are you … *hup!* … gonna punish me daddy?"

"For playing hooky and lying, yes. You know the rules. No more shows for two weeks. No sodas for the same period."

Scott gulped. "You gonna keep my things?"

"I don't know yet."

"Well … g'night, daddy. G'night, mom."

After the small figure had gone upstairs, Paradine dragged a chair to the table and carefully scrutinized the box. He poked thoughtfully at the fused gadgetry. Jane watched.

"What is it, Denny?"

"Dunno. Who'd leave a box of toys down by the creek?"

"It might have fallen out of a car."

"Not at that point. The road doesn't hit the creek north of the railroad trestle. Empty lots—nothing else." Paradine lit a cigarette. "Drink, honey?"

"I'll fix it." Jane went to work, her eyes troubled. She brought Paradine a glass and stood behind him, ruffling his hair with her fingers. "Is anything wrong?"

"Of course not. Only—where did these toys come from?"

"Johnsons's didn't know, and they get their stock from New York."

"I've been checking up, too," Paradine admitted. "That doll"—he poked it—"rather worried me. Custom jobs, maybe, but I wish I knew who'd made 'em."

"A psychologist? That abacus—don't they give people tests with such things?"

Paradine snapped his fingers. "Right! And say! There's a guy going to speak at the university next week, fellow named Holloway, who's a child psychologist. He's a big shot, with quite a reputation. He might know something about it."

"Holloway? I don't—"

"Rex Holloway. He's … hm-m-m! He doesn't live far from here. Do you suppose he might have had these things made himself?"

Jane was examining the abacus. She grimaced and drew back. "If he did, I don't like him. But see if you can find out, Denny."

Paradine nodded. "I shall."

He drank his highball, frowning. He was vaguely worried. But he wasn't scared—yet.

Rex Holloway was a fat, shiny man, with a bald head and thick spectacles, above which his thick, black brows lay like bushy caterpillars. Paradine brought him home to dinner one night a week later. Holloway did not appear to watch the children, but nothing they did or said was lost on him. His gray eyes, shred and bright, missed little.

The toys fascinated him. In the living room the three adults gathered around the table, where the playthings had been placed. Holloway studied them carefully as he listened to what Jane and Paradine had to say. At last he broke his silence.

"I'm glad I came here tonight. But not completely. This is very disturbing, you know."

"Eh?" Paradine stared, and Jane's face showed her consternation. Holloway's next words did not calm them.

"We are dealing with madness."

He smiled at the shocked looks they gave him. "All children are mad, from an adult viewpoint. Ever read Hughes' 'High Wind in Jamaica'?"[1]

"I've got it." Paradine secured the little book from its shelf. Holloway

1 A 1929 novel by Richard Hughes, in which children are kidnapped by pirates. The quotation that follows is verbatim from the novel, with minor punctuation differences.

extended a hand, took it, and flipped the pages till he had found the place he wanted. He read aloud:

"'Babies of course are not human—they are animals, and have a very ancient and ramified culture, as cats have, and fishes, and even snakes; the same in kind as these, but much more complicated and vivid, since babies are, after all, one of the most developed species of the lower vertebrates. In short, babies have minds which work in terms and categories of their own which cannot be translated into the terms and categories of the human mind.'"

Jane tried to take that calmly, but couldn't. "You don't mean that Emma—"

"Could you think like your daughter?" Holloway asked. "Listen: 'One can no more think like a baby than one can think like a bee.'"

Paradine mixed drinks. Over his shoulder he said, "You're theorizing quite a bit, aren't you? As I get it, you're implying that babies have a culture of their own, even a high standard of intelligence."

"Not necessarily. There's no yardstick, you see. All I say is that babies think in other ways than we do. Not necessarily *better*—that's a question of relative values. But with a different manner of extension—" He sought for the words, grimacing.

"Fantasy," Paradine said, rather rudely, but annoyed because of Emma. "Babies don't have different senses from ours."

"Who said they did?" Holloway demanded. "They use their minds in a different way, that's all. But it's quite enough!"

"I'm trying to understand," Jane said slowly. "All I can think of is my Mixmaster. It can whip up batter and potatoes, but it can squeeze oranges, too."[1]

"Something like that. The brain's a colloid, a very complicated machine. We don't know much about its potentialities. We don't even know how much it can grasp. But it *is* known that the mind becomes conditioned as the human animal matures. It follows certain familiar theorems, and all thought thereafter is pretty well based on patterns taken for granted. Look at this." Holloway touched the abacus. "Have you experimented with it?"

"A little," Paradine said.

"But not much. Eh?"

"Well—"

"Why not?"

"It's pointless," Paradine complained. "Even a puzzle has to have some logic. But those crazy angles—"

"Your mind has been conditioned to Euclid," Holloway said. "So this—thing—bores us, and seems pointless. But a child knows nothing of Euclid. A different sort of geometry from ours wouldn't impress him as being illogical. He believes what he sees."

---

1 The Mixmaster kitchen mixer appliance, introduced in 1930 by what would become the Sunbeam Products company, was known especially for the many attachments you could add to it.

"Are you trying to tell me that this gadget's got a fourth-dimensional extension?" Paradine demanded.

"Not visually, anyway," Holloway denied. "All I say is that our minds, conditioned to Euclid, can see nothing in this but an illogical tangle of wires. But a child—especially a baby—might see more. Not at first. It'd be a puzzle, of course. Only a child wouldn't be handicapped by too many preconceived ideas."

"Hardening of the thought-arteries," Jane interjected.

Paradine was not convinced. "Then a baby could work calculus better than Einstein? No, I don't mean that. I can see your point, more or less clearly. Only—"

"Well, look. Let's suppose there are two kinds of geometry—we'll limit it, for the sake of the example. Our kind, Euclidean, and another, which we'll call *x*. *X* hasn't much relationship to Euclid. It's based on different theorems. Two and two needn't equal four in it; they could equal y^2, or they might not even *equal*. A baby's mind is not yet conditioned, except by certain questionable factors of heredity and environment. Start the infant on Euclid—"

"Poor kid," Jane said.

Holloway shot her a quick glance. "The basis of Euclid. Alphabet blocks. Math, geometry, algebra—they come much later. We're familiar with that development. On the other hand, start the baby with the basic principles of our *x* logic."

"Blocks? What kind?"

Holloway looked at the abacus. "It wouldn't make much sense to us. But we've been conditioned to Euclid."

Paradine poured himself a stiff shot of whiskey. "That's pretty awful. You're not limiting to math."

"Right! I'm not limiting it at all. How can I? I'm not conditioned to *x* logic."

"There's the answer," Jane said, with a sigh of relief. "Who is? It'd take such a person to make the sort of toys you apparently think these are."

Holloway nodded, his eyes, behind the thick lenses, blinking. "Such people may exist."

"Where?"

"They might prefer to keep hidden."

"Supermen?"

"I wish I knew. You see, Paradine, we've got yardstick trouble again. By our standards these people might seem super-doopers in certain respects. In others they might seem moronic. It's not a quantitative difference; it's qualitative. They *think* different. And I'm sure we can do things they can't."

"Maybe they wouldn't want to," Jane said.

Paradine tapped the fused gadgetry on the box. "What about this? It implies—"

"A purpose, sure."

"Transportation?"

"One thinks of that first. If so, the box might have come from anywhere."

"Where—things are—*different?*" Paradine asked slowly.

"Exactly. In space, or even time. I don't know; I'm a psychologist. Unfortunately I'm conditioned to Euclid, too."

"Funny place it must be," Jane said. "Denny, get rid of those toys."

"I intend to."

Holloway picked up the crystal cube. "Did you question the children much?"

Paradine said, "Yeah. Scott said there were people in that cube when he first looked. I asked him what was in it now."

"What did he say?" The psychologist's eyes widened.

"He said they were building a place. His exact words. I asked him who—people? But he couldn't explain."

"No, I suppose not," Holloway muttered. "It must be progressive. How long have the children had these toys?"

"About three months, I guess."

"Time enough. The perfect toy, you see, is both instructive and mechanical. It should do things, to interest a child, and it should teach, preferably unobtrusively. Simple problems at first. Later—"

"*X* logic," Jane said, white-faced.

Paradine cursed under his breath. "Emma and Scott are perfectly normal!"

"Do you know how their minds work—now?"

Holloway didn't pursue the thought. He fingered the doll. "It would be interesting to know the conditions of the place where these things came from. Induction doesn't help a great deal, though. Too many factors are missing. We can't visualize a world based on the *x* factor—environment adjusted to minds thinking in *x* patterns. This luminous network inside the doll. It could be anything. It could exist inside us, though we haven't discovered it yet. When we find the right stain—" He shrugged. "What do you make of this?"

It was a crimson globe, two inches in diameter, with a protruding knob upon its surface.

"What could anyone make of it?"

"Scott? Emma?"

"I hadn't even seen it till about three weeks ago. Then Emma started to play with it." Paradine nibbled his lip. "After that, Scott got interested."

"Just what do they do?"

"Hold it up in front of them and move it back and forth. No particular pattern of motion."

"No Euclidean pattern," Holloway corrected. "At first they couldn't understand the toy's purpose. They had to be educated up to it."

"That's horrible," Jane said.

"Not to them. Emma is probably quicker at understanding *x* than Scott, for her mind isn't yet conditioned to this environment."

Paradine said, "But I can remember plenty of things I did as a child. Even as a baby."

"Well?"

"Was I—mad—then?"

"The things you don't remember are the criterion of your madness," Holloway retorted. "But I use the word 'madness' purely as a convenient symbol for the variation from the known human norm. The arbitrary standard of sanity."

Jane put down her glass. "You've said that induction was difficult, Mr. Holloway. But it seems to me you're making a great deal of it from very little. After all, these toys—"

"I am a psychologist, and I've specialized in children. I'm not a layman. These toys mean a great deal to me, chiefly because they mean so little."

"You might be wrong."

"Well, I rather hope I am. I'd like to examine the children."

Jane rose in alarm. "How?"

After Holloway had explained, she nodded, though still a bit hesitantly. "Well, that's all right. But they're not guinea pigs."

The psychologist patted the air with a plump hand. "My dear girl! I'm not a Frankenstein.[1] To me the individual is the prime factor—naturally, since I work with minds. If there's anything wrong with the youngsters, I want to cure them."

Paradine put down his cigarette and slowly watched blue smoke spiral up, wavering in an unfelt draft. "Can you give a prognosis?"

"I'll try. That's all I can say. If the undeveloped minds have been turned into the *x* channel, it's necessary to divert them back. I'm not saying that's the wisest thing to do, but it probably is from our standards. After all, Emma and Scott will have to live in this world."

"Yeah. Yeah. I can't believe there's much wrong. They seem about average, thoroughly normal."

"Superficially they may seem so. They've no reason for acting abnormally, have they? And how can you tell if they—think differently?"

"I'll call 'em," Paradine said.

"Make it informal, then. I don't want them to be on guard."

Jane nodded toward the toys. Holloway said, "Leave the stuff there, eh?"

But the psychologist, after Emma and Scott were summoned, made no immediate move at direct questioning. He managed to draw Scott unobtrusively into the conversation, dropping key words now and then. Nothing so obvious as a word-association test—co-operation is necessary for that.

The most interesting development occurred when Holloway took up the abacus. "Mind showing me how this works?"

1 Victor Frankenstein from Mary Wollstonecraft Shelley's novel *Frankenstein; or, the Modern Prometheus* (1818).

Scott hesitated. "Yes, sir. Like this—" He slid a bead deftly through the maze, in a tangled course, so swiftly that no one was quite sure whether or not it ultimately vanished. It might have been merely legerdemain. Then, again—

Holloway tried. Scott watched, wrinkling his nose.

"That right?'

"Uh-huh. It's gotta go *there*—"

"Here? Why?"

"Well, that's the only way to make it work."

But Holloway was conditioned to Euclid. There was no apparent reason why the bead should slide from this particular wire to the other. It looked like a random factor. Also, Holloway suddenly noticed, this wasn't the path the bead had taken previously, when Scott had worked the puzzle. At least, as well as he could tell.

"Will you show me again?"

Scott did, and twice more, on request. Holloway blinked through his glasses. Random, yes. And a variable. Scott moved the bead along a different course each time.

Somehow, none of the adults could tell whether or not the bead vanished. If they had expected to see it disappear, their reactions might have been different.

In the end nothing was solved. Holloway, as he said good night, seemed ill at ease.

"May I come again?"

"I wish you would," Jane told him. "Any time. You still think—"

He nodded. "The children's minds are not reacting normally. They're not dull at all, but I've the most extraordinary impression that they arrive at conclusions in a way we don't understand. As though they used algebra while we used geometry. The same conclusion, but a different method of reaching it."

"What about the toys?" Paradine asked suddenly.

"Keep them out of the way. I'd like to borrow them, if I may—"

That night Paradine slept badly. Holloway's parallel had been ill-chosen. It led to disturbing theories. The *x* factor— The children were using the equivalent of algebraic reasoning, while adults used geometry.

Fair enough. Only—

Algebra can give you answers that geometry cannot, since there are certain terms and symbols which cannot be expressed geometrically. Suppose *x* logic showed conclusions inconceivable to an adult mind?

"Damn!" Paradine whispered. Jane stirred beside him.

"Dear? Can't you sleep either?"

"No." He got up and went into the next room. Emma slept peacefully as a cherub,[1] her fat arm curled around Mr. Bear. Through the open doorway Paradine could see Scott's dark head motionless on the pillow.

---

1 A form of angel, often represented in Christian art as a baby or very young child with wings.

Jane was beside him. He slipped his arm around her.

"Poor little people," she murmured. "And Holloway called them mad. I think we're the ones who are crazy, Dennis."

"Uh-huh. We've got jitters."

Scott stirred in his sleep. Without awakening, he called what was obviously a question, though it did not seem to be in any particular language. Emma gave a little mewling cry that changed pitch sharply.

She had not wakened. The children lay without stirring.

But Paradine thought, with a sudden sickness in his middle, it was exactly as though Scott had asked Emma something, and she had replied.

Had their minds changed so that even—sleep—was different to them?

He thrust the thought away. "You'll catch cold. Let's get back to bed. Want a drink?"

"I think I do," Jane said, watching Emma. Her hand reached out blindly toward the child; she drew it back. "Come on. We'll wake the kids."

They drank a little brandy together, but said nothing. Jane cried in her sleep, later.

Scott was not awake, but his mind worked in slow, careful building. Thus—

"They'll take the toys away. The fat man ... listava dangerous maybe. But the Ghoric direction won't show ... evankrus dun hasn't-them. Intransdection ... bright and shiny. Emma. She's more khopranik-high now than ... I still don't see how to ... thavarar lixery dist—"

A little of Scott's thoughts could still be understood. But Emma had become conditioned to *x* much faster.

She was thinking, too.

Not like an adult or a child. Not even like a human. Except, perhaps, a human of a type shockingly unfamiliar to *genus homo*.

Sometimes Scott himself had difficulty in following her thoughts.

If it had not been for Holloway, life might have settled back into an almost normal routine. The toys were no longer active reminders. Emma still enjoyed her dolls and sand pile, with a thoroughly explicable delight. Scott was satisfied with baseball and his chemical set. They did everything other children did, and evinced few, if any, flashes of abnormality. But Holloway seemed to be an alarmist.

He was having the toys tested, with rather idiotic results. He drew endless charts and diagrams, corresponded with mathematicians, engineers, and other psychologists, and went quietly crazy trying to find rhyme or reason in the construction of the gadgets. The box itself, with its cryptic machinery, told nothing. Fusing had melted too much of the stuff into slag. But the toys—

It was the random element that baffled investigation. Even that was a matter of semantics. For Holloway was convinced that it wasn't really random. There just weren't enough known factors. No adult could work the abacus, for example. And Holloway thoughtfully refrained from letting a child play with the thing.

The crystal cube was similarly cryptic. It showed a mad pattern of colors, which sometimes moved. In this it resembled a kaleidoscope. But the shifting of balance and gravity didn't affect it. Again the random factor.

Or, rather, the unknown. The *x* pattern. Eventually Paradine and Jane slipped back into something like complacence, with a feeling that the children had been cured of their mental quirk, now that the contributing cause had been removed. Certain of the actions of Emma and Scott gave them every reason to quit worrying.

For the kids enjoyed swimming, hiking, movies, games, the normal functional toys of this particular time-sector. It was true that they failed to master certain rather puzzling mechanical devices which involved some calculation. A three-dimensional jigsaw globe Paradine had picked up, for example. But he found that difficult himself.

Once in a while there were lapses. Scott was hiking with his father one Saturday afternoon, and the two had paused at the summit of a hill. Beneath them a rather lovely valley was spread.

"Pretty, isn't it?" Paradine remarked.

Scott examined the scene gravely. "It's all wrong," he said.

"Eh?"

"I dunno."

"What's wrong about it?

"Gee—" Scott lapsed into puzzled silence. "I dunno."

The children had missed their toys, but not for long. Emma recovered first, though Scott still moped. He held unintelligible conversations with his sister, and studied meaningless scrawls she drew on paper he supplied. It was almost as though he was consulting her, anent difficult problems beyond his grasp.

If Emma understood more, Scott had more real intelligence, and manipulatory skill as well. He built a gadget with his Meccano set, but was dissatisfied. The apparent cause of his dissatisfaction was exactly why Paradine was relieved when he viewed the structure. It was the sort of thing a normal boy would make, vaguely reminiscent of a cubistic ship.

It was a bit too normal to please Scott. He asked Emma more questions, though in private. She thought for a time, and then made more scrawls with an awkwardly clutched pencil.

"Can you read that stuff?" Jane asked her son one morning.

"Not read it, exactly. I can tell what she means. Not all the time, but mostly."

"Is it writing?"

"N-no. It doesn't mean what it *looks* like."

"Symbolism," Paradine suggested over his coffee.

Jane looked at him, her eyes widening. "Denny—"

He winked and shook his head. Later, when they were alone, he said,

"Don't let Holloway upset you. I'm not implying the kids are corresponding in an unknown tongue. If Emma draws a squiggle and says it's a flower, that's an arbitrary rule—Scott remembers that. Next time she draws the same sort of squiggle, or tries to—well!"

"Sure," Jane said doubtfully. "Have you noticed Scott's been doing a lot of reading lately?"

"I noticed. Nothing unusual, though. No Kant or Spinoza."

"He browses, that's all."

"Well, so did I, at his age," Paradine said, and went off to his morning classes. He lunched with Holloway, which was becoming a daily habit, and spoke of Emma's literary endeavors.

"Was I right about symbolism, Rex?"

The psychologist nodded. "Quite right. Our own language is nothing but arbitrary symbolism now. At least in its application. Look here." On his napkin he drew a very narrow ellipse. "What's that?"

"You mean what does it represent?"

"Yes. What does it suggest to you? It could be a crude representation of—what?"

"Plenty of things," Paradine said. "Rim of a glass. A fried egg. A loaf of French bread. A cigar."

Holloway added a little triangle to his drawing, apex joined to one end of the ellipse. He looked up at Paradine.

"A fish," the latter said instantly.

"Our familiar symbol for a fish. Even without fins, eyes or mouth, it's recognizable, because we've been conditioned to identify this particular shape with our mental picture of a fish. The basis of a rebus.[1] A symbol, to us, means a lot more than what we actually see on paper. What's in your mind when you look at this sketch?"

"Why—a fish."

"Keep going. What do you visualize—everything!"

"Scales," Paradine said slowly, looking into space. "Water. Foam. A fish's eye. The fins. The colors."

"So the symbol represents a lot more than just the abstract idea *fish*. Note the connotation's that of a noun, not a verb. It's harder to express actions by symbolism, you know. Anyway—reverse the process. Suppose you want to make a symbol for some concrete noun, say *bird*. Draw it."

Paradine drew two connected arcs, concavities down.

"The lowest common denominator," Holloway nodded. "The natural tendency is to simplify. Especially when a child is seeing something for the first time and has few standards of comparison. He tries to identify the new thing with what's already familiar to him. Ever notice how a child draws the ocean?" He didn't wait for an answer; he went on.

1 A puzzle in which words or whole phrases are represented by a picture combined with a letter.

"A series of jagged points. Like the oscillating line on a seismograph. When I first saw the Pacific, I was about three. I remember it pretty clearly. It looked—tilted. A flat plain, slanted at an angle. The waves were regular triangles, apex upward. Now I didn't *see* them stylized that way, but later, remembering, I had to find some familiar standard of comparison. Which is the only way of getting any conception of an entirely new thing. The average child tries to draw these regular triangles, but his co-ordination's poor. He gets a seismograph pattern."

"All of which means what?"

"A child sees the ocean. He stylizes it. He draws a certain definite pattern, symbolic, to him, of the sea. Emma's scrawls may be symbols, too. I don't mean that the world looks different to her—brighter, perhaps, and sharper, more vivid and with a slackening of perception above her eye level. What I do mean is that her thought-processes are different, that she translates what she sees into abnormal symbols."

"You still believe—"

"Yes, I do. Her mind has been conditioned unusually. It may be that she breaks down what she sees into simple, obvious patterns—and realizes a significance to those patterns that we can't understand. Like the abacus. She saw a pattern in that, though to us it was completely random."

Paradine abruptly decided to taper off these luncheon engagements with Holloway. The man was an alarmist. His theories were growing more fantastic than ever, and he dragged in anything, applicable or not, that would support them.

Rather sardonically he said, "Do you mean Emma's communicating with Scott in an unknown language?"

"In symbols for which she hasn't any words. I'm sure Scott understands a great deal of those—scrawls. To him, an isosceles triangle may represent any factor, though probably a concrete noun. Would a man who knew nothing of algebra understand what H_2O meant? Would he realize that the symbol could evoke a picture of the ocean?"

Paradine didn't answer. Instead, he mentioned to Holloway Scott's curious remark that the landscape, from the hill, had looked all wrong. A moment later, he was inclined to regret his impulse, for the psychologist was off again.

"Scott's thought-patterns are building up to a sum that doesn't equal this world. Perhaps he's subconsciously expecting to see the world where those toys came from."

Paradine stopped listening. Enough was enough. The kids were getting along all right, and the only remaining disturbing factor was Holloway himself. That night, however, Scott evinced an interest, later significant, in eels.

There was nothing apparently harmful in natural history. Paradine explained about eels.

"But where do they lay their eggs? Or do they?"

"That's still a mystery. Their spawning grounds are unknown. Maybe the Sargasso Sea, or the deeps, where the pressure can help them force the young out of their bodies."

"Funny," Scott said, thinking deeply.

"Salmon do the same thing, more or less. They go up rivers to spawn." Paradine went into detail. Scott was fascinated.

"But that's *right*, dad. They're born in the river, and when they learn how to swim, they go down to the sea. And they come back to lay their eggs, huh?"

"Right."

"Only, they wouldn't *come* back," Scott pondered. "They'd just send their eggs—"

"It'd take a very long ovipositor," Paradine said, and vouchsafed some well-chosen remarks upon oviparity.

His son wasn't entirely satisfied. Flowers, he contended, sent their seeds long distances.

"They don't guide them. Not many find fertile soil."

"Flowers haven't got brains, though. Dad, why do people live *here*?"

"Glendale?"

"No—*here*. This whole place. It isn't all there is, I bet."

"Do you mean the other planets?"

Scott was hesitant. "This is only—part—of the big place. It's like the river where the salmon go. Why don't people go on down to the ocean when they grow up?"

Paradine realized that Scott was speaking figuratively. He felt a brief chill. The—ocean?

The young of the species are not conditioned to live in the completer world of their parents. Having developed sufficiently, they enter that world. Later they breed. The fertilized eggs are buried in the sand, far up the river, where later they hatch.

And they learn. Instinct alone is fatally slow. Especially in the case of a specialized genus, unable to cope even with this world, unable to feed or drink or survive, unless someone has foresightedly provided for those needs.

The young, fed and tended, would survive. There would be incubators and robots. They would survive, but they would not know how to swim downstream, to the vaster world of the ocean.

So they must be taught. They must be trained and conditioned in many ways.

Painlessly, subtly, unobtrusively. Children love toys that do things—and if those toys teach at the same time—

In the latter half of the nineteenth century an Englishman sat on a grassy bank near a stream. A very small girl lay near him, staring up at the sky. She had discarded a curious toy with which she had been playing, and now was murmuring a wordless little song, to which the man listened with half an ear.

"What was that, my dear?" he asked at last.

"Just something I made up, Uncle Charles."

"Sing it again." He pulled out a notebook.

The girl obeyed.

"Does it mean anything?"

She nodded. "Oh, yes. Like the stories I tell you, you know."

"They're wonderful stories, dear."

"And you'll put them in a book some day?"

"Yes, but I must change them quite a lot, or no one would understand. But I don't think I'll change your little song."

"You mustn't. If you did, it wouldn't mean anything."

"I won't change that stanza, anyway," he promised. "Just what does it mean?"

"It's the way out, I think," the girl said doubtfully. "I'm not sure yet. My magic toys told me."

"I wish I knew what London shop sold those marvelous toys!"

"Mamma bought them for me. She's dead. Papa doesn't care."

She lied. She had found the toys in a box one day, as she played by the Thames. And they were indeed wonderful.

Her little song— Uncle Charles thought it didn't mean anything. (He wasn't her real uncle, she parenthesized. But he was nice.) The song meant a great deal. It was the way. Presently she would do what it said, and then—

But she was already too old. She never found the way.

Paradine had dropped Holloway. Jane had taken a dislike to him, naturally enough, since what she wanted most of all was to have her fears calmed. Since Scott and Emma acted normally now, Jane felt satisfied. It was partly wishful-thinking, to which Paradine could not entirely subscribe.

Scott kept bringing gadgets to Emma for her approval. Usually she'd shake her head. Sometimes she would look doubtful. Very occasionally she would signify agreement. Then there would be an hour of laborious, crazy scribbling on scraps of note paper, and Scott, after studying the notations, would arrange and rearrange his rocks, bits of machinery, candle ends, and assorted junk. Each day the maid cleaned them away, and each day Scott began again.

He condescended to explain a little to his puzzled father, who could see no rhyme or reason in the game.

"But why this pebble right here?"

"It's hard and round, dad. It *belongs* there."

"So is this one hard and round."

"Well, that's got vaseline on it. When you get that far, you can't *see* just a hard round thing."

"What comes next? This candle?"

Scott looked disgusted. "That's toward the end. The iron ring's next."

It was, Paradine thought, like a Scout trail through the woods, markers in a labyrinth. But here again was the random factor. Logic halted—familiar logic—as Scott's motives in arranging the junk as he did.

Paradine went out. Over his shoulder he saw Scott pull a crumpled piece of paper and a pencil from his pocket, and head for Emma, who was squatted in a corner thinking things over.

Well—

Jane was lunching with Uncle Harry, and, on this hot Sunday afternoon, there was little to do but read the papers. Paradine settled himself in the coolest place he could find, with a Collins, and lost himself in the comic strips.

An hour later a clatter of feet upstairs roused him from his doze. Scott's voice was crying exultantly, "This is it, Slug! Come on—"

Paradine stood up quickly, frowning. As he went into the hall the telephone began to ring. Jane had promised to call—

His hand was on the receiver when Emma's faint voice squealed with excitement. Paradine grimaced. What the devil was going on upstairs?

Scott shrieked, "Look out! This way!"

Paradine, his mouth working, his nerves ridiculously tense, forgot the phone and raced up the stairs. The door of Scott's room was open.

The children were vanishing.

They went in fragments, like thick smoke in a wind, or like movement in a distorting mirror. Hand in hand they went, in a direction Paradine could not understand, and as he blinked there on the threshold, they were gone.

"Emma!" he said, dry-throated. "*Scotty!*"

On carpet lay a pattern of markers, pebbles, an iron ring—junk. A random pattern. A crumpled sheet of paper blew towards Paradine.

He picked it up automatically.

"Kids. Where are you? Don't hide—"

"*Emma! SCOTTY!*"

Downstairs the telephone stopped its shrill, monotonous ringing. Paradine looked at the paper he held.

It was a leaf torn from a book. There were interlineations and marginal notes, in Emma's meaningless scrawl. A stanza of verse had been so underlined and scribbled over that it was almost illegible, but Paradine was thoroughly familiar with "Through the Looking Glass." His memory gave him the words—

'Twas brillig, and the slithy toves
  Did gyre and gimbel in the wabe.
All mimsy were the borogoves,
  And the mome raths outgrabe.[1]

1 From the poem "Jabberwocky," by Lewis Carroll, which originally appeared in his novel *Through the Looking-Glass* (1871), a sequel to *Alice in Wonderland* (1865). The character Humpty Dumpty later offers Alice an explanation, of sorts, of the poem's nonsense words.

Idiotically he thought: Humpty Dumpty explained it. A wabe is the plot of grass around a sundial. A sundial. Time— It has something to do with time. A long time ago Scotty asked me what a wabe was. Symbolism.

'Twas brillig—

A perfect mathematical formula, giving all the conditions, in symbolism the children had finally understood. The junk on the floor. The toves had to be made slithy—vaseline?—and they had to be placed in a certain relationship, so that they'd gyre and gimbel.

Lunacy!

But it had not been lunacy to Emma and Scott. They thought differently. They used *x* logic. Those notes Emma had made on the page—she'd translated Carroll's words into symbols both she and Scott could understand.

The random factor had made sense to the children. They had fulfilled the conditions of the time-span equation. *And the mome raths outgrabe—*

Paradine made a rather ghastly little sound, deep in his throat. He looked at the crazy pattern on the carpet. If he could follow it, as the kids had done—but he couldn't. The pattern was senseless. The random factor defeated him. He was conditioned to Euclid.

Even if he went insane, he still couldn't do it. It would be the wrong kind of lunacy.

His mind had stopped working now. But in a moment the stasis of incredulous horror would pass— Paradine crumpled the page in his fingers. "Emma, Scotty," he called in a dead voice, as though he could expect no response.

Sunlight slanted through the open windows, brightening the golden pelt of Mr. Bear. Downstairs the ringing of the telephone began again.

Ray Bradbury (1920–2012)

One of the best-known and prolific mid-twentieth-century SF authors, Ray Bradbury was influenced by the pulps of the previous generation, but he expanded on them with more explicit social and political commentary, thus arguably setting the stage for later New Wave writers. He is perhaps best known for his anti-censorship novel *Fahrenheit 451* (1953)—a book that was itself banned in different jurisdictions and partially censored in some editions by its publisher, Ballantine.

Note on the text: This story appeared in different versions in 1950, including one in *Collier's Magazine* (6 May 1950) and the version used here, from *The Martian Chronicles*, a collection of stories or a "fix-up" novel (in which stories were stitched together into a longer work). In the *Collier's* version, the story takes place on the 28th and 29th of April 1985 in an unspecified city, rather than 4th and 5th of August 2026 in Allendale, CA, and includes a two-paragraph description of the construction of the house and of the nuclear war, along with other differences throughout. The first two paragraphs in the *Collier's* version are as follows:

> The house was a good house and had been planned and built by the people who were to live in it, in the year 1980. The house was like many another house in that year; it fed and slept and entertained its inhabitants, and made a good life for them. The man and wife and their two children lived at ease there, and lived happily, even while the world trembled. All of the fine things of living, the warm things, music and poetry, books that talked, beds that warmed and made themselves, fires that built themselves in the fireplaces of evenings, were in this house, and living there was a contentment.
>
> And then one day the world shook and there was an explosion followed by ten thousand explosions and red fire in the sky and a rain of ashes and radioactivity, and the happy time was over.

"There Will Come Soft Rains" (1950)[1]

In the living room the voice-clock sang, *Tick-tock, seven o'clock, time to get up, time to get up, seven o'clock!* as if it were afraid nobody would. The morning house lay empty. The clock ticked on, repeating and repeating its sounds into the emptiness. *Seven-nine, breakfast time, seven-nine!*

In the kitchen the breakfast stove gave a hissing sigh and ejected from its

1 The stories in *The Martian Chronicles* take place between January 1999 and October 2026, with the month and year preceding the title of each story. This story is preceded by "August 2026."

warm interior eight pieces of perfectly browned toast, eight eggs sunnyside up, sixteen slices of bacon, two coffees, and two cool glasses of milk.

"Today is August 4, 2026," said a second voice from the kitchen ceiling, "in the city of Allendale, California." It repeated the date three times for memory's sake. "Today is Mr. Featherstone's birthday. Today is the anniversary of Tilita's marriage. Insurance is payable, as are the water, gas, and light bills."

Somewhere in the walls, relays clicked, memory tapes glided under electric eyes.

Eight-one, tick-tock, eight-one o'clock, off to school, off to work, run, run, eight-one! But no doors slammed, no carpets took the soft tread of rubber heels. It was raining outside. The weather box on the front door sang quietly: "Rain, rain, go away; rubbers, raincoats for today ..." And the rain tapped on the empty house, echoing.

Outside, the garage chimed and lifted its door to reveal the waiting car. After a long wait the door swung down again.

At eight-thirty the eggs were shriveled and the toast was like stone. An aluminum wedge scraped them into the sink, where hot water whirled them down a metal throat which digested and flushed them away to the distant sea. The dirty dishes were dropped into a hot washer and emerged twinkling dry.

Nine-fifteen, sang the clock, time to clean.

Out of warrens in the wall, tiny robot mice darted. The rooms were acrawl with the small cleaning animals, all rubber and metal. They thudded against chairs, whirling their mustached runners, kneading the rug nap, sucking gently at hidden dust. Then, like mysterious invaders, they popped into their burrows. Their pink electric eyes faded. The house was clean.

Ten o'clock. The sun came out from behind the rain. The house stood alone in a city of rubble and ashes. This was the one house left standing. At night the ruined city gave off a radioactive glow which could be seen for miles.

Ten-fifteen. The garden sprinklers whirled up in golden founts, filling the soft morning air with scatterings of brightness. The water pelted windowpanes, running down the charred west side where the house had been burned evenly free of its white paint. The entire west face of the house was black, save for five places. Here the silhouette in paint of a man mowing a lawn. Here, as in a photograph, a woman bent to pick flowers. Still farther over, their images burned on wood in one titanic instant, a small boy, hands flung into the air; higher up, the image of thrown ball, and opposite him a girl, hands raised to catch a ball which never came down.

The five spots of paint—the man, the woman, the children, the ball—remained. The rest was a thin charcoaled layer.[1]

---

1 On 6 August 1945, the US dropped an atomic bomb on Hiroshima, Japan, followed by another in Nagasaki on 9 August. In the aftermath of the immense destruction caused by these weapons, "shadows" of objects and of people were found. These shadows were created by the objects and people's bodies blocking the surface behind them from some of the radiation and heat of the explosion.

The gentle sprinkler rain filled the garden with falling light.

Until this day, how well the house had kept its peace. How carefully it had inquired, "Who goes there? What's the password?" and, getting no answer from the lonely foxes and whining cats, it had shut up its windows and drawn shades in an old-maidenly preoccupation with self-protection which bordered on a mechanical paranoia.

It quivered at each sound, the house did. If a sparrow brushed a window, the shade snapped up. The bird, startled, flew off! No, not even a bird must touch the house!

The house was an altar with ten thousand attendants, big, small, servicing, attending, in choirs. But the gods had gone away, and the ritual of the religion continued senselessly, uselessly.

Twelve noon.

A dog whined, shivering, on the front porch.

The front door recognized the dog voice and opened. The dog, once large and fleshy, but now gone to bone and covered with sores, moved in and through the house, tracking mud. Behind it whirred angry mice, angry at having to pick up mud, angry at inconvenience.

For not a leaf fragment blew under the door but what the wall panels flipped open and the copper scrap rats flashed swiftly out. The offending dust, hair, or paper, seized in miniature steel jaws, was raced back to the burrows. There, down tubes which fed into the cellar, it was dropped into the sighing vent of an incinerator which sat like evil Baal[1] in a dark corner.

The dog ran upstairs, hysterically yelping to each door, at last realizing, as the house realized, that only silence was here.

It sniffed the air and scratched the kitchen door. Behind the door, the stove was making pancakes which filled the house with a rich baked odor and the scent of maple syrup.

The dog frothed at the mouth, lying at the door, sniffing, its eyes turned to fire. It ran wildly in circles, biting at its tail, spun in a frenzy, and died. It lay in the parlor for an hour.

Two o'clock, sang a voice.

Delicately sensing decay at last, the regiments of mice hummed out as softly as blown gray leaves in an electrical wind.

Two-fifteen.

The dog was gone.

In the cellar, the incinerator glowed suddenly and a whirl of sparks leaped up the chimney.

Two thirty-five.

Bridge tables sprouted from patio walls. Playing cards fluttered onto pads in a shower of pips. Martinis manifested on an oaken bench with egg salad sandwiches. Music played.

1 Baal was a Canaanite god, decried as a demon or false god in the Abrahamic religions.

But the tables were silent and the cards untouched.

At four o'clock the tables folded like great butterflies back through the paneled walls.

Four-thirty.

The nursery walls glowed.

Animals took shape: yellow giraffes, blue lions, pink antelopes, lilac panthers cavorting in crystal substance. The walls were glass. They looked out upon color and fantasy. Hidden films clocked through well-oiled sprockets, and the walls lived. The nursery floor was woven to resemble a crisp, cereal meadow. Over this ran aluminum roaches and iron crickets, and in the hot still air butterflies of delicate red tissue wavered among the sharp aroma of animal spoors! There was the sound like a great matted yellow hive of bees within a dark bellows, the lazy bumble of a purring lion. And there was the patter of okapi feet and the murmur of a fresh jungle rain, like other hoofs, falling upon the summer-starched grass. Now the walls dissolved into distances of parched weed, mile on mile, and warm endless sky. The animals drew away into thorn brakes and water holes.

It was the children's hour.

Five o'clock. The bath filled with clear hot water.

Six, seven, eight o'clock. The dinner dishes manipulated like magic tricks, and in the study a *click*. In the metal stand opposite the hearth where a fire now blazed up warmly, a cigar popped out, half an inch of soft gray ash on it, smoking, waiting.

Nine o'clock. The beds warmed their hidden circuits, for nights were cool here.

Nine-five. A voice spoke from the study ceiling:

"Mrs. McClellan, which poem would you like this evening?"

The house was silent.

The voice said at last, "Since you express no preference, I shall select a poem at random." Quiet music rose to back the voice. "Sara Teasdale. As I recall, your favorite …

"There will come soft rains and the smell of the ground,
And swallows circling with their shimmering sound;

And frogs in the pools singing at night,
And wild plum trees in tremulous white;

Robins will wear their feathery fire,
Whistling their whims on a low fence-wire;

And not one will know of the war, not one
Will care at last when it is done.

Not one would mind, neither bird nor tree,
If mankind perished utterly;

And Spring herself, when she woke at dawn,
Would scarcely know that we were gone."[1]

The fire burned on the stone hearth and the cigar fell away into a mound of quiet ash on its tray. The empty chairs faced each other between the silent walls, and the music played.

At ten o'clock the house began to die.

The wind blew. A falling tree bough crashed through the kitchen window. Cleaning solvent, bottled, shattered over the stove. The room was ablaze in an instant!

"Fire!" screamed a voice. The house lights flashed, water pumps shot water from the ceilings. But the solvent spread on the linoleum, licking, eating, under the kitchen door, while the voices took it up in chorus: "Fire, fire, fire!"

The house tried to save itself. Doors sprang tightly shut, but the windows were broken by the heat and the wind blew and sucked upon the fire.

The house gave ground as the fire in ten billion angry sparks moved with flaming ease from room to room and then up the stairs. While scurrying water rats squeaked from the walls, pistoled their water, and ran for more. And the wall sprays let down showers of mechanical rain.

But too late. Somewhere, sighing, a pump shrugged to a stop. The quenching rain ceased. The reserve water supply which had filled the baths and washed the dishes for many quiet days was gone.

The fire crackled up the stairs. It fed upon Picassos and Matisses[2] in the upper halls, like delicacies, baking off the oily flesh, tenderly crisping the canvases into black shavings.

Now the fire lay in beds, stood in windows, changed the colors of drapes!

And then, reinforcements.

From attic trapdoors, blind robot faces peered down with faucet mouths gushing green chemical.

The fire backed off, as even an elephant must at the sight of a dead snake. Now there were twenty snakes whipping over the floor, killing the fire with a clear cold venom of green froth.

---

1 Sara Teasdale (1884–1923) was a Pulitzer Prize winning American poet. "There Will Come Soft Rains" appears in her collection *Flame and Shadow* (1920). In the *Collier's* version of Bradbury's story, the poem could arguably be said to have more resonance, since that version is set in Spring rather than Fall.

2 Pablo Picasso (1881–1973) and Henri Matisse (1868–1954): two of the most famous and influential artists of the twentieth century.

But the fire was clever. It had sent flame outside the house, up through the attic to the pumps there. An explosion! The attic brain which directed the pumps was shattered into bronze shrapnel on the beams.

The fire rushed back into every closet and felt of the clothes that hung there.

The house shuddered, oak bone on bone, its bared skeleton cringing from the heat, its wire, its nerves revealed as if a surgeon had torn the skin off to let the red veins and capillaries quiver in the scalded air. Help, help! Fire! Run, run! Heat snapped mirrors like the first brittle winter ice. And the voices wailed Fire, fire, run, run, like a tragic nursery rhyme, a dozen voices, high, low, like children dying in a forest, alone, alone. And the voices fading as the wires popped their sheathings like hot chestnuts. One, two, three, four, five voices died.

In the nursery the jungle burned. Blue lions roared, purple giraffes bounded off. The panthers ran in circles, changing color, and ten million animals, running before the fire, vanished off toward a distant steaming river....

Ten more voices died. In the last instant under the fire avalanche, other choruses, oblivious, could be heard announcing the time, playing music, cutting the lawn by remote-control mower, or setting an umbrella frantically out and in the slamming and opening front door, a thousand things happening, like a clock shop when each clock strikes the hour insanely before or after the other, a scene of maniac confusion, yet unity; singing, screaming, a few last cleaning mice darting bravely out to carry the horrid ashes away! And one voice, with sublime disregard for the situation, read poetry aloud in the fiery study, until all the film spools burned, until all the wires withered and the circuits cracked.

The fire burst the house and let it slam flat down, puffing out skirts of spark and smoke.

In the kitchen, an instant before the rain of fire and timber, the stove could be seen making breakfasts at a psychopathic rate, ten dozen eggs, six loaves of toast, twenty dozen bacon strips, which, eaten by fire, started the stove working again, hysterically hissing!

The crash. The attic smashing into the kitchen and parlor. The parlor into cellar, cellar into sub-cellar. Deep freeze, armchair, film tapes, circuits, beds, and all like skeletons thrown in a cluttered mound deep under.

Smoke and silence. A great quantity of smoke.

Dawn showed faintly in the east. Among the ruins, one wall stood alone. Within the wall, a last voice said, over and over again and again, even as the sun rose to shine upon the heaped rubble and steam:

"Today is August 5, 2026, today is August 5, 2026, today is ..."

James H. Hill (b. 1916; date of death unknown)

The hundreds of stories written by James H. Hill for the *The Afro-American* newspaper had fallen into obscurity before being recovered by academic Brooks E. Hefner, who discusses Hill in his study *Black Pulp: Genre Fiction in the Shadow of Jim Crow* (2021). As of this writing, there is still little known of Hill's life, and what is known comes from Dr. Hefner's research and an *Afro-American* article, from 4 August 1945: born in 1916 (according to his draft card), he was married to Dororthy Harris Hill by 1940; in addition to his writing work, he also served as a union organizer for the Congress of Industrial Organizations. Hefner notes that in the two decades following his first publication in 1935, Hill would "publish over three hundred stories and serial installments in the newspaper" (124). Hefner compares this writing pace to another famed African American SF author, George S. Schuyler (see the introduction to this anthology); like Schuyler, Hill's works and those of others writing for Black newspapers and journals point to the wider publishing arena for SF in the middle decades of twentieth century, well beyond the traditionally considered pulps, and to the long and rich history of what would later be called Afrofuturism.[1]

Note on the text: "The Space Ship," which seems at first to trade in several of what were already pulp clichés, also gestures to Hill's larger engagement with politics and culture, citing as it does the contemporary fascination with UFOs, the Cold War, ecological injustice, racist laws and policing, and several other contemporary issues. The story was published in four installments of the "Afro Magazine" section of *The Afro-American*, between 16 September and 7 October 1950. Each installment, starting with the second, includes a recap of the story so far (reproduced in notes, here). Each also included an illustration, with a full-page illustration introducing the first section, signed "Yancey" (likely Francis Yancey, who illustrated others of Hill's works) (Fig. 5). Some newspaper typesetting choices and obvious errors have been silently adjusted, judgements made where the text was unclear, and substantive changes noted; otherwise, the original text is followed.

1 Information on Hill comes from Dr. Hefner's book and from my email correspondence with him, and I thank him for both.

'Red Cross on Front Lines in Korea'—Hicks—See Pg. 3

AFRO Magazine

Sept. 16, 1950

SPACE SHIP

OPERATION SMOG

Part I—"The Gray Men"

The half-century meeting of the Astro Physical Society of the World was not attended by the Russians this year. In fact, the Soviet Union had had no representation since 1948 when the young Doctors Sergei Gronsk and Nikoli Belikov had been present on behalf of the U.S.S.R.

Last year, when Dr. Morton Alderhoff had sent invitations to Gronsk and Belikov, to attend the meeting being held in Copenhagen, he had received the terse reply that Doctors Gronsk and Belikov had disappeared. There were no details.

To the forty-three members of the society, it was another instance of Iron Curtain tactics, and their attitude toward the Soviet paralleled that of the members of the United Nations when the Russian delegation walks out without cause or explanation.

A Physical Chemist

Dr. Philip Browne, a native of Haiti, who had become a naturalized American in 1945, was the lone colored member of A-P S W. On the very top floor of a New York office building, he worked as a physical chemist for the McHugh Plastics Corporation.

He listened with quiet patience as Dr. Eric Jungstrom, one of the Scandinavian members, switched from the discussion of ex-

(Continued on Page 2)

YANCEY

A FOUR-PART SERIAL

Fig. 5: Francis Yancey. Illustration to "The Space Ship." *The Afro-American*, 16 Sept. 1950.

"The Space Ship" (1950)

OPERATION SMOG

PART I

"The Gray Men"

THE half-century meeting of the Astro-Physical Society of the World was not attended by the Russians this year. In fact, the Soviet Union had had no representation since 1948,[1] when the young Doctors Sergei Gronsk and Nikoli Belikov had been present on behalf of the U.S.S.R.

Last year, when Dr. Morton Alderhoff had sent invitations to Gronsk and Belikov, to attend the meeting being held in Copenhagen, he had received the terse reply that Doctors Gronsk and Belikov had disappeared. There were no details.

To the forty-three members of the society, it was another instance of Iron Curtain[2] tactics, and their attitude toward the Soviet paralleled that of the members of the United Nations when the Russian delegation walks out without cause or explanation.[3]

A Physical Chemist

Dr. Philip Browne, a native of Haiti,[4] who had become a naturalized American in 1945, was the lone colored member of the A-P S.W. On the very top floor of a New York office building, he worked as a physical chemist for the McHugh Plastics Corporation.

He listened with quiet patience as Dr. Eric Jungstrom, one of the Scandinavian members, switched from the discussion of extragalactic universes, to a scathing denunciation of Russian policy.

Browne, himself, needed no interpreter from Jungstrom's discussion. He was proficient in eleven languages, including Bella-Russian and Neapolitan Italian.

He was, too, the most imaginative of the group, and his antipathy toward the Soviet was not as deep-dyed as that of the others. He had seen too many

1 The Union of Soviet Socialist Republics, which grew out of the 1917 Russian Revolution and subsequent Civil War (1917–22), was a communist state, and global superpower, from 1922 to 1991. With the US, and later the North Atlantic Treaty Organization (NATO, founded in 1949), as its primary antagonists, it engaged in the so-called Cold War and nuclear arms race from c. 1947 to 1991. In addition to more openly hostile arms buildup and proxy wars, the two groups also engaged in forms of scientific and cultural competition, notably the so-called Space Race, which this story prefigures.

2 A metaphorical term commonly used during the Cold War to describe the material and cultural barriers between the USSR and the West.

3 Of note is the Soviet boycott of the United Nations from January to August 1950 (shortly before the story's publication) to protest the UN's refusal to recognize the newly formed People's Republic of China as a member nation.

4 Haiti is a Caribbean nation founded following a successful revolution (1791–1804) in which the formerly enslaved populace overthrew the French colonial government and abolished slavery. The US occupied Haiti from 1918 to 1934.

instances of suppression and regimentation in the alleged democracies to be fundamentally impressed with the political posturings of empires.

"On the very eve of our venture into interplanetary travel, we have to receive such treatment from our own colleagues!" Jungstrom ranted. "I, for one, am strongly against listing the Soviet Union as contributor to our Space-Ship, Hydra."

After a moment, during which time the interpreters translated Jungstrom's remarks, an assenting hubbub filled the great chamber.

Browne raised his hand, and the chairman, Doctor Alderhoff, recognized him.

In the perfect, somewhat stilted English of the learned immigrant, Browne said: "The attitude of the preceding speaker is understandable in view of present world crises, but I think a most salient point has been missed, gentlemen. And that is this: Sergei Gronsk and Nikoli Belikov have made more actual progress on the construction of a space-ship than any of us.

"We know they were last seen in Murmansk[1] the night of June 8, 1948, tinkering with a spheroid-type ship, the Krona. We know also, that a violent blast shook Murmansk that same night and that neither the doctors nor the Krona have been heard from since."

But the very blond Jungstrom was obstinate. "Then why didn't the Russians say they were killed in an explosion, and why didn't they send other astro-physicists?" he said by way of interpreter.

Alferhoff's gavel rapped for order once, and Browne proceeded.

No Evidence

"It is my opinion that the Russians simply don't know—do not have any evidence to support the statement that Gronsk and Belikov were killed!" He was silent a moment, trying to divine the expectant looks on his colleagues' faces.

Then he drew himself up to his full height and took a deep breath, for he was about to make a startling announcement—one which might indicate to his confreres that he was ready for a padded cell.

"In fact," he said at last, "I am of the opinion that Gronsk and Belikov succeded in bursting through the ring of gravity in the Krona!"

While they gasped in astonishment and exchanged meaningful glances and directed sympathy toward the Haitian-American, the latter reached into his leather briefcase and withdrew a sheaf of documents and photographs.

After the initial consternation had spent itself, Browne laughed quietly. "Believe me, gentlemen, I have not been reading Flash Gordon and Buck Rogers.[2] But consider it from this point: When Admiral Peary was in Greenland in 1894 he discovered a meteorite which weighed

1 A city in northwestern Russia.

2 Flash Gordon and Buck Rogers were pulp SF heroes. On Buck Rogers, see the introduction to the comic strip in this anthology. Flash Gordon, largely a Buck Rogers knock-off, started life as a comic strip in 1934, before going on to his own film and television career.

thirty-six-and-a-half tons;[1] then there's the Hoba iron,[2] which weighs from fifty to seventy tons—the largest ever found. Now if these bodies can penetrate our atmosphere at speeds of over forty-miles a second without being burned to useless ashes, is it not possible to reverse the procedure?

Pictured in Magazine

"I have here a magazine—an American magazine of international prominence." He held it up for all to view. "It carries an article—and pictures of all the so-called 'Flying Saucers.' All of you, I'm sure, are familiar with the disc-like forms which used to be attributed to delirium tremens.[3]

"One of the pictures was taken by a Robert Kirk, near Chicago; William Rhodes took one at Tucson; Betty Malles took one over Hawthorne, California,[4] but—" he paused and the expression on his smooth brown face was grave, "—no one had a camera handy the night one appeared over Donora, Pennsylvania; or if one was handy, there was no infra-red film with which to photograph it.

"Yet hundreds of Donora's citizens saw the disc—and a hundred or more died in a mysterious emanation which industrial scientists have called a 'smog,' for want of a better name."[5] His tone grew ominous. "The smog and the disc, gentlemen—and the missing spheroid Krona!"

Dr. Philip Browne's implications were clear. But even so, it sounded fantastic, bordering on madness. It implied also that Gronsk and Belikov were alive, flying around in space, and experimenting with a new kind of death radiation.

The session was over at four in the afternoon, and when Browne came out in the New York sunshine to meet Rosanna Daniels, his svelte brown fiancee,

---

1 Robert Peary (1856–1920) was an American explorer of the Arctic. In 1894, he was led to the Innaanganeq meteorite in Greenland (also called the Cape York meteorite) by Inuit who had known and used its material for centuries. Peary exploited and abused Inuit communities who helped him.

2 A large meteorite located in Namibia.

3 A physical condition caused by alcohol withdrawal.

4 While the editor has yet to find a magazine article that contains all the photos referenced, the details that Hill provides were reported at the time in both the mainstream and pulp press. In its first issue (Spring 1948), *Fate* magazine published "Mystery of the Flying Disks," which included the now-famous photos by William Rhodes (1916–2007) of a purported UFO in Tucson, printed earlier in *The Arizona Republic*. Photos by Bette Malles appeared with the article "Amateur Photographer Snaps Weird Disk in Sky" in *The Los Angeles Times* (12 March 1950), while Robert W. Kirk is the subject of the skeptical article "Reports Seeing Flying Saucer; Takes 3 Photos" (*Chicago Tribune*, 20 March 1950). The popular article "Flying Saucers are Real," by Donald Keyhoe (1897–1988), appeared in the Jan. 1950 issue of *True Magazine* (turned into a book of the same title later that year), but does not include these photos. Later, one of Malles's photos and one of Kirk's would appear in *Flying Saucers on the Attack* (1954) by Harold T. Wilkins (1891–1960). All of these publications followed the so-called "Flying Saucer Craze" of 1947.

5 The Donora Smog was an air pollution event in Pennsylvania in 1948, when toxic gases were released by a US Steel plant. Approximately twenty people died during the initial four-day event, with estimates of fifty more dying shortly after, while thousands were made ill. It is noted as an early event that led to the eventual development of the Clean Air Act (passed in 1963); it is now memorialized in the Donora Smog museum (see McPhee).

he was followed by Mart Kramer, the well-known Washington reporter.

Kramer was an intense man, of medium build, with a startling shock of iron-gray hair and gray, lackluster eyes. He caught Browne by the sleeve just as Rosanna rounded the corner from the parking lot next to the hotel where the conclave was being held. Browne recognized him at once. Kramer had been allowed to attend all of the Astro-Physical Society's meetings since their inception five years ago.

Then How Come?

"Riddle me this," the reporter said, bringing out a pack of cigarettes. "If, as you implied, Gronsk and Belikov are alive and kicking what would be the purpose of their smog attack?"

Browne shook his head. "I could only guess at that. Maybe they've discovered a new gas or a new germ somewhere in the universe and are experimenting."

"Just where in the universe?"

"Mars, Venus—maybe just the moon."

Kramer smiled like an indulgent parent listening to a juvenile rehash of Jack-and-the-Beanstalk.[1] "You'll forgive me," he said, "but you speak of those places like the average person speaks of California or Honolulu."

"The average person thought a two-ton blockbuster was a terrible weapon until we let go a considerably smaller atom bomb,"[2] Browne returned. He looked about then and greeted Rosanna.

Kramer bowed to her and she nodded. "Really, dear, you should be getting away from those stuffy old geniuses," she said. "You look so very tired."

"You should see those stuffy old geniuses after Philip finished talking," Kramer interposed, offering both a cigarette.

Neither of them accepted, however, and the reporter nodded and went his way.

In the booth of the restaurant Rosanna said: "What did Kramer mean by his remark?"

Philip sighed and briefly told Rosanna what he had said at today's session.

She thought about it a moment, toying with her health salad. "Don't you think it sounds a little far-fetched?"

"I'll Have Proof!"

"Of course," he laughed. "But one of these nights—tonight maybe—I'll have indisputable proof that Gronsk and Belikov are alive!"

For a moment, Rosanna's fork wavered over her plate and her fawn-colored eyes searched his face for some hint that he was making a joke.

To the mute query in her eyes he said: "No, darling. It's no jest. I'm quite serious. Three nights ago, by ultra-micro-wave, I even talked with them!"

1 English fairy tale.

2 A two-ton blockbuster was a large bomb used in World War II.

Rosanna's fork clattered to the table and her eyes distended in their lovely sockets as she watched the impassive expression on Philip's face.

He said: "You should not be so alarmed, Rosanna. I would have been called an unmitigated liar if I'd have mentioned that in today's session; but it's true."

Finally Rosanna averted her eyes to the table. "It's hard to comprehend, Philip."

"Much harder for you than my colleagues; but I couldn't stand it if you didn't believe me. Tell you what: I've a two-way set in my laboratory in the McHugh suite on the top floor of the Keyes Building. I have a key and can go there any time.

"The owners never quite figured why I needed those two powerful generators, but I use them to project and receive strong signals in the ionosphere and beyond. For instance, when the Navy aimed an Americanized version of the V-2[1] straight up I could hear its ticker when it was eighty miles up. It never got beyond the gravitational pull however. Would you like to go to the laboratory with me tonight after the show?"

Rosanna seemed delighted. "Why, of course!" she had always been awed and fascinated by the great glittering masses of dials and screens and prisms and labyrinthine wirings of the physicists.

On the roof of the Keyes Building, young Dr. Philip Browne directed his bowl antennae toward the planet Mars; but nothing happened that night, nor the next.

Success at Last

On the third night, however, a humming in his radar-screen riveted the attention of them both. Philip twisted a tuning dial and stepped up the output, and the quartz screen began to glow an unholy green. There was a shimmering as he cut in an auxiliary grid and a red spot appeared in the sea of green—a red spot which gradually took the shape of a tiny elliptical disc!

Rosanna was sitting tensely, now unaware that she was fiercely squeezing Philip's free arm. "What do you make of it?" she asked hoarsely. Philip's eyes flicked over the dials. "Could be our missing physicists. According to my celerinometer, they're approaching at a rate of thirty-seven miles a second. If it's a meteor it'll burn itself out or at least split up. If it's the Krona, with its multiple refrigerated skins, it might—"

He didn't finish the explanation because the soft orange bulb beside the screen began to flash a steady Morse Code.[2] It was international Morse and Philip jotted down the words as the disc grew larger on the screen.

1 The V-2 was a supersonic, guided ballistic missile, the first of its kind capable of hitting long-range targets. Developed by the Nazis in World War II, after the war it became foundational in the development of rockets for space launches.

2 Created by and named for American inventor and artist Samuel Morse (1791–1872), Morse Code uses a series of short and long electronic signals to represent different letters. It was first used for another of Morse's famous inventions, the telegraph.

"Received signal Browne ... We're living dead only a year's food supply tablets left ... Mars hell ..."

Rosanna read the words and sat rigid, half incredulous.

"Coming in on your signal direction," the bulb flashed. "Forget Project Hydra. Gronsk and Belikov!"

A cold perspiration filmed Philip's brow. He was tense as he turned to his fiancee. He extended his hand. "Come, darling—to the roof."

The Krona looked for all the world like a giant flying manta ray as it zoomed in over Long Island Sound and whisked toward Manhattan, leaving great vapor trails in its wake.

It traveled so fast that those who saw it coming in over the sound weren't sure that their eyes weren't playing tricks on them. But as it settled, like a monstrous bird over the flat roof of the Keyes Building, the New Yorkers who saw it merely passed it off as some press-agent's publicity stunt.

Philip held Rosanna in the lee of a chimney spire as the great black ship settled its bottom on the roof. He remembered that the Krona had a bright beryllium hull, but the heat of atmospheric friction had blackened it. Even the cockpit bulb was black for several moments.

Gradually, it cleared and for the first time since the Astro-Physical Conclave of nineteen-forty-eight, held in Potsdam, Philip Browne looked upon the faces of Doctors Sergei Gronsk and Nikoli Belikov! And the faces were those of desperate men and were the horrible, sickening gray of the long-dead![1]

PART II

"Death Fog"

When Dr. Philip Browne took the first look at the men behind the pyralin-domed[2] cockpit of the Krona, he had the sudden urge to flee—to take Rosanna and put as much distance as possible between them and the saucer-like space-ship. It would have been the prudent thing to do; but the scientific mind being ever a-thirst for new knowledge made him venture closer to the still-closed pit.

Both of the missing doctors were wearing heavy spun-glass and rubber pressurized suits onto which could be fitted large head-globes which were

---

1 The first installment ends here. The following week's installment begins with the following:

THE STORY SO FAR: DR. PHILIP BROWNE, young Haitian-American astro-physicist, tells the members of the Astro-Physical Society of the World that he believes two Russian members, who disappeared in 1948 are still alive and have penetrated the ionosphere successfully.

One night, in company with his fiancee, ROSANNA DANIELS, he contacts the two Russian physicists, DRS. GONSK [sic] AND BELIKOV with a micro-short-wave set. They come in with their flying disc ship and land on the building where he has a laboratory on the top floor. When they raise the hood of their ship, the Krona, he sees that they have turned a strange brittle gray color. NOW READ ON:—

2 A cellulose nitrate plastic developed by Du Pont in the 1920s.

equipped with powerful binoculars, camera, speaking tubes, oxygen tubes. In a way, they looked like ultra-modern divers, and their movements were about as awkward.

What Did It Mean?

Philip and Rosanna watched as they laboriously donned and sealed the heavy head-pieces. He thought about the code-light winking beside his screen. "We're living dead." What did it mean?

Rosanna did not approach the ship. She stayed close to the chimney-spire, one well-manicured hand to her throat.

There was a coughing sound as the glass dome slid upward, and for one horrible moment strange blue veins stood out in the parchment-grey faces behind the globes and the two young astro-physicists gasped for breath. But in a moment, they seemed to be breathing normally again.

Philip got the weird feeling as they struggled for air that their stiff-looking faces would crumble from the exertion.

Under ordinary circumstances it would seem that the two strange visitors would be quite warm in their heavy equipment, but the temperature and atmosphere in a pressurized suit can be what the wearer desires it to be. And these two looked cold.

Belikov spoke first, and his voice was heavily laden with mechanical overtones through the miniature speaker. His face, Philip noted, was unfriendly. "Why did you persist in trying to reach us?" he queried in his native tongue. Without giving the amazed brown man a chance to reply, he went on: "If you suspected we were alive, how many others may suspect the same thing?"

"How Many Know?"

"How many know that we are alive?" snapped Gronsk, and there was no mistaking the venom in the taller man's eyes.

An unnamed terror shook Rosanna now, but her voice was stuck in her throat.

"So far as I know, I'm the only one," Philip answered in their language. "To be frank they thought I'd taken momentary leave of my senses when I suggested that the two of you were alive in Tuesday's session."

Belikov's voice grew an even sharper edge. "You mean you got on the floor and said you believed we were alive!"

Bewilderment was a pulsing thing in Philip's dark eyes. "But I thought it a great tribute to you—both of you. I even remarked that you were much farther advanced in the knowledge of space-ship construction than the rest of us."

The two robot-like men exchanged glances, and for a moment, their expressions relaxed.

"Why are you so upset about it?" Philip wanted to know. "If you really got to Mars and have come back you're international heroes!"

There was a pause. Then: "We can never return to earth and live like normal men again," Belikov said. "Look at us! We reached Mars all right; but we were foolish enough to get out without our pressure suits. Our lungs shrivelled much and our blood ran blue. We managed to get back into the ship, but it was too late. We can only survive on pure oxygen now!"

Philip's eyes were bright with awe. "Tell me—is there really animal life on Mars?"

For a moment, the eerie gray faces of the two Soviet physicists were implacable. Then Gronsk's face broke into an odd smile. Philip's flesh crawled and it took an effort to keep from shrinking back in terror as the mere act of smiling seemed to threaten to crumble the man's features.

Ignoring the brown man's question, Gronsk said; "With two pairs of human lungs we might be like other humans again."

Pistol Appears

Despite the heat of the late summer night the icy hand of fear made Philip shiver; and before he could comment on Gronsk's remarks there was a strange-looking pistol in the latter's covered right hand.

Rosanna screamed, but could not move from the chimney-spire. She could not understand the conversation (which was being held in Russian) but her feminine instincts could divine a sinister purpose in the two weird men in the space-ship.

Belikov's voice was low and sibilant. "This is greater luck than we anticipated. We have two of you—two pairs of lungs. We must ask you to accompany us to Phobos!"

Philip was at once terrified and angry, for the weapon in Gronsk's fist was aimed at Rosanna—not at him! Why did these strange creatures want to go to Mars's greater moon, Phobos? Why not Deimos, the lesser—or Mars itself?

"A blast from [t]his gun and the flesh shrivels and dies in less than five seconds," Gronsk warned.

"Your beautiful lady will turn to a blackened, shriveled mummy before your eyes. Tell her to get in! In a way you and the lady are honored. You will be instrumental in preparing the two greatest physicists in the universe for their second coming!"

Rosanna could not move, and Philip was so unnerved that it required superhuman effort for him to move over to the chimney, lift his fiancee and carry her to the Krona. Not until the hatch-cover slid into place did Gronsk holster the curious pistol.

The control-cabin of the Krona seemed superheated to Philip and Rosanna, who sat huddled together as the space-ship arched up through the stratosphere with such speed that forward motion kept them jammed against a cushioned wall.

"Unfortunately," Belikov said, "we have no more pressurized suits. But the after-cabin is pressurized and there are oxygen helmets. We'll keep this altitude until you get back there. Because of the folding, laminated skins of this cabin there is a seepage of pressure. In time you would bleed to death, and we have need for both of you at our destination point."

Like a Convict

Philip translated for Rosanna as briefly as possible and struggled to his feet. When he and the girl passed through the air-lock to the rear cabin, he felt curiously like a convict walking through the little green door to the electric chair. Only the convict's type of death was a certainty. Philip was not sure what theirs would be like.

They lacked privacy even in this small bare cabin, for Gronsk followed them inside with the pistol unholstered again. Here too the heat was stifling and Philip and Rosanna were in a welter of perspiration. The globe-like oxygen helmets helped their breathing. At last Rosanna said: "I can stand this heat no longer. If I don't get out of these clothes I'll die!"

Gronsk, who understood but could speak no English worth mentioning, went to one side of the cabin, opened a semi-parabolic door. From a small drawer he took two small garments and tossed them to Rosanna.

To Philip he said: "The bathing suit I bought for my Katrine the day we exploded from Murmansk." The colored physical chemist thought he saw something akin to tears in Gronsk's eyes.

Then with a gallantry neither of them expected, Gronsk turned his back and indicated that Philip should do likewise—with the pistol, of course.

It was a dubious kind of privacy, but Rosanna had no other choice; and though the two men did not turn during her change of costume, she exposed as little of her charms as possible during the process. Indeed, she was more exposed after the change than during it!

Philip, too, was more comfortable in shorts, shoes, and topshirt, and with a resigned sigh, he began to question Gronsk about a number of things, which, to this point, had been conjecture and theory.

Can Reproduce

"There are humanoid creatures on Mars," Gronsk said. "But they are androgynes—like earthy[1] flowers—able to reproduce themselves without a partner. They're small, hairless, with thick hides and great moon faces; and so far they cannot understand our words—nor our gestures."

"Would you say their civilization was as advanced as ours, or more so?"

"More advanced. The canals you see from the average observatory telescope are really jet-train tubes, much like the pneumatic change-tubes[2] in modern

1 Perhaps a typesetter's error for "earthly."

2 Popular commercially in the late nineteenth and early twentieth centuries, pneumatic tubes used compressed air or a partial vacuum to move containers between locations. In this case, they would have been used to move cash between the front-line customer service location and a centralized cash room.

department stores. They can circumnavigate the nearly nine thousand miles of the planet in four hours.

"Further, their mentality—if we're to call it that—seems to be advanced to such a degree that speech is unnecessary. Mental telepathy seems to be their mode of communication. I never heard a sound from them the whole year I was away."

"Year? You were away since nineteen-forty-eight?"

Gronsk smiled and shook his head. "How quickly earth-beings forget! I was speaking about the Martian Year, of course."

Philip lowered his eyes with embarrassment. "Of course. Six hundred and eighty-seven earth days." When he raised his eyes he noticed that the pistol was still aimed at Rosanna.

He said: "What kind of new germ did you spread over Donora, Pennsylvania, back in forty-eight?"

The sudden change of question caught Gronsk unprepared to manufacture a fabrication. Almost automatically, he said: "The so-called 'Smog' wasn't germ warfare. It's a Martian carbon gas we call belligen. We will use much of it in our 'second coming.'"

"But why?"

Gronsk snorted. "Why? It's a silly question—why! We are, first of all, Russian, just as you are American. We must show the world the real might of the Soviet Union—the greatest might in the universe—the might which can channel the undreamed-of power of the stars into our cause." He paused then and laughed.

Korean War Amusing[1]

"I cannot help but find the present 'Korean War' amusing. Really when you see what fearsome destruction we'll bring back to earth that little war will sound like a cap pistol going off against a Long Tom.[2] But then—you, nor the charming lady will be there to witness it. Better for you. First the smog; then ultimatums; and if they're not met we'll rain such destruction on the western part of the earth that much of it may rip off into space!"

Philip was awed at the terrible picture Gronsk painted, and his deep fear was reflected in the eyes of his intended. "I believe" he said, "that you would even depose your Uncle Joe!"[3]

Gronsk stiffened and his gray face seemed ready to cave in. "And why not? Nikoli and I have found this power. The Martians seem to have no objections to our using it—besides: We have four other young scientists on Phobos with us.

1 The Korean War (1950–53) was fought between North and South Korea in the immediate aftermath of World War II, and is generally seen as the first "proxy war" between the Cold War antagonists, the US and the USSR. An armistice was declared, but to this day there is no peace treaty between the two sides. This was also the first war in which the US employed racially integrated armed services.

2 The Long Tom was a large-calibre field gun first used by the US in World War II.

3 A common nickname for Joseph Stalin (1878–1953), the leader of the USSR (1924–53).

"And (you'll find this surprising) we have your Hydra—the ship that your astronomical society built. One of our more daring young men bribed the guard at Tiajuana[1] with American dollars and took off in it. Needless to say, the six men who comprised the guard were killed. What? You're surprised? I said you'd be!"

Dr. Philip Browne was truly astonished; but for the moment he was glad that his captor knew nothing of mental telepathy.

Otherwise he might have divined that the prisoner was entertaining thoughts of escape. A very slim chance to be sure; but if only he could devise some means whereby he might get inside the Hydra … He knew every inch of her sixty-two-feet length—the porous refrigerated aluminum nose, the magneto-steering device, the quadruple titanium skins....

Gronsk must have thought Philip was suffering the first pangs of necromania, for he said: "Don't dwell too much on your death. It will be easy and painless—for both of you."

"We're Landing"

A red light flashed above the air-lock door in a series of signals then, and Gronsk said: "Brace yourselves in the wall straps. We're landing on Phobos!"

Philip shook his head sadly. "If only I could sit in the pit of the Hydra just once more...."

Gronsk shrugged. "Even we still have in our hearts the simple amenities for the condemned. You shall sit in the pit of the Hydra. You shall also die in it!"

A blackness with a kind of palpable texture swarmed over the four when they swung out of the Krona. Philip half-expected that they would float—as one does in the ionosphere when beyond the pull of gravity. They seemed to be standing on a rocky substance, and before they could take three strides a giant circle of light came up around them.

A young gauntleted man, wearing a bizarre headpiece, came out to meet them. He strode very proudly through the swirling darkness which the powerful lights could not altogether dispel.

"That is Anton Torkyo, passionate adherent to our cause," Belikov said. "Since Sergei promised it, I will have him take you to the Hydra."

Philip tried to tell Rosanna of his plan, but young Anton must have suspected something and walked between them. He was totally unprepared for the earthly right cross that Philip smacked against his fine jaw.[2]

---

1 Tijuana, Mexico.

2 The second instalment ends here. The third begins with the following summary:

THE STORY SO FAR: DR. PHILIP BROWNE, young Haitian American astro-physicist, tells the members of the Astro-Physical Society of the World that he believes the Russian members, GRONSK and BELIKOV, who disappeared in 1948, are still alive and may have successfully penetrated the ionosphere.

One night, with his fiancee, ROSANNA DANIELS, PHILIP contacts the two missing (*continued*)

PART III

"Hell's Gauntlet"

When the desperation wallop had dropped young Anton to the rocky sod of Phobos, the larger of Mars' two moons, Dr. Philip Browne was grateful for the fog-like blackness. It even seemed to muffle the sound of their running feet as they sped toward the semi-circle of space-ships.

There were three disc-like ships, fashioned after the Krona, but much smaller, and on one end was the Hydra, which Philip had last seen in New Mexico on earth. It was built more along conventional lines, with short, swept back wings, solid tungsten skid, giant reaction tube. But it had made the flight from earth to Phobos without any apparent mishap.

Hard to Believe

It was still crazy; still incredulous, Philip thought as he pressed the button which slid back the laminated pyralin hood, half-pushed Rosanna inside and climbed in himself. Who would believe that astral overdrive could make a craft surpass the speed of light? Render obsolete the Law of Limitation? It was staggering even to the imagination.

Outside a thunderclap sounded as Philip closed the cover of the Hydra. A split-second later, the ship trembled under a blow.

"They've discovered Anton!" Philip exclaimed.[1] "They're firing on us!" Rosanna broke out in hysterical weeping. "What are we going to do?"

Philip pulled the primer-rocket toggle and closed his eyes a moment. "Lord God of the Universe, guide us to Thy firmament!"

His eyes were great dark pools in his face. Perspiration was beginning to seep out from under the oxygen globe; but his hands were steady on the controls. He knew that before they got very far the other ships would be pouncing on them.

Quickly Philip set about charting a course which would take him close to Deimos, the lesser moon and out into the mysterious void toward the earth's moon.

Ships Upon Them

But before they could cover the seven thousand miles between the two moons of Mars the swift disc ships were upon them.

Russians by micro-wave and they come in with their saucer-like ship and kidnap PHILIP and ROSANNA for the purpose of getting their lungs to replace the lungs which shriveled inside them in Martian atmosphere.

They land on the Mars moon, Phobos, where PHILIP strikes one of his captors on the jaw and runs for the Hydra, the space-ship built by the A-P Society and stolen by the Russians. NOW READ ON:—

1 This word could be either "explained" or "exclaimed," as in the original it was incorrectly typeset as "exclained."

The Krona poured a withering concentration of disintegration rays from seven swiveling gun-points and Philip was glad that the other ships mounted only one gun apiece. The Hydra itself didn't have a weapon as such, but there was an Atom-Gun in the nose. It had been built in there for the purpose of blasting aerolites,[1] meteorites, and other vagrant astral bodies that got in the path.

But there were only seven charges in the A-gun, and the terrific recoil would slow them up, waste precious liquid oxygen fuel.

They whipped past Deimos so fast that in seconds the small moon, five miles in diameter, was no bigger than a golf-ball.[2] Only in passing other objects, however, is speed discernible. Until a star or moon or some other object loomed into view, they seemed to be standing still—to be suspended in space.

"If only we hold together until we hit the ionosphere," Philip said as the four enemy ships continued to blast at them. "One thing," he said grimly. "If Gronsk and Belikov need lungs they'll have to get them elsewhere."

Rosanna had lost her hysteria now. She sat very close to Philip helping him to manipulate the multiple controls as he directed.

Suddenly the girl's voice caught in her throat. She was pointing at a huge star that seemed to puff huge rings of light from its outer rim—massive bright clouds of fierce heat and light that were almost blinding. "What star is that?" she said at last.

"The greatest of them all," he replied. "It's the sun, and it's still some seventy million miles away."

The fury of the Soviet wolf-pack was unabated, and the Hydra shuddered under a glancing blast in her port wing.

But Rosanna was pointing at the alto-scope needle. It was beginning to waver.

"Bring On Your Saucers!"

Philip's face brightened. "We must be nearing the ionosphere!" he said. "Now—bring on your saucers. We may not pack their power, but we can out-maneuver them!"

Rosanna clutched his arm. "I hope you're right. That one was dangerously close!"

Philip cut in the forward rockets then, to check forward speed, and the four attacking saucers flashed by like comets.

Philip turned a knob and the ugly snout of an A-gun protruded from the nose of the Hydra. He eased off the forward rockets, fed a little more sauce to the combustion chamber and caught up with the wolf-pack ten miles above the earth.

---

1 Aerolite: "stony meterorite" (*OED*).

2 According to NASA, more recent measurements put Deimos's diameter, on average, closer to 7.5 miles, or 12 kilometres (see "Martian Moon Deimos").

They cut around for an encircling movement, obviously sure that the A-gun was of no use in battle, and opened fire again.

Philip barreled the Hydra above the barrage, lined up one of the smaller saucers in his sight and let go the atom charge.

There was a stentorian[1] explosion, attended by a flash of lightning as the fearsome weapon went off in the atmosphere; and the saucer vanished in a shower of bright silvery dust.

The recoil had been terrific, however, and Philip thought the safety belts would eviscerate them both. Rosanna smiled up at him bravely, however. "Give it to 'em, Phil!" she urged.

"Okay. Loose the belt and brace your feet. Hold onto the hand-grabs!"

The seven evil eyes of the Krona winked maliciously at them again, and this time, Philip sent the Hydra through a long rille,[2] doubled back on the evil mantaray and loosed two charges.

Giant Boiling

Again there was that violent flashing of thunder and lightning—a giant boiling of the turbulent atmosphere, and the evil work of the lung-less Soviet physicists was at an end. The Krona dissolved into fine powder that seemed to stay suspended in a thin, undulating mass that covered roughly two acres of atmosphere.

The other two saucers, seeing the Krona dissolve like that, tried to turn and flee, but the Hydra corralled them, herded them back toward the western hemisphere of earth.

Once, at six miles up, the three of them passed a flight of B-29's returning from a raid on a rail-head in North Korea.[3]

They passed the big bombers with such speed that the bomb crews complained only of hearing a strange noise en route to Teajon.[4] They didn't see anything!

Philip and Rosanna were exuberant as they crossed Honolulu and headed toward California. It was soon after that that the two prize captives, apparently in a suicide pact, rammed each other and disappeared in the choppy waters of the Pacific.

"Damn!" Philip exploded. "Those saucers would have been concrete proof of my contentions the other day."

"And verification of a trip that was really out of this world," added Rosanna. "Now if I breathe one word about the journey they'll clap me in the nearest booby-hatch."[5]

---

1 Stentorian: "very loud and far-reaching" (*OED*).

2 "a groove or narrow channel" (*OED*).

3 The Boeing B-29 Superfortress was a large, propeller-driven bomber airplane used heavily by the US in World War II, including the world's first nuclear attacks on Hiroshima and Nagasaki, Japan.

4 Taejon, now Daejeon, South Korea, was the site of a battle (16–20 July 1950) early in the Korean War.

5 Derogatory slang for a psychiatric hospital.

They took off their oxygen globes now, for they were no longer necessary, and they both had another problem now.

What were they going to do about clothes? Day was breaking, and unless they landed on a beach …

"Fuel's just about gone," Philip announced. "I doubt we'll make it to Denver."

"But what am I going to do for clothes?" Rosanna wanted to know.

"You're lucky you still have your pretty neck and a whole hide."

"You could do with a pair of trousers yourself."

"I'll be glad to get back to earth raw, if need be."

Unorthodox Reception

They did make it to Denver, however—almost to the airport. What they could not understand was that a crowd of police seemed to be awaiting them as they came in cross-wind—a very unorthodox way to land any heavier-than-air craft.

"We're heroes!" Rosanna cried. "That is—a hero and a heroine! Now let's see: What shall I say when they—"

"Rosanna!" The tenor of his voice caused her to turn around suddenly. "It doesn't look like a reception committee to me. They don't generally greet heroes by waving sub-machine guns!"

Rosanna's mouth popped open. There was indeed no brass band nor a velvet carpet. There were thirty-odd, very tough-looking Denver gendarmes, and those who were not bearing tommy-guns[1] were swinging those extra-long night-sticks that the Denver policemen carry.

"I—don't understand!" Rosanna stammered.

"We will—in a moment."

A big, red-faced police captain sauntered up to the space-ship and wrinkled his nose at the colored occupants, though his light-gray eyes did linger over-long on Rosanna's opulent, lightly-clad charms.

The cop said: "All right, Joe, who are you and what are you doing in this here ship?"

With a start Philip remembered that all of his identification papers were in his wallet and his wallet was in his coat pocket, and that it, along with the Krona, was now a part of silver dust floating around somewhere in the earth's atmosphere.

"Well, speak up! Who are you?" roared the policeman.

"He's Doctor Philip Browne," Rosanna said testily, "and he just saved this stinking old world of ours!"

The captain swung his gaze to her. It lingered on a choice section of her anatomy. "So, you two've been skylarking around in a stolen airship! And you've been drinking!" he shot at the outraged girl.

1 Thompson submachine guns.

Philip squeezed her hand to check a further outburst. "I am Dr. Philip Browne," Philip said. "I'm a member of the Astro-Physical Society of the World, and I helped to design and build this ship."

No Authorization?

"Just the same, you weren't authorized to fly it. Where's your identification?"

Philip sighed. "I don't have any. I—seem to have lost it."

The policeman drew up his shoulders. "In that case we'll see that you don't lose yourself in one of our nice dry cells while Dr. Alderhoof is flying out here."

"Alderhoff," Philip corrected.

"All right—Alderhoff. And who's the girl?"

"Miss Rosanna Daniels, my fiancee."

"Been swimming?"

"No—just flying."

The captain sighed. "All right, put on the rest of your clothes and come with me—both of you. This is a valuable piece of property you've been playing with—and for a whole week!"

A week! Philip was startled. It couldn't have been a week! They had had a few food tablets in the Krona and more in the Hydra, but it didn't seem as though they'd eaten more than five or six times. Out in space, however, there was no way to compute time by lightness and darkness; and if asked what day it was they might be sent to a psychopathic ward.

Finally Philip said: "These are all the clothes we have. The others were lost overboard. My wallet was in my suit."

The policeman pursed his lips and scowled darkly at Philip. The young physicist shook his head. "It's not what you're thinking, officer. We've been perfectly decent."

The captain grinned wryly. "Sure, sure, and maybe now I can dream up another charge to go along with grand larceny. The Mann Act is still in effect, you know."[1]

"But I didn't transport this young lady over any state line for immoral purposes," Philip protested.

"Tell it to the judge!" snarled the officer.[2]

---

1 Also known as the White-Slave Traffic Act of 1910, the Mann Act made it a felony to transport a woman across state lines for "the purpose of prostitution or debauchery, or for any other immoral purpose." However, it was also used to persecute people in consenting relationships, including between people who weren't married, and between interracial couples. The most famous of the latter was the prosecution of Black heavyweight boxing champion Jack Johnson (1878–1946) in 1912.

2 The third section concludes here. The fourth and final installment begins with:

THE STORY SO FAR: DR. PHILIP BROWNE, young Haitian-American astro-physicist, tells the members of the Astro-Physical Society of the World, that he believes the Russian members, GRONSK and BELIKOV, who disappeared in 1948, are still alive and may have penetrated the ionosphere.

One night, with his fiancee, ROSANNA DANIELS, PHILIP contacts the missing Russians, who

[PART IV]

"The Iron Fist"

On the way to the Denver Police Detention Quarters, Philip and Rosanna learned that today was Tuesday, the twenty-ninth. That meant that the Hydra had been stolen on the twenty-second.

On the twenty-second! But that was impossible. That had been the day that he had gotten the floor at the conclave and propounded his theories about flying saucers, the smog, and the missing Soviet physicists. In fact, it wasn't until Thursday night that he had contacted Gronsk and Belikov.

By the time he reached the lock-up he was in a more jovial mood, though a few hours in durance vile[1] did not particularly appeal to him. One thing was certain. He could certainly prove he hadn't stolen the Hydra, although he couldn't prove where he'd retrieved it from. The whole astronomical society would back him up on the former.

Confident

In low tones he told Rosanna of his convictions and assured her that as soon as Alderhoff arrived and made the identification all would be well again.

But it was Mart Kramer, the D.C. reporter, who arrived at the gaol first.

Still in his shorts and shirt, Philip was sitting on the hard bench of a dingy cell, reading a newspaper. There were only three lines in Kramer's syndicated column concerning the missing space-ship.

Philip never thought he'd be as happy to see Kramer as he was that day. There was an expression of wonderment in the reporter's gray lackluster eyes when they beheld the colored physicist calmly reading his newspaper.

"Phil!" he cried. "It's really you!"

The police captain, in shirt-sleeves now, was with the reporter. "Then this guy's really on the level, I guess," he said grudgingly. "You got quite a reputation with that column of yours, Mr. Kramer."

"I've known him for five years. Where's your duds?"

"Claims he lost 'em outta that stolen airship," the captain interposed.

Kramer ran a hand through his hair. It was obvious to Philip that he wanted the captain out of the way so that he could begin to fire a barrage of questions.

---

come in their saucer-like ship and kidnap PHILIP and ROSANNA for their lungs—to replace theirs which they claimed shriveled in the Martian atmosphere, making it necessary for them to always breathe pure oxygen to live.

They land on one of the Mars moons, Phobos, where Philip knocks out one his captors and escaped in the space-ship Hydra, a product of the A-P Society. A violent interplanetary fight ensues in the heavens until the combatants reach the earth's ionosphere.

Then PHILIP brings his Atom-Gun into play and blasts two of his pursuers to powder. The other two crash in a suicide pact. PHILIP and ROSANNA expect a royal welcome when they land at Denver later; but instead they are clapped in jail and PHILIP is charged with stealing the Hydra and carrying his fiancee across the state lines for immoral purposes. NOW READ ON—

1 In durance vile: "Forced confinement, imprisonment; constraint" (*OED*).

"Would you be a good guy, captain, and have one of your boys dash out and get the doctor some clothes." He produced a tooled-leather wallet and peeled off two fifty-dollar bills.

"While you've got it out, have the matron get some clothes for my fiancee. She's a perfect thirty-six and wears a size five shoe on a double-A last.[1] Me? I'll take a banker's gray, single breasted, size 42 long. Thirty-four inch pant legs."

"How did it Happen?"

When the officer was gone, Kramer pulled up a chair beside the cell and said: "Am I full of riddles, Phil! First: How could you steal the Hydra and be at a meeting of the Astro-Physical society at the same time? Second: Where did you get the message I found in the waste-basket in your laboratory atop the Keyes building? Third: How did you and your girl friend get out without being seen by the watchman on duty that Thursday-Friday morning? I am all agog Phil!"

Philip frowned. "I'm afraid that what I have to say wouldn't 'un-gog' you. But let's see: I'll try to answer your questions in chronological order. One—I did not steal the Hydra.

"Two—I don't know what message you're talking about. Three—the watchman in the Keyes Building is a notorious sleeper who sets an alarm clock every hour so that he won't miss his rounds."

Kramer gave him a fishy stare. "You haven't answered a single riddle! Come on—give!" Suddenly Kramer raised his brow, snapped his fingers. "Where did you find the Hydra?"

Philip shrugged his shoulders. "The important thing was finding it." He was determined that they wouldn't be sending for the men with the white coats. Besides a banker's gray became him more than a strait-jacket.

Kramer sighed and crossed his legs. "All right. Suppose I tell you doc!"

Philip settled back on the hard bench. "Suppose you do."

The lackluster eyes took on a hardness then and the reporter's jaw-muscles bunched. "I think it was all a great hoax," he began. "Of course I wanted a story—a bona-fide story from you. I believe that you didn't steal the Hydra—but I think you engineered the theft with some confederate of yours."

Illogical Conclusion

Philip's mouth popped open. "For what purpose? What could I do with it? It was the only one of its kind—a half-million-dollar space ship identifiable almost anywhere. What kind of logic is that?"

"You geniuses aren't always logical. Maybe you just wanted to joy-ride. Maybe you wanted to see if the ship really would break through the ionosphere."

1 A "last" is a term for the mould used to make shoes. In this case, a "double-A last" indicates a very narrow shoe.

"You're second-guessing—and very badly," Philip cut in.

There was a minor commotion near the entrance of the lock-up, and both Kramer and Philip turned to see what had occurred.

The jaunty, middle-aged Dr. Alderhoff had arrived, and there were four other members of the Astro-Physical Society with him, one of whom Philip didn't recognize.

"Who's the big, bald man with the Lenin mustache and goatee," he wanted to know.

"The new Soviet representative," Kramer supplied. "Doctor Varga." Kramer smirked. "Two days with the society now, and already he's delivering ultimatums. You'd think he was a U.N. delegate!"

The new clothes and the delegation arrived at Philip's cell at the same time. The Haitian-American got permission from the jailer to repair to an anteroom while he shaved and changed.

When he had finished the delegation came into the anteroom, Alderhoff in the lead, and clearly upset. Doctor Varga scowled darkly at everyone, including the police sergeant in attendance.

Alderhoff's greeting was almost paternal in its warmth. "Philip, boy, where have you been? I know you can explain everything satisfactorily."

"He is a fakir!" The booming voice was heavy with an accent. "That ship we saw can't possibly be the Hydra! A replica, perhaps, but not the Hydra."

Philip's face was impassive now as he looked into the piercing black eyes of Doctor Varga. In them was the look of maniacal fury he had seen in other eyes a short time ago when two gray men talked bravely of a second coming.

"I think," Philip said, "that we should go to a cloister of our own, if my release has been obtained. Besides, I'm very tired and will not wake up until the day after tomorrow."

A Knockout

"A very sensible idea," Alderhoff commented. "Oh, here comes Miss Daniels."

Rosanna was a knockout in green and brown. Her ensemble must have set Kramer back another hundred dollars.

"We're flying East on the next plane, dear," Philip said to her. "Think you're up to it?"

"No. I've had enough flying for one lifetime. I'm going to try to wangle a lower berth on the Burlington to Chicago; then I'll catch another train from there."

"Make it two," Philip said, taking her by the arm. Suddenly he turned to Alderhoff. "I just remembered. I haven't a cent. How about a few hundred till I get to New York?"

Philip had a lot of time to sleep and a lot of time to think on the way to New York. The central figure of his cogitations was Doctor Casmir Varga. Why had he been so sure that the real Hydra was elsewhere—or destroyed?

Why had the Soviet Union suddenly decided to send an astro-physicist of their own to replace Belikov and Gronsk? Why had he been delivering ultimatums to the rest of the society members?

Rosanna, on the other hand, was pushing the nightmare of interstellar flight and conflict to the back of her mind. She wanted to forget the harrowing ugly scenes of a short time ago and concentrate more fully on her profession as a concert pianist.

She found, however, that she was beginning to have a lower regard for Russian music, and such an attitude was very unhealthy in a musician.

On the day the Liberty Limited[1] brought Philip and Rosanna to New York, a special session of the astronomical society was held in the Chantilly Room of the Van Astor Hotel[2] in downtown Manhattan.

As usual, the only reporter present was Mart Kramer, the scribe, who was still nursing a peeve against Philip.

Rosanna had gone home to her apartment for further recuperation and Philip found himself the center of attraction. Every member was present, and not a few of them cast meaningful scowls in Philip's direction.

Mystery Confounds

Dr. Alderhoff rapped his gavel for order and opened the session. "In view of certain unusual occurrences we are met again in a special session. We hope to get to the bottom of a mystery concerning the society's space-ship, the Hydra, and the later disappearance of our Doctor Philip Browne."

But it was Doctor Varga who took the floor. He waved a big paw in a deprecatory gesture as Philip started to rise.

"He is a liar and a fakir," Varga boomed. "I know his kind. Exhibitionists. The Hydra—"

The sharp rapping of the gavel intervened. Kramer strained forward, pencil poised above pad.

"Doctor Varga!" Alderhoff said sharply. "After all, you should be used to protocol."

Varga's lip curled in a sneer. "Protocol, rules, amenities—bah! Soon we will make the rules and you all will jump like puppets when we pull the strings!"

Philip frowned. "Mr. Chairman, I think I can restore order if you'll allow me a few words with Dr. Varga alone—over by the window."

Dr. Alderhoff bit his lip. "It's a bit irregular—but if it'll restore order—"

Dr. Varga thrust out his heavy jaw. "Say what you want so all of us can hear, fakir!" he roared.

"All right," Philip snapped. "I was going to tell you to pull in your horns, Varga, because what you think is on Phobos isn't there anymore!"

The Soviet doctor staggered back as though struck with a blow to the

---

1 The Liberty Limited train, operated by Pennsylvania Railroad, ran between Washington, DC, and Chicago, where passengers could then take the Broadway Limited to New York.

2 Perhaps the Hotel Astor, built in 1904, or a fictional hotel modelled on it.

midriff, his eyes gaping, his mouth working like a gaffed bass. Very weakly he sank into a chair and perspiration began to bead his brow.

Dead Silence

The other members of the society, as well as Kramer, were amazed at the tableau. A dead silence hung over the room for a long moment.

Philip's voice broke it again. "Gentlemen, you have every right to my report, but believe me, I am loth to give it because it will sound so utterly fantastic." Then, eliminating no detail and embellishing none, he gave a full account of what had transpired between the Thursday night he went to the roof of the Keyes Building and his landing at Denver, adding: "But if a word of it ever got out to the public—well—"

Varga was crying now—like a small boy. "But I cannot understand it! We are superior. Yet, everything he said dovetails—even to the black fog of the Phobos moon!"

Then he settled back in his chair and began to whimper.

When the session was over, Kramer came over to him. "I want to apologize, Phil. I'll admit if you'd told me that story in that Denver calaboose I'd a thought you'd blown your cork or'd been hitting the hop.[1]

"In fact, the only way I can believe it now is the way you took the wind out of Varga's sails when you mentioned Phobos. And when you talked so authoritatively about his gray-faced, lungless comrades, he paled so much I just had to believe you." He sighed. "Still, I have no story. At least, none that I can print."

Philip laughed. "Then why don't you send it in as fiction—to a science-fiction magazine?"

Kramer shook his head. "Even fiction has to be plausible. Still, maybe I'll try it."

Later, in Rosanna's apartment, Philip lay in his fiancee's arms and said: "You know, dear, this is a weird, crazy world we're in."

"I know it is," she said, kissing him. "And I want it to stay that way. I'd hate like the dickens to be an androgyne and have to make love to myself."

1 Hitting the hop: "to use drugs, especially heroin or opium" (Dalzell and Victor 91).

Arthur C. Clarke (1917–2008)

One of the giants of SF in the so-called "Golden Age," and recognized as a "Grand Master" by the Science Fiction Research Association, Arthur C. Clarke is also often hailed as the originator of the idea of using geostationary satellites for communications purposes. Clarke's fiction, including the well-known novel and Stanley Kubrick-directed film *2001: A Space Odyssey* (both 1968), often deals with the intersections of religion and technology, as in what is likely his most famous statement that "any sufficiently advanced technology is indistinguishable from magic," something he says he "dealt with" in many publications, including *2001* (Clarke, "Clarke's Third Law on UFO's"). A gay man at a time when homosexual acts were still illegal in the UK, Clarke moved to Sri Lanka in 1956, and lived there until his death, having been awarded the Sri Lankabhimanya, that country's highest civilian honour in 2005, following his knighthood in 1998.

Note on the text: This story was first published in *Star Science Fiction Stories*, edited by famed SF editor and author Frederik Pohl (1953; this was later referred to as "No. 1" when *Star Science Fiction Stories* became a series). The text follows the first British edition with minor corrections from later versions.

"The Nine Billion Names of God" (1953)

"This is a slightly unusual request," said Dr. Wagner, with what he hoped was commendable restraint. "As far as I know, it's the first time anyone's been asked to supply a Tibetan monastery with an Automatic Sequence Computer. I don't wish to be inquisitive, but I should hardly have thought that your—ah—establishment had much use for such a machine. Could you explain just what you intend to do with it?"

"Gladly," replied the Lama,[1] readjusting his silk robe and carefully putting away the slide rule[2] he had been using for currency conversions. "Your Mark V Computer can carry out any routine mathematical operation involving up to ten digits. However, for our work we are interested in *letters,* not numbers. As we wish you to modify the output circuits, the machine will be printing words, not columns of figures."

"I don't quite understand ..."

"This is a project on which we have been working for the last three centuries—since the lamasery was founded, in fact. It is somewhat alien to your way of thought, so I hope you will listen with an open mind while I explain it."

1 A spiritual leader in Tibetan Buddhism.

2 A mechanical device, made of two or more rulers that slide together, which can be used to perform such mathematical tasks as multiplication, division, and logarithms.

"Naturally."

"It is really quite simple. We have been compiling a list which shall contain all the possible names of God."

"I beg your pardon?"

"We have reason to believe," continued the Lama imperturbably, "that all such names can be written with not more than nine letters in an alphabet we have devised."

"And you have been doing this for three centuries?"

"Yes: we expected it would take us about fifteen thousand years to complete the task."

"Oh," Dr. Wagner looked a little dazed. "Now I see why you wanted to hire one of our machines. But exactly what is the *purpose* of this project?"

The Lama hesitated for a fraction of a second and Wagner wondered if he had offended him. If so, there was no trace of annoyance in the reply.

"Call it ritual, if you like, but it's a fundamental part of our belief. All the many names of the Supreme Being—God, Jehovah, Allah, and so on—they are only man-made labels. There is a philosophical problem of some difficulty here, which I do not propose to discuss, but somewhere among all the possible combinations of letters which can occur are what one may call the *real* names of God. By systematic permutation of letters, we have been trying to list them all."

"I see. You've been starting at AAAAAAAAA … and working up to ZZZZZZZZZ …"

"Exactly—though we use a special alphabet of our own. Modifying the electromatic typewriters to deal with this is, of course, trivial. A rather more interesting problem is that of devising suitable circuits to eliminate ridiculous combinations. For example, no letter must occur more than three times in succession."

"Three? Surely you mean two."

"Three is correct: I am afraid it would take too long to explain why, even if you understood our language."

"I'm sure it would," said Wagner hastily. "Go on."

"Luckily, it will be a simple matter to adapt your Automatic Sequence Computer for this work, since once it has been programed properly it will permute each letter in turn and print the result. What would have taken us fifteen thousand years it will be able to do in a hundred days."

Dr. Wagner was scarcely conscious of the faint sounds from the Manhattan streets far below. He was in a different world, a world of natural, not man-made, mountains. High up in their remote aeries these monks had been patiently at work, generation after generation, compiling their lists of meaningless words. Was there any limit to the follies of mankind? Still, he must give no hint of his inner thoughts. The customer was always right …

"There's no doubt," replied the doctor, "that we can modify the Mark V to print lists of this nature. I'm much more worried about the problem of installation and maintenance. Getting out to Tibet, in these days, is not going to be easy."

"We can arrange that. The components are small enough to travel by air—that is one reason why we chose your machine. If you can get them to India, we will provide transport from there."

"And you want to hire two of our engineers?"

"Yes, for the three months which the project should occupy."

"I've no doubt that Personnel can manage that." Dr. Wagner scribbled a note on his desk pad. "There are just two other points—"

Before he could finish the sentence the Lama had produced a small slip of paper.

"This is my certified credit balance at the Asiatic Bank."

"Thank you. It appears to be—ah—adequate. The second matter is so trivial that I hesitate to mention it—but it's surprising how often the obvious gets overlooked. What source of electrical energy have you?"

"A diesel generator providing 50 kilowatts at 110 volts. It was installed about five years ago and is quite reliable. It's made life at the lamasery much more comfortable, but of course it was really installed to provide power for the motors driving the prayer wheels."

"Of course," echoed Dr. Wagner. "I should have thought of that."

The view from the parapet was vertiginous, but in time one gets used to anything. After three months, George Hanley was not impressed by the two-thousand-foot swoop into the abyss or the remote checkerboard of fields in the valley below. He was leaning against the wind-smoothed stones and staring morosely at the distant mountains whose names he had never bothered to discover.

This, thought George, was the craziest thing that had ever happened to him. "Project Shangri-La," some wit back at the labs had christened it. For weeks now the Mark V had been churning out acres of sheets covered with gibberish. Patiently, inexorably, the computer had been rearranging letters in all their possible combinations, exhausting each class before going on to the next. As the sheets had emerged from the electromatic typewriters, the monks had carefully cut them up and pasted them into enormous books. In another week, heaven be praised, they would have finished. Just what obscure calculations had convinced the monks that they needn't bother to go on to words of ten, twenty, or a hundred letters, George didn't know. One of his recurring nightmares was that there would be some change of plan, and that the High Lama (whom they'd naturally called Sam Jaffe, though he didn't look a bit like him)[1] would suddenly announce that the project would be extended to approximately 2060 A.D. They were quite capable of it.

George heard the heavy wooden door slam in the wind as Chuck came out on to the parapet beside him. As usual, Chuck was smoking one of the

1 Sam Jaffe (1891–1984) was an American actor who had recently appeared as a professor and scientist in the SF film—destined to become a classic of the form—*The Day the Earth Stood Still* (1951).

cigars that made him so popular with the monks—who, it seemed, were quite willing to embrace all the minor and most of the major pleasures of life. That was one thing in their favor: they might be crazy, but they weren't bluenoses.[1] Those frequent trips they took down to the village, for instance …

"Listen, George," said Chuck urgently. "I've learned something that means trouble."

"What's wrong? Isn't the machine behaving?" That was the worst contingency George could imagine. It might delay his return, than which nothing could be more horrible. The way he felt now, even the sight of a TV commercial would seem like manna from heaven. At least it would be some link with home.

"No—it's nothing like that." Chuck settled himself on the parapet, which was unusual because normally he was scared of the drop. "I've just found what all this is about."

"What d'ya mean—I thought we knew."

"Sure—we know what the monks are trying to do. But we didn't know *why*. It's the craziest thing—"

"Tell me something new," growled George.

"—but old Sam's just come clean with me. You know the way he drops in every afternoon to watch the sheets roll out. Well, this time he seemed rather excited, or at least as near as he'll ever get to it. When I told him that we were on the last cycle he asked me, in that cute English accent of his, if I'd ever wondered what they were trying to do. I said, 'Sure'—and he told me."

"Go on: I'll buy it."

"Well, they believe that when they have listed all His names—and they reckon that there are about nine billion of them—God's purpose will be achieved. The human race will have finished what it was created to do, and there won't be any point in carrying on. Indeed, the very idea is something like blasphemy."

"Then what do they expect us to do? Commit suicide?"

"There's no need for that. When the list's completed, God steps in and simply winds things up … bingo!"

"Oh, I get it. When we finish our job, it will be the end of the world."

Chuck gave a nervous little laugh.

"That's just what I said to Sam. And do you know what happened? He looked at me in a very queer way, like I'd been stupid in class, and said, 'It's nothing as trivial as *that*.'"

George thought this over for a moment.

"That's what I call taking the Wide View," he said presently. "But what d'ya suppose we should do about it? I don't see that it makes the slightest difference to us. After all, we already knew that they were crazy."

---

1 Here, "any excessively moralistic person" (*OED*), as opposed to the more common usage: someone from Nova Scotia, Canada.

"Yes—but don't you see what may happen? When the list's complete and the Last Trump doesn't blow—or whatever it is they expect—*we* may get the blame. It's our machine they've been using. I don't like the situation one little bit."

"I see," said George slowly. "You've got a point there. But this sort of thing's happened before, you know. When I was a kid down in Louisiana we had a crackpot preacher who said the world was going to end next Sunday. Hundreds of people believed him—even sold their homes. Yet when nothing happened, they didn't turn nasty, as you'd expect. They just decided that he'd made a mistake in his calculations and went right on believing. I guess some of them still do."

"Well, this isn't Louisiana, in case you hadn't noticed. There are just two of us and hundreds of these monks. I like them, and I'll be sorry for old Sam when his lifework backfires on him. But all the same, I wish I was somewhere else."

"I've been wishing that for weeks. But there's nothing we can do until the contract's finished and the transport arrives to fly us out."

"Of course," said Chuck thoughtfully, "we could always try a bit of sabotage."

"Like hell we could! That would make things worse."

"Not the way I meant. Look at it like this. The machine will finish its run four days from now, on the present twenty-hours-a-day basis. The transport calls in a week. O.K.—then all we need to do is to find something that wants replacing during one of the overhaul periods—something that will hold up the works for a couple of days. We'll fix it, of course, but not too quickly. If we time matters properly, we can be down at the airfield when the last name pops out of the register. They won't be able to catch us then."

"I don't like it," said George. "It will be the first time I ever walked out on a job. Besides, it would make them suspicious. No. I'll sit tight and take what comes."

"I *still* don't like it," he said, seven days later, as the tough little mountain ponies carried them down the winding road. "And don't you think I'm running away because I'm afraid. I'm just sorry for those poor old guys up there, and I don't want to be around when they find what suckers they've been. Wonder how Sam will take it?"

"It's funny," replied Chuck, "but when I said good-bye I got the idea he knew we were walking out on him—and that he didn't care because he knew the machine was running smoothly and that the job would soon be finished. After that—well, of course, for him there just isn't any After That...."

George turned in his saddle and stared back up the mountain road. This was the last place from which one could get a clear view of the lamasery. The squat, angular buildings were silhouetted against the afterglow of the sunset: here and there, lights gleamed like portholes in the side of an ocean liner.

Electric lights, of course, sharing the same circuit as the Mark V. How much longer would they share it, wondered George. Would the monks smash up the computer in their rage and disappointment? Or would they just sit down quietly and begin their calculations all over again?

He knew exactly what was happening up on the mountain at this very moment. The High Lama and his assistants would be sitting in their silk robes, inspecting the sheets as the junior monks carried them away from the typewriters and pasted them into the great volumes. No one would be saying anything. The only sound would be the incessant patter, the never-ending rainstorm of the keys hitting the paper, for the Mark V itself was utterly silent as it flashed through its thousands of calculations a second. Three months of this, thought George, was enough to start anyone climbing up the wall.

"There she is!" called Chuck, pointing down into the valley. "Ain't she beautiful!"

She certainly was, thought George. The battered old DC 3[1] lay at the end of the runway like a tiny silver cross. In two hours she would be bearing them away to freedom and sanity. It was a thought worth savoring like a fine liqueur. George let it roll round his mind as the pony trudged patiently down the slope.

The swift night of the high Himalayas was now almost upon them. Fortunately, the road was very good, as roads went in this region, and they were both carrying torches. There was not the slightest danger, only a certain discomfort from the bitter cold. The sky overhead was perfectly clear and ablaze with the familiar, friendly stars. At least there would be no risk, thought George, of the pilot being unable to take off because of weather conditions. That had been his only remaining worry.

He began to sing, but gave it up after a while. This vast arena of mountains, gleaming like whitely hooded ghosts on every side, did not encourage such ebullience. Presently George glanced at his watch.

"Should be there in an hour," he called back over his shoulder to Chuck. Then he added, in an afterthought: "Wonder if the computer's finished its run. It was due about now."

Chuck didn't reply, so George swung round in his saddle. He could just see Chuck's face, a white oval turned toward the sky.

"Look," whispered Chuck, and George lifted his eyes to heaven. (There is always a last time for everything.)

Overhead, without any fuss, the stars were going out.

1 The Douglas DC-3 was an early commercial airplane that was also used by the military in World War II.

Fig. 6: Gredno Mahasm. Illustration to "The World Well Lost." *Universe Science Fiction*, no. 1, 1953.

Theodore Sturgeon (1918–85)

Theodore Sturgeon's memoir, *Argyll* (titled after his stepfather's nickname), details his youthful reading of pulp SF works, which his stepfather threw away because "That's what we do with garbage," instead insisting his stepson read more classic literature (36). From this origin, Sturgeon became what could be best referred to as a "science fiction writer's science fiction writer"; his work has been repeatedly praised by many SF authors and fans, but he never achieved the popular, name-recognition fame of some of his contemporaries (despite writing popular episodes of the original *Star Trek* series). In his memorial to Sturgeon, famed SF author and critic Samuel R. Delany notes that Sturgeon's work "is the single most important body of science fiction by an American today" ("Theodore Sturgeon, *In Memoriam*" 63–64). "The World Well Lost" is often described as one of the earliest known SF stories to deal directly with themes of queer sexuality and homophobia.

Note on the text: The story was published in 1953 in both Sturgeon's collection *E Pluribus Unicorn* (Abelard) and the inaugural issue of *Universe Science Fiction* (June 1953). The current text follows the appearance in *Universe,* which was illustrated by Gredno Mahasm (Fig. 6).

"The World Well Lost" (1953)

ALL the world knew them as loverbirds, though they were certainly not birds, but humans. Well, say humanoids. Featherless bipeds. Their stay on earth[1] was brief, a nine-day wonder. Any wonder that lasts nine days on an earth of orgasmic trideo shows; time-freezing pills; synapse-inverter fields which make it possible for a man to turn a sunset to perfumes, a masochist to a fur-feeler; and a thousand other euphorics—why, on such an earth, a nine-day wonder is a wonder indeed.

Like a sudden bloom across the face of the world came the peculiar magic of the loverbirds. There were loverbird songs and loverbird trinkets, loverbird hats and pins, bangles and baubles, coins and quaffs and tidbits. For there was that about the loverbirds which made a deep enchantment. No one can be told about a loverbird and feel this curious delight. Many are immune even to a solidograph. But watch loverbirds, only for a moment, and see what happens. It's the feeling you had when you were twelve, and summer-drenched, and you kissed a girl for the very first time and knew a breathlessness you were sure could never happen again. And indeed it never could—unless you watched loverbirds. Then you are spellbound for four quiet seconds, and

1 In both book and magazine publications, "earth" is inconsistently capitalized or not; the original typography has been retained.

suddenly your very heart twists, and incredulous tears sting and stay; and the very first move you make afterward, you make on tiptoe, and your first word is a whisper.

This magic came over very well on trideo, and everyone had trideo; so for a brief while the earth was enchanted.

There were only two loverbirds. They came down out of the sky in a single brassy flash, and stepped out of their ship, hand in hand. Their eyes were full of wonder, each at the other, and together at the world. They seemed frozen in a full-to-bursting moment of discovery; they made way for one another gravely and with courtesy, they looked about them and in the very looking gave each other gifts—the color of the sky, the taste of the air, the pressures of things growing and meeting and changing. They never spoke. They simply *were* together. To watch them was to know of their awestruck mounting of staircases of bird notes, of how each knew the warmth of the other as their flesh supped silently on sunlight.

They stepped from their ship, and the tall one threw a yellow powder back to it. The ship fell in upon itself and became a pile of rubble, which collapsed into a pile of gleaming sand, which slumped compactly down to dust and then to an airblown emulsion so fine that Brownian movement itself hammered it up and out and away. Anyone could see that they intended to stay. Anyone could know by simply watching them that next to their wondrous delight in each other came their delighted wonder at earth itself, everything and everybody about it.

Now, if terrestrial culture were a pyramid, at the apex (where the power is) would sit a blind man, for so constituted are we that only by blinding ourselves, bit by bit, may we rise above our fellows. The man at the apex has an immense preoccupation with the welfare of the whole, because he regards it as the source and structure of his elevation, which it is, and as an extension of himself, which it is not. It was such a man who, in the face of immeasurable evidence, chose to find a defense against loverbirds, and fed the matrices and coordinates of the loverbird image into the most marvelous calculator that had ever been built.

The machine sucked in symbols and raced them about, compared and waited and matched and sat still while its bulging memory, cell by cell, was silent, was silent—and suddenly, in a far corner, resonated. It grasped this resonance in forceps made of mathematics, snatched it out (translating furiously as it snatched) and put out a fevered tongue of paper on which was typed:

DIRBANU

Now this utterly changed the complexion of things. For earth ships had ranged the cosmos far and wide, with few hindrances. Of these hindrances, all could be understood but one, and that one was Dirbanu, a transgalactic planet which shrouded itself in impenetrable fields of force whenever an earthship approached. There were other worlds which could do this, but in each case the crews knew why it was done. Dirbanu, upon discovery, had prohibited landings from the very first until an ambassador could be sent to Terra. In due time one did arrive (so reported the calculator, which was the only entity that remembered the episode) and it was obvious that Earth and Dirbanu had much in common. The ambassador, however, showed a most uncommon disdain of Earth and all its works, curled his lip and went wordlessly home, and ever since then Dirbanu had locked itself tight away from the questing Terrans.

Dirbanu thereby became of value, and fair game, but we could do nothing to ripple the bland face of her defenses. As this impregnability repeatedly proved itself, Dirbanu evolved in our group mind through the usual stages of being: the Curiosity, the Mystery, the Challenge, the Enemy, the Enemy, the Enemy, the Mystery, the Curiosity, and finally That-which-is-too-faraway-to-bother-with, or the Forgotten.

And suddenly, after all this time, Earth had two genuine natives of Dirbanu aboard, entrancing the populace and giving no information. This intolerable circumstance began to make itself felt throughout the world—but slowly, for this time the blind men's din was cushioned and soaked by the magic of the loverbirds. It might have taken a very long time to convince the people of the menace in their midst had there not been a truly startling development:

A direct message was received from Dirbanu.

The collective impact of loverbird material emanating from transmitters on Earth had attracted the attention of Dirbanu, which promptly informed us that the loverbirds were indeed their nationals, that in addition they were fugitives, that Dirbanu would take it ill if Earth should regard itself as a sanctuary for the criminals of Dirbanu but would, on the other hand, find it in its heart to be very pleased if Earth saw fit to return them.

So from the depths of its enchantment, Terra was able to calculate a course of action. Here at last was an opportunity to consort with Dirbanu on a friendly basis—great Dirbanu which, since it had force fields which Earth could not duplicate, must of necessity have many other things Earth could use; mighty Dirbanu before whom we could kneel in supplication (with purely-for-defense bombs hidden in our pockets) with lowered heads (making invisible the knife in our teeth) and ask for crumbs from their table (in order to extrapolate the location of their kitchens).

Thus the loverbird episode became another item in the weary procession of proofs that Terra's most reasonable intolerance can conquer practically anything, even magic.

Especially magic.

So it was that the loverbirds were arrested, that the *Starmite* 439 was fitted out as a prison ship, that a most carefully screened crew was chosen for her, and that she struck starward with the cargo that would gain us a world.

* * *

Two men were the crew—a colorful little rooster of a man and a great dun bull of a man. They were, respectively, Rootes, who was Captain and staff, and Grunty, who was midship and inboard corps. Rootes was cocky, springy, white and crisp. His hair was auburn and so were his eyes, and the eyes were hard. Grunty was a shambler with big gentle hands and heavy shoulders half as wide as Rootes was high. He should have worn a cowl and rope-belted habit. He should, perhaps, have worn a burnoose. He did neither, but the effect was there. Known only to him was the fact that words and pictures, concepts and comparisons were an endless swirling blizzard inside him. Known only to him and Rootes was the fact that he had books, and books, and books, and Rootes did not care if he had or not. Grunty he had been called since he first learned to talk, and Grunty was name enough for him. For the words in his head would not leave him except one or two at a time, with long moments between. So he had learned to condense his verbal messages to breathy grunts, and when they wouldn't condense, he said nothing.

They were primitives, both of them, which is to say that they were doers, while Modern Man is a thinker and/or a feeler. The thinkers compose new variations and permutations of euphoria, and the feelers repay the thinkers by responding to their inventions. The ships had no place for Modern Man, and Modern Man had only the most casual use for the ships.

Doers can cooperate like cam and pushrod, like ratchet and pawl, and such linkage creates a powerful bond. But Rootes and Grunty were unique among crews in that these machine parts were not interchangeable. Any good captain can command any good crew, surroundings being equivalent. But Rootes would not and could not ship out with anyone but Grunty, and Grunty was just that dependent. Grunty understood this bond, and the fact that the only way it could conceivably be broken would be to explain it to Rootes. Rootes did not understand it because it never occurred to him to try, and had he tried, he would have failed, since he was inherently non-equipped for the task. Grunty knew that their unique bond was, for him, a survival matter. Rootes did not know this, and would have rejected the idea with violence.

So Rootes regarded Grunty with tolerance and a modified amusement. The modification was an inarticulate realization of Grunty's complete dependability. Grunty regarded Rootes with … well, with the ceaseless, silent flurry of words in his mind.

There was, beside the harmony of functions and the other link, understood only by Grunty, a third adjunct to their phenomenal efficiency as a crew. It was organic, and it had to do with the stellar drive.

Reaction engines were long forgotten. The so-called "warp" drive was used only experimentally and on certain crash-priority war-craft where operating costs were not a factor. The *Starmite* 439 was, like most interstellar craft, powered by an RS plant. Like the transistor, the Referential Stasis generator is extremely simple to construct and very difficult indeed to explain. Its mathematics approaches mysticism and its theory contains certain impossibilities which are ignored in practice. Its effect is to shift the area of stasis of the ship and everything in it from one point of reference to another. For example, the ship at rest on the Earth's surface is in stasis in reference to the ground on which it rests. Throwing the ship into stasis in reference to the center of the earth gives it instantly an effective speed equal to the surface velocity of the planet around its core—some one thousand miles per hour. Stasis referential to the sun moves the Earth out from under the ship at the Earth's orbital velocity. GH stasis "moves" the ship at the angular velocity of the sun about the Galactic Hub. The galactic drift can be used, as can any simple or complex mass center in this expanding universe. There are resultants and there are multipliers, and effective velocities can be enormous. Yet the ship is constantly in stasis, so that there is never an inertia factor.

The one inconvenience of the RS drive is that shifts from one referent to another invariably black the crew out, for psychoneural reasons. The blackout period varies slightly between individuals, from one to two and a half hours. But some anomaly in Grunty's gigantic frame kept his blackout periods down to thirty or forty minutes, while Rootes was always out for two hours or more. There was that about Grunty which made moments of isolation a vital necessity, for a man must occasionally be himself, which in anyone's company Grunty was not. But after stasis shifts Grunty had an hour or so to himself while his commander lay numbly spread-eagled on the blackout couch, and he spent these in communions of his own devising. Sometimes this meant only a good book.

This, then, was the crew picked to man the prison ship. It had been together longer than any other crew in the Space Service. Its record showed a metrical efficiency and a resistance to physical and psychic debilitations previously unheard of in a trade where close confinement on long voyages had come to be regarded as hazards. In space, shift followed shift uneventfully, and planetfall was made on schedule and without incident. In port Rootes would roar off to the fleshpots, in which he would wallow noisily until an hour before takeoff, while Grunty found, first, the business office, and next, a bookstore.

They were pleased to be chosen for the Dirbanu trip. Rootes felt no remorse at taking away Earth's new delight, since he was one of the very few who was immune to it. ("Pretty," he said at his first encounter.) Grunty simply grunted, but then, so did everyone else. Rootes did not notice, and Grunty did not remark upon the obvious fact that though the loverbirds' expression of awestruck wonderment in each other's presence had, if anything, intensified, their extreme pleasure in Earth and the things of Earth had vanished. They were locked, securely but comfortably, in the after cabin behind a new transparent door, so that their every move could be watched from the main cabin and control console. They sat close, with their arms about one another, and though their radiant joy in the contact never lessened, it was a shadowed pleasure, a lachrymose beauty like the wrenching music of the wailing wall.

The RS drive laid its hand on the moon and they vaulted away. Grunty came up from blackout to find it very quiet. The loverbirds lay still in each other's arms, looking very human except for the high joining of their closed eyelids, which nictated upward rather than downward like a Terran's. Rootes sprawled limply on the other couch, and Grunty nodded at the sight. He deeply appreciated the silence, since Rootes had filled the small cabin with earthy chatter about his conquests in port, detail by hairy detail, for two solid hours preceding their departure. It was a routine which Grunty found particularly wearing, partly for its content, which interested him not at all, but mostly for its inevitability. Grunty had long ago noted that these recitations, for all their detail, carried the tones of thirst rather than of satiety. He had his own conclusions about it, and, characteristically, kept them to himself. But inside, his spinning gusts of words could shape themselves well to it, and they did. "And man, she moaned!" Rootes would chant. "And take money? She *gave* me money. And what did I do with it? Why, I bought up some more of the same." *And what you could buy with a shekel's worth of tenderness, my prince!* his silent words sang. "… across the floor and around the rug until, by damn, I thought we're about to climb the wall. Loaded, Grunty-boy, I tell you, I was loaded!" *Poor little one* ran the hushed susurrus, *thy poverty is as great as thy joy and a tenth as great as thine empty noise.* One of Grunty's greatest pleasures was taken in the fact that this kind of chuntering was limited to the first day out, with barely another word on the varied theme until the next departure, no matter how many months away that might be. *Squeak to me of love, dear mouse,* his words would chuckle. *Stand up on your cheese and nibble away at your dream.* Then, wearily, *But oh, this treasure I carry is too heavy a burden, in all its fullness, to be so tugged at by your clattering vacuum!*

Grunty left the couch and went to the controls. The preset courses checked against the indicators. He logged them and fixed the finder control to locate a certain mass-nexus in the Crab Nebula. It would chime when it was ready. He set the switch for final closing by the push-button beside his couch, and went aft to wait.

He stood watching the loverbirds because there was nothing else for him to do.

They lay quite still, but love so permeated them that their very poses expressed it. Their lax bodies yearned each to each, and the tall one's hand seemed to stream toward the fingers of his beloved, and then back again, like the riven tatters of a torn fabric straining toward oneness again. And as their mood was a sadness too, so their pose, each and both, together and singly expressed it, and singly each through the other silently spoke of the loss they had suffered, and how it ensured greater losses to come. Slowly the picture suffused Grunty's thinking, and his words picked and pieced and smoothed it down, and murmured finally, *Brush away the dusting of sadness from the future, bright ones. You've sadness enough for now. Grief should live only after it is truly born, and not before.*

His words sang,

Come fill the cup and in the fire of spring
Your winter garment of repentance fling.
The bird of time has but a little way
To flutter—and the bird is on the wing.

and added *Omar Khayyam, born circa 1073*, for this, too, was one of the words' functions.[1]

And then he stiffened in horror; his great hands came up convulsively and clawed the imprisoning glass …

They were smiling at him.

They were smiling, and on their faces and on and about their bodies there was no sadness.

They had *heard* him!

He glanced convulsively around at the Captain's unconscious form, then back to the loverbirds.

That they should recover so swiftly from blackout was, to say the least, an intrusion; for his moments of aloneness were precious and more than precious to Grunty, and would be useless to him under the scrutiny of those jewelled eyes. But that was a minor matter compared to this other thing, this terrible fact that they *heard*.

Telepathic races were not common, but they did exist. And what he was now experiencing was what invariably happened when humans encountered one. He could only send; the loverbirds could only receive. And they *must not* receive him! No one must. No one must know what he was, what he thought. If anyone did, it would be a disaster beyond bearing. It would mean no more flights with Rootes. Which, of course, meant no flights with anyone. And how could he live—where could he go?

He turned back to the loverbirds. His lips were white and drawn back in a snarl of panic and fury. For a blood-thick moment he held their eyes. They drew closer to one another, and together sent him a radiant, anxious, friendly look that made him grind his teeth.

Then, at the console, the finder chimed.

Grunty turned slowly from the transparent door and went to his couch. He lay down and poised his thumb over the push-button.

He *hated* the loverbirds, and there was no joy in him. He pressed the button, the ship slid into a new stasis, and he blacked out.

---

1 Omar Khayyam (1048–1131), famed Persian poet, mathematician, and astronomer. Poetry attributed to him became famous in the English-speaking world with the publication of Edward FitzGerald's translation, published in book form as the *Rubáiyát of Omar Khayyám* (1859), where *Rubáiyát* refers to a collection of ruba'i, or Persian-language quatrains. The quoted version comes from a later edition, evidenced by "To fly" being replaced with "To flutter."

★ ★ ★

The time passed.

"Grunty!"

"?"

"You feed them this shift?"

"Nuh."

"Last shift?"

"Nuh."

"What the hell's matter with you, y'big dumb bastich? What you expect them to live on?"

Grunty sent a look of roiling hatred aft. "Love," he said.

"Feed 'em," snapped Rootes.

Wordlessly Grunty went about preparing a meal for the prisoners. Rootes stood in the middle of the cabin, his hard small fists on his hips, his gleaming auburn head tilted to one side, and watched every move. "I didn't used to have to tell you anything," he growled, half pugnaciously, half worriedly. "You sick?"

Grunty shook his head. He twisted the tops of two cans and set them aside to heat themselves, and took down the water suckers.

"You got it in for those honeymooners or something?"

Grunty averted his face.

"We get them to Dirbanu alive and healthy, hear me? They get sick, you get sick, by God. I'll see to that. Don't give me trouble, Grunty. I'll take it out on you. I never whipped you yet, but I will."

Grunty carried the tray aft. "You hear me?" Rootes yelled.

Grunty nodded without looking at him. He touched the control and a small communication window slid open in the glass wall. He slid the tray through. The taller loverbird stepped forward and took it eagerly, gracefully, and gave him a dazzling smile of thanks. Grunty growled low in his throat like a carnivore. The loverbird carried the food back to the couch and they began to eat, feeding each other little morsels.

★ ★ ★

A new stasis, and Grunty came fighting up out of blackness. He sat up abruptly, glanced around the ship. The Captain was sprawled out across the cushions, his compact body and outflung arm forming the poured-out, spring-steel laxness usually seen only in sleeping cats. The loverbirds, even in deep unconsciousness, lay like hardly separate parts of something whole, the small one on the couch, the tall one on the deck, prone, reaching, supplicating.

Grunty snorted and hove to his feet. He crossed the cabin and stood looking down on Rootes.

The hummingbird is a yellowjacket, said his words. *Buzz and dart, hiss and flash away. Swift and hurtful, hurtful …*

He stood for a long moment, his great shoulder muscles working one against the other, and his mouth trembled.

He looked at the loverbirds, who were still motionless. His eyes slowly narrowed.

His words tumbled and climbed, and ordered themselves:

I through love have learned three things,
Sorrow, sin and death it brings.
Yet day by day my heart within
Dares shame and sorrow, death and sin….[1]

And dutifully he added *Samuel Ferguson, born 1810.* He glared at the loverbirds, and brought his fist into his palm with a sound like a club on an anthill. They had heard him again, and this time they did not smile, but looked into each other's eyes and then turned together to regard him, nodding gravely.

* * *

Rootes went through Grunty's books, leafing and casting aside. He had never touched them before. "Buncha crap," he jeered. "Garden of the Plynck. Wind in the Willows. Worm Ouroborous.[2] Kid stuff."

Grunty lumbered across and patiently gathered up the books the Captain had flung aside, putting them one by one back into their places, stroking them as if they had been bruised.

"Isn't there nothing in here with pictures?"

Grunty regarded him silently for a moment and then took down a tall volume. The Captain snatched it, leafed through it. "Mountains," he growled. "Old houses." He leafed. "Damn boats." He smashed the book to the deck. "Haven't you got *any* of what I want?"

Grunty waited attentively.

"Do I have to draw a diagram?" the Captain roared. "Got that ol' itch, Grunty. You wouldn't know. I feel like looking at pictures, get what I mean?"

Grunty stared at him, utterly without expression, but deep within him a panic squirmed. The Captain never, *never* behaved like this in mid-voyage. It was going to get worse, he realized. Much worse. And quickly.

He shot the loverbirds a vicious, hate-filled glance. If they weren't aboard …

1 From the traditional Irish Gaelic poem, "The Coolin" (also written as "The Coolun") or, "The Fair-Haired Girl," translated into English by Samuel Ferguson (1810–86) as noted in the subsequent line.

2 *The Garden of the Plynk* (1920): children's fantasy novel by American author Karle Wilson Baker (1878–1960); *Wind in the Willows* (1908): children's novel by British author Kenneth Grahame (1859–1932); *Worm Ouroborous* (1922): fantasy novel by English writer E.R. Eddison (1882–1945).

There could be no waiting. Not now. Something had to be done. Something …

"Come on, come on," said Rootes. "Goddlemighty Godfrey, even a dead-butt like you must have *something* for kicks."

Grunty turned away from him, squeezed his eyes closed for a tortured second, then pulled himself together. He ran his hand over the books, hesitated, and finally brought out a large, heavy one. He handed it to the Captain and went forward to the console. He slumped down there over the file of computer tapes, pretending to be busy.

The Captain sprawled onto Grunty's couch and opened the book. "Michelangelo,[1] what the hell," he growled. He grunted, almost like his shipmate. "Statues," he half-whispered, in withering scorn. But he ogled and leafed at last, and was quiet.

The loverbirds looked at him with a sad tenderness, and then together sent beseeching glances at Grunty's angry back.

The matrix-pattern for Terra slipped through Grunty's fingers, and he suddenly tore the tape across, and across again. A filthy place, Terra. *There is nothing*, he thought, *like the conservatism of license.* Given a culture of sybaritics,[2] with an endless choice of mechanical titillations, and you have a people of unbreakable and hidebound formality, a people with few but massive taboos, a shockable, narrow, prissy people obeying the rules—even the rules of their calculated depravities—and protecting their treasured, specialized pruderies. In such a group there are words one may not use for fear of their fanged laughter, colors one may not wear, gestures and intonations one must forego, on pain of being torn to pieces. The rules are complex and absolute, and in such a place one's heart may not sing lest, through its warm free joyousness, it betrays one.

And if you must have joy of such a nature, if you must be free to be your pressured self, then off to space … off to the glittering black loneliness. And let the days go by, and let the time pass, and huddle beneath your impenetrable integument,[3] and wait, and wait, and every once in a long while you will have that moment of lonely consciousness when there is no one around to see; and then it may burst from you and you may dance, or cry, or twist the hair on your head till your eyeballs blaze, or do any of the other things your so unfashionable nature thirstily demands.

It took Grunty half a lifetime to find this freedom: No price would be too great to keep it. Not lives, nor interplanetary diplomacy, nor Earth itself were worth such a frightful loss.

---

1 Michelangelo (1475–1564), Italian Renaissance artist, sculptor, and poet, best known for his sculpture *David* and for biblical scenes painted on the ceiling of the Sistine Chapel. Importantly for this story, Michelangelo's sexuality has long been a topic of discussion and research, often focussed on his love poems dedicated to a young man.

2 "Characterized by or devoted to sensuous luxury or pleasure" (*OED*); derived from the inhabitants of Sybaris, a Greek city in what is now Italy, about whom there were several classical Greek fables.

3 "That with which anything is covered, enclosed, or clothed" (*OED*).

He would lose it if anyone knew, and the loverbirds knew.

He pressed his heavy hands together until the knuckles crackled. Dirbanu, reading it all from the ardent minds of the loverbirds; Dirbanu flashing the news across the stars; the roar of reaction, and then Rootes, Rootes, when the huge and ugly impact washed over him …

So let Dirbanu be offended. Let Terra accuse this ship of fumbling, even of treachery—anything but the withering news the loverbirds had stolen.

⋆ ⋆ ⋆

Another new stasis, and Grunty's first thought as he came alive in the silent ship was *It has to be soon.*

He rolled off the couch and glared at the unconscious loverbirds. The helpless loverbirds.

Smash their heads in.

Then Rootes … what to tell Rootes?

The loverbirds attacked him, tried to seize the ship?

He shook his head like a bear in a beehive. Rootes would never believe that. Even if the loverbirds could open the door, which they could not, it was more than ridiculous to imagine those two bright and slender things attacking anyone—especially not so rugged and massive an opponent.

Poison? No—there was nothing in the efficient, unfailingly beneficial food stores that might help.

His glance strayed to the Captain, and he stopped breathing.

Of course!

He ran to the Captain's personal lockers. He should have known that such a cocky little hound as Rootes could not live, could not strut and prance as he did, unless he had a weapon. And if it was the kind of weapon that such a man would characteristically choose—

A movement caught his eye as he searched.

The loverbirds were awake.

That wouldn't matter.

He laughed at them, a flashing, ugly laugh. They cowered close together and their eyes grew very bright.

They knew.

He was aware that they were suddenly very busy, as busy as he. And then he found the gun.

It was a snug little thing, smooth and intimate in his hand. It was exactly what he had guessed, what he had hoped for—just what he needed. It was silent. It would leave no mark. It need not even be aimed carefully. Just a touch of its feral radiation and throughout the body the axones[1] suddenly

1 Axone (var. of axon): "a filamentous process of a nerve cell carrying outgoing nerve impulses, usually single and often very long" (*OED*).

refuse to propagate nerve impulses. No thought leaves the brain, no slightest contraction of heart or lung occurs again, ever. And afterward, no sign remains that a weapon has been used.

He went to the serving window with the gun in his hand. *When he wakes, you will be dead,* he thought. *Couldn't recover from stasis blackout. Too bad. But no one's to blame, hm? We never had Dirbanu passengers before. So how could we know?*

The loverbirds, instead of flinching, were crowding close to the window, their faces beseeching, their delicate hands signing and signaling, frantically trying to convey something.

He touched the control, and the panel slid back.

The taller loverbird held up something as if it would shield him. The other pointed at it, nodded urgently, and gave him one of those accursed, hauntingly sweet smiles.

Grunty put up his hand to sweep the thing aside, and then checked himself.

It was only a piece of paper.

All of the cruelty of humanity rose up in Grunty. *A species that can't protect itself doesn't deserve to live.* He raised the gun.

And then he saw the pictures.

Economical and accurate, and for all their subject, done with the ineffable grace of the loverbirds themselves, the pictures showed three figures:

Grunty himself, hulking, impassive, the eyes glowing, the tree-trunk legs and hunched shoulders.

Rootes, in a pose so characteristic and so cleverly done that Grunty gasped. Crisp and clean, Rootes' image had one foot up on a chair, both elbows on the high knee, the head half turned. The eyes fairly sparkled from the paper.

And a girl.

She was beautiful. She stood with her arms behind her, her feet slightly apart, her face down a little. She was deep-eyed, pensive, and to see her was to be silent, to wait for those downcast lids to lift and break the spell.

Grunty frowned and faltered. He lifted a puzzled gaze from these exquisite renderings to the loverbirds, and met the appeal, the earnest, eager, hopeful faces.

The loverbird put a second paper against the glass.

There were the same three figures, identical in every respect to the previous ones, except for one detail: they were all naked.

He wondered how they knew human anatomy so meticulously.

Before he could react, still another sheet went up.

The loverbirds, this time—the tall one, the shorter one, hand in hand. And next to them a third figure, somewhat similar, but tiny, very round, and with grotesquely short arms.

Grunty stared at the three sheets, one after the other. There was something … something …

And then the loverbird put up the fourth sketch, and slowly, slowly, Grunty began to understand. In the last picture, the loverbirds were shown exactly as before, except that they were naked, and so was the small creature beside them. He had never seen loverbirds naked before. Possibly no one had.

Slowly he lowered the gun. He began to laugh. He reached through the window and took both the loverbirds' hands in one of his, and they laughed with him.

⋆ ⋆ ⋆

Rootes stretched easily with his eyes closed, pressed his face down into the couch, and rolled over. He dropped his feet to the deck, held his head in his hands and yawned. Only then did he realize that Grunty was standing just before him.

"What's the matter with you?"

He followed Grunty's grim gaze.

The glass door stood open.

Rootes bounced to his feet as if the couch had turned white-hot. "Where—what—"

Grunty's crag of a face was turned to the starboard bulkhead. Rootes spun to it, balanced on the balls of his feet as if he were boxing. His smooth face gleamed in the red glow of the light over the airlock.

"The lifeboat … you mean they took the lifeboat? They got away?"

Grunty nodded.

Rootes held his head. "Oh, fine," he moaned. He whipped around to Grunty. "And where the hell were you when this happened?"

"Here."

"Well, what in God's name happened?" Rootes was on the trembling edge of foaming hysteria.

Grunty thumped his chest.

"You're not trying to tell me you let them go?"

Grunty nodded, and waited—not for very long.

"I'm going to burn you down," Rootes raged. "I'm going to break you so low you'll have to climb for twelve years before you get a barracks to sweep. And after I get done with you I'll turn you over to the Service. What do you think they'll do to you? What do you think they're going to do to *me?*"

He leapt at Grunty and struck him a hard, cutting blow to the cheek. Grunty kept his hands down and made no attempt to avoid the fist. He stood immovable, and waited.

"Maybe those were criminals, but they were Dirbanu nationals," Rootes roared when he could get his breath. "How are we going to explain this to Dirbanu? Do you realize this could mean war?"

Grunty shook his head.

"What do you mean? You know something. You better talk while you can. Come on, bright boy—what are we going to tell Dirbanu?"

Grunty pointed at the empty cell. "Dead," he said.

"What good will it do us to say they're dead? They're not. They'll show up again some day, and—"

Grunty shook his head. He pointed to the star chart. Dirbanu showed as the nearest body. There was no livable planet within thousands of parsecs.

"They didn't go to Dirbanu!"

"Nuh."

"Damn it, it's like pulling rivets to get anything out of you. In that lifeboat they go to Dirbanu—which they won't—or they head out, maybe for years, to the Rim stars. That's all they can do!"

Grunty nodded.

"And you think Dirbanu won't track them, won't bring 'em down?"

"No ships."

"They have ships!"

"Nuh."

"The loverbirds told you?"

Grunty agreed.

"You mean their own ship that they destroyed, and the one the ambassador used were all they had?"

"Yuh."

Rootes strode up and back. "I don't get it. I don't begin to get it. What did you do it for, Grunty?"

Grunty stood for a moment, watching Rootes' face. Then he went to the computing desk. Rootes had no choice but to follow. Grunty spread out the four drawings.

"What's this? Who drew these? *Them?* What do you know. *Damn!* Who is the chick?"

Grunty patiently indicated all of the pictures in one sweep. Rootes looked at him, puzzled, looked at one of Grunty's eyes, then the other, shook his head, and applied himself to the pictures again. "This is more like it," he murmured. "Wish I'd 'a known they could draw like this." Again Grunty drew his attention to all the pictures and away from the single drawing that fascinated him.

"There's you, there's me. Right? Then this chick. Now, here we are again, all buff naked. Damn, what a carcass. All right, all right, I'm going on. Now, this is the prisoners, right? And who's the little fat one?"

Grunty pushed the fourth sheet over. "Oh," said Rootes. "Here everybody's naked too. Hm."

He yelped suddenly and bent close. Then he rapidly eyed all four sheets in sequence. His face began to get red. He gave the fourth picture a long, close scrutiny. Finally he put his finger on the sketch of the round little alien. "This is … a … a Dirbanu—"

Grunty nodded. "Female."

"Then those two—they were—"

Grunty nodded.

"So that's it!" Rootes fairly shrieked in fury. "You mean we been shipped out all this time with a coupla God damned *fairies?* Why, if I'd a' known that I'd a' killed 'em!"

"Yuh."

Rootes looked up at him with a growing respect and considerable amusement. "So you got rid of 'em so's I wouldn't kill 'em, and mess everything up?" He scratched his head. "Well, I'll be billy-bedamned. You got a think-tank on you after all. Anything I can't stand, it's a fruit."

Grunty nodded.

"God," said Rootes, "It figures. It really figures. Their females don't look anything like the males. Compared with them, our females are practically identical to us. So the ambassador comes, and sees what looks like a planet full of queers. He knows better but he can't stand the sight. So back he goes to Dirbanu, and Earth gets brushed off."

Grunty nodded.

"Then these pansies here run off to Earth, figuring they'll be at home. They damn near made it, too. But Dirbanu calls 'em back, not wanting the likes of them representing their planet. I don't blame 'em a bit. How would you feel if the only Terran on Dirbanu was a fluff? Wouldn't you want him out of there, but quick?"

Grunty said nothing.

"And now," said Rootes, "we better give Dirbanu the good news."

He went forward to the communicator.

It took a surprisingly short time to contact the shrouded planet. Dirbanu acknowledged and coded out a greeting. The decoder over the console printed the message for them:

GREETINGS STARMITE 439. ESTABLISH ORBIT. CAN YOU DROP PRISONERS TO DIRBANU? NEVER MIND PARACHUTE.

"Whew," said Rootes. "Nice people. Hey, you notice they don't say come on in. They never expected to let us land. Well, what'll we tell 'em about their lavender lads?"

"Dead," said Grunty.

"Yeah," said Rootes. "That's what they want anyway." He sent rapidly.

In a few minutes the response clattered out of the decoder.

STAND BY FOR TELEPATH SWEEP. WE MUST CHECK. PRISONERS MAY BE PRETENDING DEATH.

"Oh-oh," said the Captain. "This is where the bottom drops out."

"Nuh," said Grunty, calmly.

"But their detector will locate—oh—I see what you're driving at. No life, no signal. Same as if they weren't here at all."

"Yuh."

The coder clattered.

DIRBANU GRATEFUL. CONSIDER MISSION COMPLETE. DO NOT WANT BODIES. YOU MAY EAT THEM.

Rootes retched. Grunty said, "Custom."

The decoder kept clattering.

NOW READY FOR RECIPROCAL AGREEMENT WITH TERRA.

"We go home in a blaze of glory," Rootes exulted. He sent,

TERRA ALSO READY. WHAT DO YOU SUGGEST?

The decoder paused, then:

TERRA STAY AWAY FROM DIRBANU AND DIRBANU WILL STAY AWAY FROM TERRA. THIS IS NOT A SUGGESTION. TAKES EFFECT IMMEDIATELY.

"Why that bunch of bastards!"

Rootes pounded his codewriter, and although they circled the planet at a respectful distance for nearly four days, they received no further response.

* * *

The last thing Rootes had said before they established the first stasis on the way home was: "Well, anyway—it does me good to think of those two queens crawling away in that lifeboat. Why, they can't even starve to death. They'll be cooped up there for *years* before they get anywhere they can sit down."

It still rang in Grunty's mind as he shook off the blackout. He glanced aft to the glass partition and smiled reminiscently. "For years," he murmured. His words curled up and spun, and said,

... Yes; love requires the focal space
Of recollection or of hope,
Ere it can measure its own scope.
Too soon, too soon comes death to show
We love more deeply than we know!

Dutifully, then, came the words: *Coventry Patmore, born 1823.*[1]

He rose slowly and stretched, revelling in his precious privacy. He crossed to the other couch and sat down on the edge of it.

For a time he watched the Captain's unconscious face, reading it with great tenderness and utmost attention, like a mother with an infant.

His words said, *Why must we love where the lightning strikes, and not where we choose?*

And they said, *But I'm glad it's you, little prince. I'm glad it's you.*

He put out his huge hand and, with a feather touch, stroked the sleeping lips.

1 Coventry Patmore (1823–96), English poet. "Victories of Love" (1862) is the final part of his long poetic work *Angel in the House*.

Judith Merril (1923–97)

Judith Josephine Grossman, under the pseudonym Judith Merril, wrote and edited science fiction for several decades, starting in the mid-1940s. As an author, she is best known for her short stories, but her contributions as an editor of SF are nearly unparalleled, and it is not an overstatement to say that she helped to shape the field throughout the 1950s and 1960s. She edited both *The Year's Greatest Science Fiction and Fantasy* and the *Annual of the Year's Best S-F* for a combined total of over a decade, and she is also often credited with bringing the British "New Wave" movement to North American audiences with her collection *England Swings SF* (1968). Moving to Canada from the US as part of the wave of expatriates during the Vietnam War, she helped mould Canadian SF fandom and study. (For example, she wrote and presented over 100 "mini-documentaries" introducing *Doctor Who* episodes on the public broadcaster TVOntario [Merril and Pohl-Weary xiv].) Significantly, she donated over 5,000 books to the Toronto Public Library, founding what was initially called the "Spaced Out Library," later renamed the Merril Collection, one of the most significant public collections of SF in the world. In terms of her writing, as Canadian author Emily Pohl-Weary—who is also Merril's granddaughter—writes, "My grandmother was not a particularly prolific fiction writer. The importance of her contribution to the literary world rests in the subjects she broached," including issues concerning political repression of leftists in the McCarthy-era US, women's sexuality and motherhood, and racism, among others (Merril and Pohl-Weary 2).

Note on the text: Selected for inclusion in *The Best American Short Stories: 1955*, "Dead Center" was initially published in the *Magazine of Fantasy and Science Fiction* (vol. 7, no. 5, Nov. 1954), for which Merril would later serve as book-review editor. The version here follows that initial publication, where the editorial introduction to the story reads:

> *This is Judith Merril's first story in F&SF, but I don't think it's necessary to say much in introducing her to our readers. I'll just remind you that her first story,* That Only a Mother *(Astounding, 1948), and her first novel,* SHADOW ON THE HEARTH *(Doubleday, 1950), revealed a fresh and individual talent for showing the direct emotional impact of science upon private lives; that her anthologies, of which the latest,* BEYOND THE BARRIERS OF SPACE AND TIME, *has just been published by Random House, are distinguished by admirable taste and diligent originality; that her 1950 novel is the basis of David Davidson's celebrated TV-play,* Atomic Attack, *now used by Civil Defense as a cautionary lesson — and add that this new novelet embodies all the poignancy and personal immediacy of the best Merril in its moving observation of those usually forgotten figures: the family of the First Man in the Moon.* (3)

"Dead Center" (1954)

THEY gave him sweet ices, and kissed him all round, and the Important People who had come to dinner all smiled in a special way as his mother took him from the living room and led him down the hall to his own bedroom.

"Great kid you got there," they said to Jock, his father, and "Serious little bugger, isn't he?" Jock didn't say anything, but Toby knew he would be grinning, looking pleased and embarrassed. Then their voices changed, and that meant they had begun to talk about the important events for which the important people had come.

In his own room, Toby wriggled his toes between crisp sheets, and breathed in the powder-and-perfume smell of his mother as she bent over him for a last hurried goodnight kiss. There was no use asking for a story tonight. Toby lay still and waited while she closed the door behind her and went off to the party, click-tap, tip-clack, hurrying on her high silver heels. She had heard the voices change back there too, and she didn't want to miss anything. Toby got up and opened his door just a crack, and set himself down in back of it, and listened.

In the big square living room, against the abstract patterns of gray and vermilion and chartreuse, the men and women moved in easy patterns of familiar acts. Coffee, brandy, cigarette, cigar. Find your partner, choose your seat. Jock sprawled with perfect relaxed contentment on the low couch with the deep red corduroy cover. Tim O'Heyer balanced nervously on the edge of the same couch, wreathed in cigar smoke, small and dark and alert. Gordon Kimberly dwarfed the big easy chair with the bulking importance of him. Ben Stein, shaggy and rumpled as ever, was running a hand through his hair till it too stood on end. He was leaning against a window frame, one hand on the back of the straight chair in which his wife Sue sat, erect and neat and proper and chic, dressed in smart black that set off perfectly her precise blonde beauty. Mrs. Kimberly, just enough overstuffed so that her pearls gave the appearance of *actually* choking her, was the only stranger to the house. She was standing near the doorway, politely admiring Toby's personal art gallery, as Allie Madero valiantly strove to explain each minor masterpiece.

Ruth Kruger stood still a moment, surveying her room and her guests. Eight of them, herself included, and all Very Important People. In the familiar comfort of her own living room, the idea made her giggle. Allie and Mrs. Kimberly both turned to her, questioning. She laughed and shrugged, helpless to explain, and they all went across the room to join the others.

"Guts," O'Heyer said, through the cloud of smoke. "How do you do it, Jock? Walk out of a setup like this into … God knows what?"

"Luck," Jock corrected him. "A setup like this helps. I'm the world's pampered darling and I know it."

"Faith is what he means," Ben put in. "He just gets by believing that last year's luck is going to hold up. So it does."

"Depends on what you mean by *luck*. If you think of it as a vector sum composed of predictive powers and personal ability and accurate information and ..."

"Charm and nerve and ..."

"Guts," Tim said again, interrupting the interrupter.

"All right, all of them," Ben agreed. "*Luck* is as good a word as any to cover the combination."

"We're all lucky people." That was Allie, drifting into range, with Ruth behind him. "We just happened to get born at the right time with the right dream. Any one of us, fifty years ago, would have been called a wild-eyed visiona—"

"Any one of us," Kimberly said heavily, "fifty years ago, would have had a different dream — in time with the times."

Jock smiled, and let them talk, not joining in much. He listened to philosophy and compliments and speculations and comments, and lay sprawled across the comfortable couch in his own living room, with his wife's hand under his own, consciously letting his mind play back and forth between the two lives he lived: this, here ... and the perfect mathematic bleakness of the metal beast that would be his home in three days' time.

He squeezed his wife's hand, and she turned and looked at him, and there was no doubt a man could have about what the world held in store.

When they had all gone, Jock walked down the hall and picked up the little boy asleep on the floor, and put him back into his bed. Toby woke up long enough to grab his father's hand and ask earnestly, out of the point in the conversation where sleep had overcome him:

"Daddy, if the universe hasn't got any ends to it, how can you tell where you are?"

"Me?" Jock asked. "I'm right next to the middle of it."

"How do you *know*?"

His father tapped him lightly on the chest.

"Because that's where the middle is." Jock smiled and stood up. "Go to sleep, champ. Good night."

And Toby slept, while the universe revolved in all its mystery about the small center Jock Kruger had assigned to it.

"Scared?" she asked, much later, in the spaceless silence of their bedroom.

He had to think about it before he could answer. "I guess not. I guess I think I ought to be, but I'm not. I don't think I'd do it at all if I wasn't *sure*." He was almost asleep, when the thought hit him, and he jerked awake and saw she was sure enough lying wide-eyed and sleepless beside him. "*Baby!*" he said, and it was almost an accusation. "Baby, *you're* not scared, are you?"

"Not if you're not," she said. But they never could lie to each other.

II

Toby sat on the platform, next to his grandmother. They were in the second row, right in back of his mother and father, so it was all right for him to wriggle a little bit, or whisper. They couldn't hear much of the speeches back there, and what they did hear mostly didn't make sense to Toby. But every now and then Grandma would grab his hand tight all of a sudden, and he understood what the whole thing was about: it was because Daddy was going away again.

His Grandma's hand was very white, with little red and tan dots in it, and big blue veins that stood out higher than the wrinkles in her skin, whenever she grabbed at his hand. Later, walking over to the towering skyscraping rocket, he held his mother's hand; it was smooth and cool and tan, all one color, and she didn't grasp at him the way Grandma did. Later still, his father's two hands, picking him up to kiss, were bigger and darker tan than his mother's, not so smooth, and the fingers were stronger, but so strong it hurt sometimes.

They took him up in an elevator, and showed him all around the inside of the rocket, where Daddy would sit, and where all the food was stored, for emergency, they said, and the radio and everything. Then it was time to say goodbye.

Daddy was laughing at first, and Toby tried to laugh, too, but he didn't really want Daddy to go away. Daddy kissed him, and he felt like crying because it was scratchy against Daddy's cheek, and the strong fingers were hurting him now. Then Daddy stopped laughing and looked at him very seriously. "You take care of your mother, now," Daddy told him. "You're a big boy this time."

"Okay," Toby said. Last time Daddy went away in a rocket, he was not-quite-four, and they teased him with the poem in the book that said, *James James Morrison Morrison Weatherby George Dupree, Took great care of his mother, though he was only three....*[1] So Toby didn't much like Daddy saying that now, because he knew they didn't really mean it.

"Okay," he said, and then because he was angry, he said, "Only she's supposed to take care of me, isn't she?"

Daddy and Mommy both laughed, and so did the two men who were standing there waiting for Daddy to get done saying goodbye to him. He wriggled, and Daddy put him down.

"I'll bring you a piece of the moon, son," Daddy said, and Toby said, "All right, fine." He reached for his mother's hand, but he found himself hanging onto Grandma instead, because Mommy and Daddy were kissing each other, and both of them had forgotten all about him.

He thought they were never going to get done kissing.

---

1 From the poem "Disobedience," published in the collection *When We Were Very Young* (1924), by English author A.A. Milne (1882–1956), best known for his children's books *Winnie-the-Pooh* (1926) and *The House at Pooh Corner* (1928).

Ruth Kruger stood in the glass control booth with her son on one side of her, and Gordon Kimberly breathing heavily on the other side. *Something's wrong*, she thought, *this time something's wrong*. And then, swiftly, *I mustn't think that way!*

Jealous? she taunted herself. Do you *want* something to be wrong, just because this one isn't all yours, because Argent did some of it?

But if anything is wrong, she prayed, let it be now, right away, so he can't go. If anything's wrong let it be in the firing gear or the … what? Even now, it was too late. The beast was too big and too delicate and too precise. If something went wrong, even now, it was too late. It was …

You didn't finish that thought. Not if you were Ruth Kruger, and your husband was Jock Kruger, and nobody knew but the two of you how much of the courage that had gone twice round the moon, and was about to land on it, was yours. When a man knows his wife's faith is *unshakable*, he can't help coming back. (But: "Baby! *You're* not scared, are you?")

Twice around the moon, and they called him Jumping Jock. There was never a doubt in anyone's mind who'd pilot the KIM-5, the bulky beautiful beast out there today. Kruger and Kimberly, O'Heyer and Stein. It was a combo. It won every time. *Every* time. Nothing to doubt. No room for doubt.

"Minus five …" someone said into a mike, and there was perfect quiet all around. "Four … three …"

(But he held me too tight, and he laughed too loud.…)

"… two … one …"

(Only because he thought *I* was scared, she answered herself.)

"… Mar—"

You didn't even hear the whole word, because the thunder-drumming roar of the beast itself split your ears.

Ringing quiet came down and she caught up Toby, held him tight, tight.…

"Perfect!" Gordon Kimberly sighed. "*Per*fect!"

So if anything *was* wrong, it hadn't showed up yet.

She put Toby down, then took his hand. "Come on," she said. "I'll buy you an ice-cream soda." He grinned at her. He'd been looking very strange all day, but now he looked real again. His hair had got messed up when she grabbed him.

"We're having cocktails for the press in the conference room," Kimberly said. "I think we could find something Toby would like."

"Wel-l-l-l …" She didn't want a cocktail, and she didn't want to talk to the press. "I think maybe we'll beg off this time.…"

"I think there might be some disappointment —" the man started; then Tim O'Heyer came dashing up.

"Come on, babe," he said. "Your old man told me to take personal charge while he was gone." He leered. On him it looked cute. She laughed. Then she looked down at Toby. "What would you rather, Tobe? Want to go out by ourselves, or go to the party?"

"I don't care," he said.

Tim took the boy's hand. "What we were thinking of was having a kind of party here, and then I think they're going to bring some dinner in, and anybody who wants to can stay up till your Daddy gets to the moon. That'll be pretty late. I guess you wouldn't want to stay up late like that, would you?"

Somebody else talking to Toby like that would be all wrong, but Tim was a friend, Toby's friend too. Ruth still didn't want to go to the party, but she remembered now that there had been plans for something like that all along, and since Toby was beginning to look eager, and it *was* important to keep the press on their side …

"You win, O'Heyer," she said. "Will somebody please send out for an ice-cream soda? Cherry syrup, I think it is this week …" She looked inquiringly at her son. "… and … *strawberry* ice cream?"

Tim shuddered. Toby nodded. Ruth smiled, and they all went in to the party.

"Well, young man!" Toby thought the redheaded man in the brown suit was probably what they called a reporter, but he wasn't sure. "How about it? You going along next time?"

"I don't know," Toby said politely. "I guess not."

"Don't you want to be a famous flier like your Daddy?" a strange woman in an evening gown asked him.

"I don't know," he muttered, and looked around for his mother, but he couldn't see her.

They kept asking him questions like that, about whether he wanted to go to the moon. Daddy said he was too little. You'd think all these people would know that much.

Jock Kruger came up swiftly out of dizzying darkness into isolation and clarity. As soon as he could move his head, before he fully remembered why, he began checking the dials and meters and flashing lights on the banked panel in front of him. He was fully aware of the ship, of its needs and strains and motion, before he came to complete consciousness of himself, his weightless body, his purpose, or his memories.

But he was aware of himself as a part of the ship before he remembered his name, so that by the time he knew he had a face and hands and innards, these parts were already occupied with feeding the beast's human brain a carefully prepared stimulant out of a nippled flask fastened in front of his head.

He pressed a button under his index finger in the arm rest of the couch that held him strapped to safety.

"Hi," he said. "Is anybody up besides me?"

He pressed the button under his middle finger and waited.

Not for long.

"Thank God!" a voice crackled out of the loudspeaker. "You really conked out this time, Jock. Nothing wrong?"

"Not so I'd know it. You want … How long was I out?"

"Twenty-three minutes, eighteen seconds, takeoff to reception. Yeah. Give us a log reading."

Methodically, in order, he read off the pointers and numbers on the control panel, the colors and codes and swinging needles and quiet ones that told him how each muscle and nerve and vital organ of the great beast was taking the trip. He did it slowly and with total concentration. Then, when he was all done, there was nothing else to do except sit back and start wondering about that big blackout.

It shouldn't have happened. It never happened before. There was nothing in the compendium of information he'd just sent back to Earth to account for it.

A different ship, different … different men. Two and a half years different. Years of easy living and … growing old? Too old for this game?

Twenty-three minutes!

Last time it was under ten. The first time maybe 90 seconds more. It didn't matter, of course, not at takeoff. There was nothing for him to do then. Nothing now. Nothing for four more hours. He was there to put the beast back down on …

He grinned, and felt like Jock Kruger again. Identity returned complete. *This* time he was there to put the beast down where no man or beast had ever been before. This time they were going to the moon.

III

Ruth Kruger sipped at a cocktail and murmured responses to the admiring, the curious, the envious, the hopeful, and the hate-full ones who spoke to her. She was waiting for something, and after an unmeasurable stretch of time Allie Madero brought it to her.

First a big smile seeking her out across the room, so she knew it had come. Then a low-voiced confirmation.

"Wasn't it … an awfully long time?" she asked. She hadn't been watching the clock, on purpose, but she was sure it was longer than it should have been.

Allie stopped smiling. "Twenty-three," she said.

Ruth gasped. "What …?"

"*You* figure it. I can't."

"There's nothing in the ship. I mean nothing was changed that would account for it." She shook her head slowly. This time she didn't know the ship well enough to talk like that. There *could* be something. Oh, *Jock*! "I don't know," she said. "Too many people worked on that thing. I …"

"Mrs. Kruger!" It was the redheaded reporter, the obnoxious one. "We just got the report on the blackout. I'd like a statement from you, if you don't mind, as designer of the ship—"

"I am not the designer of this ship," she said coldly.

"You worked on the design, didn't you?"

"Yes."

"Well, then, to the best of your knowledge …?"

"To the best of my knowledge, there is no change in design to account for Mr. Kruger's prolonged unconsciousness. Had there been any such prognosis, the press would have been informed."

"Mrs. Kruger, I'd like to ask you whether you feel that the innovations made by Mr. Argent could—"

"Aw, lay off, will you?" Allie broke in, trying to be casual and kidding about it; but behind her own flaming cheeks, Ruth was aware of her friend's matching anger. "How much do you want to milk this for, anyhow? So the guy conked out an extra ten minutes. If you want somebody to crucify for it, why don't you pick on one of us who doesn't happen to be married to him?" She turned to Ruth before the man could answer. "Where's Toby? He's probably about ready to bust from cookies and carbonation."

"He's in the lounge," the reporter put in. "Or he was a few minutes—"

Ruth and Allie started off without waiting for the rest. The redhead had been talking to the kid. No telling how many of them were on top of him now.

"I thought Tim was with him," Ruth said hastily, then she thought of something, and turned back long enough to say: "For the record, Mr. … uh … I know of no criticism that can be made of any of the work done by Mr. Argent." Then she went to find her son.

There was nothing to do and nothing to see except the instrument meters and dials to check and log and check and log again. Radio stations all around Earth were beamed on him. He could have kibitzed[1] his way to the moon, but he didn't want to. He was thinking.

Thinking back, and forward, and right in this moment. Thinking of the instant's stiffness of Ruth's body when she said she wasn't scared, and the rambling big house on the hill, and Toby politely agreeing when he offered to bring him back a piece of the moon.

Thinking of Toby growing up some day, and how little he really knew about his son, and what would they do, Toby and Ruth, if anything …

He'd never thought that way before. He'd never thought anything except to know he'd come back, because he couldn't stay away. It was always that simple. He couldn't stay away now, either. That hadn't changed. But as he sat there, silent and useless for the time, it occurred to him that he'd left something out of his calculations. *Luck*, they'd been talking about. Yes, he'd had luck. But—what was it Sue had said about a vector sum?—there was more to figure in than your own reflexes and the beast's strength. There was the *outside*. Space … environment … God … destiny. What difference does it make what name you give it?

1 Kibitz: here likely used to mean "any talk, chat; conversation" (*OED*).

He couldn't *stay* away … but maybe he could be *kept* away.

He'd never thought that way before.

"You tired, honey?"

"No," he said. "I'm just sick of this party. I want to go home."

"It'll be over pretty soon, Tobe. I think as long as we stayed this long, we better wait for … for the end of the party."

"It's a silly party. You said you'd buy me an ice-cream soda."

"I did, darling," she said patiently. "At least, if I didn't *buy* it, I got it for you. You had it, didn't you?"

"Yes, but you *said* we'd go *out* and have one."

"Look, why don't you just put your head down on my lap and …"

"I'm no *baby*! Anyhow I'm not tired."

"All right. We'll go pretty soon. You just sit here on the couch, and you don't have to talk to anybody if you don't feel like it. I'll tell you what. I'll go find you a magazine or a book or something to look at, and—"

"I don't *want* a magazine. I want my own book with the pirates in it."

"You just stay put a minute, so I can find you. I'll bring you something."

She got up and went out to the other part of the building where the officers were, and collected an assortment of leaflets and folders with shiny bright pictures of mail rockets and freight transports and jets and visionary moon rocket designs, and took them back to the little lounge where she'd left him.

She looked at the clock on the way. Twenty-seven more minutes. There was *no* reason to believe that anything was wrong.

They were falling now. A man's body is not equipped to sense direction *toward* or *from*, *up* or *down*, without the help of landmarks or gravity. But the body of the beast was designed to know such things; and Kruger, at the nerve center, knew everything the beast knew.

Ship is extension of self, and self is—extension or limitation?—of ship. If Jock Kruger is the center of the universe—remember the late night after the party, and picking Toby off the floor?—then ship is extension of self, and the man is the brain of the beast. But if ship *is* universe—certainly continuum; that's universe, isn't it?—then the weakling man-thing in the couch is a limiting condition of the universe. A human brake. He was there to make it stop when it didn't "want" to.

Suppose it wouldn't stop? Suppose it had decided to be a self-determined, free-willed universe?

Jock grinned, and started setting controls. His time was coming. It was measurable in minutes, and then in seconds … *now!*

His hand reached for the firing lever (but *what* was she scared of?), groped, and touched, hesitated, clasped, and pulled.

Grown-up parties at home were fun. But other places, like this one, they were silly. Toby half-woke-up on the way home, enough to realize his Uncle Tim was driving them, and they weren't in their own car. He was sitting on the front seat next to his mother, with his head against her side, and her arm around him. He tried to come all the way awake, to listen to what they were saying, but they weren't talking, so he started to go back to sleep.

Then Uncle Tim said, "For God's sake, Ruth, he's safe, and whatever happened certainly wasn't *your* fault. He's got enough supplies to hold out till ..."

"Shh!" his mother said sharply, and then, whispering, "I know."

Now he remembered.

"Mommy ..."

"Yes, hon?"

"Did Daddy go to the moon all right?"

"Y ... yes, dear."

Her voice was funny.

"Where is it?"

"Where's what?"

"The moon."

"Oh. We can't see it now, darling. It's around the other side of the earth."

"Well, when is he going to come *back?*"

Silence.

"*Mommy ... when?*"

"As soon as ... just as soon as he can, darling. Now go to sleep."

And now the moon was up, high in the sky, a gilded football dangling from Somebody's black serge lapel. When she was a little girl, she used to say she loved the man in the moon, and now the man in the moon loved her too, but if she was a little girl still, somebody would tuck her into bed, and pat her head and tell her to go to sleep, and she would sleep as easy, breathe as soft, as Toby did....

But she wasn't a little girl, she was all grown up, and she married the man, the man in the moon, and sleep could come and sleep could go, but sleep could never stay with her while the moonwash swept the window panes.

She stood at the open window and wrote a letter in her mind and sent it up the path of light to the man in the moon. It said:

"Dear Jock: Tim says it wasn't my fault, and I can't explain it even to him. I'm sorry, darling. Please to stay alive till we can get to you. Faithfully yours, Cassandra."

IV

The glasses and ashes and litter and spilled drinks had all been cleared away. The table top gleamed in polished stripes of light and dark, where the light came through the louvered plastic of the wall. The big chairs were empty, waiting, and at each place, arranged with the precision of a formal dinner-setting, was the inevitable pad of yellow paper, two freshly-sharpened pencils, a small neat pile of typed white sheets of paper, a small glass ashtray and a shining empty water glass. Down the center of the table, spaced for comfort, three crystal pitchers of ice and water stood in perfect alignment.

Ruth was the first one there. She stood in front of a chair, fingering the little stack of paper on which someone (Allie? She'd have had to be up early to get it done so quickly) had tabulated the details of yesterday's events. "To refresh your memory," was how they always put it.

She poured a glass of water, and guiltily replaced the pitcher on the exact spot where it had been; lit a cigarette, and stared with dismay at the burnt match marring the cleanliness of the little ashtray; pulled her chair in beneath her and winced at the screech of the wooden leg across the floor.

Get it over with! She picked up the typed pages, and glanced at them. Two at the bottom were headed "Recommendations of U.S. Rocket Corps to Facilitate Construction of KIM-VIII." That could wait. The three top sheets she'd better get through while she was still alone.

She read slowly and carefully, trying to memorize each sentence, so that when the time came to talk, she could think of what had happened this way, from outside, instead of remembering how it had been for *her.*

There was nothing in the report that she didn't already know.

Jock Kruger had set out in the KIM-VII at 5:39 p.m., C.S.T., just at sunset. First report after recovery from blackout came at 6:02-plus. First log readings gave no reason to anticipate any difficulty. Subsequent reports and radioed log readings were, for Kruger, unusually terse and formal, and surprisingly infrequent; but earth-to-ship contact at twenty-minute intervals had been acknowledged. No reason to believe Kruger was having trouble at any time during the trip.

At 11:54, an attempt to call the ship went unanswered for 56 seconds. The radioman here described Kruger's voice as "irritable" when the reply finally came, but all he said was, "Sorry. I was firing the first brake." Then a string of figures, and a quick log reading—everything just what you'd expect.

Earth acknowledged, and waited.

Eighteen seconds later:

"Second brake." More figures. Again, everything as it should be. But twenty seconds after that call was completed:

"This is Kruger. Anything wrong with the dope[1] I gave you?"

"Earth to Kruger. Everything okay in our book. Trouble?"

"Track me, boy. I'm off."

"You want a course correction?"

"I can figure it quicker here. I'll keep talking as I go. Stop me if I'm wrong

1 Informal term for information.

by your book." More figures, and Kruger's calculations coincided perfectly with the swift work done at the base. Both sides came to the same conclusion, and both sides knew what it meant. The man in the beast fired once more, and once again, and made a landing.

There was no reason to believe that either ship or pilot had been hurt. There was no way of finding out. By the best calculations, they were five degrees of arc around onto the dark side. And there was no possibility at all, after that second corrective firing that Kruger had enough fuel left to take off again. The last thing Earth had heard, before the edge of the moon cut off Kruger's radio, was:

"Sorry, boys. I guess I fouled up this time. Looks like you'll have to come and ..."

One by one, they filled the seats: Gordon Kimberly at one end, and the Colonel at the other; Tim O'Heyer to one side of Kimberly, and Ruth at the other; Allie, with her pad and pencil poised, alongside Tim; the Colonel's aide next down the line, with his little silent stenotype[1] in front of him; the Steins across from him, next to Ruth. With a minimum of formality, Kimberly opened the meeting and introduced Col. Swenson.

The Colonel cleared his throat. "I'd like to make something clear," he said. "Right from the start, I want to make this clear. I'm here to help. Not to get in the way. My presence does not indicate any—*criticism* on the part of the Armed Services. We are entirely satisfied with the work you people have been doing." He cleared his throat again, and Kimberly put in:

"You saw our plans, I believe, Colonel. Everything was checked and approved by your outfit ahead of time."

"Exactly. We had no criticism then, and we have none now. The rocket program is what's important. Getting Kruger back is important, not just for ordinary humanitarian reasons—pardon me, Mrs. Kruger, if I'm too blunt—but for the sake of the whole program. Public opinion, for one thing. That's your line, isn't it, Mr. O'Heyer? And then, *we have to find out what happened!*

"I came down here today to offer any help we can give you on the relief ship, and to make a suggestion to facilitate matters."

He paused deliberately this time.

"Go ahead. Colonel," Tim said. "We're listening."

"Briefly, the proposal is that you all accept temporary commissions while the project is going on. Part of that report in front of you embodies the details of the plan. I hope you'll find it acceptable. You all know there is a great deal of—necessary, I'm afraid—*red tape*, you'd call it, and 'going through channels,' and such in the Services. It makes cooperation between civilian and military groups difficult. If we can all get together as one outfit 'for the duration,' so to speak ..."

1 A form of typewriter used for generating shorthand notes.

This time nobody jumped into the silence. The Colonel cleared his throat once more.

"Perhaps you'd best read the full report before we discuss it any further. I brought the matter up now just to—to let you know the *attitude* with which we are submitting the proposal to you ..."

"Thank you. Colonel." O'Heyer saved him. "I've already had a chance to look at the report. Don't know that anyone else has, except of course Miss Madero. But I personally, at least, appreciate your attitude. And I think I can speak for Mr. Kimberly too...."

He looked sideways at his boss; Gordon nodded.

"What I'd like to suggest now," O'Heyer went on, "since I've seen the report already, and I believe everyone else would like to have a chance to bone up some—perhaps you'd like to have a first-hand look at some of our plant, Colonel? I could take you around a bit....?"

"Thank you. I would like to." The officer stood up, his gold Rocket Corps uniform blazing in the louvered light. "If I may say so, Mr. O'Heyer, you seem remarkably sensible, for a—well, a *publicity* man."

"That's all right. Colonel." Tim laughed easily. "I don't even think it's a dirty word. You seem like an all-right guy yourself—for an *officer*, that is."

They all laughed then, and Tim led the blaze of glory out of the room while the rest of them settled down to studying the R.C. proposals. When they had all finished, Kimberly spoke slowly, voicing the general reaction:

"I hate to admit it, but it makes sense."

"They're being pretty decent about it, aren't they?" Ben said. "Putting it to us as a proposal instead of pulling a lot of weight."

He nodded. "I've had a little contact with this man Swenson before. He's a good man to work with. It ... makes sense, that's all."

"On paper, anyhow," Sue put in.

"Well, Ruth ..." the big man turned to her, waiting. "You haven't said anything."

"I ... it seems all right to me," she said, and added: "Frankly, Gordon, I don't know that I ought to speak at all. I'm not quite sure why I'm here."

Allie looked up sharply, questioning, from her notes; Sue pushed back her chair and half-stood. "My God, you're not going to back out on us now?"

"I ... look, you all know I didn't do any of the real work on the last one. It was Andy Argent's job, and a good one. I've got Toby to think about, and ..."

"Kid, we *need* you," Sue protested. "Argent can't do this one; this is going to be another Three, only more so. Unmanned, remote-control stuff, and no returning atmosphere-landing problems. This is up your alley. It's ..." She sank back; there was nothing else to say.

"That's true, Ruth." Tim had come back in during the last outburst. Now he sat down. "Speed is what counts, gal. That's why we're letting the gold braid in on the job—we are, aren't we?" Kimberly nodded; Tim went on: "With you on the job, we've got a working team. With somebody new—well, you know what a ruckus we had until Sue got used to Argent's blueprints, and how Ben's pencil notes used to drive Andy wild. And we can't even use him this time. It's not his field. He did do a good job, but we'd have to start in with somebody new all over again …" He broke off, and looked at Kimberly.

"I hope you'll decide to work with us, Ruth," he said simply.

"If … obviously, if it's the best way to get it done *quick*, I will," she said. "Twenty-eight hours a day if you like."

Tim grinned. "I guess we can let the braid back in now …?" He got up and went to the door.

Another Three, only more so … Sue's words danced in her mind while the Colonel and the Colonel's aide marched in, and took their places, while voices murmured politely, exchanging good will.

Another Three—the first ship she had designed for Kimberly. The ship that made her rich and famous, but that was nothing, because it was the ship that brought Jock to her, that made him write the letter, that made her meet him, that led to the Five and Six and now …

"I've got some ideas for a manned ship," he'd written. "If we could get together to discuss it some time …"

"… pleasure to know you'll be working with us, Mrs. Kruger." She shook her head sharply, and located in time and place.

"Thank you. Colonel. I want to do what I can, of course …"

V

James James Morrison's mother put on a golden gown …

Toby knew the whole thing, almost, by heart. The little boy in the poem *told* his mother not to *go down to the end of the town*, wherever that was, unless she took him along. And she said she wouldn't, but she put on that golden gown and went, and thought she'd be back in time for tea. Only she wasn't. She never came back at all. *Last seen wandering vaguely* … *King John said he was sorry* …

Who's King John? And what time is tea?

Toby sat quietly beside his mother on the front seat of the car, and looked obliquely at the golden uniform she wore, and could not find a way to ask the questions in his mind.

Where was James James's *father?* Why did James James have to be the one to keep his mother from going down to the end of the town?

"Are you in the Army now, Mommy?" he asked.

"Well … sort of. But not for long, darling. Just till Daddy comes home."

"When is Daddy coming home?"

"Soon. Soon, I hope. Not too long."

She didn't sound right. Her voice had a cracking sound like Grandma's, and other old ladies. She didn't look right, either, in that golden-gown uniform.

When she kissed him goodbye in front of the school, she didn't *feel* right. She didn't even *smell* the same as she used to.

"'Bye, boy. See you tonight," she said—the same words she always said, but they sounded different.

"'Bye." He walked up the driveway and up the front steps and down the corridor and into the pretty-painted room where his teacher was waiting. Miss Callahan was nice. Today she was *too* nice. The other kids teased him, and called him teacher's pet. At lunch time he went back in the room before anybody else did, and made pictures all over the floor with the colored chalk. It was the worst thing he could think of to do. Miss Callahan made him wash it all up, and she wasn't nice any more for the rest of the afternoon.

When he went out front after school, he couldn't see the car anywhere. It was true then. His mother had put on that golden gown, and now she was gone. Then he saw Grandma waving to him out of *her* car, and he remembered Mommy had said Grandma would come and get him. He got in the car, and she grabbed at him like she always did. He pulled away.

"Is Daddy home yet?" he asked.

Grandma started the car. "Not yet," she said, and she was crying. He didn't dare ask about Mommy after that, but she wasn't home when they got there. It was a long time after that till dinner was ready.

She came home for dinner, though.

"You have to allow for the human factor...."

Nobody had said it to her, of course. Nobody would. She wondered how much tougher it made the job for everybody, having her around. She wondered how she'd stay sane, if she didn't have the job to do.

Thank God Toby was in school now! She couldn't do it, if it meant leaving him with someone else all day—even his grandmother. As it was, having the old lady in the house so much was nerve-racking.

I ought to ask her if she'd like to sleep here for a while, Ruth thought, and shivered. Dinner time was enough.

Anyhow, Toby liked having her there, and that's what counted.

I'll have to go in and see his teacher. Tomorrow, she thought. I've got to make time for it tomorrow. Let her know ... but of course she knew. Jock Kruger's family's affairs were hardly private. Just the same, I better talk to her....

Ruth got out of bed and stood at the window, waiting for the moon. Another ten minutes, fifteen, twenty maybe, and it would edge over the hills on the other side of town. The white hands on the clock said 2:40. She had to get some sleep. She couldn't stand here waiting for the moon. Get to sleep now, before it comes up. That's better....

Oh, *Jock!*

"... the human factor ..." They didn't know. She wanted to go tell them all, find somebody right away, and shout it. "*It's not his fault. I did it!*"

"You're *not scared, are you, baby?*"

Oh, no! No, no! Don't be silly. Who, me? Just stiff and trembling. The cold, you know …?

Stop that!

She stood at the window, waiting for the moon, the man, the man in the moon.

Human factor … well, there wouldn't be a human factor in this one. If she went out to the field on takeoff day and told KIM-VIII she was scared, it wouldn't matter at all.

Thank God I can do something, at least!

Abruptly, she closed the blind, so she wouldn't know when it came, and pulled out the envelope she'd brought home; switched on the bed light, and unfolded the first blueprints.

It was all familiar. Just small changes here and there. Otherwise, it was the Three all over again—the first unmanned ship to be landed successfully on the moon surface. The only important difference was that this one had to have some fancy gadgetry on the landing mech. Stein had given her the orbit calcs today. The rest of the job was hers and Sue's: design and production. Between them, they could do it. What they needed was a goldberg[1] that would take the thing once around low enough to contact Jock, if … to contact him, that's all. Then back again, prepared for him to take over the landing by remote, according to instructions, if he wanted to. If he could. If his radio was working. If …

Twice around, and then down where they figured he was, if he hadn't tried to bring it down himself.

It was complicated, but only quantitatively. Nothing basically new, or untried. And no *human* factors to be allowed for, once it was off the ground.

She fell asleep, finally, with the light still on, and the blind drawn, and the blueprints spread out on the floor next to the bed.

Every day, she drove him to school, dressed in her golden gown. And every afternoon, he waited, telling himself she was sure to come home.

That was a very silly little poem, and he wasn't three, he was six now.

But it was a long time since Daddy went away.

"I'd rather not," she said stiffly.

"I'm sorry, Ruth. I know—well, I *don't* know, but I can imagine how you feel. I hate to ask it, but if you can do it at all … just be there and look confident, and … *you* know."

Look confident! I couldn't do it for Jock, she thought; why should I do it for *them*? But of course that was silly. They didn't know her the way Jock did.

1 Likely a reference to "Rube Goldberg machines," devices drawn by American cartoonist Rube Goldberg (1883–1970) which generally accomplished simple tasks automatically but in very complicated ways. Here, it seems simply to mean an automated system.

They couldn't read her smiles, or sense a barely present stiffness, or know anything except what she chose to show on the front of her face.

"Look confident? What difference does it make, Tim? If the thing works, they'll all know soon enough. If ..."

She stopped.

"All right. I'll be blunt. If it *doesn't* work, it's going to make a hell of a difference what the public feeling was at the time it went off. If we have to try again. If—damn it, you want it straight, all right! If we can't save Jock, we're not going to give up the whole thing! We're not going to let space travel wait another half century while the psychological effects wear off. *And Jock wouldn't want us to!* Don't forget that. It was his dream, too. It was yours, once upon a time. If ..."

"All *right!*" She was startled by her voice. She was screaming, or almost.

"All right," she said bitterly, more quietly. "If you think I'll be holding up progress for fifty years by not dragging Toby along to a launching, I'll come."

"Oh, Ruth, I'm sorry. No, it's not that important. And I had no business talking that way. But listen, babe, you used to understand this—the way I feel, the way Jock fel—feels. Even a guy like Kimberly. You used to feel it too. Look: the single item of you showing your face at the takeoff doesn't amount to much. Neither does one ounce of fuel. But either one could be the little bit that makes the difference. Kid, we got to put *everything* we've got behind it this time."

"All right," she said again. "I told you I'd come."

"You do understand, don't you?" he pleaded.

"I don't know, Tim. I'm not sure I do. But you're right. I would have, once. Maybe—I don't know. It's different for a woman, I guess. But I'll come. Don't worry about it."

She turned and started out.

"Thanks, Ruth. And I *am* sorry. Uh—want me to come and pick you up?"

She nodded. "Thanks." She was glad she wouldn't have to drive.

VI

He kept waiting for a chance to ask her. He couldn't do it in the house before they left, because right after she told him where they were going, she went to get dressed in her golden uniform, and he had to stay with Grandma all the time.

Then Mr. O'Heyer came with the car, and he couldn't ask because, even though he sat up front with Mommy, Mr. O'Heyer was there too.

When they got to the launching field, there were people around all the time. Once he tried to get her off by himself, but all she did was think he had to go to the bathroom. Then, bit by bit, he didn't *have* to ask, because he could tell from the way they were all talking, and the way the cameras were all pointed at her all the time, like they had been at Daddy the other time.

Then there was the speeches part again, and this time *she* got up and talked, so that settled it.

He was glad he hadn't asked. They probably all thought he knew. Maybe they'd even told him, and he'd forgotten, like he sometimes did. "Mommy," he listened to himself in his mind, "Mommy, are you going to the moon too?" Wouldn't that sound silly!

She'd come back for him, he told himself. The other times, when Daddy went some place—like when they first came here to live, and Daddy went first, then Mommy, and then they came back to get him, and some other time, he didn't remember just what—but when Daddy went away, Mommy always went to stay with him, and then they *always* came to get him too.

It wasn't any different from Mommy going back to be with Daddy at a party or something, instead of staying in his room to talk to him when she put him to bed. It didn't feel any worse than that, he told himself.

Only he didn't believe himself.

She never did tell me! I wouldn't of forgotten that! She should *of told me!*

She did not want to make a speech. Nobody had warned her that she would be called upon to make a speech. It was bad enough trying to answer reporters coherently. She stood up and went forward to the microphone dutifully, and shook hands with the President of the United States, and tried to look confident. She opened her mouth and nothing came out.

"Thank you," she said finally, though she didn't know just what for. "You've all been very kind." She turned to the mike, and spoke directly into it. "I feel that a good deal of honor is being accorded me today which is not rightfully mine. We gave ourselves a two-month limit to complete a job, and the fact that it was finished inside of six weeks instead …"

She had to stop because everybody was cheering, and they wouldn't have heard her.

"… that fact is not something for which the designer of a ship can be thanked. The credit is due to all the people at Kimberly who worked so hard, and to the Rocket Corps personnel who helped so much. I think …"

This time she paused to find the right words. It had suddenly become very important to level with the crowd, to tell them what she honestly felt.

"I think it is I who should be doing the thanking. I happen to be a designer of rockets, but much more importantly, to me, I am Jock Kruger's wife. So I want to thank everyone who helped …"

Grandma's hand tightened around his, and then pulled away to get a handkerchief, because she was crying. Right up here on the platform! Then he realized what Mommy had just said. She said that being Jock Kruger's wife was more important to her than anything else.

It was funny that Grandma should feel bad about that. Everybody else seemed to think it was a right thing to say, the way they were yelling and clapping and shouting. It occurred to Toby with a small shock of surprise that maybe Grandma sometimes felt bad about things the same way he did.

He was sort of sorry he wouldn't have much chance to find out more about that.

She broke away from the reporters and V.I.P.'s, and went and got Toby, and asked him did he want to look inside the rocket before it left.

He nodded. He was certainly being quiet today. Poor kid—he must be pretty mixed up about the whole thing by now.

She tried to figure out what was going on inside the small brown head, but all she could think of was how *much* like Jock he looked today.

She took him up the elevator inside the rocket. There wasn't much room to move around, of course, but they'd rigged it so that all the big shots who were there could have a look. She was a little startled to see the President and her mother-in-law come up together in the next elevator, but between trying to answer Toby's questions, and trying to brush off reporters, she didn't have much time to be concerned about such oddities.

She had never seen Toby so intent on anything. He wanted to know *everything*. Where's this, and what's that for? And where are you going to sit, Mommy?

"I'm not, hon. You know that. There isn't room in this rocket for …"

"Mrs. Kruger, pardon me, but …"

"Just a minute, *please*."

"Oh, I'm sorry."

"What was it you wanted to know now, Tobe?" There were too many people; there was too much talk. She felt slightly dizzy. "Look, hon, I want to go on down." It was hard to talk. She saw Mrs. Kruger on the ramp, and called her, and left Toby with her. Down at the bottom, she saw Sue Stein, and asked her if she'd go take over with Toby and try to answer his questions.

"Sure. Feeling rocky, kid?"

"Kind of." She tried to smile.

"You better go lie down. Maybe Allie can get something for you. I saw her over there.…" She waved a vague hand. "You look like hell, kid. Better lie down." Then she rushed off.

He got away from Grandma when Sue Stein came and said Mother wanted her to show him everything. Then he said he was tired and got away from *her*. He could find his Grandma all right, he said.

He'd found the spot he wanted. He could just about wriggle into it, he thought.

The loudspeaker crackled over her head. Five minutes now.

The other women who'd been fixing their hair and brightening their lipstick snapped their bags shut and took a last look and ran out, to find places where they could see everything. Ruth stretched out on the couch and closed her eyes. Five minutes now, by herself, to get used to the idea that the job was done.

She had done everything she could do, including coming here today. There was nothing further she could do. From now on, or in five minutes' time, it was out of anyone's hands, but—Whose? And Jock's, of course. Once the relief rocket got there, it was up to him.

If it got there.

If he was there for it to get to.

The way they had worked it, there was a chance at least they'd know the answer in an hour's time. If the rocket made its orbit once, and only once, it would mean he was alive and well and in control of his own ship, with the radio working, and …

And if it made a second orbit, there was still hope. It *might* mean nothing worse than that his radio was out. But that way they would have to wait …

God! It could take months, if the calculations as to where he'd come down were not quite right. If … *if* a million little things that would make it harder to get the fuel from one rocket to the other.

But if they only saw one orbit …

For the first time, she let herself, forced herself to, consider the possibility that Jock was dead. That he would not come back.

He's not dead, she thought. I'd know it if he was. Like I knew something was wrong last time. Like I'd know it now if …

"Sixty seconds before zero," said the speaker.

But there is! She sat bolt upright, not tired or dizzy any more. Now she had faced it, she didn't feel confused. There was something … something dreadfully *wrong*.…

She ran out, and as she came on to the open field, the speaker was saying, "Fifty-one."

She ran to the edge of the crowd, and couldn't get through, and had to run, keep running, around the edges, to find the aisle between the cords.

Stop it! she screamed, but not out loud, because she had to use all her breath for running.

And while she ran, she tried to think.

"Minus forty-seven."

She couldn't make them stop without a reason. They'd think she was hysterical …

"… forty-five …"

Maybe she was, at that. Coolly, her mind considered the idea and rejected it. No; there was a problem that hadn't been solved, a question she hadn't answered.

But *what* problem? What …

"Minus forty."

She dashed down between the ropes, toward the control booth. The guard stepped forward, then recognized her, and stepped back. The corridor between the packed crowds went on forever.

"Minus thirty-nine ... eight ... thirty-seven."

She stopped outside the door of Control, and tried to think, think, *think!* What *was* it? What could she tell them? How could she convince them? She *knew*, but they'd want to know what, why ...

You just didn't change plans at a moment like this.

But if they fired the rocket before she figured it out, before she remembered the problem, and then found an answer, it was as good as murdering Jock. They could never get another one up quickly enough if anything went wrong this time.

She pushed open the door.

"Stop!" she said. "Listen, you've got to stop. Wait! There's something ..."

Tim O'Heyer came and took her arm, and smiled and said something. Something soothing.

"Minus nineteen," somebody said into a microphone, quietly.

She kept trying to explain, and Tim kept talking at her, and when she tried to pull away she realized the hand on her arm wasn't just there to comfort her. He was keeping her from making trouble. He ...

Oh, God! If there was just some way to make them understand! If she could only remember *what* was wrong ...

"Minus three ... two ..."

It was no use.

She stopped fighting, caught her breath, stood still, and saw Tim's approving smile, as the word and the flare went off together:

"Mark!"

Then, in a dead calm, she looked around and saw Sue.

"Where's Toby?" she asked.

She was looking in the reserved grandstand seats for Mrs. Kruger, when she heard the crowd sigh, and looked up and saw it happening.

VII

The crash fire did not damage the inside of the rocket at all. The cause of the crash was self-evident, as soon as they found Toby Kruger's body wedged into the empty space between the outer hull of the third stage, and the inner hull of the second.

The headlines were not as bad as might have been expected. Whether it was the tired and unholy calm on Ruth Kruger's face that restrained them, or Tim O'Heyer's emergency-reserve supply of Irish whisky that convinced them, the newsmen took it easy on the story. All America couldn't attend the funeral, but a representative hundred thousand citizens mobbed the streets when the boy was buried; the other hundred and eighty million saw the ceremonies more intimately on their TV sets.

Nobody who heard the quiet words spoken over the fresh grave—a historic piece of poetry to which the author, O'Heyer, could never sign his name—nobody who heard that simple speech remained entirely unmoved. Just where or when or with whom the movement started is still not known; probably it began spontaneously in a thousand different homes during the brief ceremony; maybe O'Heyer had something to do with that part of it, too. Whichever way, the money started coming in, by wire, twenty minutes afterwards; and by the end of the week "Bring Jock Back" was denting more paychecks than the numbers racket and the nylon industry combined.

The KIM-IX was finished in a month. They didn't have Ruth Kruger to design this time, but they didn't need her: the KIM-VIII plans were still good. O'Heyer managed to keep the sleeping-pill story down to a tiny back-page notice in most of the papers, and the funeral was not televised.

Later, they brought back the perfectly preserved, emaciated body of Jock Kruger, and laid him to rest next to his wife and son. He had been a good pilot and an ingenious man. The moon couldn't kill him; it took starvation to do that.

They made an international shrine of the house, and the garden where the three graves lay.

Now they are talking of making an interplanetary shrine of the lonely rocket on the wrong side of the moon.

Sun Ra (1914–93)

Sun Ra was a jazz musician and poet who said he experienced a physical and spiritual journey to Saturn that inspired his work. Born in Birmingham, Alabama as Herman Blount, Ra was later drafted into the US army, shortly after the US entered World War II, but as a conscientious objector he refused to serve and was subsequently arrested before being given a medical release. He later moved to Chicago, where he changed his name and formed the musical collective known as the Arkestra. Fully immersed in larger Black political and cultural movements in the US, Sun Ra's work is foundational to Afrofuturism, as well as to the wider place of SF in popular music culture.

Note on the text: The poem was published on the back of what seems to be a later-issued cover of the album *Super-Sonic Jazz*, released in 1957; it was also included in the liner notes for the 1959 album *Jazz in Silhouette.* (These liner notes have been reprinted by the Corbett vs Dempsey gallery as part of a catalogue of Sun Ra's work.) The poem has been reprinted in Sun Ra's *Collected Works, Vol. 1: Immeasurable Equation* (2005, ed. Adam Abraham), which uses the 1957 date. The version below follows that on the album cover, which is identical to the 1959 liner notes with the exception of the added final line, included on the album and in later reproductions. The image of Sun Ra (Fig. 7), a promotional photo by Impulse! Records and ABC/Dunhill Records for the 1973 rerelease of his album *The Magic City*, highlights the importance of SF and Afrofuturist imagery in his artistic self-presentation.

"The Space Age Cannot Be Avoided" (1957)

The prophets of the past belong to the past,
The space prophets of the greater future
Belong to the greater future.

The greater future is the age of the Space Prophet,
The scientific airy-minded second man:
The prince of the power of the air.
The air is music.
The music is power.
The power of the past was its music,
The greater power of the future greater
Greater music is art,
Is its greater music:
Art is the foundation of any living culture.
Living culture is skilled culture

Skilled dutifulness, aim and care
And love of beauty is the only way to produce art.

Skilled culture is the new weapon of nations,
The new measure of determination as to whether a nation
Is ready to be a greater nation is art.
A nation without art is a nation without a lifeline.
Art is the lifeline because art is the airy concept
Of greater living. It is the airy foundation of the airy
Kingdom of the future.
Tomorrow Beyond Tomorrow is the greater kingdom,
THE KINGDOM OF THE SPACE AGE …

Fig. 7: Impulse! Records and ABC/Dunhill Records. Promotional image of Sun Ra, 1973.

Muriel Spark (1918–2006)

Scottish author Muriel Spark began writing professionally following World War II, when she held a position in the Newsroom of the Department of Political Intelligence (for which James Bond creator Ian Fleming also worked). This office, among other tasks, produced propaganda for the war effort. The position would influence her later writing (as detailed by Simon Cooke), and points toward the fascination in her work with the tenuous but always present divisions between reality and fiction. Best known for her novel *The Prime of Miss Jean Brodie* (1961), Spark was not a science fiction author *per se*, but her interest in the interaction of fantasy and reality lends itself to the form, as made clear in "Miss Pinkerton's Apocalypse," a story that also satirizes how gendered assumptions feed into such discussions.

Note on the text: "Miss Pinkerton's Apocalypse" first appeared in Spark's collection *The Go-Away Bird and Other Stories* (1958), which is the source of the text reproduced here.

"Miss Pinkerton's Apocalypse" (1958)

ONE evening, a damp one in February, something flew in at the window. Miss Laura Pinkerton, who was doing something innocent to the fire, heard a faint throbbing noise overhead. On looking up, "George! come here! come quickly!"

George Lake came in at once, though sullenly because of their quarrel, eating a sandwich from the kitchen. He looked up at the noise then sat down immediately.

From this point onward their story comes in two versions, his and hers. But they agree as to the main facts; they agree that it was a small round flattish object, and that it flew.

"It's a flying object of some sort," whispered George eventually.

"It's a saucer," said Miss Pinkerton, keen and loud, "an antique piece. You can tell by the shape."

"It can't be an antique, that's absolutely certain," George said.

He ought to have been more tactful, and would have been, but for the stress of the moment. Of course it set Miss Pinkerton off, she being in the right.

"I know my facts," she stated as usual, "I should hope I know my facts. I've been in antique china for twenty-three years in the autumn," which was true, and George knew it.

The little saucer was cavorting round the lamp.

"It seems to be attracted by the light," George remarked, as one might distinguish a moth.

Promptly, it made as if to dive dangerously at George's head. He ducked, and Miss Pinkerton backed against the wall. As the dish tilted on its side, skimming George's shoulder, Miss Pinkerton could see inside it.

"The thing might be radio-active. It might be dangerous." George was breathless. The saucer had climbed, was circling high above his head, and now made for him again, but missed.

"It is not radio-active," said Miss Pinkerton, "it is Spode."[1]

"Don't be so damn silly," George replied, under the stress of the occasion.

"All right, very well," said Miss Pinkerton, "it is not Spode. I suppose you are the expert, George, I suppose you know best. I was only judging by the pattern. After the best part of a lifetime in china—"

"It must be a forgery," George said unfortunately. For, unfortunately, something familiar and abrasive in Miss Pinkerton's speech began to grind within him. Also, he was afraid of the saucer.

It had taken a stately turn, following the picture rail in a steady career round the room.

"Forgery, ha!" said Miss Pinkerton. She was out of the room like a shot, and in again carrying a pair of steps.

"I will examine the mark," said she, pointing intensely at the saucer. "Where are my glasses?"

Obligingly, the saucer settled in a corner; it hung like a spider a few inches from the ceiling. Miss Pinkerton adjusted the steps. With her glasses on she was almost her sunny self again, she was ceremonious and expert.

"Don't touch it, don't go near it!" George pushed her aside and grabbed the steps, knocking over a blue glass bowl, a Dresden figure,[2] a vase of flowers and a decanter of sherry; like a bull in a china shop, as Miss Pinkerton exclaimed. But she was determined, and struggled to reclaim the steps.

"Laura!" he said desperately. "I believe it is Spode. I take your word."

The saucer then flew out of the window.

They acted quickly. They telephoned to the local paper. A reporter would come right away. Meanwhile, Miss Pinkerton telephoned to her two scientific friends—at least, one was interested in psychic research and the other was an electrician. But she got no reply from either. George had leaned out of the window, scanning the rooftops and the night sky. He had leaned out of the back windows, had tried all the lights and the wireless. These things were as usual.

The news man arrived, accompanied by a photographer.

"There's nothing to photograph," said Miss Pinkerton excitably. "It went away."

"We could take a few shots of the actual spot," the man explained.

---

1 An English brand of pottery and bone china, founded by Josiah Spode (1733–97), characterized by blue glazed patterning.

2 Porcelain figurines generally made at a factory in Meissen, near Dresden (in what is now Germany), starting in the eighteenth century.

Miss Pinkerton looked anxiously at the result of George and the steps.

"The place is a wreck."

Sherry from the decanter was still dripping from the sideboard.

"I'd better clear the place up. George, help me!" She fluttered nervously, and started to pack the fire with small coals.

"No, leave everything as it is," the reporter advised her. "Did the apparition make this mess?"

George and Miss Pinkerton spoke together.

"Well, indirectly," said George.

"It wasn't an apparition," said Miss Pinkerton.

The reporter settled on the nearest chair, poising his pencil and asking, "Do you mind if I take notes?"

"Would you mind sitting over here?" said Miss Pinkerton. "I don't use the Queen Annes,[1] normally. They are very frail pieces."

The reporter rose as if stung, then perched on a table which Miss Pinkerton looked at uneasily.

"You see, I'm in antiques," she rattled on, for the affair was beginning to tell on her, as George told himself. In fact he sized up that she was done for; his irritation abated, his confidence came flooding back.

"Now, Laura, sit down and take it easy." Solicitously he pushed her into an easy chair.

"She's overwrought," he informed the pressmen in an audible undertone.

"You say this object actually flew in this window?" suggested the reporter.

"That is correct," said George.

The camera-man trained his apparatus on the window.

"And you were both here at the time?"

"No," Miss Pinkerton said. "Mr. Lake was in the kitchen and I called out, of course. But he didn't see inside the bowl, only the outside, underneath where the manufacturer's mark is. I saw the pattern so I got the steps to make sure. That's how Mr. Lake knocked my things over. I saw inside."

"I am going to say something," said George.

The men looked hopefully towards him. After a pause, George continued, "Let us begin at the beginning."

"Right," said the reporter, breezing up.

"It was like this," George said. "I came straight in when Miss Pinkerton screamed, and there was a white convex disc, you realize, floating around up there."

The reporter contemplated the spot indicated by George.

"It was making a hell of a racket like a cat purring," George told him.

"Any idea what it really was?" the reporter inquired.

George took his time to answer. "Well, yes," he said, "and no."

---

1 An eighteenth-century furniture design, named for Anne, who reigned as Queen of England, Scotland, and Ireland (1702–07), and of Great Britain and Ireland (1707–14).

"Spode ware," said Miss Pinkerton.

George continued, "I'm not up in these things. I'm extremely sceptical as a rule. This was a new experience to me."

"That's just it," said Miss Pinkerton. "Personally, I've been in china for twenty-three years. I recognised the thing immediately."

The reporter scribbled and inquired, "These flying discs appear frequently in China?"

"It was a saucer. I've never seen one flying before," Miss Pinkerton explained.

"I am going to ask a question," George said.

Miss Pinkerton continued, "Mr. Lake is an art framer. He handles old canvases but next to no antiques."

"I am going to ask. Are you telling the story or am I?" George said.

"Perhaps Mr. Lake's account first and then the lady's," the reporter ventured.

Miss Pinkerton subsided crossly while he turned to George.

"Was the object attached to anything? No wires or anything? I mean, someone couldn't have been having a joke or something?"

George gave a decent moment to the possibility.

"No," he then said. "It struck me, in fact, that there was some sort of Mind behind it, operating from outer space. It tried to attack me, in fact."

"Really, how was that?"

"Mr. Lake was not attacked," Miss Pinkerton stated. "There was no danger at all. I saw the expression on the pilot's face. He was having a game with Mr. Lake, grinning all over his face."

"Pilot?" said George. 'What are you talking about—pilot!"

Miss Pinkerton sighed. "A tiny man half the size of my finger," she declared. "He sat on a tiny stool. He held the little tiny steering-wheel with one hand and waved with the other. Because, there was something like a sewing-machine fixed near the rim, and he worked the tiny treadle with his foot. Mr. Lake was not attacked."

"Don't be so damn silly," said George.

"You don't mean this?" the reporter asked her with scrutiny.

"Of course I do."

"I would like to know something," George demanded.

"You only saw the under-side of the saucer, George."

"You said nothing about any pilot at the time," said George. "I saw no pilot."

"Mr. Lake got a fright when the saucer came at him. If he hadn't been dodging he would have seen for himself."

"You mentioned no pilot," said George. "Be reasonable."

"I had no chance," said she. She appealed to the camera-man. "You see, I know what I'm talking about. Mr. Lake thought he knew better, however. Mr. Lake said, 'It's a forgery.' If there's one thing I do know, it's china."

"It would be most unlikely," said George to the reporter. "A steering-wheel and a treadle machine these days, can you credit it?"

"The man would have fallen out," the camera-man reflected.

"I must say," said the reporter, "that I favour Mr. Lake's long-range theory. The lady may have been subject to some hallucination, after the shock of the saucer."

"Quite," said George. He whispered something to the photographer. "Women!" Miss Pinkerton heard him breathe.

The reporter heard him also. He gave a friendly laugh. "Shall we continue with Mr. Lake's account, and then see what we can make of both stories?"

But Miss Pinkerton had come to a rapid decision. She began to display a mood hitherto unknown to George. Leaning back, she gave way to a weak and artless giggling. Her hand fluttered prettily as she spoke between gurgles of mirth. "Oh, what a mess! What an evening! We aren't accustomed to drink, you see, and now oh dear, oh dear!"

"Are you all right, Laura?" George inquired severely.

"Yes, yes, yes," said Miss Pinkerton, drowsy and amiable. "We really oughtn't have done this, George. Bringing these gentlemen out. But I can't keep it up, George. Oh dear, it's been fun though."

She was away into her giggles again. George looked bewildered. Then he looked suspicious.

"It's definitely the effect of this extraordinary phenomenon," George said firmly to the Press.

"It was my fault, all my fault," spluttered Miss Pinkerton.

The reporter looked at his watch. "I can quite definitely say you saw a flying object?" he asked. "And that you were both put out by it?"

"Put down that it was a small, round, flattish object. We both agree to that," George said.

A spurt of delight arose from Miss Pinkerton again.

"Women, you know! It always comes down to women in the finish," she told them. "We had a couple of drinks."

"Mr. Lake had rather more than I did," she added triumphantly.

"I assure you," said George to the reporter.

"We might be fined for bringing the Press along, George. It might be an offence," she put in.

"I assure you," George insisted to the photographer, "that we had a flying saucer less than an hour ago in this room."

Miss Pinkerton giggled.

The reporter looked round the room with new eyes; and with the air of one to whom to understand all is to forgive all, he folded his notebook. The camera-man stared at the pool of sherry, the overturned flowers, the broken glass and china. He packed up his camera, and they went away.

George gave out the tale to his regular customers. He gave both versions, appealing to their reason to choose. Farther up the road at her corner shop, Miss Pinkerton smiled tolerantly when questioned. "Flying saucer? George is very artistic," she would say, "and allowances must be made for imaginative folk." Sometimes she added that the evening had been a memorable one, "Quite a party!"

It caused a certain amount of tittering in the neighbourhood. George felt this; but otherwise, the affair made no difference between them. Personally, I believe the story, with a preference for Miss Pinkerton's original version. She is a neighbour of mine. I have reason to believe this version because, not long afterwards, I too received a flying visitation from a saucer. The little pilot, in my case, was shy and inquisitive. He pedalled with all his might. My saucer was Royal Worcester,[1] fake or not I can't say.

1 A porcelain manufacturer from Worcester, England, that can be traced back to 1751.

REVOLUTIONS AND NEW WAVES: 1960–1980S

Pamela Zoline (b. 1941)

Pamela Zoline is an American author, artist, and political and arts activist whose best-known SF was written while she was living in the UK. As part of the group of authors associated with Michael Moorcock's tenure as editor of *New Worlds* magazine, she is firmly associated with the so-called New Wave, especially for her most famous story, reproduced here, which is among the most recognized of the period. Beyond her writing, Zoline is best known as a founder of the Telluride Institute, which supports cultural and artistic, environmental, and political events and festivals.

Note on the text: Republished often, the story originally appeared in *New Worlds* (July 1967), with the author listed as "P. A. Zoline" and with the following biography: "P. A. Zoline is a painter who has exhibited at the Tate Gallery, the United States Embassy (in the London Group), and elsewhere. Born in Chicago, she now lives in Camden Town. *The Heat Death of the Universe* is her first story" (64). The version here follows the initial magazine publication, but obvious typographical errors that were corrected in Zoline's later collection, published in the UK as *Busy about the Tree of Life and Other Stories* and in the US as *The Heat Death of the Universe and Other Stories* (1988), are likewise corrected here.

"The Heat Death of the Universe" (1967)

1. ONTOLOGY: That branch of metaphysics which concerns itself with the problems of the nature of existence or being.

2. Imagine a pale blue morning sky, almost green, with clouds only at the rims. The earth rolls and the sun appears to mount, mountains erode, fruits decay, the Foraminifera[1] adds another chamber to its shell, babies' fingernails grow as does the hair of the dead in their graves, and in egg timers the sands fall and the eggs cook on.

3. Sarah Boyle thinks of her nose as too large, though several men have cherished it. The nose is generous and performs a well calculated geometric curve, at the arch of which the skin is drawn very tight and a faint whiteness of bone can be seen showing through, it has much the same architectural tension and sense of mathematical calculation as the day after Thanksgiving breastbone on the carcass of turkey; her maiden name was Sloss, mixed German, English and Irish descent; in grade school she was very bad at playing softball and, besides being chosen last for the team, was always made to play center field,

1 Single-celled organisms that live primarily in the sea.

no one could ever hit to center field; she loves music best of all the arts, and of music, Bach, J.S.;[1] she lives in California, though she grew up in Boston and Toledo.

4. BREAKFAST TIME AT THE BOYLE'S HOUSE ON LA FLORIDA STREET, ALAMEDA, CALIFORNIA, THE CHILDREN DEMAND SUGAR FROSTED FLAKES.

With some reluctance Sarah Boyle dishes out Sugar Frosted Flakes to her children, already hearing the decay set in upon the little milk white teeth, the bony whine of the dentist's drill. The dentist is a short, gentle man with a moustache who sometimes reminds Sarah of an uncle who lives in Ohio. One bowl per child.

5. If one can imagine it considered as an abstract object, by members of a totally separate culture, one can see that the cereal box might seem a beautiful thing. The solid rectangle is neatly joined and classical in proportions, on it are squandered wealths of richest colours, virgin blues, crimsons, dense ochres, precious pigments once reserved for sacred paintings and as cosmetics for the blind faces of marble gods. Giant size. Net Weight 16 ounces, 250 grams. "They're tigeriffic!" says Tony the Tiger.[2] The box blatts[3] promises: Energy, Nature's Own Goodness, an endless pubescence. On its back is a mask of William Shakespeare[4] to be cut out, folded, worn by thousands of tiny Shakespeares in Kansas City, Detroit, Tucson, San Diego, Tampa. He appears at once more kindly and somewhat more vacant than we are used to seeing him. Two or more of the children lay claim to the mask, but Sarah puts off that Solomon's decision[5] until such time as the box is empty.

6. A notice in orange flourishes states that a Surprise Gift is to be found somewhere in the package, nestled amongst the golden flakes. So far it has not been unearthed, and the children request more cereal than they wish to eat, great yellow heaps of it, to hurry the discovery. Even so, at the end of the meal, some layers of flakes remain in the box and the Gift must still be among them.

---

1 Johann Sebastian Bach (1685–1750), German composer regularly cited as one of the most important and influential in the history of European music.

2 Tony the Tiger was the cartoon mascot for Kellog's Frosted Flakes Cereal, best known for his stylized catchphrase "They're great!" as read by famed singer and voice actor Thurl Ravenscroft (1914–2005). "Tigeriffic," more generally spelled "tiggerific," is more closely associated with the character Tigger in the Disney cartoon adaptations of A.A. Milne's Winnie-the-Pooh stories.

3 Blat: "To bleat, or make similar sounds. Also figurative, to talk noisily or impulsively" (*OED*).

4 William Shakespeare (c. 1564–1616), English playwright and poet.

5 Solomon, biblical king of Israel and Judah, and successor to King David. "Solomon's decision" alludes to the story recounted in 1 Kings 3:16–28. Two women who live in the same house each gave birth; one of the infants dies, and each woman claims the remaining child as her own. Solomon orders the child be cut in two, and when only one woman begs for the child's life to be spared, even if it means she must give up her claim, Solomon declares her to be the mother.

7. There is even a Special Offer of a secret membership, code and magic ring; these to be obtained by sending in the box top with 50¢.

8. Three offers on one cereal box. To Sarah Boyle this seems to be oversell. Perhaps something is terribly wrong with the cereal and it must be sold quickly, got off the shelves before the news breaks. Perhaps it causes a special, cruel Cancer in little children. As Sarah Boyle collects the bowls printed with bunnies and baseball statistics, still slopping half full of milk and wilted flakes, she imagines *in her mind's eye* the headlines, "Nation's Small Fry Stricken, Fate's Finger Sugar Coated, Lethal Sweetness Socks Tots."

9. Sarah Boyle is a vivacious and intelligent young wife and mother, educated at a fine Eastern college, proud of her growing family which keeps her busy and happy around the house.

10. BIRTHDAY.
Today is the birthday of one of the children. There will be a party in the late afternoon.

11. CLEANING UP THE HOUSE. ONE.
Cleaning up the kitchen. Sarah Boyle puts the bowls, plates, glasses and silverware into the sink. She scrubs at the stickiness on the yellow-marbled formica table with a blue synthetic sponge, a special blue which we shall see again. There are marks of children's hands in various sizes printed with sugar and grime on all the table's surfaces. The marks catch the light, they appear and disappear according to the position of the observing eye. The floor sweepings include a triangular half of toast spread with grape jelly, bobby pins, a green band-aid, flakes, a doll's eye, dust, dog's hair and a button.

12. Until we reach the statistically likely planet and begin to converse with whatever green-faced, teleporting denizens thereof—considering only this shrunk and communication-ravaged world—can we any more postulate a separate culture? Viewing the metastasis of Western Culture it seems progressively less likely. Sarah Boyle imagines a whole world which has become like California, all topographical imperfections sanded away with the sweet smelling burr of the plastic surgeon's cosmetic polisher; a world populace dieting, leisured, similar in pink and mauve hair and rhinestone shades. A land Cunt Pink and Avocado Green, brassiered and girdled by monstrous complexities of Super Highways; a California endless and unceasing, embracing and transforming the entire globe, California, California!

13. INSERT ONE. ON ENTROPY.
ENTROPY: A quantity introduced in the first place to facilitate the calculations, and to give clear expressions to the results of thermodynamics.

Changes of entropy can be calculated only for a reversible process, and may then be defined as the ratio of the amount of heat taken up to the absolute temperature at which the heat is absorbed. Entropy changes for actual irreversible processes are calculated by postulating equivalent theoretical reversible changes. The entropy of a system is a measure of its degree of disorder. The total entropy of any isolated system can never decrease in any change; it must either increase (irreversible process) or remain constant (reversible process). The total entropy of the Universe therefore is increasing, tending towards a maximum, corresponding to complete disorder of the particles in it (assuming that it may be regarded as an isolated system). See *heat death of the Universe.*

14. CLEANING UP THE HOUSE. TWO.

Washing the baby's diapers. Sarah Boyle writes notes to herself all over the house; a mazed wild script larded with arrows, diagrams, pictures; graffiti on every available surface in a desperate/heroic attempt to index, record, bluff, invoke, order and placate. On the fluted and flowered white plastic lid of the diaper bin she has written in Blushing Pink Nitetime lipstick a phrase to ward off fumey ammoniac despair. "The nitrogen cycle is the vital round of organic and inorganic exchange on earth. The sweet breath of the Universe." On the wall by the washing machine are Yin and Yang signs, mandalas,[1] and the words, "Many young wives feel trapped. It is a contemporary sociological phenomenon which may be explained in part by a gap between changing living patterns and the accommodation of social services to these patterns." Over the stove she had written "Help, Help, Help, Help, Help."

15. Sometimes she numbers or letters the things in a room, writing the assigned character on each object. There are 819 separate moveable objects in the living room, counting books. Sometimes she labels objects with their names, or with false names, thus on her bureau the hair brush is labeled HAIR BRUSH, the cologne, COLOGNE, the hand cream, CAT. She is passionately fond of children's dictionaries, encyclopaedias, ABCs and all reference books, transfixed and comforted at their simulacra of a complete listing and ordering.

16. On the door of a bedroom are written two definitions from reference books, "GOD: An object of worship"; "HOMEOSTASIS: Maintenance of constancy of internal environment."

17. Sarah Boyle washes the diapers, washes the linen, Oh Saint Veronica,[2]

1 In Chinese philosophy, yin and yang are opposing forces that nonetheless operate together to create the cycles of existence and balance in the universe. Mandalas are symbolic geometric shapes that, in various religious and spiritual traditions, are used as part of meditative and other spiritual practices.

2 In Christian tradition, Saint Veronica was a witness to Christ carrying his cross to the site of his crucifixion; sympathizing with his suffering, she gave him her veil to wipe his face, which miraculously imparted the image of his face to the cloth.

changes the sheets on the baby's crib. She begins to put away some of the toys, stepping over and around the organizations of playthings which still seem inhabited. There are various vehicles, and articles of medicine, domesticity and war; whole zoos of stuffed animals, bruised and odorous with years of love; hundreds of small figures, plastic animals, cowboys, cars, spacemen, with which the children make sub and supra worlds in their play. One of Sarah's favourite toys is the Baba, the wooden Russian doll which, opened, reveals a smaller but otherwise identical doll which opens to reveal, etc., a lesson in infinity at least to the number of seven dolls.

18. Sarah Boyle's mother has been dead for two years. Sarah Boyle thinks of music as the formal articulation of the passage of time, and of Bach as the most poignant rendering of this. Her eyes are sometimes the colour of the aforementioned kitchen sponge. Her hair is natural spaniel brown; months ago on an hysterical day she dyed it red, so now it is two-toned with a stripe in the middle, like the painted walls of slum buildings or old schools.

19. INSERT TWO. THE HEAT DEATH OF UNIVERSE.
The second law of thermodynamics can be interpreted to mean that the ENTROPY of a closed system tends toward a maximum and that its available ENERGY tends toward a minimum. It has been held that the Universe constitutes a thermodynamically closed system, and if this were true it would mean that a time must finally come when the Universe "unwinds" itself, no energy being available for use. This state is referred to as the "heat death of the Universe." It is by no means certain, however, that the Universe can be considered as a closed system in this sense.

20. Sarah Boyle pours out a Coke from the refrigerator and lights a cigarette. The coldness and sweetness of the thick brown liquid make her throat ache and her teeth sting briefly, sweet juice of my youth, her eyes glass with the carbonation, she thinks of the Heat Death of the Universe. A logarithmic of those late summer days, endless as the Irish serpent twisting through jewelled manuscripts forever, tail in mouth, the heat pressing, bloating, doing violence.[1] The Los Angeles sky becomes so filled and bleached with detritus that it loses all colour and silvers like a mirror, reflecting back the fricasseeing earth. Everything becoming warmer and warmer, each particle of matter becoming more agitated, more excited until the bonds shatter, the glues fail, the deodorants lose their seals. She imagines the whole of New York City

---

1 This description echoes that of the ouroboros, an ancient image, commonly used in medieval manuscripts, of a serpent or dragon eating its own tail, often presented as a stylized circle. Used in some traditions to represent the cycle of life and death, it relates to Zoline's earlier use of the yin and yang symbol. The reference to a specific Irish serpent could also point to Irish legends, including the serpent or dragon-like Oilliphéist, or to the legend of Saint Patrick driving snakes from Ireland.

melting like a Dali[1] into a great chocolate mass, a great soup, the Great Soup of New York.

21. CLEANING UP THE HOUSE. THREE.

Beds made. Vacuuming the hall, a carpet of faded flowers, vines and leaves which endlessly wind and twist into each other in a fevered and permanent ecstasy. Suddenly the vacuum blows instead of sucks, spewing marbles, dolls' eyes, dust, crackers. An old trick. "Oh my god," says Sarah. The baby yells on cue for attention/changing/food. Sarah kicks the vacuum cleaner and it retches and begins working again.

22. AT LUNCH ONLY ONE GLASS OF MILK IS SPILLED.

At lunch only one glass of milk is spilled.

23. The plants need watering, Geranium, Hyacinth, Lavender, Avocado, Cyclamen. Feed the fish, happy fish with china castles and mermaids in the bowl. The turtle looks more and more unwell and is probably dying.

24. Sarah Boyle's blue eyes, how blue? Bluer far and of a different quality than the Nature metaphors which were both engine and fuel to so much of precedent literature. A fine, modern, acid, synthetic blue; the shiny cerulean of the skies on postcards sent from lush subtropics, the natives grinning ivory ambivalent grins in their dark faces; the promising, fat, unnatural blue of the heavy tranquillizer capsule; the cool, mean blue of that fake kitchen sponge; the deepest, most unbelievable azure of the tiled and mossless interiors of California swimming pools. The chemists in their kitchens cooked, cooled and distilled this blue from thousands of colourless and wonderfully constructed crystals, each one unique and nonpareil; and now that colour, hisses, bubbles, burns in Sarah's eyes.

25. INSERT THREE. ON LIGHT.

LIGHT: Name given to the agency by means of which a viewed object influences the observer's eyes. Consists of electro-magnetic radiation within the wavelength range 4×10^{-5} cm. to 7×10^{-5} cm. approximately;[2] variations in the wave-length produce different sensations in the eye, corresponding to different colours. See colour vision.

26. LIGHT AND CLEANING THE LIVING ROOM.

All the objects (819) and surfaces in the living room are dusty, grey common

1 Salvador Dalí (1904–89): famous Spanish surrealist painter. One of his best-known works, "The Persistence of Memory" (1931), shows pocket watches melting over objects in a landscape.

2 This is a roughly accurate measurement of the wavelengths of the visible spectrum of light, from violet to red, respectively.

dust as though this were the den of a giant, moulting mouse. Suddenly quantities of waves or particles of very strong sunlight speed in through the window, and everything incandesces, multiple rainbows. Poised in what has become a solid cube of light, like an ancient insect trapped in amber, Sarah Boyle realizes that the dust is indeed the most beautiful stuff in the room, a manna for the eyes. Duchamp,[1] that father of thought, has set with fixative some dust which fell on one of his sculptures, counting it as part of the work. "That way madness lies, says Sarah," says Sarah. The thought of ordering a household on Dada principles balloons again. All the rooms would fill up with objects, newspapers and magazines would compost, the potatoes in the rack, the canned green beans in the garbage can would take new heart and come to life again, reaching out green shoots towards the sun. The plants would grow wild and wind into a jungle around the house, splitting plaster, tearing shingles, the garden would enter in at the door. The goldfish would die, the birds would die, we'd have them stuffed; the dog would die from lack of care, and probably the children—all stuffed and sitting around the house, covered with dust.

27. INSERT FOUR. DADA.

DADA (Fr., hobby-horse) was a nihilistic precursor of Surrealism, invented in Zurich during World War I, a product of hysteria and shock lasting from about 1915 to 1922. It was deliberately anti-art and anti-sense, intended to outrage and scandalize, and its most characteristic production was the reproduction of the *Mona Lisa* decorated with a moustache and the obscene caption LHOOQ (read: *elle a chaud au cul*[2]) "by" Duchamp. Other manifestations included Arp's[3] collages of coloured paper cut out at random and shuffled, ready-made objects such as the bottle drier and the bicycle wheel "signed" by Duchamp, Picabia's[4] drawings of bits of machinery with incongruous titles, incoherent poetry, a lecture given by 38 lecturers in unison, and an exhibition in Cologne in 1920, held in an annexe to a café lavatory, at which a chopper was provided for spectators to smash the exhibits with—which they did.

28. TIME PIECES AND OTHER MEASURING DEVICES.

In the Boyle house there are four clocks; three watches (one a Mickey Mouse watch which does not work); two calendars and two engagement books; three rulers; a yard stick; a measuring cup; a set of red plastic measuring spoons which includes a tablespoon, a teaspoon, a one-half teaspoon, one-fourth teaspoon and one-eighth teaspoon; an egg timer; an oral thermometer

1 Marcel Duchamp (1887–1968) was a conceptual artist affiliated with the Dada movement (see entry 27 in the story). One of his most famous works is *Fountain*, which consists of a urinal signed "R Mutt" (of note in relation to this story are later arguments that the sculpture was actually the work of Elsa von Freytag-Loringhoven [1874–1927]).

2 elle a chaud au cul (Fr.): "she has a hot ass."

3 Jean Arp (born Hans Peter Wilhelm Arp; 1886–1966), French-German artist associated with Dada.

4 Francis Picabia (1879–1953), French artist of the Dada circle.

and a rectal thermometer; a Boy Scout compass; a barometer in the shape of a house, in and out of which an old woman and an old man chase each other forever without fulfilment; a bathroom scale; an infant scale; a tape measure which can be pulled out of a stuffed felt strawberry; a wall on which the children's heights are marked; a metronome.

29. Sarah Boyle finds a new line in her face after lunch while cleaning the bathroom. It is as yet barely visible, running from the midpoint of her forehead to the bridge of her nose. By inward curling of her eyebrows she can etch it clearly as it will come to appear in the future. She marks another mark on the wall where she has drawn out a scoring area. Face Lines and Other Intimations of Mortality, the heading says. There are thirty-two marks, counting this latest one.

30. Sarah Boyle is a vivacious and witty young wife and mother, educated at a fine Eastern college, proud of her growing family which keeps her happy and busy around the house, involved in many hobbies and community activities, and only occasionally given to obsessions concerning Time/Entropy/Chaos and Death.

31. Sarah Boyle is never quite sure how many children she has.

32. Sarah thinks from time to time; Sarah is occasionally visited with this thought; at times this thought comes upon Sarah, that there are things to be hoped for, accomplishments to be desired beyond the mere reproductions, mirror reproduction of one's kind. The babies. Lying in bed at night sometimes the memory of the act of birth, always the hue and texture of red plush theatre seats, washes up; the rending which always, at a certain intensity of pain, slipped into landscapes, the sweet breath of the sweating nurse. The wooden Russian doll has bright, perfectly round red spots on her cheeks, she splits in the centre to reveal a doll smaller but in all other respects identical with round bright red spots on her cheeks, etc.

33. How fortunate for the species, Sarah muses or is mused, that children are as ingratiating as we know them. Otherwise they would soon be salted off for the leeches they are, and the race would extinguish itself in a fair sweet flowering, the last generations' massive achievement in the arts and pursuits of high civilization. The finest women would have their tubes tied off at the age of twelve, or perhaps refrain altogether from the Act of Love? All interests would be bent to a refining and perfecting of each febrile sense, each fluid hour, with no more cowardly investment in immortality via the patchy and too often disappointing vegetables of one's own womb.

34. INSERT FIVE. LOVE.

LOVE: a typical sentiment involving fondness for, or attachment to, an object, the idea of which is emotionally coloured whenever it arises in the mind, and capable, as Shand[1] has pointed out, of evoking any one of a whole gamut of primary emotions, according to the situation in which the object is placed, or represented; often, and by psychoanalysts always, used in the sense of *sex-love* or even *lust* (q.v.).

35. Sarah Boyle has at times felt a unity with her body, at other times a complete separation. The mind/body duality considered. The time/space duality considered. The male/female duality considered. The matter/energy duality considered. Sometimes, at extremes, her Body seems to her an animal on a leash, taken for walks in the park by her Mind. The lamp posts of experience. Her arms are lightly freckled, and when she gets very tired the places under her eyes become violet.

36. Housework is never completed, the chaos always lurks ready to encroach on any area left unweeded, a jungle filled with dirty pans and the roaring of giant stuffed toy animals suddenly turned savage. Terrible glass eyes.

37. SHOPPING FOR THE BIRTHDAY CAKE.

Shopping in the supermarket with the baby in front of the cart and a larger child holding on. The light from the ice cube tray shaped fluorescent lights is mixed blue and pink and brighter, colder, and cheaper than daylight. The doors swing open just as you reach out your hand for them, Tantalus,[2] moving with a ghastly quiet swing. Hot dogs for the party. Potato chips, gum drops, a paper table cloth with birthday designs, hot dog buns, catsup, mustard, picalilli, balloons, instant coffee Continental style, dog food, frozen peas, ice cream, frozen lima beans, frozen broccoli in butter sauce, paper birthday hats, paper napkins in three colours, a box of Sugar Frosted Flakes with a Wolfgang Amadeus Mozart[3] mask on the back, bread, pizza mix. The notes of a just graspable music filter through the giant store, for the most part by-passing the brain and acting directly on the liver, blood and lymph. The air is delicately scented with aluminum. Half and half cream, tea bags, bacon, sandwich meat, strawberry jam. Sarah is in front of the shelves of cleaning

---

1 Likely a reference to English psychologist Alexander F. Shand (1858–1936), and specifically his *Foundations of Character* (1920).

2 Tantalus is a figure from Greek mythology who was punished by the gods for telling their secrets, for bringing ambrosia and nectar from Olympus to give to his people, and for killing and cooking his son and trying to feed him to the gods. His punishment was to stand in a pool of water underneath a fruit tree, but never to be able to eat the fruit or drink the water, as both moved away from him when he tried to reach them.

3 Wolfgang Amadeus Mozart (1756–91), often hailed as one of the greatest composers of the Classical period in the European tradition.

products now, and the baby is beginning to whine. Around her are whole libraries of objects, offering themselves. Some of that same old hysteria that had incarnadined her hair rises up again, and she does not refuse it. There is one moment when she can choose direction, like standing on a chalk drawn X, a hot cross bun, and she does not choose calm and measure. Sarah Boyle begins to pick out, methodically, deliberately and with a careful ecstasy, one of every cleaning product which the store sells. Window Cleaner, Glass Cleaner, Brass Polish, Silver Polish, Steel Wool, eighteen different brands of Detergent, Disinfectant, Toilet Cleanser, Water Softener, Fabric Softener, Drain Cleanser, Spot Remover, Floor Wax, Furniture Wax, Car Wax, Carpet Shampoo, Dog Shampoo, Shampoo for people with dry, oily and normal hair, for people with dandruff, for people with grey hair. Tooth Paste, Tooth Powder, Denture Cleaner, Deodorants, Antiperspirants, Antiseptics, Soaps, Cleansers, Abrasives, Oven Cleansers, Makeup Removers. When the same products appear in different sizes Sarah takes one of each size. For some products she accumulates whole little families of containers: a giant Father bottle of shampoo, a Mother bottle, an Older Sister bottle just smaller than the Mother bottle, and a very tiny Baby Brother bottle. Sarah fills three shopping carts and has to have help wheeling them all down the aisles. At the check-out counter her laughter and hysteria keep threatening to overflow as the pale blonde clerk with no eyebrows like the *Mona Lisa* pretends normality and disinterest. The bill comes to $57.53 and Sarah has to write a check. Driving home, the baby strapped in the drive-a-cot and the paper bags bulging in the back seat, she cries.

38. BEFORE THE PARTY.

Mrs. David Boyle, mother-in-law of Sarah Boyle, is coming to the party of her grandchild. She brings a toy, a yellow wooden duck on a string, made in Austria; the duck quacks as it is pulled along the floor. Sarah is filling paper cups with gum drops and chocolates, and Mrs. David Boyle sits at the kitchen table and talks to her. She is talking about several things, she is talking about her garden which is flourishing except for a plague of rare black beetles, thought to have come from Hong Kong, which are undermining some of the most delicate growths at the roots, and feasting on the leaves of other plants. She is talking about a sale of household linens which she plans to attend on the following Tuesday. She is talking about her neighbour who has Cancer and is wasting away. The neighbour is a Catholic woman who had never had a day's illness in her life until the Cancer struck, and now she is, apparently, failing with dizzying speed. The doctor says her body's chaos, chaos, cells running wild all over, says Mrs. David Boyle. When I visited her she hardly *knew* me, can hardly *speak,* can't keep herself *clean,* says Mrs. David Boyle.

39. Sometimes Sarah can hardly remember how many cute, chubby little children she has.

40. When she used to stand out in center field far away from the other players, she used to make up songs and sing them to herself.

41. She thinks of the end of the world by ice.

42. She thinks of the end of the world by water.

43. She thinks of the end of the world by nuclear war.

44. There must be more than this, Sarah Boyle thinks, from time to time. What could one do to justify one's passage? Or less ambitiously, to change, even in the motion of the smallest mote, the course and circulation of the world? Sometimes Sarah's dreams are of heroic girth, a new symphony using laboratories of machinery and all invented instruments, at once giant in scope and intelligible to all, to heal the bloody breach; a series of paintings which would transfigure and astonish and calm the frenzied art world in its panting race; a new novel that would refurbish language. Sometimes she considers the mystical, the streaky and random, and it seems that one change, no matter how small, would be enough. Turtles are supposed to live for many years. To carve a name, date and perhaps a word of hope upon a turtle's shell, then set him free to wend the world, surely this one act might cancel out absurdity?

45. Mrs. David Boyle has a faint moustache, like Duchamp's *Mona Lisa*.

46. THE BIRTHDAY PARTY.
Many children, dressed in pastels, sit around the long table. They are exhausted and overexcited from games fiercely played, some are flushed and wet, others unnaturally pale. This general agitation, and the paper party hats they wear, combine to make them appear a dinner party of debauched midgets. It is time for the cake. A huge chocolate cake in the shape of a rocket and launching pad and covered with blue and pink icing is carried in. In the hush the birthday child begins to cry. He stops crying, makes a wish and blows out the candles.

47. One child will not eat hot dogs, ice cream or cake, and asks for cereal. Sarah pours him out a bowl of Sugar Frosted Flakes, and a moment later he chokes. Sarah pounds him on the back and out spits a tiny green plastic snake with red glass eyes, the Surprise Gift. All the children want it.

48. AFTER THE PARTY THE CHILDREN ARE PUT TO BED.
Bath time. Observing the nakedness of children, pink and slippery as seals, squealing as seals, now the splashing, grunting and smacking of cherry flesh on raspberry flesh reverberate in the pearl tiled steamy cubicle. The nakedness of children is so much more absolute than that of the mature. No musky curling hair to indicate the target points, no knobbly clutch of plane and fat

and curvature to ennoble this prince of beasts. All well-fed naked children appear edible, Sarah's teeth hum in her head with memory of bloody feastings, prehistory. Young humans appear too like the young of other species for smugness, and the comparison is not even in their favour, they are much the most peeled and unsupple of those young. Such pinkness, such utter nuded pinkness; the orifices neatly incised, rimmed with a slightly deeper rose, the incessant demands for breast, time, milks of many sorts.

49. INSERT SIX. WEINER ON ENTROPY.

In Gibbs'[1] Universe order is least probable, chaos most probable. But while the Universe as a whole, if indeed there is a whole Universe, tends to run down, there are local enclaves whose direction seems opposed to that of the Universe at large and in which there is a limited and temporary tendency for organization to increase. Life finds its home in some of these enclaves.

50. Sarah Boyle imagines, in her mind's eye, cleaning and ordering the whole world, even the Universe. Filling the great spaces of Space with a marvellous sweet smelling, deep cleansing foam. Deodorizing rank caves and volcanoes. Scrubbing rocks.

51. INSERT SEVEN. TURTLES.

Many different species of carnivorous Turtles live in the fresh waters of the tropical and temperate zones of various continents. Most Northerly of the European Turtles (extending as far as Holland and Lithuania) is the European Pond Turtle (*Emys orbicularis*). It is from 8 to 10 inches long and may live a hundred years.

52. CLEANING UP AFTER THE PARTY.

Sarah is cleaning up after the party. Gum drops and melted ice cream surge off paper plates, making holes in the paper tablecloth through the printed roses. A fly has died a splendid death in a pool of strawberry ice cream. Wet jelly beans stain all they touch, finally becoming themselves colourless, opaque white like flocks of tamed or sleeping maggots. Plastic favours mount half-eaten pieces of blue cake. Strewn about are thin strips of fortune papers from the Japanese poppers. Upon them are printed strangely assorted phrases selected by apparently unilingual Japanese. Crowds of delicate yellow people[2] spending great chunks of their lives in producing these most ephemeral of objects, and inscribing thousands of fine papers with absurd and incomprehensible messages. "The very hairs of your head are all numbered," reads one. Most of the balloons have popped. Someone has planted a hot dog in the

1 Josiah Willard Gibbs (1839–1903), American scientist most commonly associated with the study of thermodynamics.

2 A racist slur referring to people of Asian heritage.

daffodil pot. A few of the helium balloons have escaped their owners and now ride the ceiling. Another fortune paper reads, "Emperor's horses meet death worse, numbers, numbers."

51. She is very tired, violet under the eyes, mauve beneath the eyes. Her uncle in Ohio used to get the same marks under his eyes. She goes to the kitchen to lay the table for tomorrow's breakfast, then she sees that in the turtle's bowl the turtle is floating, still, on the surface of the water. Sarah Boyle pokes at it with a pencil but it does not move. She stands for several minutes looking at the dead turtle on the surface of the water. She is crying again.

54. She begins to cry. She goes to the refrigerator and takes out a carton of eggs, white eggs, extra large. She throws them one by one on to the kitchen floor which is patterned with strawberries in squares. They break beautifully. There is a Secret Society of Dentists, all moustached, with Special Code and Magic Rings. She begins to cry. She takes up three bunny dishes and throws them against the refrigerator, they shatter, and then the floor is covered with shards, chunks of partial bunnies, an ear, an eye here, a paw; Stockton, California, Acton, California, Chico, California, Redding, California, Glen Ellen, California, Cadix, California, Angels Camp, California, Half Moon Bay. The total ENTROPY of the Universe therefore is increasing, tending towards a maximum, corresponding to complete disorder of the particles in it. She is crying, her mouth is open. She throws a jar of grape jelly and it smashes the window over the sink. Her eyes are blue. She begins to open her mouth. It has been held that the Universe constitutes a thermodynamically closed system, and if this were true it would mean that a time must finally come when the Universe "unwinds" itself, no energy being available for use. This state is referred to as the "heat death of the Universe." Sarah Boyle begins to cry. She throws a jar of strawberry jam against the stove, enamel chips off and the stove begins to bleed. Bach had twenty children, how many children has Sarah Boyle? Her mouth is open. Her mouth is opening. She turns on the water and fills the sinks with detergent. She writes on the kitchen wall, "William Shakespeare has Cancer and lives in California." She writes, "Sugar Frosted Flakes are the Food of the Gods." The water foams up in the sink, overflowing, bubbling on to the strawberry floor. She is about to begin to cry. Her mouth is opening. She is crying. She cries. How can one ever tell whether there are one or many fish? She begins to break glasses and dishes, she throws cups and cooking pots and jars of food which shatter and break and spread over the kitchen. The sand keeps falling, very quietly, in the egg timer. The old man and woman in the barometer never catch each other. She picks up eggs and throws them into the air. She begins to cry. She opens her mouth. The eggs arch slowly through the kitchen, like a baseball, hit high against the spring sky, seen from far away. They go higher and higher in the stillness, hesitate at the zenith, then begin to fall away slowly, slowly, through the fine, clear air.

Philip K. Dick (1928–82)

It would be difficult to exaggerate the influence Philip K. Dick has had on contemporary science fiction. A prolific writer, many of his more than forty novels were later turned into films; most famously *Do Androids Dream of Electric Sheep?* (1968) was adapted as *Blade Runner* (1982). Dick's works often address the difficulties of perception and include characters who have trouble distinguishing fantasy from reality or the "real" from the simulated. This central theme is expressed in representations of mental illness, drug use, alternate realities, religious revelation, and more. In doing so, he draws not only on his own experiences, but also on the fraught politics of the Cold War, the social and political upheavals of the 1960s and later, and the blossoming of literary postmodernism. The Philip K. Dick Award for the best original science fiction paperback in the United States is named for him. Dick himself received multiple awards, including the Hugo Award and the British Science Fiction Award.

Note on the text: The text used here follows its original publication in *The Magazine of Fantasy and Science Fiction* (vol. 37, no. 4, Oct. 1969), with minor typos in the original corrected silently; its editorial introduction reads:

> *Short fiction by Philip Dick is a rare event these days, mostly because of his concentration on novels, the most recent of which is* UBIK *(Doubleday). His most well-known book is probably the brilliant parallel-world story,* THE MAN IN THE HIGH CASTLE. *Mr. Dick's first story here since "We Can Remember It For You Wholesale" (April 1966) is about Garson Poole, who was not exactly human, but who possessed an overwhelmingly human—and dangerous—sense of curiosity.*

"The Electric Ant" (1969)

At four-fifteen in the afternoon, T.S.T., Garson Poole woke up in his hospital bed, knew that he lay in a hospital bed in a three-bed ward and realized in addition two things: that he no longer had a right hand and that he felt no pain.

They have given me a strong analgesic, he said to himself as he stared at the far wall with its window showing downtown New York. Webs in which vehicles and peds darted and wheeled glimmered in the late afternoon sun, and the brilliance of the aging light pleased him. It's not yet out, he thought. And neither am I.

A fone lay on the table beside his bed; he hesitated, then picked it up and dialed for an outside line. A moment later he was faced by Louis Danceman, in charge of Tri-Plan's activities while he, Garson Poole, was elsewhere.

"Thank god you're alive," Danceman said, seeing him; his big, fleshy face with its moon's surface of pock marks flattened with relief. "I've been calling all—"

"I just don't have a right hand," Poole said.

"But you'll be okay. I mean, they can graft another one on."

"How long have I been here?" Poole said. He wondered where the nurses and doctors had gone to; why weren't they clucking and fussing about him making a call?

"Four days," Danceman said. "Everything here at the plant is going splunkishly. In fact we've splunked orders from three separate police systems, all here on Terra. Two in Ohio, one in Wyoming. Good solid orders, with one third in advance and the usual three-year lease-option."

"Come and get me out of here," Poole said.

"I can't get you out until the new hand—"

"I'll have it done later." He wanted desperately to get back to familiar surroundings; memory of the mercantile squib looming grotesquely on the pilot screen careened at the back of his mind; if he shut his eyes he felt himself back in his damaged craft as it plunged from one vehicle to another, piling up enormous damage as it went. The kinetic sensations ... he winced, recalling them. I guess I'm lucky, he said to himself.

"Is Sarah Benton there with you?" Danceman asked.

"No." Of course; his personal secretary—if only for job considerations—would be hovering close by, mothering him in her jejune, infantile way. All heavy-set women like to mother people, he thought. And they're dangerous; if they fall on you they can kill you. "Maybe that's what happened to me," he said aloud. "Maybe Sarah fell on my squib."

"No, no; a tie rod in the steering fin of your squib split apart during the heavy rush-hour traffic and you—"

"I remember." He turned in his bed as the door of the ward opened; a white-clad doctor and two blue-clad nurses appeared, making their way toward his bed. "I'll talk to you later," Poole said, and hung up the fone. He took a deep, expectant breath.

"You shouldn't be foning quite so soon," the doctor said as he studied his chart. "Mr. Garson Poole, owner of Tri-Plan Electronics. Maker of random ident darts that track their prey for a circle-radius of a thousand miles, responding to unique enceph wave patterns. You're a successful man, Mr. Poole. But, Mr. Poole, you're not a man. You're an electric ant."

"Christ," Poole said, stunned.

"So we can't really treat you here, now that we've found out. We knew, of course, as soon as we examined your injured right hand; we saw the electronic components and then we made torso x-rays and of course they bore out our hypothesis."

"What," Poole said, "is an 'electric ant'?" But he knew; he could decipher the term.

A nurse said, "An organic robot."

"I see," Poole said. Frigid perspiration rose to the surface of his skin, across all his body.

"You didn't know," the doctor said.

"No." Poole shook his head.

The doctor said, "We get an electric ant every week or so. Either brought in here from a squib accident—like yourself—or one seeking voluntary admission ... one who, like yourself, has never been told, who has functioned along side humans, believing himself—itself—human. As to your hand—" He paused.

"Forget my hand," Poole said savagely.

"Be calm." The doctor leaned over him, peered acutely down into Poole's face. "We'll have a hospital boat convey you over to a service facility where repairs, or replacement, on your hand can be made at a reasonable expense, either to yourself, if you're self-owned, or to your owners, if such there are. In any case you'll be back at your desk at Tri-Plan, functioning just as before."

"Except," Poole said, "now I know." He wondered if Danceman or Sarah or any of the others at the office knew. Had they—or one of them—purchased him? Designed him? A figurehead, he said to himself; that's all I've been. I must never really have run the company; it was a delusion implanted in me when I was made ... along with the delusion that I am human and alive.

"Before you leave for the repair facility," the doctor said, "could you kindly settle your bill at the front desk?"

Poole said acidly, "How can there be a bill if you don't treat ants here?"

"For our services," the nurse said. "Up until the point we knew."

"Bill me," Poole said, with furious, impotent anger. "Bill my firm." With massive effort he managed to sit up; his head swimming, he stepped haltingly from the bed and onto the floor. "I'll be glad to leave here," he said as he rose to a standing position. "And thank you for your humane attention."

"Thank you, too, Mr. Poole," the doctor said. "Or rather I should say just Poole."

At the repair facility he had his missing hand replaced.

It proved fascinating, the hand; he examined it for a long time before he let the technicians install it. On the surface it appeared organic—in fact, on the surface, it was. Natural skin covered natural flesh, and true blood filled the veins and capillaries. But, beneath that, wires and circuits, miniaturized components, gleamed ... looking deep into the wrist he saw surge gates, motors, multi-stage valves, all very small. Intricate. And—the hand cost forty frogs. A week's salary, insofar as he drew it from the company payroll.

"Is this guaranteed?" he asked the technicians as they fused the "bone" section of the hand to the balance of his body.

"Ninety days, parts and labor," one of the technicians said. "Unless subjected to unusual or intentional abuse."

"That sounds vaguely suggestive," Pool said.

The technician, a man—all of them were men—said, regarding him keenly, "You've been posing?"

"Unintentionally," Poole said.

"And now it's intentional?"

Poole said, "Exactly."

"Do you know why you never guessed? There must have been signs … clickings and whirrings from inside you, now and then. You never guessed because you were programed not to notice. You'll now have the same difficulty finding out why you were built and for whom you've been operating."

"A slave," Poole said. "A mechanical slave."

"You've had fun."

"I've lived a good life," Poole said. "I've worked hard."

He paid the facility its forty frogs, flexed his new fingers, tested them out by picking up various objects such as coins, then departed. Ten minutes later he was aboard a public carrier, on his way home. It had been quite a day.

At home, in his one-room apartment, he poured himself a shot of Jack Daniel's[1] Purple Label—sixty years old—and sat sipping it, meanwhile gazing through his sole window at the building on the opposite side of the street. Shall I go to the office? he asked himself. If so, why? If not, why? Choose one. Christ, he thought, it undermines you, knowing this. I'm a freak, he realized. An inanimate object mimicking an animate one. But—he felt alive. Yet … he felt differently, now. About himself. Hence about everyone, especially Danceman and Sarah, everyone at Tri-Plan.

I think I'll kill myself, he said to himself. But I'm probably programed not to do that; it would be a costly waste which my owner would have to absorb. And he wouldn't want to.

Programed. In me somewhere, he thought, there is a matrix fitted in place, a grid screen that cuts me off from certain thoughts, certain actions. And forces me into others. I am not free. I never was, but now I know it; that makes it different.

Turning his window to opaque, he snapped on the overhead light, carefully set about removing his clothing, piece by piece. He had watched carefully as the technicians at the repair facility had attached his new hand: he had a rather clear idea, now, of how his body had been assembled. Two major panels, one in each thigh; the technicians had removed the panels to check the circuit complexes beneath. If I'm programed, he decided, the matrix probably can be found there.

The maze of circuitry baffled him. I need help, he said to himself. Let's see … what's the fone code for the class BBB computer we hire at the office?

He picked up the fone, dialed the computer at its permanent location in Boise, Idaho.

---

1 Jack Daniel's is a brand of US whiskey. The use of label colours to indicate age is more commonly associated with Johnnie Walker, whose "Black Label" whiskey is aged 12 years.

"Use of this computer is prorated at a five frogs per minute basis," a mechanical voice from the fone said. "Please hold your mastercreditchargeplate before the screen."

He did so.

"At the sound of the buzzer you will be connected with the computer," the voice continued. "Please query it as rapidly as possible, taking into account the fact that its answer will be given in terms of a microsecond, while your query will—" He turned the sound down, then. But quickly turned it up as the blank audio input of the computer appeared on the screen. At this moment the computer had become a giant ear, listening to him—as well as fifty thousand other queriers throughout Terra.

"Scan me visually," he instructed the computer. "And tell me where I will find the programing mechanism which controls my thoughts and behavior." He waited. On the fone's screen a great active eye, multi-lensed, peered at him; he displayed himself for it, there in his one-room apartment.

The computer said, "Remove your chest panel. Apply pressure at your breastbone and then ease outward."

He did so. A section of his chest came off; dizzily, he set it down on the floor.

"I can distinguish control modules," the computer said, "but I can't tell which—" It paused as its eye roved about on the fone screen. "I distinguish a roll of punched tape mounted above your heart mechanism.[1] Do you see it?" Poole craned his neck, peered. He saw it, too. "I will have to sign off," the computer said. "After I have examined the data available to me I will contact you and give you an answer. Good day." The screen died out.

I'll yank the tape out of me, Poole said to himself. Tiny ... no larger than two spools of thread, with a scanner mounted between the delivery drum and the take-up drum. He could not see any sign of motion; the spools seemed inert. They must cut in as override, he reflected, when specific situations occur. Override to my encephalic processes. And they've been doing it all my life.

He reached down, touched the delivery drum. All I have to do is tear this out, he thought, and—

The fone screen relit. "Mastercreditchargeplate number 3-BNX-882-HQR446-T," the computer's voice came. "This is BBB-307DR recontacting you in response to your query of sixteen seconds lapse, November 4, 1992. The punched tape roll above your heart mechanism is not a programing turret but is in fact a reality-supply construct. All sense stimuli received by your central neurological system emanate from that unit and tampering with it would

1 At the time of this story's publication, punched tape, made of either paper or plastic, was used both for telecommunications purposes and to program and transfer data, using binary code, to and from computers.

be risky if not terminal." It added, "You appear to have no programing circuit. Query answered. Good day." It flicked off.

Poole, standing naked before the fone screen, touched the tape drum once again, with calculated, enormous caution. I see, he thought wildly. Or do I see? This unit—

If I cut the tape, he realized, my world will disappear. Reality will continue for others, but not for me. Because my reality, my universe, is coming to me from this minuscule unit. Fed into the scanner and then into my central nervous system as it snailishly unwinds.

It has been unwinding for years, he decided.

Getting his clothes, he redressed, seated himself in his big armchair—a luxury imported into his apartment from Tri-Plan's main offices—and lit a tobacco cigarette. His hands shook as he laid down his initialed lighter; leaning back, he blew smoke before himself, creating a nimbus of gray.

I have to go slowly, he said to himself. What am I trying to do? Bypass my programing? But the computer found no programing circuit. Do I want to interfere with the reality tape? And if so, *why?*

Because, he thought, if I control that, I control reality. At least so far as I'm concerned. My subjective reality ... but that's all there is. Objective reality is a synthetic construct, dealing with a hypothetical universalization of a multitude of subjective realities.

My universe is lying within my fingers, he realized. If I can just figure out how the damn thing works. All I set out to do originally was to search for and locate my programing circuit so I could gain true homeostatic functioning: control of myself. But with this—

With this he did not merely gain control of himself; he gained control over everything.

And this sets me apart from every human who ever lived and died, he thought somberly.

Going over to the fone he dialed his office. When he had Danceman on the screen he said briskly, "I want you to send a complete set of microtools and enlarging screen over to my apartment. I have some microcircuitry to work on." Then he broke the connection, not wanting to discuss it.

A half hour later a knock sounded on his door. When he opened up he found himself facing one of the shop foremen, loaded down with microtools of every sort. "You didn't say exactly what you wanted," the foreman said, entering the apartment. "So Mr. Danceman had me bring everything."

"And the enlarging-lens system?"

"In the truck, up on the roof."

Maybe what I want to do, Poole thought, is die. He lit a cigarette, stood smoking and waiting as the shop foreman lugged the heavy enlarging screen, with its power-supply and control panel, into the apartment. This is suicide, what I'm doing here. He shuddered.

"Anything wrong, Mr. Poole?" the shop foreman said as he rose to his feet, relieved of the burden of the enlarging-lens system. "You must still be rickety on your pins from your accident."

"Yes," Poole said quietly. He stood tautly waiting until the foreman left.

Under the enlarging-lens system the plastic tape assumed a new shape: a wide track along which hundreds of thousands of punch-holes worked their way. I thought so, Poole thought. Not recorded as charges on a ferrous oxide layer but actually punched-free slots.

Under the lens the strip of tape visibly oozed forward. Very slowly, but it did, at uniform velocity, move in the direction of the scanner.

The way I figure it, he thought, is that the punched holes are *on* gates. It functions like a player piano;[1] solid is no, punch-hole is yes. How can I test this?

Obviously by filling in a number of the holes.

He measured the amount of tape left on the delivery spool, calculated—at great effort—the velocity of the tape's movement, and then came up with a figure. If he altered the tape visible at the in-going edge of the scanner, five to seven hours would pass before that particular time period arrived. He would in effect be painting out stimuli due a few hours from now.

With a microbrush he swabbed a large—relatively large—section of tape with opaque varnish ... obtained from the supply kit accompanying the microtools. I have smeared out stimuli for about half an hour, he pondered. Have covered at least a thousand punches.

It would be interesting to see what change, if any, overcame his environment, six hours from now.

Five and a half hours later he sat at Krackter's, a superb bar in Manhattan, having a drink with Danceman.

"You look bad," Danceman said.

"I am bad," Poole said. He finished his drink, a Scotch sour, and ordered another.

"From the accident?"

"In a sense, yes."

Danceman said, "Is it—something you found out about yourself?"

Raising his head, Poole eyed him in the murky light of the bar.

"Then you know."

"I know," Danceman said, "that I should call you 'Poole' instead of 'Mr. Poole.' But I prefer the latter, and will continue to do so."

"How long have you known?" Poole said.

"Since you took over the firm. I was told that the actual owners of Tri-Plan,

1 A "self-playing" piano for which the music was encoded, as in early computers, on punched paper or metal rolls.

who are located in the Prox System,[1] wanted Tri-Plan run by an electric ant whom they could control. They wanted a brilliant and forceful—"

"The real owners?" This was the first he had heard about that. "We have two thousand stockholders. Scattered everywhere."

"Marvis Bey and her husband Ernan, on Prox 4, control fifty-one percent of the voting stock. This has been true from the start."

"Why didn't I know?"

"I was told not to tell you. You were to think that you yourself made all company policy. With my help. But actually I was feeding you what the Beys fed to me."

"I'm a figurehead," Poole said.

"In a sense, yes." Danceman nodded. "But you'll always be 'Mr. Poole' to me."

A section of the far wall vanished. And with it, several people at tables nearby. And—

Through the big glass side of the bar, the skyline of New York City flickered out of existence.

Seeing his face, Danceman said, "What is it?"

Poole said hoarsely, "Look around. Do you see any changes?"

After looking around the room, Danceman said, "No. What like?"

"You still see the skyline?"

"Sure. Smoggy as it is. The lights wink—"

"Now I know," Poole said. He had been right; every punch-hole covered up meant the disappearance of some object in his reality world. Standing, he said, "I'll see you later, Danceman. I have to get back to my apartment; there's some work I'm doing. Goodnight." He strode from the bar and out onto the street, searching for a cab.

No cabs.

Those, too, he thought. I wonder what else I painted over. Prostitutes? Flowers? Prisons?

There, in the bar's parking lot, Danceman's squib. I'll take that, he decided. There are still cabs in Danceman's world; he can get one later. Anyhow it's a company car, and I hold a copy of the key.

Presently he was in the air, turning toward his apartment.

New York City had not returned. To the left and right vehicles and buildings, streets, ped-runners, signs … and in the center nothing. How can I fly into that? he asked himself. I'd disappear.

Or would I? He flew toward the nothingness.

Smoking one cigarette after another he flew in a circle for fifteen minutes … and then, soundlessly, New York reappeared. He could finish his trip. He stubbed out his cigarette (a waste of something so valuable) and shot off in the direction of his apartment.

---

1 The solar system of the star Proxima Centauri; this setting appears in many of Dick's works. It is the next closest star to our own.

If I insert a narrow opaque strip, he pondered as he unlocked his apartment door, I can—

His thoughts ceased. Someone sat in his living room chair, watching a captain kirk[1] on the TV. "Sarah," he said, nettled.

She rose, well-padded but graceful. "You weren't at the hospital, so I came here. I still have that key you gave me back in March after we had that awful argument. Oh … you look so depressed." She came up to him, peeped into his face anxiously. "Does your injury hurt that badly?"

"It's not that." He removed his coat, tie, shirt, and then his chest panel; kneeling down he began inserting his hands into the microtool gloves. Pausing, he looked up at her and said, "I found out I'm an electric ant. Which from one standpoint opens up certain possibilities, which I am exploring now." He flexed his fingers and, at the far end of the left waldo, a micro screwdriver moved, magnified into visibility by the enlarging-lens system. "You can watch," he informed her. "If you so desire."

She had begun to cry.

"What's the matter?" he demanded savagely, without looking up from his work.

"I—it's just so sad. You've been such a good employer to all of us at Tri-Plan. We respect you so. And now it's all changed."

The plastic tape had an unpunched margin at top and bottom; he cut a horizontal strip, very narrow, then, after a moment of great concentration, cut the tape itself four hours away from the scanning head. He then rotated the cut strip into a right-angle piece in relation to the scanner, fused it in place with a micro heat element, then reattached the tape reel to its left and right sides. He had, in effect, inserted a dead twenty minutes into the unfolding flow of his reality. It would take effect—according to his calculations—a few minutes after midnight.

"Are you fixing yourself?" Sarah asked timidly.

Poole said, "I'm freeing myself." Beyond this he had several other alterations in mind. But first he had to test his theory; blank, unpunched tape meant no stimuli, in which case the *lack* of tape …

"That look on your face," Sarah said. She began gathering up her purse, coat, rolled-up aud-vid magazine. "I'll go; I can see how you feel about finding me here."

"Stay," he said. "I'll watch the captain kirk with you." He got into his shirt. "Remember years ago when there were—what was it?—twenty or twenty-two TV channels? Before the government shut down the independents?"

---

1 James Tiberius Kirk was the captain of the starship *Enterprise* in the original television series *Star Trek* (1966–69). By seemingly making Kirk's name a stand-in for generic science fiction television, Dick is perhaps ahead of his time in imagining the future popularity of the series, which would spawn several films and other media productions that continue as of this writing, despite the original series being cancelled twice in its initial run.

She nodded.

"What would it have looked like," he said, "if this TV set projected all channels onto the cathode ray screen *at the same time?* Could we have distinguished anything, in the mixture?"

"I don't think so."

"Maybe we could learn to. Learn to be selective; do our own job of perceiving what we wanted to and what we didn't. Think of the possibilities, if our brain could handle twenty images at once; think of the amount of knowledge which could be stored during a given period. I wonder if the brain, the human brain—" He broke off. "The human brain couldn't do it," he said, presently, reflecting to himself. "But in theory a quasi-organic brain might."

"Is that what you have?" Sarah asked.

"Yes," Poole said.

They watched the captain kirk to its end, and then they went to bed. But Poole sat up against his pillows, smoking and brooding. Beside him, Sarah stirred restlessly, wondering why he did not turn off the light.

Eleven-fifty. It would happen anytime, now.

"Sarah," he said, "I want your help. In a very few minutes something strange will happen to me. It won't last long, but I want you to watch me carefully. See if I—" He gestured. "Show any changes. If I seem to go to sleep, or if I talk nonsense, or—" He wanted to say, if I disappear. But he did not. "I won't do you any harm, but I think it might be a good idea if you armed yourself. Do you have your anti-mugging gun with you?"

"In my purse." She had become fully awake now; sitting up in bed, she gazed at him with wild fright, her ample shoulders tanned and freckled in the light of the room.

He got her gun for her.

The room stiffened into paralyzed immobility. Then the colors began to drain away. Objects diminished until, smoke-like, they flitted away into shadows. Darkness filmed everything as the objects in the room became weaker and weaker.

The last stimuli are dying out, Poole realized. He squinted, trying to see. He made out Sarah Benton, sitting in the bed: a two-dimensional figure that doll-like had been propped up, there to fade and dwindle. Random gusts of dematerialized substance eddied about in unstable clouds; the elements collected, fell apart, then collected once again. And then the last heat, energy and light dissipated; the room closed over and fell into itself, as if sealed off from reality. And at that point absolute blackness replaced everything, space without depth, not nocturnal but rather stiff and unyielding. And in addition he heard nothing.

Reaching, he tried to touch something. But he had nothing to reach with. Awareness of his own body had departed along with everything else in the universe. He had no hands, and even if he had, there would be nothing for them to feel.

I am still right about the way the damn tape works, he said to himself, using a nonexistent mouth to communicate an invisible message.

Will this pass in ten minutes? he asked himself. Am I right about that, too? He waited … but knew intuitively that his time sense had departed with everything else. I can only wait, he realized. And hope it won't be long.

To pace himself, he thought, I'll make up an encyclopedia; I'll try to list everything that begins with an "a." Let's see. He pondered. Apple, automobile, acksetron, atmosphere, Atlantic, tomato aspic, advertising—he thought on and on, categories slithering through his fright-haunted mind.

All at once light flickered on.

He lay on the couch in the living room, and mild sunlight spilled in through the single window. Two men bent over him, their hands full of tools. Maintenance men, he realized. They've been working on me.

"He's conscious," one of the technicians said. He rose, stood back; Sarah Benton, dithering with anxiety, replaced him.

"Thank god!" she said, breathing wetly in Poole's ear. "I was so afraid; I called Mr. Danceman finally about—"

"What happened?" Poole broke in harshly. "Start from the beginning and for god's sake speak slowly. So I can assimilate it all."

Sarah composed herself, paused to rub her nose, and then plunged on nervously, "You passed out. You just lay there, as if you were dead. I waited until two-thirty and you did nothing. I called Mr. Danceman, waking him up unfortunately, and he called the electric-ant maintenance—I mean, the organic-roby maintenance people, and these two men came about four forty-five, and they've been working on you ever since. It's now six fifteen in the morning. And I'm very cold and I want to go to bed; I can't make it in to the office today; I really can't." She turned away, sniffling. The sound annoyed him.

One of the uniformed maintenance men said, "You've been playing around with your reality tape."

"Yes," Poole said. Why deny it? Obviously they had found the inserted solid strip. "I shouldn't have been out that long," he said. "I inserted a ten minute strip only."

"It shut off the tape transport," the technician explained. "The tape stopped moving forward; your insertion jammed it, and it automatically shut down to avoid tearing the tape. Why would you want to fiddle around with that? Don't you know what you could do?"

"I'm not sure," Poole said.

"But you have a good idea."

Poole said acridly, "That's why I'm doing it."

"Your bill," the maintenance man said, "is going to be ninety-five frogs. Payable in installments, if you so desire."

"Okay," he said; he sat up groggily, rubbed his eyes and grimaced. His head ached and his stomach felt totally empty.

"Shave the tape next time," the primary technician told him. "That way it won't jam. Didn't it occur to you that it had a safety factor built into it? So it would stop rather than—"

"What happens," Poole interrupted, his voice low and intently careful, "if no tape passes under the scanner? No tape—nothing at all. The photocell shining upward without impedance?"

The technicians glanced at each other. One said, "All the neuro circuits jump their gaps and short out."

"Meaning what?" Poole said.

"Meaning it's the end of the mechanism."

Poole said, "I've examined the circuit. It doesn't carry enough voltage to do that. Metal won't fuse under such slight loads of current, even if the terminals are touching. We're talking about a millionth of a watt along a cesium channel perhaps a sixteenth of an inch in length. Let's assume there are a billion possible combinations at one instant arising from the punch-outs on the tape. The total output isn't cumulative; the amount of current depends on what the battery details for that module, and it's not much. With all gates open and going."

"Would we lie?" one of the technicians asked wearily.

"Why not?" Poole said. "Here I have an opportunity to experience everything. Simultaneously. To know the universe in its entirety, to be momentarily in contact with all reality. Something that no human can do. A symphonic score entering my brain outside of time, all notes, all instruments sounding at once. And all symphonies. Do you see?"

"It'll burn you out," both technicians said, together.

"I don't think so," Poole said.

Sarah said, "Would you like a cup of coffee, Mr. Poole?"

"Yes," he said; he lowered his legs, pressed his cold feet against the floor, shuddered. He then stood up. His body ached. They had me lying all night on the couch, he realized. All things considered, they could have done better than that.

At the kitchen table in the far corner of the room, Garson Poole sat sipping coffee across from Sarah. The technicians had long since gone.

"You're not going to try any more experiments on yourself, are you?" Sarah asked wistfully.

Poole grated, "I would like to control time. To reverse it." I will cut a segment of tape out, he thought, and fuse it in upside down. The causal sequences will then flow the other way. Thereupon I will walk backward down the steps from the roof field, back up to my door, push a locked door open, walk backward to the sink, where I will get out a stack of dirty dishes. I will seat myself at this table before the stack, fill each dish with food produced from my stomach … I will then transfer the food to the refrigerator. The next day I will take the food out of the refrigerator, pack it in bags, carry the bags to a supermarket, distribute the food here and there in the store. And at last, at the front counter, they will pay me money for this, from their cash register. The food will be packed with other food in big plastic boxes, shipped out of the city into the hydroponic plants on the Atlantic, there to be joined back to trees and bushes or the bodies of dead animals or pushed deep into the ground. But what would all that prove? A video tape running backward ... I would know no more than I know now, which is not enough.

What I want, he realized, is ultimate and absolute reality, for one microsecond. After that it doesn't matter, because all will be known; nothing will be left to understand or see.

I might try one other change, he said to himself. Before I try cutting the tape. I will prick new punch-holes in the tape and see what presently emerges. It will be interesting because I will not know what the holes I make mean.

Using the tip of a microtool, he punched several holes, at random, on the tape. As close to the scanner as he could manage ... he did not want to wait.

"I wonder if you'll see it," he said to Sarah. Apparently not, insofar as he could extrapolate. "Something may show up," he said to her. "I just want to warn you; I don't want you to be afraid."

"Oh dear," Sarah said tinnily.

He examined his wristwatch. One minute passed, then a second, a third. And then—

In the center of the room appeared a flock of green and black ducks. They quacked excitedly, rose from the floor, fluttered against the ceiling in a dithering mass of feathers and wings and frantic in their vast urge, their instinct, to get away.

"Ducks," Poole said, marveling. "I punched a hole for a flight of wild ducks."

Now something else appeared. A park bench with an elderly, tattered man seated on it, reading a torn, bent newspaper. He looked up, dimly made out Poole, smiled briefly at him with badly made dentures, and then returned to his folded-back newspaper. He read on.

"Do you see him?" Poole asked Sarah. "And the ducks." At that moment the ducks and the park bum disappeared. Nothing remained of them. The interval of their punch-holes had quickly passed.

"They weren't real," Sarah said. "Were they? So how—"

"You're not real," he told Sarah. "You're a stimulus-factor on my reality tape. A punch-hole that can be glazed over. Do you also have an existence in another reality tape, or one in an objective reality?" He did not know; he couldn't tell. Perhaps Sarah did not know, either. Perhaps she existed in a thousand reality tapes; perhaps on every reality tape ever manufactured. "If I cut the tape," he said, "you will be everywhere and nowhere. Like everything else in the universe. At least as far as I am aware of it."

Sarah faltered, "I am real."

"I want to know you completely," Poole said. "To do that I must cut the tape. If I don't do it now, I'll do it some other time; it's inevitable that eventually I'll do it." So why wait? he asked himself. And there is always the possibility that Danceman has reported back to my maker, that they will be making moves to head me off. Because, perhaps, I'm endangering their property—myself.

"You make me wish I had gone to the office after all," Sarah said, her mouth turned down with dimpled gloom.

"Go," Poole said.

"I don't want to leave you alone."

"I'll be fine," Poole said.

"No, you're not going to be fine. You're going to unplug yourself or something, kill yourself because you've found out you're just an electric ant and not a human being."

He said, presently, "Maybe so." Maybe it boiled down to that.

"And I can't stop you," she said.

"No." He nodded in agreement.

"But I'm going to stay," Sarah said. "Even if I can't stop you. Because if I do leave and you do kill yourself, I'll always ask myself for the rest of my life what would have happened if I had stayed. You see?"

Again he nodded.

"Go ahead," Sarah said.

He rose to his feet. "It's not pain I'm going to feel," he told her. "Although it may look like that to you. Keep in mind the fact that organic robots have minimal pain-circuits in them. I will be experiencing the most intense—"

"Don't tell me any more," she broke in. "Just do it if you're going to, or don't do it if you're not."

Clumsily—because he was frightened—he wriggled his hands into the microglove assembly, reached to pick up a tiny tool: a sharp cutting blade. "I am going to cut a tape mounted inside my chest panel," he said, as he gazed through the enlarging-lens system. "That's all." His hand shook as it lifted the cutting blade. In a second it can be done, he realized. All over. And—I will have time to fuse the cut ends of tape back together, he realized. A half hour at least. If I change my mind.

He cut the tape.

Staring at him, cowering, Sarah whispered, "Nothing happened."

"I have thirty or forty minutes."

He reseated himself at the table, having drawn his hands from the gloves. His voice, he noticed, shook; undoubtedly Sarah was aware of it, and he felt anger at himself, knowing that he had alarmed her. "I'm sorry," he said, irrationally; he wanted to apologize to her. "Maybe you ought to leave," he said in panic; again he stood up. So did she, reflexively, as if imitating him; bloated and nervous she stood there palpitating. "Go away," he said thickly. "Back to the office where you ought to be. Where we both ought to be." I'm going to fuse the tape-ends together, he told himself; the tension is too great for me to stand.

Reaching his hands toward the gloves he groped to pull them over his straining fingers. Peering into the enlarging screen, he saw the beam from the photoelectric gleam upward, pointed directly into the scanner; at the same time he saw the end of the tape disappearing under the scanner ... he saw this, understood it; I'm too late, he realized. It has passed through. God, he thought, help me. It has begun winding at a rate greater than I calculated. So it's *now* that—

He saw apples and cobblestones and zebras. He felt warmth, the silky texture of cloth; he felt the ocean lapping at him and a great wind, from the north, plucking at him as if to lead him somewhere. Sarah was all around him, so was Danceman, New York glowed in the night, and the squibs about him scuttled and bounced through night skies and daytime and flooding and drought. Butter relaxed into liquid on his tongue, and at the same time hideous odors and tastes assailed him: the bitter presence of poisons and lemons and blades of summer grass. He drowned; he fell; he lay in the arms of a woman in a vast white bed which at the same time dinned shrilly in his ear: the warning noise of a defective elevator in one of the ancient, ruined downtown hotels. I am living, I have lived, I will never live, he said to himself, and with his thoughts came every word, every sound; insects squeaked and raced, and he half sank into a complex body of homeostatic machinery located somewhere in Tri-Plan's labs.

He wanted to say something to Sarah. Opening his mouth he tried to bring forth words—a specific string of them out of the enormous mass of them brilliantly lighting his mind, scorching him with their utter meaning.

His mouth burned. He wondered why.

Frozen against the wall, Sarah Benton opened her eyes and saw the curl of smoke ascending from Poole's half-opened mouth. Then the roby sank down, knelt on elbows and knees, then slowly spread out in a broken, crumpled heap. She knew without examining it that it had "died."

Poole did it to itself, she realized. And it couldn't feel pain; it said so itself. Or at least not very much pain; maybe a little. Anyhow, now it is over.

I had better call Mr. Danceman and tell him what's happened, she decided. Still shaky, she made her way across the room to the fone; picking it up, she dialed from memory.

It thought I was a stimulus-factor on its reality tape, she said to herself. So it thought I would die when it "died." How strange, she thought. Why did it imagine that? It had never been plugged into the real world; it had "lived" in an electronic world of its own. How bizarre.

"Mr. Danceman," she said, when the circuit to his office had been put through. "Poole is gone. It destroyed itself right in front of my eyes. You'd better come over."

"So we're finally free of it."

"Yes, won't it be nice?"

Danceman said, "I'll send a couple of men over from the shop." He saw past her, made out the sight of Poole lying by the kitchen table. "You go home and rest," he instructed Sarah. "You must be worn out by all this."

"Yes," she said. "Thank you, Mr. Danceman." She hung up and stood, aimlessly.

And then she noticed something.

My hands, she thought. She held them up. Why is it I can see through them?

The walls of the room, too, had become ill-defined.

Trembling, she walked back to the inert roby, stood by it, not knowing what to do. Through her legs the carpet showed, and then the carpet became dim, and she saw, through it, further layers of disintegrating matter beyond.

Maybe if I can fuse the tape-ends back together, she thought. But she did not know how. And already Poole had become vague.

The wind of early morning blew about her. She did not feel it; she had begun, now, to cease to feel.

The winds blew on.

Gil Scott-Heron (1949–2011)

A spoken-word poet and jazz musician, Gil Scott-Heron has been credited as a foundational inspiration for later rap and hip-hop artists. His piece, "The Revolution Will Not Be Televised," from the same album as "Whitey on the Moon," has become a cultural touchstone for both its liberatory, revolutionary message and its trenchant critique of US politics and media. "Whitey on the Moon" continues this analysis, juxtaposing US space exploration with the realities of racism and inequity in the US.

Note on the text: This spoken-word poem originally appeared on Scott-Heron's debut album, *Small Talk at 125th and Lenox* (1970). The version here uses for its copy text the print version, from his book, *Now and Then.... The Poems of Gil Scott-Heron* (2000). It is largely the same as the recorded version, except the latter includes "Airmail special" as the penultimate line.

"Whitey on the Moon" (1970)

A rat done bit my sister Nell.
  (with Whitey on the moon)
Her face and arms began to swell.
  (and Whitey's on the moon)
I can't pay no doctor bill.
  (but Whitey's on the moon)
Ten years from now I'll be payin' still.
  (while Whitey's on the moon)
The man jus' upped my rent las' night.
  ('cause Whitey's on the moon)
No hot water, no toilets, no lights.
  (but Whitey's on the moon)
I wonder why he uppin' me?
  ('cause Whitey's on the moon?)
I wuz already payin' 'im fifty a week.
  (with Whitey on the moon)
Taxes takin' my whole damn check,
Junkies make me a nervous wreck,
The price of food is goin' up,
An' as if all that crap wuzn't enough:
A rat done bit my sister Nell.
  (with Whitey on the moon)
Her face an' arm began to swell.
  (but Whitey's on the moon)
Was all that money I made las' year

 (for Whitey on the moon?)
How come there ain't no money here?
 (Hmm! Whitey's on the moon)
Y'know I jus' 'bout had my fill
 (of Whitey on the moon.)
I think I'll sen' these doctor bills
 (to Whitey on the moon.)

James Tiptree Jr. (Alice Bradley Sheldon; 1915–87)

Writing as James Tiptree Jr., Alice Sheldon (née Alice Bradley) was a celebrated SF author from the US, who served in Intelligence for the US armed forces during World War II. Sheldon's work has been placed in relief and somewhat overwritten by the debates about, and revelation in 1977 of, her gender. The most famous example of the debate is from SF author Robert Silverberg's introduction to Tiptree's collection *Warm Worlds and Otherwise* (1975), where he acknowledges that "Tiptree" might be a pseudonym, but finds the idea that "Tiptree is female" to be "absurd, for there is something ineluctably masculine about Tiptree's writing" (xii), later characterizing the stories as "lean, muscular, supple" (xv). This moment of SF history, as noted SF critic Wendy Gay Pearson writes, "brings into question simplistic notions about male versus female style" (171); further, it is important to note that Sheldon's works do challenge gendered assumptions even as they explore other issues. The Hugo and Nebula nominated story below, for example, addresses the entanglements of sexual desire, xenophobia and bigotry, exploration and colonialism, and links all these not only to an analysis of the generic expectations of SF itself, but also to the larger literary landscape, as evidenced through the text's allusion, in its title and beyond, to John Keats's Romantic-era ballad "La Belle Dame Sans Merci" (1820).

Note on the text: There are several small changes between the story's original publication in *The Magazine of Fantasy and Science Fiction* (March 1972) and later editions; the original publication is used here, though the version in Tiptree's collection *Ten Thousand Light-Years from Home* (1973) was consulted for minor typographical corrections. In the magazine publication, the story is preceded by the following editorial:

> In most sf, man's reaction to alien ranges from a middle ground of open-minded tolerance to an extreme of repulsion or insularity. There is another extreme, way over to the other side of that middle ground; it is rarely considered, and it is the subject of Mr. Tiptree's unusual new story. (68)

"And I Awoke and Found Me Here on the Cold Hill's Side" (1972)[1]

HE was standing absolutely still by a service port, staring out at the belly of the *Sirian* docking above us. He had on a gray uniform and his reddish-gray hair was cut short. I took him for a station engineer.

That was bad. Newsmen strictly don't belong in the bowels of Big Junction. But there was no place else to get a shot of the alien ship.

I turned my holocam to show its big World Media insigne and started my bit about What It Meant to the People Back Home who were paying for it all.

"—It may be routine work to you, sir, but we owe it to them to share—"

His face came around slow and tight, and his gaze passed over me from a peculiar distance.

"The color, the drama," he repeated dispassionately. His eyes focused on me. "You consummated fool."

"Could you tell me what races are coming in, sir? If I could even get a view—"

He waved me to the port, deadpan. Greedily I angled the lenses up at the long blue hull blocking out the starfield. Beyond her I could see the bulge of a black and gold ship.

"That's a Foramen," he said. "There's a freighter from Belye on the other side, you'd call it Arcturus. Not much traffic right now."

"You're the first person who's said two sentences to me since I've been here, sir. What are those colorful little craft?"

"Procya," he shrugged. "They're always around. Like us."

I squashed my face on the vitrite, peering. The walls clanked. Somewhere overhead the Sirians were off-loading into their private sector of Big Junction. The man glanced at his wrist.

"Are you waiting to go out, sir?"

His grunt could have meant anything.

"Where are you from on Earth?" he asked me in his hard tone.

I started to tell him and suddenly saw that he had forgotten my existence. His eyes were on nowhere, and his head was slowly bowing forward onto the port frame.

"Go home," he said thickly. I caught a strong smell of tallow.

"Hey, sir!" I grabbed his arm; he was in rigid tremor. "Steady, man."

"I'm waiting … waiting for my wife. My loving wife." He gave a short ugly laugh. "Where are you from?"

I told him again.

"Go home," he mumbled. "Go home and make babies. While you still can."

One of the early GR casualties, I thought.

1 The title repeats the final two lines of the penultimate stanza of "La Belle Dame Sans Merci" (1820) by John Keats (1795–1821).

"Is that all you know?" Scorn animated him. "Fools. Dressing in their styles. *Gnivo* suits. *Aoleelee* music. Oh, I see your newscasts," he sneered. "Nixi parties. A year's salary for a *Garph'tha*. Gamma radiation—go home. Read history. *Fountain pens and bicycles* ..."

He started a slow slide downward in the half G. My only informant. We struggled confusedly; he wouldn't take one of my sobertabs but I finally got him along the service corridor to a bench in an empty loading bay. He fumbled out a little vacuum cartridge. As I was helping him unscrew it, a brindled creature in starched whites put his head in the bay.

"I can be of assistance, yes?" His eyes popped. It was a Procya. I started to thank him but the red-haired man cut me off.

"Get lost. Out."

The creature withdrew, its big eyes moist. The man stuck his pinky in the cartridge and put it up his nose, gasping deep in his diaphragm. Then he looked toward his wrist.

"What time is it?"

I told him.

"News," he said. "A message for the eager, hopeful human race. All right. A word about those lovely, lovable aliens we all love so much." He looked at me. "Shocked, aren't you, newsboy?"

I had him figured now. Alien menace, plot to take over Earth.

"Aaugh, Christ, they couldn't care less." He took another deep gasp, shuddered and straightened. "The hell with generalities. What time d'you say it was? ... All right, I'll tell you how I learned it. The hard way. While we wait for my loving wife. You can bring that little recorder out of your sleeve, too. Play it over to yourself some time. When it's too late." He chuckled almost normally; his voice had become light and facile. An educated voice. "You ever heard of supernormal stimuli?"

"No," I said. "Wait a minute. White sugar?"

"Near enough. Y'know Little Junction bar in D.C.? No, you're an Aussie, you said. Well, I'm from Burned Barn, Nebraska."

He took a breath, consulting some vast disarray of the soul. This was going to be a longie.

"When I was eighteen I drifted into Little Junction by accident. No. Correct that. You don't go into Little Junction by accident, any more than you first shoot up on skag by accident. You go into Little Junction because you've been craving it, dreaming about it, grooving on every hint and clue about it, back there in Burned Barn since before you had hair in your pants. Whether you know it or not. Once you're out of Burned Barn, you can no more help going into Little Junction than a sea worm can help rising to the moon.[1]

---

1 Palola worms, a species of marine worm from around the Pacific Islands, spawn in Spring or Summer during the waning moon; their back half breaks off from the rest of their bodies and rises to the surface of the water, allowing sperm and eggs to be released and mixed.

"I was a big lad with a brand-new liquor ident in my pocket. It was early; there was an empty spot beside some humans at the bar. Little Junction isn't an embassy bar, y'know. I found out later where the high-caste aliens go—when they go out. The New Rive, the Curtain by the Georgetown Marina.

"And they go by themselves. Oh, once in a while they do the Cultural Exchange bit with a few frosty couples of other aliens and some stuffed humans. Galactic Amity with a ten-foot pole.

"Little Junction was the place where the lower orders went, the single clerks and drivers, out for kicks. Including, my friend, the perverts. The ones who can take humans. Into their beds, that is."

He chuckled grimly and sniffed his finger again, not looking at me.

"Ah, yes. Little Junction is Galactic Amity night, every night. I ordered … what? A margharita. I didn't have the nerve to ask the snotty spade[1] bartender for one of the alien liquors glowing behind the bar. It was dim. I was trying to stare everywhere at once without showing it. I remember those white bone-heads—Lyrans, that is. And a mess of green veiling I decided was a multiple being from some place. I caught a couple of human glances in the bar mirror. Hostile flicks. I didn't get the message, then.

"Suddenly an alien pushed right in beside me. Before I could get over my paralysis, I heard this blurry voice:

"'You air a futeball enthushiash?'

"An alien had spoken to me. An *alien,* a being from the stars. Had spoken. To me.

"Oh, god, I had no time for football, but I would have claimed a passion for paper-folding, for Dumb Crambo[2]—anything to keep him talking. I asked him about his home-planet sports, I insisted on buying his drinks. I listened raptly while he spluttered out a play-by-play account of a game I wouldn't have turned a dial for. The 'Grain Bay Pashkers.'[3] Yeah. And I was dimly aware of trouble among the humans on my other side.

"Suddenly this woman—I'd call her a girl now—this girl said something in a high nasty voice and swung her stool into the arm I was holding my drink with. We both turned around together.

"Christ, I can see her now. The first thing that hit me was *discrepancy.* She was a nothing—but terrific. Transfigured. Oozing it, radiating it.

"The next thing was I had a horrifying hard-on just looking at her.

"I scrooched over so my tunic hid it, and my spilled drink trickled down, making everything worse. She pawed vaguely at the spill, muttering. I just

1 A racist anti-Black epithet.

2 Crambo is a word game in which a player thinks of a word, and then tells the other players words it rhymes with. Players try to guess the initial word not by saying it, but by defining it. In Dumb Crambo, instead of saying the meaning aloud, the other players act out the meaning, in the manner of charades.

3 The Green Bay Packers are an American football team from Green Bay, Wisconsin, founded in 1919.

stared at her trying to figure out what had hit me. An ordinary figure, sort of a soft avidness in the face. Eyes heavy, satiated-looking. She was totally sexualized. I remember her throat pulsed. She had one hand up touching her scarf, which had slipped off her shoulder. I saw angry bruises there. That really tore it. I understood at once those bruises had some sexual meaning.

"She was looking past my head with her face like a radar dish. Then she made an 'Ah-h-h-h' sound that had nothing to do with me and grabbed my forearm as if it were a railing. One of the men behind her laughed. The woman said, 'Excuse me,' in a ridiculous voice and slipped out behind me. I wheeled around after her, nearly upsetting my futeball friend, and saw that some Sirians had come in.

"That was my first look at Sirians in the flesh, if that's the word. God knows I'd memorized every news shot, but I wasn't prepared. That tallness, that cruel thinness. That appalling alien arrogance. Ivory-blue, these were. Two males in immaculate metallic gear. Then I saw there was a female with them. An ivory-indigo exquisite with a permanent faint smile on those bone-hard lips.

"The girl who'd left me was ushering them to a table. She reminded me of a goddamn dog that wants you to follow it. Just as the crowd hid them, I saw a man join them too. A big man, expensively dressed, with something wrecked about his face.

"Then the music started and I had to apologize to my furry friend. And the Sellice dancer came out and my personal introduction to hell began."

The red-haired man fell silent for a minute. Self-pitying bastard, I thought. Something wrecked about the face; it fit.

He sensed my distaste, pulled his face together.

"First I'll give you the only coherent observation of my entire evening. You can see it here at Big Junction, always the same. Outside of the Procya, it's humans with aliens, right? Very seldom aliens with other aliens, never aliens with humans. It's the humans who want in."

I nodded, but he wasn't talking to me. His voice had that soft druggy fluency.

"Ah, yes, my Sellice. My first Sellice.

"They aren't really well built, y'know, under those cloaks. No waist to speak of and short-legged. But they flow when they walk.

"This one flowed out into the spotlight, cloaked to the ground in violet silk. You could only see a fall of black hair and tassels over a narrow face like a vole. She was a mole-grey. They come in all colors; their fur is like a flexible velvet all over; only the color changes startlingly around their eyes and lips and other places ... Erogenous zones! Ah, man, with them it's not zones.

"She began to do what we'd call a dance, but it's no dance, it's their natural movement. Like smiling, say, with us. The music built up, and her arms snaked forward letting the cloak fall apart little by little. She was naked under it. The spotlight started to pick up her body markings, moving in the slit of the cloak. Her arms floated apart and I saw more and more.

"She was fantastically marked and the markings were writhing. Not like body paint—alive. Smiling, that's a good word for it. As if her whole body was smiling sexually, beckoning, winking, urging, pouting, speaking to me. You've seen a classic Egyptian belly dance? Forget it—that's a sorry, stiff thing compared to what any Sellice can do. This one was ripe, near term.

"Her arms went up and those blazing lemon-colored curves pulsed, waved, everted, contracted, evolved unbelievably welcoming, promising permutations. *Come do it to me, do it, do it here and here and here and now.* You couldn't see the rest of her, only a wicked flash of mouth. Every human male in the room was aching to ram it to that burning, melting target. The other aliens were quiet too, except one of the Sirians who was chewing out a waiter.

"I was a basket case before she was halfway through … I won't bore you with what happened next. Before it was over there were several fights and I got cut. My money ran out on the third night, and she was gone next day.

"I didn't have time to find out about the Sellice cycle then, mercifully. That came after I went back to campus and discovered you had to have a degree in solid-state electronics to apply for off-planet work. I was a premed but I got that degree. It only took me as far as First Junction then.

"Oh, god, First Junction. I thought I was in Heaven—the alien ships coming in and our freighters going out. I saw them all, all but the real exotics, the tankies. You only see a few of them a cycle, even here. And the Yyeire. You've never seen that.

"Go home, boy. Go home to your version of Burned Barn … The first Yyeir I saw, I dropped everything and started walking after it like a starving hound, just breathing. You've seen the pix of course … Like lost dreams. *Man is in love and loves what vanishes*[1] … It's the scent, you can't guess that. I followed until I ran into a slammed port. I spent half a cycle's credits sending the creature the wine they call stars' tears … Later I found out it was a male. That made no difference at all. You can't have sex with them, y'know. No way. They breed by light or something, no one knows exactly. There's a story about a man who got hold of a Yyeir woman and tried. They had him skinned. Stories …"

He was starting to wander.

"What about that girl in the bar, did you see her again?"

He came back from somewhere.

"Oh, yes. I saw her. She'd been making it with the two Sirians, y'know. The males do it in pairs. Said to be the total sexual thing for a woman, if she can stand the damage from those beaks. I wouldn't know. She talked to me a couple of times after they finished with her. No use for men whatever. She drove off P Street bridge … The man, poor bastard, he was trying to keep that Sirian bitch happy single-handed. Money helps, for a while. I don't know where he ended."

---

1 A line from W.B. Yeats's poem "Nineteen Hundred and Nineteen" (1928).

He glanced at his wrist again. I saw the pale bare place where a watch had been and told him the time.

"Is that the message you want to give Earth? Never love an alien?"

"Never love an alien ..." He shrugged. "Yeah. No. Ah, Christ, can't you see? Everything going out, nothing coming back. Like the poor damned Polynesians. We're gutting Earth, to begin with. Swapping raw resources for junk. Alien status symbols. Ball-point pens and mickey mouse watches."

"Well, there is concern over the balance of trade. Is that your message?"

"The balance of trade." He rolled it sardonically. "Did the Polynesians have a word for it, I wonder? You don't see, do you? All right, why are you here? I mean you, personally. How many guys did you climb over—"

He went rigid, hearing footsteps outside. The Procya's hopeful face appeared around the corner. The red-haired man snarled at him and he backed out. I started to protest.

"No sweat, that stupid bastard loves it. And it's the only pleasure we have left ... Don't you see, man? That's us. That's the way we look to them, to the real ones."

"But—"

"And now we're getting the cheap C-drive, we'll be all over just like the Procya. For the pleasure of serving as freight monkeys and junction crews. Oh, they appreciate our ingenious little service stations, the beautiful star folk. They don't *need* them, y'know. Just an amusing convenience. D'you know what I do here with my two degrees? What I did at First Junction: hull cleaning. A swab. Sometimes I get to replace a tube fitting."

I muttered something. The self-pity was getting heavy.

"Bitter? Man, it's a *good* job. Sometimes I get to talk to one of them." His face twisted. "My wife works as a—Oh, hell, you wouldn't know. I'd trade—I *have* traded—everything Earth offered me for just that chance. To see them. To speak to them. Once in a while to touch one. Once in a great while to find one low enough, perverted enough to want to touch me ..."

His voice trailed off and suddenly came back strong.

"And so will you!" He glared at me. "Go home! Go home and tell them to quit it. Close the ports. Burn every god-lost alien thing before it's too late! That's what the Polynesians didn't do."

"But surely—"

"But surely be damned! Balance of trade, my festering feet. Balance of *life,* man. I don't know if our birth rate is going; that's not the point. Our soul is leaking out; we're bleeding to death!"

He took a breath and lowered his tone.

"What I'm trying to tell you, this is a trap. We've hit the supernormal stimulus. Man is exogamous—all our history is one long drive to find and impregnate the stranger. Or get impregnated by him, it works for women, too. Anything different colored, different nose, ass, anything, man *has* to screw it or die trying. That's a drive, y'know, it's built in. Because it works fine as long as the stranger is human. For millions of years that kept the genes circulating. But now we've met aliens we can't screw, and we're about to die trying ... Do you think I can touch my wife?"

"But—"

"Look. Y'know, if you give a bird a fake egg like its own but bigger and brighter marked, it'll roll its own egg out of the nest and sit on the fake? That's what we're doing."

"You're too much in the sex bag, man, you're freaked on it."

"Sex? Yeah. No ... It's deeper." He rubbed his head, trying to clear the drugs. "Sex is only part of it, there's more. I've seen Earth missionaries, teachers, sexless people. Teachers—they end cycling waste or pushing floaters, but they're hooked. They stay. I saw one fine-looking old woman, she was servant to a Cu'ushbar kid. A defective; his own people would have let him die. That wretch was swabbing up its vomit as if it was holy water. Man, it's deep ... Some cargo-cult[1] of the soul. We're built to dream outwards ... They laugh at us. They don't have it."

There were sounds of movement in the next corridor. The dinner crowd was starting. I had to get rid of him and get there. Suddenly a side door opened and a figure started towards us.

At first I thought it was an alien, and then I saw it was a woman wearing an awkward body-shell. She seemed to be limping slightly. Behind her I could glimpse the dinner-bound throng passing the open door.

The man got up as she turned into the bay. They didn't greet each other.

"The station employs only happily wedded couples," he told me with that ugly laugh. "We give each other ... comfort."

He took one of her hands. She flinched as he drew it over his arm and let him turn her passively, not looking at me. "Forgive me if I don't introduce you. My wife appears fatigued."

I saw that one of her shoulders was brutally scarred.

"Tell them," he said, turning to go. "Go home and tell them." Then his head snapped back toward me, and he added quietly, "And stay away from the Syrtis desk or I'll kill you."

They went away up the corridor.

I changed tapes hurriedly with one eye on the figures passing that open door. Suddenly among the humans and Procya I caught a glimpse of two sleek scarlet shapes. My first real aliens. I snapped the recorder shut and hurried to fall in behind them.

---

1 Cargo cult is a derogatory term for a number of spiritual practices among Melanesian peoples, generally arising after interactions with European colonizers.

Joanna Russ (1937–2011)

An American author best known for her feminist SF novel *The Female Man* (1975), Joanna Russ is also known for the fantasy-inflected tales collected as *The Adventures of Alyx* (1976), and her non-fiction and critical works, including her foundational work of feminist criticism, *How to Supress Women's Writing* (1983). The story printed here won the Nebula Award, and she received the Hugo, Locus, and other honours for both her fiction and her scholarship. The story here connects to *The Female Man* in that both describe Whileaway, an all-women society, but the versions differ in several ways from each other.

Note on the text: The source-text is that of the first publication in *Again, Dangerous Visions*, edited by Harlan Ellison (1972). There, the story is followed by Russ's Afterword, in which she explains the impetus for writing the story; she writes, in part,

> I have read SF stories about manless worlds before; they are either full of busty girls in wisps of chiffon who slink about writhing with lust [...] or the women have set up a static, beelike society in imitation of some presumed primitive matriarchy. These stories are written by men. Why women who have been alone for generations should "instinctively" turn their sexual desires toward persons of whom they have only intellectual knowledge, or why female people are presumed to have an innate preference for Byzantine rigidity I don't know. [...] I had read a very fine SF novel, Ursula Le Guin's *The Left Hand of Darkness*,[1] in which all the characters are humanoid hermaphrodites, and was wondering at the obduracy of the English language, in which everybody is "he" or "she" and "it" is reserved for typewriters. But how can one call a hermaphrodite "he," as Miss Le Guin does? I tried (in my head) changing all the masculine pronouns to feminine ones, and marveled at the difference. And then I wondered why Miss Le Guin's native "hero" is male in *every* important sexual encounter of his life except that with the human man in the book. Weeks later the Daemon suddenly whispered, "Katy drives like a maniac," and I found myself on Whileaway, on a country road at night. (260–62)

"When it Changed" (1972)

KATY drives like a maniac; we must have been doing over 120 km/hr on those turns. She's good, though, extremely good, and I've seen her take the whole car apart and put it together again in a day. My birthplace on Whileaway was largely given to farm machinery and I refuse to wrestle with a five-gear shift

1 For information on Le Guin, see p. 376.

at unholy speeds, not having been brought up to it, but even on those turns in the middle of the night, on a country road as bad as only our district can make them, Katy's driving didn't scare me. The funny thing about my wife, though: she will not handle guns. She has even gone hiking in the forests above the 48th parallel without firearms, for days at a time. And that *does* scare me.

Katy and I have three children between us, one of hers and two of mine. Yuriko, my eldest, was asleep in the back seat, dreaming twelve-year-old dreams of love and war: running away to sea, hunting in the North, dreams of strangely beautiful people in strangely beautiful places, all the wonderful guff you think up when you're turning twelve and the glands start going. Some day soon, like all of them, she will disappear for weeks on end to come back grimy and proud, having knifed her first cougar or shot her first bear, dragging some abominably dangerous dead beastie behind her, which I will never forgive for what it might have done to my daughter. Yuriko says Katy's driving puts her to sleep.

For someone who has fought three duels, I am afraid of far, far too much. I'm getting old. I told this to my wife.

"You're thirty-four," she said. Laconic to the point of silence, that one. She flipped the lights on, on the dash—three km. to go and the road getting worse all the time. Far out in the country. Electric-green trees rushed into our headlights and around the car. I reached down next to me where we bolt the carrier panel to the door and eased my rifle into my lap. Yuriko stirred in the back. My height but Katy's eyes, Katy's face. The car engine is so quiet, Katy says, that you can hear breathing in the back seat. Yuki had been alone in the car when the message came, enthusiastically decoding her dot-dashes (silly to mount a wide-frequency transceiver near an I.C. engine, but most of Whileaway is on steam). She had thrown herself out of the car, my gangly and gaudy offspring, shouting at the top of her lungs, so of course she had had to come along. We've been intellectually prepared for this ever since the Colony was founded, ever since it was abandoned, but this is different. This is awful.

"Men!" Yuki had screamed, leaping over the car door. "They've come back! Real Earth men!"

We met them in the kitchen of the farmhouse near the place where they had landed; the windows were open, the night air very mild. We had passed all sorts of transportation when we parked outside, steam tractors, trucks, an I.C. flatbed, even a bicycle. Lydia, the district biologist, had come out of her Northern taciturnity long enough to take blood and urine samples and was sitting in a corner of the kitchen shaking her head in astonishment over the results; she even forced herself (very big, very fair, very shy, always painfully blushing) to dig up the old language manuals—though I can talk the old tongues in my sleep. And do. Lydia is uneasy with us; we're Southerners and too flamboyant. I counted twenty people in that kitchen, all the brains of

North Continent. Phyllis Spet, I think, had come in by glider. Yuki was the only child there.

Then I saw the four of them.

They are bigger than we are. They are bigger and broader. Two were taller than me, and I am extremely tall, 1m, 80cm in my bare feet.[1] They are obviously of our species but *off*, indescribably off, and as my eyes could not and still cannot quite comprehend the lines of those alien bodies, I could not, then, bring myself to touch them, though the one who spoke Russian—what voices they have!—wanted to "shake hands," a custom from the past, I imagine. I can only say they were apes with human faces. He seemed to mean well, but I found myself shuddering back almost the length of the kitchen—and then I laughed apologetically—and then to set a good example (*interstellar amity*, I thought) did "shake hands" finally. A hard, hard hand. They are heavy as draft horses. Blurred, deep voices. Yuriko had sneaked in between the adults and was gazing at *the men* with her mouth open.

He turned *his* head—those words have not been in our language for six hundred years—and said, in bad Russian:

"Who's that?"

"My daughter," I said, and added (with that irrational attention to good manners we sometimes employ in moments of insanity), "My daughter, Yuriko Janetson. We use the patronymic. You would say matronymic."

He laughed, involuntarily. Yuki exclaimed, "I thought they would be *good-looking!*" greatly disappointed at this reception of herself. Phyllis Helgason Spet, whom someday I shall kill, gave me across the room a cold, level, venomous look, as if to say: *Watch what you say. You know what I can do.* It's true that I have little formal status, but Madam President will get herself in serious trouble with both me and her own staff if she continues to consider industrial espionage good clean fun. Wars and rumors of wars, as it says in one of our ancestor's books.[2] I translated Yuki's words into *the man's* dog-Russian, once our *lingua franca*, and *the man* laughed again.

"Where are all your people?" he said conversationally.

I translated again and watched the faces around the room; Lydia embarrassed (as usual), Spet narrowing her eyes with some damned scheme, Katy very pale.

"This is Whileaway," I said.

He continued to look unenlightened.

"Whileaway," I said. "Do you remember? Do you have records? There was a plague on Whileaway."

He looked moderately interested. Heads turned in the back of the room, and I caught a glimpse of the local professions-parliament delegate; by morning every town meeting, every district caucus, would be in full session.

---

1 5'11".

2 Matthew 24.6.

"Plague?" he said. "That's most unfortunate."

"Yes," I said. "Most unfortunate. We lost half our population in one generation."

He looked properly impressed.

"Whileaway was lucky," I said. "We had a big initial gene pool, we had been chosen for extreme intelligence, we had a high technology and a large remaining population in which every adult was two-or-three experts in one. The soil is good. The climate is blessedly easy. There are thirty millions of us now. Things are beginning to snowball in industry—do you understand?—give us seventy years and we'll have more than one real city, more than a few industrial centers, full-time professions, full-time radio operators, full-time machinists, give us seventy years and not everyone will have to spend three quarters of a lifetime on the farm." And I tried to explain how hard it is when artists can practice full-time only in old age, when there are so few, so very few who can be free, like Katy and myself. I tried also to outline our government, the two houses, the one by professions and the geographic one; I told him the district caucuses handled problems too big for the individual towns. And that population control was not a political issue, not yet, though give us time and it would be. This was a delicate point in our history; give us time. There was no need to sacrifice the quality of life for an insane rush into industrialization. Let us go our own pace. Give us time.

"Where are all the people?" said the monomaniac.

I realized then that he did not mean people, he meant *men*, and he was giving the word the meaning it had not had on Whileaway for six centuries.

"They died," I said. "Thirty generations ago."

I thought we had poleaxed him. He caught his breath. He made as if to get out of the chair he was sitting in; he put his hand to his chest; he looked around at us with the strangest blend of awe and sentimental tenderness. Then he said, solemnly and earnestly:

"A great tragedy."

I waited, not quite understanding.

"Yes," he said, catching his breath again with that queer smile, that adult-to-child smile that tells you something is being hidden and will be presently produced with cries of encouragement and joy, "a great tragedy. But it's over." And again he looked around at all of us with the strangest deference. As if we were invalids.

"You've adapted amazingly," he said.

"To what?" I said. He looked embarrassed. He looked inane. Finally he said, "Where I come from, the women don't dress so plainly."

"Like you?" I said. "Like a bride?" for the men were wearing silver from head to foot. I had never seen anything so gaudy. He made as if to answer and then apparently thought better of it; he laughed at me again. With an odd exhilaration—as if we were something childish and something wonderful, as if he were doing us an enormous favor—he took one shaky breath and said, "Well, we're here."

I looked at Spet, Spet looked at Lydia, Lydia looked at Amalia, who is the head of the local town meeting, Amalia looked at I don't know who. My throat was raw. I cannot stand local beer, which the farmers swill as if their stomachs had iridium linings, but I took it anyway, from Amalia (it was her bicycle we had seen outside as we parked), and swallowed it all. This was going to take a long time. I said, "Yes, here you are," and smiled (feeling like a fool), and wondered seriously if male Earth people's minds worked so very differently from female Earth people's minds, but that couldn't be so or the race would have died out long ago. The radio network had got the news around-planet by now and we had another Russian speaker, flown in from Varna; I decided to cut out when *the man* passed around pictures of his wife, who looked like the priestess of some arcane cult. He proposed to question Yuki, so I barreled her into a back room in spite of her furious protests, and went out on the front porch. As I left, Lydia was explaining the difference between parthenogenesis[1] (which is so easy that anyone can practice it) and what we do, which is the merging of ova. That is why Katy's baby looks like me. Lydia went on to the Ansky process and Katy Ansky, our one full-polymath genius and the great-great-I don't know how many times great-grandmother of my own Katharina.

A dot-dash transmitter in one of the outbuildings chattered faintly to itself: operators flirting and passing jokes down the line.

There was a man on the porch. The other tall man. I watched him for a few minutes—I can move very quietly when I want to—and when I allowed him to see me, he stopped talking into the little machine hung around his neck. Then he said calmly, in excellent Russian, "Did you know that sexual equality has been re-established on Earth?"

"You're the real one," I said, "aren't you? The other one's for show." It was a great relief to get things cleared up. He nodded affably.

"As a people, we are not very bright," he said. "There's been too much genetic damage in the last few centuries. Radiation. Drugs. We can use Whileaway's genes, Janet." Strangers do not call strangers by the first name.

"You can have cells enough to drown in," I said. "Breed your own."

He smiled. "That's not the way we want to do it." Behind him I saw Katy come into the square of light that was the screened-in door. He went on, low and urbane, not mocking me, I think, but with the self-confidence of someone who has always had money and strength to spare, who doesn't know what it is to be second-class or provincial. Which is very odd, because the day before, I would have said that was an exact description of me.

"I'm talking to you, Janet," he said, "because I suspect you have more popular influence than anyone else here. You know as well as I do that parthenogenetic culture has all sorts of inherent defects, and we do not—if we can help

1 Parthenogenesis is a form of asexual reproduction without fertilization. Other women's separatist utopian works likewise employ parthenogenesis or other forms of asexual reproduction, the most famous of which is Charlotte Perkins Gilman's *Herland* (1915).

it—mean to use you for anything of the sort. Pardon me; I should not have said 'use.' But surely you can see that this kind of society is unnatural."

"Humanity is unnatural," said Katy. She had my rifle under her left arm. The top of that silky head does not quite come up to my collarbone, but she is as tough as steel; he began to move, again with that queer smiling deference (which his fellow had showed to me but he had not) and the gun slid into Katy's grip as if she had shot with it all her life.

"I agree," said the man. "Humanity is unnatural. I should know. I have metal in my teeth and metal pins here." He touched his shoulder. "Seals are harem animals," he added, "and so are men; apes are promiscuous and so are men; doves are monogamous and so are men; there are even celibate men and homosexual men. There are homosexual cows, I believe. But Whileaway is still missing something." He gave a dry chuckle. I will give him the credit of believing that it had something to do with nerves.

"I miss nothing," said Katy, "except that life isn't endless."

"You are—?" said the man, nodding from me to her.

"Wives," said Katy. "We're married." Again the dry chuckle.

"A good economic arrangement," he said, "for working and taking care of the children. And as good an arrangement as any for randomizing heredity, if your reproduction is made to follow the same pattern. But think, Katharina Michaelason, if there isn't something better that you might secure for your daughters. I believe in instincts, even in Man, and I can't think that the two of you—a machinist, are you? and I gather you are some sort of chief of police—don't feel somehow what even you must miss. You know it intellectually, of course. There is only half a species here. Men must come back to Whileaway."

Katy said nothing.

"I should think, Katharina Michaelason," said the man gently, "that you, of all people, would benefit most from such a change," and he walked past Katy's rifle into the square of light coming from the door. I think it was then that he noticed my scar, which really does not show unless the light is from the side: a fine line that runs from temple to chin. Most people don't even know about it.

"Where did you get that?" he said, and I answered with an involuntary grin, "In my last duel." We stood there bristling at each other for several seconds (this is absurd but true) until he went inside and shut the screen door behind him. Katy said in a brittle voice, "You damned fool, don't you know when we've been insulted?" and swung up the rifle to shoot him through the screen, but I got to her before she could fire and knocked the rifle out of aim; it burned a hole through the porch floor. Katy was shaking. She kept whispering over and over, "That's why I never touched it, because I knew I'd kill someone, I knew I'd kill someone." The first man—the one I'd spoken with first—was still talking inside the house, something about the grand movement to re-colonize and re-discover all that Earth had lost. He stressed the advantages to Whileaway: trade, exchange of ideas, education. He too said that sexual equality had been re-established on Earth.

Katy was right, of course; we should have burned them down where they stood. Men are coming to Whileaway. When one culture has the big guns and the other has none, there is a certain predictability about the outcome. Maybe men would have come eventually in any case. I like to think that a hundred years from now my great-grandchildren could have stood them off or fought them to a standstill, but even that's no odds; I will remember all my life those four people I first met who were muscled like bulls and who made me—if only for a moment—feel small. A neurotic reaction, Katy says. I remember everything that happened that night; I remember Yuki's excitement in the car, I remember Katy's sobbing when we got home as if her heart would break, I remember her lovemaking, a little peremptory as always, but wonderfully soothing and comforting. I remember prowling restlessly around the house after Katy fell asleep with one bare arm flung into a patch of light from the hall. The muscles of her forearms are like metal bars from all that driving and testing of her machines. Sometimes I dream about Katy's arms. I remember wandering into the nursery and picking up my wife's baby, dozing for a while with the poignant, amazing warmth of an infant in my lap, and finally returning to the kitchen to find Yuriko fixing herself a late snack. My daughter eats like a Great Dane.

"Yuki," I said, "do you think you could fall in love with a man?" and she whooped derisively. "With a ten-foot toad!" said my tactful child.

But men are coming to Whileaway. Lately I sit up nights and worry about the men who will come to this planet, about my two daughters and Betta Katharinason, about what will happen to Katy, to me, to my life. Our ancestors' journals are one long cry of pain and I suppose I ought to be glad now but one can't throw away six centuries, or even (as I have lately discovered) thirty-four years. Sometimes I laugh at the question those four men hedged about all evening and never quite dared to ask, looking at the lot of us, hicks in overalls, farmers in canvas pants and plain shirts: *Which of you plays the role of the man?* As if we had to produce a carbon copy of their mistakes! I doubt very much that sexual equality has been re-established on Earth. I do not like to think of myself mocked, of Katy deferred to as if she were weak, of Yuki made to feel unimportant or silly, of my other children cheated of their full humanity or turned into strangers. And I'm afraid that my own achievements will dwindle from what they were—or what I thought they were—to the not-very-interesting curiosa of the human race, the oddities you read about in the back of the book, things to laugh at sometimes because they are so exotic, quaint but not impressive, charming but not useful. I find this more painful than I can say. You will agree that for a woman who has fought three duels, all of them kills, indulging in such fears is ludicrous. But what's around the corner now is a duel so big that I don't think I have the guts for it; in Faust's words: *Verweile doch, du bist so schoen!*[1] Keep it as it is. Don't change.

---

1 "Stay a while, you are so beautiful" (Ger.), spoken by Faust to Mephistopheles in the play *Faust* by Johann Wolfgang von Goethe (1749–1832). Faust makes a bargain with Mephistopheles that if there is ever a moment when he is perfectly satisfied, then at that moment Mephistopheles can take his soul.

Sometimes at night I remember the original name of this planet, changed by the first generation of our ancestors, those curious women for whom, I suppose, the real name was too painful a reminder after the men died. I find it amusing, in a grim way, to see it all so completely turned around. This too shall pass. All good things must come to an end.

Take my life but don't take away the meaning of my life.

For-A-While.

Ursula K. Le Guin (1929–2018)

One of the most celebrated authors of the later decades of the twentieth century, Ursula K. Le Guin wrote works that explored the political possibilities of the utopian form. Far from perfect, the societies she painted in such well-known novels as *The Dispossessed: An Ambiguous Utopia* (1974), *The Left Hand of Darkness* (1969), and *The Word for World is Forest* (1972), as well as in her long-running *Earthsea* series, consider issues of revolution, gender, and colonialism, among many others, from political, social, and interpersonal perspectives. This complex approach led to numerous awards and honours both within SF (with multiple Hugos, Nebula, and Locus awards) and from the wider cultural field (including being named a "Living Legend" by the Library of Congress, receiving the Medal for Distinguished Contribution to American Letters from the National Book Foundation, and being shortlisted for a Pulitzer).

Note on the text: There are minor differences between the text in its original publication in the magazine *New Dimensions 3*, used as the foundation for this version, and the one in Le Guin's collection *The Wind's Twelve Quarters* (1975). In the original and later versions, the subtitle always follows in parentheses.

In her introduction to this story in her collection, Le Guin discusses the concept of the scapegoat in Fyodor Dostoyevsky's novel *The Brothers Karamazov* (1879–80) and in the writings of psychologist William James (1842–1910). She quotes James, who asks what would happen "if the hypothesis were offered us of a world in which Messrs. Fourier's and Bellamy's and Morris's utopias should all be outdone, and millions kept permanently happy on the one simple condition that a certain lost soul on the far-off edge of things should lead a life of lonely torment." This passage became the impetus for the story; the name of the town, meanwhile, "came from a road sign: Salem (Oregon) backwards" (*The Wind's Twelve Quarters* 275–76).[1]

"The Ones Who Walk Away from Omelas (Variations on a Theme by William James)" (1973)

WITH a clamor of bells that set the swallows soaring, the Festival of Summer came to the city Omelas, bright-towered by the sea. The rigging of the boats in harbor sparkled with flags. In the streets between houses with red roofs and painted walls, between old moss-grown gardens and under avenues of trees,

1 The passage Le Guin quotes is from James's essay "The Moral Philosopher and the Moral Life" (1891). Charles Fourier (1772–1837), Edward Bellamy (1850–98), and William Morris (1834–96) were all social reformers and socialists who wrote influential utopian works.

past great parks and public buildings, processions moved. Some were decorous: old people in long stiff robes of mauve and gray, grave master workmen, quiet, merry women carrying their babies and chatting as they walked. In other streets the music beat faster, a shimmering of gong and tambourine, and the people went dancing, the procession was a dance. Children dodged in and out, their high calls rising like the swallows' crossing flights over the music and the singing. All the processions wound toward the north side of the city, where on the great watermeadow called the Green Fields boys and girls, naked in the bright air, with mudstained feet and ankles and long, lithe arms, exercised their restive horses before the race. The horses wore no gear at all but a halter without bit. Their manes were braided with streamers of silver, gold, and green. They blew out their nostrils and pranced and boasted to one another; they were vastly excited, the horse being the only animal who has adopted our ceremonies as his own. Far off to the north and west the mountains stood up half-encircling Omelas on her bay. The air of morning was so clear that the snow still crowning the Eighteen Peaks burned with white-gold fire across the miles of sunlit air, under the dark blue of the sky. There was just enough wind to make the banners that marked the race course snap and flutter now and then. In the silence of the broad green meadows one could hear the music winding through the city streets, farther and nearer and ever approaching, a cheerful faint sweetness of the air that from time to time trembled and gathered together and broke out into the great joyous clanging of the bells.

Joyous! How is one to tell about joy? How describe the citizens of Omelas?

They were not simple folk, you see, though they were happy. But we do not say the words of cheer much any more. All smiles have become archaic. Given a description such as this one tends to make certain assumptions. Given a description such as this one tends to look next for the King, mounted on a splendid stallion and surrounded by his noble knights, or perhaps in a golden litter borne by great-muscled slaves. But there was no king. They did not use swords, or keep slaves. They were not barbarians. I do not know the rules and laws of their society, but I suspect that they were singularly few. As they did without monarchy and slavery, so they also got on without the stock exchange, the advertisement, the secret police, and the bomb. Yet I repeat that these were not simple folk, not dulcet shepherds, noble savages, bland utopians. They were not less complex than we. The trouble is that we have a bad habit, encouraged by pedants and sophisticates, of considering happiness as something rather stupid. Only pain is intellectual, only evil interesting. This is the treason of the artist: a refusal to admit the banality of evil and the terrible boredom of pain. If you can't lick 'em, join 'em. If it hurts, repeat it. But to praise despair is to condemn delight, to embrace violence is to lose hold of everything else. We have almost lost hold; we can no longer describe happy man, nor make any celebration of joy. How can I tell you about the people of Omelas? They were not naive and happy children—though their children were, in fact, happy. They were mature, intelligent, passionate adults whose lives were not wretched. O miracle! But I wish I could describe it better. I wish I could convince you. Omelas sounds in my words like a city in a fairy tale, long ago and far away, once upon a time. Perhaps it would be best if you imagined it as your own fancy bids, assuming it will rise to the occasion, for certainly I cannot suit you all. For instance, how about technology? I think that there would be no cars or helicopters in and above the streets; this follows from the fact that the people of Omelas are happy people. Happiness is based on a just discrimination of what is necessary, what is neither necessary nor destructive, and what is destructive. In the middle category, however—that of the unnecessary but undestructive, that of comfort, luxury, exuberance, etc.—they could perfectly well have central heating, subway trains, washing machines, and all kinds of marvelous devices not yet invented here, floating light-sources, fuelless power, a cure for the common cold. Or they could have none of that: it doesn't matter. As you like it. I incline to think that people from towns up and down the coast have been coming in to Omelas during the last days before the Festival on very fast little trains and doubledecked trams, and that the train station of Omelas is actually the handsomest building in town, though plainer than the magnificent Farmers Market. But even granted trains, I fear that Omelas so far strikes some of you as goody-goody. Smiles, bells, parades, horses, bleh. If so, please add an orgy. If an orgy would help, don't hesitate. Let us not, however, have temples from which issue beautiful nude priests and priestesses already half in ecstasy and ready to copulate with whosoever, man or woman, lover or stranger, desires union with the deep godhead of the blood, although that was my first idea. But really it would be better not to have any temples in Omelas—at least, not manned temples. Religion yes, clergy no. Surely the beautiful nudes can just wander about, offering themselves like divine soufflés to the hunger of the needy and the rapture of the flesh. Let them join the processions. Let tambourines be struck above the copulations, and the glory of desire be proclaimed upon the gongs, and (a not unimportant point) let the offspring of these delightful rituals be beloved and looked after by all. One thing I know there is none of in Omelas is guilt. But what else should there be? I thought at first there were no drugs, but that is puritanical. For those who like it, the faint insistent sweetness of *drooz* may perfume the ways of the city, *drooz* which first brings a great lightness and brilliance to the mind and limbs, and then after some hours a dreamy languor, and wonderful visions at last of the very arcana and inmost secrets of the Universe, as well as exciting the pleasure of sex beyond all belief; and it is not habit-forming. For more modest tastes I think there ought to be beer. What else, what else belongs in the joyous city? The sense of victory, surely, the celebration of courage. But as we did without clergy, let us do without soldiers. The joy built upon successful slaughter is not the right kind of joy; it will not do; it is fearful and it is trivial. A boundless and generous contentment, a magnanimous triumph felt not against some outer enemy but in communion with the finest and fairest in the souls of all men everywhere and the splendor of the world's summer: this is what swells the hearts of the people of Omelas, and the victory they celebrate is that of life. I really don't think many of them need to take *drooz*.

Most of the processions have reached the Green Fields by now. A marvelous smell of cooking goes forth from the red and blue tents of the provisioners. The faces of small children are amiably sticky; in the benign gray beard of a man a couple of crumbs of rich pastry are entangled. The youths and girls have mounted their horses and are beginning to group around the starting line of the course. An old woman, small, fat, and laughing, is passing out flowers from a basket, and tall young men wear her flowers in their shining hair. A child of nine or ten sits at the edge of the crowd, alone, playing on a wooden flute. People pause to listen, and they smile, but they do not speak to him, for he never ceases playing and never sees them, his dark eyes wholly rapt in the sweet, thin magic of the tune.

He finishes, and slowly lowers his hands holding the wooden flute.

As if that little private silence were the signal, all at once a trumpet sounds from the pavilion near the starting line: imperious, melancholy, piercing. The horses rear on their slender legs, and some of them neigh in answer. Sober-faced, the young riders stroke the horses' necks and soothe them, whispering, "Quiet, quiet, there my beauty, my hope ..." They begin to form in rank along the starting line. The crowds along the race course are like a field of grass and flowers in the wind. The Festival of Summer has begun.

Do you believe? Do you accept the festival, the city, the joy? No? Then let me describe one more thing.

In a basement under one of the beautiful public buildings of Omelas, or perhaps in the cellar of one of its spacious private homes, there is a room. It has one locked door, and no window. A little light seeps in dustily between cracks in the boards, secondhand from a cobwebbed window somewhere across the cellar. In one corner of the little room a couple of mops, with stiff, clotted, foul-smelling heads, stand near a rusty bucket. The floor is dirt, a little damp to the touch, as cellar dirt usually is. The room is about three paces long and two wide: a mere broom closet or disused toolroom. In the room a child is sitting. It might be a boy or a girl. It looks about six, but actually is nearly ten. It is feebleminded. Perhaps it was born defective, or perhaps it has become imbecile through fear, malnutrition, and neglect. It picks its nose and occasionally fumbles vaguely with its toes or genitals, as it sits hunched in the corner farthest from the bucket and the two mops. It is afraid of the mops. It finds them horrible. It shuts its eyes, but it knows the mops are still standing there; and the door is locked; and nobody will come. The door is always locked, and nobody ever comes, except that sometimes—the child has no understanding of time or interval—sometimes the door rattles terribly and opens, and a person, or several people, are there. One of them may come in and kick the child to make it stand up. The others never come close, but peer in at it with frightened, disgusted eyes. The food bowl and the water jug are hastily filled, the door is locked, the eyes disappear. The people at the door never say anything, but the child, who has not always lived in the toolroom, and can remember sunlight and its mother's voice, sometimes speaks. "I will be good," it says. "Please let me out. I will be good!" They never answer. The child used to scream for help at night, and cry a good deal, but now it only makes a kind of whining, "eh-haa, eh-haa," and it speaks less and less often. It is so thin there are no calves to its legs; its belly protrudes; it lives on a half-bowl of cornmeal and grease a day. It is naked. Its buttocks and thighs are a mass of festered sores, as it sits in its own excrement continually.

They all know it is there, all the people of Omelas. Some of them have come to see it, others are content merely to know it is there. They all know that it has to be there. Some of them understand why, and some do not, but they all understand that their happiness, the beauty of their city, the tenderness of their friendships, the health of their children, the wisdom of their scholars, the skill of their makers, even the abundance of their harvest and the kindly weathers of their skies, depend wholly on this child's abominable misery.

This is usually explained to children when they are between eight and twelve, whenever they seem capable of understanding; and most of those who come to see the child are young people, though often enough an adult comes, or comes back, to see the child. No matter how well the matter has been explained to them, these young spectators are always shocked and sickened at the sight. They feel disgust, which they had thought themselves superior to. They feel anger, outrage, impotence, despite all the explanations. They would like to do something for the child. But there is nothing they can do. If the child were brought up into the sunlight out of that vile place, if it were cleaned and fed and comforted, that would be a good thing, indeed; but if it were done, in that day and hour all the prosperity and beauty and delight of Omelas would wither and be destroyed. Those are the terms. To exchange all the goodness and grace of every life in Omelas for that single, small improvement: to throw away the happiness of thousands for the chance of the happiness of one: that would be to let guilt within the walls indeed.

The terms are strict and absolute; there may not even be a kind word spoken to the child.

Often the young people go home in tears, or in a tearless rage, when they have seen the child and faced this terrible paradox. They may brood over it for weeks or years. But as time goes on they begin to realize that even if the child could be released, it would not get much good of its freedom: a little vague pleasure of warmth and food, no doubt, but little more. It is too degraded and imbecile to know any real joy. It has been afraid too long ever to be free of fear. Its habits are too uncouth for it to respond to humane treatment. Indeed after so long it would probably be wretched without walls about it to protect it, and darkness for its eyes, and its own excrement to sit in. Their tears at the bitter injustice dry when they begin to perceive the terrible justice of reality, and to accept it. Yet it is their tears and anger, the trying of their generosity and the acceptance of their helplessness, which are perhaps the true source of the splendor of their lives. Theirs is no vapid, irresponsible happiness. They know that they, like the child, are not free. They know compassion. It is the existence of the child, and their knowledge of its existence, that makes possible the nobility of their architecture, the poignancy of their music, the profundity of their science. It is because of the child that they are so gentle with children. They know that if the wretched one were not there sniveling in the dark, the other one, the flute player, could make no joyful music as the young riders line up in their beauty for the race in the sunlight of the first morning of summer.

Now do you believe in them? Are they not more credible? But there is one more thing to tell, and this is quite incredible.

At times one of the adolescent girls or boys who go to see the child does not go home to weep or rage, does not, in fact, go home at all. Sometimes also a man or a woman much older falls silent for a day or two, and then leaves home. These people go out into the street, and walk down the street alone. They keep walking, and walk straight out of the city of Omelas, through the beautiful gates. They keep walking across the farmlands of Omelas. Each one goes alone, youth or girl, man or woman. Night falls; the traveler must pass down village streets, between the houses with yellow-lit windows, and on out into the darkness of the fields. Each alone, they go west or north, toward the mountains. They go on. They leave Omelas, they walk ahead into the darkness, and they do not come back. The place they go toward is a place even less imaginable to most of us than the city of happiness. I cannot describe it at all. It is possible that it does not exist. But they seem to know where they are going, the ones who walk away from Omelas.

Samuel R. Delany (b. 1942)

With works ranging from the 1960s to the time of this writing, Samuel R. Delany holds a unique and central place in the history of contemporary SF and in literary and critical fields more generally: identified as a founding author of Afrofuturism (the term being coined by Mark Dery in an interview with Delany and other Black creators), an innovator in space opera and the New Wave, as well as a deeply significant figure in queer SF and queer theory, Delany's influence is immense. His first novel, *The Jewels of Aptor* (1962), was finished when he was nineteen and published by the time he was twenty, and was followed by eight more SF novels over the next six years. Born in Harlem, NY, Delany was immersed in Black cultural and political life in that city and the larger US—he is only two generations removed from slavery in the US (his grandfather was born into the system of slavery), and his aunts, Sarah L. Delany (1889–1999) and A. Elizabeth Delany (1891–1995), organized a picket of a re-release of the film *Birth of a Nation* in New York in 1925. He has also published works that explore queer life and culture, including *Times Square Red/Times Square Blue* (1999) and the autobiographical graphic novel *Bread and Wine: An Erotic Tale of New York* (1999). All these foci come together in many of his works, including the story below and his most recent SF novel, *Through the Valley of the Nest of Spiders* (2012). He is also well known for his sword-and-sorcery fantasy series, known collectively as *Return to Nevèrÿon*, which includes the novel *The Tale of Plagues and Carnivals* (included in the 1985 collection *Flight from Nevèrÿon*), which has been identified as one of the first novels to deal explicitly with AIDS and the first from a major publisher.

Note on the text: Written in 1976, this story wasn't published until May 1987, in an issue of the fanzine *New Moon*, edited by Janice M. Bogstad. It reached a wider audience in a double issue of the academic journal *Mississippi Review* dedicated to the topic of cyberpunk (1988),[1] and in Delany's collection *Aye, and Gomorrah, and Other Stories* (2003). The text used here follows a previously unpublished version sent by Delany for this anthology. In addition to several smaller changes from the earlier versions, Delany included the two images (Fig. 8 and Fig. 9), including notes to one. Additionally, he sent the following introduction:

> Sometime in 1965, when I returned from San Francisco to set up my new apartment on 82nd Street, I saw an announcement that some science fiction writers had started a writing club and, under the name of Chip, I went down to wherever they met—I was wearing a green jumpsuit; I believe one of the men who showed up was older than I was, and we all started talking about what we wanted to write.

1 This issue later became the foundation for the collection *Storming the Reality Studio: A Casebook of Cyberpunk and Postmodern Science Fiction* (1992), edited by Larry McCaffery.

"Well," I said, "why don't we all go home, and when we meet in a couple of weeks again, we'll read our stories to each other, and we can criticize each other."

I came back for the next session with the text of "Among the Blobs," an experimental story I thought might be amusing. Basically, it describes an orgasm, and the real hero is the nameless young fellow on the subway, and the imaginary hero that he sometimes thinks of himself becoming is Bat Durston, a name I picked off the back of *Galaxy* magazine, who used to boast about the fact that they never published any science fiction like *that.* As far as I was concerned when I was a kid, with the Lensmen, Campbell's *Cloak of Aesir,*[1] that's exactly the kind of science fiction I started out loving. Somehow, between the second and third meeting, they figured out who I was ... After the first round of criticism of another story, one of them asked me very guardedly, "Are you *Samuel* Delany...?" Somehow, after that, the whole group completely broke up and couldn't meet again. I wish I could remember who the guys in the group were.

But that's the tale behind the tale.

—Philadelphia
November 2022

"Among the Blobs" (writ. 1976; pub. 1987)

(1) "I'M terribly sorry, ma'am. I'm sorry." He swayed, one arm raised, torso stalled in the torque of its own turning. His name was Joe. To one side of his back was, not a pain nor even a feeling, but rather a sensational ghost, an unformed blob, where she had lurched against his army jacket, or he had backed into her tweed. "Are you all right?" She probably couldn't hear because of the subway car's roar. "You okay?"

"Yes." (Was she confused a little, a little bewildered?) "That's all right." Swaying by the pole, her fuchsia scarf pulled through something gold, amoeboid, and splattered with ruby glass, she looked like one of the black Miss Subways.[2] He had no idea if she were five years older or five years younger than he.

Joe turned, because after all, all he'd done was bump her a little; or she'd bumped him. But I could have smiled, he thought, reaching for and missing and then getting the next hanger. He knew his smile was good.

(2) And Bat D—,[3] in a rocket of luciprene-6 with vytrol fittings, careened

1 "Lensmen" refers to a series of novels by E. E. "Doc" Smith (1890–1965); *Cloak of Aesir* is a 1952 story collection by John W. Campbell (1910–71).

2 "Miss Subways" was a long-running beauty contest and advertising campaign run by the New York Subways Advertising Company, starting in 1941. The first Black Miss Subways, Thelma Potter, was selected in 1947 (see Fig. 8).

3 See Fig. 9.

[1, 2]

Fig. 8: "Meet Miss Subways: Thelma Porter," 1948. Image provided by Samuel R. Delany.

at ballistic speeds through interstellar night. Flakes had fallen off the black, letting in light: stars. Bat was dubious and alert, with the belly feeling that is both anxiety and enthusiasm. His would be the first human encounter with the Blob—which had been reported flûtchüláting (a form of communication? digestion? play?) in sector E-3. Till this report Bat D—, of the blazing death-laser, slayer of twenty-seven seven-foot Uranites, hero of the Kpt rebellion on Fomalhaut-G, had poohed the existence of Blobs, but the closer his luciprene hull swooped toward Galactic Council, the more indubitable seemed the Blob's particular order of ontological resolution—what an earlier, less vulgar epoch would have called her "reality."

(3) And Joe, on the Broadway Local,[3] headed for Forty-Second, wearing a Pendleton[4] that didn't look it because his friend Joe—another Joe—had been

1 Gershwin's slushy harmonies (which survive in such unexpected places as some of the compositions of John Adams) always seem to me to weigh down the music, sapping rather than adding energy, and to be a musical equivalent of "hedging-ones-bets," originality-wise. "Rhapsody in Blue" just makes me cringe — to my ears, it's one with the neither-one-nor-the-other condescending "Raga-Rock" recordings of the late 1960s, or, from another age, 1930s and '40s "socially aware" orchestral music pieces like late Ruth Crawford Seeger works ("Rissolty, Rossolty," for example). But it all comes down to taste, don't it, though? (Note by Bill Bamberger, Delany's publisher); George Gershwin (1898–1937) and Ruth Crawford Seeger (1901–53), both US composers.

2 As to Gershwin, when George Gershwin and Igor Stravinsky both lived in what was my third NYC neighborhood, the Upper West Side (center of New York leftist activity and the arts, for many, many years), the self-taught Gershwin came knocking on Stravinsky's 103rd Street apartment door and asked if he could take composition lessons from the famous Russian recently arrived.

Stravinsky, very popular in both France and Russia and hoping to become the same here, already knew Gershwin's work and its success. "Young man," he said, "I think I'm the one who ought to be taking composition lessons from you."

"Rhapsody in Blue" along with some Ellington, was the only orchestral music my dad had in his jazz collection. (Delany's note); Igor Stravinsky (1882–1971), Russian composer.

3 Part of the BMT Broadway Line (mentioned a few lines later) of the New York Subway system.

4 Pendleton Woollen Mills made blankets and jackets, including for the US military during World War II.

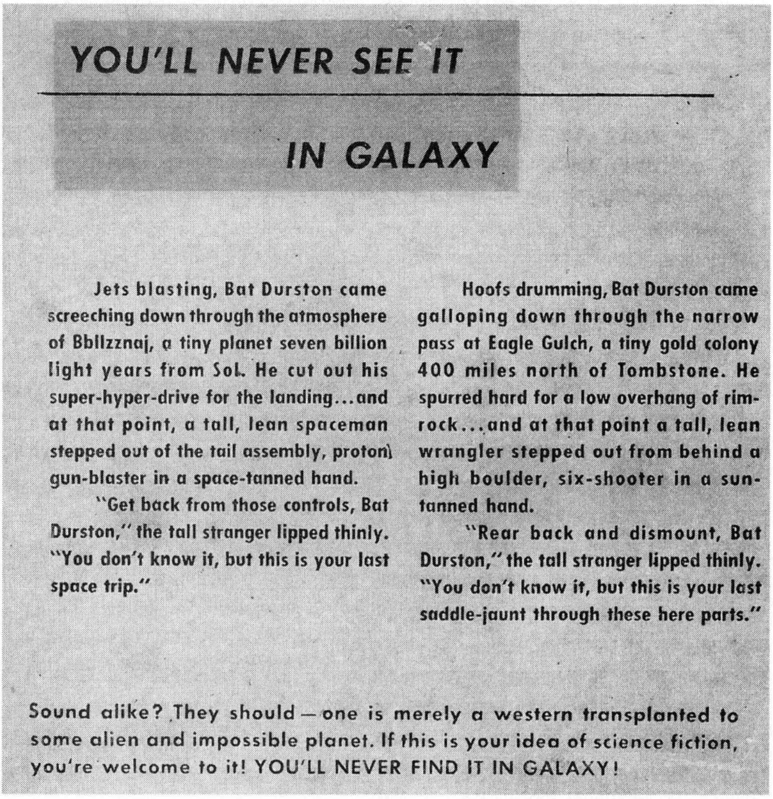

Fig. 9: A portion of the back cover of *Galaxy Science Fiction*, vol. 1, no. 1, October 1950. Image provided by Samuel R. Delany.

in with his truck the day before yesterday, and the two of them had worked on the transmission six hours up at the Dyckman Street garage.

One train door stuck.

Army jacket open, Joe hammered up the concrete steps to the station concourse, loped under pipes and fluorescent fixtures, passed the rack of phone booths, the doughnut emporium. Another twenty-five steps and the florist concession pressed dull plants against glass; then down past the stall of Latin records, across from the hot-dog/pasteles/piña-colada/Coca-Cola/cuchifrito[1] counter, and toward the BMT.

Joe had been moving all this time through the late rush-hour crowds, which crowds we have not mentioned till now because he was just about to separate himself from them. Joe thought of these crowds as a Blob, to which he was by and large indifferent.

1 piña-colada: a rum, pineapple, and coconut drink; pasteles and cuchifrito are both Puerto Rican dishes.

Neither the Blob nor Joe's indifference, however, were impregnable to analysis. There were the men, of whom he was vaguely resentful, because if he stood too close to one in the crush, or sat too close to one on a subway seat—too much body contact—they might suspect he was not a heterosexual lustful-panting-monster, and the grapevine had it they could get hostile toward the other kind. There were the women, of whom he was vaguely resentful, because, since everyone knew all men *were* heterosexual lustful-panting-monsters, if he bumped one or brushed one (not to mention stood too near or sat too close) he had to apologize, be appallingly polite, and generally come on far more deferentially than any normal human should be expected to to establish that, indeed, he was *not* a heterosexual lustful-panting-monster. At twenty-six, actually, he knew how to deal with the men: stand or sit where you want and fuck 'em. They could move. The women, however, confused him a little, bewildered him. And women were a subject about which the grapevine was distressingly un- (if not ill-) informed. Resentment, however vague, is not pleasant; hence the indifference in which he traveled.

At the blue and white column, Joe swung left toward the john.

The wooden gate—not, this time, "Closed for Cleaning"—was wedged back, askew on its hinges. Some time ago they'd painted the tiled entrance hall blue. Hand-sized paint flakes had fallen away. The antiseptic with which the place was flushed every other day had blistered what paint remained. Sometimes it left fumes so strong you couldn't stay inside long enough to take an honest leak.

In front of five of the ten porcelain urinals—most of the brass flush-treadles lay without tension on the red-tiled floor—

(4) Half the Galactic Council was in attendance. It was a highly formalized gathering. Members came and went according to an arcane protocol Bat D— still did not understand. Each member entered the High and Icy Hall (here and there still crossed with traces of unbreathable fumes) to linger, silently and intently for an arbitrary while, before what looked to Bat D— for all the world like something from a book on Twentieth-Century toilet fixtures.

The members of the Council were laboring to express the Blob.

The Blob was not impregnable to analysis: it was a largely mucusoid emulsion contained in a selectively permeable membrane within which drifted a nucleus, various nucleoli, vacuoles, ribosomes, mitochondria, and chloroplasts, the whole a symbiotic intrusion of eukaryotic and prokaryotic cells[1] from a less vulgar moment in the pluroma when all was closer than it is today to organic soup, to inorganic matter.

1 "nucleoli ... mitochondria": all parts of cells; "chloroplasts": organelles of plant cells central to photosynthesis; "eukaryotic and prokaryotic cells": the two main forms of cell—the former has a nucleus and is the type of complex cell found in plants and animals, while the latter lacks a nucleus and is characteristic of bacteria as single-cell organisms.

The Council members, minds on high matters, manipulated their computers.

The Blob was, appropriately, near Betelgeuse.[1]

And Betelgeuse was in E-3.

(5) Joe lingered at the next-to-the-end urinal. He had a thing for older guys with big, heavily veined cocks and small hands with overlong nails; and the guy to his left, at the end urinal (Pushing sixty? But that was all right), was probably a librarian. He wore a dumb-silly coat with a fur collar you couldn't button up. Or a designer. The black portfolio leaned on the wall behind them. But that was all right.

A bum lurched through the door (probably not as old as this guy beside him with those long, long nails the color of aluminum in winterlight. In his own too wide, too horny hand, at the memory only a second old—rather than at what was beside him—Joe hardened), mustache full of mucus, missing a lot of hair over one ear, missing shirt buttons; and the breast pocket gone. His pants leg was ripped, knee to cuff, showing a shin like soap. The bum looked around: "Aw, Jesus Christ, nothin' in here but a bunch of … I mean ever'body in here is one of them fuckin' … Hey you there, I bet you're one of …"

To Joe's right, two members of the Galactic Council glanced at each other, smiled. One shook his head. Hands down before white porcelain, busy with calculations, they manipulated and manipulated.

Wilson, the deaf-mute hustler, fists pouched in his frayed wind-breaker, came bopping in. Joe knew him because Wilson had once tried to score from Joe, who had bought him a cup of coffee at the hot dog counter across the concourse and explained to him—Joe had two aunts who had been born deaf and with whom he had stayed for a year in Portland when he was ten, which is how he knew the deaf-and-dumb sign language—that at this particular spot there was just too much of it walking around for free to make it worth a working man's time. Wilson came around the bum ("Hey, *you* ain't interested in these fuckin' faggots,[2] huh …?"), surveyed the Council Members at their stalls, and left.

"Shit …!" The bum turned, started out, stumbled into the jamb. An incoming Member—a subway worker Joe had seen here a few times before—steadied him:

"Hey, *watch* it, old man …"

The worker moved the bum out to arm's length and looked down to see a dripping cuff; and the shin was wet. Not having made it to a stall, the bum lurched out, leaving sneaker piss-prints on the chalky floor.

Joe turned back to the man beside him: gray hair, Vandyke[3] beard, glasses …

---

1 Betelgeuse is a star, visible from Earth in the constellation Orion. It has a long history of representation in SF as the star of an inhabited system.

2 A derogatory term for gay men.

3 The Vandyke is a facial-hair style characterized by both a moustache and a goatee.

They exchanged glances, anxious, enthusiastic, eye to lens, lens to groin. That crank (Joe had grown up in Seattle), those nails: Joe felt the warmth of orgasm heating the backs of his knees—

(6) The salmon light of Betelgeuse slanted through the clear wall of Sumpter[1] VII, the Fort named—jokingly—by the first generation of galactic anthropologists, how many years ago now ...? And where were they today: reduced to inert jelly during the tragic Kpt. Now, this Blob ...? Bat D— walked across reddened tiles of luciprene-57 past the Fort's transparent north facade, that looked out across the magnetic sands webbed with molten ammonia runulets worming the hyborean[2] chill, toward the sheer range called Chroma—because of the pink, fuchsia, and vermilion clays streaking its silver slopes. Warily, Bat turned from the window-wall to round a partition studded with ruby vytrol—

She quivered there within the high, luminous geometries of Sumpter VII, contracting her gargantuan bulk inward from those bloated pseudopods into which her viscid soap-collared stuffs had spread. Nucleoli and vacuoles and just plain bubbles puckered her membrane. She could sense him, Bat could tell. Languorously, she heaved herself forward.

Bat D—'s thumb snapped open the cover of his Naugahyde[3] holster. He tugged loose his death-laser, its handle of black ivory worked into rare scrimshaw[4] by the Little Folk of Antares-10,[5] its symmetrically veined and partitioned barrel molded of clear lucite casting resin by Jonas & Barboli of Fenton, Pennsylvania. Carefully, Bat raised the gun—

The Blob said: "Burble, burble ... burble." She flattened her amoeboid volume slightly, then heaved again.

Bat fired—and a pseudopod, a little charred, smoking a little, dropped from the ceiling and knocked the death-laser fifteen feet to crack the partition. Ruby vytrol chattered to the floor, glittered on the tiles.

Bat D—, terrified and exuberant, stepped back. The Blob, enraged, hurled herself. Bat D— shrieked and flung up his arms. She smacked him, knee to chin, with a strange and violet warmth that flattened him to the ground. She rolled across him, was in him at every orifice—ears, urethra, anus, mouth, nostrils. She was without him. She was within him. She rolled through him. She flowed around him.

---

1 Fort Sumter was a military installation in South Carolina, and the site of the first battle of the US Civil War. The spelling here could also be a pun on "sump" as in a "sump pump." "Sumpter" is also an archaic term for a pack animal.

2 In other versions, Delany uses "hyperborian," referring to a far-northern land from Greek myth; Hyborean, or Hyborian, was derived from the myth by Robert E. Howard (1906–36) as the setting for his Conan the Barbarian stories.

3 Fake leather made from vinyl.

4 Commonly associated with whaling, scrimshaw is an art form that involves carving intricate works onto ivory or bone.

5 Antares is a star visible from Earth in the Scorpio constellation, and a common site in science fiction.

While he lay, gloriously stalled within her circling torque, with her within him within her, the Blob said: "Honey, what's *with* this shit resenting strange niggers on the subway? *That* sort of double-think[1] earns you no popcorn coupons from the Big Movie Theatre in the sky. Try to imagine an older, less vulgar epoch. Just be your own sweet self—you *have* a lovely smile. But Lord, this luciprene is getting to me. Tastes like old airplane glue!"

For a moment Bat D— thought he would really die. But the Blob withdrew. Letting a howl that resembled nothing so much as the Twentieth-Century war-whoop of Sheena, Queen of the Jungle,[2] she flung herself at Fort Sumpter VII's north wall—

It shattered!

Eyes still tight, Bat heard fragments thud outward on the sand, clatter inward to the floor.

Moments later when, panting and weak, he pulled himself erect beside the jagged pane—already frosting with ammonia from the hyborean chill—the Blob, a football field away, was flûtchüláting (a method of transportation? reproduction? art?) across the black sands, making her erratic path between runulets, toward the Chroma's ceramic and silver.

(7) Joe leaned his forehead on the tile above the urinal, taking deep breaths.

The man beside him zipped his fly, squeezed Joe's jacketed elbow (with that *fine* hand), and whispered: "You know, fellow, you really get into it, don't you?" (One of the Council's feyer members had actually applauded. Another had gotten scared and run.) "You're too much.... Maybe I'll see you in here again sometime—?"

Without lifting his head, Joe grinned; and nodded—because when, on the odd Thursday you found somebody that much what you were into, it took a minute to get it back together. Faint pain pulsed in his spleen—he'd cum that hard. He stuffed himself back in his fly, took another breath, looked up—

The man, and his portfolio, were gone.

On the urinal edge, semen trailed the glaze.

Joe shouldered out between two more arriving members (the blue door was marked E-3) and nearly bumped the incoming policeman. Joe grinned at the cop, nodded; automatically, the cop smiled, nodded back—then apparently remembered himself and frowned.

But Joe was already making it down the concrete ramp to the RR[3]—when two high-school girls collided with him from behind. As he turned, "I'm sorry!" started up behind his teeth, but he chewed and chomped it into, "Hello ..." And smiled.

---

1 "Doublethink" was coined by George Orwell (1903–50) in his novel *Nineteen Eighty-Four* (1949). Here, given the use of the racial epithet and the general content of the dialogue, the story could also be playing on the concept of "double consciousness" as described in *The Souls of Black Folk* (1903) by African American civil rights leader, sociologist, historian, and philosopher W.E.B. Du Bois (1868–1963).

2 A comic book character created in 1938 by Will Eisner (1917–2005) and Jerry Iger (1903–90).

3 Part of the BMT Broadway Line of the New York Subway system.

One girl giggled over her packages. The other, with more packages, blinked.

After a moment the blinking one said, hesitantly: "Oh … excuse me."

"That's okay," Joe said. "What *are* all those?"

The packages were part of an exhibit they were setting up at the Brooklyn Public Library on the history of Puerto Rico. They talked about it through three trains. When they did say good-bye, all three of them were grinning a lot—grinning too much, Joe decided once he was in the car.

Well, old habits die hard. So kill a little harder. Interesting kids, Joe thought. Maybe he should check out the exhibit. Perhaps next Wednesday, after he'd finished standing around at Unemployment. And he would be at the Fourteenth Street john in ten minutes—unless he stopped in at Twenty-third, which, the grapevine had it, was sort of kicky this month.

—*New York*
February 1976

J.G. Ballard (1930–2009)

Born to English parents living in Shanghai, James Graham Ballard was, with his family, held in the Lunghua Civil Assembly Centre internment camp during the Japanese occupation in World War II. His novel, *Empire of the Sun* (1984), is in part based on this experience. After the war, he moved to the UK, joined the Royal Air Force, and was stationed in Moose Jaw, Saskatchewan. While there, as he details in his autobiography *Miracles of Life* (2008), he discovered SF in pulp magazines, and began writing surrealist-influenced SF works, often with a psychological focus. He framed this approach as a study of "inner space," as opposed to outer space, a distinction that would often be used to describe New Wave SF (and, like many New Wave authors, Ballard would publish in *New Worlds* magazine under editor Michael Moorcock). In addition to *Empire of the Sun*, he is best known for his novels *Crash* (1973) and the climate-fiction SF novel *The Drowned World* (1962).

Note on the text: This work originally appeared in the magazine *Bananas: The Literary Newspaper* (Summer 1977) before being reprinted in the magazine *Re/Search* (no. 8/9, 1984), which is the version used for the text here, though minor typographical corrections in Ballard's collection *War Fever* (1990) are silently adopted. Because a large number of "entries" in this piece include historical, geographical, and other "real-world" referents (interspersed with the fictional), annotation is impossible. Classroom activities around these references can prove very useful.

"The Index" (1977)

Editor's note. From abundant internal evidence it seems clear that the text printed below is the index to the unpublished and perhaps suppressed autobiography of a man who may well have been one of the most remarkable figures of the 20th century. Yet of his existence nothing is publicly known, although his life and work appear to have exerted a profound influence on the events of the past fifty years. Physician and philosopher, man of action and patron of the arts, sometime claimant to the English throne and founder of a new religion, Henry Rhodes Hamilton was evidently the intimate of the greatest men and women of our age. After World War II he founded a new movement of spiritual regeneration, but private scandal and public concern at his growing megalomania, culminating in his proclamation of himself as a new divinity, seem to have led to his downfall. Incarcerated within an unspecified government institution, he presumably spent his last years writing his autobiography, of which this index is the only surviving fragment.

A substantial mystery still remains. Is it conceivable that all traces of his activities could be erased from our records of the period? Is the suppressed autobiography itself a disguised roman à clef, in which the fictional hero exposes the secret identities of his historical contemporaries? And what is the true role of the indexer himself, clearly a close friend of the writer, who first suggested that he embark on his autobiography? This ambiguous and shadowy figure has taken the unusual step of indexing himself into his own index. Perhaps the entire compilation is nothing more than a figment of the overwrought imagination of some deranged lexicographer. Alternatively, the index may be wholly genuine, and the only glimpse we have into a world hidden from us by a gigantic conspiracy, of which Henry Rhodes Hamilton is the greatest victim.

A

Acapulco, 143
Acton, Harold, 142–7, 213
Alcazar, Siege of, 221–5
Alimony, HRH pays, 172, 247, 367, 453
Anaxagoras, 35, 67, 69–78, 481
Apollinaire, 98
Arden, Elizabeth, 189, 194, 376–84
Autobiography of Alice B. Toklas, The (Stein), 112
Avignon, birthplace of HRH, 9–13; childhood holidays, 27; research at Pasteur Institute of Ophthalmology, 101; attempts to restore anti-Papacy, 420–35

B

Bal Musette, Paris, 98
Balliol College, Oxford, 69–75, 231
Beach, Sylvia, 94–97
Berenson, Bernard, conversations with HRH, 134; offer of adoption, 145; loan of Dürer etching, 146; lawsuit against HRH, 173–85
Bergman, Ingrid, 197, 234, 267
Biarritz, 123
Blixen, Karen von (Isak Dinesen), letters to HRH, declines marriage proposal, 197
Byron, Lord, 28, 76, 98, 543

C

Cambodia, HRH plans journey to, 188; crashes aircraft, 196; writes book about, 235; meetings with Malraux, 239; capture by insurgents, 253; escape, 261; writes second book about, 283
Cap d'Antibes, 218

William Gibson (b. 1948)

Born in the United States, William Gibson moved to Canada in 1967 as part of the wave of Americans moving north to evade the military draft for the war in Vietnam (though Gibson himself was never drafted). A life-long science fiction fan, he received an English degree from the University of British Columbia, where professor and Hugo-winning SF critic Dr. Susan Wood (1948–80) encouraged him to write and publish his first SF story. Gibson is most often cited as an originator and foremost author of cyberpunk, which combines a digital, near-future aesthetic with both the aesthetics and politics of punk music and culture. Such works—exemplified in Gibson's best-known, and first, novel *Neuromancer* (1984)—emphasize a "lived-in" future that eschews earlier techno-utopian visions for a more dystopian representation of digital and other technologies. "The Gernsback Continuum" offers a thesis statement, of sorts, for the need to move from the pulp utopianism of early pulp SF to the decaying near-future of cyberpunk. The description of the "dream Tucson" in the story bears a striking resemblance to one of the unsigned illustrations—possibly by Frank R. Paul (1884–1963)—for Gernsback's novel *Ralph 124C41+* as it appeared in *Amazing Stories Quarterly* (Winter 1929) (Fig. 10). Other classic SF imagery Gibson draws on includes the film *Metropolis* (1927), as seen in the set photograph by Horst von Harbou (1879–1953) of the city in the film (Fig. 11).

Note on the text: The story first appeared in the anthology *Universe 11*, edited by Terry Carr (1981), before being reprinted in Gibson's collection *Burning Chrome* (1986). The version used here follows the *Universe 11* text. Carr introduces it with the following:

> Science fiction has a long tradition of fascinating stories about 'alternative time-streams,' or worlds in which events small or large changed the course of history. Methods of visiting or perceiving these worlds have varied greatly. In 'The Gernsback Continuum,' William Gibson suggests that it might be accomplished by the increased concentration of psychological fixation. His alternative world is a peculiar one, but one that you're likely to find oddly familiar.
>
> This story is William Gibson's second sale, the first having been to the semiprofessional magazine *UnEarth*; subsequently he's sold stories to *New Worlds*, *Omni*, and (in collaboration with John Shirley) *Shadows*. Born in the United States, he now lives in Canada with his wife and one child. (81)

"The Gernsback Continuum" (1981)

MERCIFULLY, the whole thing is starting to fade, to become an episode. When I do still catch the odd glimpse, it's peripheral; mere fragments of mad-doctor chrome, confining themselves to the corner of the eye. There was that flying-wing liner over San Francisco last week, but it was almost translucent. And the shark-fin roadsters have gotten scarcer, and freeways discreetly avoid unfolding themselves into the gleaming eighty-lane monsters I was forced to drive last month in my rented Toyota. And I know that none of it will follow me to New York; my vision is narrowing to a single wavelength of probability. I've worked hard for that. Television helped a lot.

I suppose it started in London, in that bogus Greek taverna in Battersea Park Road, with lunch on Cohen's corporate tab. Dead steam-table food and it took them thirty minutes to find an ice bucket for the retsina. Cohen works for Barris-Watford, who publish big, trendy "trade" paperbacks: illustrated histories of the neon sign, the pinball machine, the windup toys of Occupied Japan.[1] I'd gone over to shoot a series of shoe ads; California girls with tanned legs and frisky day-glow[2] jogging shoes had capered for me down the escalators of St. John's Wood and across the platforms of Tooting Bec.[3] A lean and hungry young agency had decided that the mystery of London Transport would sell waffle-tread nylon runners. They decide; I shoot. And Cohen, whom I knew vaguely from the old days in New York, had invited me to lunch the day before I was due out of Heathrow. He brought along a very fashionably dressed young woman named Dialta Downes, who was virtually chinless and evidently a noted pop-art historian. In retrospect, I see her walking in beside Cohen under a floating neon sign that flashes THIS WAY LIES MADNESS in huge sans-serif capitals.[4]

Cohen introduced us and explained that Dialta was the prime mover behind the latest Barris-Watford project, an illustrated history of what she called "American Streamlined Moderne." Cohen called it "raygun Gothic." Their working title was *The Airstream Futuropolis: The Tomorrow That Never Was.*

There's a British obsession with the more baroque elements of American pop culture, something like the weird cowboys-and-Indians fetish of the West Germans or the aberrant French hunger for old Jerry Lewis films. In Dialta

1 Following World War II, Japan was occupied by Allied forces, primarily the US, from 1945 to 1952. Many toys and collectibles from this period were stamped "Made in Occupied Japan."

2 DayGlo is a brand of brightly-coloured, fluorescent paint. It is commonly associated with the psychedelic counter-culture 1960s, when the company took on the current name, but was popularly used in several different products. The spelling of the term was corrected to "Day-Glo" in the *Burning Chrome* version of the story.

3 St. John's Wood and Tooting Bec are both areas in London, England, and stations of the London Underground; the former is the site of Abbey Road Studios, made famous by The Beatles.

4 A popular phrase that originates in William Shakespeare's *Tragedy of King Lear* (1606), where the titular character says, "That way madness lies" (Act 3, Sc. 4).

Downes this manifested itself in a mania for a uniquely American form of architecture that most Americans are scarcely aware of. At first I wasn't sure what she was talking about, but gradually it began to dawn on me. I found myself remembering Sunday morning television in the Fifties.

Sometimes they'd run old eroded newsreels as filler on the local station. You'd sit there with a peanut butter sandwich and a glass of milk, and a static-ridden Hollywood baritone would tell you that there was A Flying Car in Your Future. And three Detroit engineers would putter around with this big old Nash with wings, and you'd see it rumbling furiously down some deserted Michigan runway. You never actually saw it take off, but it flew away to Dialta Downes's never-never land, true home of a generation of completely uninhibited technophiles. She was talking about those odds and ends of "futuristic" thirties and forties architecture you pass daily in American cities without noticing: the movie marquees ribbed to radiate some mysterious energy, the dime stores faced with fluted aluminum, the chrome-tube chairs gathering dust in the lobbies of transient hotels. She saw these things as segments of a dream world, abandoned in the uncaring present; she wanted me to photograph them for her.

The thirties had seen the first generation of American industrial designers; until the thirties, all pencil sharpeners had looked like pencil sharpeners—your basic Victorian mechanism, perhaps with a curlicue of decorative trim. After the advent of the designers, some pencil sharpeners looked as though they'd been put together in wind tunnels. For the most part, the change was only skin deep; under the streamlined chrome shell, you'd find the same Victorian mechanism. Which made a certain kind of sense, because the most successful American designers had been recruited from the ranks of Broadway theater designers. It was all a stage set, a series of elaborate props for playing at living in the future.

Over coffee, Cohen produced a fat manila envelope full of glossies. I saw the winged statues that guard the Hoover Dam, forty-foot concrete hood ornaments leaning steadfastly into an imaginary hurricane. I saw a dozen shots of Frank Lloyd Wright's Johnson's Wax Building, juxtaposed with the covers of old *Amazing Stories* pulps, by an artist named Frank R. Paul; the employees of Johnson's Wax must have felt as though they were walking into one of Paul's spray-paint pulp utopias.[1] Wright's building looked as though it had been designed for people who wore white togas and lucite[2] sandals. I hesitated over one sketch of a particularly grandiose prop-driven airliner, all wing, like a fat symmetrical boomerang with windows in unlikely places. Labeled arrows

1 Frank Lloyd Wright (1867–1959), famed American architect who designed the Johnson Wax Headquarters, in Racine, Wisconsin, completed in 1939. Frank R. Paul (1884–1963), American artist best known for his illustrations and covers for Hugo Gernsback's *Amazing Stories* magazine.

2 Lucite is a type of plastic developed in the 1930s that became increasingly popular in jewellery, furniture, and other items in the subsequent decades.

indicated the locations of the grand ballroom and two squash courts. It was dated 1936.

"This thing couldn't have flown ...?" I looked at Dialta Downes.

"Oh, no, quite impossible, even with those twelve giant props; but they loved the look, don't you see? New York to London in less than two days, first-class dining rooms, private cabins, sun decks, dancing to jazz in the evening ... The designers were populists, you see; they were trying to give the public what it wanted. What the public wanted was the future."

I'd been in Burbank for three days, trying to suffuse a really dull-looking rocker with charisma, when I got the package from Cohen. It is possible to photograph what isn't there; it's damned hard to do, and consequently a very marketable talent. While I'm not bad at it, I'm not exactly the best, either, and this poor guy strained my Nikon's[1] credibility. I got out, depressed, because I do like to do a good job, but not totally depressed, because I did make sure I'd gotten the check for the job, and I decided to restore myself with the sublime artiness of the Barris-Watford assignment. Cohen had sent me some books on thirties design, more photos of streamlined buildings, and a list of Dialta Downes's fifty favorite examples of the style in California.

Architectural photography can involve a lot of waiting; the building becomes a kind of sundial, while you wait for a shadow to crawl away from a detail you want, or for the mass and balance of the structure to reveal itself in a certain way. While I was waiting, I thought myself into Dialta Downes's America. When I isolated a few of the factory buildings on the ground glass of the Hasselblad,[2] they came across with a kind of sinister totalitarian dignity, like the stadiums Albert Speer[3] built for Hitler. But the rest of it was relentlessly tacky: ephemeral stuff extruded by the collective American subconscious of the thirties, tending mostly to survive along depressing strips lined with dusty motels, mattress wholesalers, and small used-car lots. I went for the gas stations in a big way.

During the high point of the Downes Age, they put Ming the Merciless[4] in charge of designing California gas stations. Favoring the architecture of his native Mongo, he cruised up and down the coast erecting raygun emplacements in white stucco. Lots of them featured superfluous central towers ringed with those strange radiator flanges that were a signature motif of the style, and made them look as though they might generate potent bursts of raw technological enthusiasm, if you could only find the switch that turned them on. I

1 Nikon is a Japanese camera company, founded in 1917.

2 Hasselblad is a Swedish camera company that released its first consumer camera in 1948.

3 Albert Speer (1905–81), Nazi Minister of Armaments and War Production; also an architect, he designed the Nazi rally grounds in Nuremberg, Germany, where he was later convicted of war crimes and crimes against humanity.

4 Ming the Merciless was the principal villain, and racist Orientalist stereotype, in the Flash Gordon comic strip.

Fig. 10: [Frank R. Paul]. Illustration for Ralph *124C41+*.
Amazing Stories Quarterly, 1929.

shot one in San Jose an hour before the bulldozers arrived and drove right through the structural truth of plaster and lathing and cheap concrete.

"Think of it," Dialta Downes had said, "as a kind of alternate America: a 1980 that never happened. An architecture of broken dreams."

And that was my frame of mind as I made the stations of her convoluted socioarchitectural cross in my red Toyota—as I gradually tuned in to her image of a shadowy America-that-wasn't, of Coca-Cola plants like beached submarines, and fifth-run movie houses like the temples of some lost sect that had worshiped blue mirrors and geometry. And as I moved among these secret ruins, I found myself wondering what the inhabitants of that lost future would think of the world I lived in. The thirties dreamed white marble and slipstream chrome, immortal crystal and burnished bronze, but the rockets on the covers of the Gernsback pulps had fallen on London in the dead of night, screaming. After the war, everyone had a car—no wings for it—and the promised superhighway to drive it down, so that the sky itself darkened, and the fumes ate the marble and pitted the miracle crystal....

And one day, on the outskirts of Bolinas, when I was setting up to shoot a particularly lavish example of Ming's martial architecture, I penetrated a fine membrane, a membrane of probability....

Ever so gently, I went over the Edge—

And looked up to see a twelve-engined thing like a bloated boomerang, all wing, thrumming its way east with an elephantine grace, so low that I could count the rivets in its dull silver skin, and hear—maybe—the echo of jazz.

I took it to Kihn.

Merv Kihn, free-lance journalist with an extensive line in Texas pterodactyls, redneck UFO contactees, bush-league Loch Ness monsters, and the Top Ten conspiracy theories in the loonier reaches of the American mass mind.

"It's good," said Kihn, polishing his yellow Polaroid shooting glasses on the hem of his Hawaiian shirt, "but it's not *mental;* lacks the true quill."

"But I saw it, Mervyn." We were seated poolside in brilliant Arizona sunlight. He was in Tucson waiting for a group of retired Las Vegas civil servants whose leader received messages from Them on her microwave oven. I'd driven all night and was feeling it.

"Of course you did. Of course you saw it. You've read my stuff; haven't you grasped my blanket solution to the UFO problem? It's simple, plain and country simple: people"—he settled the glasses carefully on his long hawk nose and fixed me with his best basilisk glare—"*see* ... things. People see these things. Nothing's there, but people *see* them anyway. Because they need to, probably. You've read Jung,[1] you should know the score.... In your case, it's so obvious: you admit you were thinking about this crackpot architecture, having fantasies

1 Carl Jung (1875–1961), noted Swiss psychotherapist most associated with the concept of the collective unconscious.

... Look, I'm sure you've taken your share of drugs, right? How many people survived the Sixties in California without having the odd hallucination? All those nights when you discovered that whole armies of Disney technicians had been employed to weave animated holograms of Egyptian hieroglyphs into the fabric of your jeans, say, or the times when—"[1]

"But it wasn't like that."

"Of course not. It wasn't like that at all; it was 'in a setting of clear reality,' right? Everything normal, and then there's the monster, the mandala, the neon cigar. In your case, a giant Tom Swift[2] airplane. It happens *all the time.* You aren't even crazy. You know that, don't you?" He fished a beer out of the battered foam cooler beside his deck chair.

"Last week I was in Virginia. Grayson County. I interviewed a sixteen-year-old girl who'd been assaulted by a *bar hade.*"

"A what?"

"A bear head. The severed head of a bear. This *bar hade,* see, was floating around on its own little flying saucer, looked kind of like the hubcaps on cousin Wayne's vintage Caddy. Had red, glowing eyes like two cigar stubs and telescoping chrome antennas poking up behind its ears." He burped.

"It assaulted her? How?"

"You don't want to know; you're obviously impressionable. 'It was cold'"—he lapsed into his bad southern accent—"'and metallic.' It made electronic noises. Now that is the real thing, the straight goods from the mass unconscious, friend; that little girl is a witch. There's just no place for her to function in this society. She'd have seen the devil, if she hadn't been brought up on 'The Bionic Man' and all those 'Star Trek' reruns.[3] She is clued into the main vein. And she knows that it happened to her. I got out ten minutes before the heavy UFO boys showed up with the polygraph."

I must have looked pained, because he set his beer down carefully beside the cooler and sat up.

"If you want a classier explanation, I'd say you saw a semiotic ghost. All these contactee stories, for instance, are framed in a kind of sci-fi imagery that permeates our culture. I could buy aliens, but not aliens that look like fifties' comic art. They're semiotic phantoms, bits of deep cultural imagery that have

---

1 The discussion of hallucinogens and jeans echoes a passage in *The Doors of Perception* (1954), by British author Aldous Huxley, where he describes staring at his trousers while high on mescaline. Huxley is also known for his SF dystopia *Brave New World* (1932).

2 Tom Swift was the teenage inventor hero of a series of over one hundred children's science fiction novels, produced by the Stratemeyer Syndicate publishing company, which also published the Nancy Drew and Hardy Boys series. The original Tom Swift Series was published between 1910 and 1941.

3 The Bionic Man was the colloquial name for the cybernetically enhanced main character of the series *The Six Million Dollar Man* (1973–78), loosely based on Martin Caidin's novel *Cyborg* (1972). The original *Star Trek* series, created by Gene Roddenberry—the first in arguably one of the best-known science fiction franchises in history—ran from 1966 to 1969, when it was cancelled, only to return as a series of movies after the first successful fan-run revival campaign.

split off and taken on a life of their own, like the Jules Verne airships that those old Kansas farmers were always seeing. But you saw a different kind of ghost, that's all. That plane was part of the mass unconscious, once. You picked up on that, somehow. The important thing is not to worry about it."

I did worry about it, though.

Kihn combed his thinning blond hair and went off to hear what They had had to say over the radar range lately, and I drew the curtains in my room and lay down in air-conditioned darkness to worry about it. I was still worrying about it when I woke up. Kihn had left a note on my door; he was flying up north in a chartered plane to check out a cattle-mutilation rumor ("muties," he called them; another of his journalistic specialties).

I had a meal, showered, took a crumbling diet pill that had been kicking around in the bottom of my shaving kit for three years, and headed back to Los Angeles.

The speed limited my vision to the tunnel of the Toyota's headlights. The body could drive, I told myself, while the mind maintained. Maintained and stayed away from the weird peripheral window dressing of amphetamine and exhaustion, the spectral, luminous vegetation that grows out of the corners of the mind's eye along late-night highways. But the mind had its own ideas, and Kihn's opinion of what I was already thinking of as my "sighting" rattled endlessly through my head in a tight, lopsided orbit. Semiotic ghosts. Fragments of the Mass Dream, whirling past in the wind of my passage. Somehow this feedback-loop aggravated the diet pill, and the speed-vegetation along the road began to assume the colors of infrared satellite images, glowing shreds blown apart in the Toyota's slipstream.

I pulled over, then, and a half-dozen aluminum beer cans winked goodnight as I killed the headlights. I wondered what time it was in London, and tried to imagine Dialta Downes having breakfast in her Hampstead flat, surrounded by streamlined chrome figurines and books on American culture.

Desert nights in that country are enormous; the moon is closer. I watched the moon for a long time and decided that Kihn was right. The main thing was not to worry. All across the continent, daily, people who were more normal than I'd ever aspired to be saw giant birds, Bigfeet, flying oil refineries; they kept Kihn busy and solvent. Why should I be upset by a glimpse of the nineteen-thirties pop imagination loose over Bolinas? I decided to go to sleep, with nothing worse to worry about than rattlesnakes and cannibal hippies, safe amid the friendly roadside garbage of my own familiar continuum. In the morning I'd drive down to Nogales and photograph the old brothels, something I'd intended to do for years. The diet pill had given up.

The light woke me, and then the voices.

The light came from somewhere behind me and threw shifting shadows inside the car. The voices were calm, indistinct, male and female, engaged in conversation.

My neck was stiff and my eyeballs felt gritty in their sockets. My leg had gone to sleep, pressed against the steering wheel. I fumbled for my glasses in the pocket of my work shirt and finally got them on.

Then I looked behind me and saw the city.

The books on thirties design were in the trunk; one of them contained sketches of an idealized city that drew on *Metropolis* and *Things to Come*,[1] but squared everything, soaring up through an architect's perfect clouds to zeppelin docks and mad neon spires. That city was a scale model of the one that rose behind me. Spire stood on spire in gleaming ziggurat steps that climbed to a central golden temple-tower ringed with the crazy radiator flanges of the Mongo gas stations. You could hide the Empire State Building in the smallest of those towers. Roads of crystal soared between the spires, crossed and recrossed by smooth silver shapes like beads of running mercury. The air was thick with ships: giant wing-liners, little darting silver things (sometimes one of the quicksilver shapes from the sky bridges rose gracefully into the air and flew up to join the dance), mile-long blimps, hovering dragonfly things that were gyrocopters …

I closed my eyes tight and swung around in the seat. When I opened them, I willed myself to see the mileage meter, the pale road dust on the black plastic dashboard, the overflowing ashtray.

"Amphetamine psychosis," I said. I opened my eyes. The dash was still there, the dust, the crushed filter tips. Very carefully, without moving my head, I turned the headlights on.

And saw them.

They were blond. They were standing beside their car, an aluminum avocado with a central shark-fin rudder jutting up from its spine and smooth black tires like a child's toy. He had his arm around her waist and was gesturing toward the city. They were both in white: loose clothing, bare legs, spotless white sun shoes. Neither of them seemed aware of the beams of my headlights. He was saying something wise and strong, and she was nodding, and suddenly I was frightened, frightened in an entirely different way. Sanity had ceased to be an issue; I knew, somehow, that the city behind me was Tucson—a dream Tucson thrown up out of the collective yearning of an era. That it was real, entirely real. But the couple in front of me lived in it, and they frightened me.

They were the children of Dialta Downes's '80-that-wasn't; they were Heirs to the Dream. They were white, blond, and they probably had blue eyes. They were American. Dialta had said that the Future had come to America first, but had finally passed it by. But not here, in the heart of the Dream. Here,

1 Arguably the first "blockbuster" science fiction film, *Metropolis* is a 1927 German silent film directed by Fritz Lang (1890–1976). *Things to Come* is a 1936 British film written by H.G. Wells (for information on Wells, see his story "The Star" in this volume, p. 91) and directed by William Cameron Menzies (1896–1957).

we'd gone on and on, in a dream logic that knew nothing of pollution, the finite bounds of fossil fuel, or foreign wars it was possible to lose. They were smug, happy, and utterly content with themselves and their world. And in the Dream, it was *their* world.

Behind me, the illuminated city: searchlights swept the sky for the sheer joy of it. I imagined them thronging the plazas of white marble, orderly and alert, their bright eyes shining with enthusiasm for their floodlit avenues and silver cars.

It had all the sinister fruitiness of Hitler Youth[1] propaganda.

I put the car in gear and drove forward slowly, until the bumper was within three feet of them. They still hadn't seen me. I rolled the window down and listened to what the man was saying. His words were bright and hollow as the pitch in some Chamber of Commerce brochure, and I knew that he believed in them absolutely.

"John," I heard the woman say, "we've forgotten to take our food pills." She clicked two bright wafers from a thing on her belt and passed one to him. I backed onto the highway and headed for Los Angeles, wincing and shaking my head.

I phoned Kihn from a gas station. A new one, in bad Spanish Modern. He was back from his expedition and didn't seem to mind the call.

"Yeah, that is a weird one. Did you try to get any pictures? Not that they ever come out, but it adds an interesting *frisson* to your story, not having the pictures turn out...."

But what should I do?

"Watch lots of television, particularly game shows and soaps. Go to porn movies. Ever see *Nazi Love Motel*? They've got it on cable, here. Really awful. Just what you need."

What was he talking about?

"Quit yelling and listen to me. I'm letting you in on a trade secret: really bad media can exorcise your semiotic ghosts. If it keeps the saucer people off my back, it can keep these Art Deco futuroids off yours. Try it. What have you got to lose?"

Then he begged off, pleading an early-morning date with the Elect.

"The who?"

"These oldsters from Vegas; the ones with the microwaves."

I considered putting a collect call through to London, getting Cohen at Barris-Watford and telling him his photographer was checking out for a protracted season in the Twilight Zone.[2] In the end, I let a machine mix me a

1 The Hitler Youth was a paramilitary youth group founded by the Nazis. "Fruitiness" can be read here as a homophobic slur (see Tyler Stevens's reading of the story in relation to *Neuromancer*, esp. 420–23).

2 *The Twilight Zone* was an influential American SF television series created by Rod Serling (1924–75). The original series aired from 1959 to 1964.

Fig. 11: Horst von Harbou. Set photograph from *Metropolis*, 1927.

really impossible cup of black coffee and climbed back into the Toyota for the haul to Los Angeles.

Los Angeles was a bad idea, and I spent two weeks there. It was prime Downes country; too much of the Dream there, and too many fragments of the Dream waiting to snare me. I nearly wrecked the car on a stretch of overpass near Disneyland, when the road fanned out like an origami trick and left me swerving through a dozen minilanes of whizzing chrome teardrops with shark fins. Even worse, Hollywood was full of people who looked too much like the couple I'd seen in Arizona. I hired an Italian director who was making ends meet doing darkroom work and installing patio decks around swimming pools until his ship came in; he made prints of all the negatives I'd accumulated on the Downes job. I didn't want to look at the stuff myself. It didn't seem to bother Leonardo, though, and when he was finished I checked the prints, riffling through them like a deck of cards, sealed them up, and sent them air freight to London. Then I took a taxi to a theater that was showing *Nazi Love Motel,* and kept my eyes shut all the way.

Cohen's congratulatory wire was forwarded to me in San Francisco a week later. Dialta had loved the pictures. He admired the way I'd "really gotten into it," and looked forward to working with me again. That afternoon I spotted a flying wing over Castro Street, but there was something tenuous about it, as though it were only half there. I rushed into the nearest newsstand and gathered up as much as I could find on the petroleum crisis and the nuclear energy hazard. I'd just decided to buy a plane ticket for New York.

"Hell of a world we live in, huh?" The proprietor was a thin black man with bad teeth and an obvious wig. I nodded, fishing in my jeans for change, anxious to find a park bench where I could submerge myself in hard evidence of the human near-dystopia we live in. "But it could be worse, huh?"

"That's right," I said, "or even worse, it could be perfect."

He watched me as I headed down the street with my little bundle of condensed catastrophe.

Charles R. Saunders (1946–2020)

Born in the United States, Charles Robert Saunders moved to Canada after being drafted into the US military for the war in Vietnam. Originally living in Ontario, after being invited to Halifax to participate in the Hal-Con SF convention he settled in Nova Scotia, where he wrote for the *Halifax Daily News*. He is best known for his "sword and soul" African fantasy novels, specifically *Imaro* (1981) and its sequels. These works sought to challenge the centrality of whiteness and explicit racism in such "African" and other adventure stories as Edgar Rice Burroughs's *Tarzan of the Apes* (1912) and Robert E. Howard's *Conan the Barbarian* tales of the 1930s (on the initial printing of *Imaro*, the publisher included the description "The Epic Novel of a Black Tarzan," which Saunders did not want, and a lawsuit by the estate of Edgar Rice Burroughs led to the entire first printing being pulped). Building on his newspaper work, Saunders also published books relating specifically to the history of the African Nova Scotian community, including *Share and Care: The Story of the Nova Scotia Home for Colored Children* (1994) and *Black and Bluenose: The Contemporary History of a Community* (1999).

Note on the text: This story was originally published, with illustrations, in the fanzine *Potboiler* (1982). It was later reprinted, with emendations by Saunders (mostly grammatical or for clarity), in the online magazine *Innsmouth Free Press* (2010). This version follows the later publication, though the original was consulted for substantive differences.

"Jeroboam Henley's Debt" (1982)

THE October moon limned the old house and its surrounding copse of trees in a wan white glare. A lowslung black sedan slowly approached the driveway, then turned in. The sound the car's motor made before its driver switched off the ignition was reminiscent of the growl of an impatient beast.

The door on the driver's side opened; when he emerged, it was as though a segment of the shadowy machine had detached itself and assumed the shape of a tall, muscular man. As the driver, whose name was Theotis Nedeau, started up the porch steps, an outside light flared on, illuminating his face. Even in the light, his complexion was of a singularly dusky hue.

With a sharp squeal of hinges, the screen door flew open and a short, rotund man bounded onto the porch to greet his visitor.

"Theotis!" he cried. "It's been so long since you wired from Toronto. My God, I thought something had happened to you...."

About to catch his friend in an impulsive embrace, the smaller man, whose name was Jeremiah Henley, suddenly stepped back. For he recognized the grim set of the dark man's mouth and the glint in his narrowed eyes.

Anticipating Henley's next thought, Nedeau broke his silence.

"I was ... delayed ... at a gas station outside of Chatham."

Suppressed fury crackled like static electricity in his voice.

"You'd better come in and have a drink, Theotis," Henley suggested.

"Maybe I'd better."

Together, the two men hauled Nedeau's two suitcases out of the trunk of the new-model 1933 Auburn and carried them into the house. Though the suitcases were of similar weight, Henley had to labour with the one he'd chosen, while Nedeau bore his own burden easily. Once again, Henley recalled his friend's phenomenal athletic prowess, how Nedeau had set football records that still stood and had once held his own sparring three rounds with Harry Wills, the black heavyweight even the great Jack Dempsey never dared to meet.[1]

And he remembered a night more than a dozen years ago in Virginia, when he and Nedeau had been stopped by a policeman wanting to know exactly how a couple of "Nigras" had come by such a fine motorcar as the one they were in without having stolen it. Nedeau had flattened the policeman with one blow and they'd fled the state with a posse of cracker[2] cops on their tail all the way up to the gates of the black college they'd been attending.

It had taken virtually all of the Dean of Men's powers of diplomacy to forestall a major racial incident. And an abrupt increase in Howard University's[3] endowment, courtesy of Nedeau's mysteriously moneyed father, had saved Theotis from summary expulsion.

Now, Theotis Nedeau had been "delayed."

Henley shivered a little as he ensconced his friend in an overstuffed chair in the living room. Then he poured two tumblers of bourbon.

"Are Emma and the boys here?" Nedeau asked.

"No," Henley replied. "They're staying with my in-laws in Dresden, north of here. They'll be safe there."

Nedeau nodded somberly. Silence fell between the two seated figures as they sipped their bourbon. They were a study in contrast. Nedeau was black as polished ebony. The immaculate dark suit he wore barely hid the mesomorphic lines of his physique. Henley was of a *café-au-lait* complexion, with a neatly trimmed mustache and carefully pomaded hair. There were lines of worry in his face and deep shadows smudged the skin beneath his eyes. His lounging suit, though expensively tailored, was unpressed.

More than a decade had passed since the former college roommates had seen each other. Even so, they had maintained a regular correspondence. It

1 Harry Wills (1889–1958) was a Black boxer who, when the sport was segregated, was the World Colored Heavyweight Champion in 1914, 1916, and 1918. There was a popular effort to have Wills fight the white heavyweight champion Jack Dempsey (1895–1983), which nearly came to pass in 1926, but Dempsey did not follow through.

2 An epithet for a white person, especially for poor whites from the Southern US.

3 Howard University is a Historical Black University in Washington DC, founded in 1867. It holds a significant place in the history of the Civil Rights Movement.

was Henley's most recent letter, followed by an urgent telegram, that had brought Nedeau more than a thousand miles northward to Ontario....

Nedeau finished his drink, then began to talk in a flat, uninflected tone.

"I had some problems with directions," he said. "Up to a point, the guards at the Niagara Falls border crossing were helpful—after I signed a statement swearing that I won't remain in Canada longer than two weeks."

Henley shook his head. He knew the intensity of Nedeau's race pride, but it was no secret that the Canadian government officially discouraged "coloured immigration." It wasn't Nedeau's pride that was at stake now, though.

"It wasn't difficult to find my way to Toronto, where I wired you to let you know I was coming, and from there to Chatham," Nedeau continued. "But I became confused a few miles west of Chatham. I saw a gas station on the side of the road, and pulled in to ask for directions. Before I could say anything, the attendant said, 'We don't serve your kind here.' When I mentioned that I only wanted directions to Henleyville, he pulled a gun, flashed a deputy's badge and forced me out of my car. He said he was going to arrest me for car theft."

Nedeau's fists clenched.

"He was disappointed to find that all my identification was in order—including my auto registration. But he wasn't done. He asked what I wanted in Henleyville. I told him I intended to visit an old friend. When he asked who the friend was, I was tempted to tell him it was none of his concern. But I wanted to arrive here as quickly as I could. So, I mentioned your name. For a moment, I thought he was going to shoot me. Then, strangely enough, he gave me the directions and walked back into the station without another word."

"That would be Lorne Cooder," Henley murmured half to himself. "I wouldn't be surprised if he paid us a visit tonight. Listen, Theotis, I'm sorry about...."

"Forget it," Nedeau said.

His eyes wandered to the wall above an ornate mantelpiece. There was a large square of wallpaper several shades lighter than the surrounding area, as though a picture that had hung there for a long time had suddenly been removed.

"What happened to the portrait?" Nedeau asked.

Henley started violently. His eyes widened with something akin to terror as he looked at Nedeau. Then Henley remembered their many late-night conversations about his illustrious grandfather—Jeroboam Henley.

Jeroboam Henley was a slave who had escaped to the North of the United States, then assisted fellow runaways in fleeing to sanctuary in Canada via the network of abolitionists known as the "Underground Railroad."[1] Henley himself had finally emigrated from Ohio to Canada in protest against the passage

1 The Underground Railroad was a network of abolitionists who helped enslaved people in the US escape to the so-called "free states," as well as to Canada and Europe.

of the Fugitive Slave Law by the U.S. Congress shortly before the start of the Civil War.[1]

Settling in Ontario, Henley built a house and founded a self-contained community of ex-slaves. He had disdained the mass migration of blacks back to the U.S. when slavery was abolished there, and the diminished community he had founded eventually bore his name.

As Jeroboam Henley's grandson, Jeremiah had been something of a celebrity even at Howard, a college replete with the scions of illustrious men of colour. He had told Nedeau of the large portrait of old Jeroboam—who had died before Jeremiah was born—that hung over the mantelpiece of the ancestral home. Thus, it was not surprising that Nedeau remembered it now.

"I burned it," Jeremiah Henley said.

⋆ ⋆ ⋆

Now, it was Nedeau's turn to express shock, though for him that expression was limited to a raising of his brows followed by an intense, thoughtful gaze.

"Jeremiah," he said, "I think you'd better swallow that drink of yours, pour yourself another, then start from the beginning. I won't be able to help you until I know the whole story."

Nodding jerkily, Henley complied. There was a tremor in his hands as he finished his first drink. When he finished the second, the trembling was gone.

"It began a few weeks ago," he said. "No—even before that. I had trouble sleeping. And when I did sleep, I tossed and yelled so much that Emma took to going downstairs and sleeping on the couch. If it was nightmares, I couldn't remember them. At least, not until *that night*....

"As usual, I couldn't get to sleep. But I must have dozed off somehow, because the next thing I remember, I was sitting up in bed and Emma wasn't there. I decided to go down to the living room to talk to her. I got out of bed, went down the hall ... *but my feet wouldn't let me go down the stairs!* I found myself walking past the children's room, toward the walled-over end of the hall where the stairs to the attic are supposed to be. I tried to stop myself—I had always dreaded that part of the house since my father whipped me within an inch of my life just for asking about it—but my legs wouldn't obey me.

"The closer I got to the end of the hall, the more fear I felt. My eyes were getting used to the dark, but I still wanted to put on the hall lights. I couldn't stop myself from walking in a straight line toward the hidden attic stairs. I decided I must be dreaming—but never before had I known I was dreaming while the dream was still going on.

1 The Fugitive Slave Act was a law passed by the US Congress in 1850. Intended as a compromise between slaveholding and free states to avoid a civil war, it stripped rights from self-freed, formerly enslaved people living in free states, permitting recapture by their former enslavers. It failed as a compromise, and the US Civil War followed, from 1861 to 1865, which eventually resulted in the abolition of chattel slavery across the US.

"When I got to the end of the hall, my hands—of their own accord—pressed against certain sections of the wall. Then the whole wall slid back, not making any sound at all! I'll tell you, Theotis, I've never been more scared in my life than I was then—not even when those crackers chased us out of Virginia. I hadn't even thought of that part of the house since the beating my father gave me. And now I was at the stairs, and my feet were carrying me up into that dark attic....

"Once I got up there, though, it wasn't all that dark. There's a big dormer window in the attic and there weren't any shades to block the moonlight. The place was piled high with boxes, crates and trunks. There were black shadows between the piles. My feet carried me straight toward one of those shadows. I knelt down. My hands reached out. My fingers worked at the fastenings of a small chest I couldn't see. I opened the lid of the chest, reached in and pulled out a thick, leather-bound book of some sort. I went to the light of the window and opened the book. By then, I was in control of my actions—and I knew I wasn't dreaming.

"The moon was full. By its light, I could clearly see the writing in the book. It was a diary—my grandfather's diary."

Henley drew the back of one hand across his brow. The hand came away wet. Silently, Nedeau waited for him to continue.

"It was actually more of a record than a diary. My grandfather kept detailed listings of all the runaway slaves who passed through his 'station' on the Underground Railroad. There were scores of names. Everyone knows Jeroboam Henley helped many of his people to freedom.

"But some of the names were—*crossed out.* I didn't know what that meant until I paged further through the book, and found a special section in the back. The names that had been crossed out earlier were repeated—with monetary values entered next to them. It was like a ledger.

"Suspicion dawned ... a sickening suspicion that was confirmed as I read further and understood more fully. With each word I read, a part of me died.

"Not all of the runaways who came to my grandfather's house in Ohio went on to Canada, Theotis. You know what that man was doing? *He was selling his own people to a plantation owner in Louisiana!* Not all of them, mind you. Just the ones who met the plantation owner's specifications. They had to be native African, and by the 1850s, you couldn't find many of those—so my grandfather said.

"He drugged their food, then tied them up and turned them over to the plantation owner's Northern agent, who lived in the town under the guise of a freight operator. The whites paid my grandfather well and they kept his secret. They needed him. He was the only one, other than Harriet Tubman,[1] that the runaways trusted implicitly—*damn him!*

1 Harriet Tubman (c. 1822–1913), born into slavery, freed herself and became one of the foremost abolitionists and leaders of the Underground Railroad, also serving in the Union Army during the US Civil War.

"There were hints in the diary that the plantation owner had some sort of hold over my grandfather. There were also suggestions that the slaves were used as sacrifices to some sort of god or devil named 'Shub-Niggurath.'"[1]

"I don't like the sound of that name," Nedeau interrupted.

"Neither do I!" Henley flared. "But it sure as hell didn't bother my grandfather! All he could think about was the money the plantation owner paid him! Hell, he loved it! The greedy son of a bitch!"

Overcome with emotion, Henley held his face in his hands.

"Damn," Nedeau said softly. "Jeremiah, I'm really sorry to hear that. You must have—"

"That's not all of it!" Henley cried. "There was a final name on the list of the ones my grandfather betrayed. It was an African name ... 'Gbomi.' He was a witch doctor of some kind, so my grandfather said. When this Gbomi realized he had been drugged, he called down a curse on my grandfather. My grandfather laughed as the African mumbled and slurred in his native tongue while being bound. He took his blood money from the plantation owner's agent and thought no more about Gbomi—not until things began to happen at night in that Ohio town.

"Strange things ... a black face appearing in people's windows ... cattle, sheep and dogs slaughtered mysteriously, horribly, drained of blood ... splayed foot prints leading to my grandfather's house....

"The town turned against my grandfather. The people were stirred up by an element which had always been opposed to his antislavery activities. The plantation owner and his agent soon let my grandfather know that he was of no further use to them. He panicked. He fled to Canada, using his opposition to the Fugitive Slave Law as a smokescreen. But he was really running from Gbomi.

"When I finished with that damnable diary, my eyes were sore from the strain of reading by moonlight. I felt as betrayed as those slaves my grandfather sold. Then the anger came, driving everything else before it. I walked out of that attic. This time, *I* was the one controlling my actions. Enraged as I was, I still managed to step quietly, so as not to awaken my sons.

"I kept walking until I got to the living room. Emma was there, sleeping on the couch. There was a low fire in the fireplace. It got higher when I set my grandfather's diary in the flames. Then I looked over to the mantel and saw his portrait. I took it down and put it in the fireplace, frame and all.

"By the time Emma woke up, both the diary and the portrait were nothing but ashes. Emma looked at the empty wall, then at the fireplace, then at me. And she ran sobbing from the room. She gathered up the boys and left. She thought I was crazy. Maybe I was that night. Maybe I still am....

1 Shub-Niggurath is an ancient god created by in H.P. Lovecraft as part of his larger Cthulhu mythos; the name is first used in "The Dunwich Horror" (1928), but is expanded upon in "The Whisperer in Darkness" (1930), where she is also referred to as "The Black Goat of the Woods. [...] The Goat with a Thousand Young!" (*Weird Tales*, August 1931, p. 43). For more information on Lovecraft and his mythos, see his story in this anthology, p. 190.

"It was not long after that night that things began to happen here—things similar to the events that forced Jeroboam Henley out of Ohio. That's why I need you, Theotis. You're the only one who can help me. Don't you see? He's come back. By all that's holy and unholy, Theotis, *he's come back*!"

"Who?" Nedeau asked quietly.

Nonplussed, Henley cried, "What do you mean, 'Who?'"

"Who do you think has come back?" Nedeau pressed. "Gbomi—or your grandfather?"

Before Henley could reply, a sudden crashing sound splintered the short silence. Both men sprang to their feet. The roar of a car motor faded in the distance as Henley and Nedeau rushed to the shattered front window. Henley bent to pick something up from the shards of glass, while Nedeau wrenched the front door open and raced outside. Only a few moments passed before he returned, his face set in a scowl of frustration.

"Couldn't get the bastard's licence number," he muttered.

"I know who it is," Henley said. "Remember, I said we'd get a visit from Lorne Cooder tonight."

Nedeau looked at him. Never before had he heard such bitterness in his friend's tone. Wordlessly, Henley handed Nedeau the red house brick that had been thrown through the window. There was a note attached:

NIGGER—[1]

If your black friend has come to take you out of here, tell him it had better be sooner than later!

The note bore no signature.

"It's come to this," Henley said. "My neighbours show their true colours at last—lily white. It was fine for us back in the old days, when the escaped slaves came up here and the Canadians took them in so that they could fling their 'true adherence to the principles of freedom' in the faces of the Americans. But when slavery was over, we became 'niggers' again. And when something goes wrong...."

"Whoever wrote that note was right in one sense," Nedeau cut in.

"What do you mean?"

"We have no time to lose," Nedeau said as he reached for the handle of one of his suitcases. "Let's go."

"Go where?" Henley asked numbly.

"Upstairs. To the attic."

"After what you just heard about my grandfather, you're still going to help me?"

"Do you think you're to blame for what your grandfather did?"

Henley left the question unanswered.

---

1 Saunders uses this anti-Black epithet to highlight the racism of the community and as part of his larger critique of racism in Weird and other genre fiction. See the introduction to H.P. Lovecraft in this anthology (p. 190).

★ ★ ★

For only the second time in his life, Jeremiah Henley stood in the cobwebbed attic of his ancestral home. Despite Nedeau's presence, Henley was experiencing even more anxiety than he had the night something outside himself had guided him to a secret better left buried with its bearer.... Except for the flicker of a row of three tapers, the attic was shrouded in darkness. Nedeau had covered the single window with a heavy quilt. Henley watched uncertainly while Nedeau carefully arranged the apparatus he had extracted from his suitcase.

Nedeau poured a sackful of sand into a shallow metal tray and spread it evenly across the bottom. From another, smaller sack he poured a fine black powder into a wooden bowl carved with geometric African designs. He took special care not to allow any of the powder to touch his skin.

Henley felt a queer sense of detachment as he observed his friend's preparations. He remembered Nedeau's almost obsessive absorption with African culture back in college, as well as how spitefully Nedeau had been ridiculed for it. All things African had been shunned by Howard students then; even the smattering of Africans attending the college were derided as "Home Boys." More than once, Henley had privately defended Nedeau's affinity for the "Home Boys." Publicly, Nedeau had always been more than capable of defending himself.

Now, Nedeau was a professor in the Howard history department and taught courses in African lore. He had even spent a year in the Gold Coast,[1] a British West African colony. Henley thought of the letters he had received with Gold Coast postage—long, enthusiastic missives full of near-incomprehensible reports of Nedeau's studies of the magic of West African *ju-ju*[2] men....

"I hope this voodoo of yours works," Henley said, for no reason other to break a silence that was becoming intolerable.

Nedeau looked at him. He had removed his coat and shirt, and his bare torso was even more impressive than Henley recalled. It was Nedeau's eyes, however, that caused Henley to recoil in dismay.

"Voodoo!" He spat the word as if it were a curse. "It would take more time than I have to explain to you the difference between that half-baked Haitian superstition and the true magic of Africa."[3]

1 The Gold Coast was a British Colony in West Africa from 1821 until it won its independence, as Ghana, in 1957.

2 Ju-ju refers to both the practice of imbuing objects with spiritual power and the objects so imbued, as part of the religious practice of various peoples of Western Africa and among the African diaspora (see Changa).

3 Voodoo (also vodou) is a set of religious practices commonly associated with Haiti, and generally seen as arising from the confluence of West African and Christian traditions among the Black diasporic communities of the region; it is often associated with the effects of and resistance to slavery. It is regularly presented in a stereotyped and racist manner in western culture, which Nedeau seems to continue here.

Scowling, he returned to his preparations. Henley, who remained seated on a dusty trunk, could not suppress a gasp of shock when Nedeau drew a pair of long, white bones from the suitcase.

"Leopard, not human," Nedeau said. "They were given to me by a powerful *malam*[1]—what the ignorant would call a 'witch doctor' or '*ju-ju* man'—because I spoke on his behalf in a case brought against him by a District Commissioner. We will need them tonight.

"From the hints I gathered in your letter—confirmed by our conversation downstairs—I would say you are being stalked by a *semando*[2]—a dead-sending."

"You mean a ... zombie?"

"Worse than that. Your grandfather's enemy must have been a powerful *malam* indeed to have launched a curse that has spanned two generations."

"What is a *semando*, if it isn't a zombie?"

"A *semando* is a dead thing shaped and motivated by the will of the *malam*. The animal killings are typical of a *semando*'s work, for it needs blood to build its potency to the point where it can fulfill its ultimate purpose—vengeance."

Henley shuddered. "How can such a—*thing*—be stopped?"

"With the powder in that bowl. It is *kaliloze*,[3] meaning that it's deadly to any supernatural thing it touches. It will be the only thing that will save us when I summon the *semando* here."

"What?" Henley cried. "Have you gone insane?"

"It's the only way, man. We can't go out to seek the creature; it's a thing of the night and it would be suicidal to attempt to face it in its own element. I must lure it here, where I'll at least have a chance to get to it with the *kaliloze*. And it *will* come. I have only to call it, using this oracle of sand and the bones of power. The *semando* will come, for what it wants is here—you."

"God!" Henley exclaimed. "This is so senseless—unreal! Savage ceremonies *here*, in 1933...."

Nedeau stood up, towering over Henley.

"You asked for my help," he grated. "If you don't want it, say so now. If you do, then you'll keep your mouth shut until this thing is over with."

Henley, well aware of the meaning of his friend's tone, fell silent. He was beginning to fear Theotis Nedeau....

---

1 A malam is a West African term for "a learned man; a scribe, teacher, or healer" (*OED*).

2 The editor, as yet, has not found the term "semando" in this context elsewhere, though James H. Neal's sensationalist colonial memoir *Jungle Magic* (1966) uses "semando" to refer to what is more commonly called the Asamando, which, "According to Akan cosmology ... is the ancestral world or the land of the spirits" (Blay, p. 69). For discussions of different representations of the zombie in relation to race, colonialism, and other topics, see *Decolonizing the Undead*, edited by Champion, Douglas, and Shapiro.

3 The closest correlates to Saunders's use of this term that the editor has found are kaliloze guns, "originally made of wood or human limb bone and are believed to have been used by the Mawiko people (Mbunda, Luvale, Chokwe and Luchazi) against witches [...]. According to Reynolds, the traditional gun has its origin in the precolonial times and the use of gun powder was borrowed from European traders and explorers" (Mufuzi 51, 65).

Holding the leopard bones like a pair of drumsticks, Nedeau squatted before the sand-filled tray. Then he began to strike the sand with the bones, beating out a rhythmic pattern that slid and twisted like a serpent of sound through Henley's mind. While he drummed, he chanted, singing a litany in a language Henley hadn't heard before.

Nervously, Henley kept his eyes on Nedeau. Though the attic was unheated, beads of perspiration were forming on Nedeau's bare chest. Reflected candlelight transformed the droplets into shimmering liquid gems. Henley moved his gaze to the sand in the tray. The yellow grains bounced and shifted to the rhythm of the pounding bones. He could almost see *shapes* appearing in the leaping sand—the shapes of graves opening at midnight....

The din of the drumming and the cacophony of the chant seemed an assault on Henley's sanity, inexorably dragging him back to things he did not want to remember and never wanted to know. Just as he was about to shout at Nedeau to stop, a rending crash surmounted the sound of the rite.

Immediately, the drumming ceased. Nedeau's voice fell silent. He sat stock-still, like an ebony carving, his eyes fixed in a set stare at something Henley could not see.

Then the footsteps came. Footsteps that ascended the stairs at a steady, measured pace. Footsteps that grew louder as the thing that made them slowly approached the door of the attic. Footsteps that rose and fell with a squamous, sucking sound....

The footsteps stopped.

"For God's sake, Theotis," Henley shouted. "*It's here*!"

Nedeau did not move.

The attic door banged inward. Dimly, the light from the floor below illuminated the hulking, indistinct silhouette filling the doorway. The figure moved closer, catching the wavering glimmer of the candles.

Henley screamed.

The *semando* was a grotesque, misshapen thing formed of mephitic grave-mud that oozed with each sickening step it took. But it was not the lurching travesty of a body that bulged Henley's eyes and clove his tongue to the roof of his mouth. It was the face.

Crudely molded and distorted as its features were, Henley had seen them before—in the portrait that had hung over the mantelpiece downstairs. It was the face of his grandfather, Jeroboam Henley....

Blunt, malformed fingers reached clawlike for Henley's throat as the *semando* drew nearer. Henley could not move; sheer horror rooted him to his seat.

"*Theotis!*" he shrieked, as if the sheer sound of his terror could halt the advance of the thing with his grandfather's face.

Then a lithe, shadowy form leaped between Henley and the approaching hell-creature. It was Nedeau, cradling the wooden bowl of *kaliloze* powder in his hands. With a swift, smooth motion, Nedeau flung the bowl's contents full into the face of the *semando*.

For a single, timeless moment, the dust hung like a black miasma, enveloping the head of the *semando*. Then it spread across the death-sending's carcass like a swarm of tiny, voracious insects.

The *semando* halted its advance. Its mouth opened, but no sound issued forth. Then the mud began to slough from its form, pooling viscously on the floorboards. Mixed with the malodorous mire was the animal blood that had lent the *semando* its macabre semblance of life. Only a skeleton remained. Then that, too, collapsed, leaving only a tangle of smeared bits of calcium behind.

"You did it, Theotis!" Henley cried, his voice weak with relief. "You destroyed the thing Gbomi sent to kill me."

"It served its purpose," Nedeau said quietly.

"What do you mean?" Henley asked.

Before Henley could move, Nedeau's hands shot out and enclosed the smaller man's throat in a clasp of steel. Henley struggled with a strength born of desperation, but Nedeau held him easily. He tightened his grip, choking off Henley's outcries. But Henley's betrayed, innocent eyes mirrored the man's final question: *Why*?

Nedeau told him. "I never mentioned much about my family back in Louisiana, Jeremiah. I never told you how we came by our name. 'Nedeau' means 'born of the water' in Creole French. In the Yoruba language of West Africa, the word for 'born of the water' is … 'Gbomi.' Gbomi—*my grandfather*. It is Gbomi who has returned, not Jeroboam Henley. Gbomi is *in me*."

Nedeau's voice was calm and steady, betraying no indication of the effort it took to keep Henley helpless in his grasp. His face was as impassive as a mask.

In a strangled voice, Henley managed to croak, "For … God's sake … Theotis … I'm … your … *friend*!"

Something softened in Nedeau's face then. His eyes blinked; his fingers began to relax.… Then, abruptly, his features contorted. An unholy flame kindled in his eyes. His lips drew back from his teeth in a rictus of sheer hatred. And the voice that issued from Nedeau's throat was not his own. The accent was thick, alien, but the words were as plain as the dates chiseled on a tombstone.

"Hen-lee … now, you die!"

Nedeau's fingers constricted. Henley's eyes popped. His tongue protruded. His cries of pain were crushed in his throat. With an abrupt wrench, Nedeau snapped Jeremiah Henley's neck. When his hands opened, a new corpse dropped to the floor beside another, far older one.

Calmly, Nedeau put on his shirt and coat. Before departing the attic, he overturned the still-burning tapers. For a moment, he watched the flames spread among the musty crates and boxes. Then he hurried down the stairs.

★ ★ ★

The Henley house blazed like a giant pyre against the night sky. Seated in his black sedan, Theotis Nedeau watched the conflagration. He knew the fire would soon be spotted even in this isolated countryside, and the man who had thrown the brick through Henley's window would return before long. By then, Nedeau would be gone, safely and anonymously back across the border while Canadian authorities sorted vainly through the maze of fictitious identification he had provided them.

His face remained expressionless as he remembered an earlier killing … the death in the Gold Coast of a man whose grandfather had sold a *malam* named Gbomi to the captain of a Yankee slave ship so many years ago. The Gold Coast man was innocent … innocent like Jeremiah Henley. Nedeau regretted those deaths.

But there was another man behind the mask of Theotis Nedeau's face … the other who had been there since the day Nedeau participated in a calling-of-the-ancestors rite in the Gold Coast. Though his bones rotted in a secret graveyard in a Louisiana bayou, the spirit of Gbomi had spanned an ocean to join with, and ultimately overwhelm, that of his grandson.

It was Gbomi who taught Nedeau the *malam*'s way[1]: all generations were part of a single continuum, ancestors and descendants all as one. Until the debts of the forebears were paid, they must be borne by the progeny.…

One more death remained to be dealt … that of the grandson of the Louisiana slave-owner who had attempted to steal the spirit of an African *malam*, then slain the *malam* as a sacrifice to a god with an unspeakable name. One more death and perhaps then, the relentless shade of Gbomi would be placated. Perhaps then, only Theotis Nedeau would dwell behind the eyes that now turned from the burning house and began to study a road map of Louisiana.

Gbomi would not allow Theotis Nedeau to weep for his friend.…

1 In the original publication, this reads "It was Gbomi who taught him in the African way."

THE DIGITAL AGE AND ITS DISCONTENTS: 1980s–2000s

William F. Wu (b. 1951)

William F. Wu is an American author noted for his 1992 story collection, *Wong's Lost and Found Emporium and Other Oddities*, his works that are part of the expanded *Foundation* and *Robot* universe, building on Isaac Asimov's original texts, and a series of stories about the character Jack Hong, a hitchhiker who follows a Chinese mythological unicorn around the United States encountering various supernatural figures and learning about Chinese-American history. Wu holds a PhD from the University of Michigan, and has also published the scholarly study *The Yellow Peril: Chinese Americans in American Fiction, 1850–1940* (1982).

Note on the text: First published in *Amazing Stories* (1983), this story would be adapted into a *Twilight Zone* episode in 1985. The version below follows the original publication, which also includes the following biography: "The author was born in Kansas City 31 years ago. His dissertation, at the University of Michigan, was on Chinese-American stereotypes in American popular fiction. He is a war-gamer, now living in Kansas" (107).

"Wong's Lost and Found Emporium" (1983)

THE sharp clicking of high heels echoed in the dark shop. The brisk footsteps on the unpolished wooden floor slowed and became irregular and uncertain as my new visitor saw some of the stuff on the shelves. They always did that.

I was on a different aisle. The shop was very big, though crammed with all kinds of objects to the point where every shelf was crowded and overflowing. Most of the stuff was inanimate, or at least dead. However, many of the beasties still stirred when adequately provoked. The inanimate objects included everything from uncut diamonds to nail-clippers to bunny bladders. Still more of the sealed crates and boxes and bottles contained critters, or other things, that might or might not be counted among the living. I had no idea and didn't care, either. For instance, whoever had hung big wooden crates from the ceiling—and there were plenty, up where they couldn't endanger anybody—must have had a good reason.

The edges of the shop were a little mysterious. I tried not to go too far down any of the aisles except the two big perpendicular corridors that ended in doors to the outside. They formed a cross in the center of the shop. The farther from the middle I went in any direction, the darker the place became, and colder. On a few occasions, I had had to go out to shelf space on the fringe that was mostly empty, and in almost complete darkness. All the edges were like that, except for the four doors at each end of those main corridors.

I didn't dare venture into the real darkness, where nothing was visible. Cold stale air seemed to be all it contained, but I wasn't going to investigate. I also had a suspicion that the shop kept growing of its own accord, outward into that nothingness. I had seen for myself that new stuff spontaneously appeared on all the shelves; but if the shop had been finite in size, it would have been absolutely crammed to the ceiling. Instead, I guessed, it simply extended its aisles and plain wooden shelves outward somehow, always providing just enough new empty space to avoid total chaos. The place was weird enough where I was; I didn't see any need to wander off the edge of the world or something.

I was seeking my destiny in this world, or at least I had been hoping to when I first came in here. My visitor was probably doing the same right now.

I came around the corner into one of the two main corridors, where the light was a little better. For a second, I thought I heard someone in one of the aisles, but that sort of thing happened all the time. Some of the live beings thumped and slithered in their containers occasionally.

My customer was a woman with snow-white hair, slender and well-dressed with a good tan. She wore a peach-colored suit and four gold chains around her neck. One hand with long, peach-colored fingernails clutched a small handbag. She looked like a shrivelled peach in a light snowfall.

"Oh—uh. I'm looking for Mr. Wong, I guess." She smiled cautiously.

"That's me," I said, walking forward briskly. After I had been here a while, I had put my signs on the four doors, saying **Wong's Lost and Found Emporium**.

She looked me over in some surprise; they always seemed to expect a doddering old geezer with a wispy white beard and an opium pipe, muttering senilities to the spirit world. I wore a blue T-shirt, fading Levi's, and Adidas indoor track shoes. After all, I'd only been here a few months, though time was different in here than on the outside. This was that kind of place.

"Oh, I'm sorry." She smiled apologetically, fidgeting now with all ten peach fingernails scratching at her purse.

"The name is Wong," I said casually, "but you can call me Mr. Double-you for short."

She didn't get the joke—they never do.

"Thank you. I, uh, was told that … this is an unusual shop? Where one can find something … she lost?"

"If you lost it, I got it." Like most of the others, she needed more encouragement. I waited for her to ask.

"I mean … well, I suppose this will sound silly, but … I'm not looking for a thing, exactly, not a solid object, I don't suppose you have a … second chance?" She forced herself to laugh, a little, like it was a joke. "Well, no, I'm sorry. I really just need a restroom, and—"

"Of course I have it," I said. "If you lost a chance at something, it's here. Follow me."

I looked around the floor and pointed to the little blue throw rug. "Have to watch out for this. It slips."

She smiled politely, but I could see her shaking with anticipation.

I glanced around the shelves, looking for the little spot of white. "What's your name?" It didn't matter, but asking made me sound official.

"I'm Mrs. Barbara Patricia Whitford and I live here in Boca.[1] Um—I was born in New York in 1926. I grew up ..."

I didn't care. A bit of white light was shining on a shoulder-high shelf across the main corridor from me. "This way," I said, signalling over my shoulder. She shut up and followed me.

As we walked, the light moved ahead of us toward the object she wanted to recover. I had no idea how it worked—I had figured it out by trial and error, or I might say by accident. I had come in here myself looking for something I had lost, but the place had had no one in it. Now, I was waiting for the proprietor, but everyone else who came in thought I was in charge. So I was.

"What kind of chance was it?" I asked over my shoulder, like it was shoe size or something. It might be a long walk.

"Well," she said, just a little breathless behind me. "I always wanted to be an artist—a painter. I didn't get started until fifteen years ago, when I started taking lessons in acrylics. And even oils. I got pretty good, even if I do say so. Several of my paintings sold at art fairs and I was just getting a few exhibited, even. I got discouraged, though. It was so hard to keep going."

The white light turned down another aisle, more cramped and dimly lit than the last. The light was brighter in these shadows, but she couldn't see it. Only I could. I had tested that on earlier customers. Unfortunately, I couldn't see my own.

A shadow shifted in the corner of my eye that was not mine or hers, but I ignored it. If something large was loose in here, it was apparently shy. It was nothing new.

"Six or seven years ago," she continued, "all of my friends were going back to school. It was easier than painting— I went for my Master's; and since I was just going to go, I didn't really have to hurry, or worry about grades. It was the thing to do, and so much easier than painting. Only, I didn't care about it." Her voice caught, and she paused to swallow. "I do care about my painting. Now, well, I just would like to have the chance I missed, when my skills were still sharp and I had more time and business connections. It—I know it sounds small. But it's the only thing I've ever accomplished. And I don't have time to start over."

She started crying.

I nodded. The white light had come to a stop, playing across a big open wooden box on an upper shelf. "Just a moment. I'll get it. It's very important to get exactly the right one, because if you get the wrong object, you're still stuck with it."

She nodded, watching me start to climb up the wooden shelves.

1 Boca Raton, Florida.

"For instance, if I gave you someone else's lost chance to work a slow freighter to Sakhalin Island,[1] why, it would just happen. You'd have to go."

"I would? ... *oh*. Well, be careful." She sniffled. "No, uh, glove cleaner or anything like that.[2] If you know what I mean."

The shelves were dusty and disgusting. My fingers caught cobwebs and brushed against small feathery clumps that were unidentifiable in the shadowy aisle. Tiny feet scurried away from me on the shelves as I climbed, prodding aside old jars with my feet. Faint shuffling noises came from inside some of them.

I finally got my head up to the shelf with the little light. It was now sitting on a transparent cylindrical container inside the wooden box. Inside, ugly brown lumps swirled around in a thick, emerald-green solution.

The box had several similar containers and a lot of miscellaneous junk. I grabbed one of the smaller pieces at random and stuck it in my pants pocket. Then I tucked the swirling green cylinder under one arm and started down.

When I had reached the floor, I held it up. Her eyes grew wide when she saw the liquid spinning inside. "Okay," I said. "When you open this, the contents will evaporate very quickly. You have to breathe in the vapor before it disappears, or the chance is lost forever." I had done this before.

She took it from me, glowing like a half-lit wino.

"You can do it here if you want," I said, "but the light's better in the main corridors."

She nodded and followed me as close as one dog behind another.

We turned along the main corridor, and I walked at a good clip back toward my beat-up steel desk and battered piano stool. They were near the junction of the main corridors. This was her business.

Before I got there, I heard a slight gasp behind me and turned around. She had slipped on the throw rug and as I turned, her slender legs were struggling for balance. Her arms reflexively made a sharp upward movement and her precious transparent cylinder was tossed out to one side.

The woman let out a wail as it sailed away and smashed on the hard floorboards. She clattered after it clumsily in her high heels. When she finally reached it, she bent over and started sniffing around like a bowser at a barbeque.

I got up stiffly and walked over.

"Did I get it? Did I get it?" She whimpered frantically.

"Doubt it," I said, sniffing around. If the stuff had lingered long enough for her to inhale it, I would have smelled some residual scent.

1 An island in Northeast Asia that lies between Russia and Japan.

2 In John Collier's short story "The Chaser" (1940), a man buys an inexpensive love potion from an "old man" in an apartment on Pell Street (in Chinatown in New York, though this isn't made explicit in the story); before selling him the love potion, the old man first tells him about an expensive poison, which is referred to as "glove-cleaner" (14), with the implication that the man will return later for it. Collier's story served as the basis for a 1960 *Twilight Zone* episode of the same title.

"Oh, *no*—I ... uh ... but, but — " She started to cry.

Criers bore me. I had a vague sense that I was expected to be sympathetic, but I had lost that ability. That's what I was here for, in fact.

"Wait a minute," I said, tapping her on the shoulder. I reached into my pocket for the other lost object I had taken from her box. It was a metal ring with four or five keys on it and a leather circle with "BPW" stamped in gold. The keys looked fairly new; I figured she had lost them some time in the last decade or so. "Here," I said. "You lost these, too."

"What?" She looked up between sobs.

I gave her the keys. "I'm glad you came. Have a nice day."

"What?" She stared at the keys. "It was the *only* thing I ever accomplished," she whimpered. "Ever." She turned away, in shock, her wide eyes fixed blankly on her old car keys. "It was my very last chance." She squeaked in a high, tiny voice.

"That way." I took her shoulders and aimed her down the corridor that led to a shopping mall in Florida.

She staggered away, snuffling.

I sat down disgustedly on a nearby stool. My time was almost up. I had to leave soon in order to get any sleep at home and then show up at work tomorrow. Without savings, I couldn't afford to leave my job, even for something as important as this. If the proprietor had been coming back, then he, she, or it would probably have returned by now. The dual passages of time in here and outside meant that I had spent over two months here, and I had only spent one week of sick days and vacation days back in New York, on the other side of one of the doors.

I had even taken my job on a loading dock in Chinatown just to be near this shop. That was why I had moved to New York. When a friend had first told me about this establishment, she had warned me of the trickiest part—the doors could not always be located. Different people could find them at their own times, sometimes. The door in New York appeared, when it did, in the back hall of a small, second-story Chinatown restaurant. Most of the time, the hall ended in two restroom doors. For a select few, though, it occasionally had three, and now the mystic third door bore my sign.

I had checked the spot often; and when I had found the door, I had phoned in immediately for a week off, begging an emergency. It had taken some arguing, but I had managed. The presence of the restaurant had allowed me to stay so long, since I sneaked food out when night fell in New York. Naturally, the shop had a few misplaced refrigerators and other appliances; a few even worked.

Once I left this place, I might not find the door again for years—if ever.

I kicked in annoyance at a random bit of crud on the floor. It unfolded five legs and scurried away under a nearby shelf. Well, I had left a mark; the doors all bore my handmade signs, minor amusement though they were.

At least my stay had been eventful. My first customer after I had figured out how the place worked had been a tall slender Chinese guy from the San Francisco corridor. The door there was in the back of a porno shop. He had been in his fifties and wore a suit that had been in style in 1961, when it was last pressed. Something about him suggested Taiwan.

He had come looking for the respect of his children, which he had of course lost. I found him a box with five frantic mice in it; what he had to do was pet them until they calmed down. However, while he was gingerly poking at them, a boa constrictor glided silently out of the shadows unnoticed. It ate all the mice and then quietly slithered away. The guy got hysterical. I almost pointed out that snakes have to eat, too, but actually I didn't care about the snake, either. I'm strictly neutral.

My youngest visitor had been a little boy, maybe about ten, who came in through the boarded-up gas station in Bosworth, Missouri. It was a one-stoplight town that didn't send me much company. The kid wore jeans and a blue Royals baseball cap. He was looking for a dog whistle he had lost. I found it for him. Nothing happened to him or it. That was okay with me, too.

I sighed and stood up. No one else would be coming in. As I rose, I saw a large shadow out of the corner of my eye and glanced toward it, expecting it to slide away among the shelves as usual. Instead, it stayed where it was. I was looking at a young woman of Asian descent, wrapped up in a long white crocheted shawl. She also wore a denim skirt and striped knee socks.

"You're sickening." She spoke with elegant disgust, in [a] New York accent.

I knew that, but I didn't like hearing it. "You've been here a while, haven't you?"

"I think about two days." She brushed back her hair with one hand. It was cut short and blunt. "You were asleep when I came in."

That was a relief. She didn't belong here any more than I did. On the other hand, she had apparently been watching me.

"Where've you been sleeping?" I asked out of curiosity. On my first day, I had spent several hours locating a sleeping bag.

"I found an air mattress," she said, still angrily. "I just meant to sleep until you woke up, but you had a—a client when I got up. After I saw the way you treated him—and all the rest of them—I decided not to approach you at all. Don't you have any feelings for them? When something goes wrong? You could at least try to help them."

"I don't sabotage anybody. Whatever happens, happens—good or bad or indifferent."

She tossed her short hair, probably less to move it than for the disdain it conveyed. "I can't stand it. Why are you so callous?"

I shrugged. "What do you care? Anyhow, some go away happy."

"*What?*" She looked astonished. "Can't you even understand simple—" She stopped and shook her head. "Maybe you'll understand selfishness. Suppose *I* want what I came for. I can't get any help from you if I have trouble."

"Well, I guess that's logi—"

I stopped when she reached for a big stoppered metal bottle, on the shelf next to her. She heaved it at me, and I only had time to spin around. It hit my shoulder blade, hard, and bounced unharmed to the floor.

I whirled back toward her, ready to grab it and throw it back at her, but she was already striding quickly toward me.

"What's *wrong* with you?" She demanded. "I want to know! Why are you so callous?" She snatched up the metal container from the floor in front of me and held it wrapped in her shawl. "Tell me *now!*" she screamed, right in front of me.

I leaned forward and spoke, glaring into her eyes. "*I* came in here looking for my compassion. I lost it years ago, bit by bit. I lost it when I was eight, and other kids chased me around the playground for no visible reason—and they weren't playing. When I started junior high and got beat up in gym class because the rest of the school was white, like my grade school. When I ran for student congress and had my posters covered with swastikas and **KKK** symbols. And that was *before* I got out into the world on my own. You want to hear about my *adult* life?"

I paused to catch my breath. She backed away from me.

"I've lost more of my compassion every year of my life for every year I can remember, until I don't have any more. Well, it's here, but I can't find it."

She stood speechless in front of me. Letting her have it all at once accomplished that much, at least.

"Maybe you were in the wrong town," she muttered.

"You think I *like* being like this? Hating the memories of my life and not caring what happens to anybody? I said I've lost my compassion, not my conscience."

She walked back and put the metal bottle back in its place on the shelf. "I can find it," she said quietly.

"What?"

"I've been watching you. When you get something for someone, you follow the little white light that appears."

"You can see that?"

"Of course I can—anybody can. You think you're special? We just can't see our own. *I* figured that out."

"Well ... so did I," I said lamely.

"So, I could get your compassion for you."

"Yeah?" I didn't think she would, considering all she'd said.

"Only you have to get what I want, first."

"You don't trust me, remember?"

She smiled smugly. It looked grotesque, as though she hadn't smiled in ages. "I can trust you. Because you know that if you don't give me what I want, I won't give you your compassion. Besides, if all goes well, your lack of compassion won't make any difference."

"Well, yeah. I guess so." I hadn't considered a deal with another customer before. Until now, I had just been waiting for the no-show proprietor, and then given up even on that.

"Well?" she demanded, still with that weird forced smile.

"Uh—yeah, okay." It was my last chance. I glanced around and found her spot of white light behind me on a lower shelf. "This way."

She walked next to me, watching me carefully as the white light led us down the crowded aisle. A large porcelain vase emitted guttural mutterings on an upper shelf as we passed. Two small lizards from the Florida corridor and something resembling a T-bone steak with legs were drinking at a pool of shiny liquid in the middle of the floor. The viscous liquid was oozing slowly out of a cracked green bottle. We stepped over it and kept going.

The light finally stopped on the cork of a long-necked blue bottle at the back of a bottom shelf. I stopped and looked down at it, wondering if this deal had an angle I hadn't figured.

"Well?" She forced herself to smile again. It gave her a sort of tortured visage.

"What is it, anyway?" I tried to sound casual.

"You don't need to know. I know that, too."

"Suppose I don't get it till you tell me."

"I won't tell you. And you won't get what you want."

She couldn't have known I had to leave soon, but she was still my last chance. I would be getting home late as it was. Besides, she was the sort who might really want more compassion in the world.

"Hurry up," she said.

I knelt down and looked at the bottle. She might have guessed what I had focused on; but with all the other junk jammed around it, she couldn't be sure. Well, I knew she had compassion herself, already. She wouldn't want to regain any lost tendencies that were nasty, like cruelty or vengefulness, so I was not in personal danger.

I took the bottle by the long neck and stood up. "It's in here, whatever it is. If it's a material object, you just open the bottle and spill it out. If it's a chance, or a personal trait, you have to uncork the bottle and inhale the fumes as they come out."

She was already taking the bottle from me, carefully in both hands. I backed away as she sank her teeth into the cork and yanked it out with a pop. White vapor issued from the bottle. She started taking deep breaths in through her nose, with her eyes closed.

I backed away, smelling something like rotten lettuce mixed with wet gerbil fur.

She kept on breathing until the vapors ran out. Then she re-corked the bottle and smiled at me, looking relaxed and natural. "Well! You're still sickening, but that was it, all right." She laughed gently. "Wow, that stuff stunk. Smelled like rotting cabbage and wet cat fur, didn't it?"

"Wha—?" I laughed, surprised at her sudden good humor. "It sure did."

"Okay, brown eyes. I see your little spot of light. Follow the swaying rear." She sashayed past me and walked casually down another dark aisle, humming to herself.

At one point, something on a shelf caught her eye and she stopped to giggle at it. It was a large brown and white snake, shoved into a jar of some kind of clear solution. She paused to make a face, imitating the snake's motionless expression. Here, of course, one never knew if a pickled snake was really pickled snake or something else temporarily in that guise. Anyway, she made a funny face and then laughed delightedly. After that, we pushed on.

When she stopped again, she was looking up at a shelf just within her reach. "There it is." She chuckled, without moving to take anything.

"Yeah?" I was suddenly afraid of that laugh.

She looked at me and laughed again.

"What's so funny?"

She shook her head and reached up on tiptoe with both hands. When she came down, she was cradling four sealed containers in her arms. One was a short-necked brown bottle encrusted with dry sand. Two were sealed jars of smoky glass and the last was a locked wooden box engraved with smile faces. She squatted on the floor Asian style and set them down.

"One of these holds your lost compassion." She looked up and laughed. "Guess which one."

My stomach tightened. I could not be sure of getting my compassion back this way. After my general insensitivity to people here, I didn't think I would ever be allowed back in, either.

"We had a deal," I said weakly. "You were going to give it to me."

"I have; it's right here. Besides, you should talk. And remember—if you inhale someone else's lost chance to wrestle an alligator or something, you'll wrestle it." She clapped her hands and laughed.

I stared at her. Maybe I deserved it, but I couldn't figure out what had happened to her. She had been concerned and compassionate before I had given her the long-necked bottle, and she certainly didn't seem angry or self-righteous now. I wondered what she had regained.

"Well?" She giggled at me and stood up. "One of them is it. That's a better chance than you gave anyone."

I looked down at the containers. She had no more idea what was in three of them than I did. "I have no intention of opening any of these," I said.

She shrugged, still grinning. "Have it your way, brown eyes. I'm leaving." She started strolling away.

"Wait."

She turned and walked away backwards, facing me. "What?"

"Uh—" I couldn't think of anything.

"Bye!"

"No—uh, hey, what *did* I give back to you, anyway?"

"Oh!" She laughed. "My sense of humor." She was still backpedaling.

"I'll do it! Wait a minute."

She stopped and folded her arms. "You'll really do it?"

"Come on. Come on back here while I do this." I wasn't sure why I wanted company, but I did.

She came back, grinning. "If you got the guts, brown eyes, you can open 'em all."

I smiled weakly. "They could all be good."

She smirked. "Sure—it's possible."

I looked down at the four containers. The wooden box seemed more likely to hold a tangible object than a lost quality. Though this place had few reliable rules, I decided to leave the box alone. The brown bottle with the short neck had such a heavy layer of sand that its contents were hidden. I knelt down and looked over the two smoky jars.

"Come on, sweetie." She started tapping her foot.

Quickly, before I could reconsider, I grabbed both jars, stood, and smashed them down on the floor. The glass shattered and two small billows of blue-gray smoke curled upward.

She stepped back.

I leaned forward, waited for the smoke to reach me, and inhaled. One strand smelled like charcoal-broiled Kansas City steak; the other, like the inside of a new car. I breathed both in, again and again, until the vapors were gone.

After a moment, I blinked and looked around. "I don't feel any different."

"Sure you do." She smiled. "Just go on as normal, and it'll come clear."

"Okay." I bent down and picked up the box and the bottle. "Where were these? I'll put 'em back. There's a broom—"

"You?" She laughed gaily. "Well, that's something. "You mean you're actually going to straighten up this place?"

"No, I—well. I've been in charge; I suppose I should do something...." I replaced the items where she pointed.

"Integrity."

"What?"

"You've got your integrity back, for one."

"Oh, I don't know...." I looked at her for a moment and then gazed up the dark aisle toward the light from one of the main corridors. "I guess I did lose that, too.... Otherwise, I couldn't have been so cruel to people, even without compassion. They trusted me." I started walking up the aisle.

She followed, watching me closely. "So what are you going to do?"

"I guess I'll stay and run the shop." It just came out naturally. I hadn't even realized I was going to say it. "The ... other thing I got back is kind of minor. For a long time, I used to try to remember the details of a fishing trip in the mountains my family went on, back when I was little. I knew I had a great time, but that was all. Now, all of a sudden, I can remember it completely."

She cocked her head to one side. "Was it still really wonderful?"

I considered my new memories a moment. "Yeah."

"Aw ..." She looked at me, smiling. "I can't help it, brown eyes. I give in. It's in that brown thing, with the sand all over it."

Excitement surged in my chest. "*Thanks!*" I reached up with trembling fingers and snatched it off the shelf.

"Careful—"

I fumbled it away. It hit my shoulder, bounced to the floor, and cracked. It rolled, and before I could bend down to grab it, it was under a bottom shelf. I dropped to the floor and slid my face under the shelf. The cracked bottle was hissing in the darkness as the special vapors escaped. I couldn't smell anything. It was too far from me.

I reached for it with one hand. It was wedged against something and stuck. I could touch it, but I couldn't get enough of a hold to pull it back.

I remained on the floor, inhaling frantically, motionless until the hissing stopped. Then, suddenly feeling heavy all over, I managed to stand up.

"What happened?" She smiled hopefully.

"It's gone," I muttered. "It ... sure was over quick." I hesitated, then added, "Thanks anyhow." Stunned, I eased past her and started walking. I could hear her follow me.

We came out into the main corridor. I picked up the little blue throw rug and hung it on a nearby hook. Then I turned, all the way around, surveying my shop. "Maybe it was no accident."

"You were nervous, that's all—"

"I don't mean that. I mean my finding the door to this place when I most needed it, and staying until ... someone came in to find my stuff."

"You think your new integrity adds up to something, it sounds like."

"My destiny."

She laughed, then tapered off when I looked at her calmly. "You serious?"

I shrugged. "This place is mine. I knew that, somehow, when I put my signs up. And now I owe this shop my best attention."

"With integrity."

I shrugged again. Taking care of the shop and its customers was important; the reasons I felt that way were not.

"I ... think I got news for you, brown eyes."

"I don't want any news." I was still in shock from disappointment. It was justice of a sort, but it wasn't pleasant.

"You have your compassion back. I'm sure of it. You can't help it."

"But you said it was in the bottle I broke—"

"It was, as a separate quality. Only, I think your integrity comes with a little compassion in a package deal. Forces it on you."

I looked up at her, hopeful. "Really?"

"You could try it." She pointed down the Florida corridor. What'shername, the peach-colored former artist lady, had never made it out the door. She was sitting near it, slumped on the floor, an incongruous position for a woman of her age and dignity. The skirt of her suit was smudged and rumpled under her, exposing more of her legs than it was supposed to.

"This is your shop now," said my companion. She put a hand on my shoulder.

I didn't say anything.

"You can't just let a customer sit there, can you?"

"No—not any more. A matter of—integrity."

"In this case, it's the same as compassion. I don't see how you can help her, but if you try—"

"I know how."

"Huh?"

"I lost one chance to help her." I smiled, suddenly understanding the true potential of this place. "If you'll go down the aisles and find it, we can fix up that customer after all."

She winked. "You got it, brown eyes."

Octavia E. Butler (1947–2006)

Octavia E. Butler is one of the most influential science fiction authors of the latter decades of the twentieth century and the early decades of the twenty-first; her works often focus on issues of social power, exploitation, and the necessity of dismantling social hierarchies in favour of more complex, hybrid communities. Butler was the first science fiction author to be awarded the MacArthur "Genius" Fellowship in 1995, and the first Black woman to win the Nebula and Hugo awards, the latter of which includes the Hugo for best short story for "Speech Sounds." Butler's work regularly deals with issues of race and gender, perhaps most famously in her novel *Kindred* (1979). She is the author of multiple series of novels, including the *Patternist* series (which starts with her first-published novel, *Patternmaster* [1976]), the *Xenogenesis* series, and the *Parable* series.

Note on the text: The version used here follows the initial publication in *Isaac Asimov's Science Fiction Magazine* (1983), except for small typographical corrections made in later editions. The original publication includes the following introduction:

> Octavia E. Butler is the author of *Mind of My Mind*, *Patternmaster*, *Kindred*, and *Wild Seed*, and on the basis of these books, she's developed a well-deserved following. Her new novel, *Clay's Ark*, due out in January of 1984, from St. Martin's Press, can only cause her circle of admirers to grow. We're delighted, therefore, to be able to publish one of her rare short stories, and are determined to see more from her. (26)

"Speech Sounds" (1983)

THERE was trouble aboard the Washington Boulevard bus. Rye had expected trouble sooner or later in her journey. She had put off going until loneliness and hopelessness drove her out. She believed she might have one group of relatives left alive—a brother and his two children twenty miles away in Pasadena. That was a day's journey one-way, if she were lucky. The unexpected arrival of the bus as she left her Virginia Road home had seemed to be a piece of luck—until the trouble began.

Two young men were involved in a disagreement of some kind, or, more likely, a misunderstanding. They stood in the aisle, grunting and gesturing at each other, each in his own uncertain "T" stance as the bus lurched over the potholes. The driver seemed to be putting some effort into keeping them off balance. Still, their gestures stopped just short of contact—mock punches, hand-games of intimidation to replace lost curses.

People watched the pair, then looked at each other and made small anxious sounds. Two children whimpered.

Rye sat a few feet behind the disputants and across from the back door. She watched the two carefully, knowing the fight would begin when someone's nerve broke or someone's hand slipped or someone came to the end of his limited ability to communicate. These things could happen any time.

One of them happened as the bus hit an especially large pothole and one man, tall, thin, and sneering, was thrown into his shorter opponent.

Instantly, the shorter man drove his left fist into the disintegrating sneer. He hammered his larger opponent as though he neither had nor needed any weapon other than his left fist. He hit quickly enough, hard enough to batter his opponent down before the taller man could regain his balance or hit back even once.

People screamed or squawked in fear. Those nearby scrambled to get out of the way. Three more young men roared in excitement and gestured wildly. Then, somehow, a second dispute broke out between two of these three—probably because one inadvertently touched or hit the other.

As the second fight scattered frightened passengers, a woman shook the driver's shoulder and grunted as she gestured toward the fighting.

The driver grunted back through bared teeth. Frightened, the woman drew away.

Rye, knowing the methods of bus drivers, braced herself and held on to the crossbar of the seat in front of her. When the driver hit the brakes, she was ready and the combatants were not. They fell over seats and onto screaming passengers, creating even more confusion. At least one more fight started.

The instant the bus came to a full stop, Rye was on her feet, pushing the back door. At the second push, it opened and she jumped out, holding her pack in one arm. Several other passengers followed, but some stayed on the bus. Buses were so rare and irregular now, people rode when they could, no matter what. There might not be another bus today—or tomorrow. People started walking, and if they saw a bus they flagged it down. People making intercity trips like Rye's from Los Angeles to Pasadena made plans to camp out, or risked seeking shelter with locals who might rob or murder them.

The bus did not move, but Rye moved away from it. She intended to wait until the trouble was over and get on again, but if there was shooting, she wanted the protection of a tree. Thus, she was near the curb when a battered, blue Ford on the other side of the street made a U-turn and pulled up in front of the bus. Cars were rare these days—as rare as a severe shortage of fuel and of relatively unimpaired mechanics could make them. Cars that still ran were as likely to be used as weapons as they were to serve as transportation. Thus, when the driver of the Ford beckoned to Rye, she moved away warily. The driver got out—a big man, young, neatly bearded with dark, thick hair. He wore a long overcoat and a look of wariness that matched Rye's. She stood several feet from him, waiting to see what he would do. He looked at the bus, now rocking with the combat inside, then at the small cluster of passengers who had gotten off. Finally he looked at Rye again.

She returned his gaze, very much aware of the old forty-five automatic her jacket concealed. She watched his hands.

He pointed with his left hand toward the bus. The dark-tinted windows prevented him from seeing what was happening inside.

His use of the left hand interested Rye more than his obvious question. Left-handed people tended to be less impaired, more reasonable and comprehending, less driven by frustration, confusion, and anger.

She imitated his gesture, pointing toward the bus with her own left hand, then punching the air with both fists.

The man took off his coat revealing a Los Angeles Police Department uniform complete with baton and service revolver.

Rye took another step back from him. There was no more LAPD, no more *any* large organization, governmental or private. There were neighborhood patrols and armed individuals. That was all.

The man took something from his coat pocket, then threw the coat into the car. Then he gestured Rye back, back toward the rear of the bus. He had something made of plastic in his hand. Rye did not understand what he wanted until he went to the rear door of the bus and beckoned her to stand there. She obeyed mainly out of curiosity. Cop or not, maybe he could do something to stop the stupid fighting.

He walked around the front of the bus, to the street side where the driver's window was open. There, she thought she saw him throw something into the bus. She was still trying to peer through the tinted glass when people began stumbling out the rear door, choking and weeping. Gas.

Rye caught an old woman who would have fallen, lifted two little children down when they were in danger of being knocked down and trampled. She could see the bearded man helping people at the front door. She caught a thin old man shoved out by one of the combatants. Staggered by the old man's weight, she was barely able to get out of the way as the last of the young men pushed his way out. This one, bleeding from nose and mouth, stumbled into another and they grappled blindly, still sobbing from the gas.

The bearded man helped the bus driver out through the front door, though the driver did not seem to appreciate his help. For a moment, Rye thought there would be another fight. The bearded man stepped back and watched the driver gesture threateningly, watched him shout in wordless anger.

The bearded man stood still, made no sound, refused to respond to clearly obscene gestures. The least impaired people tended to do this—stand back unless they were physically threatened and let those with less control scream and jump around. It was as though they felt it beneath them to be as touchy as the less comprehending. This was an attitude of superiority and that was the way people like the bus driver perceived it. Such "superiority" was frequently punished by beatings, even by death. Rye had had close calls of her own. As a result, she never went unarmed. And in this world where the only likely common language was body language, being armed was often enough. She had rarely had to draw her gun or even display it.

The bearded man's revolver was on constant display. Apparently that was enough for the bus driver. The driver spat in disgust, glared at the bearded man for a moment longer, then strode back to his gas-filled bus. He stared at it for a moment, clearly wanting to get in, but the gas was still too strong. Of the windows, only his tiny driver's window actually opened. The front door was open, but the rear door would not stay open unless someone held it. Of course, the air conditioning had failed long ago. The bus would take some time to clear. It was the driver's property, his livelihood. He had pasted old magazine pictures of items he would accept as fare on its sides. Then he would use what he collected to feed his family or to trade. If his bus did not run, he did not eat. On the other hand, if the inside of his bus were torn apart by senseless fighting, he would not eat very well either. He was apparently unable to perceive this. All he could see was that it would be some time before he could use his bus again. He shook his fist at the bearded man and shouted. There seemed to be words in his shout, but Rye could not understand them. She did not know whether this was his fault or hers. She had heard so little coherent human speech for the past three years, she was no longer certain how well she recognized it, no longer certain of the degree of her own impairment.

The bearded man sighed. He glanced toward his car, then beckoned to Rye. He was ready to leave, but he wanted something from her first. No. No, he wanted her to leave with him. Risk getting into his car when, in spite of his uniform, law and order were nothing—not even words any longer.

She shook her head in a universally understood negative, but the man continued to beckon.

She waved him away. He was doing what the less-impaired rarely did—drawing potentially negative attention to another of his kind. People from the bus had begun to look at her.

One of the men who had been fighting tapped another on the arm, then pointed from the bearded man to Rye, and finally held up the first two fingers of his right hand as though giving two thirds of a Boy Scout salute. The gesture was very quick, its meaning obvious even at a distance. She had been grouped with the bearded man. Now what?

The man who had made the gesture started toward her.

She had no idea what she intended, but she stood her ground. The man was half-a-foot taller than she was and perhaps ten years younger. She did not imagine she could outrun him. Nor did she expect anyone to help her if she needed help. The people around her were all strangers.

She gestured once—a clear indication to the man to stop. She did not intend to repeat the gesture. Fortunately, the man obeyed. He gestured obscenely and several other men laughed. Loss of verbal language had spawned a whole new set of obscene gestures. The man, with stark simplicity, had accused her of sex with the bearded man and had suggested she accommodate the other men present—beginning with him.

Rye watched him wearily. People might very well stand by and watch if he tried to rape her. They would also stand and watch her shoot him. Would he push things that far?

He did not. After a series of obscene gestures that brought him no closer to her, he turned contemptuously and walked away.

And the bearded man still waited. He had removed his service revolver, holster and all. He beckoned again, both hands empty. No doubt his gun was in the car and within easy reach, but his taking it off impressed her. Maybe he was all right. Maybe he was just alone. She had been alone herself for three years. The illness had stripped her, killing her children one by one, killing her husband, her sister, her parents....

The illness, if it was an illness, had cut even the living off from one another. As it swept over the country, people hardly had time to lay blame on the Soviets (though they were falling silent along with the rest of the world), on a new virus, a new pollutant, radiation, divine retribution.... The illness was strokeswift in the way it cut people down and strokelike in some of its effects. But it was highly specific. Language was always lost or severely impaired. It was never regained. Often there was also paralysis, intellectual impairment, death.

Rye walked toward the bearded man, ignoring the whistling and applauding of two of the young men and their thumbs-up signs to the bearded man. If he had smiled at them or acknowledged them in any way, she would almost certainly have changed her mind. If she had let herself think of the possible deadly consequences of getting into a stranger's car, she would have changed her mind. Instead, she thought of the man who lived across the street from her. He rarely washed since his bout with the illness. And he had gotten into the habit of urinating wherever he happened to be. He had two women already—one tending each of his large gardens. They put up with him in exchange for his protection. He had made it clear that he wanted Rye to become his third woman.

She got into the car and the bearded man shut the door. She watched as he walked around to the driver's door—watched for his sake because his gun was on the seat beside her. And the bus driver and a pair of young men had come a few steps closer. They did nothing, though, until the bearded man was in the car. Then one of them threw a rock. Others followed his example, and as the car drove away, several rocks bounced off it harmlessly.

When the bus was some distance behind them. Rye wiped sweat from her forehead and longed to relax. The bus would have taken her more than halfway to Pasadena. She would have had only ten miles to walk. She wondered how far she would have to walk now—and wondered if walking a long distance would be her only problem.

At Figuroa and Washington[1] where the bus normally made a left turn, the

1 The corner of Figueroa Street and Washington Boulevard in downtown Los Angeles.

bearded man stopped, looked at her, and indicated that she should choose a direction. When she directed him left and he actually turned left, she began to relax. If he was willing to go where she directed, perhaps he was safe.

As they passed blocks of burned, abandoned buildings, empty lots, and wrecked or stripped cars, he slipped a gold chain over his head and handed it to her. The pendant attached to it was a smooth, glassy, black rock. Obsidian. His name might be Rock or Peter or Black, but she decided to think of him as Obsidian. Even her sometimes useless memory would retain a name like Obsidian.

She handed him her own name symbol—a pin in the shape of a large golden stalk of wheat. She had bought it long before the illness and the silence began. Now she wore it, thinking it was as close as she was likely to come to Rye. People like Obsidian who had not known her before probably thought of her as Wheat. Not that it mattered. She would never hear her name spoken again.

Obsidian handed her pin back to her. He caught her hand as she reached for it and rubbed his thumb over her calluses.

He stopped at First Street and asked which way again. Then, after turning right as she had indicated, he parked near the Music Center.[1] There, he took a folded paper from the dashboard and unfolded it. Rye recognized it as a street map, though the writing on it meant nothing to her. He flattened the map, took her hand again, and put her index finger on one spot. He touched her, touched himself, pointed toward the floor. In effect, "We are here." She knew he wanted to know where she was going. She wanted to tell him, but she shook her head sadly. She had lost reading and writing. That was her most serious impairment and her most painful. She had taught history at UCLA. She had done freelance writing. Now she could not even read her own manuscripts. She had a house full of books that she could neither read nor bring herself to use as fuel. And she had a memory that would not bring back to her much of what she had read before.

She stared at the map, trying to calculate. She had been born in Pasadena, had lived for fifteen years in Los Angeles. Now she was near L.A. Civic Center. She knew the relative positions of the two cities, knew streets, directions, even knew to stay away from freeways which might be blocked by wrecked cars and destroyed overpasses. She ought to know how to point out Pasadena even though she could not recognize the word.

Hesitantly, she placed her hand over a pale orange patch in the upper right corner of the map. That should be right. Pasadena.

Obsidian lifted her hand and looked under it, then folded the map and put it back on the dashboard. He could read, she realized belatedly. He could probably write, too. Abruptly, she hated him—deep, bitter hatred. What did

---

1 Originally opened in 1964, the Music Center in Los Angeles "was dedicated as 'A Living Memorial to Peace.'" It was expanded in both 1967 and, after this story's publication, 2003 ("History of the Music Center").

literacy mean to him—a grown man who played cops and robbers? But he was literate and she was not. She never would be. She felt sick to her stomach with hatred, frustration, and jealousy. And only a few inches from her hand was a loaded gun.

She held herself still, staring at him, almost seeing his blood. But her rage crested and ebbed and she did nothing.

Obsidian reached for her hand with hesitant familiarity. She looked at him. Her face had already revealed too much. No person still living in what was left of human society could fail to recognize that expression, that jealousy.

She closed her eyes wearily, drew a deep breath. She had experienced longing for the past, hatred of the present, growing hopelessness, purposelessness, but she had never experienced such a powerful urge to kill another person. She had left her home, finally, because she had come near to killing herself. She had found no reason to stay alive. Perhaps that was why she had gotten into Obsidian's car. She had never before done such a thing.

He touched her mouth and made chatter motions with thumb and fingers. Could she speak?

She nodded and watched his milder envy come and go. Now both had admitted what it was not safe to admit, and there had been no violence. He tapped his mouth and forehead and shook his head. He did not speak or comprehend spoken language. The illness had played with them, taking away, she suspected, what each valued most.

She plucked at his sleeve, wondering why he had decided on his own to keep the LAPD alive with what he had left. He was sane enough otherwise. Why wasn't he at home raising corn, rabbits, and children? But she did not know how to ask. Then he put his hand on her thigh and she had another question to deal with.

She shook her head. Disease, pregnancy, helpless, solitary agony … no.

He massaged her thigh gently and smiled in obvious disbelief.

No one had touched her for three years. She had not wanted anyone to touch her. What kind of world was this to chance bringing a child into even if the father were willing to stay and help raise it? It was too bad, though. Obsidian could not know how attractive he was to her—young, probably younger than she was, clean, asking for what he wanted rather than demanding it. But none of that mattered. What were a few moments of pleasure measured against a lifetime of consequences?

He pulled her closer to him and for a moment she let herself enjoy the closeness. He smelled good—male and good. She pulled away reluctantly.

He sighed, reached toward the glove compartment. She stiffened, not knowing what to expect, but all he took out was a small box. The writing on it meant nothing to her. She did not understand until he broke the seal, opened the box, and took out a condom. He looked at her and she first looked away in surprise. Then she giggled. She could not remember when she had last giggled.

He grinned, gestured toward the back seat, and she laughed aloud. Even in her teens, she had disliked back seats of cars. But she looked around at the empty streets and ruined buildings, then she got out and into the back seat. He let her put the condom on him, then seemed surprised at her eagerness.

Sometime later, they sat together, covered by his coat, unwilling to become clothed near-strangers again just yet. He made rock-the-baby gestures and looked questioningly at her.

She swallowed, shook her head. She did not know how to tell him her children were dead.

He took her hand and drew a cross in it with his index finger, then made his baby-rocking gesture again.

She nodded, held up three fingers, then turned away, trying to shut out a sudden flood of memories. She had told herself that the children growing up now were to be pitied. They would run through the downtown canyons with no real memory of what the buildings had been or even how they had come to be. Today's children gathered books as well as wood to be burned as fuel. They ran through the streets chasing each other and hooting like chimpanzees. They had no future. They were now all they would ever be.

He put his hand on her shoulder and she turned suddenly, fumbling for his small box, then urging him to make love to her again. He could give her forgetfulness and pleasure. Until now, nothing had been able to do that. Until now, every day had brought her closer to the time when she would do what she had left home to avoid doing: putting her gun in her mouth and pulling the trigger.

She asked Obsidian if he would come home with her, stay with her.

He looked surprised and pleased once he understood. But he did not answer at once. Finally he shook his head as she had feared he might. He was probably having too much fun playing cops and robbers and picking up women.

She dressed in silent disappointment, unable to feel any anger toward him. Perhaps he already had a wife and a home. That was likely. The illness had been harder on men than on women—had killed more men, had left male survivors more severely impaired. Men like Obsidian were rare. Women either settled for less or stayed alone. If they found an Obsidian, they did what they could to keep him. Rye suspected he had someone younger, prettier keeping him.

He touched her while she was strapping her gun on and asked with a complicated series of gestures whether it was loaded.

She nodded grimly.

He patted her arm.

She asked once more if he would come home with her, this time using a different series of gestures. He had seemed hesitant. Perhaps he could be courted.

He got out and into the front seat without responding.

She took her place in front again, watching him. Now he plucked at his uniform and looked at her. She thought she was being asked something, but did not know what it was.

He took off his badge, tapped it with one finger, then tapped his chest. Of course.

She took the badge from his hand and pinned her wheat stalk to it. If playing cops and robbers was his only insanity, let him play. She would take him, uniform and all. It occurred to her that she might eventually lose him to someone he would meet as he had met her. But she would have him for a while.

He took the street map down again, tapped it, pointed vaguely northeast toward Pasadena, then looked at her.

She shrugged, tapped his shoulder then her own, and held up her index and second fingers tight together, just to be sure.

He grasped the two fingers and nodded. He was with her.

She took the map from him and threw it onto the dashboard. She pointed back southwest—back toward home. Now she did not have to go to Pasadena. Now she could go on having a brother there and two nephews—three right-handed males. Now she did not have to find out for certain whether she was as alone as she feared. Now she was not alone.

Obsidian took Hill Street south, then Washington west, and she leaned back, wondering what it would be like to have someone again. With what she had scavenged, what she had preserved, and what she grew, there was easily enough food for him. There was certainly room enough in a four-bedroom house. He could move his possessions in. Best of all, the animal across the street would pull back and possibly not force her to kill him.

Obsidian had drawn her closer to him and she had put her head on his shoulder when suddenly he braked hard, almost throwing her off the seat. Out of the corner of her eye, she saw that someone had run across the street in front of the car. One car on the street and someone had to run in front of it.

Straightening up. Rye saw that the runner was a woman, fleeing from an old frame house to a boarded-up storefront. She ran silently, but the man who followed her a moment later shouted what sounded like garbled words as he ran. He had something in his hand. Not a gun. A knife, perhaps.

The woman tried a door, found it locked, looked around desperately, finally snatched up a fragment of glass broken from the storefront window. With this she turned to face her pursuer. Rye thought she would be more likely to cut her own hand than to hurt anyone else with the glass.

Obsidian jumped from the car, shouting. It was the first time Rye had heard his voice—deep and hoarse from disuse. He made the same sound over and over the way some speechless people did, "Da, da, da!"

Rye got out of the car as Obsidian ran toward the couple. He had drawn his gun. Fearful, she drew her own and released the safety. She looked around to see who else might be attracted to the scene. She saw the man glance at Obsidian, then suddenly lunge at the woman. The woman jabbed his face with her glass, but he caught her arm and managed to stab her twice before Obsidian shot him.

The man doubled, then toppled, clutching his abdomen. Obsidian shouted, then gestured Rye over to help the woman.

Rye moved to the woman's side, remembering that she had little more than bandages and antiseptic in her pack. But the woman was beyond help. She had been stabbed with a long, slender, boning knife.

She touched Obsidian to let him know the woman was dead. He had bent to check the wounded man who lay still and also seemed dead. But as Obsidian looked around to see what Rye wanted, the man opened his eyes. Face contorted, he seized Obsidian's just-holstered revolver and fired. The bullet caught Obsidian in the temple and he collapsed.

It happened just that simply, just that fast. An instant later, Rye shot the wounded man as he was turning the gun on her.

And Rye was alone—with three corpses.

She knelt beside Obsidian, dry-eyed, frowning, trying to understand why everything had suddenly changed. Obsidian was gone. He had died and left her—like everyone else.

Two very small children came out of the house from which the man and woman had run—a boy and girl perhaps three years old. Holding hands, they crossed the street toward Rye. They stared at her, then edged past her and went to the dead woman. The girl shook the woman's arm as though trying to wake her.

This was too much. Rye got up, feeling sick to her stomach with grief and anger. If the children began to cry, she thought she would vomit.

They were on their own, those two kids. They were old enough to scavenge. She did not need any more grief. She did not need a stranger's children who would grow up to be hairless chimps.

She went back to the car. She could drive home, at least. She remembered how to drive.

The thought that Obsidian should be buried occurred to her before she reached the car, and she did vomit.

She had found and lost the man so quickly. It was as though she had been snatched from comfort and security and given a sudden, inexplicable beating. Her head would not clear. She could not think.

Somehow, she made herself go back to him, look at him. She found herself on her knees beside him with no memory of having knelt. She stroked his face, his beard. One of the children made a noise and she looked at them, at the woman who was probably their mother. The children looked back at her, obviously frightened. Perhaps it was their fear that reached her finally.

She had been about to drive away and leave them. She had almost done it, almost left two toddlers to die. Surely there had been enough dying. She would have to take the children home with her. She would not be able to live with any other decision. She looked around for a place to bury three bodies.

Or two. She wondered if the murderer were the children's father. Before the silence, the police had always said some of the most dangerous calls they went out on were domestic disturbance calls. Obsidian should have known that—not that the knowledge would have kept him in the car. It would not have held her back either. She could not have watched the woman murdered and done nothing.

She dragged Obsidian toward the car. She had nothing to dig with here, and no one to guard for her while she dug. Better to take the bodies with her and bury them next to her husband and her children. Obsidian would come home with her after all.

When she had gotten him onto the floor in the back, she returned for the woman. The little girl, thin, dirty, solemn, stood up and unknowingly gave Rye a gift. As Rye began to drag the woman by her arms, the little girl screamed, "No!"

Rye dropped the woman and stared at the girl.

"No!" the girl repeated. She came to stand beside the woman. "Go away!" she told Rye.

"Don't talk," the little boy said to her. There was no blurring or confusing of sounds. Both children had spoken and Rye had understood. The boy looked at the dead murderer and moved farther from him. He took the girl's hand. "Be quiet," he whispered.

Fluent speech! Had the woman died because she could talk and had taught her children to talk? Had she been killed by a husband's festering anger or by a stranger's jealous rage? And the children … they must have been born after the silence. Had the disease run its course, then? Or were these children simply immune? Certainly they had had time to fall sick and silent. Rye's mind leaped ahead. What if children of three or fewer years were safe and able to learn language? What if all they needed were teachers? Teachers and protectors.

Rye glanced at the dead murderer. To her shame, she thought she could understand some of the passions that must have driven him, whoever he was. Anger, frustration, hopelessness, insane jealousy … how many more of him were there—people willing to destroy what they could not have?

Obsidian had been the protector, had chosen that role for who knew what reason. Perhaps putting on an obsolete uniform and patrolling the empty streets had been what he did instead of putting a gun into his mouth. And now that there was something worth protecting, he was gone.

She had been a teacher. A good one. She had been a protector, too, though only of herself. She had kept herself alive when she had no reason to live. If the illness let these children alone, she could keep them alive.

Somehow she lifted the dead woman into her arms and placed her on the back seat of the car. The children began to cry, but she knelt on the broken pavement and whispered to them, fearful of frightening them with the harshness of her long unused voice.

"It's all right," she told them. "You're going with us, too. Come on." She lifted them both, one in each arm. They were so light. Had they been getting enough to eat?

The boy covered her mouth with his hand, but she moved her face away. "It's all right for me to talk," she told him. "As long as no one's around, it's all right." She put the boy down on the front seat of the car and he moved over without being told to, to make room for the girl. When they were both in the car Rye leaned against the window, looking at them, seeing that they were less afraid now, that they watched her with at least as much curiosity as fear.

"I'm Valerie Rye," she said, savoring the words. "It's all right for you to talk to me."

Pat Cadigan (b. 1953)

Pat Cadigan is a multiple-award-winning SF and Fantasy author and editor. Born in the US and currently living in the UK, Cadigan is best known for her short stories and early cyberpunk work. She has written novelizations for several films, and her work, "The Girl-Thing Who Went Out for Sushi" (2012), received a Hugo Award for Best Novelette.

Note on the text: A story that explores both sexuality and spirituality through cyberpunk's focus on what William Gibson has called "The Street" ("Rocket Radio" 10), "Angel" won the Locus award in 1988, was a finalist for the Hugo, and was nominated for both the Nebula and World Fantasy Awards. The original publication in Isaac Asimov's *Science Fiction Magazine* (May 1987), which is followed here, includes this introduction: "The author's first novel, *Mindplayers*, is due out from Bantam sometime this fall. It is based on her Pathosfinder stories—one of which, 'Nearly Departed,' appeared in our June 1983 issue" (96).

"Angel" (1987)

STAND with me awhile, Angel, I said, and Angel said he'd do that. Angel was good to me that way, good to have with you on a cold night and nowhere to go. We stood on the street corner together and watched the cars going by and the people and all. The streets were lit up like Christmas, streetlights, store lights, marquees over the all-night movie houses and bookstores blinking and flashing; shank of the evening in east midtown. Angel was getting used to things here and getting used to how I did, nights. Standing outside, because what else are you going to do. He was *my* Angel now, had been since that other cold night when I'd been going home, because where are you going to go, and I'd found him and took him with me. It's good to have someone to take with you, someone to look after. Angel knew that. He started looking after me, too.

Like now. We were standing there awhile and I was looking around at nothing and everything, the cars cruising past, some of them stopping now and again for the hookers posing by the curb, and then I saw it, out of the corner of my eye. Stuff coming out of the Angel, shiny like sparks but flowing like liquid. Silver fireworks. I turned and looked all the way at him and it was gone. And he turned and gave a little grin like he was embarrassed I'd seen. Nobody else saw it, though; not the short guy who paused next to the Angel before crossing the street against the light, not the skinny hype looking to sell the boom-box he was carrying on his shoulder, not the homeboy strutting past us with both his girlfriends on his arms, nobody but me.

The Angel said. Hungry?

Sure, I said. I'm hungry.

Angel looked past me. Okay, he said. I looked, too, and here they came, three leather boys, visor caps, belts, boots, keyrings. On the cruise together. Scary stuff, even though you know it's not looking for you.

I said, them? *Them?*

Angel didn't answer. One went by, then the second, and the Angel stopped the third by taking hold of his arm.

Hi.

The guy nodded. His head was shaved. I could see a little grey-black stubble under his cap. No eyebrows, disinterested eyes. The eyes were because of the Angel.

I could use a little money, the Angel said. My friend and I are hungry.

The guy put his hand in his pocket and wiggled out some bills, offering them to the Angel. The Angel selected a twenty and closed the guy's hand around the rest.

This will be enough, thank you.

The guy put his money away and waited.

I hope you have a good night, said the Angel.

The guy nodded and walked on, going across the street to where his two friends were waiting on the next corner. Nobody found anything weird about it.

Angel was grinning at me. Sometimes he was *the* Angel, when he was doing something, sometimes he was Angel, when he was just with me. Now he was Angel again. We went up the street to the luncheonette and got a seat by the front window so we could still watch the street while we ate.

Cheeseburger and fries, I said without bothering to look at the plastic-covered menus lying on top of the napkin holder. The Angel nodded.

Thought so, he said. I'll have the same, then.

The waitress came over with a little tiny pad to take our order. I cleared my throat. It seemed like I hadn't used my voice in a hundred years. "Two cheeseburgers and two fries," I said, "and two cups of—" I looked up at her and froze. She had no face. Like, *nothing*, blank from hairline to chin, soft little dents where the eyes and nose and mouth would have been. Under the table, the Angel kicked me, but gentle.

"And two cups of coffee," I said.

She didn't say anything—how could she?—as she wrote down the order and then walked away again. All shaken up, I looked at the Angel, but he was calm like always.

She's a new arrival, Angel told me and leaned back in his chair. Not enough time to grow a face.

But how can she breathe? I said.

Through her pores. She doesn't need much air yet.

Yah, but what about—like, I mean, don't other people *notice* that she's got nothing there?

No. It's not such an extraordinary condition. The only reason you notice is because you're with me. Certain things have rubbed off on you. But no one else notices. When they look at her, they see whatever face they expect someone like her to have. And eventually, she'll have it.

But you have a face, I said. You've always had a face.

I'm different, said the Angel.

You sure are, I thought, looking at him. Angel had a beautiful face. That wasn't why I took him home that night, just because he had a beautiful face—I left all that behind a long time ago—but it was there, his beauty. The way you think of a man being beautiful, good clean lines, deep-set eyes, ageless. About the only way you could describe him—look away and you'd forget everything except that he was beautiful. But he did have a face. He *did*.

Angel shifted in the chair—these were like somebody's old kitchen chairs, you couldn't get too comfortable in them—and shook his head, because he knew I was thinking troubled thoughts. Sometimes you could think something and it wouldn't be troubled and later you'd think the same thing and it would be troubled. The Angel didn't like me to be troubled about him.

Do you have a cigarette? he asked.

I think so.

I patted my jacket and came up with most of a pack that I handed over to him. The Angel lit up and amused us both by having the smoke come out his ears and trickle out of his eyes like ghostly tears. I felt my own eyes watering for his; I wiped them and there was that *stuff* again, but from me now. I was crying silver fireworks. I flicked them on the table and watched them puff out and vanish.

Does this mean I'm getting to *be* you, now? I asked.

Angel shook his head. Smoke wafted out of his hair. Just things rubbing off on you. Because we've been together and you're—susceptible. But they're different for you.

Then the waitress brought our food and we went on to another sequence, as the Angel would say. She still had no face but I guess she could see well enough because she put all the plates down just where you'd think they were supposed to go and left the tiny little check in the middle of the table.

Is she—I mean, did you know her, from where you—

Angel gave his head a brief little shake. No. She's from somewhere else. Not one of my—people. He pushed the cheeseburger and fries in front of him over to my side of the table. That was the way it was done; I did all the eating and somehow it worked out.

I picked up my cheeseburger and I was bringing it up to my mouth when my eyes got all funny and I saw it coming up like a whole *series* of cheeseburgers, whoom-whoom-whoom, trick photography, only for real. I closed my eyes and jammed the cheeseburger into my mouth, holding it there, waiting for all the other cheeseburgers to catch up with it.

You'll be okay, said the Angel. Steady, now.

I said with my mouth full, That was—that was *weird*. Will I ever get used to this?

I doubt it. But I'll do what I can to help you.

Yah, well, the Angel *would* know. Stuff rubbing off on me, he could feel it better than I could. He was the one it was rubbing off *from*.

I had put away my cheeseburger and half of Angel's and was working on the french fries for both of us when I noticed he was looking out the window with this hard, tight expression on his face.

Something? I asked him.

Keep eating, he said.

I kept eating, but I kept watching, too. The Angel was staring at a big blue car parked at the curb right outside the diner. It was silvery blue, one of those lots-of-money models and there was a woman kind of leaning across from the driver's side to look out the passenger window. She was beautiful in that lots-of-money way, tawny hair swept back from her face, and even from here I could see she had turquoise eyes. Really beautiful woman. I almost felt like crying. I mean, jeez, how did people get that way and me too harmless to live.

But the Angel wasn't one bit glad to see her. I knew he didn't want me to say anything, but I couldn't help it.

Who is she?

Keep eating, Angel said. We need the protein, what little there is.

I ate and watched the woman and the Angel watch each other and it was getting very—I don't know, very *something* between them, even through the glass. Then a cop car pulled up next to her and I knew they were telling her to move it along. She moved it along.

Angel sagged against the back of his chair and lit another cigarette, smoking it in the regular, unremarkable way.

What are we going to do tonight? I asked the Angel as we left the restaurant.

Keep out of harm's way, Angel said, which was a new answer. Most nights we spent just kind of going around soaking everything up. The Angel soaked it up, mostly. I got some of it along with him, but not the same way he did. It was different for him. Sometimes he would use me like a kind of filter. Other times he took it direct. There'd been the big car accident one night, right at my usual corner, a big old Buick running a red light smack into somebody's nice Lincoln. The Angel had had to take it direct because I couldn't handle that kind of stuff. I didn't know how the Angel could take it, but he could. It carried him for days afterwards, too. I only had to eat for myself.

It's the intensity, little friend, he'd told me, as though that were supposed to explain it.

It's the intensity, not whether it's good or bad. The universe doesn't know good or bad, only less or more. Most of you have a bad time reconciling this. *You* have a bad time with it, little friend, but you get through better than other people. Maybe because of the way you are. You got squeezed out of a lot, you haven't had much of a chance at life. You're as much an exile as I am, only in your own land.

That may have been true, but at least I *belonged* here, so that part was easier for me. But I didn't say that to the Angel. I think he liked to think he could do as well or better than me at living—I mean, I couldn't just look at some leather boy and get him to cough up a twenty dollar bill. Cough up a fist in the face or worse, was more like it.

Tonight, though, he wasn't doing so good, and it was that woman in the car. She'd thrown him out of step, kind of.

Don't think about her, the Angel said, just out of nowhere. Don't think about her any more.

Okay, I said, feeling creepy because it was creepy when the Angel got a glimpse of my head. And then, of course, I couldn't think about anything else hardly.

Do you want to go home? I asked him.

No. I can't stay in now. We'll do the best we can tonight, but I'll have to be very careful about the tricks. They take so much out of me, and if we're keeping out of harm's way, I might not be able to make up for a lot of it.

It's okay, I said. I ate. I don't need anything else tonight, you don't have to do any more.

Angel got that look on his face, the one where I knew he wanted to give me things, like feelings I couldn't have any more. Generous, the Angel was. But I didn't need those feelings, not like other people seem to. For awhile, it was like the Angel didn't understand that, but he let me be.

Little friend, he said, and almost touched me. The Angel didn't touch a lot. I could touch him and that would be okay, but if *he* touched somebody, he couldn't help *doing* something to them, like the trade that had given us the money. That had been deliberate. If the trade had touched the Angel first, it would have been different, nothing would have happened unless the Angel touched him back. All touch meant something to the Angel that I didn't understand. There was touching without touching, too. Like things rubbing off on me. And sometimes, when I did touch the Angel, I'd get the feeling that it was maybe more his idea than mine, but I didn't mind that. How many people were going their whole lives never being able to touch an Angel?

We walked together and all around us the street was really coming to life. It was getting colder, too. I tried to make my jacket cover more. The Angel wasn't feeling it. Most of the time hot and cold didn't mean much to him. We saw the three rough trade guys again. The one Angel had gotten the money from was getting into a car. The other two watched it drive away and then walked on. I looked over at the Angel.

Because we took his twenty, I said.

Even if we hadn't, Angel said.

So we went along, the Angel and me, and I could feel how different it was tonight than it was all the other nights we'd walked or stood together. The Angel was kind of pulled back into himself and seemed to be keeping a check on me, pushing us closer together. I was getting more of those fireworks out of the corners of my eyes, but when I'd turn my head to look, they'd vanish. It reminded me of the night I'd found the Angel standing on my corner all by himself in pain. The Angel told me later that was real talent, knowing he was in pain. I never thought of myself as any too talented, but the way everyone else had been just ignoring him, I guess I must have had something to see him after all.

The Angel stopped us several feet down from an all-night bookstore. Don't look, he said. Watch the traffic or stare at your feet, but don't look or it won't happen.

There wasn't anything to see right then, but I didn't look anyway. That was the way it was sometimes, the Angel telling me it made a difference whether I was watching something or not, something about the other people being conscious of me being conscious of them. I didn't understand, but I knew Angel was usually right. So I was watching traffic when the guy came out of the bookstore and got his head punched.

I could almost see it out of the corner of my eye. A lot of movement, arms and legs flying and grunty noises. Other people stopped to look but I kept my eyes on the traffic, some of which was slowing up so they could check out the fight. Next to me, the Angel was stiff all over. Taking it in, what he called the expenditure of emotional kinetic energy. No right, no wrong, little friend, he'd told me. Just energy, like the rest of the universe.

So he took it in and I *felt* him taking it in, and while I was feeling it, a kind of silver fog started creeping around my eyeballs and I was in two places at once. I was watching the traffic and I was in the Angel watching the fight and feeling him charge up like a big battery.

It felt like nothing I'd ever felt before. These two guys slugging it out—well, one guy doing all the slugging and the other skittering around trying to get out from under the fists and having his head punched but good, and the Angel drinking it like he was sipping at an empty cup and somehow getting it to have something in it after all. Deep inside him, whatever made the Angel go was getting a little stronger.

I kind of swung back and forth between him and me, or swayed might be more like it was. I wondered about it, because the Angel wasn't touching me. I really was getting to *be* him, I thought; Angel picked that up and put the thought away to answer later. It was like I was traveling by the fog, being one of us and then the other, for a long time, it seemed, and then after awhile I was more me than him again, and some of the fog cleared away.

And there was that car, pointed the other way this time, and the woman was climbing out of it with this big weird smile on her face, as though she'd won something. She waved at the Angel to come to her.

Bang went the connection between us dead and the Angel shot past me, running away from the car. I went after him. I caught a glimpse of her jumping back into the car and yanking at the gear shift.

Angel wasn't much of a runner. Something funny about his knees. We'd gone maybe a hundred feet when he started wobbling and I could hear him pant. He cut across a Park & Lock that was dark and mostly empty. It was back-to-back with some kind of private parking lot and the fences for each one tried to mark off the same narrow strip of lumpy pavement. They were easy to climb but Angel was too panicked. He just *went* through them before he even thought about it; I knew that because if he'd been thinking, he'd have wanted to save what he'd just charged up with for when he really needed it bad enough.

I had to haul myself over the fences in the usual way, and when he heard me rattling on the saggy chainlink, he stopped and looked back.

Go, I told him. Don't wait on me!

He shook his head sadly. Little friend, I'm a fool. I could stand to learn from you a little more.

Don't stand, run! I got over the fences and caught up with him. Let's go! I yanked his sleeve as I slogged past and he followed at a clumsy trot.

Have to hide somewhere, he said, camouflage ourselves with people.

I shook my head, thinking we could just run maybe four more blocks and we'd be at the freeway overpass. Below it were the butt-ends of old roads closed off when the freeway had been built. You could hide there the rest of your life and no one would find you. But Angel made me turn right and go down a block to this rundown crack-in-the-wall called Stan's Jigger. I'd never been in there—I'd never made it a practice to go into bars—but the Angel was pushing too hard to argue.

Inside it was smelly and dark and not too happy. The Angel and I went down to the end of the bar and stood under a blood-red light while he searched his pockets for money.

Enough for one drink apiece, he said.

I don't want anything.

You can have soda or something.

The Angel ordered from the bartender, who was suspicious. This was a place for regulars and nobody else, and certainly nobody else like me or the Angel. The Angel knew that even stronger than I did but he just stood and pretended to sip his drink without looking at me. He was all pulled into himself and I was hovering around the edges. I knew he was still pretty panicked and trying to figure out what he could do next. As close as I was, if he had to get real far away, he was going to have a problem and so was I. He'd have to tow me along with him and that wasn't the most practical thing to do.

Maybe he was sorry now he'd let me take him home. But he'd been so weak then, and now with all the filtering and stuff I'd done for him he couldn't just cut me off without a lot of pain.

I was trying to figure out what I could do for him now when the bartender came back and gave us a look that meant order or get out, and he'd have liked it better if we got out. So would everyone else there. The few other people standing at the bar weren't looking at us, but they knew right where we were, like a sore spot. It wasn't hard to figure out what they thought about us, either, maybe because of me or because of the Angel's beautiful face.

We got to leave, I said to the Angel but he had it in his head this was good camouflage. There wasn't enough money for two more drinks so he smiled at the bartender and slid his hand across the bar and put it on top of the bartender's. It was tricky doing it this way; bartenders and waitresses took more persuading because it wasn't normal for them just to give you something.

The bartender looked at the Angel with his eyes half closed. He seemed to be thinking it over. But the Angel had just blown a lot going through the fence instead of climbing over it and the fear was scuttling his concentration and I just knew that it wouldn't work. And maybe my knowing that didn't help, either.

The bartender's free hand dipped down below the bar and came up with a small club. "Faggot!" he roared and caught Angel just over the ear. Angel slammed into me and we both crashed to the floor. Plenty of emotional kinetic energy in here, I thought dimly as the guys standing at the bar fell on us, and then I didn't think anything more as I curled up into a ball under their fists and boots.

We were lucky they didn't much feel like killing anyone. Angel went out the door first and they tossed me out on top of him. As soon as I landed on him, I knew we were both in trouble; something was broken inside him. So much for keeping out of harm's way. I rolled off him and lay on the pavement, staring at the sky and trying to catch my breath. There was blood in my mouth and my nose, and my back was on fire.

Angel? I said, after a bit.

He didn't answer. I felt my mind get kind of all loose and runny, like my brains were leaking out my ears. I thought about the trade we'd taken the money from and how I'd been scared of him and his friends and how silly that had been. But then, I was too harmless to live.

The stars were raining silver fireworks down on me. It didn't help.

Angel? I said again.

I rolled over onto my side to reach for him, and there she was. The car was parked at the curb and she had Angel under the armpits, dragging him toward the open passenger door. I couldn't tell if he was conscious or not and that scared me. I sat up.

She paused, still holding the Angel. We looked into each other's eyes, and I started to understand.

"Help me get him into the car," she said at last. Her voice sounded hard and flat and unnatural. "Then you can get in, too. In the *back* seat."

I was in no shape to take her out. It couldn't have been better for her if she'd set it up herself. I got up, the pain flaring in me so bad that I almost fell down again, and took the Angel's ankles. His ankles were so delicate, almost like a woman's, like *hers*. I didn't really help much, except to guide his feet in as she sat him on the seat and strapped him in with the shoulder harness. I got in the back as she ran around to the other side of the car, her steps real light and peppy, like she'd found a million dollars lying there on the sidewalk.

We were out on the freeway before the Angel stirred in the shoulder harness. His head lolled from side to side on the back of the seat. I reached up and touched his hair lightly, hoping she couldn't see me do it.

Where are you taking me, the Angel said.

"For a ride," said the woman. "For the moment."

Why does she talk out loud like that? I asked the Angel.

Because she knows it bothers me.

"You know I can focus my thoughts better if I say things out loud," she said. "I'm not like one of your little pushovers." She glanced at me in the rear view mirror. "Just *what* have you gotten yourself into since you left, darling? Is that a boy or a girl?"

I pretended I didn't care about what she said or that I was too harmless to live or any of that stuff, but the way she said it, she meant it to sting.

Friends can be either, Angel said. It doesn't matter which. Where are you taking us?

Now it was *us*. In spite of everything, I almost could have smiled.

"Us? You mean, you and me? Or are you really referring to your little pet back there?"

My friend and I are together. You and I are *not*.

The way the Angel said it made me think he meant more than not together; like he'd been with her once the way he was with me now. The Angel let me know I was right. Silver fireworks started flowing slowly off his head down the back of the seat and I knew there was something wrong about it. There was too much all at once.

"Why can't you talk out loud to me, darling?" the woman said with fakey-sounding petulance. "Just say a few words and make me happy. You have a lovely voice when you use it."

That was true, but the Angel never spoke out loud unless he couldn't get out of it, like when he'd ordered from the bartender. Which had probably helped the bartender decide about what he thought we were, but it was useless to think about that.

"All right," said Angel, and I knew the strain was awful for him. "I've said a few words. Are you happy?" He sagged in the shoulder harness.

"Ecstatic. But it won't make me let you go. I'll drop your pet at the nearest hospital and then we'll go home." She glanced at the Angel as she drove. "I've missed you so much. I can't *stand* it without you, without you making things happen. Doing your little miracles. You knew I'd get addicted to it, all the things you could do to people. And then you just took off, I didn't know what had happened to you. And it *hurt*." Her voice turned kind of pitiful, like a little kid's. "I was in real *pain.* You must have been, too. Weren't you? Well, *weren't you?*"

Yes, the Angel said. I was in pain, too.

I remembered him standing on my corner, where I'd hung out all that time by myself until he came. Standing there in pain. I didn't know why or from what then, I just took him home, and after a little while, the pain went away. When he decided we were together, I guess.

The silvery flow over the back of the car seat thickened. I cupped my hands under it and it was like my brain was lighting up with pictures. I saw the Angel before he was my Angel, in this really nice house, the woman's house, and how she'd take him places, restaurants or stores or parties, thinking at him real hard so that he was all filled up with her and had to do what she wanted him to. Steal sometimes; other times, weird stuff, make people do silly things like suddenly start singing or taking their clothes off. That was mostly at the parties, though she made a waiter she didn't like burn himself with a pot of coffee. She'd get men, too, through the Angel, and they'd think it was the greatest idea in the world to go to bed with her. Then she'd make the Angel show her the others, the ones that had been sent here the way he had for crimes nobody could have understood, like the waitress with no face. She'd look at them, sometimes try to do things to them to make them uncomfortable or unhappy. But mostly she'd just stare.

It wasn't like that in the very beginning, the Angel said weakly and I knew he was ashamed.

It's okay, I told him. People can be nice at first, I know that. Then they find out about you.

The woman laughed. "You two are so sweet and pathetic. Like a couple of little children. I guess that's what you were looking for, wasn't it, darling? Except children can be cruel, too, can't they? So you got this—*creature* for yourself." She looked at me in the rear view mirror again as she slowed down a little, and for a moment I was afraid she'd seen what I was doing with the silvery stuff that was still pouring out of the Angel. It was starting to slow now. There wasn't much time left. I wanted to scream, but the Angel was calming me for what was coming next. "What happened to you, anyway?"

Tell her, said the Angel. To stall for time, I knew, keep her occupied.

I was born funny, I said. I had both sexes.

"A hermaphrodite!" she exclaimed with real delight.

She loves freaks, the Angel said, but she didn't pay any attention.

There was an operation, but things went wrong. They kept trying to fix it as I got older but my body didn't have the right kind of chemistry or something. My parents were ashamed. I left after awhile.

"You poor thing," she said, not meaning anything like that. "You were *just* what darling, here, needed, weren't you? Just a little nothing, no demands, no desires. For anything." Her voice got all hard. "They could probably fix you up now, you know."

I don't want it. I left all that behind a long time ago, I don't need it.

"*Just* the sort of little pet that would be perfect for you," she said to the Angel. "Sorry I have to tear you away. But I can't get along without you now. Life is so boring. And empty. And—" She sounded puzzled. "And like there's nothing more to live for since you left me."

That's not me, said the Angel. That's you.

"No, it's a lot of you, too, and you know it. You know you're addictive to human beings, you knew that when you came here—when they *sent* you here. Hey, you, *pet*, do you know what his crime was, why they sent him to this little backwater penal colony of a planet?"

Yeah, I know, I said. I really didn't, but I wasn't going to tell her that.

"What do you think about *that*, little pet neuter?" she said gleefully, hitting the accelerator pedal and speeding up. "What do you think of the crime of refusing to mate?"

The Angel made a sort of an out-loud groan and lunged at the steering wheel. The car swerved wildly and I fell backwards, the silvery stuff from the Angel going all over me. I tried to keep scooping it into my mouth the way I'd been doing, but it was flying all over the place now. I heard the crunch as the tires left the road and went onto the shoulder. Something struck the side of the car, probably the guard rail, and made it fishtail, throwing me down on the floor. Up front the woman was screaming and cursing and the Angel wasn't making a sound, but, in my head, I could hear him sort of keening. Whatever happened, this would be it. The Angel had told me all that time ago, after I'd taken him home, that they didn't last long after they got here, the exiles from his world and other worlds. Things tended to *happen* to them, even if they latched on to someone like me or the woman. They'd be in accidents or the people here would kill them. Like antibodies in a human body rejecting something or fighting a disease. At least I belonged here, but it looked like I was going to die in a car accident with the Angel and the woman both. I didn't care.

The car swerved back onto the highway for a few seconds and then pitched to the right again. Suddenly there was nothing under us and then we thumped down on something, not road but dirt or grass or something, bombing madly up and down. I pulled myself up on the back of the seat just in time to see the sign coming at us at an angle. The corner of it started to go through the windshield on the woman's side and then all I saw for a long time was the biggest display of silver fireworks ever.

It was hard to be gentle with him. Every move hurt but I didn't want to leave him sitting in the car next to her, even if she was dead. Being in the back seat had kept most of the glass from flying into me but I was still shaking some out of my hair and the impact hadn't done much for my back.

I laid the Angel out on the lumpy grass a little ways from the car and looked around. We were maybe a hundred yards from the highway, near a road that ran parallel to it. It was dark but I could still read the sign that had come through the windshield and split the woman's head in half. It said, *Construction Ahead, Reduce Speed.* Far off on the other road, I could see a flashing yellow light and at first I was afraid it was the police or something but it stayed where it was and I realized that must be the construction.

"Friend," whispered the Angel, startling me. He'd never spoken aloud to me, not directly.

Don't talk, I said, bending over him, trying to figure out some way I could touch him, just for comfort. There wasn't anything else I could do now.

"I have to," he said, still whispering. "It's almost all gone. Did you get it?"

Mostly, I said. Not all.

"I meant for you to have it."

I know.

"I don't know that it will really do you any good." His breath kind of bubbled in his throat. I could see something wet and shiny on his mouth but it wasn't silver fireworks. "But it's yours. You can do as you like with it. Live on it the way I did. Get what you need when you need it. But you can live as a human, too. Eat. Work. However, whatever."

I'm not human, I said. I'm not any more human than you, even if I do belong here.

"Yes, you are, little friend. I haven't made you any less human," he said, and coughed some. "I'm not sorry I wouldn't mate. I couldn't mate with my own. It was too … I don't know, too little of me, too much of them, something. I couldn't bond, it would have been nothing but emptiness. The Great Sin, to be unable to give, because the universe knows only less or more and I insisted that it would be good or bad. So they sent me here. But in the end, you know, they got their way, little friend." I felt his hand on me for a moment before it fell away. "I did it after all. Even if it wasn't with my own."

The bubbling in his throat stopped. I sat next to him for a while in the dark. Finally I felt it, the Angel stuff. It was kind of fluttery-churny, like too much coffee on an empty stomach. I closed my eyes and lay down on the grass, shivering. Maybe some of it was shock but I don't think so. The silver fireworks started, in my head this time, and with them came a lot of pictures I couldn't understand. Stuff about the Angel and where he'd come from and the way they mated. It was a lot like how we'd been together, the Angel and me. They looked a lot like us but there were a lot of differences, too, things I couldn't make out. I couldn't make out how they'd sent him here, either—by *light*, in, like, little bundles or something. It didn't make any sense to me, but I guessed an Angel could be light. Silver fireworks.

I must have passed out, because when I opened my eyes, it felt like I'd been laying there a long time. It was still dark, though. I sat up and reached for the Angel, thinking I ought to hide his body.

He was gone. There was just a sort of wet sandy stuff where he'd been.

I looked at the car and her. All that was still there. Somebody was going to see it soon. I didn't want to be around for that.

Everything still hurt but I managed to get to the other road and start walking back toward the city. It was like I could *feel* it now, the way the Angel must have, as though it were vibrating like a drum or ringing like a bell with all kinds of stuff, people laughing and crying and loving and hating and being afraid and everything else that happens to people. The stuff that the Angel took in, energy, that I could take in now if I wanted.

And I knew that taking it in that way, it would be bigger than anything all those people had, bigger than anything I could have had if things hadn't gone wrong with me all those years ago.

I wasn't so sure I wanted it. Like the Angel, refusing to mate back where he'd come from. He wouldn't, there, and I couldn't, here. Except now I could do something else.

I wasn't so sure I wanted it. But I didn't think I'd be able to stop it, either, any more than I could stop my heart from beating. Maybe it wasn't really such a good thing or a right thing. But it was like the Angel said: the universe doesn't know good or bad, only less or more.

Yeah. I heard *that*.

I thought about the waitress with no face. I could find them all now, all the ones from the other places, other worlds that sent them away for some kind of alien crimes nobody would have understood. I could find them all. They threw away their outcasts. I'd tell them, but here, we *kept* ours. And here's how. Here's how you live in a universe that only knows less or more.

I kept walking toward the city.

Joe Haldeman (b. 1943)

Joe Haldeman is an American SF author whose first SF novel, *The Forever War* (1974), won the Hugo, Nebula, and Locus awards for best novel. Regularly hailed as one of the best works in the subgenre of military SF, *The Forever War* draws on Haldeman's own experience as a soldier in the Vietnam War, during which he was wounded, receiving a Purple Heart for his service. Recognized as a Grand Master by the Science Fiction Writers Association, he is also a past president of that association.

Note on the text: The version here follows the poem's original publication in the anthology *In the Field of Fire*, edited by Jeanne Van Buren Dann and Jack Dann (Tor, 1987), which collects SF and fantasy responses to the Vietnam War. "DX," the only poem in the collection, is also its concluding piece.

"DX" (1987)

So every night
You build a little house

You dig a hole
and cover it with
logs

Cover with logs
with sandbags
against the
shrapnel weather

A house you
sleep beside
and hope not
to enter

Some nights you wake
to noise and light
and metal singing

Roll out of the bag
and into the house
with all the scorpions
centipedes roaches
but no bullets flying inside it

Most nights
you just sleep

deep sleep
and dreamless

mostly
from labor

This night was just sleep.

In the morning
you unbuild the house

hours of work
again
for nothing

Kick the logs away
pour out the sandbags
into the hole

Roll up the sandbags
for the next night's bit
of rural urban renewal

Eat some cold bad food
Clean your weapon
Drink instant coffee
from a can

Check the tape on
the grenades;
check the pins.
Inspect ammo clips
(Clean the top
rounds with
illegal
gasoline.)

Most carefully
repack the demolition
bag: blasting caps
TNT plastic time fuse
det cord—

ten kilograms of fragile
most instant
death

Then shoulder the heavy rucksack
Secure your weapons and tools
and follow the other primates
into the jungle

watching the trees

walk silently
as possible
through the green

watching the ground

Don't get too close
to the man in front of you

This is good advice:
Don't let the enemy
have two targets.

Remember that: don't get too close to any man.

Only a fool, or an officer,
doesn't grab the ground
at the first shot

high-pitched
rattle
of M-16s[1]

even if it's rather distant

louder
Russian rifles
answer

even if it's
a couple of klicks away

manly chug
of heavy
machine
guns

God knows which way they're shooting

grenade's
flat
bang

Like fools, or officers,
we get up off the ground and move

All that metal
flying through
the air—
and do we move away
from it?

no

We make haste
in the wrong direction

like fools or officers
we head for the
action

making lots of noise now
who cares now

but careful not to bunch up

Remember: don't get too close to any man.

---

1 The M16 assault rifle was developed for the US military and first deployed in the Vietnam War.

It's over before we get there.
The enemy, not fools
(perhaps lacking officers)
went in the proper direction.

As we approach
the abandoned enemy camp
a bit of impolite and
(perhaps to you)
incomprehensible
dialogue greets us:

"You wanna get some
X-Rays down here?
Charlie left
a motherfuckin'
DX pile
behind."

TERMS:

X-Rays are engineers,
demolition men,
us.

Charlie is the enemy.

"DX" means destroy;
A DX pile is a collection
of explosives that are no longer
trustworthy. When you leave
the camp finally, you
put a long fuse on the DX pile, and
blow it up.

(Both "motherfucker" and "DX"
are technical terms that can serve as
polite euphemisms:

"Private
you wanna
DX that
motherfucker?"

instead
of

"Private,
kill
that
man.")

We'd been lucky.
No shooting.
Just a pile of
explosive
leftovers
to dispose of.

And we'd done it before.

It was quite a pile,
though,
taller than a man

all
enough to kill
everybody
with some left over

artillery shells
mortar rounds
satchel charges
rifle grenades

festooned with
chains of
fifty-caliber
ammunition

The major wouldn't
let us
evacuate his troops
then put a long fuse on the pile

We had to stand there
nervous
and guard it

no

They'd been working hard
first they get lunch and a nap
then we can move them out
and we can blow it.

(we liked his "we")

We didn't know
it was wired for sound

it was booby-trapped

Remember: don't get too close to any man:

Don't know that Farmer
has an actual farm waiting
back in Alabama

and Don't know that
Crowder
has new grandbabies
and is headed
for retirement
when he gets home

and don't know that Doc
was a basketball champ
in his black high school
and really did want
to be a doctor

Because they all are
one short beep
of a radio detonator

away
from

a sound
so loud grey smoke
you don't
hear it blood
really

It just hits you like a car.

everywhere blood
and screaming

Doc
both his long legs
blown off
dies quickly

Sergeant Crowder
separated from one
foot
is unconscious
or stoic

Farmer had his belly spilled
but lived long enough to shout
"Professor?
Where'd they get you?" and

since I didn't have
enough breath
for a complete catalog

(foot shins knees
thigh groin genitals
arm ear scalp
and disposition)

I settled for "the balls."

Oh my God
Farmer said
then he died

Two days later
I woke up in a dirty hospital
(sewed up like Frankenstein's charge)
woke up in time
to see Crowder leave
with a sheet over his eyes

and so it was over
in a way
the whole squad DX
but me

there is nothing for it
there is nothing you can take for it
they are names on a wall now
they are compost in Arlington
and somehow I am not

but give me this

There are three other universes, like this:

In one, Farmer curses the rain
wrestles his tractor through the mud
curses the bank that owns it
and sometimes remembers
that he alone survived

In another Crowder tells grown grandchildren
for the hundredth time
over a late-night whiskey
his one war story
that beats the others all to hell

In the third Doc stands over a bloody patient
steady hand healing knife
and sometimes he recalls
blood years past and sometimes
remembers to be glad to be alive;

in these worlds
I am dead

and at peace.

Candas Jane Dorsey (b. 1952)

Canadian author Candas Jane Dorsey writes across multiple genres and forms, and currently teaches at MacEwan University in Edmonton, Alberta. In addition to her own writing, she is also a well-known editor, including of SF. She is the founding president of SF Canada, a professional association of speculative fiction authors in that country; in an interview for *Locus* magazine, she is quoted as saying "Canadians often feel like aliens, like observers, in North American culture" ("Candas Jane Dorsey: Saving the World" 8).

Note on the text: "(Learning about) Machine Sex" was first published in Dorsey's collection *Machine Sex and Other Stories* (Tesseract, 1988), and has since been anthologized in several SF and other collections. The initial publication is followed here.

"(Learning about) Machine Sex" (1988)

A NAKED woman working at a computer. Which attracts you most? It was a measure of Whitman that, as he entered the room, his eyes went first to the unfolded machine gleaming small and awkward in the light of the long-armed desk lamp; he'd seen the woman before.

Angel was the woman. Thin and pale-skinned, with dark nipples and black pubic hair, and her face hidden by a dark unkempt mane of long hair as she leaned over her work.

A woman complete with her work. It was a measure of Angel that she never acted naked, even when she was. Perhaps especially when she was.

So she has a new board, thought Whitman, and felt his guts stir the way they stirred when he first contemplated taking her to bed. That was a long time ago. And she knew it, felt without turning her head the desire, and behind the screen of her straight dark hair, uncombed and tumbled in front of her eyes, she smiled her anger down.

"Where have you been?" he asked, and she shook her hair back, leaned backward to ease her tense neck.

"What is that thing?" he went on insistently, and Angel turned her face to him, half-scowling. The board on the desk had thin irregular wings spreading from a small central module. Her fingers didn't slow their keyboard dance.

"None of your business," she said.

She saved the input, and he watched her fold the board into a smaller and smaller rectangle. Finally she shook her hair back from her face.

"I've got the option on your bioware," he said.

"Pay as you go," she said. "New house rule."

And found herself on her ass on the floor from his reflexive, furious blow. And his hand in her hair, pulling her up and against the wall. Hard.

Astonishing her with how quickly she could hurt how much. Then she hurt too much to analyze it.

"You are a bitch," he said.

"So what?" she said. "When I was nicer, you were still an asshole."

Her head back against the wall, crack. Ouch.

Breathless, Angel: "Once more and you never see this bioware." And Whitman slowly draws breath, draws back, and looks at her the way she knew he always felt.

"Get out," she said. "I'll bring it to Kozyk's office when it's ready."

So he went. She slumped back in the chair, and tears began to blur her vision, but hate cleared them up fast enough, as she unfolded the board again, so that despite the pain she hardly missed a moment of programming time.

Assault only a distraction now, betrayal only a detail: Angel was on a roll. She had her revenge well in hand, though it took a subtle mind to recognize it.

* * *

Again: "I have the option on any of your bioware." This time, in the office, Whitman wore the nostalgic denims he now affected, and Angel her street-silks and leather.

"This is mine, but I made one for you." She pulled it out of the bag. Where her board looked jerry-built, this one was sleek. Her board looked interesting; this one packaged. "I made it before you sold our company," she said. "I put my best into it. You may as well have it. I suppose you own the option anyway, eh?"

She stood. Whitman was unconsciously restless before her.

"When you pay me for this," she said, "make it in MannComp stock." She tossed him the board. "But be careful. If you take it apart wrong, you'll break it. Then you'll have to ask me to fix it, and from now on, my tech rate goes up."

As she walked by him, he reached for her, hooked one arm around her waist. She looked at him, totally expressionless. "Max," she said, "it's like I told you last night. From now on, if you want it, you pay. Just like everyone else." He let her go. She pulled the soft dirty white silk shirt on over the black leather jacket. The compleat rebel now.

"It's a little going away present. When you're a big shot in MannComp, remember that I made it. And that you couldn't even take it apart right. I guarantee."

He wasn't going to watch her leave. He was already studying the board. Hardly listening, either.

"Call it the Mannboard," she said. "It gets big if you stroke it." She shut the door quietly behind herself.

* * *

It would be easier if this were a story about sex, or about machines. It is true that the subject is Angel, a woman who builds computers like they have never been built before outside the human skull. Angel, like everyone else, comes from somewhere and goes somewhere else. She lives in that linear and binary universe. However, like everyone else, she lives concurrently in another universe less simple. Trivalent, quadrivalent, multivalent. World without end, with no amen. And so, on.

* * *

They say a hacker's burned out before he's twenty-one. Note the pronoun: he. Not many young women in that heady realm of the chip.

Before Angel was twenty-one—long before—she had taken the cybernetic chip out of a Wm Kuhns[1] fantasy and patented it; she had written the program for the self-taught AI the Bronfmanns had bought and used to gain world prominence for their MannComp lapboard; somewhere in there, she'd lost innocence, and when her clever additions to that AI turned it into something the military wanted, she dropped out of sight in Toronto and went back to Rocky Mountain House, Alberta, on a Greyhound bus.

It was while she was thinking about something else—cash, and how to get some—that she had looked out of the bus window in Winnipeg into the display window of a sex shop. Garter belts, sleazy magazines on cheap coated paper with dayglo orange stickers over the genitals of bored sex kings and queens, a variety of ornamental vibrators. She had too many memories of Max to take it lightly, though she heard the laughter of the roughnecks in the back of the bus as they topped each others' dirty jokes, and thought perhaps their humour was worth emulating. If only she could.

She passed her twentieth birthday in a hotel in Regina, where she stopped to take a shower and tap into the phone lines, checking for pursuit. Armed with the money she got through automatic transfer from a dummy account in Medicine Hat, she rode the bus the rest of the way ignoring the rolling of beer bottles under the seats, the acrid stink of the onboard toilet. She was thinking about sex.

As the bus roared across the long flat prairie she kept one hand on the roll of bills in her pocket, but with the other she made the first notes on the program that would eventually make her famous.

She made the notes on an antique NEC[2] lapboard which had been her

1 Likely William Kuhns (b. 1943), US-born Canadian writer best known for non-fiction works on technology, including *The Post-Industrial Prophets: Interpretations of Technology* (1971); he also wrote the play *The Zen of an Intelligent Machine* (1985).

2 Nippon Electric Company, a Japanese technology firm.

aunt's, in old-fashioned BASIC[1]—all the machine would support—but she unravelled it and knitted it into that artificial trivalent language when she got to the place at Rocky and plugged the idea into her Mannboard. She had it written in a little over four hours on-time, but that counted an hour and a half she took to write a new loop into the AI. (She would patent that loop later the same year and put the royalties into a blind trust for her brother, Brian, brain damaged from birth. He was in Michener Centre in Red Deer,[2] not educable; no one at Bronfmann knew about her family, and she kept it that way.)

She called it Machine Sex; working title.

* * *

Working title for a life: born in Innisfail General Hospital, father a rodeo cowboy who raised rodeo horses, did enough mixed farming out near Caroline to build his young second wife a big log house facing the mountain view. The first baby came within a year, ending her mother's tenure as teller at the local bank. Her aunt was a programmer for the University of Lethbridge, chemical molecular model analysis on the University of Calgary mainframe through a modem link.

From her aunt she learned BASIC, Pascal, COBOL and C;[3] in school she played the usual turtle games on the Apple IIe;[4] when she was fourteen she took a bus to Toronto, changed her name to Angel, affected a punk hairstyle and the insolent all-white costume of that year's youth, and eventually walked into Northern Systems, the company struggling most successfully with bionics at the time, with the perfected biochip, grinning at the proper young men in their grey three-piece suits as they tried to find a bug in it anywhere. For the first million she let them open it up; for the next five she told them how she did it. Eighteen years old by the phony records she'd cooked on her arrival in Toronto, she was free to negotiate her own contracts.

But no one got her away from Northern until Bronfmann bought Northern lock, stock and climate-controlled workshop. She had been sleeping with Northern's boy-wonder president by then for about a year, had yet to have an orgasm though she'd learned a lot about kinky sex toys. Figured she'd been screwed by him for the last time when he sold the company without telling her; spent the next two weeks doing a lot of drugs and having a lot of cheap sex in the degenerate punk underground; came up with the AI education program.

1 Beginners' All-purpose Symbolic Instruction Code, a computer programming language developed in 1963 and which gained popularity on personal computers, especially through the 1980s.

2 Originally known as the Provincial Training School, this facility opened in Red Deer, Alberta, in 1923; while later becoming a health care facility, it started as part of the eugenics program, including forced sterilization (until that practice ended in the early 1970s). See Claudia Malacrida.

3 All of these are computer programming languages.

4 An early personal computer, launched in 1983.

Came up indeed, came swaggering into Ted Kozyk's office, president of Bronfmann's MannComp subsidiary, with that jury-rigged Mannboard tied into two black-box add-ons no bigger than a bar of soap, and said, "Watch this."

Took out the power supply first, wiped the memory, plugged into a wall outlet and turned it on.

The bootstrap greeting sounded a lot like Goo. "Okay," she said, "it's ready."

"Ready for what?"

"Anything you want," she said. By then he knew her, knew her rep, knew that the sweaty-smelling, disheveled, anorectic-looking waif in the filthy, oversized silk shirt (the rebels had affected natural fabrics the year she left home, and she always did after that, even later when the silk was cleaner, more upmarket, and black instead of white) had something. Two weeks ago he'd bought a company on the strength of that something, and the board Whitman had brought him the day after the sale, even without the software to run on it, had been enough to convince him he'd been right.

He sat down to work, and hours later he was playing Go with an AI he'd taught to talk back, play games, and predict horse races and the stock market.

He sat back, flicked the power switch and pulled the plug, and stared at her.

"Congratulations," she said.

"What for?" he said; "you're the genius."

"No, congratulations, you just murdered your first baby," she said, and plugged it back in. "Want to try for two?"

"Goo," said the deck. "Dada."

It was her little joke. It was never a feature on the MannComp A-One they sold across every MannComp counter in the world.

* * *

But now she's all grown up, she's sitting in a log house near Rocky Mountain house, watching the late summer sunset from the big front windows, while the computer runs Machine Sex to its logical conclusion, orgasm.

She had her first orgasm at nineteen. According to her false identity, she was twenty-three. Her lover was a delegate to MannComp's annual sales convention; she picked him up after the speech she gave on the ethics of selling AIs to high school students in Thailand. Or whatever, she didn't care. Kozyk used to write her speeches but she usually changed them to suit her mood. This night she'd been circumspect, only a few expletives, enough to amuse the younger sales representatives and reassure the older ones.

The one she chose was smooth in his approach and she thought, well, we'll see. They went up to the suite MannComp provided, all mod cons and king-size bed, and as she undressed she looked at him and thought, he's ambitious, this boy, better not give him an inch.

He surprised her in bed. Ambitious maybe, but he paid a lot of attention to detail.

After he spread her across the universe in a way she had never felt before, he turned to her and said, "That was pretty good, eh, baby?" and smiled a smooth little grin. "Sure," she said, "it was okay," and was glad she hadn't said more while she was out in the ozone.

By then she thought she was over what Whitman had done to her. And after all, it had been simple enough, what he did. Back in that loft she had in Hull, upstairs of a shop, where she covered the windows with opaque mylar and worked night and day in that twilight. That night as she worked he stood behind her, hands on her shoulders, massaging her into further tenseness.

"Hey, Max, you know I don't like it when people look over my shoulder when I'm working."

"Sorry, baby." He moved away, and she felt her shoulders relax just to have his hands fall away.

"Come on to bed," he said. "You know you can pick that up whenever."

She had to admit he was being pleasant tonight. Maybe he too was tired of the constant scrapping, disguised as jokes, that wore at her nerves so much. All his efforts to make her stop working, slow her down so he could stay up. The sharp edges that couldn't be disguised. Her bravado made her answer in the same vein, but in the mornings, when he was gone to Northern; she paced and muttered to herself, reworking the previous day until it was done with, enough that she could go on. And after all what was missing? She had no idea how to debug it.

Tonight he'd even made some dinner, and touched her kindly. Should she be grateful? Maybe the conversations, such as they were, where she tried to work it out, had just made it worse—.

"Ah, shit," she said, and pushed the board away. "You're right, I'm too tired for this. *Demain*."[1] She was learning French in her spare time.

He began with hugging her, and stroking the long line along her back, something he knew she liked, like a cat likes it, arches its back at the end of the stroke. He knew she got turned on by it. And she did. When they had sex at her house he was without the paraphernalia he preferred, but he seemed to manage, buoyed up by some mood she couldn't share; nor could she share his release.

Afterward, she lay beside him, tense and dissatisfied in the big bed, not admitting it, or she'd have to admit she didn't know what would help. He seemed to be okay, stretched, relaxed and smiling.

"Had a big day," he said.

"Yeah?"

"Big deal went through."

"Yeah?"

"Yeah, I sold the company."

---

1 "Tomorrow" (Fr.).

"You what?" Reflexively moving herself so that none of her body touched his.

"Northern. I put it to Bronfmann. Megabucks."

"Are you joking?" but she saw he was not. "You didn't, I didn't.... Northern's *our* company."

"My company. I started it."

"I made it big for you."

"Oh, and I paid you well for every bit of that."

She got up. He was smiling a little, trying on the little-boy grin. No, baby, she thought, not tonight.

"Well," she said, "I know for sure that this is my bed. Get out of it."

"Now, I knew you might take this badly. But it really was the best thing. The R&D costs were killing us. Bronfmann can eat them for breakfast."

R&D costs meant her. "Maybe. Your clothes are here." She tossed them on the bed, went into the other room.

As well as sex, she hadn't figured out betrayal yet either; on the street, she thought, people fucked you over openly, not in secret.

This, even as she said it to herself, she recognised as romantic and certainly not based on experience. She was street-wise in every way but one: Max had been her first lover.

She unfolded the new board. It had taken her some time to figure out how to make it expand like that, to fit the program it was going to run. This idea of shaping the hardware to the software had been with her since she made the biochip, and thus made it possible and much more interesting than the other way around. But making the hardware to fit her new idea had involved a great deal of study and technique, and so far she had had limited success.

This reminded her again of sex, and, she supposed, relationships, although it seemed to her that before sex everything had been on surfaces, very easy. Now she had sex, she had had Max, and now she had no way to realize the results of any of that. Especially now, when Northern had just vanished into Bronfmann's computer empire, putting her in the position again of having to prove herself. What had Max used to make Bronfmann take the bait? She knew very clearly: Angel, the Northern Angel, would now become the MannComp Angel. The rest of the bait would have been the AI; she was making more of it every day, but couldn't yet bring it together. Could it be done at all? Bronfmann had paid high for an affirmative answer.

Certainly this time the bioware was working together. She began to smile a little to herself, almost unaware of it, as she saw how she could interconnect the loops to make a solid net to support the program's full and growing weight. Because, of course, it would have to learn as it went along—that was basic.

Angel as metaphor; she had to laugh at herself when she woke from programming hours later, Max still sleeping in her bed, ignoring her eviction notice. He'll have to get up to piss anyway, she thought; that's when I'll get him out. She went herself to the bathroom in the half-dawn light, stretching her cramped back muscles and thinking remotely, well, I got some satisfaction out of last night after all: the beginnings of the idea that might break this impasse. While it's still inside my head, this one is mine. How can I keep it that way?

New fiscal controls, she thought grimly. New contracts, now that Northern doesn't exist any more. Max can't have this, whatever it turns into, for my dowry to MannComp.

When she put on her white silks—leather jacket underneath, against the skin as street fashion would have it—she hardly knew herself what she would do. The little board went into her bag with the boxes of pills the pharmaceutical tailor had made for her. If there was nothing there to suit, she'd buy something new. In the end, she left Max sleeping in her bed; so what? she thought as she reached the highway. The first ride she hitched took her to Toronto, not without a little tariff, but she no longer gave a damn about any of that.

By then the drugs in her system had lifted her out of a body that could be betrayed, and she didn't return to it for two weeks, two weeks of floating in a soup of disjointed noise, and always the program running, unfolding, running again, unfolding inside her relentless mind. She kept it running to drown anything she might remember about trust or the dream of happiness.

When she came home two weeks later, on a hot day in summer with the Ottawa Valley humidity unbearable and her body tired, sore and bruised, and very dirty, she stepped out of her filthy silks in a room messy with Whitman's continued inhabitation; furious, she popped a system cleanser and unfolded the board on her desk. When he came back in she was there, naked, angry, working.

★ ★ ★

A naked woman working at a computer. What good were cover-ups? Watching Max after she took the new AI up to Kozyk, she was only triumphant because she'd done something Max could never do, however much he might be able to sell her out. Watching them fit it to the bioboard, the strange unfolding machine she had made to fit the ideas only she could have, she began to be afraid. The system cleanser she'd taken made the clarity inescapable. Over the next few months, as she kept adding clever loops and twists, she watched their glee and she looked at what telephone numbers were in the top ten on their modem memories and she began to realise that it was not only business and science that would pay high for a truly thinking machine.

She knew that ten years before there had been Pentagon programmers working to model predatory behaviour in AIs using Prolog[1] and its like. That

1 Prolog is a computer-programming language that was especially important in the development of artificial intelligence.

was old hat. None of them, however, knew what they needed to know to write for her bioware yet. No one but Angel could do that. So, by the end of her nineteenth year, that made Angel one of the most sought after, endangered ex-anorectics on the block.

She went to conferences and talked about the ethics of selling AIs to teenagers in Nepal. Or something. And took a smooth salesman to bed, and thought all the time about when they were going to make their approach. It would be Whitman again, not Kozyk, she thought; Ted wouldn't get his hands dirty, while Max was born with grime under his nails.

She thought also about metaphors. How, even in the new street slang which she could speak as easily as her native tongue, being screwed, knocked, fucked over, jossed, dragged all meant the same thing: hurt to the core. And this was what people sought out, what they spent their time seeking in pick-up joints, to the beat of bad old headbanger bands, that nostalgia shit. Now, as well as the biochip, Max, the AI breakthrough, and all the tailored drugs she could eat, she'd had orgasm too.

Well, she supposed it passed the time.

What interested her intellectually about orgasm was not the lovely illusion of transcendence it brought, but the absolute binary predictability of it. When you learn what to do to the nerve endings, and they are in a receptive state, the program runs like kismet. Warm boot. She'd known a hacker once who'd altered his bootstrap messages[1] to read "Warm pussy." She knew where most hackers were at; they played with their computers more than they played with themselves. She was the same, otherwise why would it have taken a pretty-boy salesman in a three-piece to show her the simple answer? All the others, just like trying to use an old MS-DOS disc to boot up one of her Mann lapboards with crystal RO/RAM.[2]

* * *

Angel forgets she's only twenty. Genius is uneven. There's no substitute for time, that relentless shaper of understanding. Etc. Etc. Angel paces with the knowledge that everything is a phase, even this. Life is hard and then you die, and so on. And so, on.

* * *

One day it occurred to her that she could simply run away.

This should have seemed elementary but to Angel it was a revelation. She

1 Bootstrap message: the message that appears when a computer starts up (commonly shortened to "boot").

2 MS-DOS: the Microsoft operating system used on most IBM and IBM-compatible PCs at the time of this story's publication; ROM: read-only memory; RAM: random-access memory.

spent her life fatalistically; her only successful escape had been from the people she loved. Her lovely, crazy grandfather; her generous and slightly avaricious aunt; and her beloved imbecile brother: they were buried deep in a carefully forgotten past. But she kept coming back to Whitman, to Kozyk and Bronfmann, as if she liked them.

As if, like a shocked dog in a learned helplessness experiment,[1] she could not believe that the cage had a door, and the door was open.

She went out the door. For old times' sake, it was the bus she chose; the steamy chill of an air-conditioned Greyhound hadn't changed at all. Bottles—pop and beer—rolling under the seats and the stench of chemicals filling the air whenever someone sneaked down to smoke a cigarette or a reef in the toilet. Did anyone ever use it to piss in? She liked the triple seat near the back, but the combined smells forced her to the front, behind the driver, where she was joined, across the country, by an endless succession of old women, immaculate in their fortrels,[2] who started conversations and shared peppermints and gum.

She didn't get stoned once.

The country unrolled strangely: sex shop in Winnipeg, bank machine in Regina, and hours of programming alternating with polite responses to the old women, until eventually she arrived,

creased and exhausted, in Rocky Mountain House.

Rocky Mountain House: a comfortable model of a small town, from which no self-respecting hacker should originate. But these days, the world a net of wire and wireless, it doesn't matter where you are, as long as you have the information people want. Luckily for Angel's secret past, however, this was not a place she would be expected to live—or to go—or to come from.

An atavism she hadn't controlled had brought her this far. A rented car took her the rest of the way to the ranch. She thought only to look around, but when she found the tenants packing for a month's holiday, she couldn't resist the opportunity. She carried her leather satchel into their crocheted, frilled guest room—it had been her room fifteen years before—with a remote kind of satisfaction.

That night, she slept like the dead—except for some dreams. But there was nothing she could do about them.

* * *

1 In an experiment designed by Martin Seligman (b. 1942), different groups of dogs were subjected to electrical shocks. One group of dogs could end the shock by performing a simple action, while another group could not. In a later stage, all dogs could stop the shock by performing a different action; the group that could not stop the shocks themselves in the earlier stage did not learn how to stop them in the later stage.

2 Fortrel is a brand of wrinkle-resistant polyester, popular for a while as a fabric for dresses.

Lightning and thunder. I should stop now, she thought, wary of power surges through the new board which she was charging as she worked. She saved her file, unplugged the power, stood, stretched, and walked to the window to look at the mountains.

The storm illuminated the closer slopes erratically, the rain hid the distances. She felt some heaviness lift. The cool wind through the window refreshed her. She heard the program stop, and turned off the machine. Sliding out the backup capsule, she smiled her angry smile unconsciously. When I get back to the Ottawa Valley, she thought, where weather never comes from the west like it's supposed to, I'll make those fuckers eat this.

Out in the corrals where the tenants kept their rodeo horses, there was animal noise, and she turned off the light to go and look out the side window. A young man was leaning his weight against the reins-length pull of a rearing, terrified horse. Angel watched as flashes of lightning strobed the hackneyed scene. This was where she came from. She remembered her father in the same struggle. And her mother at this window with her, both of them watching the man. Her mother's anger she never understood until now. Her father's abandonment of all that was in the house, including her brother, Brian, inert and restless in his oversized crib.

Angel walked back through the house, furnished now in the kitschy western style of every trailer and bungalow in this countryside. She was lucky to stay, invited on a generous impulse, while all but their son were away. She felt vaguely guilty at her implicit criticism.

Angel invited the young rancher into the house not only because this is what her mother and her grandmother would have done. Even Angel's great-grandmother, whose father kept the stopping house, which meant she kept the travellers fed, even her spirit infused in Angel the unwilling act. She watched him almost sullenly as he left his rain gear in the wide porch.

He was big, sitting in the big farm kitchen. His hair was wet, and he swore almost as much as she did. He told her how he had put a trailer on the north forty, and lived there now, instead of in the little room where she'd been invited to sleep. He told her about the stock he'd accumulated riding the rodeo. They drank Glenfiddich.[1] She told him her father had been a rodeo cowboy. He told her about his university degree in agriculture. She told him she'd never been to university. They drank more whiskey and he told her he couldn't drink that other rot gut any more since he tasted real Scotch. He invited her to see his computer. She went with him across the yard and through the trees in the rain, her bag over her shoulder, board hidden in it, and he showed her his computer. It turned out to be the first machine she designed for Northern—archaic now, compared with the one she'd just invented.

Fair is fair, she thought drunkenly, and she pulled out her board and unfolded it.

---

1 A famous brand of Scotch whisky.

"You showed me yours, I'll show you mine," she said.

He liked the board. He was amazed that she had made it. They finished the Scotch.

"I like you," she said. "Let me show you something. You can be the first." And she ran Machine Sex for him.

* * *

He was the first to see it: before Whitman and Kozyk who bought it to sell to people who already have had and done everything; before David and Jonathan, the Hardware Twins in MannComp's Gulf Islands shop, who made the touchpad devices necessary to run it properly; before a world market hungry for the kind of glossy degradation Machine Sex could give them bought it in droves from a hastily-created—MannComp-subsidiary—numbered company. She ran it for him with just the automouse on her board, and a description of what it would do when the hardware was upgraded to fit.

It was very simple, really. If orgasm was binary, it could be programmed. Feed back the sensation through one or more touchpads to program the body. The other thing she knew about human sex was that it was as much cortical as genital, or more so: touch is optional for the turn-on. Also easy, then, to produce cortical stimuli by programmed input. The rest was a cosmetic elaboration of the premise.

At first it did turn him on, then off, then it made his blood run cold. She was pleased by that: her work had chilled her too.

"You can't market that thing!" he said.

"Why not? It's a fucking good program. Hey, get it? Fucking good."

"It's not real."

"Of course it isn't. So what?"

"So, people don't need that kind of stuff to get turned on."

She told him about people. More people than he'd known were in the world. People who made her those designer drugs, given in return for favors she never granted until after Whitman sold her like a used car. People like Whitman, teaching her about sexual equipment while dealing with the Pentagon and CSIS[1] to sell them Angel's sharp angry mind, as if she'd work on killing others as eagerly as she was trying to kill herself. People who would hire a woman, on the street, as they had her during that two-week nightmare almost a year before, and use her as casually as their own hand, without giving a damn.

"One night," she said, "just to see, I told all the johns I was fourteen. I was skinny enough, even then, to get away with it. And they all loved it. Every single one gave me a bonus, and took me anyway."

1 The Pentagon is the name for the five-sided building that serves as the headquarters for the US Department of Defense; CSIS stands for Canadian Security Intelligence Service.

The whiskey fog was wearing a little thin. More time had passed than she thought, and more had been said than she had intended. She went to her bag, rummaged, but she'd left her drugs in Toronto, some dim idea at that time that she should clean up her act. All that had happened was that she had spent the days so tight with rage that she couldn't eat, and she'd already cured herself of that once; for the record, she thought, she'd rather be stoned.

"Do you have any more booze?" she said, and he went to look. She followed him around his kitchen.

"Furthermore," she said, "I rolled every one of them that I could, and all but one had pictures of his kids in his wallet, and all of them were teenagers. Boys and girls together. And their saintly dads out fucking someone who looked just like them. Just like them."

Luckily, he had another bottle. Not quite the same quality, but she wasn't fussy.

"So I figure," she finished, "that they don't care who they fuck. Why not the computer in the den? Or the office system at lunch hour?"

"It's not like that," he said. "It's nothing like that. People deserve better." He had the neck of the bottle in his big hand, was seriously, carefully pouring himself another shot. He gestured with both bottle and glass. "People deserve to have—love."

"Love?"

"Yeah, love. You think I'm stupid, you think I watched too much TV as a kid, but I know it's out there. Somewhere. Other people think so too. Don't you? Didn't you, even if you won't admit it now, fall in love with that guy Max at first? You never said what he did at the beginning, how he talked you into being his lover. Something must have happened. Well, that's what I mean: love."

"Let me tell you about love. Love is a guy who talks real smooth taking me out to the woods and telling me he just loves my smile. And then taking me home and putting me in leather handcuffs so he can come. And if I hurt he likes it, because he likes it to hurt a little and he thinks I must like it like he does. And if I moan he thinks I'm coming. And if I cry he thinks it's love. And so do I. Until one evening—not too long after my *last* birthday, as I recall—he tells me that he has sold me to another company. And this only after he fucks me one last time. Even though I don't belong to him any more. After all, he had the option on all my bioware."

"All that is just politics." He was sharp, she had to grant him that.

"Politics," she said, "give me a break. Was it politics made Max able to sell me with the stock: hardware, software, liveware?"

"I've met guys like that. Women too. You have to understand that it wasn't personal to him, it was just politics." Also stubborn. "Sure, you were naive, but you weren't wrong. You just didn't understand company politics."

"Oh, sure I did. I always have. Why do you think I changed my name? Why do you think I dress in natural fibres and go through all the rest of this bullshit?

I know how to set up power blocs. Except in mine there is only one party—me. And that's the way it's going to stay. Me against them from now on."

"It's not always like that. There are assholes in the world, and there are other people too. Everyone around here still remembers your grandfather, even though he's been retired in Camrose for fifteen years. They still talk about the way he and his wife used to waltz at the Legion Hall. What about him? There are more people like him than there are Whitmans."

"Charlotte doesn't waltz much since her stroke."

"That's a cheap shot. You can't get away with cheap shots. Speaking of shots, have another."

"Don't mind if I do. Okay, I give you Eric and Charlotte. But one half-happy ending doesn't balance out the people who go through their lives with their teeth clenched, trying to make it come out the same as a True Romance comic,[1] and always wondering what's missing. They read those bodice-ripper novels, and make that do for the love you believe in so naively." Call her naive, would he? Two could play at that game. "That's why they'll all go crazy for Machine Sex. So simple. So linear. So fast. So uncomplicated."

"You underestimate people's ability to be happy. People are better at loving than you think."

"You think so? Wait until you have your own little piece of land and some sweetheart takes you out in the trees on a moonlit night and gives you head until you think your heart will break. So you marry her and have some kids. She furnishes the trailer in a five-room sale grouping. You have to quit drinking Glenfiddich because she hates it when you talk too loud. She gets an allowance every month and crochets a cozy for the TV. You work all day out in the rain and all evening in the back room making the books balance on the outdated computer. After the kids come she gains weight and sells real estate if you're lucky. If not she makes things out of recycled bleach bottles and hangs them in the yard. Pretty soon she wears a nightgown to bed and turns her back when you slip in after a hard night at the keyboard. So you take up drinking again and teach the kids about the rodeo. And you find some square-dancing chick who gives you head out behind the bleachers one night in Trochu, so sweet you think your heart will break. What you gonna do then, mountain man?"

"Okay, we can tell stories until the sun comes up. Which won't be too long, look at the time; but no matter how many stories you tell, you can't make me forget about that thing." He pointed to the computer with loathing.

"It's just a machine."

"You know what I mean. That thing in it. And besides, I'm gay. Your little scenario wouldn't work."

She laughed and laughed. "So that's why you haven't made a pass at me yet." She wondered coldly how gay he was, but she was tired, so tired of proving

1 A generic term for romance comic books, most popular in the 1950s.

power. His virtue was safe with her; so, she thought suddenly, strangely, was hers with him. It was unsettling and comforting at once.

"Maybe," he said. "Or maybe I'm just a liar like you think everyone is. Eh? You think everyone strings everyone else a line? Crap. Who has the time for that shit?"

Perhaps they were drinking beer now. Or was it vodka? She found it hard to tell after a while.

"You know what I mean," she said. "You should know. The sweet young thing who has AIDS and doesn't tell you. Or me. I'm lucky so far. Are you? Or who sucks you for your money. Or josses you 'cause he's into denim and Nordic looks."

"Okay, okay. I give up. Everybody's a creep but you and me."

"And I'm not so sure about you."

"Likewise, I'm sure. Have another. So, if you're so pure, what about the ethics of it?"

"What *about* the ethics of it?" she asked. "Do you think I went through all that sex without paying attention? I had nothing else to do but watch other people come. I saw that old cult movie, where the aliens feed on heroin addiction and orgasm, and the woman's not allowed orgasm so she has to O.D. on smack.[1] Orgasm's more decadent than shooting heroin? I can't buy that, but there's something about a world that sells it over and over again. Sells the thought of pleasure as a commodity, sells the getting of it as if it were the getting of wisdom. And all these times I told you about, I saw other people get it through me. Even when someone finally made me come, it was just a feather in his cap, an accomplishment, nothing personal. Like you said. All I was was a program, they plugged into me and went through the motions and got their result. Nobody cares if the AI finds fulfilment running their damned data analyses. Nobody thinks about depressed and angry Mannboard ROMs. They just think about getting theirs.

"So why not get mine?" She was pacing now, angry, leaning that thin body as if the wind were against her. "Let me be the one who runs the program."

"But you won't be there. You told me how you were going to hide out, all that spy stuff."

She leaned against the wall, smiling a new smile she thought of as predatory. And maybe it was. "Oh, yes," she said. "I'll be there the first time. When Max and Kozyk run this thing and it turns them on. I'll be there. That's all I care to see."

He put his big hands on the wall on either side of her and leaned in. He smelled of sweat and liquor and his face was earnest with intoxication.

"I'll tell you something," he said. "As long as there's the real thing, it won't sell. They'll never buy it."

---

1 *Liquid Sky*, an independent film directed by Slava Tsukeman, written by Tsukeman, Anne Carlisle, and Nina V. Kerova. It debuted at the Montreal Film Festival in 1982.

Angel thought so too. Secretly, because she wouldn't give him the satisfaction of agreement, she too thought they would not go that low. *That's right,* she told herself, *trying to sell it is all right—because they will never buy it.*

But they did.

★ ★ ★

A woman and a computer. Which attracts you most? Now you don't have to choose. Angel has made the choice irrelevant.

In Kozyk's office, he and Max go over the ad campaign. They've already tested the program themselves quite a lot; Angel knows this because it's company gossip, heard over the cubicle walls in the washrooms. The two men are so absorbed that they don't notice her arrival.

"Why is a woman better than a sheep? Because sheep can't cook. Why is a woman better than a Mannboard? Because you haven't bought your sensory add-on." Max laughs.

"And what's better than a man?" Angel says; they jump slightly. "Why, your MannComp touchpads, with two-way input. I bet you'll be able to have them personally fitted."

"Good idea," says Kozyk, and Whitman makes a note on his lapboard. Angel, still stunned though she's had weeks to get used to this, looks at them, then reaches across the desk and picks up her prototype board. "This one's mine," she says. "You play with yourselves and your touchpads all you want."

"Well, you wrote it, baby," said Max. "If you can't come with your own program...."

Kozyk hiccoughs a short laugh before he shakes his head. "Shut up, Whitman," he says. "You're talking to a very rich and famous woman."

Whitman looks up from the simulations of his advertising storyboards, smiling a little, anticipating his joke. "Yeah. It's just too bad she finally burned herself out with this one. They always did say it gives you brain damage."

But Angel hadn't waited for the punch line. She was gone.

Connie Willis (b. 1945)

Connie Willis is a US author who has been writing SF and Fantasy for more than five decades; in that time, she has won more Hugo and Nebula awards than any other author. Her best-known works are a series of time-travel novels focussing on historians from Oxford University who travel to significant periods in history for research purposes, including *Doomsday Book* (1992), *To Say Nothing of the Dog* (1998), and the two-volume *Blackout* and *All Clear* (2010). Her work is also noted for its (often laugh-out-loud) humour, depth of characterization, and engagement with both larger literary history and popular culture.

Note on the text: Originally published in *Omni* (1989) where the title is preceded by "Almost anything can happen ...," "At the Rialto" was subsequently published in several anthologies both before and after it was reprinted in Willis's own collection, *Impossible Things* (1994). This version uses the original as its copy-text.

"At the Rialto" (1989)

"Seriousness of mind was a prerequisite for understanding Newtonian physics. I am not convinced it is not a handicap in understanding quantum theory."

—Excerpt from Dr. Gedanken's keynote address to the 1989
International Congress of Quantum Physicists
Annual Meeting, Hollywood[1]

I got to Hollywood around one-thirty and started trying to check into the Rialto.

"Sorry, we don't have any rooms," the girl behind the desk said. "We're all booked up with some science thing."

"I'm with the science thing," I said. "Dr. Ruth Baringer. I reserved a double."

"There are a bunch of Republicans here, too, and a tour group from Finland. They told me when I started work here that they got all these movie people, but the only one I've seen so far was that guy who played the friend of that other guy in that one movie. You're not a movie person, are you?"

1 Newtonian mechanics are founded on the three laws of motion as detailed by Isaac Newton (1624–1727). Quantum mechanics, conversely, describes the actions of atomic and subatomic nature, which behaves in ways not describable by Newtonian physics. In physics, a "gedanken" experiment is a common term for a thought experiment, from the German. The International Congress of Quantum Physicists is, like many of the scientists mentioned, fictional.

"No," I said. "I'm with the science thing. Dr. Ruth Baringer."

"My name's Tiffany," she said. "I'm not actually a hotel clerk at all. I'm just working here to pay for my transcendental posture lessons. I'm really a model-slash-actress."

"I'm a quantum physicist," I said, trying to get things back on track. "The name is Ruth Baringer."

She messed with the computer for a minute. "I don't show a reservation for you."

"Maybe it's in Dr. Mendoza's name. I'm sharing a room with her."

She messed with the computer some more. "I don't show a reservation for her either. Are you sure you don't want the Disneyland Hotel? A lot of people get the two confused."

"I want the Rialto," I said, rummaging through my bag for my notebook. "I have a confirmation number. W37420."

She typed it in. "Are you Dr. Gedanken?" she asked.

"Excuse me," an elderly man said.

"I'll be right with you," Tiffany told him. "How long do you plan to stay with us, Dr. Gedanken?" she asked me.

"Excuse me," the man said, sounding desperate. He had bushy white hair and a dazed expression, as if he had just been through a horrific experience or had been trying to check in to the Rialto.

He wasn't wearing any socks. I wondered if *he* was Dr. Gedanken. Dr. Gedanken was the main reason I'd decided to come to the meeting. I had missed his lecture on wave/particle duality last year, but I had read the text of it in the *ICQP Journal*, and it had actually seemed to make sense, which is more than you can say for most of quantum theory. He was giving the keynote address this year, and I was determined to hear it.

It wasn't Dr. Gedanken. "My name is Dr. Whedbee," the elderly man said. "You gave me the wrong room."

"All our rooms are pretty much the same," Tiffany said. "Except for how many beds they have in them and stuff."

"My room has a *person* in it!" he said. "Dr. Sleeth. From the University of Texas at Austin. She was changing her clothes." His hair seemed to get wilder as he spoke. "She thought I was a serial killer."

"And you said your name is Dr. Whedbee?" Tiffany asked, fooling with the computer once again. "I don't show a reservation for you."

Dr. Whedbee began to cry.

Tiffany got out a paper towel, wiped off the counter, and turned back to me. "May I help you?" she said.

Thursday, 7:30-9 P.M. *Opening Ceremonies.* Dr. Halvard Onofrio, University of Maryland at College Park, will speak on "Doubts Surrounding the Heisenberg Uncertainty Principle." Ballroom.

I finally got my room at five after Tiffany went off duty. Till then I sat around the lobby with Dr. Whedbee, listening to Abey Fields complain about Hollywood.

"What's wrong with Racine?" he said. "Why do we always have to go to these exotic places, like Hollywood? And St. Louis last year wasn't much better. The Institut Henri Poincaré[1] people kept going off to see the arch and Busch Stadium."

"Speaking of St. Louis," Dr. Takumi said, "have you seen David yet?"

"No," I said.

"Oh, really?" she said. "Last year at the annual meeting you two were practically inseparable. Moonlight riverboat rides and all."

"What's on the programming tonight?" I said to Abey.

"David was just here," Dr. Takumi said. "He said to tell you he was going out to look at the stars in the sidewalk."

"That's exactly what I'm talking about," Abey said. "Riverboat rides and movie stars. What do those things have to do with quantum theory? Racine would have been an appropriate setting for a group of physicists. Not like this ... this ... do you realize we're practically across the street from Grauman's Chinese Theatre? And Hollywood Boulevard's where all those gangs hang out. If they catch you wearing red or blue, they'll—"[2]

He stopped. "Is that Dr. Gedanken?" he asked, staring at the front desk.

I turned and looked. A short, roundish man with a mustache was trying to check in. "No," I said. "That's Dr. Onofrio."

"Oh, yes," Abey said, consulting his program book. "He's speaking tonight at the opening ceremonies. On the Heisenberg uncertainty principle. Are you going?"

"I'm not sure," I said, which was supposed to be a joke, but Abey didn't laugh.

"I must meet Dr. Gedanken. He's just gotten funding for a new project."

I wondered what Dr. Gedanken's new project was—I would have loved to work with him.

"I'm hoping he'll come to my workshop on the wonderful world of quantum physics," Abey said, still watching the desk. Amazingly enough, Dr. Onofrio seemed to have gotten a key and was heading for the elevators. "I think his project has something to do with understanding quantum theory."

Well, that let me out. I didn't understand quantum theory at all. I sometimes had a sneaking suspicion nobody else did either, including Abey Fields, and that they just weren't willing to admit it.

---

1 A mathematics research facility at Sorbonne University named after mathematician Henri Poincaré (1854–1912).

2 Grauman's Chinese Theatre is a movie theatre opened by Sid Grauman (1879–1959) in 1927 in Los Angeles, on the famous Hollywood Boulevard, also home to the Hollywood Walk of Fame. The gangs referred to are the Crips and the Bloods, identified by blue and red clothing, respectively, though the story likely references their representation in popular culture (such as in the 1988 film *Colors*) rather than reality.

I mean, an electron is a particle except it acts like a wave. In fact, a neutron acts like two waves and interferes with itself (or each other), and you can't really measure any of this stuff properly because of the Heisenberg uncertainty principle, and that isn't the worst of it.[1] When you set up a Josephson junction to figure out what rules the electrons obey, they sneak past the barrier to the other side, and they don't seem to care much about the limits of the speed of light either, and Schrödinger's cat is neither alive nor dead till you open the box, and it all makes about as much sense as Tiffany's calling me Dr. Gedanken.

Which reminded me, I had promised to call Darlene and give her our room number. I didn't have a room number, but if I waited much longer, she'd have left. She was flying to Denver to speak at CU and then coming on to Hollywood sometime tomorrow morning. I interrupted Abey in the middle of his telling me how beautiful Racine was in the winter and went to call her.

"I don't have a room yet," I said when she answered. "Should I leave a message on your machine, or do you want to give me your number in Denver?"

"Never mind all that," Darlene said. "Have you seen David yet?"

To illustrate the problems of the concept of wave function, Dr. Schrödinger imagines a cat being put into a box with a piece of uranium, a bottle of poison gas, and a Geiger counter. If a uranium nucleus disintegrates while the cat is in the box, it will release radiation which will set off the Geiger counter and break the bottle of poison gas. Since it is impossible in quantum theory to predict whether a uranium nucleus will disintegrate while the cat is in the box, and only possible to calculate uranium's probable half-life, the cat is neither alive nor dead until we open the box.—From "The Wonderful World of Quantum Physics," a seminar presented at the ICQP Annual Meeting by A. Fields, Ph.D., University of Nebraska at Wahoo

I completely forgot to warn Darlene about Tiffany, the model-slash-actress.

"What do you mean you're trying to avoid David?" she had asked me at least three times. "Why would you do a stupid thing like that?"

Because in St. Louis I ended up on a riverboat in the moonlight and didn't make it back until the conference was over.

"Because I want to attend the programming," I said the third time around, "not a wax museum. I am a middle-aged woman."

"And David is a middle-aged man who, I might add, is absolutely charming. In fact, he may be the last charming man left in the universe."

"Charm is for quarks,"[2] I said and hung up, feeling smug until I remembered

---

1 Described in 1927 by physicist Werner Heisenberg (1901–76), the uncertainty principle in quantum mechanics posits that the position and speed of a subatomic wave-particle (e.g., a photon or electron) cannot be described exactly. The other terms in this section, including Josephson junction and Schrödinger's cat, are described later in the story.

2 The charm quark is an elementary subatomic particle.

I hadn't told her about Tiffany. I went back to the front desk, thinking maybe Dr. Onofrio's success signaled a change. Tiffany asked, "May I help you?" and left me standing there.

After a while I gave up and went back to the red and gold sofas.

"David was here again," Dr. Takumi said. "He said to tell you he was going to the wax museum."

"There *are* no wax museums in Racine," Abey said.

"What's the programming for tonight?" I said, taking Abey's program from him.

"There's a mixer at six-thirty and the opening ceremonies in the ballroom and then some seminars."

I read the descriptions of the seminars. There was one on the Josephson junction. Electrons were able to somehow tunnel through an insulated barrier even though they didn't have the required energy. Maybe I could somehow get a room without checking in.

"If we were in Racine," Abey said, looking at his watch, "we'd already be checked in and on our way to dinner."

Dr. Onofrio emerged from the elevator, still carrying his bags. He came over and sank down on the sofa next to Abey.

"Did they give you a room with a semi-naked woman in it?" Dr. Whedbee asked.

"I don't know," Dr. Onofrio said. "I couldn't find it." He looked sadly at the key. "They gave me 1282, but the room numbers only go up to 75."

"I think I'll attend the seminar on chaos," I said.

The most serious difficulty quantum theory faces today is not the inherent limitation of measurement capability or the EPR paradox. It is the lack of a paradigm. Quantum theory has no working model, no metaphor that properly defines it.—Excerpt from Dr. Gedanken's keynote address[1]

I got to my room at six, after a brief skirmish with the bellboy-slash-actor who couldn't remember where he'd stored my suitcase and unpacked.

My clothes, which had been permanent-press all the way from MIT, underwent a complete wave-function collapse the moment that I opened my suitcase, and came out looking like Schrödinger's almost-dead cat.

By the time I had called housekeeping for an iron, taken a bath, given up on the iron, and steamed a dress in the shower, I had missed the "Mixer with Munchies" and was half an hour late for Dr. Onofrio's opening remarks.

I opened the door to the ballroom as quietly as I could and slid inside. I had

1 The Einstein–Podolsky–Rosen (EPR) paradox was proposed by Albert Einstein (1879–1955), Boris Podolsky (1896–1966), and Nathan Rosen (1909–95). In the EPR paradox, two entangled subatomic particles can affect each other, regardless of the distance between them; this would seem to violate classical physics, which says that nothing can travel faster than speed of light.

hoped they would be late getting started, but a man I didn't recognize was already introducing the speaker: "—and an inspiration to all of us in the field."

I dived for the nearest chair and sat down.

"Hi," David said. "I've been looking all over for you. Where were you?"

"Not at the wax museum," I whispered.

"You should have been," he whispered back. "It was great. They had John Wayne, Elvis,[1] and Tiffany the model-slash-actress with the brain of a pea-slash-amoeba."

"Shh," I said.

"—the person we've all been waiting to hear, Dr. Ringgit Dinari."

"What happened to Dr. Onofrio?" I asked.

"Shhh," David said.

Dr. Dinari looked a lot like Dr. Onofrio. She was short, roundish, and mustached and was wearing a rainbow-striped caftan. "I will be your guide this evening into a strange new world," she said, "a world where all that you thought you knew, all common sense, all accepted wisdom, must be discarded. A world where all the rules have changed and it sometimes seems there are no rules at all."

She sounded just like Dr. Onofrio, too. He had given this same speech two years ago in Cincinnati. I wondered if he had undergone some strange transformation during his search for room 1282 and was now a woman.

"Before I go on," Dr. Dinari said, "how many of you have already channeled?"

Newtonian physics had as its model the machine. The metaphor of the machine, with its interrelated parts, its gears and wheels, its causes and effects, was what made it possible to think *about Newtonian physics.*—Excerpt from Dr. Gedanken's keynote address

"You knew we were in the wrong place," I hissed at David when we made it out to the lobby.

When we stood up to leave, Dr. Dinari had extended her pudgy hand in its rainbow-striped sleeve and called out in a voice a lot like Charlton Heston's, "O unbelievers! Leave not, for here only is reality!"[2]

"Actually, channeling would explain a lot," David said, grinning.

"If the opening remarks aren't in the ballroom, where are they?"

"Beats me," he said. "Want to go see the Capitol Records Building? It's shaped like a stack of records."

---

1 John Wayne (1907–79), famous US actor best known for starring in Westerns. Elvis Presley (1935–77), famous US singer and actor.

2 Charlton Heston (1923–2008), US actor, famous for roles in such films as *The Ten Commandments* (1956)—in which he played Moses, which is likely being evoked here—and the classic SF films *Planet of the Apes* (1968) and *Soylent Green* (1973).

"I want to go to the opening remarks."

"The beacon on top blinks out *Hollywood* in Morse code."[1]

I went over to the front desk.

"Can I help you?" the clerk behind the desk said. "My name is Natalie, and I'm an actress—"

"Where is the ICQP meeting this evening?" I said.

"They're in the ballroom."

"I'll bet you didn't have any dinner," David said. "I'll buy you an ice cream cone. There's this great place that has the ice cream cone Ryan O'Neal bought for Tatum in *Paper Moon*."[2]

"A channeler's in the ballroom," I told Natalie. "I'm looking for the ICQP."

She fiddled with the computer. "I'm sorry. I don't show a reservation for them."

"How about Grauman's Chinese?" David said. "You want reality? You want Charlton Heston? You want to see quantum theory in action?"

He grabbed my hands. "Come with me," he said seriously.

In St. Louis I had suffered a wave-function collapse a lot like what had happened to my clothes when I opened the suitcase. I had ended up on a riverboat halfway to New Orleans that time. It happened again, and the next thing I knew I was walking around the courtyard of Sid Grauman's Chinese Theatre, eating an ice cream cone and trying to fit my feet in Myrna Loy's[3] footprints.

She must have been a midget or had her feet bound as a child. So, apparently, had Debbie Reynolds, Dorothy Lamour, and Wallace Beery.

The only footprints I came close to fitting were Donald Duck's.[4]

"I see this as a map of the microcosm," David said, sweeping his hand over the slightly irregular pavement of printed and signed cement squares.

"See, there are all these tracks. We know something's been here, and the prints are pretty much the same, only every once in a while you've got this"—he knelt down and pointed to the print of John Wayne's clenched fist—"and over here"—he walked toward the box office and pointed to the print of Betty Grable's leg—"and we can figure out the signatures, but what is this reference to 'Sid' on all these squares? And what does this mean?" He pointed at Red Skelton's square. It said, THANKS SID WE DOOD IT.[5]

"You keep thinking you've found a pattern," David said, crossing over to the

1 Developed in part by Samuel Morse (1791–1872), Morse Code is a system of encoding letters as series of long and short dashes or electrical impulses, originally designed for Morse's telegraph machines.

2 Ryan O'Neal (1941–2023) and Tatum O'Neal (b. 1963), father and daughter US actors who co-starred in the film *Paper Moon* (1973).

3 Myrna Loy (1905–93), US actor known for several hit films, including *The Thin Man* (1934) and its sequels.

4 Debbie Reynolds (1932–2016), Dorothy Lamour (1914–96), and Wallace Beery (1885–1949), all US actors. Donald Duck: Disney cartoon character that first appeared in 1934.

5 Betty Grable (1916–73), US actor, model, and singer; Red Skelton (1913–97), US actor and comedian, who starred in, among other films, the comedy *I Dood It* (1943).

other side, "but Van Johnson's square is kind of sandwiched in here at an angle between Esther Williams and Cantinflas, and who the hell is May Robson?[1] And why are all these squares empty?"

He had managed to maneuver me over behind the display of Academy Award winners. It was an accordionlike wrought-iron screen. I was in the fold between 1944 and 1945.

"And as if that isn't enough, you suddenly realize you're standing in the courtyard. You're not even in the theater."

"And that's what you think is happening in quantum theory?" I said weakly. I was backed up into Bing Crosby, who had won for Best Actor in *Going My Way*.[2] "You think we're not in the theater yet?"

"I think we know as much about quantum theory as we can figure out about May Robson from her footprints," he said, putting his hand up to Ingrid Bergman's cheek (Best Actress, *Gaslight*[3]) and blocking my escape. "I don't think we understand anything *about* quantum theory, not tunneling, not complementarity."[4] He leaned toward me. "Not passion."

The Best Movie of 1945 was *The Lost Weekend*.[5] "Dr. Gedanken understands it," I said, disentangling myself from the Academy Award winners and David. "Did you know he's putting together a new research team for a big project on understanding quantum theory?"

"Yes," David said. "Want to see a movie?"

"There's a seminar on chaos at nine," I said, stepping over the Marx Brothers.[6] "I have to get back."

"If it's chaos you want, you should stay right here," he said, stopping to look at Irene Dunne's handprints. "We could see the movie and then go have dinner. There's this place near Hollywood and Vine that has the mashed potatoes Richard Dreyfuss made into Devils Tower in *Close Encounters*."[7]

---

1 Van Johnson (1916–2008), US actor; Esther Williams (1921–2013), US actor; Cantinflas, stage name of Mexican comedian and actor Mario Fortino Alfonso Moreno Reyes (1911–93); May Robson (1858–1942), Australian American actor.

2 Bing Crosby (1902–77), US singer and actor; *Going My Way* (1944) is a musical comedy, perhaps better known now through its sequel *The Bells of St. Mary's* (1945).

3 Ingrid Bergman (1915–82), Swedish actor who also appeared in *Going My Way* and its sequel. *Gaslight* (1944): a psychological thriller in which a husband tries to convince his wife that she is insane; the film's title is now often used to characterize this form of misogynist manipulation.

4 In quantum mechanics, complementarity refers to the concept that "a complete knowledge of phenomena on atomic dimensions requires a description of both wave and particle properties" (*Britannica*). Quantum tunnelling refers to a phenomenon in which an atomic or subatomic object can pass through an energy barrier, even when the object's energy does not seem strong enough to break through that barrier.

5 *The Lost Weekend* (1945), dir. Billy Wilder, is about an alcoholic writer; in addition to the Oscar for Best Picture, it also won Best Director, Best Actor, and Best Adapted Screenplay, as well as the Grand Prix du Festival International du Film at the first Cannes Film Festival, held immediately after the end of World War II.

6 The Marx Brothers were a comedy troupe, originating in vaudeville before transitioning to film.

7 Irene Dunne (1898–1990) and Richard Dreyfuss (b. 1947), both US actors. *Close Encounters of the Third*

"I want to meet Dr. Gedanken," I said, making it safely to the sidewalk. I looked back at David.

He had gone back to the other side of the courtyard and was looking at Roy Rogers's signature.

"Are you kidding? He doesn't understand it any better than we do."

"Well, at least he's trying."

"So am I. The problem is, how can one neutron possibly interfere with itself, and why are there only two of Trigger's hoofprints here?"[1]

"It's eight fifty-five," I said. "I am going to the chaos seminar."

"If you can find it," he said, getting down on one knee to look at the signature.

"I'll find it," I said grimly.

He stood up and grinned at me, his hands in his pockets. "It's a great movie," he said.

It was happening again. I turned and practically ran across the street.

"*Benji IX* is showing," he shouted after me. "He accidentally exchanges bodies with a Siamese cat."[2]

Thursday 9–10 P.M. "The Science of Chaos." I. Durcheinander,[3] Leipzig. A seminar on the structure of chaos. Principles of chaos will be discussed, including the butterfly effect, fractals, and in-solid billowing. Clara Bow[4] Room.

I couldn't find the chaos seminar. The Clara Bow Room, where it was supposed to be, was empty. A meeting of vegetarians was next door in the Fatty Arbuckle[5] Room, and all the other conference rooms were locked. The channeler was still in the ballroom. "Come!" she commanded when I opened the door. "Understanding awaits!"

I went upstairs to bed.

I had forgotten to call Darlene. She would have left for Denver already but I called her answering machine and told it the room number in case she picked up her messages. In the morning I would have to tell the front desk to give her a key. I went to bed.

Kind (1977) is an iconic SF film directed by Steven Spielberg, in which Dreyfuss's character carves a large mound of mashed potatoes into a replica of the Devil's Tower mountain in Wyoming, where the climax of the film takes place.

1 Roy Rogers (1911–98), US actor and singer, mostly associated with Westerns. Trigger was his horse, who starred with Rogers in several films, and whom Rogers had stuffed and mounted when Trigger died in 1965.

2 Benji was a fictional dog and the hero of several films, starting with *Benji* (1974).

3 Durcheinander (Ger.) can be translated as "mixed up" or "messy," with some connotations of chaos.

4 Clara Bow (1905–65), US film actor, most known for her role in *It* (1927), which gave her the nickname, "the It girl," which also became a popular phrase to refer to a "woman who is very famous, fashionable, or successful at a particular time" (*OED*).

5 Roscoe "Fatty" Arbuckle (1887–1933), US actor and director, who faced three trials for the rape and manslaughter of Viginia Rappe (1891–1921), at the last of which he was acquitted.

I didn't sleep well. The air conditioner went off during the night, which meant I didn't have to steam my suit when I got up the next morning. I got dressed and went downstairs.

The programming started at nine o'clock with Abey Fields's "Wonderful World" workshop in the Mary Pickford[1] Room, a breakfast buffet in the ballroom, and a slide presentation on "Delayed Choice Experiments" in Cecil B. DeMille[2] A on the mezzanine level.

The breakfast buffet sounded wonderful, even though it always turns out to be urn coffee and donuts. I hadn't had anything but an ice cream cone since noon the day before, but if David were around, he would be somewhere close to the food, and I wanted to steer clear of him. Last night it had been Grauman's Chinese. Today I was likely to end up at Knott's Berry Farm.[3] I wasn't going to let that happen, even if he was charming.

It was pitch-dark inside Cecil B. DeMille A. Even the slide on the screen up front appeared to be black. "As you can see," Dr. Lvov said, "the laser pulse is already in motion before the experimenter sets up the wave or particle detector."

He clicked to the next slide, which was dark gray, "We used a Mach-Zehnder interferometer[4] with two mirrors and a particle detector. For the first series of tries we allowed the experimenter to decide which apparatus he would use by whatever method he wished. For the second series, we used that most primitive of randomizers—"

He clicked again, to a white slide with black polka dots that gave off enough light for me to be able to spot an empty chair on the aisle ten rows up. I hurried to get to it before the slide changed, and sat down.

"—a pair of dice. Alley's experiments had shown us that when the particle detector was in place, the light was detected as a particle, and when the wave detector was in place, the light showed wavelike behavior, no matter when the choice of apparatus was made."[5]

"Hi," David said. "You've missed five black slides, two gray ones, and a white with black polka dots."

"Shh," I said.

"In our two series, we hoped to ascertain whether the consciousness of the decision affected the outcome." Dr. Lvov clicked to another black slide. "As you can see, the graph shows no effective difference between the tries in which the experimenter chose the detection apparatus and those in which the apparatus was randomly chosen."

"You want to go get some breakfast?" David whispered.

---

1 Mary Pickford (1892–1979), Canadian-US Oscar-winning film actor and co-founder of United Artists.

2 Cecil B. DeMille (1881–1959), US filmmaker.

3 An amusement park in California.

4 A device that measures phase shifts, used in several research areas of quantum physics.

5 Likely a reference to US physicist Carroll Overton (C. O.) Alley Jr. (1927–2016).

"I already ate," I whispered back, and waited for my stomach to growl and give me away. It did.

"There's a great place down near Hollywood and Vine that has the waffles Katharine Hepburn made for Spencer Tracy in *Woman of the Year*."[1]

"Shh," I said.

"And after breakfast, we could go to Frederick's of Hollywood and see the bra museum."[2]

"Will you please be quiet? I can't hear."

"Or see," he said, but he subsided more or less for the remaining ninety-two black, gray, and polka-dotted slides.

Dr. Lvov turned on the lights and blinked smilingly at the audience. "Consciousness had no discernible effect on the results of the experiment. As one of my lab assistants put it, 'The little devil knows what you're going to do before you know it yourself.'"[3]

This was apparently supposed to be a joke, but I didn't think it was very funny. I opened my program and tried to find something to go to that David wouldn't be caught dead at.

"Are you two going to breakfast?" Dr. Thibodeaux asked.

"Yes," David said.

"No," I said.

"Dr. Hotard and I wished to eat somewhere that is *vraiment*[4] Hollywood."

"David knows just the place," I said. "He's been telling me about this great place where they have the grapefruit James Cagney shoved in Mae Clarke's face in *Public Enemy*."[5]

Dr. Hotard hurried up, carrying a camera and four guidebooks. "And then perhaps you would show us Grauman's Chinese Theatre?" he asked David.

"Of course he will," I said. "I'm sorry I can't go with you, but I promised Dr. Verikovsky I'd be at his lecture on Boolean logic.[6] And after Grauman's Chinese, David can take you to the bra museum at Frederick's of Hollywood."

---

1 Katharine Hepburn (1907–2003) and Spencer Tracy (1900–67), US actors who starred together in several films and became an off-screen couple for more than two decades, starting with their first film together, *Woman of the Year* (1942).

2 Frederick's of Hollywood is a US lingerie designer and brand, which opened its Bra Museum (later the Lingerie Museum) in 1987.

3 A reference to Maxwell's demon, a thought-experiment by Scottish physicist James Clerk Maxwell (1831–79), relating to entropy.

4 Truly (Fr.).

5 *The Public Enemy* (1931) was a film about noted gangster Al Capone (1899–1947) starring Cagney (1899–1986); Clarke (1910–92) was uncredited in the film in the role of Kitty.

6 Boolean logic and Boolean algebra—named for their developer, Irish mathematician George Boole (1815–64)—consist of equations or statements designed to generate a result that is either true or false. The statements use such terms as "AND," "OR," and/or "NOT" to achieve the result (see below, for example, when the narrator tries to determine if Tiffany is a model AND actress, or a model OR actress). Boolean operators are important to computer programming, and have a history of use in search engines.

"And the Brown Derby?"[1] Thibodeaux asked. "I have heard it is shaped like a chapeau."[2] They dragged him off. I watched till they were safely out of the lobby and then ducked upstairs and into Dr. Whedbee's lecture on information theory. Dr. Whedbee wasn't there.

"He went to find an overhead projector," Dr. Takumi said. She had half a donut on a plate in one hand and a Styrofoam cup in the other.

"Did you get that at the breakfast buffet?" I asked.

"Yes. It was the last one. And they ran out of coffee right after I got there. You weren't at Abey Fields's thing, were you?" She set the coffee cup down and took a bite of the donut.

"No," I said, wondering if I should try to take her by surprise or just wrestle the donut away from her.

"You didn't miss anything. He raved the whole time about how we should have had the meeting in Racine." She popped the last piece of donut in her mouth. "Have you seen David yet?"

Friday, 9–10 P.M. "The Eureka Experiment: A Slide Presentation." J. Lvov, Eureka College. Descriptions, results, and conclusions of Lvov's delayed conscious/randomized choice experiments. Cecil B. DeMille A.

Dr. Whedbee eventually came in carrying an overhead projector, the cord trailing behind him. He plugged it in. The light didn't go on.

"Here," Dr. Takumi said, handing me her plate and cup. "I have one of these at Caltech. It needs its fractal basin boundaries adjusted."[3]

She whacked the side of the projector.

There weren't even any crumbs left of the donut. There was about a millimeter of coffee in the bottom of the cup. I was about to stoop to new depths when she hit the projector again. The light came on. "I learned that in the chaos seminar last night," she said, grabbing the cup away from me and draining it. "You should have been there. The Clara Bow Room was packed."

"I believe I'm ready to begin," Dr. Whedbee said. Dr. Takumi and I sat down. "Information is the transmission of meaning," Dr. Whedbee said. He wrote MEANING or possibly INFORMATION on the screen with a green Magic Marker.

"When information is randomized, meaning cannot be transmitted, and we have a state of entropy." He wrote it under MEANING with a red Magic Marker. His handwriting appeared to be completely illegible.

"States of entropy vary from low entropy, such as the mild static on your car radio, to high entropy, a state of complete disorder, of randomness and confusion, in which no information at all is being communicated."

---

1 The Brown Derby was a restaurant in Los Angeles, opened in 1926, which was shaped like a brown derby hat. It spawned a chain of restaurants.

2 Hat (Fr.).

3 Dr. Takumi is making a physics joke about moving a complex, dynamic system (in this case, the projector) into a new state.

Oh, my God, I thought. I forgot to tell the hotel about Darlene.

The next time Dr. Whedbee bent over to inscribe hieroglyphics on the screen, I sneaked out and went down to the desk, hoping Tiffany hadn't come on duty yet. She had.

"May I help you?" she asked.

"I'm in room 663," I said. "I'm sharing a room with Dr. Darlene Mendoza. She's coming in this morning, and she'll be needing a key."

"For what?" Tiffany said.

"To get into the room. I may be in one of the lectures when she gets here."

"Why doesn't she have a key?"

"Because she isn't here yet."

"I thought you said she was sharing a room with you."

"She *will* be sharing a room with me. Her name is Darlene Mendoza."

"And your name?" she asked, hands poised over the computer.

"Ruth Baringer."

"We don't show a reservation for you."

We have made impressive advances in quantum physics in the ninety years since Planck's constant, but they have by and large been advances in technology, not theory. We can only make advances in theory when we have a model we can visualize.—Excerpt from Dr. Gedanken's keynote address

I high-entropied with Tiffany for a while on the subjects of my not having a reservation and the air-conditioning and then switched back suddenly to the problem of Darlene's key in the hope of catching her off guard. It worked about as well as Alley's delayed-choice experiments.

In the middle of my attempting to explain that Darlene was not the air-conditioning repairman, Abey Fields came up.

"Have you seen Dr. Gedanken?"

I shook my head.

"I was sure he'd come to my 'Wonderful World' workshop, but he didn't, and the hotel says they can't find his reservation," he said, scanning the lobby. "I found out what his new project is, incidentally, and I'd be perfect for it. He's going to find a paradigm for quantum theory. Is that him?" he said, pointing at an elderly man getting in the elevator.

"I think that's Dr. Whedbee," I said, but he had already sprinted across the lobby to the elevator.

He nearly made it. The elevator slid to a close just as he got there.

He pushed the elevator button several times to make the door open again, and when that didn't work, tried to readjust its fractal basin boundaries. I turned back to the desk.

"May I help you?" Tiffany said.

"You may," I said. "My roommate, Darlene Mendoza, will be arriving sometime this morning. She's a producer. She's here to cast the female lead in a new movie starring Robert Redford and Harrison Ford.[1] When she gets here, give her her key. And fix the air-conditioning."

"Yes, ma'am," she said.

The Josephson junction is designed so that electrons must obtain additional energy to surmount the energy barrier. It has been found, however, that some electrons simply tunnel, as Heinz Pagels[2] *put it, "right through the wall."*—From "The Wonderful World of Quantum Physics," A. Fields, UNW

Abey had stopped banging on the elevator button and was trying to pry the elevator doors apart.

I went out the side door and up to Hollywood Boulevard. David's restaurant was near Hollywood and Vine. I turned the other direction, toward Grauman's Chinese Theatre, and ducked into the first restaurant I saw.

"I'm Stephanie," the waitress said. "How many are there in your party?"

There was no one remotely in my vicinity. "Are you an actress-slash-model?" I asked her.

"Yes. I'm working here part-time to pay for my holistic hairstyling lessons."

"There's one of me," I said, holding up my forefinger to make it perfectly clear. "I want a table away from the window."

She led me to a table in front of the window, handed me a menu the size of the macrocosm, and put another one down across from me.

"Our breakfast specials today are papaya stuffed with salmonberries and nasturtium/radicchio salad with a balsamic vinaigrette. I'll take your order when your other party arrives."

I stood the extra menu up so it hid me from the window, opened the other one, and read the breakfast entrees. They all seemed to have *cilantro* or *lemongrass* in their names.

I wondered if *radicchio* could possibly be Californian for *donut*.

"Hi," David said, grabbing the standing-up menu and sitting down. "The sea urchin pâté looks good."

I was actually glad to see him. "How did you get here?" I asked.

"Tunneling," he said. "What exactly is extra-virgin olive oil?"

"I wanted a donut," I said pitifully.

He took my menu away from me, laid it on the table, and stood up. "There's a great place next door that's got the donut Clark Gable taught Claudette Colbert how to dunk in *It Happened One Night*."[3]

---

1 Robert Redford (b. 1936) and Harrison Ford (b. 1942), US actors. Ford is arguably best known for portraying iconic SF and adventure characters Han Solo (from the *Star Wars* franchise) and Indiana Jones in a series of films about that character.

2 Heinz Pagels (1939–88), US physicist.

3 Clark Gable (1901–60), US actor, best known as a leading actor in romantic films. Claudette Colbert (1903–96), French-born US actor who won the Academy Award for Best Actress for her role in the comedy *It Happened One Night* (1934).

The great place was probably out in Long Beach someplace, but I was too weak with hunger to resist him. I stood up. Stephanie hurried over.

"Will there be anything else?" she asked.

"We're leaving," David said.

"Okay then," she said, tearing a check off her pad and slapping it on the table. "I hope you enjoyed your breakfast."

Finding such a paradigm is difficult, if not impossible. Due to Planck's constant[1] *the world we see is largely dominated by Newtonian mechanics. Particles are particles, waves are waves, and objects do not suddenly vanish through walls and reappear on the other side. It is only on the subatomic level that quantum effects dominate.*—Excerpt from Dr. Gedanken's keynote address

The restaurant was next door to Grauman's Chinese, which made me a little nervous, but it had eggs and bacon and toast and orange juice and coffee. And donuts. "I thought you were having breakfast with Dr. Thibodeaux and Dr. Hotard," I said, dunking one in my coffee. "What happened to them?"

"They went to Forest Lawn. Dr. Hotard wanted to see the church where Ronald Reagan got married."

"He got married at Forest Lawn?"

He took a bite of my donut. "In the Wee Kirk of the Heather. Did you know Forest Lawn's got the World's Largest Oil Painting Incorporating a Religious Theme?"[2]

"So why didn't you go with them?"

"And miss the movie?" He grabbed both my hands across the table. "There's a matinee at two o'clock. Come with me."

I could feel things starting to collapse. "I have to get back," I said, trying to disentangle my hands. "There's a panel on the EPR paradox at two o'clock."

"There's another showing at five. And one at eight."

"Dr. Gedanken's giving the keynote address at eight."

"You know what the problem is?" he said, still holding on to my hands. "It isn't really Grauman's Chinese Theatre; it's Mann's, so Sid isn't even around to ask. Like, why do some pairs like Joanne Woodward and Paul Newman share the same square and other pairs don't? Like Ginger Rogers and Fred Astaire?"[3]

---

1 Planck's constant: a physical constant that is central to quantum mechanics, discovered by German physicist Max Planck (1858–1947), whose work in the field earned him a Nobel Prize.

2 Ronald Reagan (1911–2004), US actor and later US President (1981–89). His first marriage to fellow actor Jane Wyman (1917–2007) took place at the Wee Kirk o' the Heather, a church inside the Forest Lawn Memorial Park cemetery in Glendale, California. The painting referenced may be "La Vierge aux anges" ("The Virgin with Angels," also called "The Song of the Angels"), by William-Adolphe Bouguereau (1825–1905).

3 Joanne Woodward (b. 1930) and Paul Newman (1925–2008): US actors, regular co-stars, and married couple; Ginger Rogers (1911–95) and Fred Astaire: US actors and dancers who also often co-starred in films.

"You know what the problem is?" I said, wrenching my hands free. "The problem is you don't take anything seriously. This is a conference, but you don't care anything about the programming or hearing Dr. Gedanken speak or trying to understand quantum theory!" I fumbled in my purse for some money for the check.

"I thought that was what we were talking about," David said, sounding surprised. "The problem is, where do those lion statues that guard the door fit in? And what about all those empty spaces?"

Friday 2–3 P.M. *Panel Discussion on the EPR Paradox*. I. Takumi, moderator, R. Iverson, L. S. Ping. A discussion of the latest research in single-state correlations, including nonlocal influences, the Calcutta proposal, and passion. Keystone Kops Room.[1]

I went up to my room as soon as I got back to the Rialto to see if Darlene was there yet. She wasn't, and when I tried to call the desk, the phone wouldn't work. I went back down to the registration desk. There was no one there. I waited fifteen minutes and then went into the panel on the EPR paradox.

"The Einstein-Podolsky-Rosen paradox cannot be reconciled with quantum theory," Dr. Takumi was saying. "I don't care what the experiments seem to indicate. Two electrons at opposite ends of the universe can't affect each other simultaneously without destroying the entire theory of the space-time continuum."

She was right. Even if it were possible to find a model of quantum theory, what about the EPR paradox? If an experimenter measured one of a pair of electrons that had originally collided, it changed the cross-correlation of the other instantaneously even if the electrons were light-years apart.

It was as if they were eternally linked by that one collision, sharing the same square forever, even if they were on opposite sides of the universe.

"If the electrons *communicated* instantaneously, I'd agree with you," Dr. Iverson said, "but they don't; they simply influence each other. Dr. Shimony defined this influence in his paper on passion, and my experiment clearly—"

I thought of David leaning over me between the Best Pictures of 1944 and 1945, saying, "I think we know as much about quantum theory as we do about May Robson from her footprints."

"You can't explain it away by inventing new terms," Dr. Takumi said.

"I completely disagree," Dr. Ping said. "Passion at a distance is not just an invented term. It's a demonstrated phenomenon." *It certainly is*, I thought, thinking about David taking the macrocosmic menu out of the window and saying, "The sea urchin pâté looks good."

1 The Calcutta proposal may refer to work by physicists Amitava Datta, Dipanker Home (b. 1955), and Amitava Raychaudhuri (b. 1952) relating to the EPR paradox (see p. 489, note 1). "Keystone Cops" was a slapstick film serial in the early years of film (1912–17).

It didn't matter where the electron went after the collision. Even if it went in the opposite direction from Hollywood and Vine, even if it stood a menu in the window to hide it, the other electron would still come and rescue it from the radicchio and buy it a donut.

"A demonstrated phenomenon!" Dr. Takumi said. "Ha!" She banged her moderator's gavel for emphasis.

"Are you saying passion doesn't exist?" Dr. Ping said, getting very red in the face.

"I'm saying one measly experiment is hardly a demonstrated phenomenon."

"One measly experiment! I spent five years on this project!" Dr. Iverson said, shaking his fist at her. "I'll show you passion at a distance!"

"Try it, and I'll adjust your fractal basin boundaries!" Dr. Takumi said, and hit him over the head with the gavel.

Yet finding a paradigm is not impossible. Newtonian physics is not a machine. It simply shares some of the attributes of a machine. We must find a model somewhere in the visible world that shares the often bizarre attributes of quantum physics. Such a model, unlikely as it sounds, surely exists somewhere, and it is up to us to find it.— Excerpt from Dr. Gedanken's keynote address

I went up to my room before the police came. Darlene still wasn't there, and the phone and air-conditioning still weren't working. I was really beginning to get worried. I walked up to Grauman's Chinese to look for David, but he wasn't there. Dr. Whedbee and Dr. Sleeth were behind the Academy Award winners folding screen.

"You haven't seen David, have you?" I asked them.

Dr. Whedbee removed his hand from Norma Shearer's[1] cheek.

"He left," Dr. Sleeth said, disentangling herself from the Best Movie of 1929–30.

"He said he was going out to Forest Lawn," Dr. Whedbee said, trying to smooth down his bushy white hair.

"Have you seen Dr. Mendoza? She was supposed to get in this morning."

They hadn't seen her, and neither had Drs. Hotard and Thibodeaux, who stopped me in the lobby and showed me a postcard of Aimee Semple McPherson's[2] tomb. Tiffany had gone off duty. Natalie couldn't find my reservation. I went back up to the room to wait, thinking Darlene might call.

The air-conditioning still wasn't fixed. I fanned myself with a Hollywood brochure and then opened it up and read it. There was a map of the courtyard of Grauman's Chinese on the back cover. Deborah Kerr and Yul Brynner[3]

1 Norma Shearer (1902–83), Canadian-US actor.

2 Aimee Semple McPherson (1890–1944), Canadian-born US evangelical faith healer and celebrity.

3 Deborah Kerr (1921–2007), Scottish actor best known for her role in *The King and I* (1956), in which she starred opposite Russian-born US actor Yul Brynner (1920–85), also known for his role in the SF classic *Westworld* (1973).

didn't have a square together either, and Katharine Hepburn and Spencer Tracy weren't even on the map. She had made him waffles in *Woman of the Year*, and they hadn't even given them a square.

I wondered if Tiffany the model-slash-actress had been in charge of assigning the cement. I could see her looking blankly at Spencer Tracy and saying, "I don't show a reservation for you."

What exactly was a model-slash-actress? Did it mean she was a model *or* an actress or a model *and* an actress? She certainly wasn't a hotel clerk.

Maybe electrons were actually the Tiffanys of the microcosm, and that explained their wave-slash-particle duality. Maybe they weren't really electrons at all. Maybe they were just working part-time at being electrons to pay for their single-state lessons.

Darlene still hadn't called by seven o'clock. I stopped fanning myself and tried to open a window. It wouldn't budge. The problem was, nobody knew anything about quantum theory. All we had to go on were a few colliding electrons that nobody could see and that couldn't be measured properly because of the Heisenberg uncertainty principle. And there was chaos to consider, and entropy, and all those empty spaces. We didn't even know who May Robson was.

At seven-thirty the phone rang. It was Darlene. "What happened?" I said. "Where are you?"

"At the Beverly Wilshire."

"In Beverly Hills?"

"Yes. It's a long story. When I got to the Rialto, the hotel clerk—I think her name was Tiffany—told me you weren't there. She said they were booked solid with some science thing and had had to send the overflow to other hotels. She said you were at the Beverly Wilshire in Room 1027. How's David?"

"Impossible," I said. "He's spent the whole conference looking at Deanna Durbin's[1] footprints at Grauman's Chinese Theatre and trying to talk me into going to the movies."

"And are you going?"

"I can't. Dr. Gedanken's giving the keynote address in half an hour."

"He is?" Darlene said, sounding surprised. "Just a minute." There was a silence, and then she came back on and said, "I think you should go to the movies. David's one of the last two charming men in the universe."

"But he doesn't take quantum theory seriously. Dr. Gedanken is hiring a research team to design a paradigm, and David keeps talking about the beacon on top of the Capitol Records Building."

"You know, he may be on to something there. I mean, seriousness was all right for Newtonian physics, but maybe quantum theory needs a different approach. Sid says—"

---

1 Deanna Durbin (1921–2013), Canadian-born US actor.

"Sid?"

"This guy who's taking me to the movies tonight. It's a long story. Tiffany gave me the wrong room number, and I walked in on this guy in his underwear. He's a quantum physicist. He was supposed to be staying at the Rialto, but Tiffany couldn't find his reservation."

The major implication of wave/particle duality is that an electron has no precise location. It exists in a superposition of probable locations. Only when the experimenter observes the electron does it "collapse" into a location.—"The Wonderful World of Quantum Physics," A. Fields, UNW

Forest Lawn closed at five o'clock. I looked it up in the Hollywood brochure after Darlene hung up.

There was no telling where he might have gone: the Brown Derby or the La Brea Tar Pits or some great place near Hollywood and Vine that had the alfalfa sprouts John Hurt ate right before his chest exploded in *Alien*.[1]

At least I knew where Dr. Gedanken was. I changed my clothes and got in the elevator, thinking about wave/particle duality and fractals and high-entropy states and delayed-choice experiments. The problem was, where could you find a paradigm that would make it possible to visualize quantum theory when you had to include Josephson junctions and passion and all those empty spaces? It wasn't possible. You had to have more to work with than a few footprints and the impression of Betty Grable's leg.

The elevator door opened, and Abey Fields pounced on me.

"I've been looking all over for you," he said. "You haven't seen Dr. Gedanken, have you?"

"Isn't he in the ballroom?"

"No," he said. "He's already fifteen minutes late, and nobody's seen him. You have to sign this," he said, shoving a clipboard at me.

"What is it?"

"It's a petition." He grabbed it back from me. "'We the undersigned demand that annual meetings of the International Congress of Quantum Physicists henceforth be held in appropriate locations.' Like Racine," he added, shoving the clipboard at me again. "*Unlike* Hollywood."

Hollywood.

"Are you aware it took the average ICQP delegate two hours and thirty-six minutes to check in? They even sent some of the delegates to a hotel in Glendale."

"And Beverly Hills," I said absently. Hollywood, Bra museums and the Marx Brothers and gangs that would kill you if you wore red or blue and Tiffany/

1 John Hurt (1940–2017), US actor. *Alien* (1979): iconic SF-horror film. La Brea Tar Pits: area in Los Angeles comprising pits of bitumen, an important paleontological research site due to the large number of well-preserved fossils.

Stephanie and the World's Largest Oil Painting Incorporating a Religious Theme.

"Beverly Hills," Abey muttered, pulling an automatic pencil out of his pocket protector and writing a note to himself. "I'm presenting the petition during Dr. Gedanken's speech. Well, go on, sign it," he said, handing me the pencil. "Unless you want the annual meeting to be here at the Rialto next year."

I handed the clipboard back to him. "I think from now on the annual meeting might be here every year," I said, and took off running for Grauman's Chinese.

When we have that paradigm, one that embraces both the logical and the nonsensical aspects of quantum theory, we will be able to look past the colliding electrons and the mathematics and see the microcosm in all its astonishing beauty.—Excerpt from Dr. Gedanken's keynote address

"I want a ticket to *Benji IX*," I told the girl at the box office. Her name tag said, WELCOME TO HOLLYWOOD. MY NAME IS KIMBERLY.

"Which theater?" she said.

"Grauman's Chinese," I said, thinking, *This is no time for a high-entropy state.*

"Which theater?"

I looked up at the marquee. *Benji IX* was showing in all three theaters, the huge main theater and the two smaller ones on either side.

"They're doing audience reaction surveys," Kimberly said. "Each theater has a different ending."

"Which one's in the main theater?"

"I don't know. I just work here part-time to pay for my organic breathing lessons."

"Do you have any dice?" I asked, and then realized I was going about this all wrong. This was quantum theory not Newtonian. It didn't matter which theater I chose or which seat I sat down in. This was a delayed-choice experiment and David was already in flight.

"The one with the happy ending," I said.

"Center theater," she said.

I walked past the stone lions and into the lobby. Rhonda Fleming[1] and some Chinese wax figures were sitting inside a glass case next to the door to the rest rooms. There was a huge painted screen behind the concession stand.

I bought a box of Raisinets, a tub of popcorn, and a box of jujubes and went inside the theater.

It was bigger than I had imagined. Rows and rows of empty red chairs curved between the huge pillars and up to the red curtains where the screen must be. The walls were covered with intricate drawings. I stood there,

1 Rhonda Fleming (1923–2020), US actor and singer.

holding my jujubes and Raisinets and popcorn, staring at the chandelier overhead. It was an elaborate gold sunburst surrounded by silver dragons. I had never imagined it was anything like this.

The lights went down, and the red curtains opened, revealing an inner curtain like a veil across the screen.

I went down the dark aisle and sat in one of the seats. "Hi," I said, and handed the Raisinets to David.

"Where have you been?" he said. "The movie's about to start."

"I know," I said. I leaned across him and handed Darlene her popcorn and Dr. Gedanken his jujubes. "I was working on the paradigm for quantum theory."

"And?" Dr. Gedanken said, opening his jujubes.

"And you're both wrong," I said. "It isn't Grauman's Chinese. It isn't movies either, Dr. Gedanken."

"Sid," Dr. Gedanken said. "If we're all going to be on the same research team, I think we should use first names."

"If it isn't Grauman's Chinese or the movies, what is it?" Darlene asked, eating popcorn.

"It's Hollywood."

"Hollywood," Dr. Gedanken said thoughtfully.

"Hollywood," I said. "Stars in the sidewalk and buildings that look like stacks of records and hats, and radicchio and audience surveys and bra museums. And the movies. And Grauman's Chinese."

"And the Rialto," David said.

"Especially the Rialto."

"And the ICQP," Dr. Gedanken said.

I thought about Dr. Lvov's black and gray slides and the disappearing chaos seminar and Dr. Whedbee writing MEANING or possibly INFORMATION on the overhead projector. "And the ICQP," I said.

"Did Dr. Takumi really hit Dr. Iverson over the head with a gavel?" Darlene asked.

"Shh," David said. "I think the movie's starting." He took hold of my hand. Darlene settled back with her popcorn, and Dr. Gedanken put his feet up on the chair in front of him. The inner curtain opened, and the screen lit up.

Derrick Bell (1930–2011)

Derrick Bell was a well-known lawyer, civil rights leader, and professor in the US, noted especially for his role in developing Critical Race Theory as an element of legal education, activism, and practice. The first Black tenured professor at Harvard Law School, he later resigned to protest the fact that there were no women of colour among the tenured faculty. A central premise of his legal scholarship was that racism was a founding principle of US law, and as such the law's pretense to "objectivity" and "neutrality" was fundamentally impossible. In addition to—but, importantly, also as a part of—his legal scholarship, he wrote several fictional narratives, mostly SF, serving as thought experiments to highlight the ways in which race and identity (from an intersectional understanding) are at the heart of American jurisprudence. "The Space Traders" is the best known of these.

Note on the text: "The Space Traders" was first published in Bell's collection *Faces at the Bottom of the Well: The Permanence of Racism* (1992), though Bell published an earlier version in *Rutgers Law Review* (1990), as "The Chronicle of the Space Traders," within the larger piece "Racism: A Prophecy for the Year 2000," itself based on a speech from 1989. The later version reached a wider SF audience when Sheree R. Thomas included it in her groundbreaking anthology *Dark Matter: A Century of Speculative Fiction from the African Diaspora* (2000). The version from *Faces at the Bottom of the Well* is used as the source here.

"The Space Traders" (1992)

1 January. The first surprise was not their arrival. The radio messages had begun weeks before, announcing that one thousand ships from a star far out in space would land on 1 January 2000, in harbors along the Atlantic coast from Cape Cod to North Carolina. Well before dawn on that day, millions of people across North America had wakened early to witness the moment the ships entered Earth's atmosphere. However expected, to the watchers, children of the electronic age, the spaceships' approach was as awesome as had been that earlier one of three small ships, one October over five hundred years before, to the Indians of the island of Santo Domingo in the Caribbean.[1]

No, the first surprise was the ships themselves. The people who lined the beaches of New Jersey where the first ships were scheduled to arrive, saw not anything NASA might have dreamed up, but huge vessels, the size of aircraft carriers, which the old men in the crowd recognized as being pretty much like the box-shaped landing craft that carried Allied troops to the Normandy beachheads during the Second World War.

1 See John Yewell, Chris Dodge, and Jan Desirey, eds., *Confronting Columbus: An Anthology* (1992). (Bell's endnote)

As the sun rose on that cold bright morning, the people on the shore, including an anxious delegation of government officials and media reporters, witnessed a fantastic display of eerie lights and strange sound—evidently the visitors' salute to their American hosts. Almost unnoticed during the spectacle, the bow of the leading ship slowly lowered. A sizable party of the visitors—the first beings from outer space anyone on Earth had ever seen—emerged and began moving majestically across the water toward shore. The shock of seeing these beings, regal in appearance and bearing, literally walking on the waves was more thrilling than frightening. At least, no one panicked.

Then came the second surprise. The leaders of this vast armada could speak English. Moreover, they spoke in the familiar comforting tones of former President Reagan,[1] having dubbed his recorded voice into a computerized language-translation system.

After the initial greetings, the leader of the U.S. delegation opened his mouth to read his welcoming speech—only the first of several speeches scheduled to be given on this historic occasion by the leaders of both political parties and other eminent citizens, including—of course—stars of the entertainment and sports worlds. But before he could begin, the principal spokesperson for the space people (and it wasn't possible to know whether it was man or woman or something else entirely) raised a hand and spoke crisply, and to the point.

And this point constituted the third surprise. Those mammoth vessels carried within their holds treasure of which the United States was in most desperate need: gold, to bail out the almost bankrupt federal, state, and local governments; special chemicals capable of unpolluting the environment, which was becoming daily more toxic, and restoring it to the pristine state it had been before Western explorers set foot on it; and a totally safe nuclear engine and fuel, to relieve the nation's all-but-depleted supply of fossil fuel. In return, the visitors wanted only one thing—and that was to take back to their home star all the African Americans who lived in the United States.

The jaw of every one of the welcoming officials dropped, not a word of the many speeches they had prepared suitable for the occasion. As the Americans stood in stupefied silence, the visitors' leader emphasized that the proposed trade was for the Americans freely to accept or not, that no force would be used. Neither then nor subsequently did the leader or any other of the visitors, whom anchorpersons on that evening's news shows immediately labeled the "Space Traders," reveal why they wanted only black people or what plans they had for them should the United States be prepared to part with that or any other group of its citizens. The leader only reiterated to his still-dumbfounded audience that, in exchange for the treasure they had brought, they wanted to take away every American citizen categorized as black on birth certificate or other official identification. The Space Traders said they would wait sixteen

1 Ronald Reagan (1911–2004), US actor and later US President (1981–89).

days for a response to their offer. That is, on 17 January—the day when in that year the birthday of Martin Luther King, Jr.,[1] was to be observed—they would depart carrying with them every black man, woman, and child in the nation and leave behind untold treasure. Otherwise, the Space Traders' leader shrugged and glanced around—at the oil slick in the water, at the dead gulls on the beach, at the thick shadow of smog that obscured the sky on all but the windiest days. Then the visitors walked back over the waves and returned to their ships.

Their departure galvanized everyone—the delegation, the watchers on the beach, the President glued to his television screen in the White House, citizens black and white throughout the country. The President, who had been advised to stay in the White House out of concern for his security, called Congress into special session and scheduled a cabinet meeting for the next morning. Governors reconvened any state legislatures not already in session. The phones of members of Congress began ringing, as soon as the millions of people viewing the Space Traders' offer on television saw them move back across the water, and never stopped till the morning of 17 January.

There was a definite split in the nature of the calls—a split that reflected distinctly different perceptions of the Space Traders. Most white people were, like the welcoming delegation that morning, relieved and pleased to find the visitors from outer space unthreatening. They were not human, obviously, but resembled the superhuman, good-guy characters in comic books; indeed, they seemed to be practical, no-nonsense folks like regular Americans.

On the other hand, many American blacks—whether watching from the shore or on their television screens—had seen the visitors as distinctly unpleasant, even menacing in appearance. While their perceptions of the visitors differed, black people all agreed that the Space Traders looked like bad news—and their trade offer certainly was—and burned up the phone lines urging black leaders to take action against it.

But whites, long conditioned to discounting any statements of blacks unconfirmed by other whites, chose now, of course, to follow their own perceptions. "Will the blacks never be free of their silly superstitions?" whites asked one another with condescending smiles. "Here, in this truly historic moment, when America has been selected as the site for this planet's first contact with people from another world, the blacks just revert to their primitive fear and foolishness." Thus, the blacks' outrage was discounted in this crisis; they had as usual, no credibility.

And it *was* a time of crisis. Not only because of the Space Traders' offer per se, but because that offer came when the country was in dire straits. Decades of conservative, laissez-faire capitalism had emptied the coffers of all

1 Martin Luther King Jr. (1929–68), US Civil Rights leader. Martin Luther King Jr. Day is a federal holiday in the US, honoured on the third Monday in January, near King's January 15 birthday. The first MLK Day was in 1986, nearly two decades after King's assassination in 1968.

but a few of the very rich. The nation that had, in the quarter-century after the Second World War, funded the reconstruction of the free world had, in the next quarter-century, given itself over to greed and willful exploitation of its natural resources. Now it was struggling to survive like any third-world nation. Massive debt had curtailed all but the most necessary services. The environment was in shambles, as reflected by the fact that the sick and elderly had to wear special masks whenever they ventured out-of-doors. In addition, supplies of crude oil and coal were almost exhausted. The Space Traders' offer had come just in time to rescue America. Though few gave voice to their thoughts, many were thinking that the trade offer was, indeed, the ultimate solution to the nation's troubles.

2 January. The insomnia that kept the American people tossing and turning that first night of the new century did not spare the White House. As soon as the President heard the Space Traders' post-arrival proposition on television, his political instincts immediately locked into place. This was big! And it looked from the outset like a "no win" situation—not a happy crisis at the start of an election year. Even so, he had framed the outline of his plan by the time his cabinet members gathered at eight o'clock the next morning.

There were no blacks in his cabinet. Four years before, during his first election campaign, the President had made some vague promises of diversity when speaking to minority gatherings. But after the election, he thought, What the hell! Most blacks and Hispanics had not supported him or his party. Although he had followed the practice of keeping one black on the Supreme Court, it had not won him many minority votes. He owed them nothing. Furthermore, the few black figures in the party always seemed to him overly opportunistic and, to be frank, not very smart. But now, as the cabinet members arrived, he wished he had covered his bases better.

In the few hours since the Space Traders' offer, the White House and the Congress had been inundated with phone calls and telegrams. The President was not surprised that a clear majority spontaneously urged acceptance of the offer.

"Easy for them to say," he murmured to an aide. "I'll bet most of those who favor the trade didn't sign or give their names."

"On the contrary," the assistant replied, "the callers are identifying themselves, and the telegrams are signed."

At least a third of the flood of phone calls and faxes urging quick acceptance of the offer expressed the view that what the nation would give up—its African-American citizens—was as worthwhile as what it would receive. The statements accurately reflected relations at the dawn of the new century. The President had, like his predecessors for the last generation, successfully exploited racial fears and hostility in his election campaign. There had been complaints, of course, but those from his political opponents sounded like sour grapes. They, too, had tried to minimize the input of blacks so as not to frighten away white voters.

The race problem had worsened greatly in the 1990s. A relatively small number of blacks had survived the retrogression of civil rights protection, perhaps 20 percent having managed to make good in the increasingly technologically oriented society. But, without anyone acknowledging it and with hardly a peep from the press, more than one half of the group had become outcasts. They were confined to former inner-city areas that had been divorced from their political boundaries. High walls surrounded these areas, and armed guards controlled entrance and exit around the clock. Still, despite all precautions, young blacks escaped from time to time to terrorize whites. Long dead was the dream that this black underclass would ever "overcome."[1]

The President had asked Gleason Golightly, the conservative black economics professor, who was his unofficial black cabinet member, to attend the meeting. Golightly was smart and seemed to be truly conservative, not a man ready to sing any political tune for a price. His mere presence as a person of color at this crucial session would neutralize any possible critics in the media, though not in the black civil rights community.

The cabinet meeting came to order.

"I think we all know the situation," the President said. "Those extraterrestrial beings are carrying in their ships a guarantee that America will conquer its present problems and prosper for at least all of this new century."

"I would venture, sir," the Vice President noted, "that the balance of your term will be known as 'America's Golden Age.' Indeed, the era will almost certainly extend to the terms of your successor."

The President smiled at the remark, as—on cue—did the cabinet. "The VP is right, of course," the President said. "Our visitors from outer space are offering us the chance to correct the excesses of several generations. Furthermore, many of the men and women—voters all—who are bombarding us with phone calls, see an added bonus in the Space Traders' offer." He looked around at his attentive cabinet members. "They are offering not only a solution to our nation's present problems but also one—surely an ultimate one—to what might be called the great American racial experiment. That's the real issue before us today. Does the promise of restored prosperity justify our sending away fifteen percent of our citizens to Lord knows what fate?"

"There are pluses and minuses to this 'fate' issue, Mr. President." Helen Hipmeyer, Secretary of Health and Human Services, usually remained silent at cabinet meetings. Her speaking up now caused eyebrows to rise around the table. "A large percentage of blacks rely on welfare and other social services. Their departure would ease substantially the burden on our state and national budgets. Why, the cost of caring for black AIDS victims alone has been extraordinary. On the other hand, the consternation and guilt among many whites if the blacks are sent away would take a severe psychological toll,

1 The reference here is to the gospel song "We Shall Overcome," which has historic and ongoing ties to the US Civil Rights and Labour movements.

with medical and other costs which might also reach astronomical levels. To gain the benefits we are discussing, without serious side effects, we must have more justification than I've heard thus far."

"Good point, Madame Secretary," the President answered, "but there are risks at every opportunity."

"I've never considered myself a particularly courageous individual, Mr. President." It was the Secretary of the Interior, a man small in stature but with a mind both sharp and devious, who had presided over the logging of the last of the old-growth timber in the nation's national forests. "But if I could guarantee prosperity for this great country by giving my life or going off with the Space Traders, I would do it without hesitation. And, if I would do it, I think every red-blooded American with an ounce of patriotism would as well." The Secretary sat down to the warm applause of his colleagues.

His suggestion kindled a thought in the Secretary of Defense. "Mr. President, the Secretary's courage is not unlike that American men and women have exhibited when called to military service. Some go more willingly than others, but almost all go even with the knowledge that they may not come back. It is a call a country makes on the assumption that its citizens will respond. I think that is the situation we have here, except that instead of just young men and women, the country needs all of its citizens of African descent to step forward and serve." More applause greeted this suggestion.

The Attorney General asked for and got the floor. "Mr. President, I think we could put together a legislative package modeled on the Selective Service Act of 1918. Courts have uniformly upheld this statute and its predecessors as being well within congressional power to exact enforced military duty at home or abroad by United States citizens.[1] While I don't see any constitutional problems, there would likely be quite a debate in Congress. But if the mail they are receiving is anything like ours, then the pressure for passage will be irresistible."

The President and the cabinet members heard reports from agents who had checked out samples of the gold, chemicals, and machinery the Space Traders had brought. More tests would be run in the next few days, but first indications were that the gold was genuine, and that the antipollution chemicals and the nuclear fuel machine were safe and worked. Everyone recognized that the benefits to the country would be enormous. The ability to erase the country's debt alone would ease the economic chaos the Federal Reserve had staved off during the last few years only by its drastic—the opposition party called it "unscrupulous"—manipulation of the money supply. The Secretary of the Treasury confirmed that the Space Traders' gold would solve the nation's economic problems for decades to come.

1 Military Selective Service Act, 50 USCS Appx §451, et seq. See, for example, *Selective Draft Law Cases*, 245 U.S. 366 (1918). (Bell's endnote); this act, which enabled the US to create an army through a draft, or conscription, was initially enacted in 1917, for World War I.

"What are your thoughts on all this, Professor Golightly?" asked the President, nodding at the scholarly-looking black man sitting far down the table. The President realized that there would be a lot more opposition to a selective service plan among ordinary citizens than among the members of his cabinet, and hoped Golightly would have some ideas for getting around it.

Golightly began as though he understood the kind of answer the President wanted.

"As you know, Mr. President, I have supported this administration's policies that have led to the repeal of some civil rights laws, to invalidation of most affirmative action programs, and to severe reduction in appropriations for public assistance. To put it mildly, the positions of mine that have received a great deal of media attention, have not been well received in African-American communities. Even so, I have been willing to be a 'good soldier' for the Party even though I am condemned as an Uncle Tom[1] by my people. I sincerely believe that black people needed to stand up on their own feet, free of special protection provided by civil rights laws, the suffocating burden of welfare checks, and the stigmatizing influence of affirmative action programs. In helping you undermine these policies, I realized that your reasons for doing so differed from mine. And yet I went along."

Golightly stopped. He reached down for his coffee mug, took a few sips, and ran his fingers through his graying but relatively straight (what some black people call "good") hair.[2] "Mr. President, my record of support entitles me to be heard on the Space Traders' proposition. I disagree strongly with both the Secretary of the Interior and the Attorney General. What they are proposing is not universal selective service for blacks. It is group banishment, a most severe penalty and one that the Attorney General would impose without benefit of either due process or judicial review.

"It is a mark of just how far out of the mainstream black people are that this proposition is given any serious consideration. Were the Space Traders attracted by and asking to trade any other group—white women with red hair and green eyes, for example—a horrified public would order the visitors off the planet without a moment's hesitation. The revulsion would not be less because the number of persons with those physical characteristics are surely fewer than the twenty million black citizens you are ready to condemn to intergalactic exile.

"Mr. President, I cannot be objective on this proposal. I will match my patriotism, including readiness to give my life for my country, with that of the Secretary of the Interior. But my duty stops short of condemning my wife, my

---

1 Uncle Tom is the eponymous character in Harriet Beecher Stowe's abolitionist novel *Uncle Tom's Cabin; or, Life among the Lowly* (1852), and the character was also adapted in several later works. Because the character is often represented as subservient to his white oppressors, the name became an insult and a stereotype.

2 Black people's hair has long been a site for racial politics in the US and elsewhere. "Good hair" generally refers, as here, to straight hair that more closely resembles racist constructions of European beauty.

three children, my grandchildren, and my aged mother to an unknown fate. You simply cannot condemn twenty million people because they are black, and thus fit fodder for trade, so that this country can pay its debts, protect its environment, and ensure its energy supply. I am not ready to recommend such a sacrifice. Moreover, I doubt whether the Secretary of the Interior would willingly offer up his family and friends if the Space Traders sought them instead of me and mine." He paused.

"Professor Golightly," the Secretary of the Interior said, leaning forward, "the President asked you a specific question. This is not the time to debate which of us is the more patriotic or to engage in the details of the sacrifice that is a necessary component of any service for one's country."

Golightly chose to ignore the interruption. He knew, and the President knew, that his support—or, at least, his silent acquiescence—would be critical in winning undecided whites over to the selective service scheme. For their purposes, the President's media people had made Golightly an important voice on racial policy issues. They needed him now as never before.

"Mr. President," he continued, "you and your cabinet must place this offer in historical perspective. This is far from the first time this country's leaders have considered and rejected the removal of all those here of African descent. Benjamin Franklin and other abolitionists actively sought schemes to free the slaves and return them to their homeland. Lincoln examined and supported emigration programs both before and after he freed the slaves.[1] Even those Radical Republicans who drafted the Civil War amendments wondered whether Africans could ever become a part of the national scene, a part of the American people.

"As early as 1866, Michigan's Senator Jacob Merritt Howard, an abolitionist and key architect of the Fourteenth Amendment,[2] recognized the nation's need to confront the challenge posed by the presence of the former slaves, and spoke out on it, saying:

> For weal or for woe, the destiny of the colored race in this country is wrapped up with our own; they are to remain in our midst, and here spend their years and here bury their fathers and finally repose them-

1 Benjamin Franklin (1706–90), US statesman and polymath and one of the signatories to the Declaration of Independence. Franklin himself was an enslaver for the majority of his adult life, but he became active as an abolitionist late in life, and eventually became president of the Pennsylvania Abolition Society and unsuccessfully petitioned Congress, shortly before he died, to abolish slavery. Abraham Lincoln (1809–65), 16th president of the US who led the Union in the Civil War. Lincoln is remembered for his work in abolishing slavery, but his views on race and slavery varied over time. Lincoln and several abolitionists voiced support for so-called "colonization" efforts to send formerly enslaved people to Liberia, a colony in Africa supported by the American Colonization Society, though Lincoln would abandon this position shortly before his assassination (see, e.g., Foner).

2 The 14th Amendment to the US Constitution, ratified in 1868, guarantees the rights of formerly enslaved people, guarantees birthright citizenship, and forbids the passing of laws that would restrict the rights of any citizen.

> selves. We may regret it. It may not be entirely compatible with our taste that they should live in our midst. We cannot help it. Our forefathers introduced them, and their destiny is to continue among us; and the practical question which now presents itself to us is as to the best mode of getting along with them.[1]

"Now, Mr. President, after receiving your invitation to this meeting, I had no difficulty in guessing its agenda or predicting how many of you might come down in favor of accepting the Space Traders' offer, and so looked up Senator Howard's speech. I have prepared copies of it for each of you. I recommend you study it."

Golightly walked around the large table to give each cabinet member a copy of the speech. As he did so, he pointed out, "The Senator's words are grudging rather than generous, conciliatory rather than crusading. He proposed sanctuary rather than equality for blacks. And though there have been periods in which their striving for full equality seems to have brought them close to their goal, sanctuary remains the more accurate description of black citizenship."

Returning to his place, Golightly continued. "This status has provided this nation an essential stability, one you sacrifice at your peril. With all due respect, Mr. President, acceptance of the Space Traders' solution will not bring a century of prosperity to this country. Secretary Hipmeyer is correct. What today seems to you a solution from Heaven will instead herald a decade of shame and dissension mirroring the moral conflicts that precipitated this nation into its most bloody conflict, the Civil War. The deep, self-inflicted wounds of that era have never really healed. Their reopening will inevitably lead to confrontations and strife that could cause the eventual dissolution of the nation."

"You seem to assume, Professor Golightly," the Secretary of the Interior interrupted again, "that the Space Traders want African Americans for some heinous purpose. Why do you ignore alternative scenarios? They are obviously aware of your people's plight here. Perhaps they have selected them to inhabit an interplanetary version of the biblical land of milk and honey. Or, more seriously," the Secretary said, "they may offer your people a new start in a less competitive environment, or"—he added, with a slight smirk in the President's direction—"perhaps they are going to give your people that training in skills and work discipline you're always urging on them."

No one actually laughed, but all except Golightly thought the Secretary's comment an excellent response to the black professor's gloomy predictions.

"I think we get your point, Professor," the President replied smoothly, concerned not to alienate a man whose support he would need. "We will give it

1 L. Levy, K. Karst, and D. Mahoney, eds., *Encyclopedia of the American Constitution*, II (1986), 761. (Bell's endnote)

weight in our considerations. Now," he said, rising, "we need to get to work on this thing. We don't have much time." He asked the Attorney General to draw up a rough draft of the proposed legislation by the end of the day, and told the rest of his cabinet that his aides would shortly be bringing them specific assignments. "Now let's all of us be sure to keep to ourselves what was said at this meeting"—and he glanced meaningfully at Professor Golightly. "Well, that's it for now, people. Meeting adjourned."

Long after the others had departed, Gleason Golightly sat at the long conference table. His hands were folded. He stared at the wall. He had always prided himself as the "man on the inside." While speaking in support of conservative policies, those were—he knew—policies that commanded enough support to be carried out. As a black man, his support legitimated those policies and salved the consciences of the whites who proposed and implemented them. A small price to pay, Golightly had always rationalized, for the many behind-the-scenes favors he received. The favors were not for himself. Golightly, a full professor at a small but well-endowed college, neither wanted nor needed what he called "blood money." Rather, he saw that black colleges got much-needed funding; and through his efforts, certain black officials received appointments or key promotions. He smiled wryly when some of these officials criticized his conservative positions and called him "Uncle Tom." He could bear that, knowing he made a contribution few others were able—or willing—to make to the racial cause.

Booker T. Washington was his hero and had been since he was a child growing up in a middle-class family in Alabama, not far from Tuskegee, the home of Tuskegee Institute, which Washington had founded in 1881.[1] He had modeled his career on old Booker T., and while he did not have a following and had created no institutions, Golightly knew he had done more for black people than had a dozen of the loud-mouthed leaders who, he felt, talked much and produced little. But all of his life, he had dreamed of there coming a moment when his position as insider would enable him to perform some heroic act to both save his people great grief and gain for him the recognition and the love for which, despite his frequent denials, he knew he yearned.

Now, as he sat alone, he feared that this morning's meeting was that big chance, and he had failed it. The stakes of course, were larger than he would have ever imagined they might be, and yet he thought he'd had the arguments. In retrospect, though, those arguments were based on morality and assumed a willingness on the part of the President and the cabinet to be fair, or at least to balance the benefits of the Trade against the sacrifice it would require of a selected portion of the American people. Instead of outsmarting them,

1 Booker T. Washington (1856–1915), civil rights leader and educator, author of the autobiography *Up from Slavery* (1901), and first principal of the Tuskegee Institute (now Tuskegee University), founded as a Black educational institution.

Golightly had done what he so frequently criticized civil rights spokespersons for doing: he had tried to get whites to do right by black people because it was right that they do so. "Crazy!" he commented when civil rights people did it. "Crazy!" he mumbled to himself, at himself.

"Oh, Golightly, glad you're still here. I want a word with you." Golightly looked up as the Secretary of the Interior, at his most unctuous, eased himself into the seat beside him.

"Listen, old man, sorry about our differences at the meeting. I understand your concerns."

Golightly did not look at the man and, indeed, kept his eyes on the wall throughout their conversation. "What do you want, Mr. Secretary?"

The Secretary ignored Golightly's coldness. "You could tell in the meeting and from the media reports that this Trade thing is big, very big. There will be debate—as there should be in a great, free country like ours. But if I were a betting man, which I am not because of my religious beliefs, I would wager that this offer will be approved."

"I assume, Mr. Secretary, that to further the best interests of this *great, free* country of ours, you will be praying that the Trade is approved." Golightly's voice deepened ironically on the crucial words.

The Secretary's smile faded, and his eyes narrowed. "The President wants you to say whatever you can in favor of this plan."

"Why don't we simply follow your suggestion, Mr. Secretary, and tell everyone that the Space Traders are going to take the blacks to a land of milk and honey?"

The Secretary's voice hardened. "I don't think even black people are that stupid. No, Gleason, talk about patriotism, about the readiness of black people to make sacrifices for this country, about how they are really worthy citizens no matter what some may think. We'll leave the wording to you. Isn't sacrifice as proof of patriotism what your Frederick Douglass[1] argued to get President Lincoln to open up the Union army to black enlistees?"

"And then?" Golightly asked, his eyes never moving from the wall.

"We know some blacks will escape. I understand some are leaving the country already. But"—and the Secretary's voice was smooth as butter—"if you go along with the program, Gleason, and the Trade is approved, the President says he'll see to it that one hundred black families are smuggled out of the country. You decide who they are. They'll include you and yours, of course."

Golightly said nothing.

After a moment of hesitation, the Secretary got up and strode to the door. Before leaving, he turned and said, "Think about it, Golightly. It's the kind of deal we think you should go for."

---

1 Frederick Douglass (c. 1818–95), self-emancipated, formerly enslaved abolitionist, author, and world-renowned statesman and speaker.

3 January. The Anti-Trade Coalition—a gathering of black and liberal white politicians, civil rights representatives, and progressive academics—quickly assembled early that morning. Working nonstop and driven by anxiety to cooperate more than they ever had in the past, the members of the coalition had drafted a series of legal and political steps designed to organize opposition to the Space Traders' offer. Constitutional challenges to any acceptance scheme were high on the list of opposition strategies. Bills opposing the Trade were drafted for early introduction in Congress. There were plans for direct action protests and boycotts. Finally, in the event that worse came to worst, and the administration decided to carry out what gathering participants were calling the "African-American kidnapping plot," a secret committee was selected to draft and distribute plans for massive disobedience.

Now, at close to midnight, the plenary session was ready to give final approval to this broad program of resistance.

At that moment, Professor Gleason Golightly sought the floor to propose an alternative response to the Trade offer. Golightly's close connection to the conservative administration and active support of its anti-black views made him far from a hero to most blacks. Many viewed his appearance at this critical hour as an administration-sponsored effort to undermine the coalition's defensive plans and tactics. At last, though, he prevailed on the conference leaders to grant him five minutes.

As he moved toward the podium, there was a wave of hostile murmuring whose justification Golightly acknowledged: "I am well aware that political and ideological differences have for several years sustained a wide chasm between us. But the events of two days ago have transformed our disputes into a painful reminder of our shared status. I am here because, whatever our ideological differences or our socioeconomic positions, we all know that black rights, black interests, black property, even black lives are expendable whenever their sacrifice will further or sustain white needs or preferences."

Hearing Golightly admitting to truths he had long denied, served to silence the murmuring. "It has become an unwritten tradition in this country for whites to sacrifice our rights to further their own interests. This tradition overshadows the national debate about the Space Traders' offer and may well foretell our reply to it."

Oblivious of the whites in the audience, Golightly said, "I realize that our liberal white friends continue to reassure us. 'This is America,' they tell us. 'It can't happen here.' But I've noticed that those whites who are most vigorous in their assurances are least able to rebut the contrary teaching of both historic fact and present reality. Outside civil rights gatherings like this, the masses of black people—those you claim to represent but to whom you seldom listen—are mostly resigned to the nation's acceptance of the Space Traders' offer. For them, liberal optimism is smothered by their life experience.

"Black people know for a fact what you, their leaders, fear to face. Black people know your plans for legislation, litigation, and protest cannot prevail against the tradition of sacrificing black rights. Indeed, your efforts will simply add a veneer of face-saving uncertainty to a debate whose outcome is not only predictable, but inevitable. Flying in the face of our history, you are still relying on the assumption that whites really want to grant justice to blacks, really want to alleviate onerous racial conditions."

"Professor Golightly," the chairman interrupted, "the time we have allotted you has almost expired. The delegates here are weary and anxious to return to their homes so that they can assist their families through this crisis. The defense plans we have formulated are our best effort. Sir, if you have a better way, let us hear it now."

Golightly nodded. "I promised to be brief, and I will. Although you have labored here unselfishly to devise a defense against what is surely the most dangerous threat to our survival since our forebears were kidnapped from Africa's shores, I think I have a better way, and I urge you to hear it objectively and without regard to our past differences. The question is how best to counter an offer that about a third of the voters would support even if the Space Traders offered America nothing at all. Another third may vacillate, but we both know that in the end they will simply not be able to pass up a good deal. The only way we can deflect, and perhaps reverse, a process that is virtually certain to result in approval of the Space Traders' offer, is to give up the oppositional stance you are about to adopt, and forthrightly urge the country to accept the Space Traders' offer."

He paused, looking out over the sea of faces. Then there was a clamor of outraged cries: "Sell-out!" "Traitor!" and "Ultimate Uncle Tom!" The chairman banged his gavel in an effort to restore order.

Seemingly unmoved by the outburst, Golightly waited until the audience quieted, then continued. "A major, perhaps the principal, motivation for racism in this country is the deeply held belief that black people should not have anything that white people don't have. Not only do whites insist on better jobs, higher incomes, better schools and neighborhoods, better everything, but they also usurp aspects of our culture. They have 'taken our blues and gone,' to quote Langston Hughes[1]—songs that sprang from our very subordination. Whites exploit not only our music but our dance, language patterns, dress and hair styles as well. Even the badge of our inferior status, our color, is not sacrosanct, whites spending billions a year to emulate our skin tones, paradoxically, as a sign of their higher status. So whites' appropriation of what is ours and their general acquisitiveness are facts—facts we must make work for us. Rather than resisting the Space Traders' offer, let us circulate widely the rumor that the Space Traders, aware of our long fruitless struggle on this planet, are arranging to transport us to a land of milk and honey—a virtual paradise.

---

1 Langston Hughes, "Note on Commercial Theatre," in *Selected Poems of Langston Hughes* (1990), 190. (Bell's endnote); Hughes (1901–67), a US poet, is primarily associated with the Harlem Renaissance.

"Remember, most whites are so jealous of their race-based prerogatives that they oppose affirmative action even though many of these programs would remove barriers that exclude whites as well as blacks. Can we not expect such whites—notwithstanding even the impressive benefits offered by the Space Traders—to go all out to prevent blacks from gaining access to an extraterrestrial New Jerusalem? Although you are planning to litigate against the Trade on the grounds that it is illegal discrimination to limit it to black people, mark my words, our 'milk and honey' story will inspire whites to institute such litigation on the grounds that limiting the Space Traders' offer to black people is unconstitutional discrimination against whites!

"Many of you have charged that I have become expert at manipulating white people for personal gain. Although profit has not in fact motivated my actions, I certainly have learned to understand how whites think on racial issues. On that knowledge, I am willing to wage my survival and that of my family. I urge you to do the same. This strategy is, however risky, our only hope."

The murmurs had subsided into stony silence by the time Golightly left the podium.

"Does anyone care to respond to Professor Golightly's suggestion?" the chairman finally asked.

Justin Jasper, a well-known and highly respected Baptist minister, came to the microphone. "I readily concede Dr. Golightly's expertise in the psychology of whites' thinking. Furthermore, as he requests, I hold in abeyance my deep distrust of a black man whose willing service to whites has led him to become a master minstrel of political mimicry. But my problem with his plan is twofold. First, it rings hollow because it so resembles Dr. Golightly's consistent opposition in the past to all our civil rights initiatives. Once again, he is urging us to accept rather than oppose a racist policy. And, not only are we not to resist, but we are to beg the country to lead us to the sacrificial altar. God may have that power, but Dr. Golightly is not my god!"

The Reverend Jasper was a master orator, and he quickly had his audience with him. "Second, because the proposal lacks truth, it insults my soul. In the forty years I have worked for civil rights, I have lost more battles than I have won, but I have never lost my integrity. Telling the truth about racism has put me in prison and many of my co-workers into early graves.

"The truth is, Dr. Golightly, that what this country is ready to do to us is wrong! It is evil! It is an action so heinous as to give the word *betrayal* a bad name. I can speak only for myself, but even if I were certain that my family and I could escape the threat we now face by lying about our likely fate—and, Dr. Golightly, that is what you're asking us to do—I do not choose to save myself by a tactic that may preserve my body at the sacrifice of my soul. The fact is, Dr. Golightly, until my Lord calls me home, I do not want to leave this country even for a land of milk and honey. My people were brought here involuntarily, and that is the only way they're going to get me out!"

The Reverend Jasper received a standing ovation. Many people were crying openly as they applauded. After thanking them, the minister asked everyone to join in singing the old nineteenth-century hymn "Amazing Grace," which, he reminded them, had been written by an English minister, one John Newton, who as a young man and before finding God's grace, had been captain of a slave ship. It was with special fervor that they sang the verse:

Through many dangers, toils, and snares,
I have already come.
'Twas grace that brought me safe this far,
And grace will lead me home.[1]

With the hymn's melody still resonating, the coalition's members voted unanimously to approve their defensive package. The meeting was quickly adjourned. Leaving the hall, everyone agreed that they had done all that could be done to oppose approval of the Space Traders' offer. As for Golightly, his proposal was dismissed as coming from a person who, in their view, had so often sold out black interests. "He's a sad case. Even with this crisis, he's just doing what he's always done."

Again, as after the President's cabinet meeting, Golightly sat for a long time alone. He did not really mind that none of the delegates had spoken to him before leaving. But he was crushed by his failure to get them to recognize what he had long known: that without power, a people must use cunning and guile. Or were cunning and guile, based on superior understanding of a situation, themselves power? Certainly, most black people knew and used this art to survive in their everyday contacts with white people. It was only civil rights professionals who confused integrity with foolhardiness.

"Faith in God is fine," Golightly muttered to himself. "But God expects us to use the common sense He gave us to get out of life-threatening situations."

Still, castigation of black leadership could not alter the fact. Golightly had failed, and he knew it. Sure, he was smarter than they were—smarter even than most whites; but he had finally outsmarted himself. At the crucial moment, when he most needed to help his people, both whites and blacks had rejected as untrustworthy both himself and his plans.

4 January. In a nationally televised address, the President sought to reassure both Trade supporters that he was responding favorably to their strong messages, and blacks and whites opposed to the Trade that he would not ignore their views. After the usual patriotic verbiage, the President said that just-completed, end-of-century economic reports revealed the nation to be in much

1 John Newton, "Amazing Grace," in *Songs of Zion* (1981), 211. (Bell's endnote); Newton (1725–1807), best known today as the writer of "Amazing Grace," was active in the trade of enslaved people but later became an abolitionist, writing *Thoughts Upon the Slave Trade* (1788).

worse shape than anyone had imagined. He summarized what he called the "very grim figures," and added that only massive new resources would save America from having to declare bankruptcy.

"On the face of it, our visitors from outer space have initiated their relationship with our country in a most unusual way. They are a foreign power and as such entitled to the respect this nation has always granted to the family of nations on Earth; it is not appropriate for us to prejudge this extraplanetary nation's offer. Thus, it is now receiving careful study and review by this administration.

"Of course, I am aware of the sacrifice that some of our most highly regarded citizens would be asked to make in the proposed trade. While these citizens are of only one racial group, there is absolutely no evidence whatsoever to indicate that the selection was intended to discriminate against any race or religion or ethnic background.

"No decisions have been made, and all options are under review. This much seems clear: the materials the Traders have offered us are genuine and perform as promised. Early estimates indicate that, if these materials were made available to this nation, they would solve our economic crisis, and we could look forward to a century of unparalleled prosperity. Whether the Trade would allow a tax-free year for every American, as some of our citizens have hoped, is not certain. But I can promise that if the Trade is approved, I will exercise my best efforts to make such a trade dividend a reality."

Early that morning, the leaders of Fortune-500 businesses,[1] heads of banks, insurance companies, and similar entities boarded their well-appointed corporate jets and flew to a remote Wyoming hunting lodge. They understood the President supported the Trade, despite his avowals that no decision had been made. They had come to discuss the Trade offer's implications for big business.

5 January. Not content with just closing the doors on their meeting as the Anti-Trade Coalition had, the corporate leaders of America gathered for an absolutely hush-hush meeting. They were joined by the Vice President and some of the wealthier members of Congress. The surroundings were beautiful, but the gathering of white males was somber. Corporate America faced a dilemma of its own making.

Media polls as well as ones privately funded by businesses all reported tremendous public support for the Trade—unhappy but hardly unexpected news for the nation's richest and most powerful men. First, blacks represented 12 percent of the market and generally consumed much more of their income than did their white counterparts. No one wanted to send that portion of the market into outer space—not even for the social and practical benefits offered by the Space Traders.

---

1 Fortune 500 businesses are the largest US corporations, as compiled yearly by *Fortune* magazine starting in 1955.

Even those benefits were a mixed blessing. Coal and oil companies, expecting to raise their prices as supplies steadily decreased, were not elated at the prospect of an inexhaustible energy source; it could quickly put them out of business. Similarly, businesses whose profits were based on sales in black ghetto communities—or who supplied law enforcement agencies, prisons, and other such institutions—faced substantial losses in sales. The real estate industry, for example, annually reaped uncounted millions in commissions on sales and rentals, inflated by the understanding that blacks would not be allowed to purchase or rent in an area. Even these concerns were overshadowed by fears of what the huge influx of gold to pay all state debts would do to the economy or to the value of either the current money supply or gold.

Though seldom acknowledging the fact, most business leaders understood that blacks were crucial in stabilizing the economy with its ever-increasing disparity between the incomes of rich and poor. They recognized that potentially turbulent unrest among those on the bottom was deflected by the continuing efforts of poorer whites to ensure that they, at least, remained ahead of blacks. If blacks were removed from the society, working- and middle-class whites—deprived of their racial distraction—might look upward toward the top of the societal well and realize that they as well as the blacks below them suffered because of the gross disparities in opportunities and income.

Many of these corporate leaders and their elected representatives had for years exploited poor whites' ignorance of their real enemy. Now, what had been a comforting insulation of their privileges and wealth, posed a serious barrier to what a majority saw as a first priority: to persuade the country to reject the Trade. A quick survey of the media and advertising representatives present was not encouraging. "It would be quite a challenge," one network executive said, "but we simply can't change this country's view about the superiority of whites and the inferiority of blacks in a week. I doubt you could do it in a decade."

Even so, the corporate leaders decided to try. They planned to launch immediately a major media campaign—television, radio, and the press—to exploit both the integration achieved in America and the moral cost of its loss. White members of professional and college sports teams would urge rejection of the Trade "so as to keep the team together." Whites in integrated businesses, schools, churches, and neighborhoods would broadcast similar messages. The business leaders even committed large sums to facilitate campaigning by pro-choice women's groups who were strongly anti-Trade. In a particularly poignant series of ads, white spouses in interracial marriages would point out that the Trade would destroy their families, and beg the public not to support it.

Newspaper and magazine publishers promised supportive editorials, but the Vice President and other government representatives argued that the immediate political gains from accepting the Trade would translate into business benefits as well.

"With all due respect, Mr. Vice President," he was told, "that argument shows why you are in politics and we are in business. It also shows that you are not listening very closely to those of us whose campaign contributions put you in office."

"We need your financial support," the Vice President admitted, "but our polls show most white voters favor the Trade, and the administration is under increasing pressure to do the same. And, as you know, pro-Trade advocates are promising that with all government debts paid, every American would get a year without any taxes. Believe it or not, some liberal environmentalists are thinking of giving their support to the Trade as the lesser of two evils. Of course, the prospect of heating and air-conditioning homes without paying through the nose is very appealing, even to those who don't care a hoot about the environment."

"However enticing such benefits of the Trade may be," interjected a government census official, "the real attraction for a great many whites is that it would remove black people from this society. Since the first of the year, my staff and I have interviewed literally thousands of citizens across the country, and, though they don't say it directly, it's clear that at bottom they simply think this will be a better country without black people. I fear, gentlemen, that those of us who have been perpetuating this belief over the years have done a better job than we knew."

"I must add what you probably already know," the Vice President broke in, "that the administration is leaning toward acceptance of the Space Traders' offer. Now, if you fellows line up against the Trade, it could make a difference—but, in that case, the President may opt to build on the phony populist image you provided him in his first election campaign. He knows that the working- and middle-class white people in this country want the blacks to go, and if they get a chance to express their real views in the privacy of a polling place, the Trade plan will pass overwhelmingly."

"Bullshit!" roared a billionaire who had made his fortune in construction. "I'm sick of this defeatist talk! We need to get off our dead asses and get to work on this thing. Everyone says that money talks. Well dammit, let's get out there and spend some money. If this thing goes to a public referendum, we can buy whatever and whoever is necessary. It sure as hell will not be the first time," he wound up, pounding both fists on the long conference table, "and likely not the last!"

The remainder of the meeting was more upbeat. Pointedly telling the Vice President that he and the administration were caught in the middle and would have to decide whose support they most wanted in the future, the business leaders began making specific plans to suspend all regular broadcasting and, through 16 January, to air nothing but anti-Trade ads and special Trade programs. They flew out that night, their confidence restored. They controlled the media. They had become rich and successful "playing hard ball." However competitive with one another, they had, as usual, united to confront this new challenge to their hegemony. It was, as usual, inconceivable that they could fail.

6 January. Although the Television Evangelists of America also owned jets, they understood that their power lay less in these perks of the wealthy than in their own ability to manipulate their TV congregations' religious feelings. So, after a lengthy conference call, they announced a massive evangelical rally in the Houston Astrodome which would be televised over their religious cable network. They went all out. The Trade offer was the evangelists' chance to rebuild their prestige and fortunes, neither of which had recovered from the Jim and Tammy Bakker and the Jimmy Swaggart scandals.[1] They would achieve this much-desired goal by playing on, rather than trying to change, the strongly racist views of their mostly working-class television audiences. True, some of the preachers had a substantial black following, but evangelical support for the Trade would not be the evangelists' decision. Rather, these media messiahs heralded it as God's will.

The Space Traders were, according to the televised "Gospel," bringing America blessings earned by their listeners' and viewers' faithful dedication to freedom, liberty, and God's word. Not only would rejection of these blessings from space be wrong, so the preachers exhorted; it would be blasphemous. It was God's will that all Americans enjoy a tax-free year, a cleaned-up environment for years to come, and cheap heating forever. True, a sacrifice was required if they were to obtain God's bounty—a painful sacrifice. But here, too, God was testing Americans, his chosen people, to ensure that they were worthy of His bounty, deserving of His love. Each preacher drew on Scripture, tortuously interpreted, to support these statements.

A "ministry of music" quartet—four of the most popular television evangelists, all speaking in careful cadences like a white rap group—preached the major sermon. It whipped the crowd into a delirium of religious feeling, making them receptive both to the financial appeals, which raised millions, and to the rally's grande finale: a somber tableau of black people marching stoically into the Space Traders' ships, which here resembled ancient sacrificial altars. Try as they might, the producers of the pageant had had a hard time finding black people willing to act out roles they might soon be forced to experience, but a few blacks were glad to be paid handsomely for walking silently across the stage. These few were easily supplemented by the many whites eager to daub on "black face."[2]

The rally was a great success despite the all-out efforts of the media to condemn this "sacrilege of all that is truly holy." That night, millions of messages,

1 Convicted felon Jim Bakker (b. 1940) and his then wife, Tammy Faye Messner (then Bakker, 1942–2007) were Christian televangelists who became embroiled in a financial scandal (and, in Bakker's case, criminal fraud) in the late 1980s following Bakker's alleged sexual assault of and hush-money payment to Jessica Hahn (b. 1959). Jimmy Swaggart (1935–2025) was a televangelist perhaps best known for scandals involving sex workers in the late 1980s and early 1990s.

2 Blackface is a form of generally racist performance in which white people colour their faces with charcoal or grease paint. It was originally a part of nineteenth-century US minstrel shows, where white actors would perform racist stereotypes of Black people.

all urging acceptance of the Space Traders' offer, deluged the President and Congress.

7 January. Groups supporting the Space Traders' proposition had from the beginning taken seriously blacks' charges that acceptance of it would violate the Constitution's most basic protections. Acting swiftly, and with the full cooperation of the states, they had set in motion the steps necessary to convene a constitutional convention in Philadelphia.[1] ("Of course!" groaned Golightly when he heard of it.) And there, on this day, on the site of the original constitutional convention, delegates—chosen, in accordance with Article V of the Constitution,[2] by the state legislatures—quickly drafted, and by a substantial majority passed, the Twenty-seventh Amendment to the Constitution of the United States. It declared:

> Without regard to the language or interpretations previously given any other provision of this document, every United States citizen is subject at the call of Congress to selection for special service for periods necessary to protect domestic interests and international needs.

The amendment was scheduled for ratification by the states on 15 January in a national referendum. If ratified, the amendment would validate amendments to existing Selective Service laws authorizing the induction of all blacks into special service for transportation under the terms of the Space Traders' offer.

8 January. Led by Rabbi Abraham Specter, a group of Jewish church and organizational leaders sponsored a mammoth anti-Trade rally in New York's Madison Square Garden. "We simply cannot stand by and allow America's version of the Final Solution[3] to its race problem to be carried out without our strong protest and committed opposition." Thirty-five thousand Jews signed pledges to disrupt by all possible nonviolent means both the referendum and—if the amendment was ratified—the selection of blacks for 'special service.'

"Already," Rabbi Specter announced, "a secret Anne Frank[4] Committee has formed, and its hundreds of members have begun to locate hiding places in out-of-the-way sites across this great country. Blacks by the thousands can be hidden for years if necessary until the nation returns to its senses.

"We vow this action because we recognize the fateful parallel between

1 Philadelphia, Pennsylvania, was the site of the First Continental Congress in 1774, in the lead up to the American Revolutionary War.

2 Article Five of the US Constitution dictates how the Constitution can be amended.

3 The Final Solution was a phrase used by the Nazis for their planned genocide of Jews, which would become the Holocaust.

4 Anne Frank (1929–45), Jewish diarist who documented living in hiding from the Nazis in German-occupied Netherlands during World War II. She was murdered by the Nazis in the Bergen-Belsen concentration camp.

the plight of the blacks in this country and the situation of the Jews in Nazi Germany. Holocaust scholars agree that the Final Solution in Germany would not have been possible without the pervasive presence and the uninterrupted tradition of anti-Semitism in Germany. We must not let the Space Traders be the final solution for blacks in America."

A concern of many Jews not contained in their official condemnations of the Trade offer, was that, in the absence of blacks, Jews could become the scapegoats for a system so reliant on an identifiable group on whose heads less-well-off whites can discharge their hate and frustrations for societal disabilities about which they are unwilling to confront their leaders. Given the German experience, few Jews argued that "it couldn't happen here."[1]

9 January. Responding almost immediately to the Jewish anti-Trade rally, the Attorney General expressed his "grave concern" that what he felt certain was but a small group of Jews would, by acting in flagrant violation of the law of the land, besmirch the good names of all patriotic American Jews. For this reason, he said, he was releasing for publication the secret list, obtained by undercover FBI agents, of all those who had joined the Anne Frank Committee. He stated that the release was needed so that all Americans could easily distinguish this group from the majority of patriotic and law-abiding Jewish citizens.

Retaliation was quick. Within hours, men and women listed as belonging to the committee lost their jobs; their contracts were canceled; their mortgages foreclosed; and harassment of them, including physical violence, escalated into a nationwide resurgence of anti-Semitic feeling. Groups on the far right, who were exploiting the growing support for the Trade, urged: "Send the blacks into space. Send the Jews into Hell." The Jews who opposed the Trade were intimidated into silence and inaction. The leaders of Rabbi Specter's group were themselves forced into hiding, leaving few able to provide any haven for blacks.

10 January. In the brief but intense pre-election day campaign, the pro-ratification groups' major argument had an appeal that surprised even those who made it. Their message was straightforward:

> The Framers intended America to be a white country. The evidence of their intentions is present in the original Constitution. After more than a hundred and thirty-seven years of good-faith efforts to build a healthy, stable interracial nation, we have concluded—as the Framers did in the beginning—that our survival today requires that we sacrifice the rights

1 Lucy S. Dawidowicz, *The Holocaust and the Historians* (1981); Lucy S. Dawidowicz, ed., *A Holocaust Reader* (1976); Asher Cohen, Joav Gelber, and Chad Ward, eds., *Comprehending the Holocaust: Historical and Literary Research* (1988); Judith Miller, *One, By One, By One: Facing the Holocaust* (1988); Yehuda Bauer, *The Holocaust* (1978). (Bell's endnote)

of blacks in order to protect and further the interests of whites. The Framers' example must be our guide. Patriotism, and not pity, must govern our decision. We should ratify the amendment and accept the Space Traders' proposition.

In response, a coalition of liberal opponents to the Space Traders' offer sought to combine pragmatism and principle in what they called their "slippery Trade slope" argument. First, they proclaimed the strong moral position that trading away a group of Americans identifiable by race is wrong and violates our basic principles. The coalition aimed its major thrust, however, at the self-interest of white Americans: "Does not consigning blacks to an unknown fate set a dangerous precedent?" the liberals demanded. "Who will be next?"

In full-page ads, they pressed the point: "Are we cannibals ready to consume our own for profit? And if we are, the blacks may be only the first. If the Space Traders return with an irresistible offer for another group, the precedent will have been set, and none of us will be safe. Certainly not the minorities—Hispanics, Jews, Asians—and perhaps not even those of us identifiable by politics or religion or geographic location. Setting such a precedent of profit could consume us all."

Astutely sidestepping the Trade precedent arguments, the pro-Trade response focused on the past sacrifices of blacks. "In each instance," it went, "the sacrifice of black rights was absolutely necessary to accomplish an important government purpose. These decisions were neither arbitrary nor capricious. Without the compromises on slavery in the Constitution of 1787,[1] there would be no America. Nor would there be any framework under which those opposed to slavery could continue the struggle that eventually led to the Civil War and emancipation.

"And where and how might slavery have ended had a new government not been formed? On what foundation would the post-Civil War amendments been appended? Sacrifices by blacks were made, but those sacrifices were both necessary and eventually rewarding to blacks as well as the nation."

In countering the anti-Trade contention that the sacrifice of black rights was both evil and unprecedented, pro-Traders claimed, "Beginning with the Civil War in which black people gained their liberty, this nation has called on its people to serve in its defense. Many men and women have voluntarily enlisted in the armed services, but literally millions of men have been conscripted, required to serve their country, and, if necessary, to sacrifice not simply their rights but also their lives."

1 The so-called "three-fifths compromise," made at the 1787 Constitutional Convention, was designed to settle a debate between those states who enslaved Black people and those who did not over how these enslaved human beings should be counted for the purposes of determining the number of elected representatives a state would have. It was decided that an enslaved person would count only as "three-fifths" of a free person.

As for the argument that the sacrifice of black rights in political compromises was odious racial discrimination, pro-Trade forces contended that "fortuitous fate and not blatant racism" should be held responsible. Just as men and not women are inducted into the military, and even then only men of a certain age and physical and mental condition, so only some groups are destined by their role in the nation's history to serve as catalyst for stability and progress.

"All Americans are expected to make sacrifices for the good of their country. Black people are no exceptions to this basic obligation of citizenship. Their role may be special, but so is that of many of those who serve. The role that blacks may be called on to play in response to the Space Traders' offer is, however regrettable, neither immoral nor unconstitutional."

A tremendous groundswell of public agreement with the pro-Trade position drowned out anti-Trade complaints of unfairness. Powerful as would have been the notion of seeing the Space Traders' offer as no more than a fortuitous circumstance, in which blacks might be called on to sacrifice for their country, the "racial sacrifice as historic necessity" argument made the pro-Trade position irresistible to millions of voters—and to their Congressional representatives.

11 January. Unconfirmed media reports asserted that U.S. officials tried in secret negotiations to get the Space Traders to take in trade only those blacks currently under the jurisdiction of the criminal justice system—that is, in prison or on parole or probation. Government negotiators noted that this would include almost one half of the black males in the twenty- to twenty-nine-year-old age bracket.[1] Negotiators were also reported to have offered to trade only blacks locked in the inner cities. But the Space Traders stated that they had no intention of turning their far-off homeland into an American prison colony for blacks. In rejecting the American offer, the Space Traders warned that they would withdraw their proposition unless the United States halted the flight of the growing numbers of middle-class blacks who—fearing the worst—were fleeing the country.

In response, executive orders were issued and implemented, barring blacks from leaving the country until the Space Traders' proposition was fully debated and resolved. "It is your patriotic duty," blacks were told by the White House, "to allow this great issue to be resolved through the democratic process and in accordance with the rule of law." To ensure that the Trade debate and referendum were concluded in a "noncoercive environment," all blacks serving

1 In 1990, the figure was 24 percent, according to Justice Department data contained in a study funded by the Rand Corporation. The National Center on Institutions and Alternatives reported that 42 percent of the black men in the District of Columbia, aged eighteen through thirty-five, were enmeshed in the criminal justice system on any given day in 1991. (Bell's footnote, to which the following endnotes are appended: David Savage, "1 in 4 Young Blacks in Jail or in Court Control Study Says," *Los Angeles Times*, 27 February 1990, sec. A, p. 1, col. 1.; Jason DeParle, "42% of Young Black Men Are in Capital's Court System," *New York Times*, 18 April 1992, sec. A, p. 1, col. 1.)

in the military were placed on furlough and relieved of their weapons. State officials took similar action with respect to blacks on active duty in state and local police forces.

12 January. The Supreme Court, citing precedent dating back to 1849, rejected a number of appeals by blacks and their white supporters whose legal challenges to every aspect of the referendum process had been dismissed by lower courts as "political questions" best resolved by the body politic rather than through judicial review.[1]

The Supreme Court's order refusing to intervene in the Space Trader proposition was unanimous. The order was brief and *per curiam*,[2] the Court agreeing that the Space Trader litigation lacked judicially discoverable and manageable standards for resolving the issues.[3] The Court also noted that, if inducted in accordance with a constitutionally approved conscription provision, blacks would have no issues of individual rights for review. Even if the Court were to conclude that rights under the Fourteenth Amendment were deserving of greater weight than the authority of the new constitutional amendment up for ratification, the standards of national necessity that prompted the Court to approve the confinement of Japanese Americans during the Second World War,[4] would serve as sufficient precedent for the induction and transfer of African Americans to the Space Traders.

While not claiming to give weight to the public opinion polls reporting strong support for the Trade, the Court noted that almost a century earlier, in 1903, Justice Oliver Wendell Holmes had denied injunctive relief to six thousand blacks who petitioned the Court to protect their right to vote.[5] The bill alleged that the great mass of the white population intended to keep the blacks from voting; but, in view of such massive opposition, Holmes reasoned that ordering the blacks' names to be placed on the voting list would be "an empty form" unless the Court also mandated electoral supervision by "officers of the court."[6]

---

1 *Luther v. Borden*, 48 U.S. (7 How.) 1 (1849) (Court refused to determine which was the legitimate government of Rhode Island). (Bell's endnote)

2 A per curiam decision is one ascribed to the entire court, rather than individually authored or signed.

3 See *Baker v. Carr*, 369 U.S. 186 (1962) (exploring the "political question" doctrine in definitive fashion). (Bell's endnote)

4 *Korematsu v. United States*, 323 U.S. 214 (1944) (sustaining a military order under which Americans of Japanese origin were removed from designated West Coast areas). See also *Hirabayashi v. United States*, 320 U.S. 81 (1943) (upholding a military curfew imposed on persons of Japanese ancestry in the West Coast during the early months of the Second World War). (Bell's endnote); people of Japanese descent were interned in concentration camps in the US during World War II, from 1942 to 1946.

5 *Giles v. Harris*, 189 U.S. 475 (1903). (Bell's endnote); this ruling essentially allowed states to develop voter registration laws that inherently, if not explicitly, worked to deny Black citizens the right to vote. Oliver Wendell Holmes (1841–1935), US Supreme Court justice from 1902 to 1932.

6 Justice Holmes wrote: "Unless we are prepared to supervise the voting in that state by officers of the court, it seems to us that all the plaintiff could get from equity would be an empty form. (*continued*)

14 January. With the legal questions of the Trade resolved, the U.S. government announced that as a result of intensive negotiations with the Space Trader leaders, the latter had agreed to amend their offer and exclude from the Trade all black people seventy years old, and older, and all those blacks who were seriously handicapped, ill, and injured. In addition, a thousand otherwise-eligible blacks and their immediate families would be left behind as trustees of black property and possessions, all of which were to be stored or held in escrow in case blacks were returned to this country. Each of the thousand black "detainees" was required to pledge to accept a subordinate status with "suspended citizenship" until such time as the "special service inductees" were returned to the country. The administration selected blacks to remain who had records of loyalty to the conservative party and no recorded instances of militant activity. Even so, many of those blacks selected declined to remain. "We will, like the others," said one black who rejected detainee status, "take our chances with the referendum."

15 January. Many whites had, to their credit, been working day and night to defeat the amendment; but, as is the usual fate of minority rights when subjected to referenda or initiatives,[1] the outcome was never really in doubt. The final vote tally confirmed the predictions. By 70 percent to 30 percent, American citizens voted to ratify the constitutional amendment that provided a legal basis for acceptance of the Space Traders' offer. In anticipation of this result, government agencies had secretly made preparations to facilitate the transfer. Some blacks escaped, and many thousands lost their lives in futile efforts to resist the joint federal and state police teams responsible for rounding up, cataloguing, and transporting blacks to the coast.

16 January. Professor Golightly and his family were not granted detainee status. Instead, the White House promised him safe passage to Canada for all his past services even though he had not made the patriotic appeal the President had requested of him. But, at the border that evening, he was stopped and turned back. It turned out the Secretary of the Interior had called to countermand his departure. Golightly was not surprised. What really distressed him was his failure to convince the black leaders of the anti-Trade coalition to heed their own rhetoric: namely that whites in power would, given the chance, do to privileged blacks what, in fact, they had done to all blacks.

"I wonder," he murmured, half to himself, half to his wife, as they rode in a luxury limousine sent, in some irony, by the Secretary of the Interior to

Apart from damages to the individual, relief from a great political wrong, if done, as alleged, by the people of a state and the state itself, must be given by them or by the legislature and political department of the Government of the United States." (Bell's footnote, to which is appended the following endnote: "Ibid., 488," referring back to *Giles v. Harris*.)

1 See Derrick Bell, "The Referendum: Democracy's Barrier to Racial Equality," *Washington Law Review* 54 (1978):1. (Bell's endnote)

convey them to the nearest roundup point, "how my high-minded brothers at the conference feel now about their decision to fail with integrity rather than stoop to the bit of trickery that might have saved them."

"But, Gleason," his wife asked, "would our lives have really been better had we fooled the country into voting against the Trade? If the Space Traders were to depart, carrying away with them what they and everyone else says can solve our major domestic problems, wouldn't people increasingly blame us blacks for increases in debt, pollution, and fuel shortages? We might have saved ourselves—but only to face here a fate as dire as any we face in space."

"I hope your stoic outlook helps us through whatever lies ahead," Golightly responded as the car stopped. Then guards hustled him and his family toward the buses being loaded with other blacks captured at the Canadian border.

17 January. The last Martin Luther King holiday the nation would ever observe dawned on an extraordinary sight. In the night, the Space Traders had drawn their strange ships right up to the beaches and discharged their cargoes of gold, minerals, and machinery leaving vast empty holds. Crowded on the beaches were the inductees, some twenty million silent black men, women, and children, including babes in arms. As the sun rose, the Space Traders directed them, first, to strip off all but a single undergarment; then, to line up; and finally, to enter those holds which yawned in the morning light like Milton's "darkness visible."[1] The inductees looked fearfully behind them. But, on the dunes above the beaches, guns at the ready, stood U.S. guards. There was no escape, no alternative. Heads bowed, arms now linked by slender chains, black people left the New World as their forebears had arrived.

---

1 John Milton (1608–74), poet and author of the epic *Paradise Lost* (1667). This line, from near the beginning of the poem, describes Hell.

Eden Robinson (b. 1968)

Eden Robinson is an award-winning author and member of the Haisla and Heiltsuk Nations. She earned her Bachelor of Fine Arts at the University of Victoria, and her Master of Fine Arts in Creative Writing at the University of British Columbia. As of this writing, she has published five novels, including the trilogy, *Son of a Trickster* (2017), *Trickster Drift* (2018), and *The Return of the Trickster* (2021). Perhaps her most widely known works are her collection of short stories, *Traplines* (1996), and her first novel, *Monkey Beach* (2000), which was adapted as a film in 2020.

Note on the text: "Terminal Avenue" was part of the original version of *Traplines*, which Robinson wrote as her MFA thesis. As she writes in *The Sasquatch at Home: Traditional Protocols and Modern Storytelling* (2011), when working on the publication version of the book, her "editors at the time felt it did not fit the style of the collection as a whole. In its place, we put 'Queen of the North'" (p. 44, n. 17). "Terminal Avenue" was first published in the journal *Aboriginal Voices* (vol. 4, no. 3, 1997). A slightly updated version, with some wording and typographical changes, was later published in *So Long Been Dreaming: Postcolonial Science Fiction and Fantasy*, edited by Nalo Hopkinson and Uppinder Mehan (2004), and *Walking the Clouds: An Anthology of Indigenous Science Fiction*, edited by Grace L. Dillon (2012). The version here follows that in *So Long Been Dreaming*.

In *Sasquatch at Home*, Robinson describes the story as her "aboriginal sci-fi bondage response to the Oka Crisis and the Fraser River salmon wars" (p. 44, n. 17). The Oka Crisis was a months-long conflict in Quebec in 1990 that arose over a land dispute, specifically a golf course that would have included development on a Kanyen'kehà:ka (Mohawk) burial ground. The violent conflict saw the Sûreté du Québec provincial police, RCMP, and Canadian army deployed against Kanyen'kehà:ka protestors. The so-called salmon wars took place throughout much of the 1990s, when Canada and the US were engaged in a significant trade dispute over the Pacific Salmon fishery. In 1994, First Nations in British Columbia and the Northwest Indian Fisheries Commission in Washington state issued a joint statement calling for responsible fishing and conservation (see Dunagan).

"Terminal Avenue" (1996)

His brother once held a peeled orange slice up against the sun. When the light shone through it, the slice became a brilliant amber: the setting sun is this colour, ripe orange.

The uniforms of the five advancing Peace Officers are robin's egg blue, but the slanting light catches their visors and sets their faces aflame.

★

In his memory, the water of the Douglas Channel[1] is a hard blue, baked to a glassy translucence by the August sun. The mountains in the distance form a crown; *Gabiswa*, the mountain in the centre, is the same shade of blue as his lover's veins.

She raises her arms to sweep her hair from her face. Her breasts lift. In the cool morning air, her nipples harden to knobby raspberries. Her eyes are widening in indignation: he once saw that shade of blue in a dragonfly's wing, but this is another thing he will keep secret.

★

Say nothing, his mother said, without moving her lips, careful not to attract attention. They waited in their car in silence after that. His father and mother were in the front seat, stiff.

Blood plastered his father's hair to his skull; blood leaked down his father's blank face. In the flashing lights of the patrol car, the blood looked black and moved like honey.

★

A rocket has entered the event horizon of a black hole. To an observer who is watching this from a safe distance, the rocket trapped here, in the black hole's inescapable halo of gravity, will appear to stop.

To an astronaut in the rocket, however, gravity is a rack that stretches his body like taffy, thinner and thinner, until there is nothing left but x-rays.

★

In full body-armour, the five Peace Officers are sexless and anonymous. With their visors down, they look like old-fashioned astronauts. The landscape they move across is the rapid transit line, the Surreycentral Skytrain station, but if they remove their body-armour, it may as well be the moon.

The Peace Officers begin to match strides until they move like a machine. This is an intimidation tactic that works, is working on him even though he knows what it is. He finds himself frozen. He can't move, even as they roll towards him, a train on invisible tracks.

★

Once, when his brother dared him, he jumped off the high diving tower. He wasn't really scared until he stepped away from the platform. In that moment, he realized he couldn't change his mind.

---

1 An inlet/fjord on the northern coast of British Columbia.

You stupid shit, his brother said when he surfaced.

In his dreams, everything is the same, except there is no water in the swimming pool and he crashes into the concrete like a dropped pumpkin.

★

He thinks of his brother, who is so perfect he wasn't born, but chiselled from stone. There is nothing he can do against that brown Apollo's[1] face, nothing he can say that will justify his inaction. Kevin would know what to do, with doom coming towards him in formation.

But Kevin is dead. He walked through their mother's door one day, wearing the robin's egg blue uniform of the great enemy, and his mother struck him down. She summoned the ghost of their father and put him in the room, sat him beside her, bloody and stunned. Against this Kevin said, I can stop it, Mom. I have the power to change things now.

She turned away, then the family turned away. Kevin looked at him, pleading, before he left her house and never came back, disappeared. Wil closed his eyes, a dark, secret joy welling in him, to watch his brother fall: Kevin never made the little mistakes in his life, never so much as sprouted a pimple. He made up for it though by doing the unforgivable.

Wil wonders if his brother knows what is happening. If, in fact, he isn't one of the Peace Officers, filled himself with secret joy.

★

His lover will wait for him tonight. Ironically, she will be wearing a complete Peace Officer's uniform, bought at great expense on the black market, and very, very illegal. She will wait at the door of her club, Terminal Avenue, and she will frisk clients that she knows will enjoy it. She will have the playroom ready, with its great wooden beams stuck through with hooks and cages, with its expensive equipment built for the exclusive purpose of causing pain. On a steel cart, her toys will be spread out as neatly as surgical instruments.

When he walks through the door, she likes to have her bouncers, also dressed as Peace Officers, hurl him against the wall. They let him struggle before they handcuff him. Their uniforms are slippery as rubber. He can't get a grip on them. The uniforms are padded with the latest in wonderfabric so no matter how hard he punches them, he can't hurt them. They will drag him into the back and strip-search him in front of clients who pay for the privilege of watching. He stands under a spotlight that shines an impersonal cone of light from the ceiling. The rest of the room is darkened. He can see reflections of glasses, red-eyed cigarettes, the glint of ice clinking against glass, shadows

1 Ancient Greek god often depicted as the ideal of male beauty.

shifting. He can hear zippers coming undone, low moans; he can smell the cum when he's beaten into passivity.

Once, he wanted to cut his hair, but she wouldn't let him, said she'd never speak to him again if he did. She likes it when the bouncers grab him by his hair and drag him to the exploratory table in the centre of the room. She says she likes the way it veils his face when he's kneeling.

In the playroom though, she changes. He can't hurt her the way she wants him to; she is tiring of him. He whips her half-heartedly until she tells the bouncer to do it properly.

A man walked in one day, in a robin's egg blue uniform, and Wil froze. When he could breathe again, when he could think, he found her watching him, thoughtful.

She borrowed the man's uniform and lay on the table, her face blank and smooth and round as a basketball under the visor. He put a painstick against the left nipple. It darkened and bruised. Her screams were muffled by the helmet. Her bouncers whispered things to her as they pinned her to the table, and he hurt her. When she begged him to stop, he moved the painstick to her right nipple.

He kept going until he was shaking so hard he had to stop.

That's enough for tonight, she said, breathless, wrapping her arms around him, telling the bouncers to leave when he started to cry. My poor virgin. It's not pain so much as it is a cleansing.

Is it, he asked her, one of those whiteguilt things?

She laughed, kissed him. Rocked him and forgave him, on the evening he discovered that it wasn't just easy to do terrible things to another person: it could give pleasure. It could give power.

She said she'd kill him if he told anyone what happened in the playroom. She has a reputation and is vaguely ashamed of her secret weakness. He wouldn't tell, not ever. He is addicted to her pain.

To distinguish it from real uniforms, hers has an inverted black triangle[1] on the left side, just over her heart: asocialism, she says with a laugh, and he doesn't get it. She won't explain it, her blue eyes black with desire as her pupils widened suddenly like a cat's.

The uniforms advancing on him, however, are clean and pure and real.

*

Wil wanted to be an astronaut. He bought the books, he watched the movies and he dreamed. He did well in Physics, Math, and Sciences, and his mother bragged, He's got my brains.

1 An inverted black triangle was a badge used by Nazis during World War II to mark concentration camp prisoners as "asocial": this category was arbitrarily applied to many people, including unhoused people, people with disabilities, pacifists, some sex workers and queer women, as well as Roma and Sinti people.

He was so dedicated, he would test himself, just like the astronauts on TV. He locked himself in his closet once with nothing but a bag of potato chips and a bottle of pop. He wanted to see if he could spend time in a small space, alone and deprived. It was July and they had no air conditioning. He fainted in the heat, dreamed that he was floating over the Earth on his way to Mars, weightless.

Kevin found him, dragged him from the closet, and laughed at him.

You stupid shit, he said. Don't you know anything?

When his father slid off the hood leaving a snail's trail of blood, Kevin ran out of the car.

Stop it! Kevin screamed, his face contorted in the headlight's beam. Shadows loomed over him, but he was undaunted. Stop it!

Kevin threw himself on their dad and saved his life.

Wil stayed with their father in the hospital, never left his side. He was there when the Peace Officers came and took their father's statement. When they closed the door in his face and he heard his father screaming. The nurses took him away and he let them. Wil watched his father withdraw into himself after that, never quite healing.

He knew the names of all the constellations, the distances of the stars, the equations that would launch a ship to reach them. He knew how to stay alive in any conditions, except when someone didn't want to stay alive.

No one was surprised when his father shot himself.

At the funeral potlatch,[1] his mother split his father's ceremonial regalia between Wil and Kevin. She gave Kevin his father's frontlet.[2] He placed it immediately on his head and danced. The room became still, the family shocked at his lack of tact. When Kevin stopped dancing, she gave Wil his father's button blanket.[3] The dark wool held his smell. Wil knew then that he would never be an astronaut. He didn't have a backup dream and drifted through school, coasting on a reputation of Brain he'd stopped trying to earn.

Kevin, on the other hand, ran away and joined the Mohawk Warriors.[4] He was at Oka[5] on August 16 when the bombs rained down and the last Canadian reserve was Adjusted.

---

1 The Potlatch is a cultural ceremony among many Indigenous nations and peoples of the Northwest Coast, including Haisla and Heiltsuk Nations. Generally a gift-giving ceremony, communities hold them during significant moments, including births, marriages, and funerals. The Canadian government banned the Potlatch from 1885 to 1951.

2 A frontlet is a ceremonial item, worn on the forehead.

3 A ceremonial blanket decorated with abalone-shell buttons.

4 The Mohawk Warrior Society (Rotisken'rakéhte), in part a land defence and resistance group, developed in its modern form in the 1970s and was active during the Oka Crisis. They also work within the community to help elders and other community members. See Louis Karoniaktajeh Hall, *The Mohawk Warrior Society: A Handbook on Sovereignty and Survival* (2023).

5 While referring to an event in the story's timeline, this reference clearly invokes the 1990 Oka Crisis. See the "Note on the text," above.

Wil expected him to come back broken. He was ready with patience, with forgiveness. Kevin came back a Peace Officer.

Why? his aunts, his uncles, cousins, and friends asked.

How could you? his mother asked.

Wil said nothing. When his brother looked up, Wil knew the truth, even if Kevin didn't. There were things that adjusted to rapid change—pigeons, dogs, rats, cockroaches. Then there were things that didn't—panda bears, whales, flamingos, Atlantic cod, salmon, owls.

Kevin would survive the Adjustment. Kevin had found a way to come through it and be better for it. He instinctively felt the changes coming and adapted. I, on the other hand, he thought, am going the way of the dodo bird.[1]

★

There are rumours in the neighbourhood. No one from the Vancouver Urban Reserve #2 can get into Terminal Avenue. They don't have the money or the connections. Whispers follow him, anyway, but no one will ask him to his face. He suspects that his mother suspects. He has been careful, but he sees the questions in her eyes when he leaves for work. Someday she'll ask him what he really does and he'll lie to her.

To allay suspicion, he smuggles cigarettes and sweetgrass[2] from the downtown core to Surreycentral. This is useful, makes him friends, adds a kick to his evening train ride. He finds that he needs these kicks. Has a morbid fear of becoming dead like his father, talking and breathing and eating, but frightened into vacancy, a living blankness.

His identity card that gets him to the downtown core says *Occupation: Waiter.* He pins it to his jacket so that no one will mistake him for a terrorist and shoot him.

He is not really alive until he steps past the industrial black doors of his lover's club. Until that moment, he is living inside his head, lost in memories. He knows that he is a novelty item, a real living Indian: that is why his prices are so inflated. He knows there will come a time when he is yesterday's condom.

He walks past the club's façade, the elegant dining rooms filled with the glittering people who watch the screens or dance across the dimly-lit ballroom-sized floor. He descends the stairs where his lover waits for him with her games and her toys, where they do things that aren't sanctioned by the Purity laws, where he gets hurt and gives hurt.

He is greeted by his high priestess. He enters her temple of discipline and submits. When the pain becomes too much, he hallucinates. There is no preparing for that moment when reality shifts and he is free.

---

1 The dodo was a flightless bird, driven to extinction following European settlement, hunting, and the introduction of invasive species.

2 Sweetgrass is a fragrant grass sacred to many Indigenous peoples in North America.

★

They have formed a circle around him. Another standard intimidation tactic. The Peace Officer facing him is waiting for him to talk. He stares up at it. This will be different from the club. He is about to become an example.

Wilson Wilson? the Officer says. The voice sounds male but is altered by computers so it won't be recognizable.

He smiles. The name is one of his mother's little jokes, a little defiance. He has hated her for it all his life, but now he doesn't mind. He is in a forgiving mood. *Yes, that's me.*

In the silence that stretches, Wil realizes that he always believed this moment would come. That he has been preparing himself for it. The smiling-faced lies from the TV haven't fooled him, or anyone else. After the Uprisings, it was only a matter of time before someone decided to solve the Indian problem once and for all.

The Peace Officer raises his club and brings it down.

★

His father held a potlatch before they left Kitamaat, before they came to Vancouver to earn a living, after the aluminum smelter closed.[1]

They had to hold it in secret, so they hired three large seiners[2] for the family and rode to Monkey Beach.[3] They left in their old beat-up speedboat, early in the morning, when the Douglas Channel was calm and flat, before the winds blew in from the ocean, turning the water choppy. The seine boats fell far behind them, heavy with people. Kevin begged and begged to steer and his father laughingly gave in.

Wil knelt on the bow and held his arms open, wishing he could take off his lifejacket. In four hours they will land on Monkey Beach and will set up for the potlatch where they will dance and sing and say goodbye. His father will cook salmon around fires, roasted the old-fashioned way: split down the centre and splayed open like butterflies, thin sticks of cedar woven through the skin to hold the fish open, the sticks planted in the sand; as the flesh darkens, the juice runs down and hisses on the fire. The smell will permeate the beach. Camouflage nets will be set up all over the beach so they won't be spotted by planes. Family will lounge under them as if they were beach umbrellas. The

---

1 Kitamaat Village is the central community of the Haisla Nation, located at the head of Douglas Channel. The nearby municipality of Kitimat has long been tied to the aluminum industry.

2 A seiner is a type of fishing boat.

3 Monkey Beach, a beach in British Columbia, also features in and serves as the title of Robinson's first novel; the name refers to the beach's association with the B'gwus (Sasquatch). In 2006, the Bishop Bay–Monkey Beach Conservancy was created.

more daring of the family will dash into the water, which is still glacier-cold and shocking.

This will happen when they land in four hours, but Wil chooses to remember the boat ride with his mother resting in his father's arm when Wil comes back from the bow and sits beside them. She is wearing a blue scarf and black sunglasses and red lipstick. She can't stop smiling even though they are going to leave home soon. She looks like a movie star. His father has his hair slicked back, and it makes him look like an otter. He kisses her, and she kisses him back.

Kevin is so excited that he raises one arm and makes the Mohawk salute they see on TV all the time. He loses control of the boat, and they swerve violently. His father cuffs Kevin and takes the wheel.

The sun rises as they pass Costi Island, and the water sparkles and shifts. The sky hardens into a deep summer blue.

The wind and the noise of the engine prevent them from talking. His father begins to sing. Wil doesn't understand the words, couldn't pronounce them if he tried. He can see that his father is happy. Maybe he's drunk on the excitement of the day, on the way that his wife touches him, tenderly. He gives Wil the wheel.

His father puts on his button blanket, rests it solemnly on his shoulders. He balances on the boat with the ease of someone who's spent all his life on the water. He does a twirl, when he reaches the bow of the speedboat and the button blanket opens, a navy lotus. The abalone buttons sparkle when they catch the light. She's laughing as he poses. He dances, suddenly inspired, exuberant.

Later he will understand what his father is doing, the rules he is breaking, the risks he is taking, and the price he will pay on a deserted road, when the siren goes off and the lights flash and they are pulled over.

At the time, though, Wil is white-knuckled, afraid to move the boat in a wrong way and toss his father overboard. He is also embarrassed, wishing his father were more reserved. Wishing he was being normal instead of dancing, a whirling shadow against the sun, blocking his view of the Channel.

This is the moment he chooses to be in, the place he goes to when the club flattens him to the Surreycentral tiles. He holds himself there, in the boat with his brother, his father, his mother. The sun on the water makes pale northern lights flicker against everyone's faces, and the smell of the water is clean and salty, and the boat's spray is cool against his skin.

Nalo Hopkinson (b. 1960)

Born in Jamaica, Nalo Hopkinson has lived Canada for most of her life, where she is currently a professor of Creative Writing at the University of British Columbia. Best known for her SF that combines future worlds with Caribbean history, story, and knowledges, she has published several novels and stories, and has also edited collections of postcolonial SF and Caribbean fabulist fiction. Her first novel, *Brown Girl in the Ring* (1998), won the Locus award, and she was named the Damon Knight Memorial Grand Master by the Science Fiction Writers of America in 2021, becoming both the youngest person and the first Black woman to receive that recognition. In this story, the name "Nancy" and the references to spiders clearly connect this character to Anansi, to the divine trickster spider associated with weaving stories; Anansi originated with the Asante people of Ghana and moved with the diaspora, driven in part by slavery, to the Caribbean and elsewhere.

Note on the text: First published in Hopkinson's story collection *Skin Folk* (2001), this story was nominated for the 2002 World Fantasy Award for Best Short Fiction, the same year *Skin Folk* won their award for Best Collection.

"Something to Hitch Meat to" (2001)

ARTHO picked up a bone lying in the street. No reason, just one of those irrational things you do when your brain is busy with something else, like whether you remembered to buy avocados or not. The alligator-tail chain of a day care snaked past him, each toddler hanging on dutifully to one of the knots in the rope by which they were being led. One of the young, gum-popping nannies said:

"So then little Zukie draws herself up real tall, and she says, 'No, silly. The purpose of the skeleton is something to hitch meat to.' Really! I swear, I nearly died laughing, she sounded so serious."

The woman eyed him as she walked past, smiled a little, glanced down. She played with her long hair and stage-whispered to her co-worker, "God, Latino men are just so hot, don't you think?" They giggled and moved on, trailing children.

The gears of Artho's brain kicked back into realtime. He was standing at the southwest comer of King and Bay, holding a chicken thighbone. Fleshless and parched, it felt dusty between his fingers. He dropped it and wiped his hand off on his jeans. Latino? What the hell?

Streetcar coming. Artho got on, elbowing himself some rush hour standing room between an old man with a bound live chicken that lay gasping in his market basket and three loud, hormonal young women, all politics and piercings. Artho reached for a steady strap. Traffic was gridlocked. He stared blankly out the window as the streetcar inched its way past a woman struggling with two huge dogs on leashes. Bergers des Pyrenées, they were; giant, woolly animals bred for rescuing skiers trapped under alpine avalanches. They were so furry that Artho could barely make out their legs. They lumbered along in a smooth, four-on-the-floor gait. The dogs' handler tugged futilely at their leashes, barely able to keep up. The beasts could probably cover miles in effortless minutes, snowshoeing on their woolly feet. Artho fancied that they would move even faster, smoother, if you changed them to have six legs, or eight. They would glide along like enormous tarantulas. Artho looked at their handler's legs and had the oddest feeling, like when an old film skips a frame, and for an instant, you can see the hole-punched edges of the film strip, black and chitinous on the screen, and then it jerks back into place, but now you're looking at a different scene than you were before. It was like that, Artho looking at this woman walking on ordinary woman legs, then reality skipped frames, and he was seeing instead a being whose natural four-legged stance had been twisted and warped so that all it could manage was this ungainly two-legged jerking from foot to foot. Made into something it wasn't.

Alarmed, Artho blinked. He made himself relax. Tired. Too many hours at work in front of a computer screen, staring at all that skin. He leaned his head against the streetcar window and dozed, thinking hungrily of the stewed chicken and rice he would have for dinner, with avocado—his dad always called them alligator pears—on the side. He could see the fleshy avocado in his mind's eye: slit free of its bumpy rind; pegged and sitting on a plate; beads of salt melting on the sweating, creamy skin. He imagined biting into a slice, his teeth meeting in its spineless centre. His mouth watered.

It wasn't until he reached his stop that he realized he really had forgotten to buy the damned avocados. He found some tired, wrinkly ones in the comer store near his apartment. The man behind the counter, who served Artho at least twice a week when he came in for cigarettes or munchies, grumbled at the fifty dollar bill that Artho gave him, and made a big show over holding it up to the light to see if it was counterfeit. Artho had seen the same man cheerfully make change from bills that large for old women or guys in suits. He handed Artho a couple of twenties and some coins, scowling. Artho held each twenty up to the light before putting it into his pocket. "Thank you," he said sweetly to the guy, who glared. Artho took his avocados and went home. When he sliced into them, one of them was hard and black inside. He threw it out.

"So," Artho's brother said, "I'm out with the guys the other night, and ..."

"Huh? What'd you say?" Artho asked. Something was obscuring Aziman's voice in the phone, making rubbing and clicking sounds over and around his speech. "What's that noise?" Artho asked the receiver. "Like dice rolling together or something."

"One dice, two die. Or is it the other way around? Anyway, so I'm ..."

"What're you eating? I can't make out what you're saying."

"Hold on." Silence. Then Aziman came on again. "This any better?"

"Yeah. What was that?"

"This hard candy the kids brought home. Got me hooked on it. These little round white thingies, y'know? I had a mouthful of them."

"Did you spit them out?"

"Well, not round exactly. Kinda egg-shaped, but squarer than that. Is 'squarer' a word?"

"Did you spit them out?" Artho was just being pissy, and he knew it. He could tell that Aziman had gotten rid of the candies somehow. His voice was coming through clearly now.

"Yeah, Artho. Can I tell my story now?"

"Where'd you spit them?"

"What's up with you today? Down the kitchen sink."

And Aziman started in with his story again, but Artho was distracted, thinking on the tiny white candies disappearing into the drain, perhaps washed down with water.

"… so this man walks up to us, a kid really, y'know? Smart-ass yuppie corn-fed kid with naturally blond hair and a polo shirt on. Probably an MBA. And he says to me, ''sup, man?' only he says it 'mon.' I mean, I guess he's decided I'm from Jamaica or something, you know?"

"Yeah," said Artho. "I know."

"He gives me this weird handshake; grabs my thumb and then makes a fist and I'm supposed to touch my fist to his, I think, I dunno if I did it right. But he says, ''sup' again, and I realize I didn't answer him, so I just say, 'Uh, nothing much,' which I guess isn't the lingo, right? But I dunno what I'm supposed to say; I mean, you and me, we're freaking north Toronto niggers,[1] right? And this white guy's got Toronto suburbs written all over him, too. Probably never been any farther than Buffalo. So what's he trying to pull with that fake ghetto street shit anyway, you know? And he leans in close, kinda chummy like, and whispers, 'Think you could sell me some shit, man?' And I'm thinking, *Like the kind you're trying to sell me on right now?* I mean, he's asking me for dope, or something."

Artho laughed. "Yeah, happens to me, too. It's always the same lame-ass question, never changes. I just point out the meanest-looking, blackest motherfucker in the joint and say, 'Not me, man, but I bet that guy'll be able to help you out.'"

"Shit. I'll try that next time."

"Though I guess it isn't fair, you know, my doing that. It's like I'm picking on guys just 'cause they're blacker than me."

"Heh. I guess, if you want to look at things that way. You going to Mom's for Easter?"

"Is Aunt Dee going to be there?"

1 Aziman here engages a linguistic reappropriation of this anti-Black racist epithet.

But Aziman's only reply was a rustling, shucking type of noise. Then, "Shit!"

"What?"

"I stuck my hand into the bag for more candy, y'know? Just figured out what these things are."

"What?"

"Skulls. Little sugar skulls, f'chrissake."

Dead people bits. That's what the candy was. It was all in the way you looked at it.

"No," said Artho. "It'll be just like last year. I'm not going to Mom's for Easter."

A few days later it happened again, a weird unfamiliarity when Artho looked at human bodies. He was in the mall food court on his lunch hour. When he went back to work, it would be to spend the rest of the day updating the Tit for Twat site: *Horny Vixens in Heat! No Holes Barred!*

The food court was crowded. People in business suits wolfed down Jolly Meals, barked on cell phones. The buzz of conversation was a formless noise, almost soothing.

Not many empty spaces. Artho had to share a table for two with a thirtyish man in fine beige wool, engrossed in the financial pages of the *Globe & Mail* newspaper. The man had shaved his head completely. Artho liked it. There was something sensuous about the baldness, like the domed heads of penises. Cute. Artho was thinking of something to say to him, some kind of opener, when the man's ears caught his gaze. They jutted out from the side of his head like knurls of deformed cartilage. There really was nothing odd about the guy's ears—that's just how ears were—but they still gave Artho a queasy feeling. With one hand, he worried at his own ear. He looked around at other people in the food court. All their ears seemed like twisted carbuncles of flesh sprouting from the sides of their heads, odd excrescences. Nausea and doubt squirmed like larvae in Artho's chest. His fingers twitched, the ones that he would use a few minutes from now to point, click, and drag his mouse as he smoothed out the cellulite and firmed up the pecs of the perfect naked models on the screen, making them even more perfect. He closed his eyes to block out the sight of all those ugly ears.

Someone was singing. A child's voice, tuneless and repetitive, threaded its whiny way through the rumble of lunchtime chatter:

"Tain't no sin,
Take off your skin,
And dance around in your bones.
Tain't no sin ..."[1]

1 "Tain't No Sin (To Dance Around in Your Bones)," words by Edgar Leslie, music by Walter Donaldson, 1929. (Hopkinson's note)

Artho opened his eyes. Wriggly as only seven-year-olds can be, a little girl slouched beside her father at a table for four, sitting on her spine so she could kick at the centre pole supporting the table welded to its four seats. Her wiry black hair was braided into thousands of dark medusa strands. The brown bumps of her knees were ashy with dry skin. The lumpy edge of a brightly coloured Spider Man[1] knapsack jutted out from behind her back.

"Tain't no sin ..." She kicked and kicked at the pole. An old man who'd been forced to share the table with them looked up from his chow mein and gave her a strained nice-little-girl smile.

"Quit it, Nancy." Not even glancing at his daughter—was she his daughter?—her father reached out with one hand and stilled the thin, kicking legs. With his other hand he hurriedly stuffed a burger into his mouth. Green relish oozed between his fingers.

The little girl stopped kicking, but all that energy had to have some outlet. She immediately started swaying her upper body from side to side, jerking her knapsack about so that something thumped around inside it. She bobbed her head in time to her little song. Her braids flowed like cilia. She looked around her. Her gaze connected with Artho's. "Daddy," she said loudly to the man beside her, "can you see me?" She wore glasses with jam-jar-thick lenses, which refracted and multiplied her eyes. She didn't look up at her father.

And he didn't look down at her, just kept gnawing on his burger. "Can't see you at all, little girl," he mumbled. "I only think I can. You're nowhere to be seen."

She smiled at that. "I'm everywhere, though, Daddy."

Must be some kind of weird game they had between the two of them. Then she started singing again. Artho found himself swaying slightly from side to side in time with her song. He looked away. He'd always hated Spider Man. As a kid, the comic book character had frightened him. His costume made him look like a skeleton, a clattery skin-and-bone man that someone had painted red as blood.

" ... dance around in your bones!" the little girl shouted, glaring at him from the depths of her specs.

Artho leapt to his feet and dumped the remainder of his lunch in the garbage, fled the girl's irritating ditty. His table partner still had his nose buried in his paper.

As Artho walked the last few feet to the elevator of his office building, he suddenly became aware of the movement of his legs: push off with left leg, bending toes for leverage; contract right knee to extend right leg, heel first; shift weight; step onto right foot; bend right knee; repeat on the other side. For a ludicrous moment, he nearly tripped over his own feet. It was like some kind of weird jig. He stumbled into the elevator, smiled I'm-fine-really at a

---

1 Spider-Man is a comic-book superhero created by Steve Ditko (1927–2018) and Stan Lee (1922–2018); the character premiered in 1962.

plump young woman in a business suit who was gazing at him curiously. She looked away. Then he did. They stared politely at the opaque white numbers, knobbled as vertebrae, that indicated each floor. The numbers clicked over, lighting up one at a time: 10 … 11 … 12 … *Roll the bones*, thought Artho.

"Um … do you know what time it is?" the woman asked him.

He checked his watch, smiled at her. "Almost ten to one." The deep rust of the suit made her flawless cinnamon skin glow, hinted at the buxom swell of breast, belly, hip, and thigh. Yum. Artho's mouse fingers stopped twitching.

She smiled back nervously. The smile quirked friendly lines at the corners of her mouth. "Thanks. Guess I'm on time after all, then."

"Job interview?"

"Uh-huh. Marketing. Up at Joint Productions."

"The design place? Cool. They've done some great stuff."

She looked even more interested, leaned forward a little. "Oh, you work there?"

Shit. "Uh, no."

"In the building, then?"

"Yeah. Web design. For, um, Tri-Ex Media."

She frowned a little, took a bit of a step back. "Another design place?"

"Yeah, sort of. We …"

The elevator stopped and the door slid noiselessly open.

"Oh, my stop," she said. "Nice talking to you."

"Yeah. Bye." If she got the job, that'd be the last civil conversation he had with her. The people at Joint acted like Tri-Ex Media was the very source and centre of evil in the universe. She'd probably get bitten by the same bug. Artho got out at 17.

Cold air prickled his forearms into goose bumps when he opened the door to Tri-Ex Media. The office was air-conditioned year-round to protect the expensive computer equipment. The not-so-pricey staff just wore sweaters. "Close the fucking door!" growled Charlie, his boss. Artho uncurled his spine to stand tall. He stitched a smile across his face and stepped inside, gently pulling the door shut behind him. "Miss me?" he cooed at Charlie.

People just look really weird, Artho thought. He contemplated the image up on his screen: a buff, tattooed man in a shoulder stand who'd curled himself tight as a fiddlehead fern so as to suck his own cock. Well, actually, he hadn't quite been able to reach it. His searching tongue was just a few inches away. Probably would have helped if he'd been interested enough in the procedure to have a hard-on. That was where Artho came in. He giggled, began the process of stiffening and elongating the man's dick. "Virtual fluffer,[1] that's me," he said, aiming the comment at the general air.

1 Fluffer refers to a worker on the set of a pornographic film who helps performers achieve and maintain erections.

Only Glenn looked up, scowling over the top of his terminal and flicking a lank lick of Popsicle pink hair out of his eyes. "Yeah? Just keep it in your pants, Mouse Boy." He grinned a little to take the sting of the comment out.

That uncomfortable little grin. Taboo subject at work, sex. Staring all day at pictures of spread, penetrated flesh—flesh more shapely than any of them in the office had: plump, perky breasts, impossibly slim waists; muscled thighs and ever-ready cocks—but *talk* about any of it?

"Hey, Artho?" Tamara called quietly from across the room.

"Yeah?" Today her thick wool sweater had a picture on it of that guy from the Fabulous Four comics, the one who turned into fire? *Flame on*. Johnny, his name was?[1] Where in hell did Tamara find the stuff she wore?

Tamara pulled the sleeves of her sweater down over her hands, trapped them against her palm with three fingers on each hand, kept typing with the free forefingers and thumbs. "You doing anything for Easter?"

Easter again. Long-distance phone call from Vancouver Island from his father. "I long to see you and your brother," he'd say. But it never happened. And if Artho visited his mother with her stiff, dead, pressed hair and the pale pink lipstick blanching her full brown lips, she'd ask if he was still working at *that place* and whisper prayers under her breath when he said yes. Aunt Dee would be there too, with her look of fearful hunger and her Doberman's knack of going for the soft underbelly of all their relatives: *Uncle James starting to lose his hair; Cousin Melba have neither chick nor child to look after; and eh-eh, look at old Uncle Cecil, taking up with a twenty-year-old chick in his dotage*. Aziman would be sitting in the basement with the basketball game turned up loud. Holidays always made him morose about his own divorce. He'd get steadily drunker on Wincarnis Tonic Wine (sugar code 17)[2] while his boy and girl screamed and romped and fought around him. "No," Artho told Tamara. "Gonna stay home, where it's quiet."

There. The autofellatio man looked like he was sucking his own dick now. It was moderately convincing. It'd do.

Easter meant that Aziman, after fueling himself with enough of the sugary wine, would flare, shouting insults at the players on the TV, yelling at his kids to quiet down, brown face flushing burgundy with the barely contained heat. Their mother would make him and the children spend the night at her place. "You can drive tomorrow, when you cool down," she'd say. Artho hoped that one day the fire inside Aziman would come busting out, fry away the polite surface he always presented.

How did that Johnny guy's flame really work? Artho wondered. Was he always flame on the inside?

---

1 "Flame on!" is the catchphrase of the comic-book superhero Johnny Storm, aka the Human Torch, as redesigned by Stan Lee and Jack Kirby (1917–94) from an earlier character. In this form, he premiered in 1961, as part of the superhero team The Fantastic Four.

2 A spiced and fortified British wine, popular in Jamaica.

On his screen, Artho checked out the autofellatio man's skin and hair; this one was going on the "Banjee Boys" page, whatever a banjee was, and Charlie thought a light brown black man just didn't fit the image.[1] Good thing the position the man was in now obscured that aquiline nose, those thin lips. Smiling to himself, Artho painted another tattoo on the man's beefy shoulder; "nkyin kyin," the West African Adinkra[2] symbol for "always changing oneself." He bet Charlie'd never recognise it in a million years.

Charlie came huffing by, glanced at the screen. "Artho, you still working on that fucking thing? Time is money here, y'know. I want Tit for Twat uploaded before you leave tonight. And no whining at me about overtime, either."

Artho sighed. "It'll be done before five." As if. But so long as it was up and running when Charlie came in on Monday, he'd never notice.

"Better be. And make that guy blacker. Looks like a dago."[3] Charlie turned away. Stopped. Turned back and peered at the screen. Guffawed, "Jesus, Arth! He's darker than you! Well, whaddya know 'bout that? Betcha his dick's no match for yours, though. Eh? Eh?" Charlie cackled and elbowed Artho in the ribs, then shaking his head and chuckling at his own wit, stumped his way out of the office. He slammed the door behind him. Everyone jumped at the thump. People avoided Artho's eyes.

Artho sighed and got to work again with his mouse, sticking cocoa-coloured pigment to the man like tar on the Tar Baby.[4] He ignored the feeling of his ears burning. It went away eventually.

He finished blackening the man up, then opened up the working files Tit for Twat. He imported the new images, new inane text ("*When Daddy's not home, see these blond sisters work each other up!*"). The "blond" was bleach, the "sisters" Tania and Raven no relation at all, and they were doing their best straight guy's lesbian fantasy. As soon as they got out of the studio, they shucked the whole act like corn trash from corn and hugged each other goodbye before going their separate ways. Raven was a CGA[5] student, blissfully married to a quiet, balding guy with a paunch, wore hightop sneakers everywhere, showed around pictures of her kids every chance she got. And Tania, as she walked out the door, would be peeling off her false two-inch nails, muttering that her girlfriends would never let her near them with knives on the tips of her fingers.

---

1 Banjee boy is a term associated with ballroom culture, specifically Black and Latino LGBTQ+ drag and dance culture. Banjee boys are typically represented with an urban or street aesthetic.

2 Adinkra symbols are part of the Asante culture of Ghana. Each symbol generally represents a proverb or concept.

3 An ethnic epithet generally aimed at people who are assumed to be of Italian or Spanish descent.

4 Tar Baby is a figure from African American folklore, notably transcribed and altered by white author Joel Chandler Harris (1848–1908) in his *Uncle Remus* stories (1881). The term has come to mean a difficult-to-escape ("sticky") situation, but has also been used as a racist epithet. Notably, Toni Morrison titled her fourth novel *Tar Baby* (1981).

5 Certified General Accountant.

"… good weekend, Artho."

"Huh? Oh, yeah. Bye, Glenn," he said as Glenn let himself out.

Artho looked around for the first time in hours. It was well past five. He straightened up, groaning; he could feel each of his vertebrae popping as he uncurled from the computer screen. And he was freezing. Charlie was long gone. He and Tamara were the only ones left.

"Lost in the land of skin?" she chuckled at him.

"Yeah. Be done soon now, though." He set the files to render, moved to the next computer over—Rahim worked at that one, but he was gone too—and called up Tomb Raider.[1] Artho'd gotten pretty good at the game. Masquerading as the impossibly firm-breasted Lara Croft, he hunted in a nightmare landscape of demons. He was just killing a ghoul in a spray of blood and bone when the door to the office whispered open. A tiny face poked round it.

"Hey, Artho?" Tamara said, waving sweater-covered fingers at him. "Relative of yours? This isn't exactly the place for a kid, you know."

It was the little girl, the one from the food court.

"What're you doing here?" Artho blurted out. "Where's your dad?"

"Daddy's always busy making stuff," came the scratchy response from the tiny face hanging in the doorway. "We do his work for him instead."

"Huh?" was all that Artho managed in response.

"Yeah. Each one of us has different jobs. Mine is that I get to go wherever I want, keep an eye on stuff." The little girl stalked on spindly legs into the room. Her knees were still ashy, the lenses of her specs still woozily thick. The wormy mass of her long, messy braids seemed to be wriggling out from their ribbons as Artho watched.

"That's ridiculous! It's"—Artho glanced at the clock on his screen—"almost seven-thirty in the evening! You can't be more than seven years old! Who're your parents? Why are you alone?"

"So you don't know her, then?" asked Tamara. She got up, went and knelt by the child. "What's your name, little girl?" she asked sweetly.

"Didn't come for you. Came for him." And the child stomped right past an astonished Tamara. "Whatcha doin?" On the screen, Lara Croft waited to be activated by a mouse click. "Oh," said the little girl. "Do you like that?"

Artho shrugged. "It's something to do."

She turned to the other screen with its bodies frozen in mid-writhe.

"Don't look at those!" Artho said.

"Just skins sewed together," she replied, grinning. "Do you like those, then?"

"Artho, do you know this kid or not?"

Artho found himself answering the child instead of Tamara: "No, I don't like them so much. I like people to look more real."

"Well, why do you make them look not real, then?"

---

1 *Tomb Raider* was a video game featuring the player character Lara Croft. Released in 1996, it has since spawned other games as well as films and versions in other media.

From the mouths of babes and sucklings. "That's why they pay me the big bucks," he said ruefully, thinking of how far his paycheque wouldn't stretch this month.

"Do you like people making *you* be not real?"

Artho thought how he'd been late for work that morning because six taxis in a row had refused to stop for him. Thought of the guy in the corner store inspecting his money. Of Charlie elbowing him in the ribs a few hours ago. He felt a burn of rage beginning. "No, dammit!"

The ugly child just stood and stared at him from the depths of her ugly glasses.

"But it's not like I can do anything about it!" Artho said.

"Do you wanna?" She was shrugging out of her Spider Man knapsack.

He turned so he could scowl at her face straight on. "Shit, girl, what d'you think? Yes!"

Tamara giggled. Fuck, why was he talking to a kid this way? He started slamming pens and pencils around on the desk.

"Well, change things, then!" the child squealed. She lunged at Artho and swung her Spider Man knapsack right at his forehead.

It was like slo-mo; Artho could see the oddly muscular bulge of her lats powering the swing, almost had time to wonder how a seven-year-old could be that built, then he had barely focused on the red and black image of Spidey coming for him, reaching for him, when *bang*, the knapsack connected and something exploded inside Artho's skull.

Tamara yelled. Artho shouted, tried to reach for the kid through the stars flaring behind his eyes. Jesus, felt like a bag of bones the damned child had in there. "Shit, shit, shit," Artho moaned, holding his aching head. He dimly saw the child slither out of Tamara's grasp and run, no, glide out of the room on those skin-and-boneless legs. She had a big butt, too, that child; as she ran, it worked under her little plaid skirt like that of someone three times her size.

"Artho, you okay? I'm calling security."

He paid Tamara no mind. He was dizzy. He put his head down between his knees. It was wet, his forehead was *wet* where he was holding it. He was bleeding! Damned girl. He took his hand away, raised his head enough to inspect it.

"Yeah, Muhammed? Can you come up to Tri-Ex Media on 17? We got a little girl loose on this floor. No, don't know where she came from. Look, she just *hit* Artho, okay? I think he's hurt. Yes, a kid did it, she's little, maybe six, seven. Little black girl, school uniform, thick glasses. Says her parents aren't with her. Okay. Okay." She hung up. "He's coming."

There was no blood. At least, the stuff leaking out of him didn't look like blood. The liquid on his hand seemed to glow one minute and go milky the next, like a smear of syrup. "What is this shit?"

"Here, let me see." Tamara crouched down by him like she had by the little girl. Nancy. That's what her dad had called her. What kind of dad let his young kid roam around loose like that?

Tamara frowned. "Yeah, you're cut, but there's this weird … stuff coming out. Oh. Never mind, it's stopped now. How d'you feel, Artho?"

"What the hell was in that knapsack? Where'd she go?"

"I'll go see." Tamara jumped up, left the office.

Artho's head was clearing. It didn't hurt so much now. He touched where the cut was, couldn't feel one. The goop was still on his fingers, though. He rubbed the fingers together to smear the stuff away. His fingers kind of tingled.

But really, he felt a lot better now. He chuckled a little, thinking of the comic books he'd read as a kid. He'd been bitten by an overactive spider.

His computer pinged to tell him that it was done rendering. Shit. Had to get that stuff done tonight, or Charlie'd have his head. He moved back to his terminal to upload Tit for Twat. He reached for the mouse. He clicked on it, and the click felt like it traveled all the way through his arm. No, like it had come *from* his arm, down through his hand, to the mouse. Weird.

Tamara came back. "Found a little girl with her dad in the elevator. Could have been her. Looked a little bit like her, I guess. I mean, I can't tell, you know, they all look … I mean …" She stopped, blushing.

They all look alike. The superintendent of Artho's apartment building always mixed him up with Patrice who lived on the 27th floor, never mind that Patrice was dark café cru to Artho's caramel, was balding, had arms like thighs, and spoke with a strong French accent. Tamara had always been nice to Artho, though. And she knew what a bonehead she'd just been, he could tell. Right? Right. He swallowed, didn't say anything. Let Tamara believe he hadn't guessed what she'd almost said.

"Anyway," Tamara continued, "she's gone now. Muhammed's gone back to his desk. You feeling any better?"

"Yeah, thanks."

"Well." She stood there, still looking sheepish and uncomfortable. "Um, I'm going home now."

"See ya." He watched her put on her coat. He waved good-bye to her. Then he uploaded the site, ignoring the odd clicking feeling in his mouse arm. God, it made him feel clumsy. He'd have to get that checked out. Probably some kind of overuse thing. He clicked the file closed. Behind it was the autofellatio man. Hadn't he uploaded that one too? He went to do it, but the hand with the mouse slipped, and he ended up instead selecting the "changing oneself always" symbol he'd put on the man's arm as a joke. Yeah, better take that off. Just in case Charlie did figure out he'd done it. Didn't want to get his ass in trouble. He dragged the nkyin kyin symbol off the guy's arm, and what the fuck, it came all the way *off* the screen, skidded right across the keyboard, and came to rest on his thigh. Alarmed, he released the mouse. The symbol melted through the cloth into the meat of his leg. "Shit!" It tingled for a second, then faded.

Ah, fuck. Bloody weird day. He reached for the mouse again. When he clicked on it this time, something subtle changed about the autofellatio man.

Artho stared hard at the image on the screen to try to see what was different. Yes, the nkyin kyin was back on the man's shoulder. And he was a little pudgier. And were those crow's-feet around his eyes? A hint of a smile around his wide-stretched mouth?

Whatever. Artho shrugged and uploaded the damned thing, ignoring the weird feeling in his arm every time he clicked the mouse.

Enough. Time to go home. Artho grabbed his coat, locked up, and left.

By the time the elevator had made it to the first floor, Artho was feeling really odd. Not sick, really, just faintly unreal, like when he smoked a joint too fast, or took sinus meds. He sighed, hoping he wasn't going to spend the weekend with the flu. At least it'd give him an excuse to skip going to his mum's. He put his hand on the door of the building to let himself out. *Click.* When he took the hand away, the nkyin kyin symbol was on it. He peered at the handle. Had it always been ornate worked brass? In the form of some kind of bug? No, now it looked like ... a skeleton? Artho touched the handle again, double-clicked. And the handle was a plain aluminum strip once more.

Artho's skin began to prickle. Not with fear, not with fever. With hope. He rushed outside the building, put his palm against its dull brick exterior. Clicked. The walls flushed red, then purple. Fluted columns started to sprout beside the doors, which were quickly changing from sliding glass and steel to intricately joined oak. With big knockers. Artho giggled. Pretty damned tarty. He wondered if that had been the builder's original dream for the building. He double-clicked. The building reverted to its usual form.

"You're getting it."

When he turned towards the voice, Artho wasn't at all surprised to see the little girl. She was crouched down beside the steps, jam-jar glasses winking at him. Her hair knotted and unknotted itself.

"Can I change everything?" Artho asked.

"Course not, silly! Changing things isn't *your* job. You're not changing things; that'll happen anyway. You're just helping them peel off the fake skins."

"How's that work?"

"You'll just have to try it and see." She stuck her tongue out at him too. It was too pointy, and more lavender than pink. She leapt, stuck to the side of the building, started climbing smoothly up it, with two legs, with four. No wonder her behind had looked so, well, well-endowed. Must have had the other pair of legs hitched up under her skirt. The little girl was far above Artho now. He could just make out white panties with her legs sticking out of four leg holes. She climbed with two arms, with four. Ah. That well-muscled back. Artho smiled. He watched her until she disappeared into the darkness. He'd figured out who, what she was. Appeared as a skeleton sometimes, in a top hat. Watcher at the boundaries, at the crossroads. Sometimes man, sometimes woman. Always trickster. He couldn't really tell in the dark, but she seemed furrier now, or more bristly, or something. Sometimes spider? He wondered if this was the kind of thing her dad had really meant her to do.

Ah, well; she was notoriously capricious. She might decide to take her gift away again, so he'd better use it while he could. He set off for the streetcar stop, almost bouncing, dancing along in his excitement, thinking where he'd like to implant the Adinkra symbol next. On Charlie? Maybe Charlie really was the way he appeared to be. Oog. His Aunt Dee? What would Dee be like if she could peel away all that unhappiness?

How about on Aziman? All these choices. "Good evening," Artho said to the tired people waiting at the stop. One white woman clutched her purse tighter when she saw him. Hmm. Maybe he should work that nkyin kyin thing on himself; it was in him, after all. He wondered what she would see then.

N.K. Jemisin (b. 1972)

N.K. Jemisin is an American SF and fantasy author who is best known for her *Broken Earth* trilogy of novels, consisting of *The Fifth Season* (2015), *The Obelisk Gate* (2016), and *The Stone Sky* (2017), the first trilogy in which all three novels won the Hugo award, which also made her the first author to win the Hugo for Best Novel in three consecutive years. When she won the Hugo for Best Novel for *The Fifth Season*, she also became the first Black author to win that award.

Note on the text: In the original publication, in the online Canadian SF magazine *Ideomancer* (vol. 3, no. 9, 2004), the text of the message-board posts and emails were blocked off in black text boxes with light-coloured font, mimicking a computer screen. Here, the format of the republication in Jemisin's award-winning collection *How Long 'til Black Future Month?* (2018) is followed. In both versions, intentional typos are included to mimic the informal and often rapid writing that happens on message boards.

"Too Many Yesterdays, Not Enough Tomorrows" (2004)

The alarm clock buzzed at seven, right after reality rolled over. Helen tapped the snooze button for ten more minutes. When the alarm went off again, she believed for a moment that a man was in the room creeping toward her. She sat up ready to lash out with nails and fists and feet, then memory returned and she chuckled to herself. A dream. Habit. Too bad.

BLOGSTER[1] login: Welcome, TwenWen!

[Thursday, ??? feels like 10 p.m.]

Hel, you had the rapist dream too? Thought I was the only sicko! Y'know, back in college psych they said those kinds of dreams are a representation of your subconscious yearning to be rescued from your out-of-control situation. (That, or you want a penis. ^_-) Usually I try to keep mine going awhile, see if he actually manages to score. Never does. Figures; even my Freudian fantasy rapists are pissant schmucks.

In browsing news, surprise! There's yet another spec-thread running among the <u>BumBloggity brats</u>.[2] "The government did it" version 2,563,741. Wish they'd get back to aliens or God; those are more fun.

1 Blogster.com is a community blogging platform, launched around the time this story was published; "blogster" has also been used as a general term for someone who blogs.

2 The underlining in the discussions indicates hyperlinks to other pages (this is a formal element of the story; they were not active links on the web version of the story.)

BTW, gang, meet SapphoJuice (his blog). He's in a snowy reality. Has a studio, poor guy.

Hey, anybody heard from MadHadder lately?

Life, post-prolif: She climbed up from the futon and shuffled across the room, her feet chuffing along the tatami-matted floor. When she reached the kitchen, she took care to yank the fridge door open so that the glass bottles would rattle and clink. Noise made the apartment seem less empty. Then she slapped onto the counter the items that would comprise her breakfast: a cup of yogurt and a cellophaned packet of grilled fish. She rummaged awhile for the stay-fresh drink box of chai tea concentrate; she knew where it was, but rummaging helped to kill time. The milk was as fusty as ever. Irrationally she always retained the vague hope that if she got up soon enough after the roll-over, it would taste fresher. Mixing it with the chai covered the not-quite-sour taste, so she microwaved that for three minutes and then used that to wash the fish down.

Chewing, she paused and grinned to herself as she felt a bone prick the inside of her cheek. She'd eaten the packet of fish seven times lately without finding it. The bone was always there, but tiny and easy to miss. Finding it made her feel lucky.

It was going to be another beautiful day in infinity.

BLOGSTER login: Welcome, SapphoJuice!

[Cinco de myass,[1] the year 2 bajillion and 2]

SPINNYSPINNYSPINNY

Hi, all. Thanks for the warm greetings. My daily routine includes two hours of spinning around in my desk chair. My mom never used to let me do it before, so … whee!

Yes, Marguille, your guess as to the origin of my username is correct; I am indeed a squealing Herbert fanboy (sorry, Conty, not a lesbian =P). Only got Children Of in my studio, though. Sucks donkey balls. Big hairy fat ones.

Ah, c'mon, Twen, specthreading is fun and oh so good for you. Granted, it's pretty much a complete waste to wonder how and why the quantum proliferation occurred because we can't do dick to fix it … And granted, the BumBloggers do seem to have the same arguments over and over (and over and over) again … but hey, there's comfort in the routine. Right? Right? ::listens to crickets::

Hel: wow, Japan? You must have been quite the adventurer, before.

---

1 A play on "Cinco de Mayo," a celebration held in Mexico every year on 5 May, commemorating the country's victory over the French at the Battle of Puebla in Puebla, Mexico, in 1862.

Jogging; she loved it. The rhythmic pounding of the hardpack under her sneakers. The mantra of her breathing. She would never have taken up jogging if there'd still been people around to watch her, maybe point and laugh at the jiggly big-boned sistah trying to be FloJo. Before the prolif she'd only just begun to shed her self-consciousness around the Japanese. They rarely stared when she could see them, and her students had gotten used to her by then, but on the street she'd always felt the pressure of the neighbors' gazes against her back, skittering away from her peripheral vision when she turned. The days of Sambo dolls at the corner store were mostly over, but not a lot of Japanese had seen black people anywhere except on television.[1] *My parents must've felt the same during grad school in Des Moines*, she'd always told herself to put things in perspective. It hadn't helped much.

Now, free from the pressure of those gazes, she could run. She was fit and strong and free.

Around her the barren, cracked desert stretched unbroken for as far as the eye could see.

BLOGSTER login: Welcome, KT!

[Saturdayish, The House That Time Forgot]

Fighting the lonelies. Everybody still out there? Conty? Guille? Hel? Twen? (Hi, Sapp.) I haven't heard from MadHadder either. What if the silence got him?

Don't want to think about that. Topic change. Did you know Mr. Hissyfit keeps going through the rollovers, too? I guess cats *do* think.

Sappjuice, it sounds like you're living in Fimbulwinter (sp?). I've got grassy plain. It's boring, but at least I know it can't kill me. You have my e-sympathies.

She liked best the fact that the day started over after about ten hours. Incomplete reality, incomplete time. She'd stayed awake to watch the rollover numerous times, but for a phenomenon that should've been a string theorist's wet dream, it was singularly unimpressive. Like watching a security camera video loop: dull scene, flicker, resume dull scene. Though once the flicker passed, there was grilled fish and stale milk in her fridge again, and her alarm clock buzzed to declare that 7:00 a.m. had returned. Only her mind remained the same.

She usually went to bed a few hours after the second alarm. That gave her time to print out the latest novella making the rounds in cyberspace, read it in the bath, and maybe work on her own would-be masterpieces. It didn't bother

1 *The Story of Little Black Sambo* (1899), illustrated children's book by Helen Bannerman (1862–1946). Originally portraying a South Asian child, later represented as a character of African descent, the book repeats anti-Black and other racist imagery and tropes. The book, and dolls based on it, were popular in Japan in the second half of the twentieth century and beyond, though controversy caused by their racism led to the book and other merchandise being recalled, temporarily, in 1988 (see Wallace).

her that the poems she wrote erased themselves every rollover. If she wanted to keep them, she posted them online where the mingling of so many minds kept time linear. But doing that exposed the fragile words to the scrutiny of others, and sometimes it was better to just let them vanish.

She decided to post the latest one to share with her friends. The new boy wasn't a friend, not yet, but maybe he had friend-potential.

BLOGSTER login: Welcome, Marguille!

[Sunday, 5 Marguille'sMonth, 2 years A.P., 2 a.m.]

I agree with Twen; specthredding is evil. But I can't help it; been reading the Bumwankers stuff (I know, I know). my vote has always been for the government theory. $87 bil. for an "emergency fund"? Shyeah. Probly only took half that to build some knd of new super-weapon, or hotwire a particle acelerator. "I know! Let's shoot some protons at the terrorists! Yeah! Oops, we bro,ke the universe!"

But seriously … I keep thinking that somewhere out there, normal reality still exists. no, scratch that — I *know* it exists, because it's possible. Fun with quantum thery! 'Course, that means oblivion exists too. (This is what we get for letting that guy Shroedinger experiment on his cat. Should've sicked PETA on him.)

SappJuice, don't feel bad about your studio. Hel's Japanese apartment's probably half the size of yours. (What do you call half a studio? A closet? … ducks rotten tomatoes from Japan::) Anyway, it's not like the rest of us are so much better off. What difference does a few square feet make when they're the same square feet every damn day?

She got the email just before she would've gone to bed. The ding from her computer surprised her. Blogs worked, as did other forms of social media. Direct, private contact was impossible. Individual-to-individual relays—instant messaging, email—worked, but were always iffy. Most people just didn't bother to try; too disappointing. And then there were the rumors.

But she read the email anyway.

"To: Hel

From: SapphoJuice

Subject: Hi

Helen (seems so weird to say your full name),

Hope you get this. I read the poem you posted in your blog. I just wanted to say … it wasn't beautiful, but it did move me. Made me remember the way things used to be, and made me realize I don't really mind that the old world is gone. I got put in a garbage can by football players *every day* during my freshman year. My mom always used to tell me I'd never amount to anything. How could I miss that? Anyway.

I guess the only thing that bothers me now is the silence. And sometimes I don't even mind that, but sometimes the snow just gets to me. Why the hell couldn't my pocket universe have formed around an ⋆interesting⋆ environment? I could dig an endless beach, maybe an endless forest. No, I get snow. It's so quiet. It never stops falling. I can't go out far without losing the apartment in the haze. Sometimes I want to just keep walking into the white, who cares? Then I read your poem.

Sappy (yeah, I know)"

She sat at her computer savoring the newness of the moment.

BLOGSTER login: Welcome, KT!

[Ohwhocares? Someday, somewhen]

Mr. Hissyfit got out. I tried to catch him but he just ran straight away into the grass. I keep going out to call for him, but he must be too far away to hear me.

Stupid cat. Stupid goddamn cat. I can't stop crying.

She emailed SapphoJuice back and told him that she had only feared the silence once. That had been right after the prolif, when she'd still been adjusting. She'd started running and hadn't stopped; just put her head down and cranked her arms like pistons and hauled ass as fast as her legs would take her, as far as her lungs could fuel. When she'd looked around, the apartment was gone, swallowed into the cracked-earth landscape. Instant panic. The apartment was only a fragment of reality, but it was *her* fragment of reality, her only connection to the other incomplete miniverses that now made up existence. Even before the prolif, she had been happiest there.

She could admit that, now, to him. But back on the day she'd run too far, she'd been in a panic, her grip on sanity slipping by cogs. It had taken the threat of true isolation, of wandering lost through endless wastelands until thirst or exposure killed her, to make her see the apartment as haven and not prison. So half-blinded by tears she had run back, thanking God that her shoes were cheap. One of them had an uneven sole, which scuffed a little crescent-shaped mark into the dusty soil. The moon had led her home.

BLOGSTER login: Welcome Conty!

RED ALERT

[Day 975 (yeah right I actually keep count in my head)]

KT no more kidding. Fight it. Don't think about the damn cat. Go out and run—you can go pretty far from your house in the grass, can't you? Eat something. Hell, eat everything; it's not like it won't come back at rollover.

Talk to us.

The emails she sent didn't always go through. More than once she had to send them again when they bounced or, more often, simply never got a response. She saw the bounce histories in his attachments and knew that he'd had to send his multiple times, too. Just another day post-prolif.

She did not tell the others about the private correspondence, and neither did he. She knew what her friends would have said. It became something special, secret, a little titillating. As the days passed, her dreams changed. Now the man creeping about her room had a face and a much less sinister demeanor. Now he looked like a skinny, geeky teenager, whose shy smile was for her alone.

BLOGSTER login: Welcome, Marguille!
[Jan. 37 errordate errortime 12:59ok p.m.]
SILENCE.
You guys want to chat? I need some facetime. I think KT's gone.

Over the exchanges, she shared her life story with him. Growing up less than middle-class, trying to act less than upper-class. The teasing in elementary school because she "talked proper" and couldn't dance. Her first boyfriend, a white boy—she'd been too guilt-ridden to bring him home to meet her parents, and they'd broken up because of her shame. Her next boyfriend, the one she'd almost married until she found out he was cheating on her. Graduating college and feeling the isolation grow in her life. Few friends, none of them local. No lovers. She'd always been an only child, a lonely child; she was used to it. The prospect of a couple of years in Japan hadn't seemed all that daunting because what difference did it make, after all?

He told her about himself. Second generation American-born Chinese, too free-spirited for the rigidly traditional family into which he'd been born, too shy to face the world without the shield of a book. No girlfriends; the girls he'd liked had been more interested in jocks and red-blooded rich boys. Never brave enough to venture far from home, the internet had become his realm, and in it he thrived. He was a Big Name Fan in certain circles, known for his biting wit and brutal honesty. The prolif had barely slowed him down.

She worried about what might happen as the clandestine exchanges continued, but never mentioned her fears to him. She'd begun to enjoy herself too much; the "incoming mail" chime was enough to make her heart race with excitement. She had to force herself out for her daily runs.

It helped that the more they talked, the more reliable the relaying became. Pretty soon messages were going through after only two or three tries, and not bouncing at all.

IRC[1] session start: Sun? MarEMBJune datetime error

*** marguille sets mode: +o TwenWen Conty Helen sappjuice

> Log set and active! TwenWen logging!

<marguille> dunno why you're logging, twen. it's judst a chat.

<TwenWen> Not just a chat. MadHadder and KT's memorial service.

* Conty sighs.

* Helen observes a moment of silence.

<marguille> ditto. y'know … I herd more spec the other day.

* Conty groans.

* Helen sighs.

* TwenWen waits for Marguille's spec … and waits … and waits.

<TwenWen> … lagged?

<marguille> this one sounds like it's from the eggheads who did this. here it is: decoherence. when things in a quantum state are coupled to thuings outside that state, both systems collapse. no lag, 2-finger-typing lots, sorry.

<Conty> Yeah, that's egghead all right

* Helen wishes she had a nickel for every egghead spec … but where would she put them all?

*** sappjuice changes topic to "The Egghead Pyramid Scheme!"

*TwenWen giggles.

<marguille> seriously … you heard abut HafCafLatay?

<marguille> she got email from her MOM.

<marguille> as soon as she read it … poof. none of her blogfriends ever heard fm her again.

<Conty> WTF does that have to do with incoherence???

* TwenWen says, "DEcoherence. And I can use other big words, like 'marmalade'."

<Conty> Whatever. Still WTF

<sappjuice> There's spec that *we're* in a quantum state, y'know, each of us. Endless partial variations on the same world, same time …

<Conty> What, so if we ever have contact with somebody in another reality, we'll disappear?

* marguille is typing.

<marguille> the eggheds say it matters if the connection is strong or weajk. the stronger the coupling, the faster the collapse. weak couplings last a long time, maybe even stabilize. vbut with really strong couplings the collapse is nearly instant.

<TwenWen> Ooh, coupling! Wink wink nudge nudge say no more.

<TwenWen> Seriously … you're saying coupling = personal ties?

---

1 Internet Relay Chat, a form of online instant messaging often used for both discussion-based forums and private chats. Also note that in early online chats (and still on some platforms today) people would narrate versions of "IRL" (in real life) actions and reactions, as in "Conty sighs" and "Conty groans."

Coupling *to other people*?

<marguille> yep. we're already weakly connected, or we wouldn't be able to talk like this. but strong connections are emotional. HafCaf found her mom and … silence. Both of 'em.

<marguille> sucks, don't it.

<Conty> Ohdamn.

<sappjuice> Huh?

<Conty> I forgot, rollover's about to

*** Conty has been disconnected.

<marguille> Fuck.

<TwenWen> Um, I rollover in 10 mins.

<sappjuice> Maybe we should cut this short, then. Nice seeing everybody face to face, so to speak.

* Helen agrees.

* marguille sighs and waves.

<marguille> back to blogdom then. Toodles.

*** marguille has logged off.

*** TwenWen has stopped logging.

*** TwenWen has logged off.

<sappjuice> So it's just you and me. Wanna email?

<Helen> Yeah.

*** Helen has logged off.

*** sappjuice has logged off.

Session Close: Mon? Time? Deeeeeeeechgkl#@ ^^^^

Just spec, she told herself over the next few days. Too many people had expected a more dramatic apocalypse; now they cried wolf at every shadow. Some of their theories sounded right, but most were cockamamie—like Guille's implication that friendship, family, love, could be the reason that some people just disappeared. That would mean the only people still alive across the proliferated realities were those whose ties to the world had been weak from the beginning.

Those who'd lived alone. Those who'd been socially isolated. Not the completely disconnected ones; people without 'net access would've gone stark raving within days after the prolif. But the loosely connected ones, who interacted with others only when they had to, or through a screen. Those who'd maintained just enough connection to keep them sane, then. Just enough connection to keep them alive, now.

Just spec, she thought again as the alarm clock buzzed. She hadn't slept in two rollovers. *Not me.*

New habit. She sat up and reached over to her laptop, which rested on a low table beside the futon, and tapped its touchpad to wake it up. It chimed as the screen lit; she had mail.

"Helen,

I know this is risky, stupid, cheesy, whatever. But I can't help myself. I've never met you and never will, but…some things you can feel no matter what. They used to say this was all just pheromones, but that's crap. I've never smelled you and I only have my imagination to tell me what you look like. But I have to say this because it's true.

I love you.

I wish oh shit I didn't believe it but it's true"

No sig. Not even a period at the end of the last sentence. He'd had enough time to send, but not to finish first.

Not me, her mind whispered, *and not him. Please, not him.*

And as the walls of her tiny apartment began to warp and the barren landscape beyond her window vanished, she had time to click on the bookmark for her blog's "update" form and type a single line.

"The way out, or the end? Sapp's gone to see. I'm going too."

She hit "post" as reality folded into silence.

THE MULTIPLE FUTURES OF CONTEMPORARY SF: 2000S—PRESENT

Ted Chiang (b. 1967)

Ted Chiang is an American author whose parents moved to the US from Taiwan after their families had left China during that country's revolution. A computer scientist by training, as an SF writer he has published exclusively shorter works, in the form of short stories and novellas, and is arguably one of the best writers in those forms working today. He has received multiple Hugo, Nebula, and Locus awards, including the Hugo, Locus, and British Science Fiction awards for the story presented here.

Note on the text: "Exhalation" was originally published in the anthology *Eclipse Two: New Science Fiction and Fantasy* (2008), edited by Jonathan Strahan, before being published in Chiang's own collection *Exhalation: Stories* (2019). The original publication is used as the source here.

"Exhalation" (2008)

It has long been said that air (which others call argon) is the source of life. This is not in fact the case, and I engrave these words to describe how I came to understand the true source of life and, as a corollary, the means by which life will one day end.

For most of history, the proposition that we drew life from air was so obvious that there was no need to assert it. Every day we consume two lungs heavy with air; every day we remove the empty ones from our chest and replace them with full ones. If a person is careless and lets his air level run too low, he feels the heaviness of his limbs and the growing need for replenishment. It is exceedingly rare that a person is unable to get at least one replacement lung before his installed pair runs empty; on those unfortunate occasions where this has happened—when a person is trapped and unable to move, with no one nearby to assist him—he dies within seconds of his air running out.

But in the normal course of life, our need for air is far from our thoughts, and indeed many would say that satisfying that need is the least important part of going to the filling stations. For the filling stations are the primary venue for social conversation, the places from which we draw emotional sustenance as well as physical. We all keep spare sets of full lungs in our homes, but when one is alone, the act of opening one's chest and replacing one's lungs can seem little better than a chore. In the company of others, however, it becomes a communal activity, a shared pleasure.

If one is exceedingly busy, or feeling unsociable, one might simply pick up a pair of full lungs, install them, and leave one's emptied lungs on the other side of the room. If one has a few minutes to spare, it's simple courtesy to connect the empty lungs to an air dispenser and refill them for the next person. But by far the most common practice is to linger and enjoy the company of others, to discuss the news of the day with friends or acquaintances and, in passing, offer newly filled lungs to one's interlocutor. While this perhaps does not constitute air sharing in the strictest sense, there is camaraderie derived from the awareness that all our air comes from the same source, for the dispensers are but the exposed terminals of pipes extending from the reservoir of air deep underground, the great lung of the world, the source of all our nourishment.

Many lungs are returned to the same filling station the next day, but just as many circulate to other stations when people visit neighboring districts; the lungs are all identical in appearance, smooth cylinders of aluminum, so one cannot tell whether a given lung has always stayed close to home or whether it has traveled long distances. And just as lungs are passed between persons and districts, so are news and gossip. In this way one can receive news from remote districts, even those at the very edge of the world, without needing to leave home, although I myself enjoy traveling. I have journeyed all the way to the edge of the world, and seen the solid chromium wall that extends from the ground up into the infinite sky.

It was at one of the filling stations that I first heard the rumors that prompted my investigation and led to my eventual enlightenment. It began innocently enough, with a remark from our district's public crier. At noon of the first day of every year, it is traditional for the crier to recite a passage of verse, an ode composed long ago for this annual celebration, which takes exactly one hour to deliver. The crier mentioned that on his most recent performance, the turret clock struck the hour before he had finished, something that had never happened before. Another person remarked that this was a coincidence, because he had just returned from a nearby district where the public crier had complained of the same incongruity.

No one gave the matter much thought beyond the simple acknowledgement that seemed warranted. It was only some days later, when there arrived word of a similar deviation between the crier and the clock of a third district, that the suggestion was made that these discrepancies might be evidence of a defect in the mechanism common to all the turret clocks, albeit a curious one to cause the clocks to run faster rather than slower. Horologists investigated the turret clocks in question, but on inspection they could discern no imperfection. In fact, when compared against the timepieces normally employed for such calibration purposes, the turret clocks were all found to have resumed keeping perfect time.

I myself found the question somewhat intriguing, but I was too focused on my own studies to devote much thought to other matters. I was and am a student of anatomy, and to provide context for my subsequent actions, I now offer a brief account of my relationship with the field.

Death is uncommon, fortunately, because we are durable and fatal mishaps are rare, but it makes difficult the study of anatomy, especially since many of the accidents serious enough to cause death leave the deceased's remains too damaged for study. If lungs are ruptured when full, the explosive force can tear a body asunder, ripping the titanium as easily as if it were tin. In the past, anatomists focused their attention on the limbs, which were the most likely to survive intact. During the very first anatomy lecture I attended a century ago, the lecturer showed us a severed arm, the casing removed to reveal the dense column of rods and pistons within. I can vividly recall the way, after he had connected its arterial hoses to a wall-mounted lung he kept in the laboratory, he was able to manipulate the actuating rods that protruded from the arm's ragged base, and in response the hand would open and close fitfully.

In the intervening years, our field has advanced to the point where anatomists are able to repair damaged limbs and, on occasion, attach a severed limb. At the same time we have become capable of studying the physiology of the living; I have given a version of that first lecture I saw, during which I opened the casing of my own arm and directed my students' attention to the rods that contracted and extended when I wiggled my fingers.

Despite these advances, the field of anatomy still had a great unsolved mystery at its core: the question of memory. While we knew a little about the structure of the brain, its physiology is notoriously hard to study because of the brain's extreme delicacy. It is typically the case in fatal accidents that, when the skull is breached, the brain erupts in a cloud of gold, leaving little besides shredded filament and leaf from which nothing useful can be discerned. For decades the prevailing theory of memory was that all of a person's experiences were engraved on sheets of gold foil; it was these sheets, torn apart by the force of the blast, that was the source of the tiny flakes found after accidents. Anatomists would collect the bits of gold leaf—so thin that light passes greenly through them—and spend years trying to reconstruct the original sheets, with the hope of eventually deciphering the symbols in which the deceased's recent experiences were inscribed.

I did not subscribe to this theory, known as the inscription hypothesis, for the simple reason that if all our experiences are in fact recorded, why is it that our memories are incomplete? Advocates of the inscription hypothesis offered an explanation for forgetfulness—suggesting that over time the foil sheets become misaligned from the stylus which reads the memories, until the oldest sheets shift out of contact with it altogether—but I never found it convincing. The appeal of the theory was easy for me to appreciate, though; I too had devoted many an hour to examining flakes of gold through a microscope, and can imagine how gratifying it would be to turn the fine adjustment knob and see legible symbols come into focus.

More than that, how wonderful would it be to decipher the very oldest of a deceased person's memories, ones that he himself had forgotten? None of us can remember much more than a hundred years in the past, and written records—accounts that we ourselves inscribed but have scant memory of doing so—extend only a few hundred years before that. How many years did we live before the beginning of written history? Where did we come from?

It is the promise of finding the answers within our own brains that makes the inscription hypothesis so seductive.

I was a proponent of the competing school of thought, which held that our memories were stored in some medium in which the process of erasure was no more difficult than recording: perhaps in the rotation of gears, or the positions of a series of switches. This theory implied that everything we had forgotten was indeed lost, and our brains contained no histories older than those found in our libraries. One advantage of this theory was that it better explained why, when lungs are installed in those who have died from lack of air, the revived have no memories and are all but mindless: somehow the shock of death had reset all the gears or switches. The inscriptionists claimed the shock had merely misaligned the foil sheets, but no one was willing to kill a living person, even an imbecile, in order to resolve the debate. I had envisioned an experiment which might allow me to determine the truth conclusively, but it was a risky one, and deserved careful consideration before it was undertaken. I remained undecided for the longest time, until I heard more news about the clock anomaly.

Word arrived from a more distant district that its public crier had likewise observed the turret clock striking the hour before he had finished his new year's recital. What made this notable was that his district's clock employed a different mechanism, one in which the hours were marked by the flow of mercury into a bowl. Here the discrepancy could not be explained by a common mechanical fault. Most people suspected fraud, a practical joke perpetrated by mischief makers. I had a different suspicion, a darker one that I dared not voice, but it decided my course of action; I would proceed with my experiment.

The first tool I constructed was the simplest: in my laboratory I fixed four prisms on mounting brackets and carefully aligned them so that their apexes formed the corners of a rectangle. When arranged thus, a beam of light directed at one of the lower prisms was reflected up, then backward, then down, and then forward again in a quadrilateral loop. Accordingly, when I sat with my eyes at the level of the first prism, I obtained a clear view of the back of my own head. This solipsistic periscope formed the basis of all that was to come.

A similarly rectangular arrangement of actuating rods allowed a displacement of action to accompany the displacement of vision afforded by the prisms. The bank of actuating rods was much larger than the periscope, but still relatively straightforward in design; by contrast, what was attached to the end of these respective mechanisms was far more intricate. To the periscope I added a binocular microscope mounted on an armature capable of swiveling side to side or up and down. To the actuating rods I added an array of precision manipulators, although that description hardly does justice to those pinnacles of the mechanician's art. Combining the ingenuity of anatomists and the inspiration provided by the bodily structures they studied, the manipulators enabled their operator to accomplish any task he might normally perform with his own hands, but on a much smaller scale.

Assembling all of this equipment took months, but I could not afford to be anything less than meticulous. Once the preparations were complete, I was able to place each of my hands on a nest of knobs and levers and control a pair of manipulators situated behind my head, and use the periscope to see what they worked on. I would then be able to dissect my own brain.

The very idea must sound like pure madness, I know, and had I told any of my colleagues, they would surely have tried to stop me. But I could not ask anyone else to risk themselves for the sake of anatomical inquiry, and because I wished to conduct the dissection myself, I would not be satisfied by merely being the passive subject of such an operation. Auto-dissection was the only option.

I brought in a dozen full lungs and connected them with a manifold. I mounted this assembly beneath the worktable that I would sit at, and positioned a dispenser to connect directly to the bronchial inlets within my chest. This would supply me with six days' worth of air. To provide for the possibility that I might not have completed my experiment within that period, I had scheduled a visit from a colleague at the end of that time. My presumption, however, was that the only way I would not have finished the operation in that period would be if I had caused my own death.

I began by removing the deeply curved plate that formed the back and top of my head; then the two, more shallowly curved plates that formed the sides. Only my faceplate remained, but it was locked into a restraining bracket, and I could not see its inner surface from the vantage point of my periscope; what I saw exposed was my own brain. It consisted of a dozen or more subassemblies, whose exteriors were covered by intricately molded shells; by positioning the periscope near the fissures that separated them, I gained a tantalizing glimpse at the fabulous mechanisms within their interiors. Even with what little I could see, I could tell it was the most beautifully complex engine I had ever beheld, so far beyond any device man had constructed that it was incontrovertibly of divine origin. The sight was both exhilarating and dizzying, and I savored it on a strictly aesthetic basis for several minutes before proceeding with my explorations.

It was generally hypothesized that the brain was divided into an engine located in the center of the head which performed the actual cognition, surrounded by an array of components in which memories were stored. What I observed was consistent with this theory, since the peripheral subassemblies seemed to resemble one another, while the subassembly in the center appeared to be different, more heterogenous and with more moving parts. However the components were packed too closely for me to see much of their operation; if I intended to learn anything more, I would require a more intimate vantage point.

Each subassembly had a local reservoir of air, fed by a hose extending from the regulator at the base of my brain. I focused my periscope on the rearmost subassembly and, using the remote manipulators, I quickly disconnected the outlet hose and installed a longer one in its place. I had practiced this maneuver countless times so that I could perform it in a matter of moments; even so, I was not certain I could complete the connection before the subassembly had depleted its local reservoir. Only after I was satisfied that the component's operation had not been interrupted did I continue; I rearranged the longer hose to gain a better view of what lay in the fissure behind it: other hoses that connected it to its neighboring components. Using the most slender pair of manipulators to reach into the narrow crevice, I replaced the hoses one by one with longer substitutes. Eventually, I had worked my way around the entire subassembly and replaced every connection it had to the rest of my brain. I was now able to unmount this subassembly from the frame that supported it, and pull the entire section outside of what was once the back of my head.

I knew it was possible I had impaired my capacity to think and was unable to recognize it, but performing some basic arithmetic tests suggested that I was uninjured. With one subassembly hanging from a scaffold above, I now had a better view of the cognition engine at the center of my brain, but there was not enough room to bring the microscope attachment itself in for a close inspection. In order for me to really examine the workings of my brain, I would have to displace at least half a dozen subassemblies.

Laboriously, painstakingly, I repeated the procedure of substituting hoses for other subassemblies, repositioning another one farther back, two more higher up, and two others out to the sides, suspending all six from the scaffold above my head. When I was done, my brain looked like an explosion frozen an infinitesimal fraction of a second after the detonation, and again I felt dizzy when I thought about it. But at last the cognition engine itself was exposed, supported on a pillar of hoses and actuating rods leading down into my torso. I now also had room to rotate my microscope around a full three hundred and sixty degrees, and pass my gaze across the inner faces of the subassemblies I had moved. What I saw was a microcosm of auric machinery,[1] a landscape of tiny spinning rotors and miniature reciprocating cylinders.

As I contemplated this vista, I wondered, where was my body? The conduits which displaced my vision and action around the room were in principle no different from those which connected my original eyes and hands to my brain. For the duration of this experiment, were these manipulators not essentially my hands? Were the magnifying lenses at the end of my periscope not essentially my eyes? I was an everted person, with my tiny, fragmented body situated at the center of my own distended brain. It was in this unlikely configuration that I began to explore myself.

I turned my microscope to one of the memory subassemblies, and began examining its design. I had no expectation that I would be able to decipher my memories, only that I might divine the means by which they were recorded. As I had predicted, there were no reams of foil pages visible, but to my surprise

1 Gold mechanisms.

neither did I see banks of gearwheels or switches. Instead, the subassembly seemed to consist almost entirely of a bank of air tubules. Through the interstices between the tubules I was able to glimpse ripples passing through the bank's interior.

With careful inspection and increasing magnification, I discerned that the tubules ramified[1] into tiny air capillaries, which were interwoven with a dense latticework of wires on which gold leaves were hinged. Under the influence of air escaping from the capillaries, the leaves were held in a variety of positions. These were not switches in the conventional sense, for they did not retain their position without a current of air to support them, but I hypothesized that these were the switches I had sought, the medium in which my memories were recorded. The ripples I saw must have been acts of recall, as an arrangement of leaves was read and sent back to the cognition engine.

Armed with this new understanding, I then turned my microscope to the cognition engine. Here too I observed a latticework of wires, but they did not bear leaves suspended in position; instead the leaves flipped back and forth almost too rapidly to see. Indeed, almost the entire engine appeared to be in motion, consisting more of lattice than of air capillaries, and I wondered how air could reach all the gold leaves in a coherent manner. For many hours I scrutinized the leaves, until I realized that they themselves were playing the role of capillaries; the leaves formed temporary conduits and valves that existed just long enough to redirect air at other leaves in turn, and then disappeared as a result. This was an engine undergoing continuous transformation, indeed modifying itself as part of its operation. The lattice was not so much a machine as it was a page on which the machine was written, and on which the machine itself ceaselessly wrote.

My consciousness could be said to be encoded in the position of these tiny leaves, but it would be more accurate to say that it was encoded in the ever-shifting pattern of air driving these leaves. Watching the oscillations of these flakes of gold, I saw that air does not, as we had always assumed, simply provide power to the engine that realizes our thoughts. Air is in fact the very medium of our thoughts. All that we are is a pattern of air flow. My memories were inscribed, not as grooves on foil or even the position of switches, but as persistent currents of argon.

In the moments after I grasped the nature of this lattice mechanism, a cascade of insights penetrated my consciousness in rapid succession. The first and most trivial was understanding why gold, the most malleable and ductile of metals, was the only material out of which our brains could be made. Only the thinnest of foil leaves could move rapidly enough for such a mechanism, and only the most delicate of filaments could act as hinges for them. By comparison, the copper burr raised by my stylus as I engrave these words and brushed from the sheet when I finish each page is as coarse and heavy as scrap.

1 Ramify means "to cause to spread out as branches or ramifications" (*OED*).

This truly was a medium where erasing and recording could be performed rapidly, far more so than any arrangement of switches or gears.

What next became clear was why installing full lungs into a person who has died from lack of air does not bring him back to life. These leaves within the lattice remain balanced between continuous cushions of air. This arrangement lets them flit back and forth swiftly, but it also means that if the flow of air ever ceases, everything is lost; the leaves all collapse into identical pendent states, erasing the patterns and the consciousness they represent. Restoring the air supply cannot recreate what has evanesced. This was the price of speed; a more stable medium for storing patterns would mean that our consciousnesses would operate far more slowly.

It was then that I perceived the solution to the clock anomaly. I saw that the speed of these leaves' movements depended on their being supported by air; with sufficient air flow, the leaves could move nearly frictionlessly. If they were moving more slowly, it was because they were being subjected to more friction, which could occur only if the cushions of air that supported them were thinner, and the air flowing through the lattice was moving with less force.

It is not that the turret clocks are running faster. What is happening is that our brains are running slower. The turret clocks are driven by pendulums, whose tempo never varies, or by the flow of mercury through a pipe, which does not change. But our brains rely on the passage of air, and when that air flows more slowly, our thoughts slow down, making the clocks seem to us to run faster.

I had feared that our brains might be growing slower, and it was this prospect that had spurred me to pursue my auto-dissection. But I had assumed that our cognition engines—while powered by air—were ultimately mechanical in nature, and some aspect of the mechanism was gradually becoming deformed through fatigue, and thus responsible for the slowing. That would have been dire, but there was at least the hope that we might be able to repair the mechanism, and restore our brains to their original speed of operation.

But if our thoughts were purely patterns of air rather than the movement of toothed gears, the problem was much more serious, for what could cause the air flowing through every person's brain to move less rapidly? It could not be a decrease in the pressure from our filling stations' dispensers; the air pressure in our lungs is so high that it must be stepped down by a series of regulators before reaching our brains. The diminution in force, I saw, must arise from the opposite direction: The pressure of our surrounding atmosphere was increasing.

How could this be? As soon as the question formed, the only possible answer became apparent: Our sky must not be infinite in height. Somewhere above the limits of our vision, the chromium walls surrounding our world must curve inward to form a dome; our universe is a sealed chamber rather than an open well. And air is gradually accumulating within that chamber, until it equals the pressure in the reservoir below.

This is why, at the beginning of this engraving, I said that air is not the source of life. Air can neither be created nor destroyed; the total amount of air in the universe remains constant, and if air were all that we needed to live, we would never die. But in truth the source of life is *a difference in air pressure*, the flow of air from spaces where it is thick to those where it is thin. The activity of our brains, the motion of our bodies, the action of every machine we have ever built is driven by the movement of air, the force exerted as differing pressures seek to balance each other out. When the pressure everywhere in the universe is the same, all air will be motionless, and useless; one day we will be surrounded by motionless air and unable to derive any benefit from it.

We are not really consuming air at all. The amount of air that I draw from each day's new pair of lungs is exactly as much as seeps out through the joints of my limbs and the seams of my casing, exactly as much as I am adding to the atmosphere around me; all I am doing is converting air at high pressure to air at low. With every movement of my body, I contribute to the equalization of pressure in our universe. With every thought that I have, I hasten the arrival of that fatal equilibrium.

Had I come to this realization under any other circumstance, I would have leapt up from my chair and ran into the streets, but in my current situation—body locked in a restraining bracket, brain suspended across my laboratory—doing so was impossible. I could see the leaves of my brain flitting faster from the tumult of my thoughts, which in turn increased my agitation at being so restrained and immobile. Panic at that moment might have led to my death, a nightmarish paroxysm of simultaneously being trapped and spiraling out of control, struggling against my restraints until my air ran out. It was by chance as much as by intention that my hands adjusted the controls to avert my periscopic gaze from the latticework, so all I could see was the plain surface of my worktable. Thus freed from having to see and magnify my own apprehensions, I was able to calm down. When I had regained sufficient composure, I began the lengthy process of reassembling myself. Eventually I restored my brain to its original compact configuration, reattached the plates of my head, and released myself from the restraining bracket.

At first the other anatomists did not believe me when I told them what I had discovered, but in the months that followed my initial auto-dissection, more and more of them became convinced. More examinations of people's brains were performed, more measurements of atmospheric pressure were taken, and the results were all found to confirm my claims. The background air pressure of our universe was indeed increasing, and slowing our thoughts as a result.

There was widespread panic in the days after the truth first became widely known, as people contemplated for the first time the idea that death was inevitable. Many called for the strict curtailment of activities in order to minimize the thickening of our atmosphere; accusations of wasted air escalated into furious brawls and, in some districts, deaths. It was the shame of having caused these deaths, together with the reminder that it would be many centuries yet before our atmosphere's pressure became equal to that of the reservoir underground, that caused the panic to subside. We are not sure precisely how many centuries it will take; additional measurements and calculations are being performed and debated. In the meantime, there is much discussion over how we should spend the time that remains to us.

One sect has dedicated itself to the goal of reversing the equalization of pressure, and found many adherents. The mechanicians among them constructed an engine that takes air from our atmosphere and forces it into a smaller volume, a process they called "compression." Their engine restores air to the pressure it originally had in the reservoir, and these Reversalists excitedly announced that it would form the basis of a new kind of filling station, one that would—with each lung it refilled—revitalize not only individuals but the universe itself. Alas, closer examination of the engine revealed its fatal flaw. The engine itself is powered by air from the reservoir, and for every lungful of air that it produces, the engine consumes not just a lungful, but slightly more. It does not reverse the process of equalization, but like everything else in the world, exacerbates it.

Although some of their adherents left in disillusionment after this setback, the Reversalists as a group were undeterred, and began drawing up alternate designs in which the compressor was powered instead by the uncoiling of springs or the descent of weights. These mechanisms fared no better. Every spring that is wound tight represents air released by the person who did the winding; every weight that rests higher than ground level represents air released by the person who did the lifting. There is no source of power in the universe that does not ultimately derive from a difference in air pressure, and there can be no engine whose operation will not, on balance, reduce that difference.

The Reversalists continue their labors, confident that they will one day construct an engine that generates more compression than it uses, a perpetual power source that will restore to the universe its lost vigor. I do not share their optimism; I believe that the process of equalization is inexorable. Eventually, all the air in our universe will be evenly distributed, no denser or more rarefied in one spot than in any other, unable to drive a piston, turn a rotor, or flip a leaf of gold foil. It will be the end of pressure, the end of motive power, the end of thought. The universe will have reached perfect equilibrium.

Some find irony in the fact that a study of our brains revealed to us not the secrets of the past, but what ultimately awaits us in the future. However, I maintain that we have indeed learned something important about the past. The universe began as an enormous breath being held. Who knows why, but whatever the reason, I am glad that it did, because I owe my existence to that fact. All my desires and ruminations are no more and no less than eddy currents generated by the gradual exhalation of our universe. And until this great exhalation is finished, my thoughts live on.

So that our thoughts may continue as long as possible, anatomists and mechanicians are designing replacements for our cerebral regulators, capable of gradually increasing the air pressure within our brains and keeping it just higher than the surrounding atmospheric pressure. Once these are installed, our thoughts will continue at roughly the same speed even as the air thickens around us. But this does not mean that life will continue unchanged. Eventually the pressure differential will fall to such a level that our limbs will weaken and our movements will grow sluggish. We may then try to slow our thoughts so that our physical torpor is less conspicuous to us, but that will also cause external processes to appear to accelerate. The ticking of clocks will rise to a chatter as their pendulums wave frantically; falling objects will slam to the ground as if propelled by springs; undulations will race down cables like the crack of a whip.

At some point our limbs will cease moving altogether. I cannot be certain of the precise sequence of events near the end, but I imagine a scenario in which our thoughts will continue to operate, so that we remain conscious but frozen, immobile as statues. Perhaps we'll be able to speak for a while longer, because our voice boxes operate on a smaller pressure differential than our limbs, but without the ability to visit a filling station, every utterance will reduce the amount of air left for thought, and bring us closer to the moment that our thoughts cease altogether. Will it be preferable to remain mute to prolong our ability to think, or to talk until the very end? I don't know.

Perhaps a few of us, in the days before we cease moving, will be able to connect our cerebral regulators directly to the dispensers in the filling stations, in effect replacing our lungs with the mighty lung of the world. If so, those few will be able to remain conscious right up to the final moments before all pressure is equalized. The last bit of air pressure left in our universe will be expended driving a person's conscious thought.

And then, our universe will be in a state of absolute equilibrium. All life and thought will cease, and with them, time itself.

But I maintain a slender hope.

Even though our universe is enclosed, perhaps it is not the only air chamber in the infinite expanse of solid chromium. I speculate that there could be another pocket of air elsewhere, another universe besides our own that is even larger in volume. It is possible that this hypothetical universe has the same or higher air pressure as ours, but suppose that it had a much lower air pressure than ours, perhaps even a true vacuum?

The chromium that separates us from this supposed universe is too thick and too hard for us to drill through, so there is no way we could reach it ourselves, no way to bleed off the excess atmosphere from our universe and regain motive power that way. But I fantasize that this neighboring universe has its own inhabitants, ones with capabilities beyond our own. What if they were able to create a conduit between the two universes, and install valves to release air from ours? They might use our universe as a reservoir, running dispensers with which they could fill their own lungs, and use our air as a way to drive their own civilization.

It cheers me to imagine that the air that once powered me could power others, to believe that the breath that enables me to engrave these words could one day flow through someone else's body. I do not delude myself into thinking that this would be a way for me to live again, because I am not that air, I am the pattern that it assumed, temporarily. The pattern that is me, the patterns that are the entire world in which I live, would be gone.

But I have an even fainter hope: that those inhabitants not only use our universe as a reservoir, but that once they have emptied it of its air, they might one day be able to open a passage and actually enter our universe as explorers. They might wander our streets, see our frozen bodies, look through our possessions, and wonder about the lives we led.

Which is why I have written this account. You, I hope, are one of those explorers. You, I hope, found these sheets of copper and deciphered the words engraved on their surfaces. And whether or not your brain is impelled by the air that once impelled mine, through the act of reading my words, the patterns that form your thoughts become an imitation of the patterns that once formed mine. And in that way I live again, through you.

Your fellow explorers will have found and read the other books that we left behind, and through the collaborative action of your imaginations, my entire civilization lives again. As you walk through our silent districts, imagine them as they were; with the turret clocks striking the hours, the filling stations crowded with gossiping neighbors, criers reciting verse in the public squares and anatomists giving lectures in the classrooms. Visualize all of these the next time you look at the frozen world around you, and it will become, in your minds, animated and vital again.

I wish you well, explorer, but I wonder: Does the same fate that befell me await you? I can only imagine that it must, that the tendency toward equilibrium is not a trait peculiar to our universe but inherent in all universes. Perhaps that is just a limitation of my thinking, and your people have discovered a source of pressure that is truly eternal. But my speculations are fanciful enough already. I will assume that one day your thoughts too will cease, although I cannot fathom how far in the future that might be. Your lives will end just as ours did, just as everyone's must. No matter how long it takes, eventually equilibrium will be reached.

I hope you are not saddened by that awareness. I hope that your expedition was more than a search for other universes to use as reservoirs. I hope that you were motivated by a desire for knowledge, a yearning to see what can arise from a universe's exhalation. Because even if a universe's lifespan is calculable, the variety of life that is generated within it is not. The buildings we have erected, the art and music and verse we have composed, the very lives we've led: none of them could have been predicted, because none of them were inevitable. Our universe might have slid into equilibrium emitting nothing more than a quiet hiss. The fact that it spawned such plenitude is a miracle, one that is matched only by your universe giving rise to you.

Though I am long dead as you read this, explorer, I offer to you a valediction. Contemplate the marvel that is existence, and rejoice that you are able to do so. I feel I have the right to tell you this because, as I am inscribing these words, I am doing the same.

Jo Walton (b. 1964)

Born and raised in Wales, Jo Walton moved to Canada in 2002, where she currently lives. Her first publications were fantasy novels, followed by several SF and alternate history works. Her fantasy novel *Among Others* (2011), an epistolary work centred on diary entries that also includes semi-autobiographical elements, won the Hugo, Nebula, and British Fantasy Awards for best novel. She is also widely recognized for her presence in SF fandom.

Note on the text: This story was originally published online at *Tor.com* (now *Reactor*, reactormag.com) in 2009, and was republished in print several times, including in Walton's collection, *Starlings* (2017). The current version follows the paragraph formatting of the *Starlings* publication.

"Escape to Other Worlds with Science Fiction" (2009)

In the Papers (1)

NATIONAL GUARD MOVES AGAINST STRIKERS
In the seventh week of the mining strike in West Virginia, armed skirmishes and running "guerrilla battles" in the hills have led to the Governor calling in

GET AN ADVANCED DEGREE BY CORRESPONDENCE
You can reap the benefits with no need to leave the safety of your house or go among unruly college students! Only from

EX-PRESIDENT LINDBERGH REPROACHES MINERS[1]

ASTOUNDING SCIENCE FICTION
April issue on newsstands now! All new stories by Poul Anderson, Anson MacDonald and H. Beam Piper! Only 35 cents.[2]

---

1 Charles Lindbergh (1902–74), an American pilot who completed the first solo non-stop transatlantic flight, between New York and Paris, in 1927. Politically, in the years leading to World War II, he was an active member and spokesperson for the far-right, isolationist America First Committee, with which he shared antisemitic, white supremacist, and fascist views.

2 *Astounding Science-Fiction* (originally *Astounding Stories of Super-Science*, then *Astounding Stories*) is one of the best-known pulp SF magazines, and under the editorship, starting in 1937, of John W. Campbell (1910–71) is mostly associated with the so-called "Golden Age" of SF (see the introduction to this anthology). All authors mentioned are SF writers who published in *Astounding* under Campbell: Poul Anderson (1926–2001) and H. Beam Piper (1904–64) are both associated with alternate histories (like this piece). Anson MacDonald was a pseudonym used by famed SF writer Robert A. Heinlein (1907–88), one of the best-known SF authors of the period and after. He used the MacDonald pseudonym when he published *Beyond this Horizon* (1943), a novel dealing with eugenics, in *Astounding*.

SPRING FASHIONS 1960
Skirts are being worn long in London and Paris this season, but here in New York the working girls are still hitching them up. It's stylish to wear a little

HOW FAR FROM MIAMI CAN THE "FALLOUT" REACH?
Scientists say it could be a problem for years, but so much depends on the weather that

You hope to work
You hope to eat
The work goes to
The man that's neat!
BurmaShave[1]

Getting By (1)

Linda Evans is a waitress in Bundt's Bakery. She used to work as a typist, but when she was let go she was glad to take this job, even though it keeps her on her feet all day and sometimes she feels her face will crack from smiling at the customers. She was never a secretary, only in the typing pool. Her sister Joan is a secretary, but she can take shorthand and type ninety words a minute. Joan graduated from high school. She taught Linda to type. But Linda was never as clever as Joan, not even when they were little girls in the time she can just remember, when their father had a job at the plant and they lived in a neat little house at the end of the bus line. Their father hasn't worked for a long time now. He drinks up any money he can bully out of the girls. Linda stands up to him better than Joan does.

"They'd have forgiven the New Deal[2] if only it had worked," a man says to another, as Linda puts down his coffee and sandwich down in front of him.

"Worked?" asks his companion scornfully. "It was working. It would have worked and got us out of this if only people had kept faith in it."

They are threadbare old men, in mended coats. They ordered grilled cheese sandwiches, the cheapest item on the menu. One of them smiles at Linda, and she smiles back, automatically, then moves on and forgets them. She's on her feet all day. Joan teases her about flirting with the customers and falling in love, but it never seems to happen. She used to tease Joan about falling in love with her boss, until she did. It would all have been dandy except that he was a married man. Now Joan spends anguished hours with him and anguished

1 Burma-Shave was a popular brand of shaving cream noted for using sequential billboard signs that created a rhyming five- or six-line verse.

2 The New Deal is the collective name for a series of economic and social programs brought into the US in the 1930s, under President Franklin Delano Roosevelt (FDR), to stabilize the economy and spur recovery following the Great Depression, which had started with the stock market crash of 1929.

days without him. He makes her useless presents of French perfume and lace underwear. When Linda wants to sell them, Joan just cries. Both of them live in fear that she'll get pregnant, and then where will they be? Linda wipes the tables and tries not to listen to the men with their endless ifs. She has enough ifs of her own: if mother hadn't died, if she'd kept her job in the pool, if John hadn't died in the war with England, and Pete in the war with Japan.

"Miss?" one of them asks. She swings around, thinking they want more coffee. One refill only is the rule. "Can you settle a question?" he asks. "Did Roosevelt want to get us to join in the European War in 1940?"[1]

"How should I know? It has nothing to do with me. I was five years old in 1940." They should get over it and leave history to bury its own dead, she thinks, and goes back to wiping the tables.

In the Papers (2)

WITH MIRACLE-GROW YOU CAN REGAIN YOUR LOST FOLLICLES!
In today's world it can be hard to find work even with qualifications. We at Cyrus Markham's Agency have extensive experience at matching candidates to positions which makes us the unrivaled

NEW TORPEDOES THAT WORK EVEN BETTER
Radar, sonar and even television to

AT LAST YOU CAN AFFORD THE HOUSE OF YOUR DREAMS

LET SCIENCE FICTION TAKE YOU TO NEW WORLDS
New books by Isaac Asimov and Robert A. Heinlein[2] for only

ANOTHER BANK FOUNDERS IN PENNSYLVANIA

WE HAVE NOT USED THE WORD "SECEDE," SAYS TEXAS GOVERNOR
Why do Canadians act so high and mighty? It's because they know

In the Line (1)

When Tommy came out of the navy, he thought he'd walk into a job just like that. He had his veteran's discharge, which entitled him to medical treatment

1 In reality, the US entered the war under FDR following the Japanese attack on the US naval base at Pearl Harbor, Hawaii.

2 For information on Isaac Asimov, see the introduction to his story "Liar!" in this volume. On Heinlein, see the reference in the introduction as well as the earlier note in this story.

for his whole life, and he was a hero. He'd been on the carrier *Constitution*, which had won the Battle of the Atlantic practically singlehanded and had sent plenty of those Royal Navy bastards to the bottom of the sea where they belonged. He had experience in maintenance as well as gunnery. Besides, he was a proud hard-working American. He never thought he'd be lining up at a soup kitchen.

In the Papers (3)

TIME FOR A NEW TUNE
Why are the bands still playing Cole Porter?[1]

SECRETARY OF STATE LINEBARGER SAYS THE BRITS WANT PEACE

ATOMIC SECRETS

DO THE JAPANESE HAVE THE BOMB?
Sources close to the Emperor say yes, but the Nazis deny that they have given out any plans. Our top scientists are still working to

NYLONS NYLONS NYLONS

DIANETICS: A NEW SCIENCE OF THE MIND[2]

Getting By (2)

Linda always works overtime when she's asked. She appreciates the money, and she's always afraid she'll be let go if she isn't obliging. There are plenty of girls who'd like her job. They come to ask every day if there's any work. She isn't afraid the Bundts will give her job away for no reason. She's worked here for four years now, since just after the Japanese War. "You're like family," Mrs. Bundt always says. They let Olive go, the other waitress, but that was because there wasn't enough work for two. Linda works overtime and closes up the cafe when they want her to. "You're a good girl," Mrs. Bundt says. But the Bundts have a daughter, Cindy. Cindy's a pretty twelve-year old, not even in high school. She comes into the cafe and drinks a milkshake sometimes with her girlfriends, all of them giggling. Linda hates her. She doesn't know what they have to giggle about. Linda is afraid that when Cindy is old enough she'll

1 Cole Porter (1891–1964), American musician and composer, noted for his musicals.

2 Dianetics is both a text and the set of ideas it espouses, often described as a pseudoscience. It was developed by pulp SF writer L. Ron Hubbard (1911–86), and first published and supported by Campbell in *Astounding*. It would become the basis for Hubbard's later creation of Scientology.

be given Linda's job. Linda might be like family, but Cindy really is family. The bakery does all right, people have to eat, but business isn't what it was. Linda knows.

She's late going home. Joan's dressing up to go out with her married boss. She washes in the sink in the room they share. The shower is down the corridor, shared with the whole floor. It gets cleaned only on Fridays, or when Joan or Linda does it. Men are such pigs, Linda thinks, lying on her bed, her weight off her feet at last. Joan is three years older than Linda but she looks younger. It's the make-up, Linda thinks, or maybe it's having somebody to love. If only she could have fallen in love with a boss who'd have married her and taken her off to a nice little suburb. But perhaps it's just as well. Linda couldn't afford the room alone, and she'd have had to find a stranger to share with. At least Joan was her sister and they were used to each other.

"I saw Dad today," Joan says, squinting in the mirror and drawing on her mouth carefully.

"Tell me you didn't give him money?"

"Just two dollars," Joan admits. Linda groans. Joan is a soft touch. She makes more than Linda, but she never has any left at the end of the week. She spends more, or gives it away. There's no use complaining, as Linda knows.

"Where's he taking you?" she asks wearily.

"To a rally," Joan says.

"Cheap entertainment." Rallies and torchlit parades and lynchings, beating up the blacks as scapegoats for everything. It didn't help at all; it just made people feel better about things to have someone to blame. "It's not how we were brought up," Linda says. Their mother's father had been a minister and had believed in the brotherhood of man. Linda loved going to her grandparents' house when she was a child. Her grandmother would bake cookies and the whole house would smell of them. There was a swing on the old apple tree in the garden. Her father had been a union man, once, when unions had still been respectable.

"What do I care about all that?" Joan says, viciously. "It's where he's taking me, and that's all. He'll buy me dinner and we'll sing some patriotic songs. I'm not going to lynch anybody." She dabs on her French perfume, fiercely.

Linda lies back. She isn't hungry. She's never hungry. She always eats at the bakery—the Bundts don't mind—any order that was wrong, or any bread that would have been left over. Sometimes they even gave her cakes or bread to bring home. She rubs her feet. She's very lucky really. But as Joan goes out the door she feels like crying. Even if she did meet somebody, how could they ever afford to marry? How could they hope for a house of their own?

In the Papers (4)

SEA MONKEYS[1] WILL ASTOUND YOUR FRIENDS!

PRESIDENT SAYS WE MUST ALL PULL TOGETHER
In Seattle today in a meeting with

TAKE A LUXURY AIRSHIP TO THE HOLY CITY

CAN THE ECONOMY EVER RECOVER?
Since the Great Depression the country has been jogging through a series of ups and downs and the economy has been lurching from one crisis to another. Administrations have tried remedies from Roosevelt's New Deal to Lindbergh's Belt Tightening but nothing has turned things around for long. Economists say that this was only to be expected and that this general trend of downturn was a natural and inevitable

NEW HOLLYWOOD BLOCKBUSTER "REICHSMARSHALL"
STARRING MARLON BRANDO[2]

In the Line (2)

When Sue was seventeen she'd had enough of school. She had a boyfriend who promised to find her a job as a dancer. She went off with him to Cleveland. She danced for a while in a topless club, and then in a strip joint. The money was never quite enough, not even after she started turning tricks. She's only thirty-four, but she knows she looks raddled. She's sick. Nobody wants her any more. She's waiting in the line because there's nowhere else to go. They feed you and take you off in trucks to make a new start, that's what she's heard. She can see the truck. She wonders where they go.

In the Papers (5)

ARE NEW HOME PERMANENTS[3] AS GOOD AS THEY SAY?
Experts say yes!

NEW WAYS TO SAVE

---

1 A brand name for brine shrimp eggs that could be hatched in home aquariums. They were popular in the 1960s and 1970s, when they were heavily advertised in children's comic books.

2 Somewhat Americanized spelling of Reichsmarschall, a rank in the Nazi military. Marlon Brando (1924–2004), US actor and civil rights activist.

3 A style of chemical hair treatment designed to create curls or waves.

PRESIDENT SAYS: THERE IS NO WITCH-HUNT[1]
Despite what communists and union organizers may claim, the President said today

Getting By (3)

The Bundts like to play the radio in the cafe at breakfast time. They talk about buying a little television for the customers to watch, if times ever get better. Mr. Bundt says this when Linda cautiously asks for a raise. If they had a television they'd be busier, he thinks, though Linda doesn't think it would make a difference. She serves coffee and bacon and toast and listens to the news. She likes music and Joan likes Walter Winchell.[2] She should ask Joan how she reconciles that with going to rallies. Winchell famously hates Hitler.[3] Crazy. Linda can't imagine feeling that strongly about an old man on the other side of the world.

Later, when Cindy and her friends are giggling over milkshakes and Linda feels as if her feet are falling off, a man comes in and takes the corner table. He orders sandwiches and coffee, and later he orders a cake and more coffee. He's an odd little man. He seems to be paying attention to everything. He's dressed quite well. His hair is slicked back and his clothes are clean. She wonders if he's a detective, because he keeps looking out of the window, but if so he seems to pay just as much attention to the inside, and to Linda herself. She remembers what Joan said, and wants to laugh but can't. He's a strange man and she can't figure him out.

She doesn't have to stay late and close up, and the man follows her out when she leaves. There's something about him that makes her think of the law way before romance. "You're Linda," he says, outside. She's scared, because he could be anybody, but they are in the street under a street light, there are people passing, and the occasional car.

"Yes," she admits, her heart hammering. "What do you want?"

"You're not a Bundt?"

"No. They're my employers, that's all," she says, disassociating herself from them as fast as she can, though they have been good to her. Immediately she has visions of them being arrested. Where would she find another job?

"Do you know where the Bundts come from?"

"Germany," she says, confidently. Bundt's German Bakery, it says, right above their heads.

"When?"

"Before I was born. Why aren't you asking them these questions?"

---

1 In this context, the term "witch hunt" is commonly associated with the controversial anti-communist activities of US senator Joseph McCarthy (1908–57).

2 Walter Winchell (1897–1972), gossip columnist who was staunchly anti-Nazi, later a McCarthy supporter.

3 Adolf Hitler (1889–1945), dictator who led Nazi Germany and oversaw the Holocaust.

"It was 1933."

"Before I was born," Linda says, feeling more confident and taking a step away.

"Have you seen any evidence that they are Jews?"

She stops, confused. "Jews? They're German. Germans hate Jews."

"Many Jews left Germany in 1933 when Hitler came to power," the man says, though he can't be much older than Linda. "If the Bundts were Jews, and hiding their identity, then if you denounced them—"

He stops, but Linda has caught up with him now. If she denounced them she would be given their property. The business, the apartment above it, their savings. "But they're not, I've never—they serve bacon!" she blurts.

"You've never seen any evidence?" he asks, sadly. "A pity. It could be a nice business for you. You're not Jewish?"

"Welsh," she says. "My grandfather was a minister."

"I thought not, with that lovely blonde hair." It's more washed out than it should be, but her hair is the dishwater blonde it always has been, the same as Joan's, the same as their mother's.

"I might have some evidence," he says, slowly. "But any evidence I had would be from before they came here, from Germany. Some evidence that they were still Jews, if you'd seen anything, would be enough to settle it. The court would deport them back to Germany and award us their business. You could run it, I'm sure you could. You seem to be doing most of the work already."

"I just serve," she says, automatically. Then, "What sort of thing would I have noticed? If they were Jewish, I mean?"

Temptation settles over her like a film of grease and hope begins to burn in her heart for the first time in a long time.

In the Line (3)

If you're black you're invisible, even in the soup line. The others are shrinking away from me, I can't deny it. They wouldn't give us guns to fight even when the Japanese were shelling the beaches up and down the California coast. I left there then and came East, much good it did me. If I'd known how invisible I'd be here, I'd have stayed right there in Los Angeles. Nobody there ever chased after me and made me run, nobody there threatened to string me up, and I had a job that made a little money. I never thought I'd be standing in this line, because when I get to the head of it I know they'll separate me out. Nobody knows what happens to us then, they take us off somewhere and we don't come back, but I'm desperate, and what I say is, wherever it is they got to feed us, don't they? Well, don't they?

In the Papers (6)

ANOTHER FACTORY CLOSING

PEACE TALKS IN LONDON AS JAPAN AND THE REICH DIVIDE UP RUSSIA
Will there be a buffer state of "Scythia" to divide the two great powers?

BATTLE IN THE APPALACHIANS: NATIONAL GUARD REINFORCEMENTS SENT IN
President says it is necessary to keep the country together

OWNERS GUN DOWN STRIKERS IN ALABAMA
Sixty people were hospitalized in Birmingham today after

ESCAPE TO OTHER WORLDS WITH SCIENCE FICTION
New titles by Frederik Pohl and Alice Davey[1]

---

1 Frederik Pohl (1919–2013), multi-award-winning US SF writer and editor. Alice Davey: Walton is playing with multiple naming conventions here. Born Alice Bradley, becoming Alice Davey on her first marriage (and Alice Sheldon on her second), this author is perhaps best known in SF under her pseudonym James Tiptree Jr. For more details, see the introduction to her story in this volume, p. 360.

China Miéville (b. 1972)

China Miéville is an English SF and Fantasy writer known mostly for his "New Weird" works, which build on earlier Weird fiction even as they renounce the racism and other biases of the Weird as associated with H.P. Lovecraft, though arguably Miéville's work owes as much or more to English fantasy writer Mervyn Peake (1911–68). Also associated with such subgenres as urban fantasy and steampunk, Miéville's first novel was *King Rat* (1998), followed by his best known *Perdido Street Station* (2000), the first in his *New Crobozun* series (also known as the *Bas-Lag* series). Miéville is also well known for his socialist and left politics, running for Member of Parliament in the UK once, and for publishing books about the Russian Revolution and *The Communist Manifesto*, and *Between Equal Rights: A Marxist Theory of International Law* (2005), a version of his PhD dissertation at the London School of Economics.

Note on the text: Initially published by *The Guardian* newspaper as part of a selection of "Oil Stories" (2011), "Covehithe" was subsequently published in Miéville's collection *Three Moments of an Explosion* (2015), the latter of which this version follows.

"Covehithe" (2011)

THERE were a few nights in Dunwich, where the owner of the B&B[1] kept telling her guests they were lucky to have found a room. Walking Dunwich Beach, showing his daughter wintering geese through binoculars so heavy they made her laugh, the man was glad they were not in Southwold or Walberswick.[2] They were not so hemmed in by visitors. Each evening they had fish and chips or pub grub.[3] Each night after she had gone to bed he hacked into next door's WiFi to check his messages and monitor the forums.[4]

On Thursday night he woke her. It was not long after midnight.

"Come on lovey," he said. "Keep it down. Let's not get anyone else up."

"I hate you," she said into her pillow.

"I know," he said. "Come on. Don't bring your phone."

There was not much on the roads. Still, Dughan took them roundabout ways, through Blythborough, on the A145 towards Uggeshall, past stationary diggers where roads were being widened.

"Where are we going?" the girl asked, only once. She hunkered; she wouldn't ask him to turn up the heating.

1 Bed and Breakfast.

2 All of the towns mentioned in the story are in Suffolk, England.

3 I.e., food prepared in a pub.

4 Online message boards, an early form of social media.

Wrentham was on the western rim of the security zone. It went north along the A12, south on the B1127[1] to Southwold. Within it, in daylight, fields were still worked, for animal feed, and roads mostly open, but those were, legally, indulgences not rights; the area was, in the absence of an official escort, no-go after dark. Exceptional laws applied in that little triangle, the coast a six-mile hypotenuse, its midpoint Covehithe.

Dughan stopped by a pub garden south of Wrentham. He opened the door for his daughter with his finger to his lips.

"Dad," she said.

"Hush," he said. It was overcast and windy, shadows taking them and releasing them as Dughan found a way through undergrowth to the boundary ditch. They were both quiet as they crossed it. Holding their breath. Beyond, they walked eastward on the edges of the fields.

"Dad, seriously, you're crazy." He had a torch but did not turn it on. When the moon came out enough he stopped and took bearings.

"They've got guns," she said.

"That's why shhh."

"What'll they do if they catch us?"

"Feed us to wolves."

"Har har."

They went still at the sound of a helicopter. The beam passed by half a field ahead, so bright it looked solid.

The air smelt. They could hear echoes. Dughan avoided the hamlet where until recently locals had lived, which had been requisitioned, with only minor scandal. They could see lit windows. They came instead at Covehithe from the north.

He stopped her by the roofless ruin of the church, pointed, heard her gasp. She stared while moonlight got past the clouds to the holed and broken walls, onto a low newer church inside the nave of the old.[2] He smiled. When eventually she was done looking they continued through the graveyard. There was nothing at all frightening about the graves.

This close to the waves the land felt, as the girl said, misbehavicious. A good word to make her feel better. In the leafless trees of this region were cold, random and silent flares of light. Touch the soil, as Dughan did, and as his daughter did too at the sight of him, and it felt greasy, heavy, as if someone had poured cream onto loam.

"Which way are we going?"

"Careful lovey," he said. "The ground here …"

"How do you know it's tonight?"

For a while he didn't answer. "Oh," he said. "Bits and pieces." He looked over his shoulder the way they had come. "Ways and means."

---

1 A12 and B1127 are roads.

2 St. Andrew's Church is a well-known historical site in Covehithe: a medieval ruin surrounds a smaller, seventeenth-century church.

"What if they find out?" She pointed at the cottages. She rolled her eyes when he said nothing.

They continued on the road past a sign forbidding exactly this last short walk, on tarmac so old it was becoming landscape. Perspective was peculiar. The smell should have been sappy and muddy and of the sea.

"Look!" His daughter gasped. The road stopped abruptly, rag-edged, fell into nothing. He watched her inch forward. "It goes right off the cliff!"

"The sea's taking it all back," he said. "There used to be a lot more coast here. Careful." But she had lain responsibly on her stomach at a certain proximity and put only her fingertips and eyes over the tarmac rim to look down its sheer crumble at the beach.

"Is it still going?" she said. Her voice was faint, she was dipping her mouth below road-level. "Being eaten?" Dughan shrugged. Waited till she scootched back and turned to him, shrugged again.

He told her they would know within two or three hours if anything was going to happen. He did not say it was only hints and whispers he had to go on, trawlings from bulletin boards.[1] Two names he knew, erstwhile colleagues, both announcing they'd be near Ipswich next week and did any of the old crew want a drink? The latest codes were beyond him, but that query and the night's sudden burst of encrypted chatter had been reasons enough to move.

He checked his watch and sat with her at the decomposing road-end. He was cross-legged, she with her chin on her knees, hugging them. She kept looking into the sea. The noise of it lulled them as if it were designed to. There was no light but the moon and those occasional sourceless mineral glows. Somewhere some insane bird, not a nightingale, was singing.

All their layers could not keep them warm. They were shaking hard when, after less than an hour, Dughan saw movement on the beach. He motioned for his daughter to stay still and looked through his binoculars at lights jouncing on the shingle. Three sets of headlamps stopped, overlaying each other, illuminating the sea and a strip of the shore.

"It's them," he said. "They're setting up. They must've ..." The girl could tell his excitement was not wholly enthusiasm. "They've ... we're on."

He could make out nothing beyond the headlight gaze, and hear nothing but waves. He recced[2] once more but they were not observed. This cliff-top was out of bounds and they, intruders, were alone. His daughter kept watching the water. Dughan wondered if she would complain or ask how long or anything, but she did not. Twenty minutes later, it was she who pointed, who first saw something in the sea.

There were no helicopters now. Nothing so noisy. No downcast beams to light up what was coming, breaking water, way off the coast. It was only moonlit. A tower. A steeple of girders. Streaming, and rising.

---

1 I.e., the "forums" mentioned earlier.

2 Slang (primarily military) for performing reconnaissance or reconnoitring a location.

The girl stood. The metal was twisted. Off-true and angular like a skew-whiff[1] crane, resisting collapse. It did not come steadily but lurched, hauling up and landward in huge jerks. After each a swaying hesitation; then another move higher, and closer.

The lights on the beach went out. Flame ignited at the tower's tip. Sooty sepia guttering lit the shaft. The sea at its base spread flat and fell away from suddenly rising intricate blockness, black, angled and extrusioned. As if a quarried wedge of the seabed itself had come up to look.

The towerwork was on a platform. In the glow of the thing's own flame they saw edificial flanks, the concrete and rust of them, the iron of the pylon barnacled, shaggy with benthic growth now lank gelatinous bunting.

It was coming at the Covehithe cliff. Under its stains and excrescences were more regular markings, stencilled warnings. Paint remnants: an encircled H.

Another step—because these were clumsy steps with which it came—and all the main mass was out of the water and raining brine. It waded. Each concrete cylinder leg a building or a smokestack wide. The two on one side came forward together, then those on the other. Pipes dangled from its roof-high underside, clots of it fell back into the sea. It wore steel containers, ruins of housing like a bad neighborhood, old hoists, lift-shafts emptying of black water.

A few wave-widths from the beach, it hesitated. It licked the air with a house-sized flame.

"P-36," the man said. "Petrobras."[2]

One of the cars below turned its headlamps back on. The rig shied. Dughan hissed. But the lights quickly dipped and after a moment he said, "It's probably OK now."

The platform was at the level of their cliff-top. Now the girl understood its strange ungainliness. On each side, its supports merged at their base, into two horizontal struts, so it moved like a quadruped skiing. What must have been ten feet of water lapped at the struts like a puddle at a child's shoes. The rig facelessly faced north and slide-stamped along the shoreline.

"Quick," the man said. They took the cliff-edge path, a hedge to their right, the oil platform's tower lurching beside them above its leaves.

"Went down 2001," Dughan said. "Roncador field."[3]

"How many people died?"

"When it sank? No one."

"Have you … is this the first …?"

He took a moment to stop, to turn and meet her eye. They could hear the flame bursts now. Its straining metal. "I've never seen it before, lovey" he said.

The path descended.

She had been too small when her father left to imagine stories of his

---

1 I.e., askew.

2 Petrobras 36 was an Italian-built oil rig, which sunk off the coast of Brazil in 2001.

3 A large oil field in the waters off Brazil.

exploits, to be proud or afraid. All she remembered were his returnings, an exhausted, careful man who lifted her onto his lap and kissed her with wary love, brought her toys and foreign sweets. When later she had asked him what he had done on those trips, his answers were so vague guilt had hushed her. She did not ask about his injuries.

The rig was slowing. The smell was stronger and the ground, the air juddered, not only in time to its huge steps. Dughan stopped at the last path-end trees. He and his daughter hugged the trunks and watched the oil rig sway in their direction. He held her hand. The girl watched him, too, but he showed no signs of angst, no flashback, no fear.

On an autumn evening in the earlyish years of the twenty-first century, a fishing boat south-east of Halifax radioed an SOS, under attack—the transmission was unclear. Rescuers found two traumatized survivors in a wash of scattered debris. As they did, the cause of the catastrophe reached the coast. Authorities could not suppress civilian footage of what had come back.

It was the Rowan Gorilla I. That was the first. No Piper Alpha, no Deepwater Horizon; an undistinguished disaster.[1] A tripod jack-up rig lost to storms and hull-fracture in 1988, on its way to the North Sea. Scattered surely by its capsizing and by thirty years below but there, back. Cramped-looking for all its enormity, latticed legs braced half-way through its platform, jutting above it and below into the sea. In the videos the three skyward leg-halves switch and lean creaking towards each other, sway away again like cranes triple-knitting, as it walks the muck on spudcan feet. It staggered like a crippled Martian out of the water and onto Canada.

It shook the coast with its steps. It walked through buildings, swatted trucks then tanks out of its way with ripped cables and pipes that flailed in inefficient deadly motion, like ill-trained snakes, like too-heavy feeding tentacles. It reached with corroded chains, wrenched obstacles from the earth. It dripped seawater, chemicals of industrial ruin and long-hoarded oil.

Ten miles inland, a line of artillery blew the thing apart. Later they made that area a memorial park. Sections of the rig's deck they left unsalvaged, preserved amid flower beds.

By panics and fuckups, Dughan's unit had been trapped on the far side of the wounded platform, between the Rowan Gorilla I, they later realized, and the sea. A third of his comrades had been killed. Crushed, torn by wires, caught in its final explosion, bequeathing him years of dreams and memories of trodden men.

The world was still reeling, investigation barely begun, when the *Ocean*

---

1 Rowan Gorilla I was a US oil rig, launched in 1983, which sunk off the coast of Halifax, Nova Scotia, Canada, in 1988. Piper Alpha was a British rig in the North Sea, which sunk in 1988. Built in South Korea, Deepwater Horizon was owned by the US company Transocean and operated by the British BP corporation when it sunk in the Gulf of Mexico in 2010, creating the largest marine oil spill in history to the date of this writing.

Express,[1] capsized in 1976 with thirteen dead, which must have been quietly recomposing itself at the bottom of the Gulf of Mexico, stood upright in relatively shallow water and strode landward.

Fighter jets scrambled from Eglin inflicted severe damage, slowed it, and the USS *Carney*[2] torpedoed one of its supports. The rig buckled, tilted and seemed to wait kneeling like a bettered knight. The *Carney* had shelled it apart.

Dughan saw this from the *Carney*'s deck. He and several comrades had been flown in as advisors to the U.S. navy. He was combatant himself again soon enough, at the return of the *Key Biscayne*[3] off Australia, and the fire-mottled *Sea Quest*'s attempt to walk into Nigeria.

National governments subcontracted strategy to the UN Platform Event Repulsion Unit: scientists, engineers, theologians and exorcists, soldiers, veterans like Dughan of those first encounters. He learned the new motions, the vastly swaying skittishness and violence of the revenant rigs. His UNPERU colleagues strove to decode this hydrocarbon Ragnarok.[4] Twice, Dughan even boarded pitching, stinking decks to transmit to them close-up footage, from which they learned nothing. They tried to figure out what economies of sacrifice were being invoked, for what this was punishment. Ruined, lost, burnt, scuttled rigs were healing on the ocean floor and coming back. Platform, jack-up, semi-submersible: all the lost.

After the semi-sub *Sea Quest* retreated under heavy attack, descending back into the Gulf of Guinea, UNPERU turned its attention and resources to the *Ocean Ranger*, stalking the Atlantic seabed. So when, shortly after its brief first appearance, the *Sea Quest* reemerged, and continued its interrupted journey into the oil-fouled delta, they were not there to intercept. Word reached Dughan and his crew en route to Canada. They came back fast, turning their plane in mid-air.

They were escorted inland by ex-M.E.N.D.[5] guerrillas with peerless local savvy, hastily pardoned by the Nigerian government. They followed the oil rig's mashed-up trail, the rainbow-filmed liquid spoor, the tripod crater prints. In retrospect, certain qualities of the disturbed interior foreshadowed more dramatic instabilities that later petrospectral presences would bring.

Bursts from the derrick known to have been destroyed in the rig's last moments, now heat-twisted but regrown, flared above the forest. The soldiers reached the edge of the clearing the *Sea Quest* had stamped. They held fire and watched.

---

1 The details here are accurate for the sinking of this rig: the thirteen deaths occurred when an escape capsule sank.

2 The USS Carney is a US Navy destroyer, launched in 1994. The ship is named for Robert Carney (1895–1990), a US Navy admiral and NATO commander.

3 The Key Biscayne rig sank off Western Australia in 1983.

4 Ragnarök is an apocalyptic event in Norse mythology.

5 The Movement for the Emancipation of the Niger Delta is a militant group whose actions are directed against the Nigerian government and oil companies operating in the Niger Delta.

Bracing on struts still thick with coralline outgrowths, the *Sea Quest* settled into the mud. It started its drill. Pushed it into the ground and down.

For a long time it was still but for an occasional swaying tremble of some stuff low-hanging from it. Should we attack? officers kept asking. Dughan shook his head. He checked Unit Beta's images, the *Ocean Ranger* off the Labrador coast, the tip of its tower a dorsal fin. The stomach-dropping video was proof for which no one had known they were waiting: that below the waves the rigs also walked.

High overhead the *Sea Quest*'s flame was all but out: a dirty smoke plume took its place as cockscomb. "It's drinking," one of the soldiers had said to the shake of its pumps. After four hours Dughan sent out a team, joined them when the rig did not respond. Another four and they went closer still. Eleven hours after the drilling had started, the tower breathed fire again and shook and abruptly pulled its drill from the mud.

The birds that had settled to peck at its deepwater carrion were gone in one cloud. The soldiers made it back to the treeline. The *Sea Quest* rose on shaft-legs like some impossible dreaming pachyderm. It retraced its stamping passage, trees in its shadow.

The UNPERU team followed. They tried to keep locals away. They were the oil rig's escorts, back to the sea. The platform walked slowly into the water, paused a while in the chop, descended.

A clutch of dead trees jutted from the scrub like bleached markers of where Covehithe ended. A ribbon of crabgrass separated the sea and shore from Benacre Broad. A cold marsh, a roosting place for birds. The Petrobras approached.

Dughan hesitated and his daughter saw him do so. He wanted to go closer, but there was not enough cover.

The rig. It closed on her and she stopped breathing. It came near enough that she felt the envelope of cold air it brought, smelled abyssal rot and chemical cracking. Spray hit her. The weary factory's spray. It giant-walked by her hiding place sending all those Suffolk birds away, hauled into the fens to squat like a monument that had always been there.

It braced. A percussion of chains, the crack of old shells, and its drill descended.

The first platforms had returned close to where they went down. But then *Interocean II* had emerged not in the North Sea but in the harbour of a hastily evacuated Oporto, stepped daintily over the seawall like someone crossing a stile. Sedco 135F rose in the Galapagos, far from the Bay of Campeche. The many-legged barge *Ocean Prince*[1] came up not in Dogger Bank but Sardinia.

1 The *Interocean II* sank in the North Sea in 1989; Oporto is a city in Portugal. *Sedco 135F* went down in 1979 in the Gulf of Mexico, leading to the then-largest marine oil spill. The *Ocean Prince* sank in the North Sea in 1968.

Revisitors might come, drill, go back to the water, even come up again, anywhere.

Dughan's daughter had got away from him, got closer to the visitor. Had he not noticed her go? Before he knew it, he might have said, she was gone. It might be true. She was pressed against one of the dead trees. Beyond her was Petrobras, like a failed city block. Dughan whispered her name. She watched the dead and come-back rig boring.

He went to her, of course. Exhilarating to exit the cover. He was quickly there, looking with her through barkless branches. The platform was calm, its fire low. It shivered, only, tinily, all its thousands of tons. Ripples passed over the wetland, not outward but in, circles decreasing, shrinking to that point where the shaft entered the ground.

They watched. After many seconds, Dughan felt something pressed to his back. He had long enough before anyone spoke to be surprised that whoever this was had got so close without him hearing. He blamed the reek and weird industry he was watching.

A voice said: "You move and I'll fucking kill you."

When the lost rigs of the world came back, old hands claimed they had seen in the motion of the drills something reversed. Dughan doubted it: shuddering was shuddering. But most of the places where the rigs went there were no oil fields. It might have been that they were sniffing other things than oil to sustain them, but that was not so.

"Turn around," the voice said. The uniformed man who faced them was young and afraid. With a weapon pointed at him, old techniques, muscle memory came back and twitched Dughan's fingers, but he stayed still.

The man scanned them. No RPGs, no mortars, not even smaller arms. They were not oleophobe fanatics here to attack the Petrobras, nor Oil Firsters, here to kill him, his colleagues and all those who came to investigate or exploit, in their parlance, the visitations.

"Who the fuck are you?" The guard glanced over their heads at the shuffling rig. He was whispering, though Dughan knew it would make little difference now.

"We're just here to watch," the girl said gently. She was taking care of him. "My dad brought me here to watch is all. Just to see it."

The guard searched them, cack-handedly.[1] Dughan silently counted the times he could have disarmed him. The man found only binoculars, torch, and cameras. He frowned at their pictures of Suffolk, of Punch-and-Judy shows,[2] of roadside oddities. No contraband sights. "Jesus!" he said. "Move, then."

Behind them the rig shifted and he cringed at the great squelch. "What are you even doing?" he said when they had retreated to the living trees. "Do you have any idea how dangerous this is?"

1 Clumsily or awkwardly.

2 Punch and Judy were characters in well-known, traditional British puppet shows.

"I'm sorry, it was me," she said. "I just really wanted to see it up close and I begged him. I'm really sorry."

The man wiped his forehead. "Let me tell you something," he said. "Last time there was one of them here, down by Camber Sands?" The Adriatic IV. Dughan didn't say it. "There was a couple of young lads got in. Got past us. I shouldn't tell you. They were larking about. Taking pictures and that. Anyway you know what happened? They had a dog with them and it got too close, and it spooked the rig and it moved. Midway through." He waved through the copse. "It trod on the dog."

Dughan looked back up at the Petrobras's subdued high burning.

"Now come on." The guard beckoned. "Let's get back."

When their feet hit the beach sand, the girl said to him, "How long'll it be?" Just close enough to the inlet and troughs gouged by the rig's passing to afford a sightline into the broads, headlights flashed. The jeeps were visible a moment, and people.

"It'll be there half a day at least," the man said. "And it's a few months later it'll all kick off." He even smiled.

"You know," he said, "I don't know, you might probably be a bit old for it but there's like a kid's club they have here. They have activities and that."

"You saw some once, didn't you, dad?" Dughan was not angry when she said that. He marveled, really, at her.

All its research notwithstanding, UNPERU expressed as much shock as the rest of the world when, over a year after the *Ocean Ranger*'s visit, up from the still-recovering Newfoundland ground into which it had pushed its drill, the first clutch of newly-hatched oil rigs had unburied themselves.

They had emerged into the night, shaking off earth. Stood quivering on stiffening metal or cement legs. Tilted tiny helipads. Tottered finally for the sea.

"How big are they, Dad?" she said.

"You've seen films," he said. "As big as me." Dughan had gone back to Nigeria. He had waited for months, on the vagaries of gestation. At last the monitors in the delta picked up evidence of subterranean shifts. Over many hours, long before dawn, he had watched unsteady six-foot riglets burrow up out of the forest dirt. Seven of them, of all different designs; buildings, supports, struts, derricks. They waited, swaying like new calves, still wet from their tarry sacs, swinging umbrella-sized cranes.

He helped to capture two, and to usher the rest safely to the water, where the baby rigs had been tagged and released to scuttle below the waves, escorted by divers as far down as the divers could go. The two captives were taken to hangars where great tanks of brine waited. But they sickened within days and died, and fell apart into scrap and rubble.

The Oporto authorities pumped poisons into the university grounds where the Interocean II had drilled and left the earth slick and soupy. Whether that was what kept its brood from being born was never clear: those eggs were not recovered. In other coastal cities, neonate oil platforms did emerge, to gallop hectic and nervy through the streets, spreading panic.

Only the most violent post-return decommissioning could stop all this, only second deaths, from which the rigs did not come back again, kept them from where they wished to go, to drill. Once chosen, a place might be visited by any one of the wild rigs that walked out of the abyss. As if such locations had been decided collectively. UNPERU observed the nesting sites, more all the time, and kept track of the rigs themselves as best they could, of their behemoth grazing or wandering at the bottom of the world.

"What activities do they do in this club?" the girl said.

"Oh." The guard shrugged. "Stuff like, you can see the eggs on a live feed. They'll be digging down to them and they'll put cameras and thermometers and whatever. Sometimes you can even see movement through the shells. And there's colouring books and games and that." He smiled again. "Like I say, it's too young for you."

They laid eggs, so, many people said, they must have sex. There was no logic there. They were oil rigs. Dughan thought the belief exoneration of the strange prurience that endlessly turned on monoliths rutting miles down. An inhuman pornography of great slams and grinding, horrified whales veering from where one rig mounted another, warmed by hydrothermal vents.

"And no one knows what happens to the young, do they, Dad?"

Other guards came to meet them. Half-welcoming, half-peremptory. Dughan recognized none. Behind the security were the few tourists lucky to have been nearby, at accredited hotels, when Petrobras's heavy steps had registered on the scanners.

"No one knows yet," Dughan said to his daughter. "They're still very young. They're little and the sea's very big. They've got a lot of growing to do."

A guide was in the middle of a spiel. "We'll come back in the morning, when it's finished laying," she said. "You can bring your cameras then—no danger then if you forgot to turn your flash off." People laughed.

"What's wrong?" Dughan whispered.

"Do you think it's true what he said?" the girl whispered. "About the dog? That's horrible." She made a face. He stared not at the twitching Petrobras P-36 with its concrete in the mere, not at its drill ovipositor injecting slippy black rig eggs into England, but at the sea. "Maybe he was lying to scare us," the girl said.

Dughan turned and took in the length of Covehithe beach. They were out of sight, but he looked in the direction of the graveyard, and of St Andrew's stubby hall where services continued within the medieval carapace, remains of a grander church fallen apart to time and the civil war and to economics, fallen ultimately with permission.

Ken Liu (b. 1976)

Ken Liu is an American author and translator, as well as computer scientist and lawyer, who was born in China. Best known for his short stories, "The Paper Menagerie" (2011) won the Hugo, Nebula, and World Fantasy awards, and his first novel, *The Grace of Kings* (2015), the first book in an epic fantasy series, won the Locus award. He is also well-known for his award-winning translation of Chinese author Liu Cixin's novel, *The Three-Body Problem* (2008; translation 2014).

Note on the text: The story was first published online in *Lightspeed Magazine* (no. 21, Aug. 2012) before being reprinted in Liu's collection *The Paper Menagerie and Other Stories* (2016). There are a few significant differences: the original includes headings with the species' names before the sections discussing them, and one passage is altered significantly in the later publication, which is followed here, with a note to that significant difference.

"The Bookmaking Habits of Select Species" (2012)

THERE is no definitive census of all the intelligent species in the universe. Not only are there perennial arguments about what qualifies as intelligence, but each moment and everywhere, civilizations rise and fall, much as the stars are born and die.

Time devours all.

Yet every species has its unique way of passing on its wisdom through the ages, its way of making thoughts visible, tangible, frozen for a moment like a bulwark against the irresistible tide of time.

Everyone makes books.

It is said by some that writing is just visible speech. But we know such views are parochial.

A musical people, the Allatians write by scratching their thin, hard proboscis across an impressionable surface, such as a metal tablet covered by a thin layer of wax or hardened clay. (Wealthy Allatians sometimes wear a nib made of precious metals on the tip of the nose.) The writer speaks his thoughts as he writes, causing the proboscis to vibrate up and down as it etches a groove in the surface.

To read a book inscribed this way, an Allatian places his nose into the groove and drags it through. The delicate proboscis vibrates in sympathy with the waveform of the groove, and a hollow chamber in the Allatian skull magnifies the sound. In this manner, the voice of the writer is re-created.

The Allatians believe that they have a writing system superior to all others. Unlike books written in alphabets, syllabaries, or logograms, an Allatian book captures not only words, but also the writer's tone, voice, inflection, emphasis, intonation, rhythm. It is simultaneously a score and a recording. A speech sounds like a speech, a lament a lament, and a story re-creates perfectly the teller's breathless excitement. For the Allatians, reading is literally hearing the voice of the past.

But there is a cost to the beauty of the Allatian book. Because the act of reading requires physical contact with the soft, malleable surface, each time a text is read, it is also damaged and some aspects of the original irretrievably lost. Copies made of more durable materials inevitably fail to capture all the subtleties of the writer's voice, and are thus shunned.

In order to preserve their literary heritage, the Allatians have to lock away their most precious manuscripts in forbidding libraries where few are granted access. Ironically, the most important and beautiful works of Allatian writers are rarely read, but are known only through interpretations made by scribes who attempt to reconstruct the original in new books after hearing the source read at special ceremonies.

For the most influential works, hundreds, thousands of interpretations exist in circulation, and they, in turn, are interpreted and proliferate through new copies. The Allatian scholars spend much of their time debating the relative authority of competing versions, and inferring, based on the multiplicity of imperfect copies, the imagined voice of their antecedent, an ideal book uncorrupted by readers.

The Quatzoli do not believe that thinking and writing are different things at all.

They are a race of mechanical beings. It is not known if they began as mechanical creations of another (older) species, if they are shells hosting the souls of a once-organic race, or if they evolved on their own from inert matter.

A Quatzoli's body is made out of copper and shaped like an hourglass. Their planet, tracing out a complicated orbit between three stars, is subjected to immense tidal forces that churn and melt its metal core, radiating heat to the surface in the form of steamy geysers and lakes of lava. A Quatzoli ingests water into its bottom chamber a few times a day, where it slowly boils and turns into steam as the Quatzoli periodically dips itself into the bubbling lava lakes. The steam passes through a regulating valve—the narrow part of the hourglass—into the upper chamber, where it powers the various gears and levers that animate the mechanical creature.

At the end of the work cycle, the steam cools and condenses against the inner surface of the upper chamber. The droplets of water flow along grooves etched into the copper until they are collected into a steady stream, and this stream then passes through a porous stone rich in carbonate minerals before being disposed of outside the body.

This stone is the seat of the Quatzoli mind. The stone organ is filled with thousands, millions of intricate channels, forming a maze that divides the water into countless tiny, parallel flows that drip, trickle, wind around each other to represent simple values which, together, coalesce into streams of consciousness and emerge as currents of thought.

Over time, the pattern of water flowing through the stone changes. Older channels are worn down and disappear or become blocked and closed off—and so some memories are forgotten. New channels are created, connecting previously separated flows—an epiphany—and the departing water deposits new mineral growths at the far, youngest end of the stone, where the tentative, fragile miniature stalactites are the newest, freshest thoughts.

When a Quatzoli parent creates a child in the forge, its final act is to gift the child with a sliver of its own stone mind, a package of received wisdom and ready thoughts that allow the child to begin its life. As the child accumulates experiences, its stone brain grows around that core, becoming ever more intricate and elaborate, until it can, in turn, divide its mind for the use of its children.

And so the Quatzoli *are* themselves books. Each carries within its stone brain a written record of the accumulated wisdom of all its ancestors: the most durable thoughts that have survived millions of years of erosion. Each mind grows from a seed inherited through the millennia, and every thought leaves a mark that can be read and seen.

Some of the more violent races of the universe, such as the Hesperoe, once delighted in extracting and collecting the stone brains of the Quatzoli. Still displayed in their museums and libraries, the stones—often labeled simply "ancient books"—no longer mean much to most visitors.

Because they could separate thought from writing, the conquering races were able to leave a record that is free of blemishes and thoughts that would have made their descendants shudder.

But the stone brains remain in their glass cases, waiting for water to flow through the dry channels so that once again they can be read and live.

The Hesperoe once wrote with strings of symbols that represented sounds in their speech, but now no longer write at all.

They have always had a complicated relationship with writing, the Hesperoe. Their great philosophers distrusted writing. A book, they thought, was not a living mind yet pretended to be one. It gave sententious pronouncements, made moral judgments, described purported historical facts, or told exciting stories … yet it could not be interrogated like a real person, could not answer its critics or justify its accounts.

The Hesperoe wrote down their thoughts reluctantly, only when they could not trust the vagaries of memory. They far preferred to live with the transience of speech, oratory, debate.

At one time, the Hesperoe were a fierce and cruel people. As much as they delighted in debates, they loved even more the glories of war. Their philosophers justified their conquests and slaughter in the name of forward motion: War was the only way to animate the ideals embedded in the static text passed down through the ages, to ensure that they remained true, and to refine them for the future. An idea was worth keeping only if it led to victory.

When they finally discovered the secret of mind storage and mapping, the Hesperoe stopped writing altogether.

In the moments before the deaths of great kings, generals, philosophers, their minds are harvested from the failing bodies. The paths of every charged ion, every fleeting electron, every strange and charming quark, are captured and cast in crystalline matrices. These minds are frozen forever in that moment of separation from their owners.

At this point, the process of mapping begins. Carefully, meticulously, a team of master cartographers—assisted by numerous apprentices—trace out each of the countless minuscule tributaries, impressions, and hunches that commingle into the flow and ebb of thought, until they gather into the tidal forces, the ideas that made their originators so great.

Once the mapping is done, they begin the calculations to project the continuing trajectories of the traced-out paths so as to simulate the next thought. The charting of the courses taken by the great, frozen minds into the vast, dark terra incognita of the future consumes the efforts of the most brilliant scholars of the Hesperoe. They devote the best years of their lives to it, and when they die, their minds, in turn, are charted indefinitely into the future as well.

In this way, the great minds of the Hesperoe do not die. To converse with them, the Hesperoe only have to find the answers on the mind maps. Thus, they no longer have a need for books as they used to make them—which were merely dead symbols—for the wisdom of the past is always with them, still thinking, still guiding, still exploring.

And as more and more of their time and resources are devoted to the simulation of ancient minds, the Hesperoe have also grown less warlike, much to the relief of their neighbors. Perhaps it is true that some books do have a civilizing influence.

The Tull-Toks read books they did not write.

They are creatures of energy. Ethereal, flickering patterns of shifting field potentials, the Tull-Toks are strung out among the stars like ghostly ribbons. When the starships of the other species pass through, the ships barely feel a gentle tug.

The Tull-Toks claim that everything in the universe can be read. Each star is a living text, where the massive convection currents of superheated gas tell an epic drama, with the starspots serving as punctuation, the coronal loops extended figures of speech, and the flares emphatic passages that ring true in the deep silence of cold space. Each planet contains a poem, written out in the bleak, jagged, staccato rhythm of bare rocky cores or the lyrical, lingering, rich rhymes—both masculine and feminine—of swirling gas giants. And then there are the planets with life, constructed like intricate jeweled clockwork, containing a multitude of self-referential literary devices that echo and re-echo without end.

But it is the event horizon around a black hole where the Tull-Toks claim the greatest books are to be found. When a Tull-Tok is tired of browsing through the endless universal library, she drifts toward a black hole. As she accelerates toward the point of no return, the streaming gamma rays and X-rays unveil more and more of the ultimate mystery for which all the other books are but glosses. The book reveals itself to be ever more complex, more nuanced, and just as she is about to be overwhelmed by the immensity of the book she is reading, her companions, observing from a distance, realize with a start that time seems to have slowed down to standstill for her, and she will have eternity to read it as she falls forever towards a center that she will never reach.[1]

Finally, a book has triumphed over time.

Of course, no Tull-Tok has ever returned from such a journey, and many dismiss their discussion of reading black holes as pure myth. Indeed, many consider the Tull-Toks to be nothing more than illiterate frauds who rely on mysticism to disguise their ignorance.

Still, some continue to seek out the Tull-Toks as interpreters of the books of nature they claim to see all around us. The interpretations thus produced are numerous and conflicting, and lead to endless debates over the books' content and—especially—authorship.

In contrast to the Tull-Toks, who read books at the grandest scale, the Caru'ee are readers and writers of the minuscule.

Small in stature, the Caru'ee each measure no larger than the period at the end of this sentence. In their travels, they seek from others only to acquire books that have lost all meaning and could no longer be read by the descendants of the authors.

Due to their unimpressive size, few races perceive the Caru'ee as threats, and they are able to obtain what they want with little trouble. For instance, at the Caru'ee's request, the people of Earth gave them tablets and vases incised with Linear A,[2] bundles of knotted strings called *quipus*,[3] as well as an assortment of ancient magnetic discs and cubes that they no longer knew how to decipher. The Hesperoe, after they had ceased their wars of conquest, gave the Caru'ee some ancient stones that they believed to be books looted from the Quatzoli. And even the reclusive Untou, who write with fragrances and flavors, allowed them to have some old bland books whose scents were too faint to be read.

---

1 In the original 2012 version, this passage reads "just as she is about to be overwhelmed by the immensity of the book she is reading, she realizes with a start that time has slowed down to standstill, and she will have eternity to read it as she falls forever towards a center that she will never reach."

2 Linear A is an early writing system developed in the Minoan civilization and used from c. 1800 to c. 1400 BCE.

3 Quipu is a type of administrative recording system comprising knots on strings or cords. Quipus were used by the Inca and other societies and peoples in South America prior to European colonization.

The Caru'ee make no effort at deciphering their acquisitions. They seek only to use the old books, now devoid of meaning, as a blank space upon which to construct their sophisticated, baroque cities.

The incised lines on the vases and tablets were turned into thoroughfares whose walls were packed with honeycombed rooms that elaborate on the pre-existing outlines with fractal beauty. The fibers in the knotted ropes were teased apart, re-woven and re-tied at the microscopic level, until each original knot had been turned into a Byzantine complex of thousands of smaller knots, each a kiosk suitable for a Caru'ee merchant just starting out or a warren of rooms for a young Caru'ee family. The magnetic discs, on the other hand, were used as arenas of entertainment, where the young and adventurous careened across their surface during the day, delighting in the shifting push and pull of local magnetic potential. At night, the place was lit up by tiny lights that followed the flow of magnetic forces, and long-dead data illuminated the dance of thousands of young people searching for love, seeking to connect.

Yet it is not accurate to say that the Caru'ee do no interpretation at all. When members of the species that had given these artifacts to the Caru'ee come to visit, inevitably they feel a sense of familiarity with the Caru'ee's new construction.

For example, when representatives from Earth were given a tour of the Great Market built in a *quipu*, they observed—via the use of a microscope—bustling activity, thriving trade, and an incessant murmur of numbers, accounts, values, currency. One of the Earth's representatives, a descendant of the people who had once knotted the string books, was astounded. Though he could not read them, he knew that the *quipus* had been made to keep track of accounts and numbers, to tally up taxes and ledgers.

Or take the example of the Quatzoli, who found the Caru'ee repurposing one of the lost Quatzoli stone brains as a research complex. The tiny chambers and channels, where ancient, watery thoughts once flowed were now laboratories, libraries, teaching rooms, and lecture halls echoing with new ideas. The Quatzoli delegation had come to recover the mind of their ancestor, but left convinced that all was as it should be.

It is as if the Caru'ee were able to perceive an echo of the past, and unconsciously, as they built upon a palimpsest of books written long ago and long forgotten, chanced to stumble upon an essence of meaning that could not be lost, no matter how much time had passed.

They read without knowing they are reading.

Pockets of sentience glow in the cold, deep void of the universe like bubbles in a vast, dark sea. Tumbling, shifting, joining and breaking, they leave behind spiraling phosphorescent trails, each as unique as a signature, as they push and rise toward an unseen surface.

Everyone makes books.

Richard Van Camp (b. 1971)

Richard Van Camp is a Tłı̨chǫ Dene author from Fort Smith, in the Northwest Territories, in Canada, where he was awarded the Order of the Northwest Territories in 2023. A multiple-award-winning author of novels, short stories, comics and graphic novels, children's books, and non-fiction, his work has also been adapted for film. He holds degrees in creative writing from the University of Victoria and the University of British Columbia. Much of his work engages Indigenous storytelling; a cycle of works—including the short stories "Wheetago War I: Lying in Bed Together," "Wheetago War II: Summoners," "The Fleshing," and "On the Wings of this Prayer," as well as the graphic novel *Wheetago War: Roth* (the first in a series)—deals with the rise of the wheetago, also called the windigo, an Indigenous figure associated with greed and the consumption of human flesh.

Note on the text: This story, as well as "The Fleshing," appear in Van Camp's collection *Godless but Loyal to Heaven* (2013), the source of the text below.

"On the Wings of this Prayer" (2013)

THERE are two stories my great-grandfather told me. He said a long time ago before *them*—the Shark Throats, he called them, during the time of the warming world—there was a family in the way of the Tar Sands of Alberta. One day as the mother was gathering water, she stepped on teeth in the ice and muskeg.[1] The jaws of an old man, a trapper, had thawed enough to bite her. She ran but she did not escape. The woman got very sick: buttons of pus boiling through a body rash, the paling, her hands hooking to claws. She asked her husband to bring her glass after glass of water. She was thirsty and panting. He kept bringing her more, yet she never drank. She said something was coming through her. Something starving.

Her voice then turned to a low growl as she began to rock for hours hissing, "Kill me now. Kill me now or I'll kill you all before the sunrise. Do it, do it if you love me. Kill me please. Your meat is magnificent and what roars in your veins is calling me. It's calling me to drink you open and warm me so sweetly. Oh let me start with your scars and scabs. Let me. Let me taste you. You'd let me if you love me."

As her husband returned with help, she snapped at the air with her teeth and rasped before striking out wildly at all of them with her nails. After they subdued her, she begged again for all of them to kill her—before the sunrise, she insisted. They tied her fists and feet and ran for more help. When they returned, she was gone. She'd torn her binding and fled, but the strangest thing—the

1 A type of marsh or bog.

oddest thing—were the glasses of water he'd brought her. They'd all turned to ice. Her husband never saw his wife again. They think she was the first and they say she is still here as their queen, that she gives birth to them through her mouth. Hatching them through her over and over. More and more. The *boiled-faces*, we call them—*zombies*, our son said—and they remember faces.

The Tar Sands of Alberta had tailing ponds[1] and excavators, and I am sure those teeth belonged to that old trapper who lived out there before them. That old man, no matter how much money the oil companies offered him, would not budge, so they built and dug around him. He quit coming to town. There was a family who went to visit him, to bring him supplies, but he had changed. He had gone to white and had eaten his own lips and fingers. He had stepped in bear traps spiked to the floors on purpose. He could still speak and said the devil was in him now and that they had to cut him up. They had to burn his heart and scatter his ashes after they cut his head off.

They did everything he asked them to, but the land was uncovered and turned for years by excavators, tractors and the curiosity of men. We think those machines must have moved the heavy rocks that covered his limbs. We think his fingers were able to crawl back to the torso and legs and head. We don't think they burnt his heart to ashes because they saw him again and he killed many, many people by biting at them. Burning, cutting, stabbing, shooting—all of it was wasted until his family heard of him walking again, so they told the people how to stop him. And that's how we knew. That was how we knew to stop the boiled faces with the old ways.

There is a ritual to things now: a lunge shot with the Decapitator through the skull. It's a longer harpoon with a cross-axe on the hilt to ram and split the skull so zombies can't grab you. It detaches so you can begin chopping. Only good one on one. Useless against many. Scramble the brains. This blinds and confuses the body. With a quick twist, the top blade comes off to free the axe. Then you hack the right arm (the reaching one) off before the left (the grabbing one)—is to be cut. Then you take the right leg and the left before cutting the heart out. As the heart is burnt with a sharpened flare, the Known People turn, look away and chant in Apache, "*Deeyá, Deeyá*" for "Leave, leave." We believe that what is left of the soul still rises and the spirit of the person inside will know to look away, as well, so it doesn't need to see what has happened to its body. There is respect and fear in this. Then we bury the limbs far apart and weigh them down with stones. The Known People buried everything and everyone pointing north, even though we've all seen some of them come back marked and scored. (Are they unburying each other or themselves?)

I can still speak Dogrib,[2] me, but Apache is the common tongue for the

1 Engineered areas designed to capture the waste created by the extraction of bitumen from the tar sands.

2 Dogrib language, or Tłı̨chǫ Yatıì, is spoken by the Tłı̨chǫ people, primarily in what is now known as the Northwest Territories, in Canada.

Known People—or it was before the three of us were banished. For some reason, when the Hair Eaters come, it slows them when you sing or talk to them or chant in the first tongue. It's like they're listening. They weaken when you chant and that's when you take them.

All those old movies were true: body shots are wasted. Even with a shattered spine, they crawl. You'd think by now we'd be used to this, but they've a hot, sweet smell like dead fish that turns your stomach when they near. We then burn their limbs to ashes and scatter them. This is why the air tastes as it does. Their wild, rolling cry is used to paralyze, but it is not as strong as their mother's. I heard it a few times in the sky and felt the strength leave my legs, but our drums drown them out. If you drum you can stop their mewling cry, turn it to ice in their throats. Also, our little group has discovered that The Boiled Faces are terrified of butterflies. They run screaming—as if set to flames—when they see a butterfly and that's why we've camped here. Also, this is why we bottle them. All it takes is one butterfly and when one runs, they all do. It is hilarious. I laugh every time I see this. I wish I could have done The Butterfly Test to the Known People. I bet they would have all run away. I would have laughed so hard I would have thrown myself upon a Decapitator throat-first and not come back.

The zombies took our dogs first, systematically and determinedly. Once the dogs were gone we were blind and deaf to them. I miss the dogs. I can't even think of their names or I will weep. A wise hunter looked where they looked, always, and dogs always know more about storms than humans. And we used the old ways when we took one down with the dogs: we poked their halfway-human-and-mean-as-starving eyes out so they wouldn't see you the next time. We sliced the tips of their ears off and hung them high so they wouldn't hear you the next time, but they do. The new ones can.

I hear of things in the ravaged south (no word from the west), but they, I hope, are rumours: death cults who eat or rape the Shark Throats for power, building sod huts and using their stomach linings for windows. In the east, thousands of people wait with their eyes closed in fields to be taken at once so they can come back to roam together. And they say the new generation of the Boiled Faces can sing themselves back together. Let us pray that this is not true.

Here in the north, the Known People dressed their children in rabbit fur and seal skins. I'm not sure if I agree with the practice of sewing bones under the skin, but I saw that most youths' faces were tattooed in the way of *Kakiniit*,[1] ghost marks in memory of the One Sun. The Known People were greedy to learn our songs for the slowing.

If you are reading this, please know that I tell you these things because I love you and wish for the world a better way. I have sent this back to tell you this, my ancestor: the Tar Sands are ecocide. They will bring Her back. In both stories, it is the Tar Sands to blame. This is how the Wheetago will return.

---

1 Kakiniit are traditional Inuit tattoos.

As far as we can tell, the exact pinpoint is around the time when they transport one atom from one part of the world to the other.[1] This has something to do with all of everything during your time. You must stop the Tar Sands. At all costs. If you read this, there is still a spirit with a starving heart there. Waiting to be resurrected.

I've seen them chase down an older couple as they ran in deep, black snow. One Shark Throat—a newer, smaller one, one with a long beak and hooks for thumbs, raced ahead and circled back, floating over the land. He cut his way into their stomachs with his claws. The elders' stomachs opened like mouths and out poured their guts. The larger Hair Eaters began to eat their unravelling intestines as they stumbled away. It was a game to them. The younger one gripped and squeezed their grey, steaming leashes as the half-alive elders tried to scream, but all that came out of their mouths was slop. The younger one began to slowly braid their guts together while pulling them closer, nearer, playing with its food. The others feasted. The younger Hair Eater looked up and saw me and pointed but the others kept gorging. It opened its beak and let out a cry as it started to run towards me. The cry tangled my wings. Their sound: it rings through what is hollow inside you. It finds your marrow and squeezes it to weaken you. And I think once their song touches you, they can hear what you are thinking.

At night, when I sleepwalk, my soul leaves my body and I fly. I could always fly and that was why I had to save Thinksawhile. I spied on the leaders of the Known People. They were boiling and eating old moccasins and mukluks[2] and they were talking of having him fall through the ice and eating him frozen. This explained our last few meals. Oh Creator, the things we've done to survive. That night, we took the boy and his computers and left, travelling downwind, upwind and through the fog. East. Always moving east. Watching the skies for ravens as ravens follow them for what's left.

Four Blankets Woman covered my eyes with ash. "So the new ones can see you."

"Heh eh," I said. "They are getting smarter, crueler."

She rubbed my back with palms of yarrow. "We need new medicine."

"You know what was beautiful?" I said. "Those elders they tore apart, they never stopped holding hands or trying to...."

"Shhh," she said as she rested on my chest. "I know how to beat them now."

I turned. "How?"

"The new ones have beaks."

"Heh eh."

"And it has a tongue to direct sound?" I nodded.

"I will chant on this to see."

---

1 Physicists have been able to teleport quantum information from one atom to another.

2 Moccasins are traditional footwear of Indigenous people in North America, generally made from deer or other leather. Mukluks are the traditional boots of seal or caribou skin made by Inuit.

The next morning I woke to find she'd tattooed my eyelids with syllabics.[1] She'd also sliced her left breast open and marked our Decapitators with strange symbols of whips and dots. "For your weapons and wings," she said.

I closed my eyes and looked at the fire to see this magic again. "Are these from heaven?"

"*In le*," she said, stirring broth. "*Gah*.[2] The Rabbit. There are only two left and they have passed their medicine to me. They told me how to beat them and the Bitch." Thinksawhile looked up from his computer.

"This will cost us one of our lives. We have to choose carefully."

Four Blankets knew the way of the four winds. I had seen her part the clouds. She knew which root and moss to braid to make wick for cooking and heat. Her medicine was rabbit medicine. When she was thirteen, she saved the life of a doe. In turn, she was given Gah medicine. Four Blankets Woman had tattooed our tongues, so the Hair Eaters could not hear us speak. Not even in this dream.

She ran soot down her nose. "Whoever we choose will suffer, but it is the only way." The boy was young, weak. I had a blown right knee and couldn't stop talking in my sleep.

"We choose tonight," she said and left to slice her arm to ribbons. This was the cost of a Dream Thrower.

Thinksawhile went back to his computer. "I have an idea," he said. "A way to stop this. A way to undo all that's been done."

I began to braid my hair. "Tell me," I said. And he did.

Before we fled, the sick cooked for us. The sick chanted for us. Scouts left. Our son vanished. Women gave birth to things that were killed immediately (except redheads), and there was a low growl from the cancered earth that trembled us. All Known Elders turned blind. What the last hunter brought was a hand that could be bear with an eye sewn backwards into the palm. Could be human, could be them. Knuckle sockets sucked dry. I touched one and singed my finger. It burns at night when I dream.

Now the air is loaded with ash that coats us and the wings of the butterflies, and my dreams. My dreams.

The Hair Eaters have eaten all the caribou, moose, bear, fox, wolf, bison, buffalo and everything under the earth here. We are too scared to check nets as they feast on our catch underwater and wait for boats. All we have left are creatures of the air: ducks and ptarmigan, geese, swans. We eat roots pretending they are what we used to love.

This message comes from the future. From our Dream Thrower. Remember, there is a hard way and an easy way: stop the Tar Sands and that old man's body from waking up. He—not she—is the beginning of the end. May your children—our ancestors—not know a time of being born hunted as we are all hunted now.

---

1 Syllabics are a writing system used for different Indigenous languages.

2 Rabbit (Dene).

As for us, our season's done, and I miss smiling at my memories. It's getting colder now. Soon the fist of the sun will surrender to frost. We see it on the lower mountains across the way. Soon the butterflies will leave (where do they sleep at night?) and they will find us. They say some humans are farming other humans and making deals with the Hair Eaters. At night, when I lower myself to the cooling earth, as I breathe through my palms to cool my roaring head, my finger burns. I think this is how they are tracking us.

I heard a story once. It warmed even the hearts of the Known People. It was a story outside of Fort Providence. The buffalo ran with two giant horses, two Clydesdales: one white, one brown. When you approached the herd you could clap your hands and the buffalo would look one way, the horses the other. Wolves and the zombies could not come near for trampling and goring. I sometimes think about how the horses and buffalo adopted each other. What was their ritual for each other? I told that story the second night after moving with the Known People, and they marvelled until hunters from that region reported that two giant horse skulls burned among the mountains of bones. They also spoke of lakes now, filled with humans swimming in their own blood. Hundreds of women, men, children, elders, harpooned and buoyed by jerry cans to keep them floating. "It's the adrenaline," a sharpshooter who got away said. "It sweetens our blood. They keep us terrified and once we die, they tear into us. They just keep adding more and more people to these lakes. There were lines of people for miles, as far as we could see."

I saw a grey whale once, rolling in shallow water. Hundreds of Hair Eaters poured over the body biting, ripping at the barnacles and sea lice. Others clawed and reached into the eyes and blowholes. One dove into its mouth. Then others. Then more and more. It thrashed and couldn't get away. The Shark Throats ate their way from the inside until I could see its skeleton. I watched a mile away and heard it scream. Their cries are supposed to be subsonic but I heard it. I still hear it.

I've seen a pack of Hair Eaters down a pack of bison in slush. The lead bull flipped in the air as the opposing Hair Eaters forked to cut him off. As he flipped in the air, two were upon him ripping and tearing at his belly and balls. He was hollowed out completely by the time he landed, still kicking.

We wish you luck. The future is a curse. There are no human trails left. I was born running from them as they are born starving and hunting for us. Now, we carry on in fever. We carry on for you and what you do next.

Four Blankets Woman has thrown two dreams now: one for you and the other to prove it. In your time, Taiwan will shut down its biggest highway for seven suns to allow for the safe passage of one million butterflies.[1] If this is so, you will know this warning to be true. I pray you remember this when you wake up.

1 In 2007, Taiwan started such traffic measures during butterfly migration periods as part of conservation efforts.

You must remember this.

You must stop the Tar Sands. Do not bring cancer to our Mother. Do not unleash them.

On the wings of this atomized prayer, we reach to you with all we have left.

Now, they have expanded their range to the fullest here and are crossing the ice of time to reach you—you who live in the time before the sun twins, when fish only had one mouth, when moose knew who they were.

You *can* change the future.

Now wake up.

Canisia Lubrin (b. 1984)

Canisia Lubrin is a Caribbean Canadian poet who currently teaches creative writing at the University of Guelph. Her first collection of poetry, *Voodoo Hypothesis: Poems* (2017), was nominated for several awards, and in 2021 Lubrin won the US-based Windham–Campbell Literature Prize in poetry.

Note on the text: Originally published in issue 31 (2015) of *The Puritan Literary Magazine* (now called *The Ex-Puritan*), "Voodoo Hypothesis" was later published as the first poem in Lubrin's collection of the same title (2017), which was the copy text for this anthology. In the book version, Lubrin includes the following note: "This poem is after *Ultimate Mars Challenge*, a documentary that chronicles mankind's most ambitious attempt to find life in our galaxy through the Curiosity rover expedition to Mars" (94).

"Voodoo Hypothesis" (2015)

Before sight, we imagine
that while they go out in search
of God
we stay in and become god,
become: Curiosity,[1]
whose soul is a nuclear battery
because she'll pulverize Martian rock
and test for organic molecules
in her lab within a lab within
a lab. She doesn't need to know our fears
so far too grand for ontology, reckoning.

Did you not land with your rocket behind
you, hope beyond hope on the tip of your rope
with the kindness of antigravity slowing you down,
you, before me, metal and earthen. But I am here to
confirm or deny, the millions of small
things that seven minutes of success were hinged upon
when I was little more than idea and research,
in the hypnotic gestures of flame and Bunsen burner,
and into parachute

1 Curiosity was the fourth of the remote-controlled "Mars Rovers" deployed by NASA to explore the surface of the planet Mars and send data back to Earth. The rover's mission was to discover whether Mars had ever been suitable to the existence of life. Landing on Mars in 2012, Curiosity is still active as of this writing.

no one foresaw, the bag of rags at the end
of the tunnel—all memory now,
this Paraclete.[1]

Where else is a pocket
of air more deadly than the atomic bomb?
Would this only happen on Earth?
Has Mars run out of tolerance for the minutiae

of air pockets, fingerprints and worry?
Aggregates of metal, Curiosity
and her clues to calm our fears for what's coming.
Mars and her epic storms, her gargantuan
volcanoes have long ceased their trembling,
her crazy flooded planes, frozen and in cinema.
Martian life now earth and revelation's phases:
Earth problem, not Mars problem.

But why
should I unravel over all this remembering?
    Great thing about landing
    is that I've arrived

at your service, at your sand, at your valley
and unsentimental magma.
Before me screams planes like Mojave Desert, Waikiki, Nagasaki,
nothing too strange to keep Curiosity off course.
Even though the Viking missions[2] found no conclusive pulse
and we declared you dead, O Mars,
never mind that we named your heights and depths
from orbit. And from your spheres of minerals
where oceans once roared—we've learned little
of your lenience for empire.
Forgive us what Spirit uncovered in the silica of your ancient
    hot springs.

Ah, yes, we've come back home.
Phoenix told us we inherited the numberless
stories of your hydraulic pathologies

---

1 In Christian tradition, Paraclete is used when referring to the Holy Spirit (one person of the Holy Trinity of God) when serving as "advocate, intercessor; a helper or comforter" (*OED*).

2 Viking 1 and Viking 2 were NASA probes that landed on Mars in 1976, each consisting of an orbiter and a lander.

but I am Curiosity. If I kill the bitch right,
she'll take us deeper and convince us to send earthlings
to set up Earth colonies on your deserts. They won't ever
come back, but that's not so bad when we trade in
the grander scheme.
As though the colonials, the Tribe Traders
and all the pharaonic masquerades of gone times
were not fair threat. That we won't know the depth
of our homeward seas
is nothing when

the sun's still got our backs.
And while waters still vaporize before us
Curiosity will keep on until the organic secrets
of that Martian puzzle become as household to us
as carbon. Oxygen wasn't the only disaster to befall Earth,
to bless her with life.

Apollo drilled on the moon and got stuck[1]
and the harder we've drilled down here
the more we've loosened our screws.
Perhaps there'll be no one left to give
a damn about the death of our privates

unless we prove ourselves enigmas,
the alien we think we know is the alien we only dream
up starting from the bottom
of the Curious.

We wake and die through
the crowns and thorns and craned chapters,
we move too quick for understanding.
Still, through the decades we predict,
Curiosity confirms the cold-slain dust.

Then come her conches blown
in the hard-won postcards travelling
on space dust faster than a bullet
to say:

---

1 The Apollo Program was NASA's human spaceflight and moon-lander program, which succeeded in landing the first humans on the moon with Apollo 11 in 1969. Apollo 15 landed on the moon in 1971 and used a drill to collect samples, but the drill became stuck.

hey,
I'm here. I safe. Wish you were here.
See Gale Crater, Mount Sharp,[1] *just as you've said.*
Come bask with me in the wonders of a Martian. Good afternoon,
you of flowering faith. Set sail for home,
because we will all wear the consequences of this choice.
And you never should have said
goodbye.

1 Mount Sharp, also known as Aeolis Mons, is a mountain in the centre of Gale Crater on Mars. Curiosity landed on the northern edge of the crater.

Drew Hayden Taylor (b. 1962)

Drew Hayden Taylor, from Curve Lake First Nation (in Ontario, Canada), is best known as a playwright, with two dozen plays produced, including *In a World Created by a Drunken God* (2003), which was adapted as a film in 2008. In addition, he has written extensively for television, including for the iconic Canadian series *The Beachcombers* (1972–90). Beyond drama, he has written several works of non-fiction dealing with Indigenous life, often with a humourous perspective, including several works in a series that started with *Funny, You Don't Look Like One: Observations of a Blue-Eyed Ojibway* (1996). His prose fiction includes *The Night Wanderer: A Native Gothic Novel* (2007) and *Take Us to Your Chief and Other Stories* (2016).

Note on the text: The text below follows its first publication in *Take Us to Your Chief and Other Stories* (2016).

"Stars" (2016)

It was the third streak of light he'd seen that night. Those mysterious glimpses of blurred motion arching across the night sky. Lying on either side of him at their summer camp, his father and uncle were deep in their own dreams, but Nimki found the sky to be a much more interesting companion. Although he was only fourteen summers old, he felt like those distant beacons dangling far above him were ancient friends. Even though he was familiar with every pattern and configuration hanging above the trees, Nimki knew precious little else about the stars, just the stories the elders told him. They were lights from the campfires of hunters and fishermen in the next world. Perhaps one of those campfires belonged to his grandfather, who had left his body and this world two winters past. Since then, occasionally Nimki would pick a star randomly and imagine his grandfather huddled over it, licking his lips in anticipation, a fat sky grouse slowly cooking over its flames.

Next to him, his sleeping uncle rolled over onto his side with a grunt. They'd left the village three days ago in search of deer or moose, or anything sizable to feed the village. Summer was supposed to be a time of plenty, but the wildlife didn't seem to know that. Other than the odd raccoon and rabbit, the three mighty Anishinabe hunters had nothing to show for their time in the bush. Nimki's father was getting frustrated. The boy could tell because he was beginning to talk in monosyllables … a dangerous sign. His mother, back in the village, was pregnant and needed good, hearty food to produce a healthy baby. Nimki's father usually fulfilled one of the requirements of manhood by supplying the family and village with tangible supplies but this summer was proving to be a more difficult endeavour. The Creator was making them search long and hard for meat.

Once again, his uncle shifted in his sleep, trying to find a more comfortable position. This was probably the last summer his uncle would be in the village. After many years of searching, he had finally found an excellent woman willing to be his wife. But she lived in another village, several weeks' travel to the east. When the summer ended, he would leave his family ... and Nimki ... and join this new wife and her community. It was difficult to say whether Nimki or his father would ever see him again. This eventuality was making Nimki's father even more moody. So far on this trip, they had managed to avoid the uncomfortable, looming topic.

He was a good uncle, Nimki thought. It was he more than his father who had taught Nimki the proper way to make a bow and how to shoot it. His father always seemed too busy with Nimki's two brothers and his sister, or doing his duties for the village. Nimki's still-childless uncle, however, seemed to have all the time in the world and Nimki revelled in it. Fortunately, patience was one of his uncle's virtues, for Nimki was not so adept with a bow. Although he spent hours practising, the arrows never seemed to go where he wanted them to. Another point of frustration for the boy's father.

In another time and another place, knowledgeable people would be able to tell that Nimki had been born without a lens in his right eye, severely limiting his depth perception, a requirement for aiming and shooting arrows. Right now and right here, the boy merely thought he was a bad hunter. But what he lacked in ability, he made up for in determination and drive. He was fast becoming one of the best trackers in the village. You didn't need depth perception for that. Usually, it took years of training and experience to track an animal the way Nimki could. He was even better than his uncle and his father. Yet another twinge of embarrassment for his father. But it is difficult to track animals that aren't there. Regardless, that is how all three came to be here, sleeping under the canopy of stars. Except the boy was not sleeping.

Sometimes, Nimki noticed, those fires in the sky seemed to shimmer, almost flicker, the way torches sometimes do when reflected off a wavy pond or lake. And they also seemed to be of slightly different colours and sizes. Some of his ancestors must have bonfires and others just small campfires. What else could that mean?

Other times, staring up into the speckled darkness, he felt if he wished hard enough or maybe opened his mind just right, his body might lift and travel up and up, eventually disappearing amid those shimmering lights. What would he find, he wondered. Such silly thoughts, but still, why was the night sky so much more interesting than the day sky? During the day it was always blue, though occasionally masked by clouds. The sun was there with monotonous regularity, and occasionally the moon would emerge on the opposite side, with bits of it missing. There were all sorts of stories to explain all that existed above and around him. But for Nimki, nighttime was so much more interesting—yes, it was easier to see and do things in the light, but in the absence of the sun, the world above became a more fascinating place.

Pondering such thoughts as he lay nestled on a bed of moss and pine needles, Nimki continued to stare up into the darkness. It was late in the summer, so there were few mosquitos to trouble him. Sometimes his eyes would fixate on an individual beacon of brightness in the dark canopy of the sky. Other times he would unfocus his eyes as best he could and let the whole panorama flood his consciousness. On occasion, he would also wonder, could his grandfather or those other hunters way up there see his campfire? Did they wonder about him and his little fire? Such silly questions.

His family often wondered why he was always tired. It seemed to them that he was only well rested in winter, when the boy's people moved into the warm wigwams or when it was cloudy and rainy for days. Nimki had difficulty explaining his interest in the night sky. He had tried once to tell his best friend, Keesic, who just shrugged, uninterested in such ideas.

Suddenly, his eyes caught another flash of light streaking through the mottled blackness. A flaming arrow perhaps, from the world above? A falling torch that burned out before it landed on Turtle Island,[1] maybe? He wished he knew.

Tomorrow, he and the two older men would continue the hunt, and it might be a better day. Just before they'd stopped for the night, they'd discovered some deer droppings. They were a few days old, but it was still a good sign.

Tomorrow night, the sun would set and the moon would rise, as it had ever since he and the elders could remember. With it, the stars would come out again, the same, or maybe slightly different. Some moved occasionally. The sky was a very mysterious place. Nimki wasn't so mysterious. He just loved watching the stars through the trees overhead.

And sometimes he felt the stars were watching him.

⋆ ⋆ ⋆

The sound of the door slamming was still echoing across the bay, reminding Walter how far sound can travel over water. He marched across the lawn—the grass was indeed in need of cutting, as his father had yelled at him repeatedly that night, spitting droplets of beer. His mother, not really paying attention, had changed the channel on the television and turned up the volume. As usual, neither his father nor his mother rushed out the door after him to stall his angry exit, or comfort him and beg him to come back into the house. Other parents, he knew, would have followed such an angry and upset boy out of the house and through the yard, eager to cajole him into returning home with them, maybe held him the way he'd seen other parents do. Possibly even make him some hot chocolate or let him watch what he wanted on television.

Instead, the door and the screen door remained shut. As with much of his life, Walter was alone. He had nowhere to go. He couldn't go to his friend Todd's place. It would be too embarrassing to tell him his parents were drunk

1 Turtle Island is the name for North America for some Indigenous peoples.

and yelling once more. His grandparents were certainly not within walking distance. His options were limited.

So as usual, he found himself at the mound. Sometime in years past, during a construction boom on the reserve, somebody had dumped a sizable pile of earth in a small glen at the edge of their property. A lilac bush hid it from the house. The mound rose about eight feet or so from the ground, the base partially covered by an abundance of weeds. Over the years, the elements, and Walter's body, had flattened the top down to the point where a teenage boy could lie on it.

Even before the boy started climbing up the side, he was breathing heavily. Walter kept telling himself that he wasn't going to cry. Not this time. Not again. Each footstep coming down on the packed earth was another stomp holding down his emotions. With a thump, he sat down at the crest of the hill. It was a dark night, and in the distance he could hear scattered dogs barking. Luckily it hadn't rained in more than a week, so the mound was merely dusty, not muddy. Walter brought his knees up to his chest and wrapped his arms around them, peering out at his sad kingdom: the lilac bush with his parents' house behind it, a disintegrating Chrysler LeBaron parked near the treeline for parts, a school desk for a little kid that had somehow made its way onto this part of the property. Not much of a kingdom. Still, he tried to tell himself, it was better than some had.

Lying back, he took another deep breath. It was Sunday night, and another week of school would begin tomorrow. Only a few hours earlier, Walter had been at church, once again at his mother's command. She'd already given up on her husband, convinced the man was going to hell, but she was determined not to lose her son to ways not of the church. She was going to make sure her progeny knew the power and glory of the Lord, no matter what. The fact that during the rest of the week she paid no mind to the lessons of the Gospel was of little importance to the woman. Sunday night in the pews was her get-out-of-jail-free card.[1] She was probably drunk by now. The darker it got, the higher his parents' blood alcohol level. As reliable as the sun rising.

Unlike many kids, Walter looked forward to school. It got him out of here—for a few hours, anyway. The reserve was a small universe with few places to hide. Tomorrow, science class was first thing in the morning and they were studying astronomy. He liked that class. It provided fun and interesting facts. Anything fun and interesting was a bonus for him. More importantly, the class supplied a much-needed distraction. It was fodder for his imagination. A lot of the other students were bored by the math and science of the topic, but not Walter. He loved the possibilities taught in that class. Just last week, their teacher, Mr. Hughes, had told them about the recent rush to discover habitable planets in the galaxy and how scientists would find them. Evidently, there

---

1 A card in the popular board game Monopoly that allows a player to get out of the "jail" position on the board without paying any penalty. Now commonly used metaphorically, as here.

were two ways to ascertain the existence of hospitable planets: by measuring the wobble of the stars resulting from the gravity of a planet yanking on them, or the minute, almost minuscule dimming of the stars' light as a planet orbits between its sun and Earth. Some of the language used was beyond the boy, but still, Walter found it ... cool.

Mr. Hughes had spent half of last class talking about Kepler-186f. It was a planet located in the Cygnus constellation, about 490 light-years away.[1] Very far as the crow flies but in space terms just a couple blocks away. It was one of the first planets to be discovered with an orbital radius similar to Earth's in the habitable zone of another star. According to experts, it was located in what was called the Goldilocks Zone, a reference to Goldilocks and the three bears.[2] Too close to the sun: hot and unlivable. Too far away: cold and unlivable. It was just the right distance away, in this case, in the orbit of a small red dwarf. It was the first of many such discoveries in the last few years.

Walter could hear another dog barking, this time on the other side of the reserve. It sounded like one of his Uncle Dick's hounds. He hoped it wouldn't be at it all night. Studying the sky, he managed to find Cygnus. He had learned that much in class. Somewhere in that group of stars sat Kepler-186f. His teacher had said there was still a lot more to learn about the planet, but the fact that it might be Earth-like, and support life, was just amazing. Were there boys there, discontent or otherwise? Did they have the same dreams and problems as the ones here on Earth did?

Walter sighed. He hoped life there—if it did exist—was a little more interesting, and happier, than life down here. Lying there on the mound of dirt, he closed his eyes and wished he could send his spirit up into the heavens.

* * *

Eric hated the *thump thump thump* of the atmospherics. They were so loud and the vibrations rattled across the whole settlement, all four square kilometres of it. No matter where you were in the huge octagonal enclosure, you could always feel the repetitive shudder as the atmospherics converted the indigenous atmosphere into oxygen. Most citizens had grown used to it and barely noticed the rumbling anymore, but for some reason Eric could feel every single tremor every single time. Lying in bed, he could count the seconds between each successive boom—usually four and a half—and then the next one would sound.

His bunk, inserted ergonomically into the wall at the back of his father's

1 An Earth-sized planet orbiting the star Kepler-186, one of the first planets in another solar system deemed possibly habitable.

2 An English fairy tale dating to the nineteenth century. In the most popular version of the story, a young blonde girl named Goldilocks breaks into the home of three bears and eats their porridge; the first bowl is too hot, the second too cold, and the third just right.

locale (the new Keplerspeak for "apartment"). While functional in the optimal usage of apartment space, it barely gave him room to turn over in frustration. Tonight, like most nights, sleep was eluding him, chased away by the constant heartbeat of Plymroc. The name, with its connections to Old Earth, was a contraction of Plymouth Rock, a symbolic name for this new and daring settlement on a foreign planet.[1]

Feeling exasperated by his sensitivity, Eric rose and put on his jumpsuit. It looked like it would be another night of wandering the hallways and labs of Plymroc until he tired himself out and forced his body to sleep. He thought this even though he knew exactly where he was going. He went there every night he couldn't sleep. One of the technicians had even given him the security code, remarking that Eric almost spent more time there than he did.

As expected, twenty Kepler minutes later, Eric showed up at the Astronosphere. He considered this place the doorway to the galaxy. Inside its walls, the young man could access all aspects of the galaxy in a few minutes, though that was a misnomer. Time was a tricky concept in the world of astronomy. Light-years were not a measurement of time but of distance. And in the four or five minutes it would take him to load the computers and access any one of the numerous technological arrays that scanned the heavens, the information he would be looking at would be hours, weeks, years, more than likely millenniums old. But the important thing was he could look at them now, regardless of when the visible light or gamma rays or x-rays had begun their journey across the universe.

Eric's father, like many people in the settlement, had several responsibilities. He worked in hydroponics as well as metallurgical structuring. The founders of Plymroc felt that focusing on one field of expertise for the rest of your life, so far away from most Earth-like diversions, could create psychological problems. So most Keplerites juggled two professions to keep the mind active. This way, each individual could flex different parts of their cognizance.

His father had never noticed Eric's midnight absences. He was always too busy or too tired. Although it was twenty-two years old, the settlement of Plymroc was far from complete. It was a never-ending construction site with priority given to such necessities as atmospherics upgrades and water purification. Right now, the list on the original Schedule of Priorities drawn up on landing was only two-thirds finished. It was estimated another twelve to fourteen years were needed before the framework of the settlement would be finalized. It would be that long before his father and many of the other colonists would be released from their twelve-hour workdays. Eric's mother had died not long after he was born, what with the med centre being less of a priority than the atmospherics and biofood domes.

---

1 Plymouth Colony was an early English settlement in what would later become the US, created by the English Puritans who landed on board the ship *The Mayflower* in 1620. Plymouth Rock—a literal boulder—was mythologized a century later as the actual landing site.

As he had expected, the Astronosphere was empty. In an attempt to mimic Earth a much as possible, Plymroc founders kept the normal terrestrial manifestations of time on Kepler-186f. The rotation of the planet was only fifty-six minutes longer, so it didn't take much of an effort to adapt it. Plymroc was on night shift now, so he had the lab to himself, as usual.

The Astronosphere was one of the few locations in the settlement specially shielded against the pervasive pulsations of the atmospherics. Because of the delicate nature of the equipment it contained, the room had been precisely designed to act as a buffer against man- and Kepler-made vibrations—the planet had a unique hum because of pulsations emanating from its highly crystalline core. For that reason, Eric had found great peace in the Cosmicon, short for Cosmic Consciousness. The Cosmicon was a small room within the Astronosphere with digital readouts and input monitors scattered in all six directions. If you manipulated things correctly—which Eric was very adept at—you could almost make it look like you were deep in space, alone and floating, surrounded by everything the Big Bang had spit out. Making himself comfortable in the Cosmicon, Eric booted the familiar program and adjusted the levels.

For about seven months now, since he had learned and decoded the programming behind the Cosmicon, he'd been able to shut out the outside world and manoeuvre himself through the far reaches of space. Floating below him in the inkiness was the Crab Nebula; dangling overhead was the distorted Orion's Belt. To his right, the twin suns of Sirius. To his left, a magnification of the massive black hole at the centre of the galaxy.[1] And directly ahead, a strange, far-off place called Earth.

Of course, Eric had never been there. He'd been born several years after Plymroc was founded, but he'd heard the stories of the Origin. The elders of the community even jokingly referred to their exodus as "the Origin Express."[2] Few now got the joke. Eric had visited the archival web, as well as taken the yearly courses in school. Every resident had studied Earth's history, composition, location and people in school, and he had studied far more by himself, in here, alone. Although the planet was far and remote, he held it close and personal. He sure wished he could see an elephant in the flesh, but that was most definitely unlikely to happen.

It was the SATD that got the first settlers here—Space Altering Thrust Drive. It altered the fabric of space, allowing transit in a remarkably short time—though, again, time is relative. It took 490 years for light from Earth's yellow sun to reach Kepler, and it would have taken double, triple, quadruple

---

1 The Crab Nebula is, in part, the remnant of a supernova, visible from Earth in the constellation of Taurus. Orion's Belt is the name for three bright star systems visible from Earth, seemingly in a straight line, in the constellation of Orion. Sirius is a bright binary star visible in the constellation Canis Major. Current research suggests that most large galaxies have supermassive black holes at their centre.

2 A play on "Orient Express," a train that ran from Paris, France, to Istanbul, Türkiye, starting in 1883.

that amount of time for a spaceship to traverse that distance by conventional means. The SATD took only twenty years, the problem being it was a one-way trip. The drive burns itself out. The citizens of Plymroc could try to build another one to return with, but why? They would travel for twenty years to settle this planet, only to spend five years and much of their limited resources building a new SATD, then travel for another twenty years to return to Earth. Not much point in that.

Eric knew every nuance and shade of that far-off blue planet. Kepler-186f had more of a dull greenish-grey tinge to it, unlike Earth's fabulous bright cerulean. It was unlikely he would ever set foot on Earth, but there was no harm in visiting it with his eyes or mind.

The image in front of him had taken 490 years to reach Kepler-186f. Again, in galactic terms, that wasn't very long. The Earth he was looking at was very different from the Earth he knew was there now. It was like looking into a time machine. When the sun's light had bounced off the planet's surface and begun its journey across the cosmos to this hidden part of the galaxy, the human race had not even flown in planes yet. It was just a hundred or so years after somebody named Columbus had sailed across what had been thought of as an impenetrable ocean, navigating by the stars, and landed on a continent populated by people who no doubt had their own ideas about the stars and planets far above them.

Once Columbus had landed, colonies had spread, and eventually people from those same colonies had crossed what they thought was an even more difficult and impenetrable terrain—the vastness of space.

Maybe right now, looking up at him from somewhere down on that far-away planet, was another young man just like him, looking up at the heavens, stargazing.

Wouldn't that be something, Eric thought.

Dilman Dila (b. 1977)

Dilman Dila is a Ugandan SF writer and filmmaker who also works in fantasy and horror genres. His stories have been nominated for multiple awards, and his film *The Felistas Fable* (2013) received several awards, including Film of the Year, at the 2014 Uganda Film Festival. His collection of stories, *Where Rivers Go to Die* (2023), was a finalist for the 2024 Philip K. Dick Award.

Note on the text: "The Last Storyteller" was first published in 2020 (copyright 2019) in the collection *Afrofuturism*, curated by Justina Cruickshank, which focussed on works by authors from Malawi, Botswana, Nigeria, South Africa, Uganda, and Kenya. The story was republished in *Where Rivers Go to Die*, with several small and more significant edits. The later publication is followed here.

"The Last Storyteller" (2019)

SHE woke up before the sun and flew down to the lake. They still called it a lake even though it no longer had water and a city sprawled in the basin. Most houses were shaped like fish with mouths gaping at the sky, eyes glowing, while those that belonged to the leaders looked like boats. Aya perched the bruka[1] on a rock that fishermen on canoes had once used as a natural pier, but which now sat on top of a cliff. She looked down at the waking city. Particles of ice on the rock and on sculptures of dead trees around her caught the light from the fish eyes, giving it a pinkish hue. The heater threw a red glow onto her face, and it left her yearning for fresh air, as though she were stuck in a hole underground. The noise of early traffic wafted to her like music from the shakes of a thousand gourds. Bruka wings flapped in the city lights, sailing past the open fish mouths like prey fleeing predators.

She could not get his face out of her mind.

She could not remember him.

The sky brightened, and the city lights started to go out. Aya glanced at the thermometer and saw that the air outside had warmed up considerably. The ice had started to drip. She stepped out of the bruka, pulling a thermal blanket tight around her, and greedily sucked in the fresh air. She let the blanket slip off her shoulders, and the chill bit into her skin. She walked around, stumping her boots into the wet stone, hugging herself, rubbing her palms against her arms, and yet she could not get rid of his face.

The sun came up. For about an hour it would be nice and warm and friendly. She flipped on her hat's visor to protect her eyes, and the city

1 The "bruka" is a flying vessel that appears elsewhere in Dila's work. In the story "How My Father Became a God" (2015), the narrator's father invents the bruka, and names it after an eagle captured by a boy who then flew on the eagle's back.

transformed into a beautiful landscape, from nondescript steel structures, gray and gloomy in the mist, to a multitude of bright and happy colors as though an artbot had been playing with paint. The fish eyes now looked like gems—some were pearls, others diamonds, some marbles—and sunrays bounced off them like lights in a nightclub of dead civilizations. The last of the ice melted away. She could still see her breath, bluish against the warm sky, and she wished she could magically read her past in it. Then she would probably know who exactly he was.

She could not go back home. He was there. He said he was her husband.

Aya walked up a stone path under the sculpture of dead trees, and for a moment she wondered what it had felt like to sit under a real tree. Ancient poets described the music leaves made as a breeze rustled them and the song of birds perched on the branches and that it was considered good luck if a bird dropped shit on you. For more than a year she had wondered what it would feel like to fly her bruka alongside a bird. If the bird would know her ornithopter[1] was a machine or if it would mistake it for another bird. There were tales of eagles ripping drones out of the sky, but scientists and historians were not sure if the eagles thought the drones were rivals or if they foresaw their death and tried to fight back.

The first bruka took to the air nearly a decade after the last bird had gone down, so there was no way of knowing how the two would have related to each other. She had become obsessed with this relationship, and she ended up telling a story about it. She thought the protagonist was entirely from her imagination until last night, hardly ten hours after she released the veepic, when he showed up at her doorstep with an electronic flower in one hand.

It emitted a perfume that she vaguely remembered, a scent her mother had loved and hummed a tune that her nanny had sung to her when she was still in kindergarten. Her nanny claimed to have seen real bees hovering on real flowers. She claimed that they made this kind of sound as they sucked out nectar. She insisted hers was the right tune and the one they played at the museum was fake, probably from a robobee. Aya had not heard it in nearly thirty years. It soothed her, so she did not scream at seeing her protagonist in flesh and blood, nor did she slam the door in his face. She had stood there like a stone sculpture, wondering if she were having a nightmare or if someone had already seen her veepic and printed out a copy of the protagonist as some kind of joke. It had to be someone who knew her intimately, who knew how she would react to that scent and tune.

He had cut his finger and bled to prove that he was not a print. She had tried to drag up memories from the smell of his blood, and she caught

1 Ornithopters are vehicles that fly by means of flapping wings. Leonardo da Vinci (1452–1519) drew designs for some, but they also have a specific history in SF, dating at least back to Cordwainer Smith's novella *The Boy Who Bought Old Earth* (1964) and later works, from where, possibly, Frank Herbert developed them for his novel *Dune* (1965).

glimpses of an injured man lying on the floor, a knife in his chest ... but that looked like her father.

Aya turned a dial on her helmet. The visor displayed a living mural of what this area had looked like back then with water in the lake, shacks struggling for space underneath trees, bare-chested men dragging big canoes into the water, stalls with stacks of fish, women in colorful dresses cleaning the fish. She walked up a sandy footpath to a large anthill, starkly red against the green vegetation, sat on it, and watched a half-submerged boat a few paces away choking in hyacinth, bobbing in the waves, six white birds standing on it, their reflections wavy on the water. Her veepic had come to her as she looked at this boat, at the birds dipping their heads into the water in an endless loop. She had wondered what was in the water, and she had seen a corpse. Him. And the veepic had fallen into her just like that.

Now she again looked at the white birds on the boat, watched their heads dipping into the greenish water, hoping it would trigger something, a long lost memory, an image, anything, something that would tell her that she indeed was married to the man she had imagined. Surely, the mural had answers since it gave her the story.

She stared until her eyes hurt. Nothing. Not even a reliving of the trippy exhilaration she experienced when the story came to her. Nothing. Just another image of a dead civilization.

She closed her eyes tight, willing the pain to go away.

Dead? Had it even existed? Had birds really filled the skies? Had trees and plants really grown all over the planet with all kinds of animals feeding off them? Had there really been a lake with boats and fish? What if the past was a lie? What if it had always been a gray and dreary world of stone and steel with some mega sensory implant giving the universe an illusion of color and a diversity of species?

She had experienced a historical veepic once that argued that the planet existed as it was because of *life*. That an asteroid with life, which was dying because the asteroid was too small to support it, fell on a bare planet and then life found a chance to *live*, and so it engineered the formation of water, of an atmosphere, of gravity, and over billions of years it built for itself a proper home. Life.

She turned the dial on her glasses, and when she opened her eyes again, she saw the street as it actually was: no mural, no birds, no water, no beautiful lakeside. Just plain gray steel stuck on bare gray rocks.

And hunger.

She walked away from the lakeside to a large building in the distance, which gleamed in the early morning sun. It was shaped like the shacks in the motion mural, rectangular walls and roof, rectangular windows and doors, and not for the first time she wondered why her forefathers had been obsessed with geometrical houses. The other popular design, which stood next to this building, was circular with a cone-shaped roof. She walked into the circular building.

A restaurant. She turned the dial on her visor, and the bare steel benches morphed into décor from the past—the fake past. She sat on a round, three-legged stool at a round table meant for twelve people. There were two other patrons, each at a huge table that emphasized their loneliness and each with a veepic headset over their faces, as a robotic arm fed them breakfast. Aya could tell from the icon blinking in the center of the headset that the person nearest her, whose gender she could not tell, was experiencing *Birds on a Boat*. Aya stiffened, watching the zee's body language to see if zee was enjoying the veepic, excited that it had indeed topped as early statistics had suggested. "People are hungry for a human story," one comment had said, that "It was easy to get into this story because you could feel it digs into humanity in a way storybots never can." She had been skeptical about this kind of praise, but never before had she walked into a random restaurant and found someone experiencing her veepic.

Her table beeped. A menu glowed. She tapped on an icon for breakfast, and instantly a waitress strutted out of a door at the extreme end of the room with a tray of food. Even from that distance, Aya could tell she was a print. Her eyes were green, and lights from the window bounced off her chocolate-coloured mercury skin. When she was near enough Aya could hear a faint whirring from inside her and a steady *thud-thud-thud* that imitated heartbeats. The waitress gave her a smile, put the food on the table, and then glided away, her heels clicking against the steel floor. The wall opened, and the waitress vanished.

At one corner of the table, the icon of a veepic headset glowed. She tapped on it, and a yellow bag parachuted from the ceiling onto the table. She took out the headset, and the bag returned into the ceiling. She wore the headset, feeling a pinch on her nape as a sensory cable touched the implant at the base of her skull. A row of veepics presented themselves. To the left were the topping stories, with *Birds on a Boat* at number four, the only human-made story in the top fifty. The row below that was a list of veepics she had loved in the past and similar veepics she had not yet experienced from storytellers whose channels she had subscribed to. At the bottom of the screen were suggested veepics. She dithered, wondering if she could get into the number one topper, which she had not yet experienced, but she could not take him off her mind, so she decided to experience *Birds on a Boat* for the first time as a non-storyteller.

The moment she tapped on its icon, the restaurant vanished, and she …

… is sitting on a white plastic chair in a rectangular room with a dusty floor. She is pleased to find the room packed. She glances at a picture framed on the wall to sees the stats. A million experiences already and steadily counting. Music with a lot of drums and guitars throbs from a radio with creaky speakers. A bored waiter dances by himself at one end while a woman with oversized boobs and masculine beards clips her fingernails from behind a counter. Behind the woman a small service window opens to the kitchen, and Aya glimpses bare-chested cooks sweating over large saucepans on charcoal stoves. The windows are large, rectangular, with burglar-proof iron bars and yellow curtains fluttering in the breeze. Paint is peeling off the walls, which were once cream colored but are now a dusty brown. Through the windows she glimpses the world outside, houses with red brick walls and rusty iron-sheet roofs, trees whose leaves whistle in the breeze, caked with dust from the dirt road.

The table is wooden, and she feels the living warmth of the rough surface, so unlike the smooth, cold steel she is used to. The waiter brings her a menu, still dancing to the music, and she chooses a katogo[1] of goat offals cooked with matooke.[2] She watches other people as she awaits her order and is pleased to see them smile. The waiter brings her a clay bowl of steaming bananas and goat offal. She picks up the fork and stuffs food into her mouth. It is surprisingly hot. She tastes salt in the crunchy goat innards, pepper in the mushy bananas, tomatoes and onions in the soup, and it gives her a smile.

Her heartbeat quickens as he walks in. The door has a curtain made out of beads, which rattle as he brushes in. He glances at her, probably realizing she is his creator. For a moment she thinks he'll not follow the script and will come straight to her table. He gives her a slight nod and walks up to a woman eating millet porridge and a mango. The woman does not smile. These two, and the waiter and the woman behind the counter, are the only characters. The rest are real people experiencing the tale.

Magara. That was the name she gave him. Last night he said his name was Obaraf, given to a person born on a day that ice does not melt at sunrise. Akello. The name she gave her. Last night he said she was called Aya. *Her* name. They were married.

He smiles at his wife. She does not smile back. She pulls a photograph out of her bag and puts it on the table in front of him. The photograph is of him and another woman. He chuckles. A storybot would have made him protest dramatically, even theatrically, not a chuckle, as if she has told a joke. This, commentators said, made the story truly human. They could read guilt in that chuckle. Akello's reaction, again, is nothing like a storybot would come up with, not overly dramatic. She smiles, picks up a knife on the table as if she is going to cut the fruit, and stabs him in the chest. Just as if she is playfully poking him. His blood squirts onto her face, but that does not take away her smile. She leaves the knife in his chest, and he slips onto the floor. She picks up her spoon and continues to eat her porridge.

Her father died like that. Her mother had stabbed him after she caught him with another woman. He lay on the floor with the knife in his chest, his blood staining the steel tiles, little Aya watching from the doorway.

Was it really her father?

Last night he had shown him[3] the scar on his chest and said a doctor had saved his life.

---

1 A traditional Ugandan breakfast.

2 A type of banana.

3 Possibly a typo for "her."

She could not watch anymore. She took off the headset, and at once, the restaurant vanished. She was back in a steel and sterile room, eating something bland. She could no longer taste the salty, crunchy, greasy intestines, the mushy peppery bananas, the oniony soup. Her mouth was full of something spongy. She spat, and a blob of something that looked like mucus splattered on the table. The robotic arm protruding from her plate dangled in the air, holding a spoonful of goo uncertainly. Lights blinked on the plate, urging her to reconnect.

Why could she not remember him?

She hurried out of the restaurant. The sun had grown hostile. She tapped a button on her shoulder, and her pants and shirt turned into a flowing gown that swept the ground as she walked. She turned a knob on her helmet, and it became a wide-brimmed hat. She pressed another button on her shoulder, and a sensory cable snaked out of her helmet into her nape. She no longer felt the heat. There were a few more people in the street, all with flowing gowns that made them look like daytime ghosts, their heads hidden inside gadgets that made them think they were in a town of a long-dead civilization under a friendly sun with tons of birds and animals and insects living happily with humans.

Her bruka was too hot to touch even with the sensory implant warding off the sun. She used a remote control feature on her wristband to open it. She climbed in. She tapped the button on her shoulder, and the gown transformed back into pants and sleeveless shirt while the hat retreated into being just a helmet. She checked the time and saw she still had thirty minutes before the records offices would allow visitors. She watched the city below, refusing to wear a visor to see the virtual vibrancy, instead seeing it as it was—nondescript sculptures of fish and boats. Fewer brukas flew above the open mouths, racing by too fast for her to enjoy the flapping of their wings as she had when still a little child.

The minutes passed. She tried to fill her mind with things that would make her forget him at least for the moment, but she could not get his face out of her mind nor that knife scar on his chest. She thought about her mother and wondered if she still lived in the Elephant City.

Aya had never liked that city. She thought the elephantine buildings were graceless, even repulsive. The stuffed elephants in the museum did not have that many colors. They were mostly gray with white tusks. Her mother, however, had loved to sit on the top of her building, which was a calf, and watch the herd of adults around her.

Mama would definitely have answers, but Mama would want to talk about other things, things that Aya would rather stayed buried deep in her subconscious. Had she wanted her husband completely out of her mind, just as she wanted to forget her mother? It did not make sense, for she could not afford memory surgery. She could now, with her story a topper, though she would have to wait a week, until after the credits had shown up in her account. Until then, she had to continue living in the guts of a fish too small to swallow her properly.

She had not created it entirely on her own. She had used an app that made it easy to quickly create stories that could compete with bots. She did not use a cerebral implant. She refused to have that. She did not want to become only half-human. She did not mind the sensory implant. It only messed with her senses like a drug, but a cerebral implant controlled how a person thought and often led to madness and sudden death. Some storytellers preferred it to compete against bots, and though they achieved success, audiences quickly reject the stories as being more bot than human, regurgitating the same old crap that bots had been recycling for nearly a century. Yet people needed those formulaic bot tales to survive. For a human to make an equivalent would require many years of hard work, and the results were not often reliable.

Then came the app. Paromit. She had been skeptical at first. Many software programs had come before it, and none delivered; but this was a true revolution. She simply had to type in what was in her mind, and the app would render it into an image that came alive in a virtual world.

She could not have dragged him out of her memory. There was no way. She started with a random picture of a man she had found in the datanets and then kept instructing Paromit to add features to his face and remove others. She kept modifying it until the face of the protagonist came about as she saw it in her mind.

Had she really not dragged him out of her memory? Was he purely her imagination?

Mama would have answers.

No. Not Mama. She was not even sure if Mama was still alive, just because she did not get a notification from The Department of Birth and Death Registration did not mean Mama was still alive. The bots might have sent the message, and she deleted it unread. She could not think of Mama, she had to hope there were records somewhere that would give her answers.

She put on her headset and now she …

… is in the Population Records Office at the Department of BDR. She wants to check for her mother to see if she is still alive, that her answers might be more satisfying than a collection of images that might not mean anything, but she can't talk to Mama. Not just yet. There is a crowd already waiting to access records, nearly a dozen people lining up to use the six data booths.

If the credits had already been reflected in her account, she would not have had to wait. She would have paid to jump the queue. Now she must wait her turn in the line. She has the option of wandering into other interesting worlds, but she thinks she deserves the torture of watching people standing in a queue in a room that's steel gray with no walls and no floor and no ceiling, with the only furniture being six blue booths.

Everybody else has a secondary headset on, and she notices with satisfaction that several of them are experiencing *Birds on a Boat*. She wonders what scenes they started at. She would have to go check the stats to see which parts people frequented the most, maybe before the stabbing when Magara and Akello are all over themselves in love. Maybe after the stabbing when Akello is in jail and in love with her cellmate and Magara is a half-human/half-robot zombie-like creature that can barely remember the love he enjoyed before his death.

The story meanders, much like real life, and if anyone started at any scene, it would not be too hard to follow, unlike some storybot stories that tried too hard to be clever or that were incomprehensible to humans, though set in beautiful and addictive psychedelic worlds.

Her turn to use a booth comes sooner than she expected, and she is thankful for it. Her fingers tremble as they hover on the keypad. What should she search for, her own records, or his? Finally, she thinks it is safer to start with her. She searches for her marriage records.

Nothing.

She searches for any memory surgeries that she might have had.

Nothing.

She sighs in relief.

She punches in his name, searches, but gets a single line on the screen. This person has never existed.

She walks out of the booth. Her knees are weak. She walks away from the queue, but the room has no visible wall or ceiling or floor, just a blank grayness, and she has gone nearly a kilometer from the booths before she remembers where she actually is. She takes off the headset and she …

… plunged back into her bruka. The sun had grown even more hostile, and the horizon had become nothing but a white, featureless strip, the sky a sick, yellowish color, like pus.

He must be a print. Nothing else could explain him. A real-life print that bled real blood and had the scent of a real person. Maybe the machine had become so efficient that it could now print a real-life person. Maybe it had been like this all along from the beginning of time, printing out birds and animals and insects to live alongside humans until something went wrong and it could not make the prints anymore and now it had repaired the fault and was printing out real humans to replace humans.

He must be a nightmare.

Mama might know.

No. Not Mama.

Maybe Mama printed him out to force her to talk. He had, after all, told her something similar, that, when she made him the protagonist of *Birds on a Board*,[1] she subconsciously wanted him to reconcile with her. So he had come straight to talk to her. *I never stopped loving you.* His voice sounded like a rusty

1 In the first publication, this reads "Birds on a Boat," as elsewhere in the story. It has been left here to reflect the later version, and because of the mention of the board, below, which occurs in both versions.

engine struggling to come to life, the kind of voice that alcohol had ruined. *Even when I had your knife in my chest, I never stopped loving you, and you put the knife in my chest because you could not stop loving me.*

No!

She had gotten the idea one evening as she sat on the cliff, watching the fish city below, admiring the brukas flying over the boats. She had walked to the anthill and seen the half-submerged canoe, the birds, and the imaginary corpse under the boat. The story had fallen to her in one piece: how the man died, why he ended up under a submerged board, and that the birds were dipping their heads into the water to eat him. She had meant it as a metaphor of her own life. She imagined that she would die and would be rotten before the neighbours discovered her. Her house would know she was dead, of course. It would notify the Department of Births and Deaths and then chuck her into the recycle system. Her neighbours would only know of her death when a new tenant came in, probably months after she was long gone.

If she had lived in the past, however fake the past seemed, she would have had pets—a dog, a cat, maybe a bird in a cage—and upon her death, even if the neighbours did not know, her pets would have eaten her. If they did not, she would have ended up in a grave to feed maggots. It would be better to die in that imaginary past. It would have been better for something other than metal to eat her.

Somehow, he was right. She made the film to send *him* a message.

Not him, the ghost that had shown up at her doorstep, but someone else, someone who would interpret her veepic and fall in love with her and grow old with her and probably have children with her, natural children that would grow in her womb the old-fashioned way.

Her nanny had once told her a folk story, which did not require any headsets to be enjoyed, just words falling out of her tongue, about a boy who had wished to have a friend. He sat under a tree that he did not know was a home for the ancestors. A spirit heard his wish and materialized into another boy. He was overjoyed to finally have a friend, but then it was not a good spirit and the story had a horrible ending.

If he was not a print, then he was a nightmare. He was her wish coming true.

Mama would have answers.

No!

Maybe *it* printed him as a gift to her.

It. Life. The machine. It needs people like her, for stories fuel its survival. It knows of her rare ability to imagine. It knows she will make better veepics if she were happier. Her house must have known how lonely she was, that she spends days not talking to anyone, refusing to commit to a relationship with anyone, so it prints him to ease her loneliness, for it knows individual parts need to bond with other individual parts to be happy. It knows that if It prints something straight out of her imagination, she would commit to a relationship with *It.*

If she went back to the records office and this time searched for him under prints, would she know the truth?

Probably.

Probably not.

Probably he was just her imagination. Her nightmare.

Mama would have answers.

No! No! No!

She ignited the bruka and pedaled hard as it leapt into the air, its wings flapping against its body. She flew away from Fish City, away from the sun, into the harsh whiteness of the horizon. She did not have to go back to the squalor of Fish City. She had nothing she needed there. He was still in her house, squeezed inside the guts like a worm, waiting for her, but she would not go back to him.

Everything she needed was in her bruka. With the success of *Birds on a Boat*, she could find a new house on a loan. Maybe she would go to Flower City, where they ate real food that grew in special gardens protected from the sun, where they walked around without special gowns and visors because they lived in a dome that kept them safe from the environment. Surely, she could now afford it. Surely, there were enough empty apartments for her to easily get one on credit.

She would not go back home. Not to the ghost that waited for her.

Select Bibliography

This bibliography includes both a (*very*) brief selection of recommended readings in and about SF, as well as the information for works cited in the introduction, headers, and explanatory notes.

Aldiss, Brian. *Billion Year Spree: The History of Science Fiction*. Doubleday, 1973.

Anderson, Douglas A. "Stevens, Francis." *Women in Science Fiction and Fantasy*, edited by Robin Anne Reid, vol. 2, Greenwood, 2009, pp. 289-90.

Anderson, Reynaldo, and Charles E. Jones, editors. *Afrofuturism 2.0: The Rise of Astro-Blackness*. Lexington, 2016.

Arabilious: Anthology of Arab Futurism. Future Fiction, 2024.

Attebery, Brian. *Decoding Gender in Science Fiction*. Routledge, 2002.

Attebery, Brian, and Veronica Hollinger, editors. *Parabolas of Science Fiction*. Wesleyan UP, 2013.

Ballard, J.G. "Which Way to Inner Space?" *New Worlds*, vol. 118, no. 40, 1969, pp. 2–3, 116–18.

Barnes, John. "America's Remarkable Record-breaking Ships." *Marine Professional*, 16 April 2021, *Institute of Marine Science and Technology*, www.imarest.org/resource/remarkable-speed-record-breaking-ships-from-the-usa.html.

Barr, Marlene S. *Alien to Femininity: Speculative Fiction and Feminist Theory*. Greenwood, 1987.

——, editor. *Afro-Future Females: Black Writers Chart Science Fiction's Newest New-Wave Trajectory*. Ohio State UP, 2008.

Behr, Ira Steven. *The Ferengi Rules of Acquisition*. Pocket Books, 1995.

Bell, Andrea L., and Yolanda Molina-Gavilán, editors. *Cosmos Latinos: An Anthology of Science Fiction from Latin America and Spain*. Wesleyan UP, 2003.

Bell, John, and Lesley Choyce, editors. *Visions from the Edge: An Anthology of Atlantic Canadian Science Fiction and Fantasy*. Pottersfield, 1981.

Bellamy, Brent Ryan. *Remainders of the American Century: Post-Apocalyptic Novels in the Age of US Decline*. Wesleyan UP, 2021.

Blay, Yaba Amgborale. "Asamando." *Encyclopedia of African Religion*, edited by Molefi Kete Asante and Ama Mazama, Sage, 2009, p. 69.

Boontharm, Dinar. *The Sultanate of Banten AD 1750–1808: A Social and Cultural History*. 2003. University of Hull, PhD Dissertation.

Bourdieu, Paul. *Distinction: A Social Critique of the Judgement of Taste*. Translated by Richard Nice, Harvard UP, 1984.

Campbell, Ian, editor. *Arabic Science Fiction*. Palgrave Macmillan, 2018.

Canavan, Gerry, and Eric Carl Link, editors. *Cambridge History of Science* Fiction, Cambridge UP, 2019.

Canavan, Gerry, and Kim Stanley Robinson. *Green Planets: Ecology and Science Fiction*. Wesleyan UP, 2014.

Champion, Giulia, Roxanne Douglas, and Stephen Shapiro, editors. *Decolonizing the Undead: Rethinking Zombies in World-Literature, Film, and Media*. Bloomsbury, 2022.

Changa, Ibo. "Juju." *Encyclopedia of African Religion*, edited by Molefi Kete Asante and Ama Mazama, Sage, 2009, pp. 355–56.

Chu, Seo-Young. *Do Metaphors Dream of Literal Sheep? A Science-Fictional Theory of Representation*. Harvard UP, 2010.

Clarke, Arthur C. "Clarke's Third Law on UFO's." Letters to the Editor, *Science*, vol. 159, no. 3812, 1968.

Clute, John, and David Langdon, editors. *The Encyclopedia of Science Fiction*, 4th edition, Ansible Editions, 2021, https://sf-encyclopedia.com.

Collier, John. "The Chaser." *New Yorker*, 28 Dec. 1940, p. 14.

Cooke, Simon. "A 'world of method and intrigue': Muriel Spark's Literary Intelligence." *Modernist Cultures*, vol. 16, no. 4, 2021, pp. 488–508.

Cruickshank, Justina, editor. *Afrofuturism*. Heady Mix, 2019.

Csicsery-Ronay, Istvan Jr. *The Seven Beauties of Science Fiction*. Wesleyan UP, 2008.

Dalzell, Tom, and Terry Victor. *Vice Slang*. Routledge, 2008.

Decarnin, Camilla, Eric Garber, and Lyn Paleo, editors. *Worlds Apart: An Anthology of Lesbian and Gay Science Fiction and Fantasy*. Alyson, 1986.

DeGraw, Sharon. *The Subject of Race in American Science Fiction*. Routledge, 2007.

Delany, Samuel R. *The American Shore: Meditations of a Tale of Science Fiction by Thomas M. Disch—"Angouleme."* 1978. Introduced by Matthew Cheney, Wesleyan UP, 2014.

——. "Science Fiction and 'Literature'–or, The Conscience of the King." *Starboard Wine: More Notes on the Language of Science Fiction*, revised edition, Wesleyan UP, 2012, pp. 61–81.

——. "Theodore Sturgeon, *In Memoriam*." 1985. *Occasional Views*, vol. 1. Wesleyan UP, 2021, pp. 61–64.

——. *Trouble on Triton: An Ambiguous Heterotopia*. 1976. Wesleyan UP, 1996.

Dery, Mark. "Black to the Future: Interviews with Samuel R. Delany, Greg Tate, and Tricia Rose." *Flame Wars: The Discourse of Cyberculture*, edited by Mark Dery, Duke UP, 1994, pp. 179–222.

Dickson, Melissa. "Charles Wheatstone's Enchanted Lyre and the Spectacle of Sound." *Sound Knowledge: Music and Science in London, 1789–1851*, edited by J.Q. Davies and Ellen Lockhart. U of Chicago P, 2017, pp. 125–44.

Dillon, Grace L., editor. *Walking the Clouds: An Anthology of Indigenous Science Fiction*. U of Arizona P, 2012.

Dorsey, Candas Jane. "Candas Jane Dorsey: Saving the World." *Locus*, vol. 45, no. 2, 2000, pp. 8, 64–66.

Doyle, Arthur Conan. "The Adventure of the Beryl Coronet." *The Strand Magazine*, vol. 3, no. 17, 1892, pp. 511–25.

Du Bois, W.E.B. *The Souls of Black Folk*. 1903. *Writings*, edited by Nathan Huggins, Library of America, 1986, pp. 357–547.

Dunagan, Christopher. "Indians tell Canada, U.S. to put fish first." *Kitsap Sun*, 25 May 1994, pp. A1, A5.

Evans, Arthur B., editor. *Vintage Visions: Essays on Early Science Fiction*. Wesleyan UP, 2014.

Ferreira, Rachel Haywood. *The Emergence of Latin American Science Fiction*. Wesleyan UP, 2011.

Foner, Eric. *The Fiery Trial: Abraham Lincoln and American Slavery*. Norton, 2010.

Franklin, H. Bruce, editor. *Future Perfect: American Science Fiction of the 19th Century*. 4th edition, expanded and revised, Rutgers UP, 1995.

Franklin, H. Bruce. "What Is Science Fiction—And How It Grew." *Reading Science Fiction*, edited by Gunn et al., pp. 23–32.

Freedman, Carl. *Critical Theory and Science Fiction*. Wesleyan UP, 2000.

Gernsback, Hugo. "A New Sort of Magazine." *Amazing Stories*, vol. 1, no. 1, 1926, p. 3.

Gibson, Mary Ellis, editor. *Science Fiction in Colonial India, 1835–1905*. Anthem, 2019.

Gibson, William. *Neuromancer*. Ace, 1984.

——. "Rocket Radio." 1989. *Distrust that Particular Flavor*, Penguin, 2012, pp. 7–18.

Gilman, Charlotte Perkins. *Herland and Related Writings*, edited by Beth Sutton-Ramspeck. Broadview, 2012.

Gloag, John. *A Short Dictionary of Furniture*. Revised and enlarged edition, Allen and Unwin, 1969.

Goodwin, Matthew David, editor. *Latinx Rising: An Anthology of Latinx Science Fiction and Fantasy*. Ohio State UP, 2020.

Griffith, Nicola, and Stephen Pagel, editors. *Bending the Landscape: Science Fiction*. Overlook, 1998.

Gunn, James E., Marleen S. Barr, and Matthew Candelaria, editors. *Reading Science Fiction*. Palgrave, 2009.

Hall, Louis Karoniaktajeh. *The Mohawk Warrior Society: A Handbook on Sovereignty and Survival*. Edited by Philippe Blouin, Matt Peterson, Malek Rasamny and Kahentinetha Rotiskarewake. Between the Lines, 2003.

Hartwell, David G., and Glenn Grant, editors. *Northern Stars: The Anthology of Canadian Science Fiction*. Tor, 1994.

Haslam, Jason. *Gender, Race, and American Science Fiction: Reflections on Fantastic Identities*. Routledge, 2015.

——. "Science Fiction." *Cambridge Companion to the Twentieth-Century American Novel and Politics*, edited by Bryan M. Santin, Cambridge UP, 2023, pp. 142–59.

Hefner, Brooks E. *Black Pulp: Genre Fiction in the Shadow of Jim Crow*. U of Minnesota P, 2021.

Higgins, David M. *Reverse Colonization: Science Fiction, Imperial Fantasy, and Alt-Victimhood*. U of Iowa P, 2021.

"The History of The Music Center." *The Music Center*, www.musiccenter.org/about/about-us/our-story/our-history/.

Hopkins, Pauline Elizabeth. *Of One Blood*. 1902–03. Edited by Eurie Dahn and Brian Sweeney, Broadview P, 2022.

Hopkinson, Nalo, editor. *Whispers from the Cotton Tree Root: Caribbean Fabulist Fiction*. Invisible Cities, 2000.

Hopkinson, Nalo, and Uppinder Mehan, editors. *So Long Been Dreaming: Postcolonial Science Fiction and Fantasy*. Arsenal Pulp, 2004.

Isaacson, Nathaniel. *Celestial Empire: The Emergence of Chinese Science Fiction*. Wesleyan UP, 2017.

James, Edward, and Farah Mendlesohn, editors. *The Cambridge Companion to Science Fiction*. Cambridge UP, 2003.

Jameson, Fredric. *Archaeologies of the Future: The Desire Called Utopia and Other Science Fictions*. London: Verso, 2005.

Ketterer, David. *Canadian Science Fiction and Fantasy*. Indiana UP, 1992.

Kilgore, De Witt Douglas. *Astrofuturism: Science, Race, and Visions of Utopia in Space*. Philadelphia: U of Pennsylvania P, 2003.

Kincaid, Paul. "On the Origins of Genre." *Extrapolation*, vol. 44, no. 4, 2003, pp. 409–19.

Kutzera, Dale. "Star Trek: Deep Space Nine." *Cinefantastique*, vol. 27, no. 4/5, pp. 88-93, 101–02, 108–15.

Landon, Brooks. "The Gernsback Years: Science Fiction and the Pulps in the 1920s and 1930s." Canavan and Link, pp. 135–48.

Lavender, Isiah III. *Afrofuturism Rising: The Literary Prehistory of a Movement*. Ohio State UP, 2019.

——. *Race in American Science Fiction*. Indiana UP, 2011.

Lavender, Isiah III, and Lisa Yaszek, editors. *Literary Afrofuturism in the Twenty-First Century*. Ohio State UP, 2020.

Lokhorst, Gert-Jan C., and Timo T. Kaitaro. "The Originality of Descartes' Theory about the Pineal Gland." *Journal of the History of the Neurosciences*, vol. 10, no. 1, 2001, pp. 6–18.

Luckhurst, Roger. *Science Fiction*. Polity, 2005.

Malacrida, Claudia. *A Special Hell: Institutional Life in Alberta's Eugenic Years*. U of Toronto P, 2015.

Marshall, Alice Kahler. *Pen Names of Women Writers: From 1600 to the Present*. Published by the author, 1985.

"Martian Moon Deimos in High Resolution." *NASA*. 9 March 2009. https://science.nasa.gov/resource/martian-moon-deimos-in-high-resolution-2/, accessed 24 May 2025.

McCaffery, Larry, editor. *Storming the Reality Studio: A Casebook of Cyberpunk and Postmodern Science Fiction*. Duke UP, 1992.

McPhee, Andy. *The Donora Death Fog: Clean Air and the Tragedy of a Pennsylvania Mill Town.* U of Pittsburgh P, 2023.

Merril, Judith, and Emily Pohl-Weary. *Better to Have Loved: The Life of Judith Merril.* Between the Lines, 2002.

Milner, Andrew. *Locating Science Fiction.* Liverpool UP, 2012.

Minnick, Lisa Cohen. *Dialect and Dichotomy: Literary Representations of African American Speech.* U of Alabama P, 2004.

Morgan, Les B., and Ram Karan Sharma. *Croaking Frogs: A Guide to Sanskrit Metrics and Figures of Speech.* Mahodara Press, 2011.

Mufuzi, Friday. "The Practice of Witchcraft and the Changing Patterns of its Paraphernalia in the Light of Technologically Produced Goods as Presented by Livingstone Museum, 1930s–1973." *Zambia Social Science Journal*, vol. 5, no. 1, 2014, pp. 50–71.

Muñoz, José Esteban. *Cruising Utopia: The Then and There of Queer Futurity.* New York UP, 2009.

NASA Hubble Mission Team. "Hubble Takes Portrait of the 'Lost Galaxy.'" *NASA.* 21 January 2021, https://science.nasa.gov/missions/hubble/hubble-takes-portrait-of-the-a-lost-galaxy/, accessed 24 May 2025.

Nelson, Alondra. "Introduction: Future Texts." *Afrofuturism*, special issue of *Social Text*, vol. 20, no. 2, 2002, pp. 1–15.

Okorafor, Nnedi. "Africanfuturism Defined." *Nnedi's Wahala Zone Blog*, 19 Oct. 2019, https://nnedi.blogspot.com/2019/10/africanfuturism-defined.html, accessed 24 May 2025.

——. "The Big Idea: Nnedi Okorafor." *Whatever*, 17 June 2010, https://whatever.scalzi.com/2010/06/17/the-big-idea-nnedi-okorafor/, accessed 24 May 2025.

Pearson, Wendy Gay. "(Re)Reading James Tiptree Jr.'s 'And I Awoke and Found Me Here on the Cold Hill Side.'" *Daughters of Earth: Feminist Science Fiction in the Twentieth Century*, edited by Justine Larbalestier, Wesleyan UP, 2006, pp. 168–89.

Pearson, Wendy Gay, Veronica Hollinger, and Joan Gordon. *Queer Universes: Sexualities in Science Fiction.* Liverpool UP, 2008.

Pennock, Caroline Dodds. *On Savage Shores: How Indigenous Americans Discovered Europe.* Knopf, 2023.

Picker, John M. *Victorian Soundscapes.* Oxford UP, 2003.

Plutarch's Lives. Volume 1, translated and edited by John Langhorne and William Langhorne. Isaiah Thomas, 1804.

Poe, Edgar Allan. *Tales and Sketches, vol. 2: 1843–1849*, edited by Thomas Ollive Mabbott, U of Illinois P, 2000.

Rieder, John. *Colonialism and the Emergence of Science Fiction.* Wesleyan UP, 2008.

——. *SF and the Mass Cultural Genre System.* Wesleyan UP, 2017.

Roberts, Adam. *The History of Science Fiction*, 2nd edition, Palgrave, 2016.

Robinson, Eden. *The Sasquatch at Home: Traditional Protocols and Modern Storytelling*. Henry Kreisel Lecture Series. U of Alberta P, 2011.

Sargent, Pamela, editor. *More Women of Wonder: Science Fiction Novelettes by Women About Women*. Vintage, 1976.

——. *The New Women of Wonder: Recent Science Fiction Stories by Women About Women*. Vintage, 1978.

——. *Women of Wonder: Science Fiction Stories by Women about Women*. Vintage, 1975.

Sawyer, Andy, and David Seed, editors. *Speaking Science Fiction: Dialogues and Interpretations*. Liverpool, UP, 2000.

Scholes, Robert. *Structural Fabulation: An Essay on Fiction of the Future*. U of Notre Dame P, 1975.

Schuyler, George. *Black No More: Being an Account of the Strange and Wonderful Workings of Science in the Land of the Free, A.D. 1933–1940*. 1931. Northeastern UP, 1989.

Scraba, Jeffrey. "Quixotic History and Cultural Memory: Knickerbocker's *History of New York*." *Early American Studies: An Interdisciplinary Journal*, vol. 7, no. 2, 2009, pp. 389–425.

Shawl, Nisi, editor. *New Suns: Original Speculative Fiction by People of Color*. Solaris, 2019.

Smith, Hilda L., and Berenice A. Carroll, editors. *Women's Political and Social Thought: An Anthology*. Indiana UP, 2000.

"Solar System Exploration." *NASA*. https://science.nasa.gov/solar-system/, accessed 24 May 2025.

Stevens, Tyler. "'Sinister Fruitiness': *Neuromancer*, Internet Sexuality and the Turing Test." *Studies in the Novel*, vol. 28, no. 3, 1996, pp. 414–33.

Sturgeon, Theodore. *Argyll: A Memoir*. The Sturgeon Project, 1993.

Sulaiman, Sonia, editor. *Thyme Travellers: An Anthology of Palestinian Speculative Fiction*. Fernwood, 2024.

Suvin, Darko. *Metamorphoses of Science Fiction: On the Poetics and History of a Literary Genre*. 1979. Edited by Gerry Canavan, Peter Lang, 2016.

Szpara, K.M., editor. *Transcendent: The Year's Best Transgender Speculative Fiction*. Lethe, 2016.

Takács, Bogi, editor. *Transcendent 2: The Year's Best Transgender Speculative Fiction*. Lethe, 2017.

——. *Transcendent 3: The Year's Best Transgender Speculative Fiction*. Lethe, 2018.

——. *Transcendent 4: The Year's Best Transgender Speculative Fiction*. Lethe, 2019.

Taylor, Taryne Jade, Isiah Lavender III, Grace L. Dillon, and Bodhisattva Chattopadhyay, editors. *The Routledge Handbook of CoFuturisms*. Routledge, 2024.

Thomas, Sheree R., editor. *Dark Matter: A Century of Speculative Fiction from the African Diaspora*. Warner, 2000.

——, editor. *Dark Matter: Reading the Bones*. Warner, 2004.

"Those Fake Steamship Funnels." *The Literary Digest*, 3 Jan. 1931, p. 13.
Tiptree, James Jr. *Warm Worlds and Otherwise*. Introduced by Robert Silverberg. Ballantine, 1975.
Todorov, Tzvetan. *The Fantastic: A Structural Approach to a Literary Genre*. 1973, translated by Richard Howard, Cornell UP, 1975.
Truth and Reconciliation Commission of Canada. *Canada's Residential Schools: The History, Part 1 Origins to* 1939. The Final Report of the Truth and Reconciliation Commission of Canada, Volume 1. McGill-Queen's UP, 2015.
——. *They Came for the Children: Canada, Aboriginal Peoples, and the Residential Schools*. Truth and Reconciliation Commission of Canada, 2012.
Vint, Sherryl, and Mark Bould. "There Is No Such Thing as Science Fiction." Gunn et al., pp. 43–51.
Wallace, Bruce. "Once Shunned as Racist, Storybook Bestseller in Japan." *Los Angeles Times*, 12 June 2005, https://www.latimes.com/archives/la-xpm-2005-jun-12-fg-bookban12-story.html, accessed 7 May 2025.
Wilson, James Grant, and John Fiske, editors. *Appletons' Cyclopaedia of American Biography*. Appleton, 1888.
Womack, Ytasha L. *Afrofuturism: The World of Black Sci-Fi and Fantasy Culture*. Lawrence Hill, 2013.
Woolfson, M.M. "The Solar System—Its Origin and Evolution." *Quarterly Journal of the Royal Astronomy Society*, vol. 34, 1993, pp. 1–20.
Wu, William F. *The Yellow Peril: Chinese Americans in American Fiction, 1850–1940*. Archon, 1982.
Yaszek, Lisa. *The Self Wired: Technology and Subjectivity in Contemporary Narrative*. Routledge, 2002.
Yaszek, Lisa, editor. *The Future Is Female! 25 Classic Science Fiction Stories by Women, from Pulp Pioneers to Ursula K. Le Guin*. Library of America, 2018.
——. *The Future Is Female! Volume Two, The 1970s: More Classic Science Fiction Stories by Women*. Library of America, 2022.

Credits

Asimov, Isaac. "Liar," illustration by Charles Schneeman, originally published in *Astounding Science Fiction* 27.3 (May 1941): 43–55. Story Copyright © 1941 by Asimov Holdings LLC. Used in the UK by permission of William Morris Endeavor Entertainment, LLC., on behalf of the Estate of Isaac Asimov. From *I, Robot*, used by permission of Bantam Books, an imprint of Random House, a division of Penguin Random House LLC. All rights reserved.

Ballard, J.G. "The Index," also published in *The Complete Stories of J.G. Ballard*, introduction by Martin Amis, W.W. Norton, 2010. Copyright © 1977, 1990, 2001 by J.G. Ballard. Copyright © 2009 by the Estate of J.G. Ballard. Reprinted by permission of The Wylie Agency LLC., on behalf of the author's estate (Canada/UK). Used by permission of W.W. Norton & Company, Inc (US).

Bell, Derrick. "The Space Traders," originally part of "A Forum on Derrick Bell's Civil Rights Chronicles," 1989 Sanford E. Sarasohn Memorial Lecture, S*t. Louis University Law Journal* 34 (1990): 393. Reprinted with permission of the Saint Louis University Law Journal © 1990 St. Louis University School of Law, St. Louis, Missouri.

Bradbury, Ray. "There Will Come Soft Rains," *The Martian Chronicles*, Doubleday, 1950; Simon & Schuster, 2012. Copyright © 1950 by the Crowell Collier Publishing Company, renewed 1977 by Ray Bradbury. Reprinted by permission of Don Congdon Associates Inc.

Butler, Octavia E. "Speech Sounds," *Bloodchild and Other Stories*. Originally published in *Isaac Asimov's Science Fiction Magazine* (December 1983). Copyright © 1983, 1995 Octavia E. Butler. Reprinted with the permission of the Octavia E. Butler Estate and The Permissions Company, LLC, on behalf of Seven Stories Press, sevenstories.com.

Cadigan, Pat. "Angel," *Isaac Asimov's Sci Fi Magazine* (May 1987), Davis Publications. Copyright © 1987 by Pat Cadigan. Reprinted by permission of Mic Cheetham Literary Agency, on behalf of the author.

Chiang, Ted. "Exhalation," also published in *Exhalation: Stories*, Alfred A. Knopf (US); Picador (UK), 2019. Copyright © 2008 Ted Chiang. Used by permission of Alfred A. Knopf, an imprint of the Knopf Doubleday Publishing Group, a division of Penguin Random House LLC. All rights reserved. Reproduced by permission of Macmillan Publishers International Limited (UK edition).

Clarke, Arthur C. "The Nine Billion Names of God," previously published in *The Nine Billion Names of God*, Harcourt, Brace & World Inc., 1967. Copyright © 1967 Arthur C. Clarke. Reprinted by permission of the author and the author's agents, David Higham Associates and Scovil Galen Ghosh Literary Agency, Inc.

Delany, Samuel R. "Among the Blobs." Copyright © 1988 Samuel R. Delany. Reprinted by permission of Coffee House Press and The Bent Agency, on behalf of the author.

Dick, Philip K. "The Electric Ant." Copyright © 1970 by Philip K. Dick. Used by permission of The Wylie Agency LLC., on behalf of the Philip K. Dick Trust, and International Literary Properties.

Dila, Dilman. "The Last Storyteller." Reprinted courtesy of the author.

Dorsey, Candas Jane. "(Learning about) Machine Sex," from *Machine Sex and Other Stories*, Tesseract Books, 1988. Reprinted courtesy of the author.

Gibson, William. "The Gernsback Continuum," first appeared in *Universe 11*, Doubleday, 1981; reprinted in *Burning Chrome*, Harper Voyager, 2003. Copyright © 1986 William Gibson. Reprinted by permission of SLL/ Sterling Lord Literistic, Inc.

Haldeman, Joe. "DX," *In the Field of Fire*, ed. Jeanne Van Buren Dann and Jack Dann, T. Doherty Associates, 1987. Copyright © 1987 Joe Haldeman. Published by permission of Joe Haldeman c/o The Lotts Agency, Ltd.

Hill, James H. "Space Ship," originally published in *The Afro-American*, No. 6–9 (Sep–Oct 1950). Courtesy of the AFRO American Newspapers Archives.

Hopkinson, Nalo. "Something to Hitch Meat to," *Skin Folk: Stories*, Warner Books, Inc., 2001. Copyright © 2001 by Nalo Hopkinson. Reprinted by permission of Donald Maass Literary Agency, on behalf of the author.

Jemisin, N.K. "Too Many Yesterdays, Not Enough Tomorrows," *How Long 'Til Black Future Month?: Stories*, Orbit Books, 2018. Copyright © 2004 by N.K. Jemisin. Reprinted by permission of The Knight Agency, on behalf of the author.

Le Guin, Ursula K. "The Ones Who Walk Away from Omelas." First appeared in *New Dimensions 3*, 1973. Reprinted in *The Wind's Twelve*

Quarters, HarperCollins, 1975. Copyright © 1973 Ursula K. Le Guin. Reprinted by permission of Ginger Clark Literary, LLC.

Liu, Ken. "The Bookmaking Habits of Select Species," *The Paper Menagerie and Other Stories*, Gallery/Saga Press, an imprint of Simon & Schuster, 2016. Copyright © 2016 Ken Liu. Reprinted in the UK by permission of the author and the author's agents, Scovil Galen Ghosh Literary Agency, Inc. Reprinted elsewhere by permission of Simon & Schuster, LLC. All rights reserved.

Lubrin, Canisia. From *Voodoo Hypothesis: Poems*, Buckrider Books, 2017. Copyright © 2017 Canisia Lubrin. Reprinted by permission of Wolsak and Wynn Publishers Ltd.

Merril, Judith. "Dead Center," *Magazine of Fantasy and Sci Fi* (November), Fantasy House, 1954. Reprinted by permission of Virginia Kidd Literary Agency, on behalf of the author's estate.

Miéville, China. "Covehithe," from *Three Moments of an Explosion: Stories.* Copyright © 2015 by China Miéville. Canada/US: Used by permission of Del Rey Books, an imprint of Random House, a division of Penguin Random House LLC. All rights reserved. UK/EU: First published in 2015 by Macmillan, an imprint of Pan Macmillan. Reproduced by permission of Macmillan Publishers International Limited.

Padgett, Lewis. "Mimsy Were the Borogoves," illustration by W.A. Kolliker, *Astounding Science Fiction*, 30.6 (Feb. 1943), Street & Smith. Copyright © 1943 by Street & Smith Publications, renewed 1970 by C.L. Moore. Reprinted by permission of Don Congdon Associates, Inc., on behalf of the author's estate.

Paul, Frank R. Illustration for *Ralph 124C 41+* (1925), by Hugo Gernsback. Used by permission of the Frank R. Paul Estate.

Ra, Sun. "The Space Age Cannot Be Avoided." Reprinted by permission of Sun Ra LLC.

Robinson, Eden. "Terminal Avenue." Copyright © 1996 by Eden Robinson. First published in Canada by *Aboriginal Voices*. Reprinted by permission of the author.

Russ, Joanna. "When it Changed." Copyright © 1972 Joanna Russ. Reprinted by permission of Diana Finch Literary Agency, on behalf of the Russ Estate.

Saunders, Charles R. "Jeroboam Henley's Debt," originally published in *Potboiler #4* (1982); reprinted by Innsmouth Free Press (July 2010), and in *The Book of Cthulhu* (2011), ed. Ross E. Lockhart, Night Shade Books.

Scott-Heron, Gil. "Whitey on the Moon," from *Now and Then: The Poems of Gil Scott-Heron*, introduction by Kae Tempest, Canongate Books, 2019. Copyright © 1990, 2000 Gil Scott-Heron. Reprinted by permission of Canongate Books Ltd. through PLSclear.

Spark, Muriel. "Miss Pinkerton's Apocalypse," also published in *All the Stories of Muriel Spark*, New Directions Publishing, 2001; *The Complete Short Stories* by Muriel Spark, Canongate, 2011. Copyright © 1953, 1957, 1958, 1961, 1964, 1967, 1985, 1987, 1989, 1994, 1995, 1996, 1997 Muriel Spark. Reprinted by permission of New Directions Publishing Corp. and David Higham Associates.

Stone, Leslie F. "The Conquest of Gola," originally published in *Wonder Stories* 2.11 (April 1931): 1278–87. Reprinted by permission of the Estate of Leslie F. Stone.

Sturgeon, Theodore. "The World Well Lost," illustration by Gredno Mahasm, originally in *Universe Science Fiction # 1* (June 1953). Reprinted in *E Pluribus Unicorn*, first published in Great Britain by Abelard-Schuman Ltd. (1959); Panther edition (1961). Copyright © Theodore Sturgeon Literary Trust. Published by permission of the Theodore Sturgeon Literary Trust c/o The Lotts Agency, Ltd.

Taylor, Drew Hayden. "Stars," from *Take Us to Your Chief and Other Stories*, Douglas and McIntyre Ltd. Copyright © 2016 Drew Hayden Taylor. Reprinted by permission of the publisher.

Tiptree, James, Jr. "And I Awoke and Found Me Here on the Cold Hill's Side," *Magazine of Fantasy and Sci Fi* (March 1972), Mercury Press. Reprinted by permission of Virginia Kidd Literary Agency, on behalf of the author's estate.

Van Camp, Richard. "On the Wings of This Prayer," *Godless but Loyal to Heaven: Stories*, Enfield & Wizenty, 2013. Copyright © 2013 Richard Van Camp. Reprinted by permission of Great Plains Publications.

Walton, Jo. "Escape to Other Worlds with Science Fiction." Reprinted by permission of Donald Maass Literary Agency, on behalf of the author.

Willis, Connie. "At the Rialto," originally in *Omni* (1989); later in *The Best of Connie Willis: Award-Winning Stories*, Del Rey, an imprint of Penguin Random House, 2014. Published by permission of Connie Willis c/o The Lotts Agency, Ltd.

Wu, William F. "Wong's Lost and Found Emporium," originally in *Amazing Science Fiction* (May 1983) by Dragon Publishing, Available in the collection *Interlaced Pathways, Contemporary Fantasy Tales*, by William F. Wu. Reprinted by permission of the author.

Zoline, Pamela. "The Heat Death of the Universe." Copyright © 1967 Pamela Zoline. Reprinted by permission of McPherson & Company.

About the Publisher

THE word "broadview" expresses a good deal of the philosophy behind our company. Our focus is very much on the humanities and social sciences—especially literature, writing, and philosophy—but within these fields we are open to a broad range of academic approaches and political viewpoints. We strive in particular to produce high-quality, pedagogically useful books for higher education classrooms—anthologies, editions, sourcebooks, surveys of particular academic fields and sub-fields, and also course texts for subjects such as composition, business communication, and critical thinking. We welcome the perspectives of authors from marginalized and underrepresented groups, and we have a strong commitment to the environment. We publish English-language works and translations from many parts of the world, and our books are available world-wide; we also publish a select list of titles with a specifically Canadian emphasis.

broadview press